Führer

The Novel

ALLAN PRIOR

SINCLAIR-STEVENSON

This Book is dedicated to the memory of my Father, who, as Second Lieutenant Percy Prior, of the Northumberland Fusiliers, faced, on his first day in the Front Line, the 2nd Bavarian List Regiment in which Adolf Hitler served as a Corporal Meldeganger, at Arras, in the March of 1917.

A.P.

First published in Great Britain by
Sinclair-Stevenson Limited
7/8 Kendrick Mews
London SW7 3HG, England

Copyright © 1991 by Allan Prior

British Library Cataloguing in Publication Data
A CIP catalogue record for this book is available from the British Library

ISBN 1-85619-082-X

Photoset by Rowland Phototypesetting Limited
Bury St Edmunds, Suffolk
Printed and bound in Great Britain by
Clays Limited, St Ives plc.

Contents

In the Summer of 1945, as a member of the British Liberation Army, I found myself in the ruins of Hitler's Europe. France, Belgium, Germany, a trail of dust, disease, death, everywhere. In Berlin the whole edifice of the Third Reich lay buried in huge stone blocks, the Chancellery a ruin, the Unter den Linden a maze of rubble, only the Brandenburg Gate still standing. Allied and Russian soldiers picked their way wonderingly amongst it; and anything – a woman or a Luger automatic – available for the price of a few cigarettes.

That is what Adolf Hitler had done for the Germans.

I stood amongst it all, and remembered my boyhood friends, many of them dead in Hitler's War; boys I'd been at school with. They were dead and I was alive, and the War was over, and it was a miracle.

One day, I said to myself, I will write about all this.

A.P.

AUTHOR'S NOTE

The Author sits in his study and looks at the mass of words and feels he has to give some justification for a number of the scenes he has offered to his reader: but first he has to give his thanks to the giant historians of the period: to Hugh Trevor Roper, Alan Bullock, A. J. P. Taylor, Joachim Fest, David Irving, William L. Shirer, John Toland, and many others. Without their research and scholarship, much of it written close to the wartime period, no new work on Adolf Hitler, using material that has come to light since then, would be possible. Also, a novelist's aims differ from those of the historian. The novelist is after character and dramatic truth: the historian is after facts. Flights-of-fancy are not the historian's stock-in-trade!

I have been conscious, all the time, that in mixing fact (and almost every important scene in the book *is* factual) with the fiction of Hitler's life (and I submit all the fiction is merely an extension of the known facts) that I need to explain some of my novelist's 'flights-of-fancy': that is, scenes and events that no historian would be able to accept as true or false, simply because there is no hard proof, such as a document or a record.

For example: the Myth that Adolf Hitler was not *personally* and totally responsible for the Final Solution. There can really be no doubt about this. Himmler was too much of a crank and a nonentity to have commissioned anything so monstrous. Himmler was a Number Two man all his life. The lack of documentary evidence means nothing in this case. Nothing much was ever put on paper, and when it was, the real meaning was covered over by euphemism and bureaucrat-speak. The documents of the Wannsee Conference are full of it. Documents that do show Hitler's hand are: a Memo to Heydrich, acting for Hitler, on 31st. July, 1941. . . .

'I instruct you further to submit to me as soon as possible a general plan showing the measures for organisation and for action necessary to carry out the desired final solution of the Jewish question'.

And the evidence of Rudolf Hoess, Commandant of Auschwitz. He gave evidence at the Nuremberg Trials that, 'Himmler told me that the Fuhrer had given the order for a definite solution of the Jewish question. We, the SS, were to carry out that order . . . We had chosen Auschwitz because of the easy access by rail and also because the extensive site could readily be isolated . . . About 20,000 acres of the surrounding country had been cleared of all inhabitants . . . The actual compound called Birkenau, where later on the extermination camp was constructed, was situated two kilometres from the Auschwitz camp.'

And finally, Adolf Hitler's own words, in September 1942.

'I have spoken of two things: first, now that the War has been forced upon us, no array of weapons and no passage of time will bring us to defeat: and second, that if Jewry should plot another world war in order to exterminate the Aryan peoples of Europe, it would not be the Aryan peoples which would be exterminated, but Jewry'.

What on earth could be plainer that that?

For example: Hitler's relationship with his half-niece, Geli Raubal, was undoubtedly sexual. Putzi Hanfstaengl certainly saw erotic drawings by Hitler, which leave little doubt as to their relationship. Of course, Putzi may have been wrong. But the spoilt-priest, Father Bernhard Stempfle, saw them as well. Unlikely that both were wrong. And Father Stempfle was killed in suspicious circumstances, during the Night of the Long Knives. I go with the theory that Father Stempfle was done away with in case he talked, even more than he had already, about Hitler's erotic drawings of himself and Geli.

For example: Hitler and Geli Raubal: nowhere can any historian accept, as fact, that she might have been pregnant. There are no doctor's certificates or hospital-admission entries. All sorts of reasons for her suicide are hinted at in the historical works: Geli wanted to go to Vienna to study music! Hitler was too dictatorial and forbade her to lead her own life! Does a strong-minded young woman, a devout Catholic, kill herself for those reasons? I say no. William Patrick Hitler (the Fuhrer's half-nephew) insisted that the fact of Geli's pregnancy was common talk in the Raubal family, and 'family talk' has a habit of being true. I just don't think that Geli Raubal would kill herself for any other reason. According to the housekeeper, Frau Winter, she loved Adolf Hitler. He had to do something extremely repugnant (like suggest abortion?) for her to take herself from his life.

For example: Hitler's ancestry. The facts are these: Hans Frank, Senior Jurist of the Third Reich, sentenced to death at the Nuremberg Trials, wrote a short work entitled *Im Angesicht des Galgens* (In the Face of the Gallows). A born-again Roman Catholic, Frank insisted that after William Patrick Hitler wrote to the Fuhrer that 'there are things about the family's heredity that the public and the press wonder about' Hitler charged Frank to find out the full facts. Frank's findings, in his own words, are set down in this book. The foremost German historian, Joachim Fest, writes (*The Face of the Third Reich*): 'On 7th June 1837, in the house of a small farmer named Trummelschlager in Strones, the maid Maria Anna Schicklegruber, aged forty-one and single, gave birth to a son. The father was and remains unknown, and the most various and daring guesses have been made. There is some evidence to support the account given by Hans Frank during his Nuremberg statement, *and it has never been entirely disproved. . . .*'

Did Hans Frank lie as he waited for the rope? Why would he *do* that? Hitler's insane hatred of all Jews may have had its root in something very small and very human, that happened over a hundred and fifty years ago. I have used the material Hans Frank left before he was silenced for ever, because it is there. Some researchers deny Frank's account. It is all a great mystery. But one thing is certain: Adolf Hitler could not have obtained a certificate of Racial Purity under his own Nuremberg Laws!

For example: Hitler's (possible) Syphilis. The disease was much more common in the years before the First World War than it is now. Hitler diatribes lengthily in *Mein Kampf* about the awfulness of the disease and the prostitutes who used to spread it, in those times. Hitler rarely attacked anything unless he had a *personal* reason for attacking it. If anything harmed him, or he thought *might* harm him, he was on the attack at once: it was one of the prime symptoms of his paranoia. Also, his choice of Dr. Theodor Morell – a venerealogist – as his personal doctor is a very strange one, surely? Hitler was recommended to Morell by Heinrich Hoffmann, his photographer, and Nerin Gun insists (*Eva Braun, Hitler's Mistress*) that Hoffmann had been treated for this social disease by Morell.

Also, the Russian version of the last days of Hitler (*The Death of Adolf Hitler*, by Lev Bezymenski), an account of the capture of the Fuhrerbunker by a squad of Red Army front-line troops in April 1945, supports this. The Soviet doctors who inspected Hitler's charred body were not looking for evidence of Syphilis: but they do say that Dr. Kersten, Himmler's doctor, admitted that Hitler had told him he had suffered from the disease. A woman secretary (not named) is known to have remarked that, 'The Fuhrer was infected by a loose woman when he was living in Munich just before the First World War'. And, perhaps most interesting of all, some Allied venereologists, watching screen-footage of Hitler's last weeks, are of the opinion that he was suffering from the last stages of Syphilis. Again, there is no proof either way. The disease 'sleeps' and is not contagious after a short period. Dr. Theodor Morell was a famous venerealogist, who numbered amongst his patients many prominent Nazis and even the German Crown Prince himself. I know what I think.

For example: Hitler's Monorchism, or lack of one testicle. The same source (Lev Bezymenski) gives the Soviet pathologist's report as confirming this. Hitler's body was found badly charred and minus a foot, but an autopsy was performed. Nobody knows where the body is now. My guess is probably in Moscow in a refrigerated vault. Hitler's skull was damaged but not destroyed by the suicide bullet.

For example: Hitler's acute paranoia. Many observers, specifically those who knew him personally, trace his symptoms back to his experiences in his youth in Vienna. To which one can reply, plenty of people were poor in Vienna in those years and didn't become paranoid, then or later. But the child is indeed Father to the Man, and Hitler had been spoilt and cosseted by his mother and bullied and physically abused by his father. Not enough to create a monster but plenty to be going on with. Without being overly Freudian about it the fact remains that Adolf Hitler became a harsh and bitter young man, convinced that 'They' wanted to kill him, *after* the Vienna period.

I have seen it suggested that he didn't have it all that bad in Vienna, that the Men's Hostel was rather like a YMCA! Anybody who needs to know what a Victorian Men's Hostel was like should read contemporary workhouse reports. My contention is: that Hitler, rejected, starving, penniless, sleeping rough, but convinced of his own Genius and his Mission to Save the German People, first developed a 'Persecution Mania', in the years immediately before the First World War. Certainly, my German Jewish refugee friends (one an eminent psychologist) say it was commonly diagnosed by them all at the time.

The signs are classic. *Hitler saw enemies everywhere. Somebody was responsible for his situation! Socialists, Communists, Jews ... They were responsible!*

Hitler was clinically, mentally ill, I contend. And was to be so the rest of his life, getting steadily worse. But he never saw that in himself. And nobody else did. Because it ran side-by-side with his political skills and his iron will. The sudden rages: the sudden death warrants: then the periods of calm. No modern psychiatrist of any discipline would fail to see the signs.

Hitler was not alone in this affliction. Most tyrants (Stalin is another example) suffer it sooner or later.

This, in my view, is a kind of explanation of his mad and murderous behaviour.

God knows, an explanation is needed!

These are just the obvious points experts may cavil about. There are many others that historians may not accept either, but I hope (without too much hope!) that there will not be too many. I have relied, far more than a historian possibly could, on sources like newspapers of the time and magazine articles and even books like *I Was Hitler's Maid* by Pauline Kohler, and the reminiscences of Heinrich Hoffmann, Hitler's photographer, which may be less than accurate in parts but somehow have the unmistakeable tang of known experience.

Hitler's days in Vienna are not chronicled in great detail and yet the kind of life he led is there to imagine. His companions in the Men's Home, Hanisch and (especially) Greiner, I have taken some liberties with, character-wise: but not in any way that militates against the truth of Hitler's situation; quite the contrary.

Anyway, as I have found in the course of writing this book (three whole years) most historians disagree with other historians about almost anything to do with the Third Reich! Which is why, I suppose, we are all foolish enough to examine the evidence afresh from time to time. Long may we all continue to do it. The modern Atilla still fascinates us all. Is it possible to be as evil as *that* and be just *ordinary* as well? Yes, it is.

For myself, I have laid a ghost. Adolf Hitler was talked about in my very 'political' family all through my adolescence. I felt I knew him even then! I was in RAF uniform for four years because of Adolf Hitler, and wore a Home Guard uniform before that. I lost many friends in Hitler's War: a football team in which I was playing at the outbreak of War counted six young boys dead, of the eleven players, by 1945. I still miss those boys and do indeed, as the poem says, remember them as they were, for they have not grown old as we who are left grow old.

The very idea of the millions of dead one never knew swamps the imagination: the thing is almost too big to comprehend. I was in Europe at the war's end and saw something of how it must have been while Hitler held sway all across the continent and halfway into Asia. There was something evil in the air. I am glad, at last, to get the taste of it out of my mouth, and my memory.

A.P.

BOOK ONE

Adolf

I

'AN *artist*? Are you insane?'

Alois glared incredulously across the dinner-table at his son. The boy stared insolently back. Fine brown hair parted in the middle, in the style of a gentleman of the time but impervious to comb or brush, falling in a lank strand over his large pale eyes. A thin, long face on him, not of his father's making, by God! A tweed suit, too good for a boy of his age: a mother's dandy of all things!

'No, I am perfectly sane, thank you for asking,' replied the boy, coolly.

Alois breathed in, hard. This boy took no notice of anybody. He had few friends – none, really – at school or in the village. His schoolmasters complained that he was indolent and uncaring. The only good reports came from Herr Ludwig Poetsch, the Nationalist teacher of history in the Realschule in nearby Linz, in Alois's view a bit of a crank. Not that he had anything against the pedagogue speaking up for a Greater German Reich, certainly not, quite the reverse, didn't his whole life of uniformed service prove that? But Pan-Germanism? Deutschland Uber Alles? There was something airy-fairy about it. It was an idea for dreamers, like this preposterous 'artist' business. Alois was no kind of dreamer. Couldn't afford to be, with his beginnings, by Christ! Not that he necessarily believed in Christ: but in the Austrian Imperial Customs Service it paid to act as if you did.

'What makes you think you can ever be an artist?' he demanded, playing for time. The boy and the mother had sprung this on him. It was a trap of sorts. He had to sniff the air, like some old dog, see what they were after.

'Herr Poetsch thinks my paintings have merit.' The boy spoke to him as if to an equal. 'And an artist can come from anywhere, even here.'

'Does Herr Poetsch know about such things?' Alois knew the boy painted country scenes: old farm buildings, prettified-up, everything

3

wistful and romantic. No smell of pig-shit or cow-dung in these scenes. The boy looked at the countryside like a townsman. Alois could see nothing in such paintings. What were they *for*? Who would buy them, the views of old Weber's farmhouse, or the cold winter potato-fields across from the Eckart place? These landscapes were not pretty, even in spring. They were, to Alois, as to all countrymen, simply a workplace in the open air, and none the better for that. Only peasants worked outside in all weathers.

The boy had not troubled to answer his father's question, plainly thinking it foolish. So Alois asked, with po-faced guile, 'Artists make no money, do they? They starve in garrets, don't they?'

'Not the good ones.'

Alois stared angrily at his son. The boy's school reports underlined the insolent, uncaring manner. The teachers at the Realschule had given him up. None of them had seemed surprised that he had failed his School Leaving Examination. The only subjects the boy excelled in were history and this ridiculous art business. A fat lot of good art would be to any young man sitting the Civil Service Examinations at Linz in the coming summer but one; which Alois had always understood, despite his son's silent protests, would be the inevitable end of it. How could the boy, now almost fifteen years old, hope to do better? What else could he find to do in a poverty-stricken hole like Leonding? Did he want to end up as a farming hobbledehoy, working from sun-up to sun-down, ankle-deep in the shit of some manger, on a level with the animals he tended? Animals belonging to somebody else, since the Hitlers owned no land.

And in Leonding land was all that mattered.

'You'll sit the Imperial Customs Examination, just as I did, at the age of sixteen! You'll pass first-class, and you'll have a job for life. As I did.' Alois felt a sense of awesome pride as he spoke. To come from his beginnings, from the dark secret of his birth, in the old farmhouse over at Strones, from the shame of having no father, or rather having a man in the house who was not his father but who simply slept with his mother, Maria Anna Schickelgruber. To come from that. It was something.

'I'd never pass the exam,' the boy was saying.

'You would if you worked. Which you never do.'

'No, I wouldn't.'

The boy was still looking at him with the strange wide eyes, a wary but confident hunter assessing a dangerous beast. Adolf's eyes were large and a very pale blue, wide-staring and almost beautiful: his mother Klara's eyes, a girl's eyes, by God, not a man's; but not asking to be loved or fooled as a woman's might – and Alois knew about *that*. No man in the Waldviertal had bedded more women than he, nobody! No, the boy's eyes were contemptuous and superior and, amazingly, cold. And, now, murderous. As if the boy would like to kill him. Would do it without compunction or conscience.

Alois shivered: such a thought was errant, foolish, it was the hangover of the beer and cognac he had consumed at the Inn before coming home to have his meal ruined by this rebellious schoolboy and his doting mother. He glanced again at Klara. As usual, her eyes dropped away as he spoke. What a difference from his old mother! Pregnant, this one, when he married her, but her children had a name. Old Maria Anna Schickelgruber had no father to name her child. Maria Anna Schickelgruber, cook, had borne Alois at forty-one years of age, out of wedlock. He was to be her only child. She had gone to her grave and never told a living soul who the father was. Yes, the old woman had been a tough one, by Christ she had, and here was this nincompoop of a boy rebelling against the wishes of his *real* father. The boy never knew, never suspected, what a boon it was to know, what a sharp and terrible pain it was *not to know*, who your father was!

Not that Alois couldn't guess who his father was.

He could guess all right.

All the busybodies, the old women of the Waldviertal, could guess. But none of them knew for certain. Nobody knew for certain. He certainly did not, and it tore him to pieces. Alois pushed the cruel thoughts away: why did he allow himself to be plagued by them? He should have worn it all out by now. But all the good beer in Leonding and all the befuddling cognac, too, could not wash the thoughts away. He had carried the shaming secret close to his chest all his life, got to where he was despite it all, and here was this sneering youth with the murderous eyes, born when Alois was fifty, taunting him, once again.

Alois said, in a thick voice, 'Nobody here has ever been an artist. They wouldn't know how to go about it.'

'I know how to go about it.' His son's eyes did not blink. The little man isn't afraid of me, Alois thought. Or, if he is, he'll die before he shows it. All the chastisements, leather belt on bare buttocks, the red weals coming up on the white skin of the boy's arse, the woman crying soundlessly in the kitchen (the right place for her, she was useless in the bedroom), and, at the end of it, the belt thrown down on the floor, in front of the fireplace, the boy turned round face-to-face. But not a tear. Just the huge blue eyes staring at him, cold with hate. Hate, when all he was trying to do was beat some sense into the boy, as any good father should.

Alois said, 'You know a lot. How?' He was still standing, resting his belly on the edge of the table. 'Hard as a water-butt,' they said, at the Inn. The young girls liked feeling the hardness of his belly. Drunk or

5

sober, he was still a man. Unlike this little man here, this son, this nothing, this would-be *artist*, who was still speaking to him in the voice somebody might use to a mental defective. 'All I have to do is apply to the Vienna School of Art, submitting some drawings and paintings. If they accept me I could go there next year.'

Alois shook his head, disbelievingly. The dark and swirling dizziness he sometimes experienced nowadays, after a heavy drinking session, swept over him, and he sat down abruptly. His coffee-cup, half-empty, spilled over, staining the damask, but that did not matter. He was a bastard peasant, with no manners, even if his rank of Collector in the Customs Service was equivalent to that of a Kapitan in the Army. Even if he had a dark blue, gold-braided uniform to go with his grey side-whiskers and his bald, burnished and massive head.

A peasant and a bastard, they said in the Waldviertal, and a by-the-book bastard at that.

A drunk and a lecher, they said, but not to his face.

And a Customs officer of equivalent rank to that of a Kapitan in the Imperial Austrian Army, he spat back at them. All of this without a word being uttered.

Alois stared at his son, through the sudden, eye-clouding dizziness. He spoke thickly, as if he was drunk, although he knew he wasn't drunk. 'You want to go to Vienna? To live? On your own? What about the Civil Service Examination?'

'I don't want to be a civil servant. What man of ability would want to be a civil servant?'

The words expressed total contempt of Alois Hitler (Schickelgruber, Heidler, how many names did he have?), of all he had ever been or could be; of the Imperial Service; of this room, warm, cosy, furnished in velvet and heavy velour drapes, a league – by God, a league! – above those of most of the inhabitants of Leonding, poor ignorant shitkickers, just as he himself had been, before he sat down at his books and taught himself knowledge enough to pass the Examination. That Examination had given this insolent youth home, and warmth, and security. It had given him a father he knew, could point to and name, and all the impertinent little *narr* could say was, 'I don't want to be a civil servant!'

As if anybody could be one? As if it wasn't an honour! As if membership of the Imperial Customs Service did not open almost every door in the district? As if Alois had not been respectfully assessed by his superiors. He had seen the words himself, on his report: '*An excellent Officer. Exemplary in the pursuit of his duties as Collector. Few offenders escape his stern and watchful eye. A credit to the Service.*'

As if all that was *nothing*!

'No possibility of it!' Alois shouted at his son. His tongue clung drily to his mouth. 'No possibility of it at all! Vienna? Ridiculous!'

'If you are thinking about money,' the boy Adolf said, the eyes never leaving his father's face, 'there are some bursaries. I would certainly apply for one.'

'Bursaries are for the poor,' Alois shouted. 'I am an officer of the Customs Service. My son would not be granted a bursary.'

There was a silence. They all three of them knew it was true.

Klara, tentatively, broke the silence. The large pale eyes looked up – *four* of those eyes looking at him now, by God! – as she twisted the thick gold wedding-ring on the thin, nervous fingers. 'Pappi, if you could see your way? I'm sure Adolf would not disgrace you? Think how it would sound? An artist in the family? A Hitler an artist!'

Hitler? It was an invented name, a label he despised, *Hitler*, the very name was a fraud! Alois's name had been 'legitimised' by, strictly speaking, illegal means. The village priest at Dollersheim had been prevailed upon to make up Alois's entry in the parish register as 'adopted son of Georg Heidler'. Until his fortieth birthday Alois had called himself Schickelgruber, his mother's name. Now it was Hitler, but he felt no pride in it.

'An artist?' Alois repeated. He could hardly contain his contempt for his wife. Besotted, that was the trouble, totally besotted by the boy. Running away from the bedchamber to the nursery, like so many women, next thing she'd be in bed with the boy, except she wouldn't, she wasn't that honest, it all stopped at adoration and woman-like wonder.

'A Hitler. An *artist*?'

Alois said the words slowly, for maximum effect. From the kitchen he heard a cough. The little one, Paula, he realised, had been pushed out there, to finish her dinner alone, so they could get at him, the two of them, in concert. The slow-thinking, slow-witted little one, under-sized and un-pretty, that he could not bear to look at. What had he done to beget such a child? First the boy, defiant and beyond his understanding. Then the slow-witted little girl-child. It was all too much.

The mother's fault, naturally. Klara's fault, it had to be. Klara was his half-niece and it was said to make a difference. People had told him not to do it, not to plead – aye, and pay for! – the Church's dispensation, but he had wanted her, and she was young and innocent and tremulous and knew nothing of life or sex or anything else, and that had, as usual, bewitched him, and he had thought he could *teach* her; but he had been wrong about that, as he had been wrong about so many other things in this late and foolish marriage. Klara should have refused him, even if she was pregnant. It was as simple as that. She'd had plenty of reason to do it. He'd been married twice before, both wives dead of the raging consumption that was the curse of all the villages in the province. He had two other children. The son Alois, named after him, was a disappointment, had run away from home at fourteen and had since been in the hands of the police for theft. He would see prison yet, and disgrace the family name. The other child, Angela, was healthy enough, and respectably married to a civil servant. She had given him none of the problems he had with this insolent youth, now loftily telling him how he was going to live his life.

'Over my dead body,' said Alois. 'You'll be an artist over my dead body.'

The words hung in the room like a declaration of war.

The mother and the son looked at each other. The son showed nothing but the mother sighed, very gently, as if at the news of an illness or a death. Her greying head (by the Sacrament, she was only forty-five!) bowed even lower as she began to collect the dinner plates into a pile, neatly, as she did every night, preparatory to taking them into the kitchen. They had no maid: Alois did not want a plump young woman around him, to tempt his weakness. Not in his own house. Besides, he spent all he earned down at the Inn, or on his other young wenches. All that he earned, he spent, one way or another, after he had supplied this mother and his ungrateful family with good, wholesome food, a warm, comfortable home, a roof over their heads.

Not that they appreciated that. By Christ they didn't. They appreciated nothing he did.

'Leave the dishes, woman! I haven't finished!'

Alois got slowly to his feet. The dizziness had gone and in its place was the pleasurable warmth in his loins that he associated with the sex act. Or with any kind of family quarrel or upset. One thing was certain: he was in the right of it. He had been provoked beyond measure: the silly woman, with her sillier son, was out to make a fool of him in the village – his son an *artist*, were they all going mad? He would be a laughing-stock at the Inn, where he had stared down all the sly asides connected with his shameful birth. Was his father, his *real* father, John Heidler, the brother of the man who had slept in his mother's bed? Had this prosperous farmer, Johann Heidler, given his son his name but through his poorer brother, Georg, and seven long years, at that, after the boy – himself – was born?

Alois did not know.

Klara, in the long silence, picked up the dishes.

Alois swept them from her hands onto the floor, where two broke. He did not care. It made him feel good. Violence always made him feel good. He got up, knocking the chair behind him to the floor. His wife

8

did not move until he had walked round the table towards the boy. Then she cried, in a hopeless voice, 'Alois. Please.'

Pleasurably, he ignored her.

The first blow across the boy's face with his meaty and powerful open hand was the most satisfying. It felt good. It put a great many things that he had been feeling to rights. It was proper. Justified. Correct.

The boy did not fall but he staggered. His white face showed, after a moment, the red mark of his father's fingers. The eyes, however, did not close in pain or show any emotion at all. That was too much, and Alois struck him again, this time with the back of his hand on the other side of the face, aiming for the hated eyes; but the boy swayed very slightly into the blow, like a talented boxer, and the knuckle struck the hard bone of the forehead, brushing aside the silky hair. Then, suddenly, and for the first time in all the ritual chastisements, the boy struck back.

It was a blow to the midriff.

It was not a hard blow; and it bounced off the waterbutt belly. Alois grinned – he almost laughed aloud! – and then he rained blow after blow upon the boy, around the ears and the neck, and, when he could, the soft flesh of the young, defiant face. But, as he did so, he saw a thing that chilled him: the boy's eyes had a new expression in them now.

An expression of joy.

He was enjoying this as much as Alois himself was enjoying it, the old man realised. It had ceased to be a chastisement and become something else, something akin to a union, a sexual act. As he rained yet more blows on the boy's head, Alois closed his eyes to blot out the expression in those pale and beautiful eyes. A feeling of pain and desolation replaced his exhilaration, and he suddenly stopped hitting the boy.

Adolf had staggered against the sideboard, and he remained there. He was not crying although he must have been dazed and in pain. He looked steadily at Alois. Wilful, thought Alois, subdued by the force of that look: a cold will, mixed with murderous hate. Then the dizziness returned, a sudden wave of it, and he grabbed hastily at the table to steady himself; and, as he did so, he yelled, to cover his panic and fear, 'Get out, get out of the house! Don't come back till bedtime! Don't let me see your face again tonight.'

Alois turned his back on them both and sat down heavily in his leather chair by the stove. He closed his eyes and waited for the dizziness to go. When it did, with a sudden loud singing in his ears, like a nearby surf, the dining-room was empty. The broken dishes were still lying on the carpet. Nothing had been cleared from the table. From the kitchen, Alois heard hushed words, Klara's, and a loud, arrogant protest from the boy; and the slam of a door. Then, footsteps fading away into the small night sounds of the village: a dog barking far off, a cow lowing in a stall, the wind soughing.

And then silence.

Alois closed his eyes and wondered: the boy was not a complete fool, despite his stupid aspiration to be an artist. The will and wilfulness had to be explained somehow. Something was under the boy's skin.

Alois wondered uneasily if the boy had heard any of the rumours about Johann Heidler and his brother Georg who had married Adolf's grandmother, seven years after her bastard son – *himself* – was born: about the great mystery of it all? Alois shook his head. It was possible the boy had heard something, a whisper behind a hand; a voice heard, hushed, through a door; an anonymous shout in the schoolyard. It was likely that the gossipmongers and jealous shitkickers would try to get at the father through the son. Say things to him or about him they would never dare to say to Alois, protected behind his blue uniform with the gold braid and the rank conferred by the old Emperor, Franz Josef himself. Likely? More likely than not.

Well, he had lived with it. The boy would have to live with it. Maria Anna Schickelgruber was only the boy's grandmother and long since dead. The pain would be less than his own. A lot less. Alois sighed. The violence had sated him and yet, unusually, disturbed him, and the dizziness was worrying. Enough! He would go down to the Inn a little later, and wash it all away with waves of cognac.

Alois Hitler's eyes closed. He relaxed: his head fell forward on his chest; and he snored.

II

KLARA waited in the scullery, listening to Alois snoring in his chair next door. The girl Paula she hushed to silence.

At last – it seemed a long time but was probably only half an hour – she heard Alois wake, with a snort and a heavy catarrhal cough. His eternal pipes, she thought, they give him a cough in winter, but he'll never give them up. Alois had seven meerschaum pipes standing in a rack on the living-room wall, one for each day of the week, just as he had seven cut-throat razors lying in the long, black leather box on the window-sill in this very scullery where he shaved himself each morning, one for each day of the week. Alois was the one for strict routine.

At first, Klara had been proud of him as a husband. Of his rank and importance. It was after all a marriage above her station. She had been in service, a slavey to his ailing wife, when Alois had bedded her first; brusquely, in her tiny servant's attic-room. Crushed by his weight into the hard horsehair mattress, all she had been conscious of was the sudden sharp pain and the blood staining her underskirt. No decent girl wore knickers; knickers were for prostitutes, and French prostitutes at that, and were worn exclusively to pander to a man's weakness. That first sexual experience had been little different from her last one, probably a month ago now: her body dry and sore and unready, and everything over in a few short thrusts. Klara had not wanted sex then, any more than she ever did, these days. Nonetheless, she lay still and suffered. She had never pretended to enjoy it. She just lay there but what else was there to do, a man was a man, a husband was a husband?

Klara got up wearily, putting her finger to her lips, as little Paula made a move to speak. 'Stay quiet, *liebchen*,' she said, smoothing the girl's starched white pinafore. All the young children wore pinafores over their day-clothes. It was an all-purpose, classless mode of dress. A peasant's uniform, she had heard it called. Well, what else were they?

Some might put on airs and pretend otherwise, take a job in Linz, as Alois had done, first as a cobbler's apprentice at the age of twelve; finally, through his own efforts, rise to Probationary Higher Customs Collector, the highest rank open to a man of elementary education. But once a man of the Waldviertal, always one.

Klara sighed. Alois had his weaknesses, of course, but many were worse. Many men drank everything away. Many men regularly beat their wives. At least Alois seldom did that. She had much to be grateful for. Klara took the kettle from the huge pot-bellied stove and poured hot water into an enamel bowl. She put a new cake of yellow soap and a clean white hand-towel next to it, on the wooden scullery table. In this room Klara washed and ironed and cooked and spent most of her days. The dining-room (always called the kitchen) was where the family ate and lived. Otherwise, there were two bedrooms, one for herself and Alois, and one for Adolf and Paula. The whole family slept between goose-down mattresses and covers, warm and comfortable in the bitter cold nights of the harsh winters of the region. There was always food enough in the house. Klara, like all the women of the village, baked her own bread and made her own sausagemeat, and the family subsisted on thick soups and goat's milk cheese, with a roast joint every Sunday, after the morning Mass she never missed. Alois attended church only when he felt he had to, for appearance's sake. Klara knew he didn't *believe*. She had always known that. Some of his talk about the local priests, his chuckling aspersions about their personal sex-lives – as if those good and devout men ever thought of such vile things! – made her blush all over. But she wisely kept her teeth together and did not protest, for she knew that would only make Alois worse.

At the start of their marriage, she had hoped, by gentle persuasion and example, to bring him to godly ways, but now she knew that such hopes were laughable. Alois Hitler saw all women as fit candidates for the bedchamber and the kitchen and judged them accordingly. She had given him five children. It should have been enough. But two had died in infancy, and a third, her dearest Edmund, had been taken into God's arms as a young child. Klara knew that somehow these happenings were her fault. Alois made her feel that.

Adolf, at least, did not share his father's lewd and peasant ways. No, indeed. Adolf was well-mannered and respectful towards women, as she had taught him to be. Some of the wives in the village remarked on it, laughing behind their hands, at the 'little gentleman', as he deigned to hold a door open for them. Klara felt hot, just thinking of it. The rough hussies! All they wanted of a man, some of them, was what he had between his legs. Fine manners were no part of their harsh existence: they had never even met a real gentleman, except possibly when some

Army officer on furlough had condescended to pleasure himself with them. In which case, they spoke of little else for months. These shameless girls did not get pregnant, however, as she had by Alois. They knew better than that.

Some of these women (*she* knew which ones, oh yes she *did*, even if they didn't think she did!) had lain with her husband, in summer field or winter byre: mostly the young, unmarried ones, giggling and foolish and ripe for treading. Klara always knew them by the interested, contemptuous looks they gave her in the village store, the sex-mad young trollops. It was an insult and a humiliation, but she bore it because Alois was her husband and not theirs, and there was no way, short of her death, that they could take him from her.

Klara listened to Alois light a pipe in the next room, and sighed with relief. He would not be lighting a pipe if his bad temper still persisted. It meant little more than that, she knew, but at least he would not come into the scullery for his evening wash, preparatory to his second visit of the day to the Inn, still shouting about Adolf and his doings. He would smoke his pipe for at least five minutes, probably ten. It gave her a brief respite.

Klara took a rough flannel from a wooden drawer, soaked it in water from the bucket (there was no running water) and wrung it out. She added a sprinkling of vinegar to the cloth. Her head hurt. It often hurt these days. She had always been prone to headaches, as well as sharp stomach pains and a general feeling of lassitude. These symptoms she ruthlessly held down. A mother had no right to be ill. It was a mother's duty to stay well and see that her family stayed well, by feeding them properly, and seeing that they were warmly wrapped up against bad weather and generally supporting them, from the home, in the great battle of life, waged exclusively by the men of the household.

Klara closed her eyes. A tear ran down her pale cheek. She had much to be thankful for, but sometimes all she wanted to do was stay in bed. All day. Just once. All one Sunday. Not even go to Mass. This sinful thought made her groan, and she opened her eyes to see that the child, Paula, had taken the flannel from her hand and was gently setting it on her forehead. More tears filled Klara's eyes, but she beat them back. No child, not even a slow one like Paula, should see a mother's tears.

'Thank you, my little love, you're a good girl.' Klara felt the cool sting of the vinegar on her temples. It always helped, thank God, who gave her so many things to be thankful for. Even Paula, a constant worry (would she ever find a husband, how would she live after Klara had gone if she didn't?), was a boon at times like this. A brighter child might be troubled, as Adolf was, by her father's loud and bullying ways, but the little *liebchen* didn't seem to see it, she had a small tremulous smile for Alois, as for everybody else. Yet her father ignored her, most of the time, and it broke Klara's heart to see it. But the finer things of life passed men by; they were like animals really, and a prey to their natural weaknesses, where women and money and power were concerned. It was how things were ordered. Even the priests counselled, nay commanded, the women to obey their husbands in all things. This Klara knew she must do.

But Adolf would be different. Adolf *was* different.

From the age of twelve he had decided to be an artist. He had first told the dream to his mother, sitting on her bed, late at night, when his father was out lusting after some farm-wench no doubt. She took comfort in Adolf's hopes. The boy had told her, in his casual way (as if she wasn't interested, as if she didn't yearn for his confidences!), that he had discovered he could paint and draw, at school: better anyway than any other boy in his form. It had been remarked upon. Now all he needed was money for drawing-paper and pencils and colours and brushes. These were very special materials but could be bought at a shop in Linz. 'How much?' Klara had tremulously asked. Her voice was hushed, for the shadow of Alois was always present in the house, even when he wasn't there in the flesh. 'Only fifty kroner, *Mutti*,' the boy had said, airily, naming a sum she would find difficult to explain away: but she had found it and dared to spend it.

Together, they had bought the drawing and painting materials at the art shop in Linz. The male assistants, condescending in high, white collars and with macassared hair parted in the middle as was the fashion, had hummed and hawed and raised their eyebrows at the boy's certainty as to what he wanted. They, personally, would have chosen this instead of that but the boy's money was as god as anybody's and the customer was, after all, always right. So Klara had paid and the boy had unsmilingly brought his materials home. From that day to this she had bought whatever he asked for: more of the heavy drawing-paper; packets of conté chalk; charcoal-sticks; bottles of India ink; small sharp pens with tiny J-nibs; sticks of eraser; even an easel. These items filled the bedroom he shared with the little one, until he had complained of her presence, and Klara had taken to making up a makeshift bed in the passageway for Paula, and even, on cold nights, in the marital bedroom itself. Alois had shouted in protest at that – the parents' bedroom was no place for a child! – and so little Paula had to go back into her brother's room, where she still was.

Adolf had hated that but there was nothing Klara could do, and he knew it. So, often, he would come down into the scullery in the dark evenings and draw, or paint, at the long scrubbed table. These were the times Klara loved best. These were the times when she felt closest to Adolf, although

14

he rarely spoke, so immersed was he in his copying work, his eyes screwed up so closely they must give him pain. Those wonderful, satisfying evenings, preferable by far (for their closeness and warmth) to any sexual liaison, were a remembered joy to her. Klara had seen with pride the drawings pile up, seen the boy's intense work grow. There seemed to be no plan to it. No marks were to be awarded for his this work. Adolf himself was the sole arbiter of its success or failure. Sometimes, dissatisfied, he tore up the expensive sheets of paper in one of his sudden rages: he had always suffered from them. Klara felt they were a sort of illness, they were sudden and frightening and came from nowhere. Tantrums, Alois called them. Not her. They marked Adolf out as different.

Adolf painted anything that he fancied: some church portal or public archway in an illustrated magazine, or a stone column or old window of the ancient cathedral in Linz. The opera-house was one of his favourite subjects, and he often painstakingly recreated portions of the vast Baroque exterior. These drawings seemed to Klara very fine and much preferable to her son's figure-drawing, which were usually of negroes and South Sea Islanders and other such heathen-people, copied from travel-features in one of his pile of illustrated magazines.

When Adolf had finished drawing, sometimes a stint of hours, Klara would tenderly bathe his eyes in an especially-bought solution of boracic powder and warm water, hidden away in the old wooden dresser from the curious gaze of her husband. She would also give him bread and cheese and buttermilk to keep up his strength. These acts gave her a complicity in all that Adolf was doing. As he worked, she would secretly watch him. She loved the way his soft hair fell over his thin, intense face. She wished he was not so much like her, and had the thick peasant body of his father, but that might make him more like his father in temperament, and she quailed at that. Yet the work, for Adolf called these drawings and paintings *work*, not play, exhausted the boy to such an extent that she sometimes intervened, when he had been sitting crouched at the table for far too many hours. 'Don't strain yourself, *liebchen*. There's another day coming.'

At that, Adolf would turn his head and look at her as if she wasn't there, and return to the close, concise, painful copying of whatever model (architecture or landscape or head) he was engaged upon. That look, so cold and unloving, cut through Klara and she fell into an abashed silence, and disturbed the boy no more. If only his father, she thought, could see Adolf's dedication to his chosen path, then he would surely applaud the boy's efforts. But Klara knew that would not, could not, be the way of it. Alois would instantly ask why, if he could give so much time and effort to his painting and drawing, he could not give it to his schoolwork? And there was no answer to that.

When Alois asked about Adolf's painting, for even he would stop sometimes and grunt and look, and even say, 'That's good,' about a drawing the boy had done, Klara would hasten to infer it was simply a hobby, something the boy did to amuse himself, and of no real consequence. She had, of course, known that the day would come when her husband would be faced with the truth. She had dreaded that day, and shed solitary tears about it, but now – that very evening! – it had happened, and it had all gone wrong. God alone knew how, if at all, it could be righted.

Klara decided she would pray to the Blessed Virgin for a way to be shown her. If she prayed long enough and hard enough somehow, surely, the Madonna would grant Adolf what he desired, a place at the Vienna Academy of Art? What the Academy of Art was, exactly, she did not know, but a distinguished place to learn, obviously. It was what Adolf wanted and so it must, somehow, be obtained. If that was the Will of God, naturally. If it was not, then somehow she would suffer it. For suffer it they must, if Alois's mind could not be changed. And Klara knew in her heart that nothing short of a miracle – and it was surely a kind of sin to ask the Virgin for *that* – would be needed, to effect it.

Yet – she thought, defiantly – Adolf *was* different from other boys (or anyway other boys in Leonding) and deserved different treatment.

Adolf was special and cut out for a special destiny.

He knew it and she knew it.

It was a thought that kept her warm on winter nights, as she lay, waiting for Alois to come home from the Inn, stinking of cognac (and sometimes of the farm wench he had just left), and feigning sleep when he did.

Adolf was the answer to all the soreness and travail of her life.

Adolf healed every hurt, even those he thoughtlessly, man-like, inflicted on her himself, with his pride and defiance towards all authority.

Adolf was hers. There was nothing of his father in him.

He even had her eyes, the eyes that had attracted the glance of many a young farmhand in the Waldviertal, the eyes – she was sure – that had brought Alois Hitler to her bed. Now, the village girls were beginning to look at Adolf thoughtfully, those who were not secretly giggling at the thin, lanky boy with his stiff, distant bearing.

Well, they would not have him.

Adolf was hers and hers alone.

If it would have helped, she would have used sex as a weapon to influence her husband: but if anybody used sex as a weapon it was Alois. There was no use thinking along those lines, not after five children.

Prayer was the only answer. Silently, Klara prayed to the Blessed Madonna.

The door to the scullery clicked open and suddenly Alois stood there. He seemed sated with sleep and strong tobacco. Klara snatched the wet cloth from her forehead and stood up. She crossed to the stove and found more warm water, saying to the little girl, 'Paula, some plates have broken in the kitchen. Will you go and pick them up, please, and put all the pots on the tray for *Mutti*?' It was always wise to get Paula out of Alois's way.

Paula nodded, smiling ingenuously at her father. Alois ignored her and crossed to the table, taking off his four-inch white-starched collar as he did so. To Klara, that meant he was definitely going out, down to the Inn. Quickly, she darted across to the old wooden chest and found him a clean collar. This she placed at his hand as he rolled up his sleeves and immersed his face in the hot, soapy water, spluttering and gasping as the moisture stung his skin. Blindly, he groped for the warm towel, which she put in his hands.

'*Danke*,' he gasped, rubbing the towel around his red face in a series of brisk movements. He handed it back to her and turned to the small mirror above the sink. Klara passed him the large-toothed comb, from the small toilet-rack, and he carefully arranged his damp sidewhiskers and parted his hair. Then he applied a palmful of macassar oil to both. While he was doing that Klara took his jacket from its hook behind the door and quickly brushed the dandruff from the collar. It was of a dark heavy serge and went well with the new and shining collar he fastened to his flannel shirt. As she stood ready with his jacket, Alois slowly knotted his heavy woollen tie and buttoned his shirt-cuffs. Then, and only then, not looking at her but surveying himself in the small mirror, did he speak.

'Let this be understood, woman, once and for all. There is no possibility of changing my mind, none whatever. If Adolf does not sit the Customs Examination, then he will be found work of a more menial order. As you know, my friend Ernst has a bakery in Linz. He has told me he can take on an apprentice. It is hard, hot work, of course, and not too well paid, but if the boy insists on defying me and not taking up his opportunities, then he must understand what the alternatives are. You can tell him that, if you like. He takes more notice of you than he does of me.'

Alois Hitler put on his velour hat, taken from its hook behind the door, the only man in the Inn that night, save the village doctor, who would wear such headgear, and walked out into the night.

As the door slammed, Klara Hitler slumped back into the chair, drained of all hope.

Poor Adolf, she whispered, too shocked to cry. Poor, poor Adolf.

III

ADOLF wanted to scream.

But he dared not because somebody might hear him.

One day, he promised himself, he would scream when he wanted to and *other people* would tremble, not him!

As he had trembled, inwardly, when his father had shouted at him. It had been a relief when, unexpectedly, the old man had struck out. Nowadays, he rarely did that.

He knew Adolf was growing stronger, even if he was still a boy and did not yet have his full strength, whereas he, Alois, was growing older, and therefore weaker.

Sooner or later, the balance would equal up and then the world would see.

That would be *Der Tag* all right.

Oh yes it would!

Adolf walked on quickly, trembling with rage, through the darkening village street, hands stuffed in his jacket-pockets, no cap on his head, knowing he was breaking two laws. One, a man never walked with his hands in his pockets, it was unmilitary. Two, a gentleman never went outdoors without a hat. Or, in the case of a peasant, a cap or beret. He didn't care. He wasn't a peasant – by God, no! He wasn't a gentleman, either. An artist shouldn't care about such things. An artist had to live his own life, free of all the stupid rules invented by ridiculous people like his father!

He wished his father was dead.

He wished it daily.

He wished his father dead when he heard the grunting noises of sex from the next bedroom, at night. He wished his father dead when the old man shouted at his mother so violently that she trembled – literally, from head to foot. He wished the old man dead for his uncaring treatment of little Paula, who was slow but surely not retarded, not an idiot or anything like that. He wished his father dead because with Alois in the way he could see no possible realisation of his dreams. He had wished his father dead many times before, but this night he wished it with a savagery and urgency that were new; and a hopelessness and frustration that were old, as old as his hopes and dreams of being an artist. Ever since his twelfth birthday, a lifetime!

Adolf kicked a stone with vigour towards the Inn which, as he passed it, rocked with the beery male laughter that so symbolised life in the village. Back-breaking work. Ignorance. Drink. Squalor. Noise and more noise. That was the Waldviertal. That was where his own roots lay, not even here in Leonding.

He walked on, bitterly pondering. Yes, he wished his father dead: that was certain. He also wished a lot of other people were dead, the world would be better off without them! People like the nincompoop pedagogues at the Realschule in Linz. Apart from Herr Poetsch, obviously. He was fine. The only good thing was that Adolf's time at school would pass. If he had any say in the matter, he would not attend the Realschule or any other school, ever again. The Academy of Fine Arts in Vienna, that would be different, a step towards the dream; but no more time wasted studying subjects that did not interest him: mathematics; science; algebra. All that was over for him, he swore it was! The only thing that stood in his way was the iron will of his father, Alois Hitler, or Schickelgruber, as some of the villagers still called him behind his back.

Well, he, Adolf Hitler, could have an iron will, too.

If that was what it took, he would have it.

So, the Realschule would inevitably go from his life, with the passage of time. Pappi was different. He was as enduring as the unlovely cottages, bare blocks of stone, that lined the village street, fit only to keep out winter snow and summer heat, nothing beautiful about them at all. Sometimes, giant trees grew around them and softened their outline; but they were mostly durable hovels for peasants who did not care how they lived, who saw nothing of the beauty of art or architecture. Well, why would they need it, all they ever did was scrape a harsh living in the potato-and-beet-fields. The soil hereabouts was not good, it never had been, which was why new people did not come into the place. They went where the farming was easier and the welcome warmer. Strangers were not received hospitably, anything but. Scowls and silence were all they could expect. The farming community was close and profoundly inbred, cousin marrying cousin, sister marrying half-brother, in the old days. Centuries and centuries of it. It could not be good. That much showed in the number of mental defectives to be seen in the streets of every village. These village idiots, protected by the insane Commandment (Thou Shalt Not Kill), were a drain on many a homestead's resources. Yet, the creatures were often fussed over and loved, mostly by the women. The men joked with them, occasionally played lewd jokes on them. Adolf knew these thoughts were not fashionable. Liberalism had been 'in' an artistic circles all over Europe (or so Herr Poetsch said) since the French Revolution. Things like pacifism were popular now, in these 'foreign artistic circles'. Herr Poetsch's lip curled when he said the words.

'Foreign artistic circles' meant French, possibly Russian, since the Russian aristocracy was Frenchified anyway. Certainly, un-German. The taking of life, in these circles, has frowned upon, even the life of a huge-headed idiot, who had to be fed and have his arse wiped by another. It was all very puzzling, the artistic world to which he aspired. Adolf wanted to be a painter, an artist, to do in paint for Germany what the great Richard Wagner had done for Germany in music: to design an opera-house perhaps, in which the great man's music could be heard. Not one like the one in Linz, which was a monstrosity really, but something new and grand, to go with the aspirations of a Greater Germany, soon to be the most powerful country of Europe. Or so Herr Poetsch prophesied. A magnificent amphitheatre possibly, on a grand scale but as German as the ancient theatre at Delphi was Greek? Adolf's mind reeled at the thought, the burning hatred and rage momentarily forgotten. These ambitions he held to himself, which was wise of him, because he knew they would be laughed at in the Realschule or anywhere in the village, where all people did was talk to each other about the quality of the pigshit they were spreading on their crops.

'The Waldviertal – where our student Adolf's forebears come from – is a backward track of agricultural land, hard by Linz and the river Inn, that has not changed in a thousand years,' had declared Herr Poetsch, in a dry and ironic tone, as he peered sternly over his pince-nez at Adolf's classmates, sitting up at attention, arms folded as they were required to do while he instructed them. This posture was only relaxed when they were actually writing something. Even then, the pupils had to hold their pens so that Herr Poetsch could see 'air' through the arch of their fingers. Any boy whose hand had slumped sideways received a sharp blow to the head or the back of the neck. Herr Poetsch was no stricter a disciplinarian than any other master at the Realschule. He simply expected order and he got it because disorder was unthinkable, to both master and pupil.

Herr Poetsch had given a dry cough and looked directly at Adolf, his favourite pupil (he was the only master in the Realschule who felt like that about Adolf), and said, 'And some of the inhabitants of the Waldviertal have not changed in that same thousand years, either. Not so as one would notice.'

Nobody in the form laughed except Adolf.

The rest of the class turned round, scandalised, fully expecting a swift and stern retribution. Any boy who laughed – actually laughed – during a lesson could expect the leather strap to wrap around his hand six times at least. Possibly, six times across his bare arse. Astonishingly, none of that happened. Adolf was laughing (and Adolf Hitler never laughed, at anything) and so was Herr Poetsch. So the whole class laughed too, which Herr Poetsch thought too much of a good thing, and snapped 'Silence!' in a stern voice. And so, as was proper, there was instant silence.

The boys of the form took to calling Adolf 'Teacher's Pet' for a while, but they all knew that whatever Adolf Hitler was, he was not a teacher's pet. He disliked all the other masters, called them things like 'disgusting ignoramuses' or 'congenital idiots', scandalising even the bravest boys in the school. Adolf had a command of the German language denied to any of them; but he did not try to do anything with it, even at examination time. He simply sat at his desk at the back of the schoolroom, a fixed smile of contempt on his face, as if the schoolmasters were indeed 'congenital idiots' and had nothing whatever to teach him.

He was respected at the Realschule for that.

But he was a loner.

He took part in no games.

He had no friends.

Not even a special pal.

Adolf had no interest, either, in girls or in the faded pornographic photographs (mainly the property of older brothers), passed around at the back of the school latrines. Some of the boys even masturbated, in pairs, while others held the photographs where they could be seen. The first boy to come won. Adolf would have none of that.

For the very good and shaming reason – if nothing else! – that he only had one testicle. The other had never dropped. It was, he supposed, still inside his body. Mutti had always reassured him, as a very small boy, that he was as real a *mensch* as any of the other boys. Adolf had, nonetheless, developed a system of hiding the fact. Once he learned that people smiled or even laughed, upon discovering the oddity, as had a crowd of curious boys at his primary school, pointing at his willy, crying out in delight and jostling to *look*, he had taken evasive action. He never undressed in the school washroom or changing rooms. He rarely bathed in the river Inn at Linz, as some of his schoolfellows did, in the boiling days of summer; and, if he did, he swam alone. Nobody in the family ever alluded to the shaming lack, but Adolf was sure his married half-sister Angi knew, from the way she looked at him: with sympathy, even pity.

So Adolf walked alone, for that very particular reason, amongst others. To his classmates, he seemed interested only in art and old buildings. They could not pretend to understand it. He had even been seen sketching outside the Linz Opera House, drawing-block on his knee. Strangely, this gained him respect at the Realschule. Also, he was known to have a stern father like most of the boys and to defy him which few boys ever did.

Adolf knew all that and didn't care, one way or the other, what they thought about him. He didn't want the things they yearned and worked for: girls, jobs, a so-called good time, dancing and drinking. *Pappi* had had all that, and look at him! As for himself, he would never, ever, *work* at an ordinary job, particularly that of a civil servant, the last refuge of the contemptible time-serving jobsworths of the town. He would rather starve than work at a job.

He was an artist.

He would live as an artist.

Go to bed when he liked.

Get up when he liked.

It was all very simple.

Nothing stood in the way of it but his father. And Adolf could, try as he might, see no way – yet! – around that.

But he would not bend the knee.

He would not take the Civil Service Examination. Like his disgraced half-brother, Alois, rumoured to be held in prison for theft, he would run away from home first.

Sitting on the stile in the darkening gloom, Adolf day-dreamed that one day he would live like an artist, a German artist on the streets of Linz or even Vienna, a city where he had never been but longed to go, for there were to be found other artistic people, who sat in the cafés and talked about important things, like a Greater Germany or Art or, for all he knew, both at the same time. For Adolf did not see why a man should not be a German and an artist at the same time. He did not see, for instance, why a German artist should preen and posture about the cafés in the foolishly romantic way that seemed to be the only accepted mode for an artistic person – dressed as a workman, like Van Gogh, or in a velvet cloak like the little *mensch* Lautrec. A German artist need not make a fool of himself in that way. Van Gogh and Gauguin were names he had read in an arts magazine in the public library in Linz. These people did not sound quite sane, to Adolf. One had cut off his ear, and was certainly certifiable. The other had run away to the South Seas to paint naked savages. That was not sane behaviour.

No German artist should do that kind of thing to prove his seriousness. The proper subject for a German artist was surely Germany itself? By Germany, Adolf meant *Gross Deutschland*, Austria and Germany together. The Austrians had a name for being fickle and fun-loving, and Adolf distanced himself from that. Herr Poetsch said the Austrians suffered from the epidemic disease of *schlumperei* – laziness, indolence, day-dreaming. Adolf supposed he suffered from it, too. He hated to get up in the morning and he certainly had a tendency to day-dream. He would strive, as time went by, to be more Germanic, more military, more decisive in his behaviour. That was the way forward, for the nation as well as for himself. His father – at the *thought* of the old man he was almost physically sick with hatred! – had once held a post in the customs office on the German side of the river Inn, and Adolf had gone for two years to a German school. Ever since then he had regarded everything German with respect and admiration. The Germans were hard, military, profoundly sure of themselves, and certain that the future was theirs, once the Austro-Hungarian Empire of old Franz Josef came to see that they were all one nation.

Herr Poetsch said it was simply a matter of time. Austria was old and tired. Germany, led by Prussia, was young and vital. Everything Austrian was decadent, everything German was vigorous. Even the German artists, musicians, and writers were superior. Many of the Austrian writers and musicians themselves were not Austrian at all, but Jews. This was a word Herr Poetsch said in a particularly knowing and disagreeable way. Herr Poetsch said there were thousands of them in Vienna. Herr Poetsch also disapproved of Czechs and Romanians and Poles and other foreigners, and of the French (Germany's mortal enemies) naturally. Adolf knew no people of those nationalities. Yet the word Jew struck a strange, disturbing chord. He had heard it used, often, he was sure, in his early childhood. It was a dim memory and he could not be sure he remembered it properly. But it had stayed with him because of the *emotion* with which it was charged. The way the word had been spoken was like a slap across the face. But that was an old forgotten story, of no relevance now. What mattered was how to become an artist, like Richard Wagner! The great composer was not long dead, but he was already revered throughout Europe. 'Not just a musician but a musical dramatist,' Adolf had read in the obituary notice. 'Herr Wagner presented a New Art Form, a verbal drama with a Musical Structure . . . A Source of New Music in Our Time . . . and all of his Art was indelibly *German* . . .'

Adolf sighed. To have such things written about your work! Truly, it would be a great honour even to design the opera-house in which Wagner's music could be heard. He wondered if Wagner had ever felt like running away from home? Somehow, he did not think it likely. Great artists did not sell their work in the street, as he was almost prepared to do. Anyway, it might never come to that. Perhaps *Mutti* would prevail on his father, somehow or other? But how? She had no power over him in the bedchamber. Only the whores of the stables and barns had that, and none of them for long. Just the time it took to fuck them. Even a girl named Thelka, from somewhere in the Waldviertal, had, years ago, been unable to stop Alois marrying his first wife, Anna Glass, a woman of fifty, and Thelka had been pregnant! Anna had money, and Alois knew on which side his bread was buttered. Anna was dead of the consumption four years later, and his father had another young girl, a servant at the Inn, Franziska, pregnant, and had to marry her. And then consumption got her, too. Now his mother, first debauched, as far as Adolf could work out, by Alois when she was sixteen and working as a maid in his house. Alois was a brutal and elemental old man, and nothing could alter him.

A feeling of deep gloom came over Adolf.

His feelings of rage turned to self-pity.

He contemplated suicide. Not for the first time.

If necessary he would do it, he told himself. If people persisted in frustrating him, and persecuting him, he would do it.

How? he asked himself. By what method?

For God's sake, did it matter *how?*

He would do it, and that was all.

The idea of death did not frighten Adolf.

It never had and it never would.

An hour later Adolf returned, warily, to the house. He had walked round and round the village to pass the time, but now it was dark and he expected the house to be in darkness. Yet all the lights were on. He found his mother sitting in the scullery, in tears. Poor little Paula was crying. The Innkeeper, fat Herr Doetz, was standing, his hat in his hands and an apology on his lips.

'It wasn't what he drank, good Frau,' he was explaining, his pop-eyes wide in sorrow and shock. 'Only his usual glass or two of cognac.'

More like six or seven, thought Adolf, wondering: had the old swine been carried home drunk, or what?

'Not my fault! Or anybody's fault! He was laughing and joking one minute, and the next minute he was on the *floor* . . .'

Herr Doetz looked imploringly around at them all, turning his hat awkwardly in his hands.

Adolf looked from his mother to his sister to Herr Doetz, and asked: 'What has happened? Is my father ill?'

Herr Doetz shook his head.

Adolf stared at him, half-fearing, half-hoping.

'Dead,' declared Herr Doetz. 'Just like that!' He snapped his fingers, then quickly crossed himself. 'A good way to go, if a man has to go.'

Adolf felt nothing at all.

Except a vast feeling of relief.

He was free.

IV

KLARA sat in her apartment at Humboldtstrasse 31, thinking sadly that she should *never* have allowed Adolf to talk her into moving to Linz, and looked anxiously at her beloved son.

'You still do not have your School-leaving Certificate, Adolf. Will the Academy take you without it?'

Her tone was interrogatory but her look was, despite her misery, admiring. Adolf was quite the man now, sixteen years old and growing a small tooth-brush moustache. Adolf had spent the two years since *Pappi*'s death at school in Steyr, but he had emerged with no extra qualifications. He did not seem to care about such things.

'I have enough, Mutti.' He sounded, as usual, very confident. His pepper-and-salt suit (new, bought for his recent trip to Vienna) hung loosely on his thin frame, and the hard white starched collar was impeccable. Klara had dipped it into the boiling starch herself. His shirt was of good blue cotton and his shoes gleamed. Klara had cleaned them that morning, as she always did. He carried an ebony walking-stick with an ivory top, and a blue silk handkerchief peeped from his breast pocket. His hair was parted slightly to one side now that he despaired of getting the desired central parting to stay in place; his hands, as usual, were meticulously clean. His eyes looked too blue and bright for his pale cheeks. Too pale, Klara thought with a pang of fear, for a boy his age but he read and sketched and painted far too much, long into the night, now he had a room of his own and did not have to share with Paula. At least his father's death had given him the freedom to work in his own room. Klara was forbidden to clean, or even touch it.

'*Mutti*, the professors at the Academy will recognise good work when they see it. Have no fear.' Adolf sat down for a moment but he was soon up again, walking around the small, shabby room as he talked. A come-down after having her own house, this place, Klara thought, only half-listening to Adolf's words. In Leonding, she'd had a garden, too. And neighbours she knew, even if she didn't always approve of them. Here, in this city, she was alone. She forced her attention back to Adolf's words.

'I intend to get a portfolio of work together and apply for entrance to the Academy for the next semester.' As usual, these days, he *told* Klara what he intended to do. He did not consult her or ask her opinion. Also, he seemed to think that her widow's pension (half of Alois's pension) was a bank on which he could draw forever. In truth, they were near the poverty-line now, because the widow's pension was designed for the widow's upkeep only, and she had both Adolf and Paula to provide for. All that she had, besides the pension, were the few hundred Kroner savings. Alois had not been a saver. Adolf was the same. He regarded money as something to spend.

Yet Adolf was a good boy in many ways, and he had not in the end hated his father, had he? Adolf had wept at the funeral.

Raubal, his half-sister Angi's husband, had said drunkenly afterwards, in the flower-filled house, that the tears were of gratitude, not grief. Angi had been angry with Raubal over that remark, but Raubal had not taken it back. He did not like the boy, Klara knew. 'Left school now, almost a year, still loafing, as far as I can see,' Raubal had said on his last visit, glass in hand as usual. 'All he does is read library books and draw his silly sketches. And he's living in cuckoo-land. He'll never get in the Academy without a School-leaving Certificate. Not a hope.'

Those words (said months ago) had stuck in Klara's mind because of the certainty with which Raubal had spoken them. Raubal was no fool, even if he was a drunken sot on occasion. Like Adolf's father, Raubal was a customs officer. He'd passed his Examinations. He was a responsible man in a responsible post, and his words had to be heeded, even if Adolf's half-sister, the pretty Angi, no longer loved him. If she ever had, which Klara doubted. Angi had been introduced to Raubal by her father. They had worked together, that was to say Raubal had been Alois's trainee. One thing had led to another and Angi was now safely married and living in Vienna with her husband. Adolf had just returned that very day from Vienna, not knowing that Raubal had written to his mother-in-law repeating what he had said to her face, months before ... *"All Adolf has done, in all the time he has been in Vienna staying with his half-sister and myself is visit libraries, art galleries and the opera house, as if he is a young person of aristocratic station and unlimited means. He does not rise in the morning until long after I have left for my work. He reads and draws long into the night, even when he has returned late from his evening's entertainment. He is not particularly pleasant to either his half-sister or myself and gives himself many airs and graces far above his station or, for that matter, his educational attainments. The way he talks one would suppose him a professor, at the very least. I fear for him, unless he returns to school for at least one more term, obtains his School-leaving Certificate and then applies for the Customs Examination, where his father's name and even mine may help him. My advice, Mutti, is to stop giving him any more money and tell him what he must do. I am not his father but I have taken it upon myself to write to Herr Milch who has replied, telling me the job as apprentice in Linz is still open. Like Adolf's father before him, I would confront the boy with the stark choice. Study – or the bakery!"*

The letter was signed, *"Yours respectfully, Raubal."* He had added a postscript: *"I have told Adolf nothing of all this. He was after all a guest."*

Klara felt the letter, received that very morning, burning a hole in her apron pocket. She tried to concentrate on what Adolf was saying. By now, he was walking more quickly around the room, fit to wear out the carpet, which was nearly threadbare, anyway. It almost gave her one of her headaches to watch him. He did not speak as a boy who lived in a two-roomed apartment, with two beds in the living-room (the shame of it!) so that he could have (as the man of the family) the one small bedroom to himself. No. He spoke as if he was a bourgeois, a man of the middle-class.

Adolf was saying: 'Once I am accepted into the Academy, *Mutti*, I will find a room, if possible with a view of the Danube! Oh, *Mutti*, you cannot imagine what a beautiful city Vienna *is*! Such buildings! Such architecture! Of course, there is poverty and dirt, much more than here in Linz, but Linz is really just a provincial town, while Vienna is cosmopolitan, a centre of art and music and painting –'

'Adolf!' Klara could bear it no more. 'I had a letter from Angi's husband.'

The retort was instant: 'That philistine! All he does every evening is sit and get drunk. I don't know why Angi stays with him!'

Klara was shocked. 'She stays with him because he's her husband!'

'Even so,' said Adolf, 'there should be a dispensation for women who find their husbands unsatisfactory. The divorce laws are too strict. But then the Church, not the State, decides them, so of course they would be. The Catholic Church wants everything to stay the same for ever and ever.'

'Adolf! Such words are blasphemous!'

Adolf was instantly at her side on the horsehair sofa. 'Now, Mutti, all I'm saying is: things can be made better,' adding mischievously, 'You know, you could improve *this* place by getting rid of Pappi's picture?' He indicated the oil-painting of his father, in his full-dress uniform, that hung on the wall. 'Or those foul old pipes! I don't know why you keep them!'

Klara looked at him in dismay. She never knew when he was joking. The painting and the pipes were all she had left of Alois. This place was so small. She'd tried to make a home of it. Then she saw he was smiling.

'Oh *you*! You tease me?'

'Of course, Mutti, of course I only tease you.'

Klara closed her eyes. Poor dear Adolf. She feared for him. She had thought he would die the previous winter, with his lung infection. She had felt sure it was the dreaded consumption. The doctor had pondered: 'Sometimes the infection stops at a patch, doesn't go further. A steam-kettle, good light food, milk puddings, beef-tea, and bed-rest!'

Mutti had given Adolf all those things, through the fever and the coughing. Night after night at his side, sitting sleepless on a hard chair in the bedroom upstairs, changing his nightshirt when the one he wore became soaked with perspiration. Klara used the steam-kettle day and night, so that the vapour filled the bedroom and gave Adolf moist air to breathe. She could have lost him then. If that had happened, and it could have, so easily, what would she have had left to live for?

Nothing. Adolf was her life.

If he said he would get into the Academy then maybe he could. She had done a mother's duty and put Raubal's point to him. He had rejected it, and he was, Raubal must remember, the only *man* left in the family. His opinion counted, although he was not yet of age. That was the custom. And the common law, by which everybody lived.

Adolf was a man and must make his own decisions.

Yet Klara, like Raubal, feared for him.

But it was no use fearing. She must help all she could.

'You really think you will get into the Academy?'

Adolf stood up, and took a deep breath. He stared out of the window, at the blank brick wall of the apartments opposite.

'Let there be no doubt of it,' he said. 'It is all a matter of Will.' He was silent a long moment. 'And I have the Will, *Mutti*.'

Something in his voice made her look at him more closely. Raubal said this boy was a wastrel, a slacker: but he did not sound like one at that moment. He sounded more like . . . Klara could not exactly think what – a Master, possibly? Yes, that was it. Not a feeble artist sort of person. Somebody who was in charge of something. But not a man selling goods or making money. Something more. The only type of man she could think of when he spoke with that kind of dogmatic certainty was a priest.

Like a priest, she thought, looking at him in awe.

Adolf left the apartment with a light step. He had disposed of that treacherous lickspittle, his brother-in-law Raubal, for the time being at least: but he must never relax. He knew that Klara was not as enthusiastic about his plans for the future as she had been in Leonding, when she had his father to defy. In Linz, away from her own house, she had lost whatever authority and certainty she had ever possessed, and it was now up to him, as the man, to determine how things should go, not Herr Civil Servant Raubal, thank you very much! Adolf had seen about enough of Herr Raubal lording it over Angi, drinking himself silly on schnapps most nights, stumbling to bed drunk, pulling Angi after him, into the bedroom, his eyes on Adolf, sitting in the chair, reading a book, laughing at him, and Angi laughing, too. Most women were good only for the bedroom or the kitchen. It was ridiculous to expect anything else. As his father had so truly said, they were with the moon.

Adolf supposed that educated women of the upper class – the sort one saw walking into the Sacher Hotel, covered in furs and carrying tiny pomeranian dogs, or languishing in the boxes at the Linz Opera House – were surely different creatures from the working-class women like his mother, who were all that he knew. These women would surely be able to carry on a conversation about politics or art with the men in their lives? Otherwise, why would the men tolerate them and their expensive ways? It surely could not be for sex alone, for sex could be had, easily enough, at the many discreet brothels in the city. Adolf had never visited a brothel, and doubted if he ever would. He did not relish the idea of some curious whore examining his single testicle and even (the idea appalled him) laughing at the sight, as the children in the primary school had laughed. Perhaps all women were much the same, frivolous and foolish and born to be flattered, as, God help him, he flattered *Mutti*. Yet Mutti was simple and good, and the women in the boxes at the opera were – or *looked* – another breed, with their blonde hair carefully dressed, and their velvet gowns, and ropes of pearls thick around their throats. From time to time he noted them looking at him over the tops of their fans. His friend Gustl would point out that this was happening, but Adolf ignored his amused glances and sometimes harshly shushed Gustl to silence. He was at the opera to listen to the music, not to flirt with rich women; but he always took back the reprimand with a smile.

For Gustl was his friend, his only friend. Adolf's step lightened as he walked along the street, satchel over his shoulder. One or two passers-by smiled at him, taking him for a student. A group of four young Austrian army officers, in perfect step, in shakos and braid and trailing sabres, stared at him insolently and forced him to step aside and make room for them. Insolent creatures, Adolf fumed to himself, sniggering birdbrains every one, mechanical puppets on a string, waiting for the next order. The Austrian Empire was in a mess, there was no doubt of that.

Its time was over, it had gone on far too long. It was time that Austria and Germany became one, with the Prussians in charge. Then Europe would see some changes.

He would tell Gustl about these so-called military men, pour out his scorn for them. Adolf had first met Gustl – short for August – at a performance of *Lohengrin* at the Opera House in Linz. They had both been standing because they could not afford the price of a seat, and got into conversation about the production. Gustl was friendly, an ordinary young artisan, and yet not exactly ordinary, for he loved music and played it, too, and how many workers did that? He was quiet and humorous, but very reserved, but he and Adolf had hit it off from the start. A few words about the performance (Adolf had not liked it much, although it was his favourite opera) and then they were out in the cool evening streets, walking together like two old friends, down the Landstrasse. Adolf did most of the talking. Gustl was obviously in awe of him, but Adolf did not mind that. Gustl had been surprised when he learned Adolf wasn't a student, and more surprised – astonished even – when he heard that Adolf followed no trade or profession, and no longer attended school. An amazing state of affairs for any young man to be in! For himself, Gustl confessed, with some shame, he worked for his father in the upholstery shop – the smell Adolf could doubtless detect from his hands was glue. It was impossible to get rid of it.

Adolf did not deny he could smell the foul glue, which was made from the skins and hoofs of animals and always retained a fleshy odour.

He simply nodded and forgot about it.

This made Gustl happy. Most people laughed.

Adolf, he soon found, had very little sense of humour. Irony, of course; but not humour.

Together, that first evening, almost a year ago now, the young men had walked and talked (or rather Adolf talked) about the opera they had just seen. Gustl knew his music – it was the only thing in the world he cared about – but he was so astonished by the torrent of words that came from his new-found friend that he simply listened, struck dumb.

Adolf had told him, waving his arms as they walked: 'Whenever I listen to Wagner I feel a different man! I feel intoxicated, drunk on that divine music! Wagner alone takes me back to the blissful times of German antiquity, to the Ideal World, as it must have been then, as in the times of the Teutonic Knights! For me, there is only Wagner! Others I can listen to, even enjoy, but to me Wagner contains everything I hold dear, everything I *desire* . . .'

Adolf had seen at once he had an audience in Gustl and had talked on in the same way, impressing him with his erudition, but most of all with his opinions, which brooked no argument or contradiction, even when Gustl, moved by something dismissive Adolf had said about Verdi, interposed, 'What about *Aida*?'

'*Aida*? Very well. *Aida* is a good piece.'

Adolf kept walking, still talking, so loudly and intensely that passersby, strolling in the cool evening air, would look sharply towards him, then, realising that what he was talking about was *music*, would smile to one another and walk on. Then Adolf added, or rather shouted, 'But what about *Traviata, Rigoletto, Trovatore*? Nothing but ice-cream confections! No body, no philosophy, unlike the divine Wagner!' He added, sternly, 'And what ridiculous stories! What would those Italians do without their daggers?'

At this, Gustl laughed loudly, and Adolf looked suprised, then pleased, and they walked on, arm in arm, two firm friends from that day. Adolf had not seen his friend for weeks, since he had been in Vienna, and wondered how Gustl was getting on without him? Gustl had real talent, he played the viola with genuine warmth and feeling, but he lacked ambition and the character to confront his father and demand his freedom from the upholstery shop. Adolf had told him many times that he should try for the Music Academy in Vienna, as he himself would certainly try for Art – try, he would succeed! Gustl, of course, had his School-leaving Certificate, as he had not, but alas he had no backbone, no real belief in himself; and also, like most Austrian boys, he was afraid of his father. Something, Adolf thought, will have to be done about poor Gustl. Adolf loped on. His long stride was tireless, since walking was the only exercise he ever took, covering the ground eagerly, so ready was he to tell his friend of all that he had seen and heard in Vienna: the operas, the music, the crowds in the Prater, the different peoples, of all races – but all belonging to the vast Austrian Empire – to be seen on every boulevard. Studious Czechs; dark Ruthenians; Magyars, some still in peasant dress, as if they had just walked off their farms, others uneasy in cheap city clothes, already assimilated into the life of one of the great cities of the world. Poles, too, slant-eyes showing their Slavic origins; Croats and Slovenes; Italians and poor Galician Jews with dreadlocks, many of them selling trinkets in the streets from wooden trays hung about their necks. There was everything to see in Vienna, riches and poverty, beauty and ugliness. He had hardly begun to explore it before it was time to come home. Mostly, he had walked around looking at the buildings, the Vienna Opera House, the Parliament Buildings, everything so Gothic and grand. His mind reeled at the thought of it all, all there, waiting for him to explore.

Of one thing Adolf was certain.

Vienna was where he must go, and soon.

The city had everything he needed.

He would not wait until the examination for the Academy of Fine Art. He would simply go!

The idea thrilled through him.

But the *money*?

Adolf strode on, crossing the streets, ignoring the cabbies, shouting at them to get out of the way. *Mutti* could be talked round, he was sure of it. No staying with Angi and Raubal this time. That was not to be thought of. He would find somewhere of his own, a decent room. He would be all alone, nobody to answer to, to explore that rich, wondrous city.

Yet, he needed a friend, one friend. Everybody needed one friend. He needed Gustl.

Adolf turned down a narrow, cobbled alley, and went into the upholsterer's shop. It was six o'clock in the evening but the workmen were still busily engaged, as if it were six in the morning, the hour at which they had started work. Clouds of choking dust rose from the soiled old couches and armchairs and mattresses they rent asunder and repaired. The men were stripped down to their singlets and trousers and long soiled aprons, but all were wearing some form of headgear, mostly caps. One or two had large, coloured handkerchiefs tied around their faces to protect them from the dust of the confined workshop. Space was expensive in the centre of Linz, and eight men worked in the place, no larger than a living-room. The dust was so thick that Adolf almost gagged. Why couldn't somebody devise a way of cleaning mattresses and couches and chairs *in situ*, instead of waiting until they had accumulated the dust of years? Gustl had told him that upholsterers had short lives. Most of them died in their thirties or forties, because of the dust. They breathed it in every minute of every hour of every working day, six days a week.

'Adolf, you're back!'

Gustl was looking up from his work, ripping off the stained cover of an old horsehair mattress – stained with what, the blood of childbirth? Adolf shuddered. Gustl threw down his tools and clapped Adolf on the back and rushed him out into the cobbled alley, where Adolf could breathe again. Even out there Adolf could smell the pungent odour of the glue, which stuck to his friend's face, hair and bare forearms, drying into a hard white film that sometimes, so Gustl told him, took the skin away with it when it was peeled off.

But now here was Gustl, at last, his young, frank face beaming at the sheer pleasure of seeing his friend again.

'Adolf! You're early! I have to go home and change!'

'These workmen should have better conditions,' said Adolf. 'It is a disgrace to a civilised nation that men should work in such places. They should have a place, also, to eat their sandwiches, instead of just sitting down and eating them in all that dust.' Adolf stepped back onto the pavement as a gig rushed by, the horses foaming at the whip as the driver, in rusty top-hat and frockcoat, swore ritually at them.

'The workmen are lucky to have lunch, bread and sausage is all they bring,' said Gustl. 'But they are better off than many. Many have no work, Adolf. The men do not complain.'

'No,' said Adolf, bitterly, 'because they dare not. Your father pays them a pittance. It is wrong. You know I have told him so?'

Gustl sighed. 'Don't you understand, Adolf, my father is very little better off than his men. Look at him in there, he works alongside them. Same conditions, same dust.'

'And you?' asked Adolf. 'Do you intend to stay here until your lungs rot of the dust?'

'I don't know,' said Gustl, sadly. Sometimes his friend depressed him. It was complaints, always complaints. 'My father can't do without me. And I must work.' Greatly daring, he added, 'Unlike some people, who are luckier than I am!'

Adolf's thin face darkened. Gustl sighed again. He should really know better by now. His friend had no sense of humour, did not see a joke, ever. In many ways it was difficult, but in others quite admirable. 'Anyway,' Gustl added quickly, 'I got your postcards, they were wonderful! You seem to have had the time of your life in Vienna?'

Adolf nodded. 'I saw a lot of excellent examples of architecture. It is indeed a magnificent city, but there's something rotten about it, too. Something ... undisciplined. We Austrians are letting too many foreigners into the country, and they mostly head for Vienna. All any of them need is a few kroner and we let them in. If you think unemployment is bad in Linz, you should see Vienna. There are beggars at every street corner.' Adolf was about to add: prostitutes too, many of them under-age, he was sure, and therefore in blatant defiance of the law: but he did not say that, for Gustl might show interest in such a low and degrading phenomenon, and he did not wish to discuss it.

'I intend to go and live there as soon as I can,' he said.

Gustl stared at him. 'When?'

'When I reach an arrangement with *Mutti*.'

'Before the examination for the Academy?'

'Of course. Linz has very little more to offer me.'

Gustl's heart sank. He realised how much he depended on Adolf for friendship and support. Without him, Linz would indeed be a dull place and the upholstery shop a very prison. He was so struck down by the prospect that he simply said, miserably, 'I'll get my coat and you can

33

walk home with me. My mother might give us coffee and a sandwich.'

Adolf nodded, looking a little put-out that his news had not been more enthusiastically received. Gustl went to get his coat and came out with it slung over his shoulder. He looked every inch a workman, with the stains of the glue all over his shirt (he had taken off his filthy apron), and even his hair stank.

'This place is no good to you,' Adolf said, as they began to walk. 'You must leave it and come with me to Vienna, to study music!'

Gustl laughed out loud at the idea.

'Fat chance of that ever happening,' he said, wondering if his friend (so smart and neat and gentlemanly) ever felt ashamed of being seen in his company. If he did, he never showed any sign of it.

'Not a chance in hell,' Gustl repeated.

Adolf looked pensive. 'Let us see,' he said.

Gustl's mother gave them coffee and bread and sausage, and, when Adolf had gone to wash his hands at the kitchen sink, said in a whisper, 'What eyes your friend has!'

Gustl patted her hand and said, 'All the young girls say that about him, but I'm sorry, he isn't interested, Mutti!'

Gustl's mother coloured and took her hand away. 'What nonsense! I was just commenting, that's all.' And they both laughed and were still laughing when Adolf came back in. He looked at them suspiciously and Gustl remembered how wary Adolf was about other people. He felt that people were, mostly, enemies, whereas Gustl felt they were mostly friends. The only thing that worried Gustl about Adolf were his sudden, terrible rages. They could be about anything: but they were always personal, concerning some small slight, real or fancied. They were quite frightening to see. Adolf went white and shook violently, and his eyes grew huge. Gustl understood none of it. But Adolf was his friend, so he ignored it, as best he could.

Now, Adolf, very correctly, was thanking Gustl's mother for the food. 'You know, Frau Kubicek, you have a most talented son?'

'He plays his viola very well, I know,' said Frau Kubicek, a pretty, motherly woman. 'Is that what you mean?'

'Certainly,' said Adolf, as if he was Gustl's schoolmaster. 'It is a talent that should be nurtured, don't you think?'

'How?' asked Frau Kubicek, a realist.

'By tuition, naturally,' replied Adolf.

'He is already going once a week to Herr Frankel. Is that what you mean, Adolf?'

'That is certainly good.' He nodded, magisterially. 'But not enough.

34

He needs more, and better, tuition. Then who knows what he could be?'

Frau Kubicek glanced uneasily at her son. 'Adolf, my son works for his father. I cannot see that changing.'

'Perhaps not.' He picked up his satchel. 'We'll have to go now or there will be no light left,' he said to Gustl, who had hastily washed and changed into street clothes.

Gustl's mother called, down the stairs, 'Don't be late, will you, Adolf? Gustl has to go to work in the morning!'

Adolf stiffened, but he turned back and bowed slightly. 'We all have our work, good Frau.'

'Take no notice of my mother. She doesn't understand that you study so hard,' said Gustl, once they were out in the street, walking fast towards the Frienberg, their destination, an open parkland. There, Adolf had an open-air 'study', where he would read his books, sketch, write his poems and paint his water-colours. He spoke to Gustl about whatever he was currently reading, telling him of the particularly fine thought in the work, or criticising it when he found it wanting. Adolf's reading was catholic and seemed to have no plan, no direction. He had read the classical authors already, Gustl knew, and discoursed on them at length: Goethe's *Faust*; Schiller's *William Tell*; Dante's *Divine Comedy*.

Gustl had found all these hard work at school. He asked Adolf why he read such difficult, if elevating work? Was it just for the Art itself?

Adolf shook his head, the hank of hair falling over his eyes. 'These are great writers. They *change* the way people think. Look, for instance, at Goethe . . .' At that moment Adolf was approached by an elderly and destitute working-man, begging for bread, not an uncommon sight in Linz, or any other large town in Austria.

'Meinherren, I have lost my job and have nowhere to sleep. I am sixty years old and nobody will hire me.' The old man stood at attention as he recited his litany, his workman's cap in his hand, his ragged clothing a testimony to the truth of his words. He had no teeth and his beard was a week old. 'I have not eaten for two days.'

Adolf would have walked on. Why hand out money one did not have to some tramp who would probably drink it anyway? Gustl fumbled in his pocket, found a few coins and put them in the old man's hand. He became aware of Adolf shouting: 'A man who all his life has worked for the State, as every working man in the States does, and has to beg his bread in the street, just because he's old! There should be a State pension for every elderly citizen!'

Gustl did not know whether he preferred this outburst to the dissection of Goethe's *Faust* he had just escaped. He wanted to hear about Vienna. 'Tell me about the Opera House? Is it as grand as people say?'

Adolf shrugged. 'There is a majesty about it. It is only when one is inside the place, listening to the music, when the mighty sounds flow through the hall, that a man feels the grandeur of it! If one can forget the dreadful gold and velvet which overlays the entire interior of the place, rather like some gigantic brothel!'

Adolf had never been in a brothel. Nor had Gustl.

'Which operas did you see?' asked Gustl.

'*Tristan, The Flying Dutchman* . . .' Adolf's voice rose, as he talked with fervour about the productions. When they reached the Frienberg they sat down on the grass and Adolf took from his satchel some of the paintings he had completed in Vienna. As usual, they were carefully drawn, but Gustl noticed Adolf had entirely dropped 'figures' from his work and now concentrated exclusively on buildings and architecture. He wondered if Adolf really cared as much about painting as he insisted he did, or whether his real bent lay with the look of things, of buildings and bridges? With the work of an architect, in fact? But to be an architect one needed specialist training, in a school of architecture, to learn (Gustl supposed) about such things as weights and stresses and building materials. Adolf had no interest in how anything worked. All he ever looked for was the broad outlines of a subject. The fiddling detail, the hard work of learning, the why and how of things, soon bored him. It was all very puzzling. Gustl looked at his friend and wondered, as he did, from time to time, what would be his eventual fate?

One thing was certain.

Adolf was no ordinary youth.

Sitting there, in his shirtsleeves, in the warmth of the evening sun, Gustl admired the passing pairs of girls, walking arm in arm, who studiously ignored Adolf and himself, but still walked close enough for them to see the glint of the sun on their golden hair (or what showed of it from under their straw hats), the shine of the sun on their bare forearms, the shape of their legs through the thin white cotten dresses they uniformly wore. Gustl sighed. It was no use proposing to Adolf that they pick up with a likely pair of girls. He would have been outraged at the idea. Gustl had once hinted at something of the sort and Adolf had responded fiercely. If Gustl wanted to waste his evenings and his own valuable time, already over-booked, for such empty-headed frivolity, then he should find himself another companion!

Gustl had never suggested it again and it occurred to him Adolf was a little shy of girls.

Anyway, what was the point?

These were respectable girls and even if they were picked up it would all end in coffee or lemonade at some café, and a lot of giggling and talk about nothing much. He had his Music and Adolf had his Art and there was plenty of time for girls, in the years ahead. They would never have their youth again, and as Adolf said, youth was the time to learn, to dare, to think for oneself, before the stultifying experience of marriage and family descended on a man. Not that Adolf was against marriage. It was simply, he said, not for him.

'Never?' Gustl had asked.

'Never,' said Adolf, firmly.

And with that Gustl had to be content.

For himself, all that was far in the future, but he had no doubt it was in the prospectus. Adolf was different, in that as in so many ways. Gustl knew he meant what he said. Adolf always meant what he said. Not, he had added, to Gustl's questioning frown, that he had anything against marriage as such. Marriage was a splendid institution and the Race could not go on without it. It should, indeed, be encouraged. He did not need it, that was all, never would. Gustl, on the other hand, probably would, sooner or later, and good luck to him!

Gustl had smiled and said no more. Adolf knew him better than he knew himself. He was an easy-going person, he supposed, a good listener, as, to be a friend of Adolf's, one needed to be. He remembered their first meetings together: Adolf's room at his mother's apartment, a choking wasteland of paper and cardboard models. Prominent was a cardboard facsimile, to scale, of the theatre he was designing and planning at the Mountain House on the Lichtenburg. There wasn't one, and why did Adolf think there ever could be a need for one, Gustl wondered? Adolf also had a plan, blueprints and all, painstakingly drawn, to rebuild the massive Bank of Upper Austria, sitting squat and untouchable in the Town Centre of Linz. Adolf was only concerned that his design should fit in with the remaining late-Gothic edifices around it. As far as Gustl could imagine, the Bank of Upper Austria would stand there for ever. Why should anybody want to tear it down?

Adolf said it was unsightly and a disgrace to the Provincial Capital of a great nation, which Linz was.

Adolf's ideas always involved *change*. Change was a constant factor in his life. He had shown Gustl a large sheaf of papers, drawings, estimates, suggestions, to change the entire face of the city of Linz! He had designed a new Concert Hall (the sketches and drawings were there, before the bemused eyes of Gustl) as were plans for an underground railway, of all things, to run from the suburbs into the centre of the City. At this, Gustl goggled. Linz was a busy provincial town but why did it need an underground railway? 'It will grow,' Adolf said, confidently, 'then it will need such transporation. You don't think it will remain this size for ever, do you? Have you looked at the latest population figures for Austria?'

Gustl hadn't but he nodded as if he had, and nodded again at Adolf's outline-plans for a mountain-railway to run all the way up to the Peak of the Lichtenburg!

'The ramblers and hikers need not walk all the way and be tired out before they get there! And the old will be able to see the magnificent views they can no longer climb up to see!'

Gustl had looked at Adolf as at a visionary – which he supposed Adolf was – and asked the obvious question, one that his practical father, the upholsterer, might have asked.

'How is all this going to happen?'

Adolf frowned, dismissively. 'It will happen. Depend on it. You will see it happen. It is inevitable!'

And the odd thing was, Gustl had believed him.

He still did.

As they lay on the grass, in the waning sunlight, Adolf spoke of his own plans. Adolf had given up his proposed sketching in favour of talk. It was a decision he often made, if he had an audience. 'I'm going to Vienna. I have decided you must come with me, so we must arrange that!'

'How do we do that?' asked Gustl, amused, shaking his head.

'I talk to your father,' said Adolf.

Gustl was at first alarmed. Then, he laughed. 'It will be like talking to the wall.'

'We shall see,' said Adolf.

Something in the look of him gave Gustl pause: these words were not uttered in jest. Adolf never spoke in jest. Gustl felt uneasy. Adolf was likely to stride in and make his own relationship with his father similar to the one Adolf had had with his own father. He didn't want that. Adolf had talked to him of violent scenes, often physical, between them. The last thing Gustl wanted was that kind of life. His father was kindly, if narrow-minded, and he didn't want to upset him.

'I don't think that would be a very good idea, Adolf.'

Adolf looked at him in surprise. 'Why, what harm can it do? He can only say no.'

And Gustl had to concede that there was truth in that.

'Don't blame me if he bites your head off,' he said, chewing on a piece of grass, and watching the girls walking in the sun in their cotton dresses.

'He won't do that,' Adolf said.

The next evening Adolf appeared at Gustl's apartment. He carried a bunch of assorted flowers for Gustl's mother, which she accepted with delight. Adolf refused food but accepted coffee, and had plainly timed his visit to coincide with the end of supper. A good time, thought Gustl admiringly. His father was in his armchair, replete with thick borsch, his pipe going well, his slippers on his feet, a cup of coffee in his hand. If there was ever a good time to talk to him, this was it. Somehow, Gustl knew that Adolf had taken all this into consideration, but he still had great foreboding about the outcome. There really wasn't any possibility that his father would allow him to go to Vienna. He needed Gustl in the upholstery shop. Then there was the money. The whole idea was something Gustl would never have put to his father. Adolf had asked him not to interrupt, but that was all. Gustl wondered, with a feeling of doom, how it would all work out.

As Frau Kubicek went out to the kitchen to put the flowers in a jar, Adolf began to speak. 'Herr Kubicek,' he began, 'do you feel you could, given the opportunity, have done better with your own life than you have? I don't mean in your personal life, in which you have plainly been blessed, but in your working life? Could you have done better, given the opportunity?'

Herr Kubicek was a pleasant but shrewd man. His cheeks were glowing now, from the food and the application of hot water and soap. His hair was still damp from the water he'd used to get rid of the accursed dust. He pondered Adolf's question, obviously regarding it as a hypothetical, if surprising, one.

'Few people in this life have the chance to use their full potential, Adolf.' He puffed at his pipe. 'I am no exception. Born in the right bed, I might be Prime Minister of the nation. I have had to just do the best I could, like most people I know.'

'Exactly,' pressed Adolf. 'The best you could? But you could have done better?'

'Yes,' said Herr Kubicek, thoughtfully. 'Of course.'

'Would you like Gustl to do better than the upholstery shop?'

Herr Kubicek was startled. 'Naturally. But how?'

'By going to Vienna with me.'

Adolf had lowered his voice, almost to a whisper. Gustl, who was used to hearing Adolf shout, was surprised. Adolf was using a tone of voice he had never heard before: soft, reasonable, almost seductive. Adolf's eyes, wide and unblinking, were on those of his father, and did not once waver. Herr Kubicek looked back into them and seemed to lose a litle of his certainty.

'To Vienna? To do what?' he asked, puzzled.

'Study music, of course. If Gustl had rich parents, there would be absolutely no question of what should happen to him. His talent on the viola is outstanding. His reading of music is beyond reproach. Ask his music teacher, Herr Frankel. He will tell you.'

Herr Kubicek shook his head like a bird-dog emerging from water. 'Herr Frankel has said nothing of this going to Vienna?'

'Only because he feels he would be putting an imposition upon you,' said Adolf smoothly. 'An imposition he feels you are financially unable to meet. Therefore, out of kindness, he says nothing.'

Gustl shifted, uneasily. Adolf was not being exactly truthful. He wasn't at all sure that Herr Frankel felt that at all. Herr Frankel had never suggested he go on to study at the Academy of Music in Vienna. Then again, he had to admit, Herr Frankel had not suggested that Gustl ought *not* to go to Vienna. So, in a way, Adolf was telling the truth, or anyway, he was not telling a direct lie.

Just the same, Gustl felt uneasy. He even opened his mouth to speak, but Adolf's eye was on him at once, and he fell silent.

Adolf talked on, with total confidence, as if he was Gustl's music-teacher himself: 'Make no mistake, Herr Kubicek, in Gustl you have an extremely talented son. If he were to go to Vienna, to try to gain admission to the Academy, and the Academy will not accept him, then nothing is lost. They will have decided, in their wisdom, that your son is not talented enough to qualify, to take his place with the very best young musicians the nation has to offer, and absolutely no disgrace in that, none at all. Many apply, few are chosen. The learned professors know which ones will go on to become musicians in the great orchestras, soloists, conductors even, and which will have to be content to teach. Either way, there is honour to be had. Gustl deserves a chance at that honour, just as much as I do in the different disciplines of art and architecture. He should, Herr Kubicek, have at least the same chance in life as I do. Anything less would be – I hesitate to say it, but I must – something of a disgrace, for talent wasted is a terrible thing, and in later years Gustl may – again I hesitate to say it, but I must – curse his ill-luck, curse even those who, in his anger, he will feel did not give him the chance to which his talent entitled him.'

Only then did Gustl notice that his mother had come into the room, the jar of flowers in her hand. She had obviously heard most of Adolf's words and had plainly been affected by them. She sat down, quiet and pensive, looking at Adolf.

Her husband, however, was made of sterner stuff, although the time it took him to reply told Gustl he had, too, been touched by Adolf's words. For himself, he felt Adolf's approach had been too direct, without subtlety. Yet the words had been uttered in that soft way that Gustl had never heard from Adolf before, and the very softness of them had obviously had an effect on both his parents.

Herr Kubicek had one damning card at his disposal and he played it at once. 'If all that is true, Adolf, and I don't deny it may be, what about the expense? What about my son, going away, leaving the business I have built up? It is there for him when I go.'

'If he lives to take it over,' Adolf said, still gently, his eyes finding Herr Kubicek's and never leaving them. 'You know as well as I do that the life of your workmen is short. Upholsterers live, on average, to the age of forty. You would surely want your son to live longer than that?'

'I have lived longer than that.' Herr Kubicek puffed on his pipe. 'He might, too.'

'I don't doubt it,' said Adolf, easily. 'But how much longer? And in what conditions? The work is hard and exacting, and only the strongest, like yourself, stand up to it.' Adolf sighed. 'Of course, if the money is all that matters, then Gustl has to fact the face that he will spend the rest of his life – what will be left of it – in the upholstery shop, and there's an end of the matter.'

Adolf closed his eyes as if exhausted and slumped back in his chair. Gustl felt quite alarmed for his friend; sweat stood out on his brow and he breathed shallowly.

'Are you all right, Adolf?' asked Frau Kubicek.

'I am fine,' said Adolf, wearily. 'Possibly a glass of water?'

'At once,' said Frau Kubicek, directing an accusing look at her husband, who avoided it and concentrated on tamping down the tobacco in his pipe, and frowning at it, in some perplexity.

Gustl could hear nothing but the soft tick of the clock on the mantel and the beating of his own heart. It was now that he realised how much he yearned for the chance to go to Vienna, how much he had denied the prompting of his own heart, never allowing himself to dream this could happen.

The silence was intolerable.

Frau Kubicek brought the glass of water to Adolf. He nodded his thanks, drained the glass and handed it back to Frau Kubicek. He closed his eyes.

The silence lengthened.

Frau Kubicek sat, where her husband could see her and stared at him, unblinkingly.

Herr Kubicek remained deep in thought for some time longer, contemplating his pipe. Then he looked up at Adolf and coughed and Adolf opened his eyes. 'I am anything but a rich man, but I am not poor either. And while I will be disappointed that Gustl will not take over my business when I go, I think I could afford to pay his fees and his keep in Vienna. The only thing I have to be sure of is that this is what Gustl wants for himself and that this is the only thing on earth he wants to do, and that he will be miserable doing anything else?'

Herr Kubicek turned to his son, with raised eyebrows, and waited.

Gustl could hear his mother's breathing step up a notch. Adolf was simply regarding him with a dreamy stare, as if he had just awakened from a dream.

'Father,' said Gustl, gently, 'it isn't that I dislike the upholstery shop. I had resigned myself to spending the rest of my life in it, or somewhere like it. But you have asked me a straight question and I can only give you a straight answer.' Gustl took a deep breath. 'Of course I want to go to Vienna, Pappi. I want it with all my heart.'

Herr Kubicek looked down, somewhat sadly, at his pipe. He sighed deeply but when he looked up he was smiling ruefully.

'Then there is no question of it.' Herr Kubicek nodded towards Adolf. 'As your young friend so rightly says, you must have your chance.' He looked at his wife and she was nodding, as tears ran down her cheek. 'You must go!'

Gustl sat there smiling at the world.

His mother put her arms around him.

Herr Kubicek blew his nose on a large linen handkerchief, stood up and shook hands with Adolf. He looked puzzled and bemused, yet exhilarated, as if something totally unexpected and spellbinding had happened to him.

For his part, Gustl embraced his father, tears in his eyes now (what the hell, even if he was a man, it wasn't every day you got your heart's desire!). But when he turned to thank Adolf, it was too late. His friend had collected his stick and was out of the door, with the protesting Frau Kubicek offering him more coffee and cake. At the door Adolf closed one eye. Gustl was shocked by that wink, but only momentarily, for after all it was only a wink and could mean anything.

Gustl shook his head. Adolf had rescued him. Adolf had given him a life. He would be eternally grateful.

Just the same, he could not help feeling that Adolf, too, had got what he wanted.

Gustl sat down thoughtfully, and shook his head.

He would never understand Adolf.

V

THAT Summer Adolf fell in love with Stephanie Schuster, the daughter of a State official, seventeen years old and still under the care of her widowed mother. Stephanie lived in the splendid middle-class suburb of Urfahr, had attended the Linz Gymnasium for Girls, and already matriculated. As such, Gustl reflected, she inhabited a different world from Adolf and himself.

Gustl watched Stephanie walk along the crowded Landstrasse, holding her satin parasol daintily with her right hand, and her skirt with her left, so that it did not – quite – brush the ground.

He wondered what Adolf was thinking about? Of course, she was blonde and slim and young, about their own age, but there was no possibility of either of them ever speaking to her.

For that, one needed an introduction.

For an introduction one needed a mutual friend.

Adolf and Stephanie had no such mutual friend.

Gustl would shrug his shoulders when Adolf gazed, cow-eyed, at the girl, as her mother, a few discreet paces away, talked to another lady of the middle-class, her eyes remaining implacably on Stephanie. The beloved object was making small talk with two extremely lustful but also extremely correct young lieutenants of the Army. There were always a few of these pompadoured wastrels (as Adolf called them) in Linz, and today was no exception.

Around the young lieutenants and the desired Stephanie the Sunday-afternoon strollers ebbed and flowed. Good burghers in stiff Sunday suits and stiffer collars, despite the oppressive heat, their good Fraus leaning heavily on their arms. The women's clothes swept the dust of the street, for to show even a glimpse of ankle was sexually shocking. The upper-arms, however, were often bare, and the decollatage sometimes worn low, especially in the evening. Breasts were not sexual objects in this age of constant childbirth and breast-feeding, so the lower limbs were the centre of all male fantasy. Neither Adolf nor Gustl had seen a girl's bare legs, nor did they expect to for some considerable time to come. Gustl sighed. Now that he was to follow Adolf to Vienna, he had hopes of somehow meeting a suitable girl, possibly a fellow-student, should he be accepted at the Academy of Music.

But all that was a dream, as yet.

It would happen though, and he had Adolf to thank for it. Gustl gazed anxiously at his friend. Everything Adolf did, he did with a frightening intensity. Whether it was reading a book, or working at one of his blueprints, Adolf seemed incapable of moderation. His latest scheme was to replace the statue of the Emperor, Franz Josef, in the Jagemaye-wald, with a 'Hall of Fame for all men who had performed Good Works for Upper Austria!' Adolf had even made up a model and a blueprint, working, as usual, long into the night to complete it.

'Why Linz?' he had asked Adolf, bemused.

'Because Linz is a city of antiquity! It has some of the finest Baroque buildings in Europe! The Cathedral is a wonder, there are three mon-astic churches, Capuchin, Urseline, Carmelite – but all that is old! We need the new! The Hall of Fame would be new!'

Gustl wondered how the lovely Stephanie, in her large-brimmed blue hat trimmed with imitation fruit, and her long, blue linen dress trailing the street, would feel about a speech like *that*? Like him, she probably never even saw the ancient beautiies of Linz, and cared not a jot for the history of the town she lived in.

Adolf said, 'Linz is a gem of the past, Gustl! The Empire still stretches from Poland to Hungary to the borders of Germany, but it is old, like Linz, and soft, like Linz, and it is in great danger of fading away, as Linz has, with its stagnant old one-man industries – like your father's upholstery shop! What good is the Empire to families living in one bug-ridden room in some of these rat-infested slums in the old town! We will change Linz.' When Gustl asked him when all this improvement would take place, Adolf had said, 'Never fear . . . You will live to see it.'

The boy who talks like that, Gustl thought, has not yet proven he is any different from anybody else. He has fallen in love with a girl he cannot have. Weary of accompanying Adolf on fruitless Sunday outings (this was the seventh, by his count), Gustl had a suggestion.

'We know one thing about Stephanie,' he said.

'And what is that?' asked Adolf, still gazing at the adored one, ten paces away.

'We know she dances. On various public occasions she will dance. We know that.'

'So?'

'So you learn to dance. Then you can approach her. Introduce yourself to her mother as Adolf Hitler, Academic Painter, and ask for the honour of a dance. What could be simpler?'

Adolf frowned. 'I'm not an Academic Painter yet.'

'You don't have to say that. You will be one, one day.'

Adolf shook his head. 'I'd have to substantiate it. Her mother would never accept any of that.'

'Very well. Learn to dance, ignore her Mama, and ask her direct. In a crowded ballroom, you might get away with it.'

'But I cannot learn to dance.'

'Why not? There are dancing academies galore. The whole nation is dance-mad,' mused Gustl.

'That is the trouble,' said Adolf, interested at once. 'This dancing craze is ridiculous. Great artists like Schubert wrote nothing but trifles for idiots to cavort to! Women in their hundreds swept along like crazed harlots by these ridiculous army officers and such!'

'Oh, I don't know,' protested Gustl. 'It's all harmless enough, surely?'

Gustl wished Adolf would move on. He felt foolish and conspicuous standing on the street-corner in his best clothes. Some of the strollers had passed them three times. Adolf should make up his mind and speak to the girl. All his talk about never marrying had turned out to be nonsense, if this Stephanie business was anything to go by. And there she stood, the minx, confident of the lecherous eyes of the sabre-clanking lieutenants, in their bright blue uniforms and braided shakos, turning her body this way and that, as she strove not to laugh at some remark one or other of the moustache-twirling lieutenants had made. For to laugh outright at a gentleman's remarks was extremely bad manners. A lady was allowed a smile, naturally, but without showing her teeth, and that was all; and not too often at that.

Gustl said, gently, 'We aren't going to get another Flower Show for another year, Adolf.'

Adolf made no reply. His eyes – so magnetic – were brighter than ever and did not blink. They never left the girl. Surely she had noticed; but if she had she made no sign. Gustl wished they had never gone to the damned Flower Show, but everybody in Linz had gone. It had all started there. The girl had thrown Adolf (like Gustl, an ordinary spectator, one of the have-nots) a red rose taken from one of the bunches of cornflowers, marguerites and poppies that adorned the carriage in which she sat, with her Mama. Adolf had caught it and held it high.

'She *smiled* at me,' Adolf said. 'Possibly she loves me?'

'It was probably meant for anybody,' replied Gustl, not very helpfully.

'She *meant* it!'

'Then go over to her, raise your hat, and introduce yourself, for God's sake!'

'No,' said Adolf. 'I will not be laughed at. A man should only introduce himself to a woman when he knows that she will be familiar with his name.'

'For that,' said Gustl, astonished, 'a man needs to be a Minister of State or a Professor, at least!'

'Ministers! Professors!' said Adolf. 'I am talking of artists and painters.' He added, after a moment, out of kindness, 'Musicians also, naturally.'

Gustl sighed, and waited for the promenade to end.

The next day Adolf took to his bed with a recurrence of his lung trouble. He coughed and sweated a lot, nursed indefatigably by Klara. After a week, Gustl visited him. Adolf was sitting up in bed, with pillows plumped up behind him, wearing a clean woollen nightshirt buttoned up to the neck. He looked pale but his fever had gone. He greeted Gustl, and picked up a cardboard model from the chair at the side of the bed. It was of a house he had designed for Stephanie. The model was painstaking in all domestic details: lighting, stoves, kitchen space. It was not the kind of house either he or Adolf could ever expect to live in. It had large airy rooms, garden-spaces, and a mock-Baroque exterior. It would have cost a small fortune to build.

'Very good. You should show it to her,' said Gustl, ironically.

Adolf put the model on the chair at the side of his sickbed. He looked at it a very long time before he spoke. 'I shan't see her again. I have been wasting my time. Love is a kind of fever, like the fever of the lungs. I have worn it out, as I have worn out my lung fever.' Adolf pointed to his clothes. 'Give me my things. I'll get up and join you downstairs. We'll have coffee and then we'll go to the Opera. *Siegfried* is on.'

'But we'll have to stand,' protested Gustl. 'Are you strong enough?'

'Certainly I'm strong enough. If a man has the will, there is nothing he cannot do. And I want to see *Siegfried*!'

Gustl handed Adolf his shirt and the pepper-and-salt tweed suit, now getting a little shabby at the elbows, since Klara's widow's pension was barely enough to feed, clothe, and pay the rent for the three of them. Adolf did not seem to realise, Klara said to Gustl downstairs, as he waited for Adolf to finish dressing, that if he had a job things would be a lot easier in the household.

'But I thought you wanted Adolf to be an artist?' said Gustl.

'I do, but can anything come of it?' answered Klara wearily, and something in her voice and her gesture made Gustl think that maybe she was ill, or tired, or both. More so even than Adolf, who seemed to have made a startling recovery. This recovery did not seem to surprise

Klara. 'He's like that,' she said. 'Lying in bed one minute, running around the town the next.' She sighed. 'His brother-in-law, Raubal, has been on to me again. The job in the bakery is still open.' She looked at Gustl, pleadingly. 'Can he earn a living, even when he *is* an artist?'

'Artist-architect,' corrected Gustl.

Klara waved her hand. 'Whatever! When our few savings are gone, and we only have the pension, what then?' She looked at her daughter, playing with her dolls in front of the pot-bellied, cast-iron stove, now cold in the summer, but still the focus of the room. 'I have the little one to think about. And what,' she whispered, looking up at the ceiling, 'will *become* of him?'

Gustl shook his head. He did not know what to say.

'Adolf will be all right,' he managed.

Klara shook her head. 'Let us hope you're right. He won't listen to anybody, that's certain.'

But when Adolf came downstairs, kissed Paula, who adored him, then his mother, and whispered in Klara's ear, Gustl noticed that she did not hesitate to open her purse and press some coins into Adolf's hand. She did not meet Gustl's eye. The two friends left after a cup of coffee and a roll with a slice of bratwurst. Adolf seemed to have recovered his appetite, too. Gustl thought: my father really can afford to send me to Linz, just about, and Adolf's mother can't. Yet he is going, and to hell with what anybody thinks or wants. Later, as they walked into the great foyer of the Opera House, and Gustl felt the anticipatory thrill of the coming performance, he said: 'Adolf, do you think it fair to take money from your mother, when she can't afford it?'

Adolf paused as the crowd – men in opera-cloaks and top hats, women in glittering gowns and chokers of pearls – passed by them and into the hall, leaving behind a wave of cigar smoke and lilac water and said, in a low, hissing voice, barely audible, to Gustl, 'I am never going to take a job. Never. Ever. Now please do not bring up the subject again!'

Gustl was taken aback by the venom in Adolf's voice but he said nothing. They filed into the gilt-and-gold main hall of the splendid theatre without a further word.

The *Siegfried* was spellbinding.

From time to time Gustl looked over at Adolf, as they stood at the back of the stalls, to remark on some aspect or other of the performance but Adolf did not look back at him. He seemed in a high fever; his eyes shone and his thin body shook, in agitation, at the roaring of the music. He looked transported, possessed. Gustl wondered if his fever had really gone or whether Wagner's music alone was causing this dramatic change in him. Even when the last chorus had echoed through the house and the final curtain-calls had been taken, to tumultuous applause, Adolf still seemed agitated and excited. As they spilled out into the cool night air, Gustl feared for his friend and suggested going home at once, but Adolf would not hear of it.

'No, no, I have to talk! I must give vent to my feelings for *Siegfried* and the great master who created him.' Adolf pointed across the square. 'Let us walk to the very top of the Frienberg. Now!'

'But you've been ill,' protested Gustl.

'Nonsense. I can do it. Come on!'

And Adolf was walking, at his usual quick pace, across the Opera Square. Gustl could do nothing but follow him.

By the time they got to the top of the Frienberg – it took them thirty minutes – Adolf was bathed in sweat. He was white-faced from his time in bed and he was shaking all over from his exertions. Gustl would never remember in detail what Adolf said then but would always recall the manner in which he spoke. It was dark now and a pale moon shone down on the faintly ridiculous figure of the youth as he stood on the lonely height and spoke for nobody but Gustl.

'The Wagnerian hero points the way to the tasks facing both Artist and People! Wagner's *Siegfried* – with his roots in the Teutonic Age of War! – is a model for the resolution and strength we need for the revitalisation of the German *Volk*! His father's shattered sword is a weapon to slay the Dragons of Wealth and Privilege! Our people are being destroyed by these Profiteers and Rationalists! Our Peasants and Farmers need a Myth to live by! The Myth of the Great Past of Germany! A Man must step forward – a Man of the *Volk*! – and speak for the *Volk* against the conspiracies of Wealth! Such a Man must take on the mantle of Siegfried himself and give the *Volk* – the workers and peasants – their History and Land back to them!'

Gustl looked at Adolf in the sudden evening breeze that had blown up, at his sweating brow and his staring eyes, at his thin, trembling lips, and feared for his friend. He would die of pneumonia if he stayed up here on the Frienberg much longer.

Just the same, he was impressed.

Who, he thought wonderingly, if Adolf was right, would Germany's saviour be?

A week later Gustl shook hands with Adolf at the smoky railway station at Linz. The local train would take four hours to get to Vienna. Adolf stood, in his pepper-and-salt suit, his hair freshly combed, and reassured Gustl that it wouldn't be long before they were together again. Gustl could not understand why Adolf had to go now, when there was a full month to his entrance examination for the Academy of Fine Arts. 'Couldn't you wait and we could go together?'

'No,' said Adolf, turning to pile his rucksack into the carriage. 'I have to get my portfolio together, to present it properly, and to prepare myself for the examination. To tell the truth, Gustl, I'm sick of Linz. It has no more to teach me.'

Gustl, for an unworthy moment, felt himself included in this general repudiation of Linz, but he recovered and shook Adolf's hand yet again, and said, 'It won't be long before we're both there together.' He crossed his fingers, behind his back. 'Always provided I get in.'

'The Academy of Music will jump at you,' said Adolf off-handedly. 'Your success is sure.'

'I'd hate to flunk it,' said Gustl. 'Don't you ever feel like that?'

'No,' said Adolf, and got in the carriage and closed the door. The express was getting up steam; guards were blowing whistles. Adolf waved at Gustl through the clouds of steam, then settled into his seat. He looked back through the window at the little town of Linz, nestling in the bend of the wide Danube, and knew that he would never live there again.

He sat back and thought of Wagner.

Adolf had read just about everything he had ever written. The man was his idol, and his music sublime! He did not care if he never heard the work of any other composer. *The Ring, Parsival* – oh, to have written such masterpieces! Wagner was not just a great composer; he was also a great German. He had made his feelings known on many subjects, particularly the need for the marriage of Germany and Austria into one nation. And of the need of the German people to keep out of their borders the intruders (Poles, Czechs, Italians, Jews) who had no real love of Austria or Germany. Adolf repeated the words of his great mentor at every opportunity, sometimes paraphrasing or changing the words but always retaining the sense of them. Adolf wondered where his ability to speak with such conviction came from, and supposed it was a low gift, of a kind. But he was, or rather would be, an Artist-Architect, and Artist-Architects never made speeches, except when they were accepting prizes for their work, and then only a mumbling, modest few words. Gazing out of the window at the rolling green lands of Lower Austria, and at the dramatic sweep of the mountains beyond – so powerful, so Germanic! – he tried to recapture the thrill he had felt the night he had shouted at Gustl on the Frienberg. The emotion, he found, could not be recaptured. Adolf felt uneasy, but he had discovered something about himself. He could make a speech, if he had to. A true and moving speech.

With such jumbled thoughts in his mind, Adolf closed his eyes, sighed, and slept all the way to Vienna.

Three weeks later Adolf presented himself at the vast examination hall at the Academy of Fine Arts in Vienna. He wore his pepper-and-salt tweed suit, the only suit he owned, but he wore it every day, unlike a worker who wore his only suit on a Sunday. Adolf knew that students and middle-class persons often had several suits, but he had only the one. There was a Viennese joke about the man who had a suit for every day of the week and tried it on of a Sunday to see if it still fitted!

That was a joke that did not amuse Adolf.

Few jokes did, and that one was a little too near the bone.

Adolf took his place at the easel and desk assigned to him and gazed keenly at the other candidates. They mostly looked as if they had more than one suit. Hair plastered-down and carefully parted, these hundred boys (there were only a dozen girls at most, tucked away in a corner at the back of the hall, where they would not distract the eye) looked to Adolf as if they were still at school. Most, he supposed, were a year younger than he was, and many were two years younger. A goodly number of the boys were extremely well-dressed (in dark serge suits, high, stiff collars and sporting fob-watches) and plainly attended the best schools in Vienna. These boys, some of whom were dark-featured and looked in some way foreign, lolled confidently about their desks, talking easily to one another, as they waited for the masters to enter the Hall and the preliminaries to begin. Adolf began to feel a little uneasy. These boys and others like them had probably been coached by the best art-teachers in the captial.

What did that matter?

Once the Examination began, they were faced with large blank sheets of drawing-paper, just as he was. It was what they set down on the paper that counted, and if that was the case, he surely had no worries? Adolf looked around the vast, dusty room, with its huge neo-classical windows – the light was magnificent, as good as any studio – and felt at home. He would be all right. These were only clever children he was up against. The Examiners would see that.

Suddenly, the candidates at the front rose to their feet, in a great rattling, echoing sound, of clattering chairs and feet, and those behind, including Adolf, did the same. The Examiners had come in.

These dignitaries were six in number and settled themselves, two down the main aisle, two down the side of the hall, and one each back and front. The Examiner at the front – in pince-nez and high collar –

introduced himself as Herr Professor Bruner and told the candidates that the Examination fell into two parts. One, a painting of any scheme or inanimate object in the artists' recollection. Two, a sketch in pencil, chalk, or ink upon the theme of 'Austria'. One hour would be allotted to each part, with a five-minute interval between. No talking or conferring was allowed, and any candidate who disobeyed that rule would be instantly disqualified. He added that these exercises did not entirely determine the candidate's fate. The portfolio they had submitted would be most strongly taken into consideration, and might well be the determining factor, in the Examiners' verdict.

Adolf had delivered his portfolio by hand, as asked, a week before. He had included all his drawings and blueprints for the improvement of Linz (including the subway and his plans for the new Opera House) plus almost all his freehand sketches and paintings. He had noticed, as he handed in the portfolio, that it was a great deal bulkier than those of other students.

All that was behind him now. He must concentrate on the task at hand. What kind of inanimate object did they mean? An apple perhaps, Adolf thought sarcastically, or an orange, or even a flower? Well, he would give them none of these things. The Cathedral at Linz was an inanimate thing and he knew it by heart. That would be his water-colour. He needed no perspective-lines or squares. It all came easily to him, for he had sketched it many times, and he knew nothing but a pleasurable feeling of satisfied effort, as first his pencil, then his brush, carefully and deliberately sketched in the exact lines of the edifice, just as he remembered it. He did not look up to see what the other candidates were doing, and it was with a feeling of surprise that he heard the bell, signifying the end of the first period. At this sound there was a long, low sigh from the candidates, then a general hubbub as they started to talk to each other all at once, silenced only by the Herr Professor holding up his hand.

'You have five minutes exactly, meinherren.' He did not include the girls in his salutation, or even look at them. 'Be prompt. Anyone late will be denied admission.'

The candidates were somewhat deflated by the tone of the Herr Professor's voice, and filed out into the quadrangle at the back of the Academy in quiet groups, withal chatting animatedly to each other. Everybody seemed to know somebody. Adolf walked away and sat on his own, on a low wall, and spoke to nobody. He was still sitting there, feeling extremely hungry, when a bell rang to signify the resumption of the sitting.

This time Adolf felt less at home.

Austria? What could such a question *mean*? Austria was pastoral?

Austria was lazy? Easy-going? Slap-dash? Decadent? Cosmopolitan? What?

Adolf drew a cartoon, in pen and ink.

The drawing depicted Austria as a flea-bitten old dog, reclining on a throne, with a crown on his head. Around him were gathered a large, belligerent, and drunken bear with a bottle in his hand, to depict the Russians; and a rather delapidated wolf with a large set of drawn fangs, to depict the French. Another character, the Prussian Eagle, multi-winged, beclawed, and much larger than the others, hovered above to give the poor old dog on the throne a helping hand. Adolf spent the entire hour on the drawing and, although no great cartoonist, considered the idea to be superior to any other he could envisage, and certainly better than anything that the snobby, milk-fed babies around him were capable of. He handed it in with some satisfaction and walked out of the Examination room into the street, with an air of triumph.

Adolf's exhilaration had not abated the next day, when he reported back in a clean collar but otherwise dressed the same, for his personal interview. He entered the portals of the massive, neo-classical building with a light step. Adolf had not slept well. He had lain awake rehearsing exactly how he would respond to the Herr Professor's words of praise for his work. A modest nod of the head would doubtless suffice. Adolf was aware of his tendency to lecture, so he sternly reproved himself on that score. Just a simple 'Danke, Herr Professor!' The object was to get into the Academy. The rest would be easy. His work was good, he knew that. There was nothing to worry about.

Adolf was ushered into the large office that served as an interview-room. The three Herr Professors sat, behind a long table, stern and unbending, bespectacled and heavy at the waist. The Chairman, Herr Professor Bruner, looked over his pince-nez at Adolf and said, 'Herr Hitler. Pray take a seat.'

Adolf did as he was bid. The Herr Professor was looking at the contents of his portfolio, Adolf realised, with some interest. He looked at the other two in turn, with a hint of amusement in his eye. Adolf braced himself for the praise to come. The Herr Professor was obviously impressed.

Adolf expected nothing less.

The Herr Professor cleared his throat. 'Herr Hitler, we are impressed by your . . . er . . . unusual architectural drawings. They are neat and competently executed and seem to us of interest . . .' He paused. 'How-ever, your painting skills and your freehand drawing skills, while gener-ally good, do not come up to the standard we have come to expect of a student in the Fine Arts faculty. We therefore have to deny your application, to thank you for it, and to wish you . . .' The Herr Professor paused, somewhat concerned at the expression on Adolf's face. He had turned down the vast majority of the candidates he had seen that day – one acceptance in ten was the average – but none had reacted as this young man had. Disappointment was usual. Sometimes there were incipient tears. Normally, a dignified acceptance. Adolescents knew, in the Herr Professor's experience, whether they were good enough. This youth obviously did not. His face had gone very pale and his eyes stared unblinkingly at the Herr Professor in a way that made him extremely uneasy. He could not think when he had seen such eyes on a young man.

Was he going to faint, the Herr Professor wondered? Or have a fit?

The Herr Professor looked beseechingly at his two companions. 'I think Herr Hitler's architectural drawings show merit? I think we should recommend him to try the Architectural College? Yes?'

Both these worthies nodded. They too could see the expression on the youth's face.

They, too, had never seen anything quite like it before. They, too, could not wait to get this very odd, rather shabby and unsuitable boy out of the room.

'Excellent,' said one of them, loudly. 'That would be the thing to do. Try the Architectural College.'

The third coughed, blinked, looked away, and then nodded agreement.

Adolf walked the half-mile to the Architectural College off the Reichstrasse in a daze, carrying his bulky portfolio. He listened in dismay to the official in the office telling him that the minimum requirement for enrolment in the College was the possession of a School-leaving Certificate, and normally to a high standard at that. The uniformed and bewhiskered official, portly in long coat with two rows of brass buttons, took some pleasure, it seemed to Adolf, in telling him this news.

Adolf, however, persisted. 'Is there any regulation against my entering, even if I have no School-leaving Certificate?'

The old fool pondered. 'No regulation, no. But it will not be accepted.'

No 'Herr' or 'my Good Herr'. Just a superior disdain. Adolf felt his face go white. 'If there is no regulation against it,' he shouted, 'then I require you to accept it, and at once, along with my form of application, which I will fill out now, if you please!'

The old fool opened his mouth to say again what he had already said three times, but seeing Adolf's face thought the better of it. He handed Adolf a long, official form of application to the College. Adolf took it to a desk and filled it out, in a cold rage. When he had done this, he returned it to the official, who glanced at it, looked surprised, then softened. 'Herr Hitler, I see your father is ... *was*? ... A Customs Officer of some standing? My apologies. I will see your application is processed at once. You will hear in perhaps a week?'

Adolf nodded, briefly, and left the College.

Now, all he could do was hope.

For the next week Adolf walked the streets of Vienna.

Fools, dolts, idiots, why had he expected anything else?

He tried not to think of the Architectural College.

One good thing: they did not require an examination, but accepted or rejected an applicant on the strength of his portfolio. Adolf, now that the cold rage of rejection had abated a little, felt some hope. By the second day he had all but convinced himself that architecture was what *really* interested him. Yes! It was the thing he cared about most, it was the discipline he should have thought of first! The professors at the Architectural College would see his talent. They must!

Adolf strode on, angrily, down the Reichsstrasse, amongst the rich and well-fed businessmen and their women (many of them mistresses, not wives, to judge by their fashionable and expensive clothes) and felt nothing but hatred for these people. The women walked into the great shops, dressed in apparel that would pay the wages of a worker for a year, trailing the fat, indulgent men behind them, these creatures very often reduced to carrying some miniature dog. Adolf watched such performances with scorn.

He viewed everything, now, with even greater scorn than ever.

If the definition of a city was that it was a town in which it was possible to lead a double life, then Vienna was certainly that. Most of these portly men were plainly married, but to somebody other than the young women they indulged in the wildly expensive shops and stores of the capital. They did not notice the army of beggars in the streets. The Handelees, penniless Jews from Galicia who sold trinkets from trays around their shoulders and seemed to be everywhere. Adolf rejected their pleas with a brusque gesture. If these poor devils were Jews, then not all Jews were rich, as Herr Poetsch at the Realschule had attested. There could be no doubt that there were too many of them, however. A stirring of his memory brought him the picture, almost forgotten, of *Pappi's* face, red and contorted, as he talked about his great injustice at the hands of the Jews ... The Handelees were the poorest of the poor, and God alone

54

knew where they slept at night. On the park-benches of the Prater, possibly. In the summer weather that would be no great hardship, but in the winter? Adolf shivered and walked on.

That week of waiting Adolf felt scorn about a lot of things. For the rich for being rich, for the poor for being poor. And mostly for those in the middle – the bourgeoisie – who sat on their fat arses in useless jobs on fat salaries and watched the great, lumbering Austro-Hungarian Empire grind to a halt! Like *Pappi*, they were *dumkopfs* who had been recruited on Metternich's principle that the worst thing Austria could ever have was a clever, well-educated Civil Service. Metternich's point was that if you did, *they* would run the Empire. Metternich did not approve of that, very correctly. So he had recruited, or caused to be recruited, applicants such as *Pappi*, who was nobody's idea – certainly not Adolf's – of an educated man! *Pappi* had wanted nothing to change, as nobody in the crowded Reichsstrasse wanted anything to change.

Ah, but it would change.

Everything had to change.

Even the Austro-Hungarian Empire had to change.

Adolf sat at a sidewalk café and ordered coffee. In Vienna a coffee could last all day. The newspapers – Vienna had six daily papers and countless magazines – were displayed on racks, and were free to customers. Adolf spent many hours reading them. It was a very civilised way – and a very cheap one – of passing the time. He would watch the Viennese middle-class, fat, lazy and talkative, endlessly discussing art and politics and science. Talk was all they ever seemed to do. Reasonable, liberal talk about how religion was dead, how science was the religion of the future, how mankind, by rational scientific thinking, could be made perfect.

Adolf did not believe it. Not for one moment. The days were long gone when Austria had held the Turks at the very gates of the city. What glorious days they must have been, although naturally, war was wasteful and should not be entered into unless absolutely necessary. Adolf swung violently between admiration for the old Austrian order that had repulsed the Turks and kept Europe Christian and the fashionable belief, held, he knew, by most educated and artistic people, that war was a savage and stupid business, and that the human race had outgrown it, despite the Franco-German War of only thirty years ago. Certainly, the liberal politicians who ran the country believed that. The old Emperor had been a prisoner of the Social Democrats most of his long reign. Their rule in the Austrian parliament amounted, now, to almost sixty years. The Social Democrats, for whom nobody in the

55

Waldviertal ever voted, had opened the floodgates, so *Die Zeit* insisted, and Adolf read, to the immigration of Poles, Czechs, Jews and other foreign races into the country. There had been, for example, almost no Jews in Vienna in 1870. Now they were one in ten of the population. What was wrong, said *Die Zeit*, was that the educated ones – it took a generation – rapidly associated themselves with the Social Democrats, once they became well-to-do, which many did, by becoming property developers and suchlike. They then entered the professions, usually through their sons. The Law Schools and Medical Colleges now had rolls in which Jewish students were in the proportion of one in four, and the number was rising.

This was all the fault, thundered *Die Zeit*, of the Social Democratic Government, which had allowed 'Open Immigration to All' for the last thirty years. A fine, humanitarian policy, no doubt. The trouble was, everybody wanted to live in Austria. Austria had excellent free schools and colleges and a liberal society. The police were not repressive and there were no pogroms. There were no second-class citizens. Anybody, from any part of the Empire, Austrian or not, could come and live in Vienna. So could anybody who wasn't in the Empire, if they possessed a very small sum of money and were not diseased. The 'Open Door' policy had doubled the population of Vienna in a decade. The starving foreigners on the streets were the living proof of it.

Adolf put down the newspaper, thoughtfully.

At the next table to Adolf sat Doctor Theodor Herzl. He was forty-two, but looked older, despite his dandified appearance. He was extremely tired. Herzl felt that his life had been for nothing. Talk, talk, talk, that was all his fellow Jews ever did. He, too, was reading *Die Zeit*, but with nothing of the approval that Adolf was. The ramblings and ravings of its editor, Schonener, were not new to him. He had been reading them for years. Did his fellow-Jews read them with the foreboding that he did? No, they did not. Their families had been in Germany and in Austria, some of them, for best part of a century. They thought of themselves as Germans and Austrians first, as Jews afterwards. Many of them had left the Faith, led by the young intellectuals: Schnitzler, Hofmannsthal, many others. That was to be expected. Intellectuals never saw what was right in front of their noses.

Pogrom!

As sure as life itself, it would come.

In Germany. In Austria, too.

The middle-class Jews wouldn't read rags like Schonener's. They thought of Schonener as a rabble-rousing Jew-baiter, which he was; but he was more than that. He was a son of the aristocracy. A lot of aristocrats thought as he did, that Jews ought to be banished from all pro-

fessions, all posts, in the vast Austrian Empire. Karl Luegar was an
anti-Semite and he was Burgomeister of Vienna! What more proof did
they want?

Herzl sighed and sipped his coffee. He must be patient. He must
realise that his views were unpleasant and unpopular. Most Jews thought
he was a crank. Even the renowned Doctor Freud had raised an eyebrow
when Herzl had outlined his plans for a Zionist State.

Teacup balanced on knee, in the stuffy, over-furnished room in the
Berggasse, Freud had asked, in an amused way, as if humouring Herzl
where exactly was the state to be founded?

'I don't know where it will be, Herr Doctor. All I know is, it has to
be!'

The massive head, the grave manner, Good God, the fellow was more
interested in being a successful doctor than in his own life!

'Because, Herr Doctor, there is not a single Gentile in this room of
yours!'

Doctor Freud had looked interested. 'What does that signify, Doctor
Herzl?'

'It signifies that you, Doctor Freud, with all your new successes and
your new professional friends – ' Herzl deliberately stressed the word
professional ' – do not meet socially with Gentiles! Now why is that, do
you suppose?'

Freud flushed. 'I do meet sometimes with Gentiles!'

'But – ?'

Freud said, 'But I often feel uncomfortable with them.'

'Are *made* to feel uncomfortable?' asked Herzl.

'Possibly.'

'Do you get all the promotion at the Hospital, to which you are
entitled?'

Herzl knew the answer to that. Freud's need for recognition, even
from – especially from – the Gentile doctors was well-known. Freud
explained it by saying it was for all Jews in the new medical-arm of his
speciality. Nonetheless, he flushed again.

'Doctor Herzl, you know I do not get all the promotion I desire. Who
does?'

'You don't get it because you are a Jew.'

'Possibly.'

'Certainly!'

'Probably.'

'Very well. You also do not mix socially, or very little, with Gentiles
because you feel uncomfortable with them. Why is that, pray?'

Freud shook his head. 'I feel more at home with my Jewish friends
and fellow-physicians. As I do with you, Doctor Herzl.'

57

Herzl set down his tea-cup. 'Why do you not feel at home with your Gentile colleagues? Is it because you feel . . . menaced?'

'Menaced?'

'Yes. Menaced.'

Freud considered the word. 'I did not say menaced, Doctor Herzl. I said uncomfortable. And I did not say always. I said sometimes.'

'I prefer menaced. Always.'

'I know you do, Doctor Herzl. We all know you do,' said Freud in a low, neutral voice, as if talking to one of his patients on his celebrated couch. Very well, Herzl thought, it was possible that the Dream was sending him mad. Possible, yes, but he did not believe it. Freud and the other people in the room could smile at him politely and pass on to talk of other, important things – the latest poem by Hofmannstahl, the latest play by Schnitzler – but they had not made the study of the situation that he had.

They had not considered (as he had, my God, his life had been consumed by it!) that there had been an anti-Semitic Party in the Austrian Parliament since 1877. There were fourteen Members elected under that ticket, and a hundred more who supported it, mostly under the thin disguise of membership of the Christian Social Party. Schonener was a Nationalist first, of course, and very probably a crank with not much of an open following. But Karl Leugar was Burgomeister of Vienna and he openly proclaimed that he and his party – the Christian Socials – were anti-Semites! And they had been elected to run Vienna!

What more did Freud – what more did any Jew! – need to know?

The Pan-German Nationalists hated the Jews. The aristocrats – many of them – hated the Jews. The working-class Intellectuals and the Catholic clergy were not, generally speaking, supporters of the Jews. Only the Social Democrats, who counted most Jews amongst their supporters, were concerned for the Jews, had given them citizenship in 1887, had always seen that they were treated the same as other citizens of the Empire: the Magyars, the Italians, the Czechs, the Poles. The Social Democrats, in Herzl's view, were finished, or near enough. Their progressive ideas were generally unpopular. Nothing, short of a War, could save them. The Christian Socials and the Nationalists would inevitably take over the government of Austria, and then what?

Pogrom!

The trouble was, the affluent, middle-class Jews in Doctor Freud's parlour had never experienced a pogrom. People's memories were short. If they would only talk to the poor Jews, the Handelees, begging on the streets of Vienna, they would learn about pogroms. These people had walked, barefoot some of them, a hundred, 500 miles, fleeing from the knout and fire-torch of the Tsarist Cossacks. Ask *them*, he felt like

58

shouting at the great Doctor Freud, but he did not, for it was very Jewish to shout, very bad-mannered to shout. Intellectual middle-class Gentiles never shouted. They reasoned.

Herzl felt that reason would get him nowhere.

He had been trying reason for years.

Herzl had reasoned, in splendid drawing-rooms in Brussels and Paris, with the Rothschilds themselves. He had said, 'I could be wrong, gentlemen, but I don't think I am. I think the Liberal World – the World of Reason! – is collapsing about us. I think Austria could go first, as she is an old Empire and unstable already. All I am asking for is a moderate support for my Dream! Gentlemen, we have to get out of Europe, many of us anyway, before the anti-Semites take over power from the Social Democrats! There are too many of us, especially in Austria, especially in Vienna. They resent us but we will not see it. We will be subjected, first, to repression, then who knows what?'

There had been silence in the splendid room, full of splendid men in splendid clothes. Nothing, they plainly felt, nothing whatever could touch *them*.

For were they not the Rothschilds?

'I am speaking of a possible Pogrom.'

He could have said a dirty word.

Nobody spoke in the elegant chamber.

The men in their expensive suits moved in their chairs, looked at the Aubusson carpet and said nothing. Sympathy hung in the air.

Theodor Herzl did not want sympathy.

He wanted action.

He tried one last time. 'A State of Israel is a possibility, if only he will believe in it! The Dream is not so far from the Deed as many people think!'

There was a long silence.

Then the oldest man present had spoken. Herzl realised that the others had waited, out of respect. This man was very old indeed, with large veins on the back of his hands, which rested on a silver-topped cane, and dark, wise eyes.

'Doctor Herzl, you say the Liberal World is collapsing?'

'I do! It is!'

'Even if it is, how many Jews believe that?'

'Almost none. They have to be convinced of it!'

'That will take time, Sir. More than that, it will take an Event.' The old one leaned forward on his stick. 'The Jew has been out of the Middle East for two thousand years. He is no longer an Oriental.' He sighed, and said in a low voice, 'To be convinced that he will find freedom in a malarial swamp in Africa, he will need an Event, Doctor Herzl.'

The whole room sighed and relaxed.

Herzl said nothing to that.

He knew how true it was.

He'd had the same reception from Jewish leaders in London. Even from Jewish workers in the East End, where he'd stood on a salt-herring barrel and shouted the truth at them, pleaded for help, aid, money for the new Jerusalem!

Jews, rich and poor alike, had said no. Only a few believed as he did.

A Pogrom, worse than any that had gone before?

Sometimes, in the darkest hours of the night, he did not believe it himself, lying in his comfortable bed, in this city where his people had been safe for almost a hundred years.

But in the light of each new morning Theodor Herzl knew that it was true. It was the burden God had given him and he would have to carry it every day of his life. He would have to go on talking, arguing, convincing. The slogan he repeated so often: *The Dream is not so far from the Deed!* The Dream had to come true. It had to.

Herzl put *Die Zeit* back on the rack, left the exact money, plus a small tip, for his pot of coffee, and walked out of the café.

He did not even notice Adolf.

Adolf was still reading the article on the Jews in *Die Zeit*. This Karl Leugar was a firebrand, a man with guts, it seemed to Adolf. He had been elected Mayor of Vienna on an anti-Semetic ticket. But the old Emperor, Franz Josef, had refused to allow him to serve. That was certainly unconstitutional, according to Leuger's supporters (mostly ex-army officers, Catholic intellectuals, aristocrats and even some businessmen), but the Emperor had been adamant. No anti-Jewish pogroms here! He had closed the Rathhaus and run the city by decree ever since.

Adolf knew little of the rights or wrongs of any of this. Yet, in his hurt and scornful mood, he felt a sympathy. Some of the candidates at the Academy, he recalled, were foreign-looking, and well-dressed, and no doubt some of them had been admitted to the College, whereas he, a pure Austrian, had not. That was not right.

No, indeed. If what *Die Zeit* said was true.

And he could not see why they should say it if it was not.

Adolf walked slowly back to his sister's apartment off the Mariahilfer-strasse, deeply disturbed. Things were indeed very wrong with the Empire. It was worse than he had imagined. He would need all his Will to surmount the difficulties being placed in front of him, some of them by people, no doubt, who should not be there at all!

Angi opened the door of her apartment herself. She tried to smile but only succeeded in looking apprehensive.

The letter lay unopened on the large table covered with velveteen cloth, in the middle of the tiny room, a single chandelier poised over it. Raubal's grinning face was there, too, but Adolf did not really take it in. His bulky portfolio lay on the table.

Slowly, trying not to tremble, Adolf opened the envelope and read the letter. It told him with regret that he could not be considered for the Architectural College since he did not have the required educational qualifications. It was signed by the Director of the College.

VI

ADOLF spent most of the next week, alone in his tiny room at Angi's apartment. The place was cramped: the main room, in which the family lived, was crowded with dark, heavy furniture. There was also a bedroom for his sister and Raubal. He had been given the box-room. Adolf did not read or draw or do any of the usual things that came as second nature to him that week. He just sat on the single-bed that almost filled the room, and gazed out of the window, seeing nothing. Opposite was the blank brick-wall of another apartment-block. Adolf spent hours just looking at it. Angi came in, dark and silently sympathetic, with delicacies to tempt his appetite: slices of dark salami or bratwurst: crusty Viennese bread, and steaming bowls of borsch. Adolf ate nothing.

He sat, brooding, hateful and burning with indignation. The idiots! Couldn't they see the merit of what he had submitted? Were they totally and terminally blind? Any fool could see his work was original, different by leagues from that of the childlike students who normally applied for entrance to the College! That, no doubt, was the trouble. The Pedagogues were used to the fact-filled boobies who normally applied, and who trembled at their every word or glance. They couldn't deal with different, original work. It was said that genius went unrecognised, or even derided, for a long time before it was accepted. That, seemingly, was to be his lot: but it was a bitter pill, a very bitter pill indeed. To have to sit and suffer, while those well-dressed, well-fed children (some of them the dark-visaged foreigners, he had no doubt) took his place, his rightful place, at the Architectural College! The official reason given for the refusal – that he did not have the basic qualifications – Adolf ignored. If they were so hidebound by bureaucratic regulations as to turn away a wonderfully gifted student, then they were not fit for the office they occupied, and should be dismissed forthwith!

Unfortunately, he had no power to dismiss them.

On the fourth day, Adolf drank a little black coffee. Angi put her hand on his shoulder – greatly daring, for she knew how he hated physical contact with other people – and whispered, 'Adolf, *liebschen*, it isn't the end of the world. There are other things you can do.' She pressed a buttered bread-roll on him. 'Please eat something. I'm worried about you. So is Raubal.'

'Raubal doesn't give a damn about me. He's glad I didn't get in.'

'No, he isn't. He's worried. We all are.'

Dear Angi, Adolf thought. She really was troubled.

Adolf was fond of Angi. Twenty-four now, married to Raubal for four years and still no sign of the child he knew she yearned for. A pretty girl, too, if a little heavy, in her flowery dress and with her dark hair set in a tidy *chignon*.

'About the College? When will you tell Mutti?' asked Angi.

Adolf shook his head. 'I'll bet Raubal has already written and told her.'

'I'm sure he hasn't,' said Angi, scandalised. Then, she reflected: 'He has written to her, though. Last night. He posted it on his way to work this morning. But I'm sure he wouldn't.'

'Of course he told her,' said Adolf, wearily. 'It would give him the greatest of pleasure. If he could get me into the Civil Service, like himself, he would be the happiest man in Vienna!'

Angi shook her head. 'If you don't get a job of some kind, Adolf, what will happen to you? You can't go on the way you are, for ever, can you?'

Adolf took her hand. 'Dearest Angi, I will not be taking any job. Either in the Customs Office or in the ridiculous bakery!' He laughed. It surprised Angi. Adolf never laughed. 'Can you see me in some bake-house, covered in flour?'

'But you'll have to do something. Will you go back to Linz?'

Adolf frowned. 'I'll never live in Linz again. This is my city, Vienna. I shall remain here, whatever happens.'

Angi said, hesitantly, 'Adolf, you know you could stay here with us as long as you like, if it was up to me? But Raubal isn't of the same mind and, unfortunately, he is the man. I'm not sure how pleased he would be if you . . .' She faltered . . . 'Well, if you wanted to stay on here, but didn't get a job?' She pressed on, not seeing the expression on Adolf's face, in the half-light. 'Of course, if you were working and were able to pay some small rent? Nothing very much. . .'

'It is all right, Angi,' said Adolf. 'I perfectly understand.'

To her horror, Adolf began to pack his rucksack, putting in the few shirts and socks he had brought with him. His collapsible easel and his portfolio, he strapped to the rucksack. Then he put the whole thing over his shoulder.

Angi watched him, helplessly: 'Adolf, I didn't mean anything. Please don't go. Please.'

'I will have to go sometime, so it might as well be now. You know it must come.'

Angi held his arm, as if to prevent him leaving. 'But Adolf, what will I tell *Mutti*? She isn't well. It will distress her.'

'I'll write and tell her I had to find another place. As I do.' He went out of the door into the living-room. Angi hurried after him.

Raubal, in his shirtsleeves, at the table, reading the *Neue Freie Presse*, looked up over it, at Adolf. 'Oh, the young artist has decided to join us, has he? And about time, young man, you can't skulk in your tent forever. Some of us who have to work can tell you . . .'

Raubal saw Adolf's rucksack and fell silent. He looked questioningly at Angi.

Angi, tears in her eyes, made a gesture of utter misery.

This annoyed Raubal. It annoyed him very much.

'So you're going home to Linz, are you? With your tail between your legs, no doubt? Well, let me, as your brother-in-law, tell you something, young Adolf: I do not rate your chances of getting into the Customs Service very highly. Not highly at all. You study the wrong things. Art? Architecture? Politics? What good will any of that ever do you?'

'It will keep me out of the Civil Service,' said Adolf icily, 'where I would have to consort with prejudiced, philistine, Pharisees like you.' He took from his pocket a bundle of ten mark notes and threw them on the table, and walked out of the door.

Half an hour later he sat in a rented room on the other side of Vienna, on the Stumpergasse, a poor working-class area, near the West Banhof. It had damp and crumbling walls, and the furniture was, he had no doubt, bug-infested, for there was a can of kerosene standing next to the ancient stove and it could only be there to kill off cockroaches and lice. There was a bunk for two, one berth above the other, some dubious-looking blankets, and a rickety table, with two hard chairs. A jug of cold water stood on the small dressing-table, and a brown-stained chamber-pot was next to the bunk. A small, grimy window gave out onto a dirty and deserted courtyard. He was in one of the poorest districts of Vienna. Noises of all kinds, babies crying, women shouting, men calling, came from other parts of the block. But it was cheap, only ten kroner a week, and, most importantly, it was all his own. Adolf reclined on the lower bunk and closed his eyes. He felt, strangely, at home.

For the first time in almost a week, he slept.

*

For the next three weeks Adolf virtually lived in the room, making it his, making it home. He bought cheap food at the local delicatessen. Bread and milk was cheapest and made his most nourishing meal of the day. The rest was bread and fish-paste. He ate an apple every day. The room came with a gas-ring and saucepan. Hot water for the cheap coffee, which was his only luxury. He ate no meat of any kind, but – if he was lucky – made a meal of vegetables that the corner-shop fruiterers almost gave away, on a Saturday night. This, Adolf discovered, was the cheapest way to shop. Only the very poor shopped then, picking up the scraps of meat the butchers insisted were good only for the dogs; the fish that would go off if kept over the weekend; the bread that would be too stale to offer customers on the Monday morning. Adolf realised that the shopkeepers, fat, aproned and jolly, performed a charity. Without their largesse (they virtually gave the food away in the very last minutes before they closed, often near to midnight) the poorest citizens of Vienna would indeed starve. Often, the baker or his boy would brush Adolf aside to give his last stale loaf of bread to some toothless, starveling scarecrow in a shawl. A form of rough justice obtained in these midnight markets and stalls and shops. It seemed to Adolf a picture of hell: the naptha-lights illuminating the crowds of starving people, sawdust and straw tramped underfoot, as they fought to get their share. There were filthy urchins, clad in rags; decent but careworn mothers of large families; unemployed men, gaunt and desperate. If a man had no work, he starved. Even the Handelees and other foreigners were there, all clamouring and pushing and shouting, no quarter asked or given, trying to attract the attention of the shopkeeper.

Adolf, in his suit and tie, was out of place here, and he felt that. However, this was an experiment, he had to suffer it. He had to find out how little it was possible to live on in Vienna. The alternative, of going back to Linz and living with *Mutti* and his sister Paula, did not seriously occur to him. He simply would not do it. That would be a denial of everything he had ever said or done. He could imagine all too easily the sneer on Raubal's fat face at the news that his tail was indeed between his legs.

Nobody would ever see that day, he swore!

So he lived in the room, holed up like some grey rat, and read his library books (he was a member of three different libraries in Vienna, all free) and totted up his money. He discovered that, with his room-rent of ten kroner a week, and allowing no money for shoes or clothing of any kind, but just for the simplest food, he could exist on thirty kroner a week. He had with him, a gift from Klara, two hundred kroner. That would somehow have to last him ten weeks. He would stay ten weeks in Vienna, in this awful room in the Stumpergasse (which, in fact, he was beginning to like) and then he would go home and put his financial terms to Klara. He would ask her for that part of her pension that was rightfully his, plus that part of Pappi's savings that remained, and he would ask for no more. From then on, he would be on his own.

Adolf estimated that he could properly ask *Mutti* for eighty kroner per month. That was something short of the thirty kroner a week he needed to live, but not by much. With his share of Pappi's savings (if Klara would give it to him) he could manage. If the alternative was Linz, then it would have to do.

He would have his independence, that was the important thing.

And one day, he would surprise them all, the sneerers like his brother-in-law, Raubal, and the boys from the Realschule who had sneered at him in the street in Linz, and all the rest of them. How could anybody expect him to go back to Linz at sixteen years of age, a failure already? It was not to be thought of.

So, Adolf made his momentous decision.

He would stay in Vienna and study architecture. He would do it without teachers. Other youths needed teachers. He did not. He would study from basic sources, not only the old but the new: the work of architects like Otto Wagner, who had designed the new Savings Bank in the Herrenstrasse. Adolf had stumped across town to look at it. Such simplicity! Otto Wagner was getting rid of the curves and curlicues of the Gothic style, and bringing Vienna into a Modernist Age. His tenements in the working-class, city-owned blocks, stark and without frills, were in direct contradiction to the Hofburg, the vast complex of the Imperial Palace that formed part of the Ringstrasse that enclosed the old town. Adolf, in the weeks that followed, walked and walked the massive boulevards of the 'Ring'. Vast, straight highways, hedged by sentinel trees, that flung themselves out from the old city, in the form of a star. Looking and sketching, sketching and looking, Adolf worked mostly in the Karntnerstrasse, where the Rathaus, the Burgotheater and the Opera House all stood, magnificent examples of modern Gothic, monuments to the majesty of the Empire. The city, viewed from this footsore level, was certainly an inspiration! His business, then, was to learn, without the benefit of moderators – teachers, lecturers, pedagogues – all that he could of his chosen profession, by studying and copying the best that could be seen. The best of old and new Baroque, with its Arab influences of curve and line, every sight-line designed so that it looked 'framed'. This was Adolf's favourite style and the Hofburg remained his favourite haunt. But in a copy of the *Architectural Review* (read, inevitably, in a café where Adolf took his one daily cup of coffee) he was surprised to read an article declaring the Ring to be 'Utilitarian,

Rational'. He had thought it merely grand. 'The Ring is heartless', declared the writer of the article, one Camillo Sitte. 'People feel dwarfed and impotent by these vast spaces.'

Adolf had not thought of that, but saw some point in it. Yet, as Otto Wagner said in rebuttal in an adjoining article: 'Architectural Art must start at one point only. *Today* – here and now! – is all that matters! The Ring brings transport and energy into the city. We do not need, any longer, to study the Gothic buildings of Italy. We must design our own. Utilitarian, if you like. Rational, if you like. Man is surely a rational creature by now? The old Beau Arts education is no longer necessary. We go our own way, the way of Urban Modernism!'

Adolf was excited by these exchanges, and made his coffee last even longer than usual, although his stomach rumbled for food. He noted without enthusiasm that Otto Wagner was the Principal of the very Architectual College that had rejected him. From that moment he felt prejudiced against Otto Wagner's Modernist line. Too plain? No facades? No small 'personal' squares as demanded by Camillo Sitte? No place, really, for the *Gemutlichkeit* – the sentimental love of all things cosy – shared by most of the citizens of the city. Or more correctly, by those citizens who earned enough kroner per month to allow them the time to have such feelings. The poverty-stricken creatures of the night, who gathered at the market-stalls, never had time, Adolf considered, for such fancy, extravagant ideas as *Gemutlichkeit*!

Adolf, mainly on account of Otto Wagner being Principal of the now hated and scorned Architectural College, finally sided with Camillo Sitte and the traditionalists. He also noted coldly that Otto Wagner – the Social Democrat – got what he wanted: the plum job of the Vienna architectural establishment. Camillo Sitte did not.

So? Even in architecture politics ruled?

Adolf began to look at the architecture around him in a slightly different way. Architects, like everybody else, were the servants of whatever political masters ruled at the Hofhaus or in the Rathaus. Top architects, no less than top generals, were political people: they had to curry favour, or otherwise impose themselves upon the politicians. It did not seem to Adolf a very honourable position to be in.

Musing on such thoughts, Adolf spent his days industriously enough. He slept well, in the horsehair mattress of his two-tiered bunk, and was only bitten by the bugs when he forgot to douse the wood-struts of the bed (and the floorboards) with kerosene. He read far into the night: Nietzche, of course, and his new favourites, Darwin and Schopenhauer. He drew a lot, and made cardboard-and-gum models of the prominent buildings of the city, and was as content as he had ever known himself to be. He had no friends, and often went for days without talking to anybody. That did not really trouble him. The only real friend he had ever had was Gustl.

Adolf was in the ninth week of his self-imposed trial when a letter arrived from Klara, telling him she was ill. He had written his stiff, formal letter to her weekly, saying how busy he was with his studies, and she had replied, weekly, just as formally, but from time to time telling him how worried she was, and urging him to come home. He had not replied to these pleas, except to say he would be home soon enough, once he had completed his work in hand, which must not, under any circumstances, be interrupted. Klara had finally stopped asking him to come home and had fallen into a plaintive style of writing, sad and almost tearful. How was he doing for laundry? He wasn't, he washed his two shirts in the tin basin: his socks, too, with hot water boiled on the stove. How was he doing for food? Not too well, he was sometimes so hungry he felt quite dizzy. For money? Adolf was down to his last few kroner when her letter came.

He packed his rucksack and took the next train to Linz. He had the fare, with only a few marks over. He arrived, apprehensive and fearful, at Blumenstrasse 9 – his mother had moved to a more airy apartment in Urfahr, a decent suburb, he wondered how?

The doctor was attending Klara when Adolf arrived. Present was his Aunt Johanna Pohl, Klara's sister, a hunchback who had never married, and lived at nearby Spital. She had been a servant all her life, and she was in tears.

One glance at Klara's yellow face and wasted body told Adolf everything.

Doctor Bloch was Jewish, dressed formally in dark suit and hat, known to the district as the People's Doctor. He was sympathetic, and seemed moved by Adolf's obvious grief.

'A week or two, no more. The cancer has gone too far,' he told Adolf in the corridor outside the apartment. 'I'm very sorry.'

'Is there nothing we can do?' asked Adolf, stricken.

'It's incurable,' answered Bloch, gently. 'I'm giving her morphine to keep the pain down. I've left instructions. I'll call in every day. There's nothing I can do, nothing anybody can do.'

Adolf said, 'Money? Would . . . ?'

'We have no cure. Believe me, we have done all we can. We tried surgery, as you know. Also iodoform, but the treatments were too painful. This way is kinder.'

'I didn't know any of that!'

'She didn't want you to.'

'But my mother is only forty-seven!'

'I know, I know. I'm very sorry.' Doctor Bloch pressed his arm, in a last gesture. He had seen many grieving sons but could not think of one sadder. Then he was gone, walking slowly down the stairs to the street, his black leather bag in his hand.

Adolf stood a long moment in the corridor, and then went back into the living-room. The living-room was now a sick-room: but there was nothing else for it. It was the only heated room in the apartment and it was November. Aunt Johanna Pohl collected her coat, pressed Adolf's hand and said, softly, 'I'll help you to look after her.' It occurred to Adolf the old hunchbacked woman was on her own now, and was surmised to have savings: but he thought no more of it, and simply thanked her.

After Aunt Johanna had gone, promising to return in two days, Adolf sat down on the chair next to the bedside. He tried to smile. 'Now then, Mutti. We'll soon have you up and about.'

Klara shook her head. The awful pallor hurt Adolf. He wanted to do something for her but could not think what. 'The doctors can be wrong!' he cried.

'No. They have done everything.' Klara fell back on the pillows. Her voice was almost a whisper. 'Adolf, I want no more treatments. I've suffered enough.'

Adolf was devastated. 'Mutti, there must be hope.'

'No.' She pressed his hand. 'Don't wish for me to live. Please.'

Adolf would not listen. 'Doctor Bloch is only a provincial physician. He is a good man but he cannot know everything.'

'Adolf, I have been in the hospital. I don't want to go back.'

'Everything is curable!' said Adolf in anguish. 'Or it ought to be!'

Klara shook her head again. 'Adolf, Paula is to go to Angi when I'm gone. Angi has agreed. She took her yesterday.'

'Angi's been here?' asked Adolf, upset.

Klara nodded. 'Raubal won't be too pleased, but Angi has a good heart, and family has to look after family, Adolf. Nobody else will.'

'No.' Adolf agreed. That was true, anyway. He could envisage a world where strangers would take care of the sick or ill or the old, but he knew it was a long way off. He nodded his head. He could only agree with that suggestion. Where else could little Paula go?

'After I'm gone,' Klara said, 'you can apply for an Orphan's Pension. It will be half of what I have been getting. It will be between Paula and you.'

Adolf said, gently, 'Mutti. We can talk about all this later. There is plenty of time.'

'No, there isn't.' Klara put her hand on his. It was very thin and claw-like. She had been ill, he realised, for weeks, and had not called him until the very end. He felt tears in his eyes but somehow resisted them.

'One half of the pension goes to Angi for little Paula. Keep the other half for yourself. Also, I will give you what there is left of Pappi's savings.' She gestured to the sideboard and Adolf took out, at her bidding, a cloth bag of coins. 'I drew it all out,' Klara said. 'There are seven hundred kroner there. I have given three hundred to Angi for Paula. It should be enough to keep you going for a while.'

Klara closed her eyes, plainly exhausted by the effort. Adolf took the official-looking *Application Form For An Orphan's Pension*, and stuffed it in his pocket, but not before he had noticed that one of the requirements was the possession of a Death Certificate, signed by a Medical Practitioner, of the Widow of the Civil Servant, deceased. Adolf got to his feet (Klara seemed to be sleeping, obviously the Doctor had just given her the morphine) and went out into the corridor. He was trembling and more upset than he ever remembered, even during his terrible fight with *Pappi*. He was brooding on the unfairness of it all, when Gustl came up the stairs.

He looked exactly the same. Adolf was glad to see him.

Gustl said, 'Adolf!' Then he lowered his voice. 'You've been in?'

Adolf nodded. He could not trust himself to speak.

'There's no hope, is there?' Gustl asked.

Adolf shook his head.

'My mother says if there's anything she can do? Come over or sit with her, or anything?'

'No,' said Adolf. 'I will sit with her.'

'All the time?'

Adolf nodded, grimly. He raised his voice. 'Until the end! Whenever it is! Those doctors! They just let her die! They do nothing! They know nothing! They don't care! Nobody cares!'

Gustl just nodded miserably. Adolf had not changed.

A week later Gustl went back to the apartment. Aunt Johanna Pohl, the hunchback sister of Klara, was out frugally shopping. He found Adolf scrubbing the floor, with a hand-brush, a pail of steamy water and a cake of yellow soap to hand. He seemed to be enjoying the exercise. 'I got sick of just sitting there, watching her. So I thought, I'll wash the floor! Stupid, but I feel better for doing it.'

Adolf's eyes were hollow from lack of sleep.

Gustl said, 'If you're finished, go into your room and rest. Go on!'

Adolf got stiffly to his feet and yawned. 'No, I'll be fine . . .'

'Go on!' said Gustl. 'I'll stay with her.'

'What a Christmas this will be,' Adolf said, in a strained voice. 'I don't think she'll see it, Gustl.'

'Go and rest.'

Adolf nodded. 'Just for an hour, that's all. Wake me then.'

Two hours later, Klara opened her eyes. She seemed very weak but quite clear in her mind.

'Gustl?'

He leaned forward to hear her better. 'Yes?'

'Be a good friend to my son when I'm gone. He has nobody else.'

Gustl pressed her hand. He had no words.

Klara died that night, while Adolf slept.

She was buried on Christmas Eve.

After the funeral, Adolf walked the streets of Linz alone. He had had enough of the family, of Raubal and the others, enough of his respectable dark clothes and the sorrow of it all. Even old Aunt Johanna Pohl, who liked him, was denied his company.

The next day he went back to Vienna.

Gustl gained admittance to the Academy of Music, as Adolf had prophesied he would. His father made him a small but adequate allowance and he joined Adolf in his room at 16 Stumpergasse. Gustl was alarmed by the poverty and smell of the place but put the best possible face on it. If Adolf was happy in these conditions, so could he be. Besides, it was cheap, and left Gustl a few kroner to go to concerts and the opera, something the frugal Herr Kubicek had not allowed for. All Gustl was concerned about was his friend. He knew that all Adolf had were the few kroner from his father's pension and the savings. What would happen when the savings had gone?

'Don't worry about me,' Adolf said. 'We are both in the same boat. We are paupers but happy ones, doing what we want to do most.'

'It was a damn shame your not getting into the Architectural College. They should have jumped at you, with your talent . . .'

Adolf held up his hand. 'Enough! That is over. As *Mutti*'s death is over. Let us not talk about such sad things. I am studying in my own way. You, Gustl, need teachers. I do not.'

And with that, Gustl had to be content.

For Gustl the next year passed in a daze.

He had never been away from home before and when he found time to think about it he missed it very much. Adolf, on the other hand, seemed to thrive, left to his own devices. Their routines were very different. Gustl had to attend the Vienna Academy of Music at strictly defined times. The Professors insisted upon practice, practice and more practice. He hugged his viola-case, mostly walking the crowded streets to the college, now and then, if it was raining, hopping on one of the fussy little tramcars that clanked along every main street in Vienna. Gustl worked at his instrument and at his sight-reading, and attended the statutory musical evenings connected with the college. Adolf came sometimes, but excused himself if the occasion seemed a grand one. 'My suit is my only suit and it is not good enough for such people,' he would say. 'I would only be your shabby friend who cannot afford a decent evening suit. You must go on your own this time, Gustl.' In truth, Gustl was in no better shape than Adolf, since they both spent money that should have gone on food on their visits to the Vienna Opera House. In that first twelve months they saw *Die Meistersingers* and *Parsival*, as well as *Trovatore*, *Rigoletto*, and *Traviata*, although Adolf scorned these last offerings by Verdi. Adolf scorned most things, in those months. A certain harshness had entered into his manner, that Gustl had not seen before. He seemed to hate a great number of things and people. The idealistic pacifism, the innocence of their early days in Linz, sitting lazily on the banks of the Danube, seemed to have gone. Gustl was smypathetic and put it down to the loss of his mother. He knew that Klara was probably the only person Adolf had ever really cared about.

Innocence, certainly, was a rarity on the streets of Vienna. Gustl was shocked by the contrast of rich and poor. Still, he did not identify himself with the poor working-men and the beggars and down-and-outs because he knew that his own spell of poverty would last only until he obtained his degree. It was the usual student's experience: hard work, poverty, talk, and a few laughs.

For his laughs, Gustl had to depend on his fellow students. Adolf never laughed. Everything was extremely serious to him. In his own way, he was working harder than Gustl. He got up late, around ten, but from then on his routine was unvarying. He walked the streets with his sketch-book, in sun, rain and wind. In the evenings, if they were not going to the cheapest seats at the opera, or to some other musical event, Gustl worked at his sight-reading and musical theory, lying on the bunk, and Adolf sat at the table, making models from the sketches he had roughed-out during the day. He would work on, long after Gustl had fallen asleep, by the light of a paraffin lamp. Adolf often worked until two or three o'clock in the morning. He was happiest in the night-hours, he told Gustl. All his thoughts came to fruition then.

Sometimes Gustl watched him, as he worked, and wondered for whom all these models, all these drawings, were being made? From time to time he would say to Adolf, 'Hey, that's good! Why don't you take it to some firm of architects and see if they'll give you a job?'

'They won't,' was Adolf's reply.

'But why not try, at least?'

'No point in it. I don't have the qualifications. I haven't been to the College. They might give me a job as a tracer, copying other people's work, but I don't want that. It would be a waste of my time.'

'Adolf, you have to eat,' Gustl pointed out, in dismay.

'I am eating well enough.'

'But when the money runs out! You're living on your father's savings now.'

'Well, yes.' Adolf had looked across the drab room towards Gustl. 'My half-sister, Angi, wrote last week, saying that Raubal was complaining how much it cost them to keep little Paula. So I have gifted my share of the Orphan's Pension to her.'

'How will you manage?'

'Don't worry about me, Gustl.'

And that was all Gustl could get out of him. Gustl worried for his friend, but could not see a way to help him. Adolf was like nobody else he knew. He certainly did not enjoy himself in the usual ways of youth. Even their sole expedition to the Prater Pleasure Gardens had been a disaster. Adolf had surveyed the garish sideshows and the huge Big Wheel and described them as 'A Viennese Babel!'

'But these people are enjoying themselves!' protested Gustl.

'It is a ridiculous waste of money and effort,' rejoined Adolf. 'Instead of wasting money on things like *this* . . .' His sweep indicated the laughing crowds; workingmen with children on their shoulders; pretty girls laughing and shrieking on the swirling rides; the noisy cheer of it all . . . 'All *this* does for people is help them to forget their misery. Most people in Vienna are on the poverty-line.' Adolf spoke academically, and Gustl almost interrupted to tell him that *they* were on the poverty-line themselves. 'The real problem in Vienna is housing,' said Adolf. 'Vienna is one vast housing problem. It needs to be torn down and built again.'

'Is that possible?'

'The city is a sink of poverty, iniquity and decay. It has a quarter of a million unemployed or homeless or both. Something will have to be done or there will be anarchy and revolution.' The lights of the Prater were behind them now and the sounds of the joyrides were fading. 'Do you know what Plato said about democracy? An interesting form of government, inevitably leading to anarchy! That is what will happen here! There is one man, one vote.' Adolf did not mention women, for they had no vote in Austria, in city or state elections. 'So there is democracy. The liberals – the Social Democrats – rule. And look at what they have given us! If large tracts of old Vienna, the slums like the one we live in were pulled down, what should be put in their place?'

73

Before Gustl could answer, Adolf said, 'Workers' flats! Built by the Government. Airy rooms. Furniture provided free. How many young couples can afford to buy furniture? Give the girl a loan for a trousseau. How many working-girls can afford a trousseau? Give a loan for a house, don't give it free. People appreciate nothing if it's free.'

'If you let a State Manufacturing Company make the furniture, it would be awful,' said Gustl. 'Give people like my father the contracts. Cloth-covered chairs, no working-people have them! Cushions, no working-people have them. Carpets even!'

Adolf nodded. 'Excellent! That would be the way.'

Good God, Gustl thought, I'm as mad as he is! How could anything like that ever come to pass? Working-men lived from hand-to-mouth all their lives, and when they grew old and weak they were lucky if they died in a warm bed, amongst their own family, not on a freezing park-bench like the poor unfortunates around them.

The only sure way to fend off such a fate, he reflected, was marriage.

'Adolf,' he said, 'don't you think about girls at all?'

'No,' Adolf replied. 'What could I offer a girl? I have no money and no position. And I have no time to waste on girls, if I had.'

'I see them look at you at the opera.'

'Who? That rich woman who sent her card to me?'

'Yes, I suppose so.' Gustl recalled the occasion. A dark-haired woman of forty, white breasts pushing dramatically against the striking black evening dress, had sent a liveried servant to present Adolf with her card. Adolf, as usual when Wagner was playing, had eyes and ears for nothing but the music. Probably his rapt and other-worldly expression had caught the married woman's roving eye, thought Gustl – he had seen the flash of a ring on her third finger. Her opera-glasses had stayed on Adolf, right through the performance. In the street, the servant, a working-man under the finery, waited, with a deadpan expression.

Adolf had peered at the card, indignantly.

'Tell the lady no. And you have my sympathy for having to carry such a message.'

For a moment the servant was too surprised to speak. Then a smile crossed his features. Gustl watched him go back to the carriage in which the woman sat, half-leaning out of the window, a long white arm drooping negligently under the weight of a huge, ermine wrap.

'What did the card say?' he'd asked, awed, as Adolf tore it up and dropped it in the straw-filled gutter. Everywhere, even the street outside the Opera, stank of horse-piss. There were as many horses, he sometimes thought, as people in the city. Their heavy, ammoniac smell was everywhere.

'I don't know. I didn't read it.' Adolf shrugged. 'Such women are worse than the whores who sell themselves for money. At least those women are honest.'

'What do you know of whores, Adolf?'

'Nothing.' Gustl thought this to be true. Adolf never seemed to lust. Never masturbated, or so he said, but everybody said that. Greatly daring, Gustl said, 'Well, if you know nothing of whores, why don't you find out? Let's go down to the Siebensternstrasse.'

The Siebensternstrasse was the brothel quarter of Vienna.

Gustl had long wanted to go and *look*, but he did not want to go alone. To his surprise, Adolf took him up on it. 'Why not? You must see the Sink for yourself! A man cannot talk about such things without experience of them!'

Gustl demurred. 'I'm not sure how safe it is, down there?'

'Last week you sat through Wedikind's *Frohlingserwavhen*! You were titillated in the theatre but you know nothing of the real thing!' Adolf talked as if he knew. 'Such creatures as *Nana* are a million miles away from the girls who actually sell their bodies for money. Men see romance in that because they cannot bear to think of it as simply a money-transaction, which is all that it ever can be!'

'Have *you* been with one of these girls?'

Adolf hesitated. 'A man must do all things that other men do, if only for the experience.'

'*Have* you?' Gustl pressed.

'A poor working-man who cannot afford to marry a respectable woman, must resort to these girls. He has no choice. You and I, who are poor, have no choice.'

Gustl was shaken. 'You *have* been with these girls?'

Adolf did not reply. Instead, he led the way briskly into the dark night. He seemed to know where he was going. Gustl followed, somewhat sorry he had spoken, and sorrier than ever, once they turned into the *Spittelbergasse* where the girls plied their trade to a clintele of working-men. 'Prostitutes at brothel-level,' Adolf explained at once, 'can have few charms for the man of money, who is able to go to expensive sporting-houses or even set up a woman in a villa in the suburbs.' The girls sat, undraped, in the illuminated windows of one-storey houses. A few were young. Most were not. Some combed their hair and regarded themselves in mirrors. Some took up lewd positions when they saw a possible client staring at them. Gustl began to feel uncomfortable, but Adolf regarded it all with the air of a man at the Zoo. When a client walked into a house, the light in the room would go out. Adolf said, 'This is purely a financial transaction. The man wants sex, the woman the money she'll probably give to a ponce.'

Adolf's voice, as usual, was very loud. People, notably two girls in the window of a house directly in front of them, were taking interest. The window was open and the girls could probably hear what Adolf was saying.

One of the naked girls leaned out of the window. She was about their own age but had bad teeth already. 'You two boys from the country, are you?' she enquired in the broadest of Viennese dialects. 'Just stay and watch, *liebschen*, and come in when you're both ready!'

Then, to Gustl's horror, the two women began to kiss and do other things, things he could not have imagined, and it was only with a tremendous effort that he tore his eyes away from the lewd scene.

Adolf, on the other hand, was watching with detached interest.

Gustl tugged at his arm. 'Adolf, come on, for God's sake, let's get out of this awful place!' Drunken working-men were looking at them and laughing.

Adolf nodded. 'You've seen all you need to see.' He turned and followed Gustl, who, looking at nobody, walked quickly out of the alley. The laughter of the drunken working-men followed them.

Adolf was undisturbed, and spoke as if discussing a social problem. 'Gustl, this is simply a market-place where sex is sold. There is no more to it than that.'

Gustl wished the whole thing could be easily dismissed like that. The truth was, as Adolf so rightly said, Vienna was a sexual sink. Temptation loomed on every street corner, in every café, in every bar. There was a theory in Vienna, Adolf told him, that the city was going to the dogs because of the licentiousness of its beautiful women. Certainly the plays presented on the stage underlined the point that the Viennese talked about sex, read about sex, watched plays about sex, indulged in sex, to a considerable excess. It was very disturbing.

The two students sauntered on through the night-time city.

They were approached outside the Hotel Kummer by a middle-aged, well-dressed man in an opera-cape, who asked them if they could help him obtain a ticket for the Opera the following night? Adolf, amused (why, wondered Gustl?) said, 'Try the Box Office in the morning?' But the man persisted, and talked of music, and Gustl was interested because he seemed to know the subject very well. On hearing Gustl was a music-student and Adolf an architectural one, he said, 'How well I remember my own student days! I was always hungry! Can I ask you to be my guest for coffee and cakes? I am staying in the hotel?'

Gustl was a little nonplussed but Adolf accepted with aplomb. 'That would be most kind,' he said. They followed the man into the hotel, Gustl shooting a glance of enquiry at Adolf, but Adolf's face was very straight, as if this were everyday. In the large hotel-lounge, a three-piece orchestra played, and waiters hurried about with large plates of the cream cakes for which Vienna was famous. The man, who did not introduce himself by his full name and occupation as yet, but simply said, 'I am called Bernd,' asked for a large plate of cakes and coffee, at once. When they came, Adolf ate four cakes and Gustl three. Gustl felt their manners were very bad, but they were both extremely hungry and no way could they afford such luxuries. As they ate the man continued to talk about music. After half-an-hour, when the cake-plate and the coffee-pot were both empty, Adolf got to his feet. The man looked a little put-out, but shook hands with both of them, Gustl thought nervously, and they left the Kummer Hotel feeling a lot better than they had when they went in.

The street was ice-cold after the warmth of the hotel. Gustl wondered what it was like to live like that all the time, in such comfort and luxury.

Adolf asked, 'Did you like that man, Gustl?'

'Very much,' said Gustl. 'A very cultured man indeed. Most artistic, with excellent musical taste.'

'And what else?' asked Adolf.

'Well, I don't know why he asked us into the hotel. I expect he was lonely or something?'

Adolf opened his palm. A calling-card with a message scribbled on it lay there. 'Yes, he was. He was also a homosexual.'

'What's a homosexual?'

Adolf tore up the card, laughed, and told him.

The days, weeks and months went by with Adolf now taking more interest in philosophy and politics than before. He still kept up his architectural work (pointless as it seemed to Gustl) but now he was apt to read out philosophical statements such as: 'Schopenhauer says that the only thing that matters is the Will to Live!'

Adolf would lean across the table, waving his spoon as they ate their bread and milk. 'The world, Gustl, is Will itself. Obstinate. Blind. Impetuous. 'All that matters is the Force of Nature and the Will to Live!'

Gustl thought that obvious but did not say so.

'Becoming! Knowing! Being! Acting!' cried Adolf, forgetting to eat in his excitement.

'Just so,' said Gustl.

'If you have the Will you can do anything!'

Gustl doubted that very much, but again did not say so.

On another occasion Adolf shouted in his excitement, 'Gustl! Nietzsche's Theory of Resentment is outstanding!' Gustl nodded, baffled. 'Nietzsche reckons there is a fundamental difference between the philosopher and the scientist. He says Professional and Academic Philosophers – all the people sitting in the Universities now! – are fools living in the Past. He says that all Middle Class Values are False! He says Philosophers should be Prophets! They should look forward, not back! He claims – are you listening, Gustl, this is most exciting! – that the accepted values of religion, morals and philosophy have lost their power in the Western World! They are over! Finished!' Adolf's eyes gleamed more than ever: 'Nietzsche insists Man needs only the Will To Power! Self-seeking, self-aggrandisement, must be the over-riding, all-embracing principle in the development of the Race!'

Gustl felt he had to say something. 'Most people like their religion. They need it.'

'Rubbish!' said Adolf. 'It's all a lot of mumbo-jumbo for illiterate peasants! Darwin has buried religion ten feet under the ground with his *Origin of Species*! He wrote that fifty years ago, proving we all belong to the same family, all the life on this planet! And the churches go on as if he never wrote a word! There never was any Garden of Eden! Man is the product of natural selection. Man evolves. It is the survival of the fittest and the weak go to the wall! Any study of nature proves that! The strongest baboon runs the tribe and has the most female baboons. The strongest man is the leader of men. Frederick the Great! Napoleon Bonaparte! Alexander! They all testify to what Nietzsche asserts. They are the higher type of human being. They are Supermen!'

Gustl finished his pap, with distaste.

'It might be best to keep those ideas to yourself, Adolf.'

'Nonsense!' said Adolf. 'I am just beginning to see how the world really works, how it really *is*!' He looked transfixed and transported by the words, almost drunk on them, so Gustl said no more. For all he knew Adolf could be right. He sometimes was.

Towards the end of their first year together, Adolf decided to write an Opera. 'I will write the words. You, Gustl, will write the music!'

Together, they hunted the second-hand shops for an old piano, and found one in a junk shop near the West Banhof, close to their room on the Stumpergasse. It was an ancient, stand-up Bechstein, battered and scratched, with deep yellow ivory keys. It looked a great deal worse than it was, as Gustl soon found out, running up and down the scales. The tone was excellent. The problem was the price. The grimy, bearded shopkeeper wanted one hundred kroner for it. Gustl had some small savings of his own, that he had brought to Vienna (sewn into his jacket and not to be touched) amounting to three hundred kroner, for emergencies only. Adolf had only whatever was left of his lump sum of seven hundred kroner. Gustl did not know how much of that was now left, but he suspected less – possibly much less – than half. It was – for both of them – madness to consider buying this or any other piano. But Adolf did not think so. 'Without it we cannot write the opera. We need a musical score and we need a piano to play it on. This seems a good piano. Let us buy it!'

'But one hundred kroner!' protested Gustl.

'We will not pay one hundred kroner,' replied Adolf, in a loud voice, 'or anything like it.' He turned and made to leave the shop. Gustl, puzzled, followed him.

The shopkeeper accosted them at the door. 'Gentlemen! Please! Make me an offer for the piano?'

Adolf pondered. 'It is out of tune. It looks terrible. It needs money spending on it to make it fit to put in a decent room! Sixty kroner!'

Thinking of their bug-ridden residence on the Stumpergasse, Gustl smiled to himself. Adolf, however, was po-faced. He waited for the shopkeeper's answer.

'You couldn't get it for that at the State Pawnshop!' cried the man who had not contradicted Adolf about the tone of the instrument. 'Then I will bid you *Guten Tag*,' said Adolf, moving to leave the shop.

'Seventy-five!' called the shopkeeper.

Adolf kept walking.

'Seventy – not a heller less!'

Adolf turned. 'If you deliver – or lend us a cart?'

'I'll lend you a cart!'

'And,' Adolf pointed, 'give us that bundle of old manuscript paper over there!'

'Take the shop!'

'Is that yes?'

'Yes, yes!'

And so it was, and the battered old piano now stood in the awful room, reducing their living-space even further. Gustl tuned it as best he could, and finally pronounced himself satisfied. Then, and only then, did he say to Adolf, 'But can we *afford* it?'

Even Adolf had to laugh at that: they both laughed hysterically. Then they wiped the tears from their eyes and began to work.

Adolf's opera was called *Wieland the Smith*. Adolf was telling a folk tale, of a Germany that was gone. *Wieland* was an archetypal German. Strong. Simple. Independent. He wanted nothing more than a rural, happy existence.

'Developers are going to drive a modern road through his village, destroying the ancient ways of the Volk,' shouted Adolf, pacing excitedly. 'So *Wieland* resists it with all his might. But the Evil Developers prove too much for him! The Modern World of Progressives and Social Democrats want a world full of people all looking and thinking the same, dancing to degenerate music, watching degenerate plays like Schnitzler's *La Ronde*, and want to convert the Volk to their degenerate ways!' Adolf paused. 'Do we allow the Road to happen, with *Wieland* dying in the process? With maximum sympathy for *Wieland*? Or not allow it to happen and have *Wieland* victorious? What do you think?'

Gustl realised that Adolf did actually think *Wieland the Smith* had a chance of a professional production. Knowing that almost every one of his colleagues at the College had an opera in his knapsack, he felt apprehensive. 'Adolf, it takes six months to get a manuscript read by Viennese theatre managers.'

'Then we have lots of copies made and send them to everybody at once' declared Adolf, never at a loss. Gustl pointed out that this was thought, in musical circles, to be unprofessional and somewhat improper, but Adolf laughed. 'The usual set of professional do-and-don'ts to discourage new talent. Nobody ever wants new talent. They only accept it when it has forced itself into the public gaze, by sheer act of Will!' His eyes shone. 'By sheer act of Will, Gustl!' He cleared the table of his cardboard models and slammed down the pile of yellowing manuscript paper. 'To work!'

For ten whole nights – Gustl was at the College all day – they worked, often until three in the morning, when Gustl had to succumb to sleep and fall exhausted on the bunk, still in his day-clothes. Adolf worked on through the night, until daylight filtered into the room. Then he would sleep until noon: get up, and work all day. Adolf was beginning to look even paler than usual, and thinner, and his skin began to have a transparent look about it.

So Gustl worked on too, heavy-eyed and yawning, transcribing the music. On and on, night after night, until he could no longer tell if the words or the music were any good or not.

It was Adolf who finally called a halt.

Gustl came back on the last day to find the table bare of manuscript-paper, and the piano-lid closed.

'What's happened?'

'It's not good enough,' said Adolf.

He was looking out of the window, sadly.

'What do we do?' asked Gustl.

'We put it away and take it out again, sometime in the future.'

They never did.

After that, Adolf turned to politics. Gustl thought it simply another fad. Another subject upon which Adolf would discourse and then discard, as he had so many other subjects: his poems; his painting; his architecture. He was doing less and less with his sketchpad, and sitting more and more, alone in the cold damp room, reading the free political-pamphlets given away on every street-corner in Vienna. One was *Ostara*, an anti-Semitic publication. Adolf said, 'According to this, the Jews have much to answer for!' Gustl, who knew no Jews, asked why. 'They take advantage of the Germanic Race in all sorts of ways. Money. Women. Everything. I have a personal reason for knowing that much, anyway, is true!' said Adolf.

'What personal reason?' asked Gustl, mystified. 'It is too personal to talk about,' Adolf said, and went on reading the scurrilous broadsheet.

'I don't understand any of that,' said Gustl.

'Or of much else. You need political instruction' said Adolf.

Later that week Adolf took the reluctant Gustl to the Parliament. They stood in the empty Visitors' Gallery, and Gustl was surprised how many of the seats in the chamber were empty. Nobody seemed to be listening to the speaker, an earnest man with a monocle and a fancy waistcoat. Deputies walked around the large, comfortable chamber, order-papers in hand, and chatted to each other in whispers.

'You see?' Adolf whispered. 'This is your so-called Democracy? These are the men paid by public taxes to represent the public! The Government can get a majority any time it likes, by calling all its members to vote.'

'But where are they?' asked Gustl.

'In the backrooms and offices of this place, making deals with one another, none of it to the benefit of the ordinary citizen!' Adolf's voice rose and a uniformed attendant approached them, raising a warning finger.

Adolf moved away from the man's stern and haughty gaze. 'Nincompoop! The Empire's full of such ridiculous, officious people! Nobodies, like my father!'

Gustl knew that Adolf still used his father's title if it seemed useful to him. In the same way that he did not deny his Catholicism if the people he was talking to were devout. It puzzled Gustl, because Adolf was always so declamatory in private. In public, he seemed concerned to be accepted as a member of the middle-class. He was always well-shaven, his collar was always clean, and the trousers of his suit still went under the dubious mattress every night, to preserve their crease. In fact, Gustl copied Adolf's manners. Bowing slightly to a lady, on introduction, with a slight click of the heels, small but very important things like that. Plainly, there were two Adolfs. The bougeois young man, and the rebellious and uncaring self-taught thinker.

As they walked out of the Parliament building, Adolf said, 'There you are, you've seen it, Gustl. It doesn't work! Something else will have to take its place!'

'What?' asked Gustl.

Adolf shrugged. 'I don't know enough about politics to tell you the answer to that question. But something.'

As they walked across the square Gustl asked Adolf the question he'd been holding back for weeks. 'Adolf. How are you for money? I mean, really?'

Adolf dodged a particularly swift gig, swore at the coachman, and said, 'I'm fine, Gustl. Don't worry about me, I will manage.'

'You always say that.' Gustl fell into step with his friend. He was indeed very concerned. 'Look, I don't have much myself, but we can both manage on what I have, somehow.'

'No, we can't. You can hardly manage as it is.'

Gustl fell silent. He knew that was all too true.

'Maybe I can get my father to help!' he suggested.

Adolf said, in a different, steely voice, 'Please, Gustl. No charity.'

Gustl shook his head. 'I'm sorry, I didn't mean it like that.'

'No, I know.' Adolf took his arm. 'Now for your second political lesson, Gustl.'

'What, another?'

'You've seen how Parliament works. Now, we go and see how politics works in the streets.'

'Where?' Gustl's feet hurt and he was hungry. He was always hungry.

'There's a Workers' Party demonstration in the Ringstrasse. It begins in one hour. It is only a mile and a half to the point at which it is due to begin. We will go there now and we will see what happens.'

Gustl felt hungrier and more footsore than ever. He had a great deal of work to do back in the room. Nonetheless, he could not deny Adolf. Adolf seemed cheerful at the idea of more strife and scorn and even danger – these Demos could get rough – and so he fell into step once more, and they joined a solid and silent throng of workingmen who were going the same way. These men wore clothes even shabbier than their own. They spoke little, and looked grim, and Gustl felt uncomfortable in their midst. Adolf, on the other hand, watched them with interest and attempted to strike up conversation with various men, but they all looked askance at his middle-class appearance: his collar and tie, and the silk handkerchief in his top-pocket, and the fact that he was wearing a suit, and of course, his *cane* – which he carried with him everywhere.

'They think I'm a police spy,' said Adolf to Gustl, in a thoughtful whisper. 'It is incorrect to come to a thing like this looking middle-class. They will not listen to you. They will not take you seriously.'

Gustl wondered what Adolf could find to say to such desperate and hungry men, but made no reply, for suddenly they were in the square, and the crush of bodies was so profound they had to struggle to breathe. Using their arms and elbows, Adolf at the front, they found themselves suddenly at a wooden barrier, erected across the Ringstrasse, to hold back the crowds. Whole squads of semi-military mounted police, armed with batons and sabres, waited at one end of the square. Adolf had never seen police in such numbers at any time. The power of the State is represented by the police, he thought, and here it is very amply demonstrated. The sullen, silent men in caps who made up the majority of the vast crowd (how many, ten thousand, twenty?) had no power, save the power of protest, and what good was that?

A long murmuring noise, like the growling of a beast roused from slumber, rose from the mass of workers. Adolf craned his head and was just able to see what had caused it. A procession of workingmen in caps had entered the square, carrying a large banner. It took a dozen of them to hold it aloft.

The banner bore one word.

Hunger.

As the procession passed through the square, foot-police in helmets, with drawn batons, waved them to a halt.

The Workers ignored them and marched on.

Twice the mounted Officer in charge of the police called to them to stop. Twice they ignored him, and marched forward.

The third time that happened, the Officer dropped his hand in a signal, and the foot-police began to hit the banner-carriers with their long, black batons. The men fell to the ground, holding their heads. Adolf could see the blood running down their faces. Some men fought back, with their bare hands and their boots, but they too were soon clubbed to the ground.

The terrible murmuring noise of the watching crowd grew louder. Stones began to fly. Some of the police were hit and staggered back holding their faces. A section of the crowd broke down a barrier and fought hand-to-hand with the foot-police. More stones flew. The whole scene had suddenly exploded into violence and chaos.

Adolf, crushed against a barrier, watched avidly, powerless to interfere. So, *this* was the street? No Members of Parliament were here to see this, but surely it mattered more than the babbling of the fawning Deputies in the Parliament?

There could be but one end to it all.

The uniformed Officer gave another signal.

The squads of mounted-police moved forward.

Adolf heard Gustl shout, 'My God, no!' but he was too transfixed to speak. He watched as the men on horseback, sabres drawn by now, slowly, systematically, cut the crowd to pieces, using the weight of the horses to send men sprawling, and striking out skilfully with the flat side of their sabres, so skilfully that men simply collapsed as they were struck, and lay still on the ground. For two or three minutes the crowd put up a fighting resistance and then it broke and ran. Adolf watched the mounted-policemen follow the running men, as they scattered across the square, selecting victims at random and striking them down with easy but terrible force.

Gustl tugged at his arm. 'Come on, Adolf! Run!'

Adolf ran, but, curiously, he was not afraid.

He was exhilarated.

Back in their room on the Stumpergasse (another hour of hard walking) Adolf and Gustl celebrated their escape from the police at the Ringstrasse, in a toast of watery coffee, accompanied by rye bread smeared with meat-paste. They had run and run to get clear of the mobs of fleeing workingmen, and youth had been on their side. They had quickly outstripped the older workers, many of whom had fallen victims to the mounted-police. Gustl could still hear the dreadful *stump* of the batons on the skulls of the running men.

Gustl felt sad. 'Those poor men. The police didn't need to do that!'

'Yes, they did,' replied Adolf, who seemed to Gustl over-excited, uplifted. 'The moment you commit yourself to use force, it must be maximum force. Anything less is a sign of weakness.'

'It was a cruel shame' objected Gustl. 'All that those men were doing was demonstrating their hunger. Don't you feel any sympathy for them?'

'Of course I do!' Adolf drank his watery coffee, greedily. 'Of course I'm on the side of the hungry and underprivileged! How could I not be? But those workers were doomed from the start. They had no leader who had the weight to argue with the police. Their leader didn't have the guts to walk in front of them and tell the Officer-in-charge that this was a lawful and legal demonstration. Somebody like that could have altered the whole course of events. But these men were leaderless. So they had no hope of getting any real notice taken of their plight!'

'The Demo was organised by the Worker's Party' said Gustl. 'They must have leaders.' Said Adolf, grimly 'whoever they were they were not in evidence, were they?' He paused, thoughtfully. 'It was a waste of time, spirit and blood.'

'But aren't you with the workers?' pressed Gustl.

'Of course I am, I've just said so,' responded Adolf. 'There's something about them, in the mass like that, something . . . exciting . . . yet, they seem like sheep, yes?'

His tone held a doubt and Gustl thought he knew what it was. Adolf, despite his low living standards – watery coffee and meat-paste for dinner – did not consider himself on a par with the poor, ignorant workless of the Demo. His father had been a Customs Officer and he still felt he belonged to a superior class. He was afraid, Gustl guessed, as everybody was who had got a few rungs up the ladder from farm or urban labourer, of falling back into the unnamed, unnumbered, anonymous ranks of the piss-poor. Gustl knew the feeling, for he had it himself.

'Yet frightening', said Adolf. 'The mob? You felt that also?' Gustl nodded.

Some weeks later, Gustl received a call-up paper for compulsory Military Service in the Austrian Army. It was not totally unexpected. Everybody got one when they attained their eighteenth birthday, if they were on house-rolls and born in Austria. It was difficult to evade, although many young men did. Some, because they were incomers and their names did not appear on the Birth-certificates from which such rolls were compiled. Others, because they ran for safety to another country. To Gustl's amazement, on seeing Gustl's disappointed and apprehensive face, Adolf proposed an odd course of action.

'Go back to Linz and take the medical examination. If you are pronounced fit, simply cross the border into Germany at Passau. It is an open border and you won't be challenged.'

'But what would I do in Germany?'

'Continue your musical studies at a German college.'

'Would they take me? Even if I could go?'

'Of course. You're a good student.'

'But wouldn't they call me up for service in the German Army?'

'No. You're not a German, you're an Austrian!' Adolf sat down at the table and gestured for Gustl to sit down, too. Gustl sat, very troubled. Here he was, doing so well in his musical studies that his Professor was sending him an occasional pupil. There was the certainty of a decent pass – possibly even a First! – in the Examination the following summer. And now this! It really was too awful. Some well-to-do students at the College got out of Military Service, Gustl presumed by family connections, probably political. None, so far as he knew, had fled to Germany to escape it, and to continue their studies there. It seemed an extreme solution, and Gustl said so.

'Why? Do you want your studies interrupted for two years or whatever time they decide to keep you in the Army?'

'Of course not. But everybody has to do it.'

'The Austrian Empire is finished. Antiquated. Moribund. To serve in it would be a total waste of your time.'

'Even so, how can I get out of it?'

'Go home to Linz and do as I say.'

'I'll have to talk to my Father about it.'

'Naturally. But he'll see the sense of it.'

Gustl was not too sure of that.

Back in Linz, Herr Kubicek was unexpectedly furious at the suggestion that his son should evade Military Service by fleeing to Germany, and after smoking a consoling pipe or two, came up with a solution. Herr Kubicek had talked to various Army acquaintances and their advice was this: Gustl should *volunteer* for the Army Reserve, which would involve him in a short period of training, and some regular yearly camps, but would avoid the long travail of compulsory Military Service, leaving him free to pursue his musical studies in Vienna.

Six weeks had passed, Gustl realised, as he returned to Vienna, humping a battered suitcase full of clean underclothes and other necessities, including food (bratwurst, pork-sausage, cooked ham) pressed on him by his mother. As he turned into the Stumpergasse, his heart lifted at the idea of seeing Adolf again. This time he was resolute. Adolf and he must share and share alike in all things. Food. Rent. Everything. He would insist on it.

Gustl found the door of their room locked, and the landlady, Frau Zakrey, a small, dark woman, middle-aged and Polish, waiting for him.

'Herr Kubicek?' Frau Zakrey held up a postcard Gustl had posted two days before. 'I had your card to say you were coming back today.'

'My card? It was addressed to my friend, Adolf?' Gustl felt aggrieved. 'Why do you have my card, Frau Zakrey?'

Frau Zakrey shrugged. 'Herr Adolf has gone.'

'Gone?' Gustl set down his case. 'When?'

'The week after you left.'

'Did he say where he was going?'

'No. He just gave me the key and left. I'm afraid I'll have to charge you the same rent as when the two of you had the room. Possibly you will find somebody else to join you?'

'No,' said Gustl slowly, 'I doubt that.' He added, 'Adolf will be at his sister Angi's.'

But he wasn't.

VII

THAT summer Adolf slept on a park-bench in the Prater. He refused to do what the habitues did, parcelling themselves in newspapers taken from the litter-bins. He had a blanket. Nobody else seemed to have a blanket, except him, and he soon realised why. A blanket (he had stolen it from the room in the Stumpergasse) had to be carried around all day. There was nowhere to leave it that was safe. Nonetheless, Adolf could not face even the cool nights of a Vienna summer without it. A cold, gusty wind blew across the Prater at dawn, and the down-and-outs shivered and turned about on their benches, even those who were numbed with the raw alcohol so many of them seemed to drink. No exception to this was Hanisch, a tramp who occupied the next bench in the Prater. Hanisch had looked at him curiously, the first night he had seen Adolf in the Prater, sitting, not lying, on his bench.

At about one in the morning, Hanisch, who was drinking from a bottle wrapped in paper, said, 'If you're going to lie down, Good Sir, lie down now, or some late-comer will give you an argument.'

'I'm locked out of my room, that's all,' said Adolf, loftily.

'I know. We all are,' said Hanisch. 'Is that a blanket in your rucksack?'

Adolf hesitated. 'Yes, it is.'

Hanisch sighed. 'Then wrap it round yourself, tight as you can. Use your rucksack as a pillow or somebody will steal it. They might anyway. Don't take your shoes off. You got any money?'

'Very little.'

'Enough for a room?'

'Not really.'

Hanisch looked at Adolf blearily but shrewdly, in the half-light from the street-lamps around the Prater. The showground rides and side-shows had closed at midnight and all that could be heard in the deserted

87

Prater was the occasional cry of a cat, or the sound of drunken cursing, from one or other of the park-benches.

'Never slept out at night before, have you?'

Adolf said, stiffly, 'I've camped out. On the mountains.'

Hanisch laughed, a wheezy dropsical sound. 'Ain't the same thing though, is it?' Adolf said nothing. All he felt was anger and bleak despair. In his pocket he had six kroner. It was enough for a bed but he needed food to survive. How could he live without food? His calculation was, he'd be out of money by the end of the week. Then he'd have to go back, cap in hand, to Angi and Raubal and ask them for charity.

It was something he knew he could never do.

Hanisch was still looking at him, over the top of his bottle of hooch. 'How much money have you got?'

'A few kroner.'

'You're rich, then. I haven't had a kroner in my hand since last Christmas. You always do all right around Christmas. Plenty of drunks, see? You from Vienna, are you?'

'No.' Adolf wished Hanisch would stop asking questions.

'My name's Hanisch.'

'Adolf.'

'Nowhere to go?'

'Nowhere I want to go.'

Hanisch nodded, and drank. The liquid, whatever it was, did not seem to have any effect on him. 'But there's somebody to go to?'

Adolf shook his head, grimly. 'Aren't there any jobs?'

Hanisch took a tin from his pocket. With a grimy finger he sorted amongst the used cigar-butts it contained, selected one, and lit it with a match taken from a pocket of the several waistcoats he seemed to be wearing. 'Plenty of them, yes, if you go to the Banhof and meet the trains and carry people's bags, that kind of job. Of course, there's plenty at it. Daresay you've seen 'em.'

Adolf nodded, appalled. He had indeed seen the down-and-outs rushing forward to greet each train, chased away by the regular porters. The idea that he might become one of them shocked Adolf. 'I couldn't do that,' he said. 'I'd die first.'

'Artist, aren't you?' said Hanisch.

'How do you know?'

'You've got a tripod in your rucksack.'

Adolf was surprised Hanisch had noticed.

'Any good, are you?'

'I'm all right.'

'Draw people, can you? Do their faces? Do likenesses and that?'

'Not really. More like a view of the Hofburg. That sort of thing.'

'Ever made any money at it?'

Adolf hesitated. 'No. Never.'

'No good, then?' Hanisch sounded disappointed.

'I haven't tried to sell them. I've been studying art and architecture.'

Hanisch looked understanding. 'Failed your exams?'

'Something like that.'

'And don't want to go back home, is that it?'

'In a way.' It was, Adolf reflected, true enough.

Hanisch nodded again, as if he now understood everything. 'Wrap up in your blanket. Put it in your rucksack tomorrow morning. Never, ever, put your rucksack down. Never. Unless it's between your legs. Never leave it, even to go a few yards away from it. Understand?'

Adolf nodded. 'I think so.'

'I'll give you a tap in the morning and show you how to live in Vienna on nothing. I'll only do it tomorrow. Then you're on your own.'

Adolf didn't know whether to be grateful or refuse the offer. Before he could decide either way, Hanisch had drained his bottle, thrown it into the air, paper and all, so that it described a shimmering arc before it splintered into a dozen fragments on the stone walkway. It was a gesture of such sudden ferocity and anarchy that Adolf was shocked.

Hanisch stretched out on his bench and pulled his tattered old coat (he seemed to have two) tightly around him.

'How old are you, My Good Sir?'

'Seventeen.'

'God, you've got a lot to learn.'

Inside a minute, Hanisch was snoring.

Adolf lay down on the hard bench, but he hardly slept at all.

There was simply no way to get comfortable. He debated putting the blanket underneath his body to take away from the unyielding hurt of the wooden bench, but that would render him too cold to sleep. He had extra socks and a shirt in his rucksack. Tomorrow, he resolved, he would wear them, like Hanisch, at night. Life with the down-and-outs was just as complicated, obviously, as life in a comfortable home, probably more so. He didn't know what he had expected, but this was not it. He wondered how long he would last out. Whatever happened, he would give it a trial. He would keep away from the places where he might run into Gustl, or anybody from the Academy of Music. He would not go, ever, near his half-sister's apartment. A million people lived in Vienna, Adolf thought, moving his hipbone around uncomfortably, he should be able to get lost in the city.

Yet, how would he live?

How would he exist without money?

The next day Hanisch showed him.

A tap on his head wakened him, and there was the dreadful face of the hobo peering down at him, an awful sight in the first rays of the sun. Hanisch was unshaven, bleary and he stank. Adolf held his breath. He was in no position to be choosy. The man might be a tramp but he had offered help and there was no sane reason to refuse it.

Adolf sat up. He ached from his neck to his toes, and his head felt fuzzy. His underclothes stuck to his body and his tongue clung to the roof of his mouth.

But Hanisch was whispering, 'Come on! Upsticks! We want to be first in line for breakfast, don't we?'

'Where?' asked Adolf.

'Place in the Tiefer Graben. Come on, we'll be late.'

'The Tiefer Graben is miles!'

'Well, if you've got a coach an' four we'll go in that, won't we? If you ain't, then we'll go on our two flat feet.'

The idea of tramping through the deserted streets of Vienna with this scarecrow was too much for Adolf.

'I have to have a wash and shave first. I can't eat unless I do!'

Hanisch looked at him with amusement. He laughed, a silent bronchial wheeze. 'Particular, ain't you? A gentleman, I can see that.' He pondered. 'If you've got ten heller to give the attendant you can stop off at the all-night lavatory in the Herrenstrasse. The attendant might even give you a towel. You can follow me on.'

Adolf wrapped up his blanket and stuffed it into his rucksack. 'That's what I'll do.'

He looked around the Prater. Most of the down-and-outs still slept. He was amazed how they could do it, what with the cold – it was in his very bones – and the hard benches. He did not think he would ever be able to sleep like that.

'Come on then,' said Hanisch, impatiently.

Adolf slung the rucksack over his shoulder and fell into step. Together the old tramp and the boy walked out of the vast green Prater, into the cool morning city, the first rays of the sun beginning to shaft their way through the tall workers' tenements looming over them. Adolf wished with all his heart that he had a bed, any bed, somewhere in this city. He reproved himself. A man could live without a bed, if he had the Will to do it.

Hanisch was talking – or rather mumbling – as they walked. Despite his age (how old was he, fifty?) he kept up a good pace, shuffling along, hardly seeming to pick up his feet at all. 'We get our breakfast at the Tiefer Graben. Then we only have to hold out till tonight.'

'Tonight? What do we do then?'

'We get some soup.'

'Where?'

'Refuge for the Roofless. I'll tell you where it is.'

Adolf was shocked again. He had never thought of the Refuge. He had, of course, read about it in the newspapers. It was a famous charity-house. Sobered, he walked on. He had elected this life, he must bear with it. Or go back and eat shit. Face the laughter and the scorn of Raubal.

That he would never do.

It was a matter of pride.

As Schopenhauer rightly said, nothing mattered but the Will. A man, as Nietschze said, must show he can take the worst the world can throw at him and conquer it. That he would do. He swore it.

'Here we are.' Hanisch pointed to the Gentlemen's Lavatory. It consisted of iron railings and steps leading down into the lavatory itself. 'Don't give him more than ten heller. Come on to the Institute at the Tiefer Graben when you're done. Don't take too long about it.'

Adolf hesitated. 'How will I know where you mean?'

Hanisch laughed his bronchial wheeze. 'You'll know.' And he trudged on down the boulevard.

Adolf descended into the lavatory, to find a lone attendant in a short white coat. 'We're closed!' he snarled, shoving an angry red face into Adolf's. He smelled of cheap schnapps.

Adolf said, 'I just want a quick wash and brush up. There's ten in it for you. I want a towel.'

The man swayed on his feet, his red-rimmed eyes assessing Adolf. 'Student are yer? Been on the piss?'

Adolf nodded. It was as good a story as any.

The man held out his palm. Adolf put ten heller in it. The man ran a basin of hot water and put a thin towel the size of a napkin next to it. A bar of yellow soap was also produced. Adolf took off his collar and tie, rolled up his sleeves and washed his face and neck thoroughly. He wiped himself dry on the towel, which was rapidly converted into a sodden rag, so thin was it, and took a razor and a small, hard tube of shaving-soap from his rucksack.

'Hey!' objected the attendant. He pointed to a sign displayed on the wall. '*No Shaving Allowed on These Premises! By Order!*'

Adolf said, evenly, 'I will be coming in every morning at about this time. I will always have ten heller for you. Do I get a shave or not?'

The attendant swayed drunkenly. What a job, Adolf thought. In this place alone, all night. No wonder the man was a drunk. 'Well?' he shouted. In Vienna or anywhere else in Austria, it always paid to shout. People, especially public-servants, took notice of a man who shouted. He was likely to be of importance.

'Yes or no, man?' Adolf yelled at the wavering drunk.

The man came to a sudden attention, clicked his heels and shouted, in reply, 'Yes. Certainly, Meinherr' To Adolf's amusement, he threw up a Prussian salute.

'Good!' shouted Adolf, and rubbed the shaving soap onto his face, getting a good hot lather. He felt better at once. The scented soap took away the frowsty smell of humanity he could detect in himself. The blade was his father's cut-throat. He had taken one, out of the case of seven, after his mother's funeral. He supposed Raubal had the other six.

'A fine razor, that one?' said the lavatory attendant.

'It belonged to my father, a Customs Officer,' said Adolf, shaving on.

'A gentleman's razor. An officer's razor,' said the lavatory attendant, handing Adolf a clean towel. 'Anybody can tell that about you, that you're a gentleman!'

Adolf left the public lavatory feeling much better. He nodded to the final salute from the attendant, and went up the stairs into the street with a lighter step.

There was a line of workless men outside the soup kitchen in the Tiefer Graben when Adolf got there. About thirty men were shuffling along, slowly, and they were, if Hanisch was to be believed, the early birds. It was barely six-thirty but the denizens of the night, Adolf realised, were afoot. For a good and simple reason. They did not lie in bed because they had no beds to lie in.

Adolf debated walking away from it all, but his stomach felt so empty it hurt. He attached himself to the end of the line, and slowly shuffled his way into the place. *Soup and Tea Institute*, read a sign over the large, open door. Once inside, Adolf saw that it was bad, but not as bad as he feared. Most of the men – there were no women – looked slumped and beaten. Men out of a job, but in the main respectable enough. A few odd tramp-like characters (Hanisch was one of them, and waved to Adolf, but he ignored him) sat here and there. These, Adolf realised, were the professionals. These were the ones who knew the ropes. These were the survivors.

The middle-aged woman at the counter passed Adolf a bowl of soup. 'Danke,' he said, and she looked surprised, and then smiled. There was nothing else. No bread. No butter. Only thin vegetable soup and a cup of tea. Adolf bore the soup carefully to a table some distance away from Hanisch. There were wooden tables and primitive furniture. Men sat smoking, if they had the makings, having finished their soup.

Adolf ate his soup very slowly.

Whoever said that a hungry man eats greedily was wrong. A hungry man eats or drinks very slowly, making every mouthful count. When

Adolf had drunk his soup, and then his tea (and they tasted much the same) he looked up to see Hanisch sitting opposite from him.

'Enjoy that?' Hanisch put a soiled cigar-butt into his mouth and lit it from yet another spare match from the recesses of his many waistcoats.

'Not much,' said Adolf.

'Better than nothing, though?'

Adolf nodded. He would not argue with that.

'You can come here every morning. That's your breakfast found. You can stay here for five nights running in the Winter. December to March. Remember it. It's free.'

Adolf nodded. He was learning. But Hanisch stank horribly. He rose. He had to get out. He would throw up the soup he'd just eaten if he didn't.

'Be at Meidling at seven this evening. The Refuge opens then. Don't be late, or you'll wait for hours.'

'What will be on the menu?' asked Adolf, ironically.

'Soup. What else?' asked Hanisch. 'You going somewhere, now?'

'A walk,' said Adolf. 'Then to the Public Library. I'm studying.'

'You don't tell me!' croaked Hanisch. He laughed again, the terrible wheezing that never broke into a cough. Adolf thought: I can never get as low as that, can I?

'What will you do all day?' he asked Hanisch, curious.

'Beg,' replied Hanisch, briefly. 'If the flatfoots allow me to live.'

Adolf nodded and pushed his way out of the crowded place. Hanisch had been right. The line was now right round the square. He walked briskly towards the Public Library. It was only when he got there that he realised it did not open for another hour and a half.

And he was hungry again, already.

So, the shortening summer days took on a pattern: a night bench in the Prater; a morning wash and shave in the lavatory; a long walk to the Tiefer Graben for soup and tea; intensive reading at the Public Library until it closed at six o'clock; another long walk to the Refuge for the Roofless in the evening. Sometimes the tramp, Hanisch, was with him, sometimes he was not. Like most tramps, Hanisch would get restless from time to time and disappear for days, or even weeks. But that first day he had taken Adolf to the Refuge for the Roofless, and Adolf knew that if Hanisch had not been with him he would have turned away, starving or not. The Refuge was a long step down from the Soup and Tea Institute. It had beds and attracted those who were really down and out. But a glance at the accommodation, sixty bunks with one blanket only, almost touching each other, in one long room was too much for him. The men were lying on their bunks, mostly fully-clothed, and they either had their boots on, or had tied them around their necks.

Property, Adolf realised, was protected with as much savagery here as it was in the world of gold and silver. Men would fight and even kill for it. He found that a confirmation of what Nietschze said: a man must survive!

Survival certainly was all that mattered here.

Hanisch, at his side, asked slyly, 'Fancy this place?'

Adolf was holding his breath against the stink of unwashed bodies and feet. 'I couldn't sleep in this. I'd rather be in the Prater.'

Hanisch wheezed, 'Come the winter you'll be glad of it.'

'Never!'

Hanisch led him out into the cool evening, past the crush of smelly, hungry men. Adolf, once in the street, breathed afresh.

'Now you know the best,' said Hanisch. 'In the Winter . . .' He smelled the cool air, '. . . and it's not far off, there are many worse places than the Refuge.'

Adolf shivered, wondering what they were, afraid to ask.

But Hanisch merely said, 'See you in the Prater,' and mooched off into the dark city, no doubt to beg his bread, or more likely his hooch, in the doorways of the main thoroughfares.

The problem with that activity, he had warned Adolf, was that sometimes an over-officious policeman would arrest a vagrant for begging. There was no law against vagrancy. Just against begging. You could, Hanisch said, find yourself in jail for a month. That was not too bad. The food, mainly swill and tea, was better than the soup at the Institute or the Refuge. The drawback was, there was no hooch and no women. There was plenty of buggery but Hanisch didn't care for that. Adolf was amazed to learn that any woman would accommodate Hanisch.

'Some old tart will oblige me,' confessed Hanisch. 'If I share my bottle with her.'

Adolf shut the picture out of his mind.

'Besides,' Hanisch added, 'I hate being closed in. That's why I got on the tramp in the first place. I can't stand being cooped up inside. Unless it's freezing your balls off, you won't find me inside, my dear Sir. I'll be under the stars. I expect I'll freeze under them one fine night.'

'What did you do before all this?' Adolf asked.

Hanisch shook his head. 'It don't matter. Down here in Hell there's no Before or After. There's just Now. Remember that, and you'll live. Think about the past and you'll die. I know. I've seen them as has done it, Good Sir.'

With that Adolf had to be content.

Hanisch was present most nights in the Prater, but in October, when it began to grow cold and Adolf woke each morning shivering, suddenly he was gone.

For the very first time, Adolf felt afraid.

He asked various of the other habitues if they had seen Hanisch but they all shook their heads. To his surprise (since he never looked at them closely and was always away from the place for his daily wash, long before they awoke) some of them were women, toothless and alcoholic certainly, but under their smelly rags, women. He found some solace in that. If these horrible creatures could survive the summers and winters of the Prater, so could he. Women were the weaker sex, insisted Nietschze, bound by their child-bearing biological role to the kitchen and the bedchamber.

Men were the warriors and the hunters.

Yet, somehow, these awful old biddies seemed to go on and on. Women, he reflected, had to be strong to bear and rear children. And they did not worry about things of the mind or soul. Women were primitive, at the last. They lived longer than men, very often. They did not war and fight. They sat still and suffered, for a very long time. As his mother had done. Pappi, after all, had gone first. The important thing for a man to remember was that his work must take precedence over everything else. Therefore his work must be done, his chosen task accomplished, before he grew old and feeble, like Hanisch, and lost his teeth and his Will.

Adolf sat in the welcoming, stuffy warmth of the Viennese Public Library. He was always the first into the Library in the morning, and the last out in the evening. He stood at the same desk, having established himself as a bona-fide student, and not a vagrant simply seeking warmth. These were ushered out by the uniformed officials, especially if they were drunk and smelled particularly badly. As Hanisch did. Adolf used the Common Reading Room, where the newspapers and magazines were locked by wooden-struts to the sloping reading-benches. A man had to stand to read and that became tiring after an hour or more. The Reference Room, on the other hand, had desks and chairs and an individual light for each desk, and rows of leather-bound books around the walls. No vagrants were admitted, although a few eccentric artists and writers were regular visitors. Nowadays his reading was no longer artistic and architectural. He had given up those subjects as irrelevant to his present needs. He had no desire, any longer, to paint, and no money for the materials anyway. He had no warm room in which to build his models of the Hofburg, and nobody to show them to, as he had shown them to Gustl.

Art and Architecture, he was beginning to realise, were luxuries.

They were subjects for self-indulgent persons, who thought such things mattered more than anything else in the world. They could be excused for thinking it, but they were, of course, wrong. The most important things in the world were a full belly, a warm bed, and a roof. Only somebody who did not have those things knew their value. Only somebody who had starved and walked the streets penniless knew what it was like to be unemployed, like a third of the population of Vienna. No job. No food. No roof.

Only the politicians could change the situation. Only the politicians – the languid men with monocles in the Parliament – could pass the legislation that gave the Volk enough to eat, a bed to sleep in, a job. Instead, they ruled the Austrian Empire as the rest of Europe ruled their subjects, as if nothing had changed since the Middle Ages, as if the Industrial Revolution had never happened! The serfs and the landless had flocked into the towns but found conditions worse than they were in the country. In the country, at least, a man was close to his relatives and food grew in the fields. There was always something to eat, even if it was only a raw turnip stolen from a farmer's field. In Vienna, nothing grew. Except dirt. Disease. Poverty. The poor got poorer, the rich got richer. Nothing got done. The politicians were impotent or did not care or both. The Social Democrats prated on about democracy and a vote for everybody, but of what use was a vote that affected nothing? Even the Christian Socials had no programme for a New Start.

And a New Start there would have to be.

With the *Volk* having the say!

With – first and most important of all – all Foreigners and Undesirables chased out of Vienna to make whatever jobs and businesses there were available for Austrians again!

Czechs, Poles, Italians, Jews – especially the Jews, who were simply fleeing Pogroms and military service in Poland and Tsarist Russia! They were doing very well in Vienna, some of them. *Die Zeit* said that some suburbs of Vienna were now seventy per cent Jewish. And these were not slums. These were fine villas and houses with trees around them. It was possible the Jews were doing all this by hard work and nothing else. But *Die Zeit* insisted they helped each other in a tribal way and took advantage not only of the Austrian Immigration Laws to enter the Empire, but of the sloppy Business and Bankruptcy Laws, and used them in their favour!

Adolf found that his hatred was beginning to focus, blindly and obsessively, more and more on the Jews. The old family rumour, half-forgotten but never entirely forgotten, came more and more into his mind as he lay sleepless and feverish on his bench in the Prater. What *had* he heard, all those years ago, in the Walviertal? . . . Nothing concrete, really. Just odd and hushed words: his grandmother in some way connected to some Jews from Gratz . . . Possibly made pregnant by one?

Nobody knew who Adolf's grandfather was. The whole thing was possible certainly. Anything, after all, was possible.

In Vienna the Jews were all too visible.

There were the poor Handelees, kaftanned, long-bearded, in the streets, peddling, begging really, selling trinkets from trays.

At least these poor creatures had *something* to sell!

Adolf did not initially feel rage against *these* Jews. It was the others, the rich ones he saw emerging from the Hotel Kummer and the Sacher that offended him. How could these *foreigners* dare to walk the streets of Vienna in laughing affluence, warmly clad and well-fed, while the *Volk* starved?

While *he* starved!

Soon, Adolf began to hate all Jews.

He also began to hate the rich.

He began to hate their shining, waterproof shoes and the grey felt spats that kept their ankles warm, and the fur-lined and fur-collared topcoats they wore, as they too walked into the Hotel Kummer or the Sacher or the Bank of Austria or the offices of a newspaper or a steamship company. He hated them for their uncaring contempt for the poor and the unemployed. He hated them for the few coins they threw – often onto the very pavement itself – to some poor, out-of-work man, not a tramp like Hanisch who expected nothing else, but some decent working-fellow down on his luck through no fault of his own. As he was.

None of it was *his* fault, Adolf knew.

It was not his fault that he now stood before the Herr Librarian in the Reference Room trying to hide the awful state of his shoes and hoping not too much of his suit showed under the smock-like coat that Pappi had worn.

In the days when he lived with Gustl, he had always taken the books home to the Stumpergasse. Now, he had to convince the Librarian (cropped head, pince-nez, a pristine white collar, dark, well-pressed suit and an odour of cologne) that he was a genuine student. His suit was threadbare and crumpled and he carried the tell-tale rucksack. It no longer bulged with the blanket because – in the greatest tragedy of the summer – one morning he awoke to find it gone.

He missed it very much. Now he used newspapers, like all the others.

He washed his shirt in the handbasin at the Gentlemen's Lavatory, once every two weeks. The Attendant allowed the shirt to dry in the towel cupboard. The same applied to his collars but he now wore them only when he entered the Library. There was no way of ironing the shirts or the collars and their condition grew gradually worse.

The hunger gnawed away at him like a beast.

Sometimes he felt so weak he made what seemed a sensible decision. He bought a large bun and a slab of cheese and simply wolfed it, in the street. In a minute – literally a minute – it was gone.

And he had half-a-crown less to live on.

When he presented himself to the Herr Librarian it was early October and already beginning to grow cold at night. If he did not get permission to study as a Student when he would have nowhere to pass the day in peace and warmth. He would quite simply be finished and death his only course of action.

Adolf was not afraid of that.

The Herr Senior Librarian looked almost mockingly over his pince-nez.

'You say you are a Student? Of what?'

'Architecture, Herr Senior Librarian,' said Adolf, giving the creature his correct rank.

'Are you at the College of Architecture?'

Adolf shook his head. 'I'm trying to get to the required standard. I was ill and fell behind. I hope to gain a place in a year or so.'

The Herr Senior Librarian looked at Adolf afresh. 'You do look a bit thin. What was it, pneumonia?'

'Bronchitis.'

'Not tuberculosis?'

'No!'

'You see, we do not allow tubercular people in here. They cough and spread germs.'

'I am not tubercular!' Adolf raised his voice.

'Please do not shout. This is not a public square.'

'My apologies.' Adolf began to sweat. He tried to calm himself down. He had no rights here, simply wants. He added, 'My father was a Customs Officer in Linz. His rank was equivalent to a kapitan in the Army.'

'Really?' The Librarian looked up from the Application Form, as if amused. 'And what was his name?'

'Herr Alois Hitler. Probationary Higher Customs Collector, attached to the Linz Division,' recited Adolf.

The Herr Librarian did not smile. He wrote it all down very slowly in his long thin and thick copperplate hand, with his J-nib.

He looked up then, and asked, idly, 'And you are still at 29 Stumpergasse?'

Adolf felt the sweat break out, a thin film, on his forehead. 'Yes, I am.'

The Librarian allowed his gaze to stray to where Adolf had left his rucksack. It was pushed guiltily behind a chair, just inside the door of the room.

'You do know that we do not accept anybody as a Reader in the Reference Room unless he has a permanent address?'

'Naturally, Herr Senior Librarian,' said Adolf, craftily, and waited. His bowels loosened. He felt – he knew! – that this effete creature was going to deny him his rightful seat in the Library. He just knew it.

'I demand to see the Principal Librarian!' he shouted. 'I demand my rights!'

The Herr Senior Librarian looked profoundly startled. 'Please do not shout!'

'I demand my rights! I am a legitimate student!'

'Of course you are, did I say you were not?'

The Herr Senior Librarian's voice was soft. The whole of the Reference Library had gone still and silent. Adolf could not see the Herr Librarian for the sudden red rage that blotted him out. Adolf swayed on his feet, and felt dizzy. Rage and hunger do not mix, he thought, desperately: I feel as if I am going to faint.

He struck the palm of one hand into the other, and fixed his pale blue eyes unblinkingly on the Herr Senior Librarian. He kept his voice low.

'Do I get a seat or not?'

The Herr Senior Librarian looked at him, alarmed.

'Are you all right? Are you ill?'

'No, I am not ill. Do I get a seat?'

The Herr Senior Librarian stared at him for a long moment. He looked again at the soiled and dirty rucksack peeping from under the chair. Then, he said, in a much softer and very different voice, 'Certainly you get the seat, my dear Sir. Here is a temporary card. You will receive a permanent one in a few days.' He quickly wrote out a card and handed it to Adolf. 'You can study from today. If there is any way I can assist you in choosing any book you may need, that is my duty. I wish you good luck in your studies.'

Adolf looked at him without expression. He was simply a bureaucrat. Adolf despised him. He nodded, took the card and sat down.

When the Herr Senior Librarian was asked why he had given a card to such an obvious vagrant, the Librarian could only say: 'He had the most beautiful blue eyes.'

*

99

In the Reference Room Adolf's reading became more catholic than ever. The books, political, military, historical, geographical, piled up on his desk. Marx, Engels, Darwin, Schopenhauer, Nietschze. Adolf read everything that smacked of power and how to acquire it. He soon abandoned Democracy as any kind of political answer for states like Austria or even Germany. In Germany and England, only men had the vote. Adolf admired the British. They were benevolent despots yet ran a huge, far-flung Empire with an iron fist, while all the time prating on about Democracy! They held down their subject races by sending an army or a gunboat.

The British did not hesitate to act, and Adolf admired that.

The Fist and the Will.

They were all that mattered.

But the British were becoming afraid of German sea-power. The Emperor Wilhelm was building a new High Seas Fleet at Wilhelmshaven and many politicians thought that it was only a matter of time before a European war broke out.

Adolf did not believe that.

A war between cousins – Edward the Seventh and Kaiser Wilhelm shared a grandmother, Queen Victoria – was unthinkable. No, the Prussians should concentrate on their old enemy, the French. Every Frenchman was a disciple of the little Emperor Bonaparte. Liberty, Equality, Fraternity – what claptrap! Waterloo had been lost by the French almost a hundred years ago; now they were making coalition noises to the British. The *Entente Cordiale*! That was a piece of perfidy by Albion! What did the Saxon English have in common with the Latin French?

One thing only.

A desire to see Germany held down.

Yet a war with the British was out of the question. Who would gain from it? No, an accommodation would be arranged between cousins, at some royal shooting-party in Scotland or in some German forest at a boar-shoot. These Royal Princes seemed to be good for very little else.

To Adolf, the whole of the so-called Western Capitalist Systems seemed to be teetering towards ruin. The European nations were headed by those same useless Princes, but their ruling politicians were mainly liberal and democratic. The soft political attitudes of these democrats inhibited the vast warrior nations – the Germans, the British – from even greater conquests and more and more power.

Plainly, Democracy and Imperialism did not mix.

But most modern European States were a mixture of both.

That was wrong.

Worse than wrong, it was insane.

Nations were like people. They were strong while they were young.

They found their peak. They prospered. They died. Nietzsche had said all that. The British had had their turn. They were a Naval power and did not need to try to be a Continental Power, like Germany, which might have further European ambitions. Germany was not at the peak of her power yet, but she was very militant, very strong. Germany had the Will. Anybody reading the Berlin newspapers, as Adolf did, even if they were a day old, in the warmth of the Vienna Library, could see that.

Adolf pondered: what was wrong?

These Empires – German, British, Tsarist – were rich beyond belief. Yet their workless were starving in the streets. As he was. Adolf sat many hours, puzzled by this paradox.

For a while he thought the Marxists had the answer.

Das Kapital, the work of the bearded Jew, Karl Marx, followed that of the German emigré, Engels, into his head. *The Communist Manifesto of 1848* was the standard book, but *Kapital* was the work that attracted him. Banned as subversive, and available in the Library to none but serious students, he had to ask for special permission to obtain a copy. The Senior Librarian, who now seemed a sort of dubious ally, handed it to him with a knowing smirk, saying, 'I wouldn't have thought *Kapital* a proper study for an architectural student?'

The insolent pederast!

What did he mean by such a remark?

Adolf scorned and hated homosexuals.

But he smiled and accepted the implied reproof.

The fact was, a man of original thought had Enemies everywhere. They were not always obviously dangerous. The Jews and homosexuals were not a personal danger, as yet. But sometimes, the enemy was very real, like Hans, the fat policeman who cruelly wakened him, if he over-slept on the bench in the Prater. He had learned the trick of sleeping on a bench by now. Never sleep on your side. The hip-bone got in the way. On a bench, you sleep on your back or you don't sleep at all. Nowadays, the bone-chilling cold was wakening him earlier and earlier.

In the warm Library Adolf read that, according to Marx, the Police and the Army were simply a repressive arm of the Capitalist state.

Without the Police and the Army the State would be at the mercy of the Workers.

That could be true, Adolf reasoned, but how did the Marxists expect to take over the Police?

The Police were Workers in uniform, that was all, insisted Marx.

They would see where their true Class Interests lay.

With the rest of the Working Class!

Adolf did not believe it for one moment.

Hans, the Policeman, who rousted them out in the mornings, would never see the workless as any kind of ally. Nor would any soldier in any army. Not, anyway, as far as a reasonable man could see. As for taking over the means of Production, Distribution and Exchange, how was *that* to be brought about?

By open rebellion, stated the old Jew in the British Museum in London.

Religion was the Opium of the People, Marx said.

Adolf did not disagree, but what would Marx put in its place? A picture of Himself?

Marx saw himself as a new Messiah! That was plain. It was Marx's religion talking. His training. Everything he knew. Communism was the new Faith. Its meeting-halls the new synagogues.

Marx was a Jew. Communism was a covert Jewish religion. A secular religion. No priests or rabbis. Commissars instead, but religion just the same. Because, like the Jew who had invented it, it was International.

What Marx was advocating was world revolution. The total abolition of Tribe. The total abolition of Nation. One Party. One World. A world run by the workers.

The rich would be eliminated.

The middle-class would be eliminated.

By God, it was bold!

Adolf had to concede that. He sat back in the library chair, smiling at the very impertinence of it.

Bold, cunning and just possibly workable, in one country at a time? Marx, as a German Jew, seemed to think the trades-unionists of Germany might rise first. Adolf knew the Austrian trade-unionists, he'd seen them at political meetings in draughty halls in Vienna. Self-important nobodies, puffing on cheap cigars and voting each other in and out of piddling little offices, local treasurer of this and local secretary of that. In the words of the English Lady Warwick, playing politics with cabbages and potatoes! If Marx thought these pot-bellied little fellows would lead a World Revolution, he was sadly mistaken!

Why, they wouldn't even strike to save their starving brothers on the streets!

They wouldn't even strike to save him, Adolf!

Adolf pondered, long, in the Reference Room, all those weeks and months, learning much from the Marxists. Their ideas of 'cells', small groups working and worming their way into control of streets, districts, through trades union and democratic processes into Parliament even, all that had much to commend it.

But *World* Revolution?

Adolf could not see it.

An Austrian Revolution, certainly?

One day the lid had to blow off that tinder-box.

But not yet.

The Army was too strong. The Police were too strong. The Churches were too strong.

But one day.

Meantime, the Marxists had no attraction for Adolf. They were Jewish. International. Foreign. They were clever, insidious, and meant, anyhow they could, to win. They had many adherents, he knew, in the pitifully small Workingmen's movements in Vienna. They had to be watched, and watched closely, for they had a lot of attractive ideas and they meant business. But, again, they were International and they were Jews.

They could, in due time, become a more dangerous enemy than the present, ramshackle Empire of Austria.

Marx the Jew was to be reckoned with.

Adolf, there and then, elected to hate and scorn all Marxists.

Outside the warm and cosy Reference Room the weather grew steadily colder. Adolf wakened one morning to rime on his hair and small moustache, and it was almost half an hour before he could feel any blood in his feet, stamp them on the ground as he might. The open parkland of the Prater was covered in a thick white frost.

The Winter was here.

Adolf wrapped up his newspapers. They were damp from the cold dew. He looked up to see Hanisch, regarding him cynically from the next bench. Hanisch was drinking the last two inches of his hooch. He did that every morning. He always kept two inches in reserve, if he could.

'It gets me moving these winter mornings,' he told Adolf. 'Without it, Good Sir, I'd die.' He offered the bottle to Adolf.

Adolf shook his head. 'I don't drink.'

Hanisch wheezed and shook his head.

'No women. No drink. Damn little grub. You're a funny one, Adolf. What are you after? Why do you sit in that Library all day? What do all those books ever do for you?'

Adolf jogged on the spot. His circulation was beginning to move. The trouble was, his hunger was coming back, too. 'Just because other people are ignorant, that is no excuse for me.'

Hanisch closed one eye. 'Winter's here, Adolf. Time to go home.

You're too thin. You're not going to see next Spring if you sleep out here any more. Take my advice. Go home.'

'I haven't got a home.'

'You have somewhere they'd take you in, yes?'

'Perhaps.'

Hanisch drank the rest of his hooch and coughed, and rose slowly to his feet. 'Go home, Good Sir.'

'No.'

Hanisch looked at him for a moment.

'I'm sleeping under the Rotunda tonight. Join me if you like. There might be a fire.'

Adolf spent that freezing night, and the next several nights, in a circle around a fire of wood, under the vast Rotunda, in the company of alcoholics. When the bottle came his way, he pretended to drink, and passed it on. Nobody asked who he was or why he was there. The alcoholics did not bother with food.

'Sorry, Adolf. If you want grub you'll have to go elsewhere,' Hanisch said.

Adolf shook his head and indicated the fire. 'It's good enough to be warm.'

'I'd be inside myself,' apologised Hanisch. 'But I can't. I suffocate.'

'No, of course. I understand.'

Adolf sat so close to the fire his thin shoes buckled and his trousers singed; but his back was chilled by the knife-keen draught swirling through the Rotunda. He began to develop a dry cough. It grew worse and it would not go away.

Finally, Hanisch spoke. 'You have to find a bed for a few nights, Adolf, or you'll die.'

'I'm all right, really.'

'You are anything but all right. Have you any money left?'

'Two kroner. I was keeping them for food,' lied Adolf. In reality he had no money left.

Hanisch shook his head. 'Spend them on a bunk in the Refuge. They'll only let you stay five nights, so there's a limit. Go tonight.'

Adolf shook his head. 'The *smell* of that place!'

'Never mind the smell. It's warm. And you'll get a breakfast. Haven't bothered with your breakfast the last two days, have you?'

Adolf shook his head. 'It didn't seem worth the walk, all the way to the Tieter Garten.'

'Feeling light-headed? Don't want to eat?'

Adolf nodded his head, slowly. 'Yes.'

'Feel as if it doesn't matter whether you eat or not?'

Adolf nodded, again.

'Haven't been to the Library for a week, right?'

Adolf nodded. Had it been a week? He couldn't remember. It didn't seem important. Not important at all. Nothing did.

'Don't care about anything, am I right?'

Adolf nodded. He didn't care. His head felt light, too. He didn't care about anything.

Nothing.

'Haven't been washing or shaving either, right?' asked Hanisch.

Adolf smiled, a comic's mirthless grimace. 'No money left. Not for that. All gone.'

Hanisch looked grim. He put his hand on Adolf's and to Adolf's astonishment a five-kroner piece was lying in his palm.

'I don't want *this*!'

'Put it away or somebody here will rob you!' Hanisch looked at the slumbering alcoholics, lying prone around the dying fire. 'Get a breakfast. Then go to the Refuge. Take a bed for the five nights. Then come back here. If I'm not here try the Warming Rooms over at the Leopoldstandt.'

'Warming Rooms? What are they?'

Hanisch grimaced. 'You'll see. But *eat*.'

'I'm not really very hungry. Truly.'

Hanisch pushed Adolf towards the entrance of the Rotunda. Outside lay a thick layer of snow.

'Go. And eat. I'll see you in five days. If I'm not here – the Leopoldstandt. It's free!'

Adolf walked out into the snow.

Inside five paces his shoes and his feet were soaking wet. A new pair of shoes were a desperate necessity.

He walked slowly, lightheadedly, all the way to the Refuge.

It took him almost two hours.

On the way he bought a piece of cheese and two sausages and a large bread roll at a baker's, although he didn't really want them. But Hanisch had said buy food. So he bought food. At the Refuge the middle-class woman gave him soup and tea and asked if he was all right? Adolf said he was, and asked if there was a bed.

'Five nights only, you know? And you're lucky, there's one or two left.' The woman smiled at Adolf. 'How old are you?'

'Almost eighteen,' answered Adolf.

'I'll sign you in and bring you your bed number,' said the woman, who reminded him a little of Klara. 'Sit down and eat, now.'

Adolf nodded, vaguely, smiling.

He sat at a table and looked at the soup.

He did not want to eat it.

To eat it would bring back the desire to eat more. To live. He did not, he realised, want to live.

The combination of the Jews, the Librarian, the Police, the Rich, had defeated him. They were lurking even now, behind every pillar in the place, waiting for him to eat, so they could torture him more.

He knew who they were. Oh yes he did!

He knew them by sight.

They were his Enemies.

'I know you!' he suddenly shouted at a workless, ragged man passing by. The man almost dropped his soup. 'I know you! Don't think I don't!'

'Well, I don't know you, you madman!' answered the shaken follow, making his way hastily to a table at the far end of the room.

The woman returned, looking at Adolf oddly.

'Eat your food, there's a good boy, and go upstairs to Bed Thirteen. Take your blanket with you.' The woman put the blanket on an empty chair. 'Now. Eat!'

'Don't want it,' mumbled Adolf.

'Eat!' said the woman, sternly. 'Eat!'

'Yes, Mutti.' mumbled Adolf.

He drank the soup and ate the sausages and the cheese and the roll. He drank the tea. Then he picked up the blanket and looked up to see the woman still there. He was surprised to see tears in her eyes.

'Sleep now,' she said. 'I'll come up with you.'

Adolf nodded, and although it was still only morning and the house-rule was that no man, unless he was ill, could go to bed before eight o'clock, was allowed to go in the vast deserted dormitory. He remembered the woman taking off his sodden socks and shoes and putting them under his hard pillow and kissing – yes, actually kissing him – on the check.

Then he fell asleep and remembered no more.

VIII

FIVE days later Adolf was in the street again.

In all that time he had never left the Refuge. He had eaten the twice-daily soup and drunk the hot, unsweetened tea. He had sat in the dining-room and although inmates were, strictly speaking, not allowed By Order to stay in the Refuge all day, the woman who reminded him of Mutti must have spoken to somebody because Adolf was left alone, sitting crouched at a table, in the far dark corner of the room, his back to the wall.

From that vantage point, he looked out for his Enemies.

They were many.

He scrutinised them as they entered.

That one, a jolly fat fellow in a rather better suit than most – no patches or food stains – was obviously a Police Informer!

There were many of those and they wanted to arrest Adolf for begging and take him to jail.

For that they needed proof.

Adolf's eye followed the Informer as he sat down and ate his soup. He would catch the man's eye and try to stare him out. Sometimes the man would look up, half-smile, and then turn away, to read – or pretend to read. These Informers were diabolically clever! His eyes would never leave the Informer until the rotten spy left the Refuge. Sometimes Adolf would get up and go to the lavatory at the same time, to make sure the Informer was not passing on his observations to somebody else.

Plainly, he was being *watched*.

Not just by the Police, bad as that was. By the Bureaucrats, too.

A very officious looking fellow in dark topcoat and hat came into the place, walked around the room, counting the chairs and comparing them to figures in his ledger. Did he expect Adolf to believe *that* was what he was really doing?

Adolf would be a fool if he believed that.

No, this Bureaucrat was obviously from the War Office and checking on Adolf's age and availability for Military Service!

Who did he think he was fooling, going around counting chairs?

Adolf determined to face him out.

He rose in his corner and called out to the man in a loud voice. It always paid to shout at these people. 'I am not yet eighteen! I cannot be called for Military Service until I am eighteen. That is the law!'

The Bureaucrat looked at Adolf, startled.

As well he might, Adolf thought.

Adolf was onto his little game.

Yes, indeed!

'Very interesting,' said the Bureaucrat, after a pause.

He looked at the woman who reminded Adolf of Mutti. She smiled wanly and shook her head.

'Very interesting indeed,' said the Bureaucrat.

He closed his ledger with a sigh, and left the dining-room. The other inmates just stared at Adolf. A few laughed. He ignored them.

Adolf sat down again and waited for the next Enemy.

He was not long in coming.

This time he was a Rich Man.

This self-important person came in, wearing a thick, dark overcoat with a fur-collar, and a top-hat. He had a large waxed moustache. His cigar was freshly lit and he called out cheerfully to the staff behind the soup counter, 'Well, Ladies! How's business today? How are you spending my money, eh? I hope none of these fine fellows has an empty belly tonight?'

Several of the down-and-outs laughed ingratiatingly at these words and were rewarded by a smile, and in some cases a hand pressed into theirs, containing, no doubt, Adolf thought, bribes.

Again, Adolf rose to his feet, in rage.

His body shook with fever and his eyes stared. He nonetheless shouted very loudly at the Rich Man, 'Do you think you can come in here and bribe these men to betray me? Do you think your dirty money will buy you anything and everything?'

The Rich Man looked nonplussed for a moment. Then he twirled his moustache between finger and thumb.

'Yes, my good Sir, as a matter of fact, I do!'

The hobos laughed aloud at that.

Several of them told Adolf to sit down and shut up. He did neither. He shouted, 'You're rich on the back of the Workers! You're a bloodsucker! But you'll never get me to work for you!'

The Rich Man smiled. 'My dear, good Sir, I wouldn't allow you to work for me for nothing!'

With that, he sprayed a few more coins around the room and departed, well-pleased, to a chorus of *'Guten Tag, Meinherr'*, and many laughs, most of them directed, Adolf knew, at himself.

The woman who reminded him of Mutti brought him an extra bowl of soup across. She laid a gentle hand on his arm. 'Don't shout, Adolf. Everything will be all right.'

'No, it won't,' Adolf said. 'You know it won't.'

'Eat your soup. You must leave tonight, you know.'

Adolf nodded. Tonight, was it? He had lost track of time.

'Have you somewhere to go?'

Adolf frowned. Hanisch had said something. What was it? Oh, yes. The Warming Rooms. Yes.

'The Warming Rooms. On the Leopoldstandt.'

The woman looked relieved. 'Go there. Go straight from here. When you've finished your soup. Go while it's light. Stay tonight. Come back here tomorrow. See me. I'll find you a bed for five more nights.'

Adolf was bemused. 'Can't I just *stay?*'

'No. Only for five nights. It's the House Rule.'

'Made by people like that Rich Man?' Adolf asserted. He was shaking again. 'To drive me out! To see I die!'

The woman looked scandalised and upset. 'No, no! That's Herr Levy. He's a Governor of this place!'

'He's a Jew then? Levy, he's a Jew?'

'Yes, Herr Levy is Jewish. He is a very good and charitable man —'

Adolf tipped the soup across the table.

'He can keep his soup! You can run around after him but I won't! I don't run around after people who want me to go out into the snow and die!'

The woman was scared of him now, Adolf could see that. She had fallen silent, the whole place had fallen silent. Few of the hobos laughed, now. They were all watching to see what he would do next.

Very well, he would show them!

'I'm not staying here to be destroyed at a time to be decided,' Adolf yelled at the grinning men. 'I'm going!'

'Adolf, please . . .' whispered the woman, trying to mop up the soup, which had spread across the wooden table-top and was slopping onto the floor.

'No! I'm going!'

Adolf picked up his rucksack, held as ever, firmly between his knees, threw it defiantly over his shoulder and marched out of the place.

A roar of delighted laughter from the hobos followed him out.

At the door Adolf turned to them and waved his fist.

'You may laugh, but you'll see I'm right!'

They laughed louder than ever.

It was very cold in the street.

They were his Enemies, the hobos. They meant to harm him, just as the Jews and the Rich and the Bureaucrats meant to harm him.

Worse than that, they meant to kill him.

All of them.

They meant to snuff him out.

Adolf trudged away in the snow, his useless shoes wet through inside a few paces, Pappi's old coat a dirty, limp rag, his shirt a stinking mess, his trousers singed and frayed, the holes in his socks yawning above the flapping shoes. Lice from the dormitory crept across his body, feeding gently. He no longer had a single kroner in his pocket.

He began to walk, very slowly, towards the Leopoldstandt.

It took Adolf two hours to get to the Warming Rooms on the Leopoldstandt. He was soaked through, dizzy and light-headed, as if with a high fever. Adolf was received with small enthusiasm, but admitted, by a stern, meat-faced male Supervisor in an overall, who looked hard at his soaking clothes, his pack, his ruined shoes. The Supervisor carried in his hand a long, thin cane.

This was a place for the lowest of the low.

A flophouse, really, operated, so the sign outside said, by *The Association For Warming Rooms and Welfare*. There was precious little welfare here, as far as Adolf could see. The inevitable plate of soup was accompanied by a piece of rye bread. He ate at one of the tables around which sat the regulars, no-hopers, down-and-outs of the lowest kind, almost all filthy and lousy. The smell was awful. There were no beds. People sat at a table and gazed vacantly at the wall or at each other.

When Adolf had finished his soup, his plate was snatched away. Surprised, he looked up to see the meat-faced Supervisor banging a spoon on the soup plate, for silence.

'You all know the Rules here,' he boomed. 'Don't you?'

To Adolf's surprise, the inmates all answered, 'Yes, Herr Supervisor!' in chorus.

'Just the same, I'll tell you again. There are one or two new people in.' The meat-faced Supervisor was a jumped-up workingman, Adolf realised, and he had spotted Adolf for some kind of delinquent, that was certain. His eye rested warningly on Adolf throughout his short speech.

'This is a Warming Room for the Destitute! It is *not* a Doss House.

You are admitted free and the only way we can fit you all in is for you all to sit up straight in your chairs and *stay awake*!'

Adolf was startled: what, *all night*?

But the Supervisor was continuing: 'Sleeping is Not Allowed! I repeat, Sleeping is Not Allowed! Talking is Not Allowed! Tuberculars are Not Allowed! Anybody coughing will have to go!' The Supervisor pointed his cane at the door. 'Women will sit in that corner!' He pointed his cane to a corner. Adolf stared. The women were already there, thirty or more of them, crowded around two tables. Some wore shawls. All were soaked through, everybody in the room was. Lank hair straggled across their faces. Their eyes stared out of their white, starved faces, at the Supervisor, showing nothing.

'Children!' the Supervisor was shouting now, 'will not occupy a chair! Children will be allowed to lie on the floor in the Women's Corner!'

Adolf craned and saw that several small children, just bundles of rags, were lying under the women's tables and on the small floor space beside them. The children did not move or cry.

'If a child cries it goes out,' shouted the Supervisor.

The two hundred people in the large room stared at him. Nobody spoke.

'If anybody uses tobacco – out!'

The people stared, wide-eyed.

'If anybody falls asleep and snores, out!'

Adolf watched a cockroach crawl across the table. None of the twenty people around the table moved to kill it. Adolf reached out and crushed it with his palm. It gave off a disgusting odour. Adolf looked up to see the eye of the Supervisor upon him.

The Supervisor leaned over the table and spoke directly to Adolf. 'Any trouble from you – out!'

Adolf stared back at him.

This man, too, was an Enemy.

That was plain.

He was surrounded by Enemies.

But careful. He had to be careful.

'You understand?' the Supervisor was shouting.

Adolf stared back at him.

'Remember! No sleeping!' the Supervisor yelled.

He glared at the inert faces in front of him for what seemed a very long time. Then he swore. 'Gutter swine,' he snarled. 'All of you. Gutter swine!' Then he walked to the door, and opened it a foot or two. A blast of freezing air shivered through the jam-packed room but nobody dared to protest. The Supervisor lit a pipe and blew the smoke into the street.

'Gutter swine. Filth,' he said, again.

Adolf knew him for an Enemy.

This man would certainly deliver him to the Police or the Military. This man would delight in doing that. The Workers had their own traitors. Plenty of them. He would have to watch this man very carefully.

Adolf kept his large blue eyes fixed on the back of the Supervisor's bullet head. After a while the Supervisor turned round, his own eyes raking the room. He saw Adolf.

'Hey, you! What you looking at?'

Adolf shook his head. Nothing.

'Eyes down! No sleeping! Eyes down!' The Supervisor's voice roared, 'Eyes down, I said!'

Adolf looked round his table.

The men lowered their eyes.

An hour went by. Two. Three.

A church clock struck the midnight hour.

Adolf looked again at the men around the table.

They were asleep on their feet, as horses or sometimes soldiers learn to sleep. Their hands supported their heads. Their elbows, resting on the table, supported their hands. Their eyes were closed. Now and then an arm would give way and the sleeper would fall forward: but never with a crash and never making a noise. He would shuffle his feet and body and recompose himself.

It was a knack and everybody at the table had mastered it, by necessity and long practice.

Except Adolf.

Slowly, Adolf's eyes closed.

He fought and fought to keep them open.

He kept them open.

They closed again.

Open.

Closed.

Suddenly, there was a loud crash in the room. People muttered, complainingly. There was a hush.

Adolf sat up, wide-awake, looking around enquiringly.

'Hey, you!'

Adolf stared at the Supervisor.

'What?'

'You're sleeping! You're noisy!'

Adolf began to speak but his rage was such that he could not breathe and instead he began to cough. And once he began, he could not stop. Tears of pain and frustration came to his eyes. He wiped them with the sleeve of his disgusting, dirty coat.

The room was half-dark but the Supervisor's face was very clear and very close to Adolf. He felt the whole room was suddenly awake, even the deep breathing of the practised sleepers had halted.

They were waiting for something.

They did not have to wait long.

The Supervisor spoke softly, almost kindly, to Adolf. 'You're a lunger, aren't you?'

'No, I'm not!'

'Don't shout at me. I say you're a lunger. I say you're out!' The Supervisor pointed his cane at the door. 'Out! Now! *Raus!*'

'No. I will not go.'

'*What-did-you-say?*'

The whole room was deathly silent.

'I said I will not go.'

The Supervisor's breath was stale with foul-smelling tobacco. He put a hand on Adolf's shoulder. 'I can send one of these people for the policeman in his box on the corner of the Leopoldstandt, if you like?'

'No,' said Adolf, suddenly cunning.

This man was the Enemy but he could be escaped from, if Adolf left, now. The Police were something else altogether. Adolf picked up his rucksack, and slung it on his back.

'Now you're being sensible.' The Supervisor's hand, as meaty as his face, guided Adolf to the door. It opened and he was propelled into the deserted Leopoldstandt, by a sudden skilled push in the small of his back. He almost fell, and turned to protest.

'Don't come back! No lungers here!'

And the door slammed.

Adolf walked very slowly for two hours, in the snow.

It was bitterly cold, the coldest night of the winter, so far, but it felt better to be out of the Warming Room. At least the air was fresh, even if it was likely to finish him off. What did that matter, anyway?

Everybody in the City was his enemy.

The Herr Professor at the College of Architecture was his Enemy.

The Librarian at the Vienna Public Library was his Enemy.

The Supervisor of the Warming Room was his Enemy.

All Enemies. All of them.

One day, he might pay them back.

Pay them back a thousandfold.

If he lived?

If he lived.

The Will, Adolf said to himself, as he trudged along the streets and streets of slums towards the Prater, the wind howling and the snow flurrying, the Will is everything. Nothing else matters.

He walked. And walked. And walked.

He ceased to think or feel.

He did not care if he died.

His old desire for Death came upon him.

If my Enemies defeat me and I die, that is no disgrace. They are simply stronger than I am.

If I survive, then I am stronger than they are.

Simple as that.

Two hours later, Adolf arrived at the Rotunda. The alcoholics' fire burned low and the bodies around it were inert. Adolf sat down near the fire and stretched his hands towards it. They were numb and he felt nothing.

Adolf sat like that for a long time before Hanisch wakened. He sat up at once, a bundle of overcoats and waistcoats and rags, and regarded Adolf seriously.

'You all right, Good Sir?'

Adolf said nothing. He could not speak. He was finished.

His Enemies had vanquished him. They had erased him from the world. There was no more to do or say. He had not the Will left to survive. He was now at one with the elements. He was a block of ice. He was nothing.

It was over.

Hanisch edged towards him, around the fire. He threw another piece of wood on to it as he moved, never leaving the ground, like some species of land-crab. In his hand he held his precious bottle of hooch.

'Adolf!'

Adolf said nothing. It was over.

'Did you go to the Warming Room?'

'Thrown out . . .' Adolf's voice was faint.

'Who by?'

'Enemy . . .' His voice was even lower. 'All my Enemies, Hanisch.'

Hanisch sighed, a long, reflective but unsurprised noise. The Enemies, was it now? 'Yes, I know. I have them too, sometimes.' Hanisch put the bottle of hooch to Adolf's lips. 'Here. Drink this.'

'No. Can't.'

'Yes, you can. It's my two inches for the morning. Drink it all. Every drop!'

'No . . .' Adolf's voice was very low, his breath almost non-existent.

Hanisch, very gently, pushed Adolf back, nudging his rucksack to take his weight. Adolf did not resist. His eyes closed.

Hanisch said, very gently, 'Don't sleep yet, Adolf. Sleep after you have drunk the water.'

'Water?'

'You're thirsty, aren't you?'

'Yes . . .'

'Then drink.'

Eyes still closed, Adolf drank. He did not cough or reject the burning hooch. It went down as if it had been water, Hanisch reflected sadly, wondering how he would face the morning without his two inches. Ah well, he'd done it before, what the hell.

Hanisch massaged Adolf's hands and took off his freezing, sopping shoes and socks and massaged his feet. He took off one of his own many waistcoats and wrapped it tightly around Adolf's feet, securing it with a tie, one of many he owned, stolen from he could not remember where. Then, and only then, did he push Adolf closer to the fire, so that the damp air rose off him in a haze.

Hanisch sat and just looked at Adolf, long into the freezing night.

When Adolf wakened, he felt very weak. His clothes were still damp but his feet, for the first time in what seemed like weeks, were warm. He soon discovered the reason. They were tightly wrapped in Hanisch's waistcoat. The sharp morning air caught his breath and he coughed. His chest hurt and he felt light-headed. He did not want to move. The heat of the wood-fire still drowsed him and the heavy pine smell of the burning wood, green branches stripped from the trees of the Prater, with some old wood to keep it going – perfumed his nostrils. Finally, he tried to sit up and found it very difficult.

Hanisch leaned over him, a tin in his hand.

Adolf looked around. The winos had gone. There was only himself and Hanisch.

'Where is everybody?'

'Never mind that. Drink.'

'What is it?'

'Bread and soup. Drink.'

Adolf drank. The soup was hot and it left a burning after-taste. He remembered thinking that perhaps it was not soup but alcohol and hot water and bread and nothing else: but the warmth of the liquid permeated his limbs, spreading its heat slowly throughout his body and even his legs and feet. It was a very pleasant, drowsy feeling and Adolf closed his eyes and slept again.

When he wakened the fire was still going and Hanisch was standing over him, looking grim. He slowly peeled the waistcoat from Adolf's feet and just as slowly he put Adolf's ragged socks, now dry, back on his feet. Hanisch's hands were shaking and it occurred to Adolf that he had not been drinking at all that day, but sitting by the fire waiting for him to waken and he wondered why Hanisch should do that for him?

Hanisch then found Adolf's shoes, dry but buckled with the heat of the fire and forced them onto Adolf's feet. Then he took off Adolf's raggedy coat and put the waistcoat under it, and put the raggedy coat back on Adolf again.

Adolf suffered this, then he asked, 'What are we going to do?'

It was then Hanisch asked: 'Show me your paintings? You *do* have some paintings, don't you?'

'In my rucksack.'

Adolf closed his eyes. He craved more of the hot soup. He could see the tin resting on two stones at the edge of the fire.

Hanisch opened the rucksack with trembling hands. He foraged inside until he found what he was looking for. He took out Adolf's sketchbook and his breath sucked in sharply as he saw the water-colours of the Hofburg and Saint Stephen's Cathedral that Adolf had made in what seemed to him, lying there, another life.

'You did these, did you?'

Adolf nodded.

'Do more if you had to? Other things?'

Adolf nodded again. 'Why?'

'Drink this soup.' Hanisch put the tin to Adolf's mouth and he drank greedily. The soup, bread and hot water and, he supposed, hooch, warmed him. He closed his eyes. That was better. Much better. He would sleep again. Then Hanisch shook him gently awake. 'No more sleep now, Good Sir!' Hanisch stamped the fire out, and put the paintings, handling them very carefully, back into Adolf's rucksack.

'Come on,' he said gently, helping Adolf to his feet. 'We have to go and see somebody, you and me, my Good Sir.'

Somehow, Adolf made it to his feet.

Shakily, and very slowly, supported by Hanisch, he managed to stagger out of the Rotunda into the snow and the cold winter sunshine.

Neumann the Jew was sceptical.

In his tiny rabbit-warren of a junk shop near the West Banhof, he crouched, surrounded by useless and worthless bric-a-brac: old clothes; rusty perambulators; broken bicycles; huge, dark, oil-paintings of fish; anything and everything, and none of it worth more than a few kroner.

He peered at Adolf's water-colours doubtfully, then looked curiously at Hanisch. 'Why have you brought him here?' he asked, softly.

'You know me,' Hanisch said. 'Don't you?'

'I do,' confirmed Neumann.

'I'm asking nothing.'

'Ah,' said Neumann in a long disbelieving breath.

'Twenty kroner, that's all. They're good, aren't they?' Hanisch asked.

'Not bad. Not bad at all,' said Neumann. 'But I can't sell these pictures. I need scenes, people, cheerful little water-colours. Can he do that?'

'Of course he can,' Hanisch insisted. 'He's an artist. He has all his painting gear with him. In his rucksack.'

They were talking as if Adolf was not there.

In a way, he wasn't.

He still felt weak, dreamy, and other-worldly but was conscious of the way he looked to Neumann, a smelly young hobo, at the end of his tether.

Neumann looked again at the water-colours.

'I *could* try with these, I suppose. You never know. I could try to sell them around the cafés and bars. Commission only, I'm afraid. No sale, no money.'

'He wouldn't mind that,' said Hanisch. 'But he'd need an advance. A few kroner against whatever you could do for him?'

Neumann shook his head, sadly. He was dark, squat. He could have been anything between forty and sixty. He was dressed in old, worn clothes. He exuded poverty.

'My dear Hanisch, I'm keeping body and soul together with great difficulty, I am not able to advance anything. Once I make a sale, that's a different matter.'

Hanisch was defeated, but only temporarily.

'He has to have help. Look at him. He won't last another week, living outside in the air.'

These words, to Adolf, had the ring of prophecy, but all this talk was a waste of time. There was no help here. Or anywhere else. Hanisch took the water-colours from Neumann's hands. 'I'll try somebody else!'

They were at the door before Neumann called them back.

'Look, I'll tell you what I'll do?' Hanisch waited. 'I'll give you twenty kroner. Between you. When he has some new work, he brings it to me, here. The twenty kroner is against that. Tell him to come and see me when he's well.'

Hanisch took the silver coins and put them in the pocket of one of his waistcoats. Neumann, though, had not finished. He was looking, for the first time, very closely at Adolf indeed.

'How ill is he? Is it his lungs?'

'No. His lungs are fine.'

'What then?'

'He needs food. And a place to sleep.'

Neumann pondered, still looking at Adolf with a keen and thoughtful gaze. 'No decent hostel will take him, looking the way he does.'

Hanisch sighed. In the little shop, heated by a small oil-stove, he was beginning to stink. Neumann shifted away from him, and said, 'Wait!'

Neumann disappeared into the dark recesses of the junk-shop. After a while, he reappeared, holding a very thick, very old, moth-eaten black coat, and a rusty, even older black hat.

'Take that rag off him,' he commanded Hanisch. 'Put this one on. It'll cover a multitude of sins, as you people say.'

The coat certainly did that. It hung down almost to Adolf's ankles. The broken shoes, sodden pulp now, squelched out from underneath it. Adolf had made a slow move like a swimmer under water, shuffling into the coat. A week, Hanisch thought? He wouldn't last another night in the streets. He said, gently, 'Put the hat on. The head loses a lot of heat.'

Adolf put the hat on.

Neumann was still looking at Adolf, thoughtfully. At last he spoke: 'Take him to Greiner at the Men's Hostel on the Mandelmanstrasse. 'Don't talk to anybody but Greiner. Say I sent you. Say I ask, can he help?'

'Do I pay him anything?'

'Give him two kroner. Give your friend here five kroner. It'll pay his first night or two. Keep the rest for yourself.'

'Thank you very much,' said Hanisch, 'for fuck all.'

'I'm twenty kroner out,' said Neumann, reasonably. 'How do I know he'll ever come back?'

Even Hanisch had to bow to that.

'He'll be back,' he said.

'I'll believe that,' said Neumann, 'when I see him.'

Unexpectedly, Neumann held out his hand to Adolf.

'I'm sorry to see you in this state, young man. Come and see me soon. Bring me some nice water-colours. Let's see if we can do something together?'

'Danke, Herr Neumann.' Adolf clicked his heels together and bowed, very slightly.

Hanisch, impressed, said to Neumann in a proprietory whisper: 'You see? He's a gentleman. I've always known that about him!'

Neumann nodded, sadly.

Hanisch stood admiringly outside the Men's Hostel in the Meldemannstrasse, half an hour later. He read the bronze plate outside the Main Entrance, slowly, aloud: '*The Men's Hostel For Those Alone in the World.* Well, that's you, Adolf. *Sponsored by the Emperor Franz Josef to Alleviate the Miserable Living Conditions of the Lower Classes.*' Hanisch

118

grinned. 'That's still you.' He read again. '*Room for Five Hundred Persons.*' He shook his head. 'Should be room for you, then!'

Adolf said nothing. He was feeling very weak indeed, and even more light-headed. He swayed and Hanisch caught his arm. 'Easy, my dear Sir. Easy does it. Come inside and sit. Don't talk. I'll do that. All right?'

Adolf nodded. Anything was all right.

He didn't care.

'This place,' said Hanisch, impressed, as they entered, 'is a Palace!' He looked around approvingly at the bare but clean Reception Area. There was the usual high, wooden, desk separating the Clerk from the reach of aggressive hobos, standard equipment in any place where Authority met Destitution. Behind it sat a stern, bespectacled Clerk. Another Bureaucrat, Another Enemy, thought Adolf, but in an academic way. They were everywhere. The Enemies were everywhere. It was useless to protest, or shout. One simply kept quiet and pretended they were not there.

Hanisch asked at the desk for Herr Greiner, in a low, ingratiating voice. The Clerk took one look at the condition of Hanisch's clothes, took in the stink and said softly, 'The Hostel is full. Also, it is for workingmen only.' He sniggered. 'Nobody earning more than fifteen hundred kroner per year is allowed in.'

Fifteen hundred kroner was a labourer's wage.

'I am not applying,' said Hanisch, frostily. 'I simply wish to speak to Herr Greiner, who is an acquaintance, if you please, Herr Manager.'

The Clerk called out. 'Greiner!'

Greiner came from behind the desk as if by magic, a bucket and mop in his hand. Hanisch, who had not known what to expect, fell into a thoughtful, watchful silence. Adolf sat on the highly polished seat. It was nothing to do with him.

'Yes?' Greiner regarded Hanisch unfavourably. He wiped his hands on the apron he was wearing, and waited. He was a big man, with a receding hair-line, and a soldierly bearing.

Hanisch motioned him over to where Adolf sat, away from the desk. 'Herr Neumann sends his regards.'

'Does he? That's nice of him.'

A good start, I don't think, thought Hanisch, but he persisted. 'He wants you to help this young man here. He isn't well. He needs a place to stay.' Hanisch lowered his voice. 'And he is by way of being employed by Herr Neumann.'

'Doing what?' asked Greiner.

'Regular work,' stressed Hanisch, keeping his voice very low, so that the Clerk would not hear. 'Very regular work, for Herr Neumann.'

'He doesn't *get* in here unless he's in regular work,' said Greiner loudly. The Clerk looked over his glasses at them, then went on writing in his huge ledger.

'He's in regular work,' insisted Hanisch. 'He's a painter. An artist. A real artist. Herr Neumann has offered him regular work.'

'On a weekly basis?' asked Greiner, loudly. 'It would have to be on a weekly basis. This is not a hostel for down-and-outs.'

He was looking at Hanisch's clothing.

Hanisch said, 'It's not for me. It's for him.'

'He looks as if he's been sleeping rough,' said Greiner, still in an accusatory voice.

'He's been ill, that's all,' responded Hanisch, softly.

'No,' said Greiner. 'I can't do it. He looks too bad. The Herr Director would never take him in, looking like that. Sorry. Even for Herr Neumann. But no.'

'Do you work here?' asked Hanisch.

'I do jobs around the place. I also work on building sites. When I can. I have a regular income between the two.'

Hanisch took the folder of paintings from Adolf's rucksack. 'Look at that work! He's a real artist!'

Greiner stared at the water-colours, bemused. He shook his head. 'I can see that. But . . . it's his clothes.'

Hanisch's hand went into his pocket. It came out with an undisclosed number of kroner in it. These coins disappeared into Greiner's hand and then into his pocket.

It all happened so quickly it might never have happened at all.

'Do what you can for him,' said Hanisch, and with that he tapped Adolf on the arm, nodded briefly, and was gone.

There was a long silence as Greiner just looked suprised. Then he sighed, and took Adolf's arm. 'Come with me. We'll see what the Herr Director has to say.'

Adolf rose and walked with him down the Reception Hall, which smelled strongly of carbolic. Together, Greiner and Adolf made their way along a highly polished corridor, towards a very grand office. From inside came the sound of a loud masculine voice, giving orders.

'Stay here,' warned Greiner. 'Don't expect anything.'

Inside, Greiner faced Herr Director Kanya across his large desk. Kanya was a very decent man even if he was a toff, and a natural class enemy of the Working Masses, with whom Greiner, as a staunch but secret Marxist, sided. History was, of course, on the side of the Workers. Greiner simply wished it would hurry up. Meantime, a man had to live as best he could.

'Got a young man out here, Herr Director,' he said. 'Comes well recommended and with a job. He's been ill so he looks bad, but I'm assured he's of excellent character, Herr Director.'

Greiner said no more. He knew his man.

The Herr Director pondered. 'Who recommended him?'

'Herr Neumann, the furniture dealer.'

The Herr Director smiled wryly. 'The one who used to live here himself?'

'The very same, Herr Director. This young fellow is an artist.'

The Herr Director looked startled. 'An artist? In what way?'

'Herr Neumann is paying him on a weekly basis, on account of the paintings he'll be doing, Herr Director.'

The Herr Director looked interested, but stern. 'Do you have any proof of this, Greiner?'

'Got his paintings. Look very good to me. Of course, I'm no expert, Herr Director.' Greiner handed over Adolf's folder. The Herr Director leafed slowly through them. He looked up. 'These seem like excellent work. You are sure Neumann is paying him on a weekly basis?'

Greiner breathed hard. 'Positive, Herr Director.'

'Hmm.' The Herr Director pondered. 'Then let's have him in, Greiner. Let's see what this artistic person looks like?'

Greiner was having severe second-thoughts about it all. A man had only so much credit with these Capitalists. Once it was used up, they cut you off. One wrong move and you were out. It would be the finish to nice little perks like the cleaning job. And this scarecrow of an artist could foul up. He seemed, for one thing, to be in a permanent daze. His face expressionless, as in many a military situation that had needed calm, Greiner gestured Adolf into the Herr Director's office.

Good Christ, he thought, what was *he* thinking about! This hobo an artist? It was not believable! The trousers, look at the trousers! The ridiculous hat he snatched off Adolf's head before he walked into the room, and threw it on a chair. No good. He had done his best, as he always did. But it would be No. It could not be anything else.

Adolf came to a halt in front of the Herr Director's vast desk, in the warm and carpeted room and waited without curiosity for whatever to happen that was going to happen.

Herr Director Kanya looked at him in some revulsion. His slow gaze travelled over Adolf's face and his clothes. Then he looked searchingly at Greiner.

'Herr . . . ? Would you mind opening your coat for me?'

Slowly, Adolf did as he was bid.

The stained and threadbare suit was revealed. So was the filthy shirt. Greiner drew in his breath. No, a rag, not a shirt, surely it had never been a shirt!

The Herr Director, again, looked hard and questioningly at Greiner. Greiner refused to meet his gaze but stared steadily ahead. Marx wrote that there was nothing to be done about the Lumpenproletariat: the tramps, hobos and prostitutes of a Capitalist System. They were expendable. This creature was one of them. He, Greiner, had done his best for him. He could not endanger his own position. He could do no more. Nor would he.

Still, the paintings were good. It was a pity.

'You did these paintings?' said the Herr Director.

Adolf answered in a dull voice. 'Yes.'

'All of them?'

'Yes.'

'Where did you study?'

'The Realschule in Linz.'

'Do you have relatives in Linz?'

'My father and mother are dead.' Adolf sighed. He would have to say it again. 'My father was a Customs Officer, Herr Director.'

The Herr Director looked surprised and startled. 'A Customs Officer? Have you no other family?'

'I do, but I cannot go to them.'

'Cannot or will not?'

'Will not.'

The Herr Director thought he saw. 'You tried your luck as an artist? Is that it? And it didn't come off?'

Adolf nodded. 'Something like that.'

'I see.' The Herr Director looked keenly at Adolf for a long moment. Then he said, 'Wait out in the corridor.'

Adolf, slowly, turned and went out.

The Herr Director pondered. 'He looks ill.'

'He isn't a lunger,' said Greiner. 'Or so he says.'

'Well, I certainly hope not!' said the Herr Director, sharply. 'Look at him, Greiner! His clothes are impossible! You know full well I can't admit anybody looking like that. The fellow looks like a tramp, man. I simply can't do it. This is a Hostel for Working-Men.' Then he added, dangerously, 'You ought to know better than to suggest I see him!'

'Sorry, Herr Director,' muttered Greiner. 'My fault, Sir.'

'Yes, it damn well *is*!' shouted the Herr Director, very angrily indeed.

The bastard, thought Greiner. They're all the same.

Then Greiner did something that surprised even himself. He took from his waistcoat pocket his heavy silver watch and put it, heavy silver chain and all, on the Herr Director's desk.

The Herr Director just looked at it.

'What's this for, Greiner?'

'Collateral, Herr Director.'

'Against what, man?'

'Ten kroner, Herr Director. To buy the man some suitable clothes!'

The Herr Director was astonished, then touched. He was also silent, wondering if this would create any kind of unsuitable precedent. Finally, he took out his purse and counted out ten silver coins. 'Find something decent for that, can you?'

'Sure of it, Herr Director.'

'How will he pay you back?'

'From his income. Sir. From his drawings'

'Very well. Tell the Clerk to sign him in. One condition!' The Herr Director paused. 'On probation for one week only. We'll see how he goes on. Yes?'

'Whatever you say, Herr Director,' answered Greiner, thinking the bloody man will shape up, by God he will, or I was never in the Army!

The Herr Director looked at the heavy timepiece, and then put it in his drawer. He would give it back to Greiner at the end of the week. A decent gesture, he thought, from a decent man. It gave you faith in Human Nature, which God knows, you sometimes needed in this place.

He would tell his wife about it over dinner.

Adolf sat on a bunk in the dormitory. Everything shone with wax. The windows were open. There was nobody there but himself and Greiner.

Greiner said, in a regimental voice, 'This is where you sleep. You have a bed, covered with a three-sectioned mattress, which you fold thus. You have a horsehair bolster for your head, which you place thus.' Greiner demonstrated. 'You have one blanket which you fold *so*. You have one clothes-rail and one china chamber-pot, which you only use to piss in of a night! All clear so far?'

Adolf nodded. He was cold from the chill draught blowing in from the open windows. Greiner said: Now, we've got to get *you* fresh and clean. Got fleas, right? Well, I had 'em when I was soldiering.' Greiner turned and strode along the vast dormitory. 'Come on, lad!'

Adolf followed him down some stairs and into the bathroom area. Nobody was about, save another man in an apron like Greiner's, swilling out the place with a mop and bucket.

'Got a right one 'ere,' called Greiner cheerfully. 'Any disinfectant about, Pieter?'

The thin, silent man handed Greiner a bottle of dark brown fluid, and moved away, Adolf thought, rather hastily. Greiner ran hot water into a large, shallow porcelain bath and poured in a dollop of the brown solution. He stirred it with a bath-brush.

'Take those rags off!' he commanded. 'All of them. Take your drawing and painting stuff out of that rucksack! Put the rucksack and everything else in *this*!' He held a brown potato-sack towards Adolf. 'Everything off!'

Adolf took off his clothes.

The long black overcoat first.

'You can keep that,' said Greiner. 'I'll have it de-loused.' As Adolf looked bemused, he explained, 'In the oven, red hot. Kills the bugs.'

Adolf took off his tweed jacket (what was left of it), the rag of a shirt, and the even greater rag of another shirt under it. He had no underclothes, they had worn out long ago. He had only the foul socks on his feet. All these items he piled into the potato-sack, which Greiner then, holding at arm's length, threw into the vast furnace of the boiler that warmed the building. The rucksack followed it. Greiner took in Adolf's skeletal frame. 'Jesus! You're thin, lad!'

His eye also took in Adolf's lack of a testicle.

But he did not remark on it.

A non-commissioned officer never makes a personal remark about a recruit's appearance, or body . . . That was what the Book said, and Greiner had lived his life by the Book.

'Right, lad, into that bath. Wash everywhere, but don't get any of that stuff in your eyes, it'll half-blind you!'

He watched as Adolf stepped gingerly into the hot and strong-smelling bath. He nodded approvingly as Adolf dunked his head into the water, and passed him a towel to make sure none of the water got into his eyes. After a few minutes he told Adolf to get out and get into an ordinary hot bath of clean water, that he had run in another cubicle.

'Stay in there till I get back. I'll be ten minutes,' said Greiner, and left Adolf soaking dreamily in the hot water. The carbolic still stung his skin but he washed it away with the foaming white soap, and felt *clean* for the first time in many weeks and months. He lay in the hot water, thinking of nothing at all, until Greiner returned, and stepped briskly into the cubicle, carrying a brown-paper bundle. He tore it open and revealed: a thick grey soldier's shirt; a pair of striped dress-trousers that went with a very old-fashioned dress-jacket; a pair of old and much-cobbled but stout black shoes; a pair of thick socks; and a set of one-piece woollen long-johns. Every item was old and second-hand, but, as Greiner said, whatever else they were, they were clean.

He gave Adolf a towel and as Adolf slowly dried himself, Greiner laid out the clothes, as for a bridegroom. 'I couldn't get any better for ten kroner, son. And it's ten kroner you owe me when Neumann starts paying you. You're on a week's probation, and I've paid your rent for you an' all, so I'm well out of pocket. Call it thirty kroner, shall we?' He paused, and added, kindly, 'So you'll 'ave to get on with yer painting an' that, won't you, lad?'

Adolf nodded. He was still weak and vague-feeling but he was warm, really warm for the first time in many, many days. And hungry. He was very, very, hungry.

Greiner, who had divination, said: 'We'll eat when the canteen opens, in an hour. Meantime, get those clothes on, lad!'

When Adolf had dressed-up, Greiner surveyed him. 'Not bad, I've seen plenty of farmlads look worse, first few days in the Regiment. Nothing fits, eh? Only two sizes, too big and too small?'

Adolf felt ridiculous in these clothes.

A month before he would have raged.

Now, he didn't care.

Greiner, whatever he was, was not an Enemy.

Or anyway, not yet.

As Adolf combed his hair in the mirror, Greiner said, 'Need a haircut, lad! We'll get somebody in the Hostel to give you a bit of a trim, later on. Now, the Rules of the Hostel! First, this here is the Bath-house! Ten Heller for Bath Towel and Apron. No walking about in the Nude! Only thirty minutes in the Tub! Only one person in a Tub at Any One Time!'

He gestured for Adolf to pick up his drawing materials and follow him. Greiner took him on a conducted tour of the vast Hostel. It was very clean and very warm. Large pipes from the vast boiler in the depths of the place, made sure of that. Greiner took him to a large room on the First Floor. It contained shelves with rows of books and many chairs, both hard and, surprisingly, some easy, plus a few couches. 'This is a Self-Help Room. For Reading, Writing, an' that. Noise of any kind is *Verboten*!' he added, noting that Adolf glanced at two men, walking in and sitting quietly down, picking up newspapers.

'These men are Inmates, but out of work, temporarily. They can use this room by day, in that case. Otherwise, they can only use it of an evening, after work.'

Adolf realised that many men at the Hostel were employed in casual work or not at all, but kept up appearances somehow. Their unemployed status was plainly winked at. He felt better for that. Greiner meantime recited: 'Men must not come into the public rooms in workclothes. They must be clean, hands and face, and well-shaven. Right?'

Adolf fingered his moustache.

'Noticed you had a razor. Not much use for it yet, though?' Greiner took Pappi's razor from his pocket and gave it back to Adolf. 'Took it 'cos I thought you might have an accident with it, state you were in!'

Wordlessly, Adolf put the cut-throat razor in his pocket of the dress-jacket, which smelled heavily of moth-balls. Greiner, he decided, thought of everything.

Greiner opened a door. The smell of cooking hit Adolf like a physical blow. 'This is the canteen. No Noisy Games or Singing! No hooch or hard liquor! Beer or Wine in moderation only! Any Drunk Behaviour and you are Out. Right?'

Adolf nodded, trying not to faint at the smell of the food.

'As to Food,' Greiner shouted, or it seemed to Adolf he shouted. 'You can buy what you can pay for, lad. The tariff isn't bad. Roast Pork and Vegetables, ten Kroner. Beer, two Kroner. Coffee, two.' He grimaced. 'Soup, Two Kroner.'

Adolf stood, as if mesmerised.

Greiner propelled him forward, towards a table, in the vast, empty canteen. He said softly, 'We're out of hours but sit down, son, and I'll see what I can do.'

Adolf sat, on a hard chair.

He waited for what seemed a long time.

He could hear the jolly, deep voice of Greiner, as he joshed and joked with the canteen women. One, a typical hausfrau, in a white apron, came out to look at Adolf, as if at a specimen. Greiner followed her out, whispered in her ear and, gripping her from behind, fondled her ample breasts, whispering the while obscene pleasantries in her ear. The woman laughed, as she fended him off, and Greiner followed her back into the kitchen, his hands reaching after her. A squeal of pleasure was heard, then a hubbub of words and female laughter, and then a chink of dishes and cutlery.

A long time seemed to go by.

Then Greiner reappeared. He looked rumpled and flushed, and two of his shirt-buttons were undone. He carried two plates of roast pork and potatoes. One he placed delicately in front of Adolf.

'Eat that, lad, and enjoy it. It's against the Rules for any Inmate to eat before mid-day, but what the fuck! An old soldier has to live off the land, eh?'

Very slowly, Adolf ate every scrap of the meat and vegetables. As he ate, he felt the strength returning to his body. A little at a time, very gradually, as if it was some kind of minor miracle. Adolf did not believe in miracles, but that was how it felt.

Greiner had finished before him and looked at Adolf as if at a new recruit. Jesus, what a man had to do for such people! They were well-educated, but they knew nothing about life. Come the Revolution, everything would be very different. Meanwhile, a man lived, indeed, as best he could.

'Enjoy that, son?'

Adolf nodded.

Greiner put ten kroner in his hand.

'That'll get you tea and soup for the next two or three days. You can go upstairs now and sleep till you feel like waking up. I'll see you're not disturbed.' He pondered. 'If you want to do your paintings in the Self-Help Room, you can. I'll clear it with the Herr Director.' Greiner smiled, a rare gesture, revealing ill-fitting Army dentures. 'Got to get you painting again, haven't we, lad, or we'll all be out of pocket, you, me, Neumann, and the Herr Director himself, am I right, lad?'

Again, Adolf simply nodded.

His head was clearing and he saw the situation, at last. He was safe here. Safe from his Enemies. They would, of course, come back. That was their way. But they had tried every way they knew to kill him. Cold. Starvation. Spying. Cunning. To erase him from the face of the Earth.

But he had survived.

He had found the Will to survive.

Adolf thought: I will stay here as long as I have to. As long as I can.

He did not know, at that moment, that he would live in the Men's Hostel on the Mandelmanstrasse for almost four years.

All he knew was that his Enemies had failed.

And he had survived.

IX

ADOLF sat in the Men's Study Room at the Men's Hostel on the Meldemannstrasse and tried to concentrate on his work: a watercolour of the Burgtheater. He was weary of the task. He had done a couple of dozen just like it in the last year. He could paint the Burgtheater in his sleep.

He looked up briefly, as Hanisch sat next to him, on a cane chair.

'Adolf? Guten morgen.'

Adolf did not deign to reply.

Hanisch moved closer. He dropped his voice so low that Adolf could only just hear him. Hanisch glanced around the room. Then, very softly, he asked his question, one he had been rehearsing all day.

'Adolf? Have you any relatives with money?'

Adolf turned and stared at the hobo. Since Hanisch had obtained permission to live in the Hostel (with Greiner's help, and who knew how many kroner it had cost Hanisch?) he had improved his appearance, anyway to the extent of wearing a relatively clean shirt, when he had one, and shaving religiously each day. Hanisch had been driven into this semi-respectability by a close call with death. He had been discovered, in a coma, freezing in the snow the previous Winter. A doctor at the Vienna General Hospital, had told him, 'Spend the next winter inside or you'll die.'

Hanisch had discovered with some surprise that he did not want to die. Even his claustrophobia had been driven away by the fear of it, at least temporarily. Even more astonishingly, his drinking had steadied somewhat. As Hanisch confessed to Adolf: 'I'm a reformed character from what I was a year ago, Adolf. It's reform or die, Good Sir. As simple as that. So here I am, resident in these splendid halls, and glad of it, Good Sir, glad of it.'

'You aren't drinking at all?'

Hanisch shook his head. 'Of course I'm drinking! How could I live if I wasn't drinking? But I'm drinking *outside* the hostel, not inside. Catch me with a bottle of hooch in *this* place!' Hanisch's grubby paw embraced the almost deserted room. In a cane chair sat Bruno, an ex-officer in a threadbare suit, a man Adolf knew to be a sexual pervert. He looked at them with interest.

Since his reappearance, and to beef up his credentials as a genuine workingman, Hanisch had worked – actually worked! – on a building-site, as a coffee-maker to the labourers. After that, for a spell, he had carried luggage at the Banhof. He had soon tired of such physical pursuits, and had taken to hawking Adolf's paintings around the café-bars of Vienna. He had been surprisingly successful. Most days he sold something. Usually, just a small watercolour of the Burgtheater or the Rathaus, mainly to a visitor of some kind, at an average price of five to ten kroner. The split was fifty-fifty, and the arrangement had kept Adolf going. Even with Greiner selling one or two paintings a week – Greiner lacked Hanisch's beggarly knowledge and was less successful – it barely kept him alive. Neumann the Jew had managed to sell a few but that had dried-up of late. Business was bad, Neumann had told Adolf that very week.

That worried Adolf, and was the driving-force behind the rages, which were recurring, now he felt a return of energy. The anxiety was due to the fact that he was now almost totally dependent on the selling-powers of Hanisch, and Hanisch was profoundly unreliable. Sales of the little paintings had been slowly falling off, due, Hanisch said, to Adolf's choice of subject. 'The market's dropped off for this stuff, people don't want it,' Hanisch had said. 'If you could give me some portraits? Of the Emperor, say, the silly old sod walking around in the Palace grounds? Something like that? I could get you twenty kroner, even twenty-five, maybe.'

Adolf had not even replied. He had long ago realised that he had no talent for figure-painting or portraits. There was no point in telling Hanisch that. Hanisch had sighed and said, with an air of finality: 'We need some sales very badly indeed. Or we could find ourselves out in the snow again.'

Adolf had physically shivered, at that.

'We have to do something, my good Sir.'

Was Hanisch suggesting Adolf join him on the Building Site again? Adolf had done that once, working as a casual labourer. The heavy work had sickened him, taken the skin off his soft hands, made him feel abused, used, foolish. He had lasted only two days. He had walked off the site, without pay, as the ganger's voice called after him, 'Hey you,

Heidler or whatever your fucking name is, where the fuck d'you think you're going?'

Adolf had not even answered.

He had walked off the site and back to the Men's Hostel, shaking with fury at his own stupidity in taking the job. He, Adolf Hitler, was not born for such donkey-work. He had raged at Hanisch about that. And now, here was Hanisch again: pestering, probing. Talking, as usual, about money. Adolf straightened his tie. It was frayed and stained and the only one he had. But a collar-and-tie marked a man out as a clerk, or better. A scarf such as Hanisch wore branded him as a manual worker or worse. Adolf dressed now in tweed jacket and knickerbockers, the attire of an artist. Nonetheless, they were a great improvement on the ridiculous top-hat and striped trousers Greiner had given him that first day at the Men's Hostel, two years before.

'So, nobody in the family with money?' asked Hanisch.

'I have a half-sister whose husband is a Civil Servant, but . . .'

'A Civil Servant?' Hanisch's hoochy breath struck Adolf in the face. He winced.

'He is an enemy. There is no help from him.'

'No?' Hanisch looked disbelieving. 'There is always help from one's relatives, in my experience, if one is . . . desperate enough?'

'Not from them.' Adolf shook his head. 'I have not seen them for a very long time.'

'Then I bet they're worried about you?' Hanisch mused. 'A Civil Servant and his wife? Respectable people? Undoubtedly, they would worry?'

'No,' Adolf repeated. 'Forget them.'

'For the moment, perhaps, but . . . A Civil Servant? There's a possibility there, I feel sure?'

Hanisch fell silent, but Adolf knew he wasn't finished.

Adolf picked up his brush, tipped it with a watery wash of off-white, and painstakingly created a cloud in the blue Viennese sky above the Burgtheater. It was now March, and still cold. The Summer was the best period in which to sell paintings. Visitors from all over the Empire poured into the city. The outdoor cafés were open and crowded. Adolf surveyed the work and cleaned his brush in clear water.

Hanisch asked, gently, 'Your Father was a Civil Servant, correct? So there *was* a pension, correct?'

Adolf nodded. 'He had a pension. It's gone.'

'No,' Hanisch persisted. 'It came to you, some of it, surely, when your Mother died?'

'I made it over to little Paula.'

Hanisch was personally aggrieved to hear that. 'And who the fuck is little Paula?'

'My sister.'

'Why did you do that, for God's sake?'

'She needed it.'

'My God, what a dumkopf you are, my Good Sir! A Benefactor, for God's sake!'

Hanisch's voice carried, and Bruno the cashiered officer and sex-pervert looked over his *Neve Frei Presse* in silent disapproval. Hanisch gave him the solo finger and the ex-officer reddened and glared long and furiously at Hanisch, then sulkily resumed his reading.

'My half-sister, Angi, needed the money,' Adolf explained, 'to keep little Paula.'

Adolf did not add that Angi had cited to the Court a sum of money Adolf had been given by Aunt Johanna Pohl the hunchback, after Mutti's funeral. It had been only a few hundred kroner. Since then, while he had been with Gustl, he had had small sums from Aunt Johanna, but nothing of any size. When he left the Stumpergasse, he had left all that behind. He had not thought of Aunt Johanna since.

'Nobody else with any money?' Hanisch came closer. Adolf edged away. Hanisch smelled. If he didn't wash more often, and be a little more careful in his alcoholic ways, the Herr Director would throw him out.

'Nobody?' Hanisch persisted. 'Nobody at all? Nobody at all in the family with any money?'

Adolf sighed. 'I have an aunt. My mother's sister, Aunt Johanna Pohl. She's over sixty. She's a hunchback. She's been a servant in other people's homes all her life, and she's got some money saved, or so they say. For a while she lived with us – but I hardly remember her. After my mother died, she gave me a few kroner.'

Hanisch almost stopped breathing. 'So?' he whispered. 'She knew you as a boy? She has money? And she likes you?'

Adolf nodded. 'As much as she likes anybody, yes, I suppose so.'

Hanisch placed his grubby hand on Adolf's sleeve, very gently.

'Aunt Johanna Pohl?' Hanisch whispered. 'I am beginning to like the sound of Aunt Johanna Pohl. I am beginning to like the sound of Aunt Johanna Pohl very much indeed, my Good Sir.'

Adolf looked at him, puzzled.

Hanisch smiled.

That night Adolf slept badly.

It was not entirely due to the heavy snoring of several of the Dormitory's sleepers, although once Greiner's loud contribution had got Adolf out of his cot. He approached the slumbering Capo with the intention of turning him onto his side.

As he had been poised to do so, the awful thing had happened. Greiner had wakened (he was lying on his back) and opening one eye – only *one* eye! – had said, 'Oh, it's you, Adolf? Fancy me, do yer?'

Adolf had stammered, 'You were snoring!'

'Didn't know you cared,' said Greiner, and bared his gums in a terrible smile. Without his teeth, he was indeed a figure from the Pit. Adolf retreated quickly, Greiner's wheezing cackle following him. Within a minute of Adolf getting back into his cot, Greiner was snoring again. Adolf felt a terrible rage possess him.

All right, Greiner had saved him from the snows, but he should not talk to him in that fashion, hinting that he, Adolf, would be happy to indulge in the buggery that certainly went on in the Dormitory from time to time – that was not to be borne, whether Greiner had helped him or not! Greiner was not to be trusted. As Hanisch was not to be trusted. Nobody in the Hostel was to be trusted. The important thing to remember was: nobody had any friends, even in here, where a man might think, surely, that privation and want would bring people together? It did not. It drove them to compete against each other ruthlessly, terribly, for what little there was to be had (food, money, sex) because they had no family or friends to assist them if they stumbled. That much was certain. Greiner and Hanisch were not enemies. Not yet.

Correction: they had not yet shown themselves to be enemies!

That was all.

Other enemies waited, out in the cold, depraved city, which was why Adolf was not anxious to encounter them, why he spent as much time as possible inside the Hostel, where, at least, he knew who his enemies were.

Finally, Adolf began to go out, forcing himself to walk along the boulevards, without looking back to see who was following or observing him: A Civil Servant from the War Ministry; a policeman; any official-seeming person, in top-hat, striped trousers, frock-coat. Such figures troubled him always, in those early walks. Gradually, the danger and fear had faded. The enemies were there, certainly. They still desired his death, his extinction. That had been proven by his experience, as he lay now, forgotten by friends and family, by everybody he had ever known, in a Hostel bed. Forgotten. Ignored. Buried alive.

Now, Hanisch the Tramp had kicked open a door to the past: Aunt Johanna Pohl!

Adolf did not know if he wished to go through that door.

He would not go!

It was as simple as that. And yet . . . The money?

Adolf gazed, sleepless, at the ceiling, listening to Greiner's loud, catarrhal snores, as the first, cold dawn-light filtered into the Men's Dormitory.

Aunt Johanna Pohl looked at Adolf with concern.

'You're so thin! Where are you living these days?'

Adolf shuffled his feet, and balanced the cup of strong hot coffee on his knee. 'In a Men's Hostel, Aunt Johanna. I'm comfortable enough.'

'A Hostel? That doesn't sound very comfortable to me!'

The old lady pushed a plate towards him. It contained several cream cakes. Adolf was particularly fond of cream cakes. However, he was not here to eat. He was here, as Hanisch had repeatedly told him, to get money. Enough, if possible, to keep him – and Hanisch – out of the killing winter snows. For the winter of Nineteen Ten had been a hard one, and it wasn't over yet.

'Have another cake?'

'No, thank you. I'm fine.'

'But you're not eating enough. Anybody can see that.'

The old servant sat opposite from Adolf in the small, stuffy, overheated room, which was overfurnished and contained a bed, pushed against one wall. She herself looked thin and none too well. A life of service had wearied her, and of course she had the added problem of the hunched back. This, she told Adolf, was her last home, a one-room apartment in Spital. None of the family ever came to see her. Angi wrote from time to time, but she had not approved of Angi getting all of her Father's pension, and citing her own small assistance to Adolf as justification for it.

'I don't understand Angi,' Aunt Johanna Pohl said. 'She brought the family's name into that Court. No need for it.'

Adolf shrugged. 'She's got Paula to look after.'

But Aunt Johanna Pohl was not letting the bone go so easily. 'Just the same. No need for it. She's your half-sister, after all.'

'Angi's all right, Aunt Johanna. I don't want her money. Let little Paula have it.' Since he had no choice, Adolf could afford to sound generous.

Aunt Johanna Pohl sniffed. 'They are all right, in their nice apartment, but you have to live in a Men's Hostel. And you the man.'

'Aunt Johanna, I don't care.'

Johanna Pohl reached out and put a large slice of gateau on Adolf's plate. 'Eat. You must eat, Adolf.'

Adolf took a bite of the gateau. 'Delicious. I haven't had such a treat for a long while.'

'All people think about,' said Aunt Johanna Pohl, 'is money.'

Money? Adolf suddenly remembered Hanisch's demand: find out how much the old lady has in the bank?

Hanisch had whispered the seductive words, his hooch-laden breath hot in Adolf's face. There had been a time when he would have ignored them, but that was before he had lived in the Hostel. Before he had seen, and smelled, exactly what poverty was. Before he had realised the truth of Schopenhauer's words: *the weak go to the wall.*

Survival. That was all that counted.

Survival and ultimately Success.

All anybody ever remembered of a man after he was dead was: was he a success in what he set out to do. Or was he a failure?

To succeed, it was necessary, first, to survive. Adolf finished the gateau and swallowed the rest of his heavily-sugared coffee. He put down the large china cup. Aunt Johanna Pohl promptly filled it up again.

'Tell me what work you are doing, Adolf?'

Adolf said, 'I am an architectural artist. I am selling my paintings.' As Aunt Johanna Pohl's face lit up, he added, hastily, 'Not too many. Not enough. But people buy them, and survive.'

'Survive?' Aunt Johanna Pohl frowned. 'That is not good, just to survive?'

Adolf shrugged. 'We all survive. In these hard times, it is enough.'

Aunt Johanna Pohl shook her grey head. An odour of snuff emanated from the black bombazine she always wore. 'Don't they feed you at the Hostel?'

'I cook my own food. I don't eat meat. I'm a vegetarian, you see.'

Aunt Johanna Pohl did not see. She did not know anybody who was a vegetarian. She was extremely concerned to hear such news. Her be-veined hands twisted the napkin on her knee. Aunt Johanna Pohl had learned 'good manners' in at least one of the houses in which she had worked. Indeed, where else but from such a house had these napkins (and the doilies under the cakes, and the antimacassars on the back of her velvet chairs) come from? Aunt Johanna Pohl did not think such acquisitions dishonest. They would have been thrown out, had she not taken them. She had been so pleased to get Adolf's letter. It was, of course, a begging-letter, dictated by Hanisch. Hanisch had said: 'She must understand you are in want and need her help. Also you must say you will call on a certain day and at what time. That way, she has the whole picture. She is *prepared*, my Good Sir!

Aunt Johanna Pohl was happy to be prepared.

Any visitor was welcome. Adolf was more than welcome.

No, nobody ever came to see her these days, as she told Adolf. She was old and most of the family lived on the family farm. Well, they would hardly know her, most of them. When you were a housekeeper to a busy family you rarely had time to keep up with visits to your own family. Yet, she had been lucky. With her disability, and consequently no hope of marriage or children, she had done as well as anybody could expect. Yet she had nobody of her own, nobody close, now she was away from the last of her adopted families, to look after, admonish, advise, help. Now, here was her dead sister's boy, God rest her soul. Here was Adolf. He had always been a moody, withdrawn boy, but he was family.

'You must eat meat, Adolf. You'll be ill.'

The boy was too thin. And she knew why. No meat? Madness!

'It is a healthy diet, Aunt Johanna. I would not eat meat even if I were rich.' Adolf smiled to take the sting out. Aunt Johanna Pohl considered it a proud remark and liked him the better for it. Naturally, he would not admit to liking meat, since he could not afford it.

'Adolf, I do not want you to be offended.' Aunt Johanna Pohl reached for her handbag. Like everything she owned, it had once belonged to somebody else, in this case her last employer, Frau Muller. A handsome, crocodile-bag too, even if the catch did not quite work as it should. 'I want to make you a little present, you see? Like I did once before?' Aunt Johanna Pohl took from her purse kroner to the value of one hundred and pressed the coins into Adolf's hand.

'Aunt Johanna. I did not come just to –'

'I know, I know,' said Aunt Johanna Pohl. 'But it will help. And you must come and see me again soon. I may be able to do a little more for you. Somebody has to look out for you, while you are getting yourself established as a painter, is that not so?'

Adolf, sitting there in his one jacket and his one pair of knickerbockers and his one good shirt (hand-washed last night, and ironed this very morning, before he started the journey) nodded. 'Well, I will not pretend it will not be most welcome.'

'What are family for?' asked Aunt Johanna Pohl. Her sallow cheeks were flushed and she smiled so warmly that it was sometimes possible, Adolf thought, to forget she was a hunchback. He understood the sadness that affliction must entail. He had his own dark physical secret, the lack of a testicle, after all. Few people were born perfect, too many rickety children and cripples! But, surely, the aim had to be a perfect species. A Race of Supermen, and the women to service them, equally perfect in all ways, as Nietzche had said. He would compensate for his own small and only rarely thought-of disability by using his brains. Poor Aunt Johanna had no such compensations, and never had.

'Danke, Aunt Johanna,' said Adolf, draining his coffee and standing up. 'That was most enjoyable.'

He still did not know what money Aunt Johanna Pohl had in the bank. Frankly, he did not care. He just wanted to get to hell out of the cramped, overheated apartment and back home to the Men's Hostel. It was the only home he had, the only real home he had ever known, he sometimes thought, if 'home' meant a place where you did as you liked.

He shook hands stiffly but correctly and cut through the old lady's protests. Why did he have to go so soon, he had only just got here?

Adolf smiled and said: 'Work to do, Aunt Johanna.'

She waved him off from the door of the flats.

Blast Hanisch, he thought. All this nonsense, for what? The old lady had very little to give. Was the effort of dressing-up, the acting worth it? Still, the jingling kroner felt good in his pocket.

At that moment Hanisch was putting one of Adolf's watercolours – yet another of the Burgtheater – in front of a dark, pretty little Viennese he knew to be a small-time actress called Zizi. She was often to be seen, always with a man, in the small bar-café near the University, a place much frequented by artists and actors and dilettantes of all kinds: not the kind of bar-café he would normally tout in. The clientèle was too educated, too knowing. They would usually turn away, contemptuously, after a quick glance at Adolf's watercolours. Some of them actually laughed. For himself, Hanisch did not care. He was in the business of selling the bloody stuff and that was all. He had not made a single sale all day, working with only a mid-day pause for alcoholic refreshment. That had been a mixture of cheap wine and methylated spirit, consumed in an alleyway.

The bar-café and the sexy little actress were his last shot. 'It's by a poor man,' whispered Hanisch. 'A man who's ill, you see?'

'Ill?' Zizi shivered prettily and glanced at her companion. A superior clerk, to Hanisch's experienced eye, a young fool: thinking he was a man because he had bought a coffee and a brandy for an out-of-work actress. Take more than that to get this one to bed, thought Hanisch the connoisseur, taking in the swell of the tight little breasts and the dark ringlets peeping out from under the bonnet and the cheap bracelets on the plump young arms.

'Ill?' repeated Zizi, holding the painting at arm's length, as if it might be infected. 'Ill? What *with*?'

'He's a lunger,' said Hanisch, cruelly. 'Like me.'

Deliberately, he breathed his hooch-laden breath directly into the girl's face.

Zizi recoiled in horror.

'Oh, take it *away*!' She thrust the painting back into Hanisch's grubby palm. 'Moritz, give him something, will you?'

Grudgingly, would-be-dandy Moritz handed Hanisch five kroner.

Hanisch just looked at it, in his palm.

Moritz made it ten kroner.

Hanisch walked out of the bar-café with a lighter step. The ten kroner could go directly for drink. Thus fortified, he would accost Adolf, back at the Hostel, and discover how things had gone with Aunt Johanna Pohl at Spital.

Hanisch, beginning his long trudge back to the Hostel, felt more hopeful than he had all day.

The satisfaction left Hanisch abruptly when he got back to the Men's Hostel. There, in the middle of the waxed and polished floor of the Dormitory, between the long rows of cots, stood Adolf. Engaged, as usual, in loud and pointless political argument, this time with Greiner, the secret Marxist – on his feet and declaiming – and the cashiered ex-officer and sex-pervert, Bruno, who was lounging on his cot, monocle fixed in his eye and his face flushed with anger.

'Adolf,' Greiner was saying, with disgust, 'you haven't lived long enough to know when to come in out of the rain! Historically, the Marxists are the only answer! The Christian Socials are useless and the Social Democrats are worse!' Greiner grinned. 'Come and talk to me about politics when you've got some hair on your cock!'

Other inmates, many in a state of undress – soiled undershirts and baggy longjohns – laughed at this sally, as they sat smoking, against the rules, and waited for Adolf to answer. A small grin lurked on many an unshaven face. Adolf was, as far as they were concerned, as good as a visit to the music-hall. His chaotic anger pleased them. It reflected their own petty resentments against the Empire, the Hostel, the Rules, and every bureaucrat or aristo who lorded it over them.

Hanisch rummaged in his voluminous coat, found a half-smoked cigar (picked up that very evening on his walk back along the Herringstrasse), popped it into his mouth and lit it with a spare match, ignited on his thumbnail, and waited, with some irritation.

The ex-officer, Bruno, was speaking now, acid and contemptuous: 'I absolutely agree with you, Greiner, when you say the Social Democrats are useless, have no balls, and will never do anything for the poor!' Bruno took out his monocle and breathed on it. 'They will never do anything for the Upper Class, either!'

This brought a derisive snort from Greiner and groans from every-body present. Greiner leaned forward, a toothpick in the corner of his mouth, in lieu of a smoke. 'Bruno, you are talking out of your arse! You're an aristo no longer! You're not in the Army any longer. You're a broken-down piss-artist, like the rest of us!' There was another laugh at that. 'Anybody can see what's needed in Austria!' Greiner lowered his voice. 'Socialism! Marxism! That's what's needed! If the Workers gain control of the means of Production, Distribution and Exchange . . .'

But Adolf had heard enough.

He held up his finger in Messianic fashion, for silence.

The silly sod, Hanisch thought, shaking his head, he's off again.

There he stands, about to go off on one of his fucking diatribes, and here I sit, feet aching, dying for a drink, which I can't have until I get out of the Hostel again, desperate to hear how he got on with little old Aunt Johanna Pohl, and now *this*!

A lank strand of hair fell across Adolf's face. It stayed there. He never troubled to push it back. It had a certain mesmeric quality about it as it danced in front of his eyes. 'My dear Sir,' Adolf said, in a low, intense voice to the surly Greiner, 'your Marxists have some good ideas, but what is the realistic possibility of putting any of them into practice?' As Greiner attempted to intervene, Adolf held up his hand again. 'A rebellion? A Workers' Revolt? Have you looked at the long history of Workers' Rebellions and Revolts, Herr Greiner? I can tell you they all have one thing in common, from Spartacus to the latest attempts in Leningrad and Moscow.' Adolf stared, his wide unblinking eyes fixed on Greiner. 'They are all put down! In a bloody and ruthless way!' Adolf laughed. In these diatribes he often chortled at his own humour. 'Do you see yourself, Herr Greiner, bare-arsed as Nature made you, hanging from a tree in the Kartnerstrasse? You would not be a pretty sight, *Comrade*!'

The down-and-outs, lounging in their dirty underclothes, laughed loudly. Hanisch was – against his will – impressed. Adolf *could* actually make crude jokes, like that. That was new. And effective, he had to admit.

'The Marxists have no chance, my dear Greiner, of taking over the State of Austria by force of arms! What arms? Where *are* these arms, where are these soldiers, with their rifles?' asked Adolf.

Greiner interrupted in his best barrack-room voice: 'The comrade-soldiers will rebel! They'll take the rifles out of the armouries and turn them on their officers! What about the French Revolution?'

The hobos grinned at each other. They respected Greiner too, as a trusty spy for the Herr Director of the Hostel. He would shop any one of them, for any infraction of the rules, unless suitably bribed, agreed. Yet he was also a Marxist, or said he was, and on the side of the Ordinary Man. Such duplicity had to be respected. Adolf was different. He talked idealism but Hanisch took it for granted he didn't mean it. He was out for Number One, like everybody else. Still, he was a good act. No doubt of that.

'The French Revolution?' Adolf was saying, or rather shouting by now. 'That was a long time ago, Herr Greiner! The French people were starving, and there was no middle-class to buttress them from the aristocrats and the court. One riot would do it, and *did*! But in Austria we have a large and prosperous middle-class –'

'Made so on the backs of the Workers!' insisted Greiner.

'Even so – and I admit that! – there is no way the Marxists are going to get power. No way at all. And if they did get it, who would lead them? *You?*'

Greiner flushed. He had reason to feel aggrieved. Here was this little nobody, this *artist*, for fuck's sake, who he had taken out of the snow, *helped*, for fuck's sake, and now *he* was telling Greiner the facts of political life and holding him up to ridicule!

'I have commanded men,' said Greiner. 'That is a fucking sight more than you have done or will ever do, young Adolf!' Greiner felt a surge of righteous anger. 'You'd run at the first shot!'

Hanisch looked up warningly, at Adolf.

He knew, and Adolf should have known, what Greiner was hinting at. Greiner knew that Adolf had been required that very week to register for Military Service in the Austrian Army. Greiner suspected that Adolf had not yet done that. Adolf showed no sign of knowing what Greiner was hinting at. He shouted: 'If the day came that I would need to lay down my life for a Greater Germany, I would do it!'

The hobos, lounging on their cots, cheered ironically. They did not believe a word of it.

Hanisch was not so sure. Adolf was mad enough for anything. Hanisch had seen his rages against people who offended him. The aristocrats and the army officers who ordered the State. The middle-class who ran it for them. The Workers who did as they were told.

Hanisch noted that Adolf had said 'Greater Germany', not 'Austria'. That was clever, a Get-out Clause. Hanisch approved. Clever.

'You'd never make a soldier, Adolf,' Greiner taunted. 'Look at you! You're all skin and bone.'

Adolf stood quite still in the middle of the waxed floor. His face was suddenly very pale. Often, Adolf would go off and eat cream cakes and sit in a café reading newspapers and political pamphlets, letting the day go by. On such days he would eat no strengthening food, meat or bread. This has been a long day for Adolf, Hanisch thought, and he had probably eaten very little. He had been all the way to Spital and back, and who knew, it might not have been worth the expense of the journey?

139

'Whose fault is it?' Adolf asked in a suddenly quiet voice, 'that nobody in this room has enough to eat? Is it ours? Is it our own fault?'

'Certainly it is,' replied Greiner, stoutly. 'Nobody in this Hostel is prepared to work. If they were they wouldn't be here!'

'I say, Herr Greiner, steady on!' exclaimed the ex-officer, Bruno. 'I've tried for twenty, thirty jobs for which I'm well-qualified, and nobody will hire me!'

'That's because you can't keep your hands off little boys, and everybody knows it,' retorted Greiner.

Bruno said, acidly, 'All that is my business and I have paid for it.' There was a silence. Every man in the room knew Bruno had been in prison for buggery. Many had been in prison themselves, if only for vagrancy. Bruno had served a longish term, for a serious offence. He had earned respect. He said, 'Our bellies are empty. Why?'

'Because,' yelled Adolf, 'the so-called Social Democrats are not interested in the Ordinary Man, and therefore do nothing for him! The Hapsburgs are – despite Bruno's pathetic support for them – finished, but they won't go away! They too are responsible for our hunger! So is the Catholic Church, which does nothing but prate on about God! What has God done for any man here? Does any man here really in his heart believe there is such a thing as God, up there in the sky?'

'Calm down,' said Greiner. 'All right. The Social Democrats? No good. Royalty? No good. The Church? No good. My dear Adolf, that only leaves you Marx and the Socialists. Who else is there?'

'What about the Christian Socials?' asked Bruno. 'They have some good ideas. At least they believe in Germany!'

'I believe in Germany!' Adolf shouted, very loudly. 'But the Christian Socials have sold the pass! They think only of the Middle Class and of getting power through Parliament! It is never going to happen. They'll never vote Greiner's friends, the Social Democrats, out of power!'

'They are no friends of *mine*,' interrupted Greiner. 'The Broad Masses are my friends – and nobody else.'

'The Broad Masses are in the Social Democratic Party,' said Adolf, in a pained, insulting voice. 'They are in the unions, such as there are any unions. They do not support you and your few Marxists.'

'They will!' shouted Greiner, raising his fist above his head. 'They will! Come the Day!'

The hobos cheered. They did not believe a word of that, either.

'No,' said Adolf, shaking his head. 'It won't happen. The Police and the Army will never let it happen. The Workers will stay in the Social Democratic Party, like so many sheep.'

'You think the workers are *sheep*?' demanded Greiner.

'Of course they are sheep!' replied Adolf, with heat. 'They march twenty deep in demonstrations and then go home to their pea soup.' He raised his finger. 'They don't understand the issues because nobody puts anything to them *simply* enough! It isn't enough, my dear Greiner, to read *Das Kapital*. You Marxists hate the Fatherland because – you *say*! – it's in the hands of the Capitalists! You say the Law holds down the *Volk*! You say Religion holds down the *Volk*! You say One World! I say *One Germany*!'

Hanisch sighed. This promised to go on for hours.

'You hate the Church yourself, you just said so,' said Greiner. 'And you think the Working-man is a sheep!' Greiner roared. 'What *do* you believe in?'

'The Working-man *is* a sheep,' shouted Adolf. 'Unless something is put to him in six simple words, he is incapable of understanding it, and not necessarily then! Yet he has the Vote! That's Democracy and it does not work!'

The hobos nodded and grumbled their assent.

'Correct, Adolf, tell the bastards' they said.

'What about the Jews?' Hanisch asked, like a hypnotist.

Adolf stood as if transfixed, absolutely still, the hypnotist's subject.

The word itself would do it. Which is why Hanisch had said it.

'The Jews?' Adolf's voice was very low and harsh. 'You ask me about the Jews?' In the last year Hanisch had noted this sudden, granite attitude towards the Jews. Even Neumann, who had helped Adolf, and still sold his paintings whenever he could, had ceased to seek out Adolf's company, so offended was he by Adolf's rank outbursts of Anti-Semitism. Or was it more than that, Hanisch wondered? Adolf's attitude towards the Jews was illogical. Adolf certainly hated the immigrant Czechs and Poles, but there was a measure of easy contempt in his attitude to such people. The Jews were something else. There was something personal in it, somewhere, had to be, and Hanisch wondered what it was?

'The Jews ... The Jews are everywhere.' Adolf was shaking his finger at the hobos. The words he spoke came from the Anti-Semitic pamphlets on sale at a dozen street-corners in the city. Adolf had read and digested them. They answered a deep-felt need. 'The Jew is behind the daubs of Modernism in the Arts!' The hobos snorted, they knew nothing of any of that. 'The Jew is behind Pornography in the Arts, only he calls it Modernism! The Jew is to be found in the extremes of Marxism, exploiting, if he can, the Ordinary Man!' Greiner roared a protest at that, but Adolf shouted on, his voice rising, as it always did, when he was contradicted or opposed. 'The Jew is to be found in Capitalism, making money from the Masses, the Jew is *everywhere*!' Adolf stared round the room. 'Even here in this place!'

The hobos cheered. They knew this was Adolf's hobby-horse. Hanisch thought he was deranged on the subject.

'Believe me, my dear Greiner,' Adolf shouted, a bead of perspiration on his forehead now, a fleck of foam on his upper lip, 'Germany must awake, and come into her own, but it will not happen while the Jew is in our midst!'

Hanisch knew that Adolf was now very near to one of his chaotic rages. Hanisch had seen these bouts grow more frequent, the longer Adolf had lived at the Men's Hostel. For a long time after his arrival, Adolf had kept his head down, had been glad of a place to live, a warm bed, something to eat. As time has passed, however, his confidence had grown, and he had started to argue with the other men about politics. When anybody persisted in arguing with him, the rage eventually showed. It was an awful rage – white face, staring eyes, trembling limbs – and it was showing now. Hanisch was almost sorry he had asked the question, but he wanted this foolish nonsense over. Adolf's rages interested him but did not disturb him. He had seen a lot of splenetics in his years on the tramp. Adolf was just another, except that he sometimes talked sense. Or what passed for sense in a place like the Men's Hostel.

Now, Adolf's voice had raised itself to the highest pitch yet. 'Germany – and that means Austria too – must *Awaken*! If she does not, then we are all doomed, all of us in this room, in this city, in all of Austria!'

A very small, dark inmate spoke for the first time. He had been in the Hostel only a few days, and nobody knew him. 'Adolf, I am a Jew but I'm an Austrian as well. That's plenty. I don't want to be a German, too? So may I please opt-out?'

The hobos hooted loudly but good-naturedly at that. The laughter went on and on. Greiner looked alarmed. This sort of noise was too much, it might well be heard in the Reception hall downstairs and bring the toffee-nosed clerk upstairs. 'All right! That's enough! No more talk! Everybody quiet down. We've got a nice number here. No need to spoil it,' said Greiner. 'All right, Adolf. It's over. Sit down and rest. You look as if you need to, lad.'

The hobos sighed and smoked and rested on their cots. The evening's entertainment was over.

Hanisch nipped out his stub of cigar and put it in a pocket. He edged over to Adolf and sat next to him, on the cot. Adolf had all but collapsed on it.

'So, how did it go at Spital, my Good Sir?'

'What?'

Adolf stared at him, that stupid open stare he had. Hanisch kept his temper, and his voice low. 'At Spital? Aunt Johanna Pohl? The money?'

Still Adolf stared at him. 'What about it?'

'How much?' Hanisch lowered his voice until it was almost inaudible. 'How much has she got in her savings account?'

Adolf shook his head, distainfully. 'She didn't say.'

'Didn't you ask her? I told you to ask her!'

'She gave me some kroner and said to come again.'

'Some kroner?' Hanisch leaned forward to see. 'How much?'

'Fifty,' said Adolf, equably. 'Here's twenty for you.' He pushed the coins into Hanisch's palm and turned away. 'Now, leave me alone. I'm tired.'

And he leaned back on his pillow and closed his eyes. His face was very pale.

Hanisch stared down at him, his patience all but gone. His words, however, although delivered in a whisper, were clear and sharp, a habit he had learned in his many short prison-spells: 'Fifty kroner! All that way for fifty kroner and a promise! My good Sir, we'll be out on our arses in the snow unless you shape up where that old lady is concerned, you hear me?'

But Adolf was asleep.

A month later Adolf went to Spital again.

It had been a hard, nay disastrous, month for the sale of his paintings. Hanisch had come back to the Men's Hostel empty-handed more days than not, complaining that nobody had money to spare for paintings that were simple replicas of what they could look at for free. They were in the market for something lively, something, possibly saucy. Adolf had snorted at this. 'I'm not a pornographer! I'm an Architectural Artist! I paint buildings, and erections of value!'

'Then I have to tell you,' said Hanisch, 'that the only erection these buyers want to see on paper is a big thick prick, halfway up some fat whore!' Hanisch was sick of pushing Adolf's paintings of churches and Cathedrals and parliamentary buildings in front of blasé Viennese who *would* buy pornography, if it was offered. 'If you could at least put a few fat, pretty women in front of these buildings, that would help,' pleaded Hanisch, the art-critic, as he threw the unsold daubs back on Adolf's cot. 'We'll sell nothing until the visitors come, in the summer.'

The problem was how to last until then.

All Adolf had done over the last week had been to lie on his cot, reading, occasionally going out to the cafés and spending what little money they had left. For Hanisch considered that Adolf's money, or half of it at least, was his. They were partners. Soon, if funds were not forthcoming, Hanisch would have to resort to begging. If that happened, and he was arrested for vagrancy, he would be thrown out of the Hostel.

The only consolation was that Adolf was in no better case. Greiner had not sold a painting of Adolf's for almost two weeks. Neumann the Jew had confessed that his last sale had been on the previous Monday, for thirty kroner. It was now Saturday. Even Adolf, who lived on bread and milk and an apple or two a day, could not last much longer. They both owed two weeks' rent. If they did not pay by the following Saturday, they were out. Herr Director Kanya allowed two weeks' arrears but was adamant that it ended there. If the current rent, *and* the arrears, were not fully paid-up by the start of the third week, an inmate had to go. This was a Workingmen's Hostel, not a Dosshouse, insisted Herr Director Kanya. If a man was working, he had wages. Therefore, he should pay his rent. If he wasn't working, then he had no right to be in a Workingmen's Hostel. It was as simple as that.

'Things, my Good Sir, have gone from worse to terrible this month,' said Hanisch, in the tone he always used with Adolf, part-wheedler, part-teacher. 'We have to do something about it, you and I, for we are in this together, are we not?'

'What are you getting at?' Adolf's large blue eyes were anything but friendly, but Hanisch was used to the hard look. He had, in his time, panhandled from the best: and the worst. 'We are two weeks behind in the rent, and if we don't pay up we're out. You can't have more than a few kroner left. Write to Aunt Johanna Pohl now and ask her to send you some money by return. Enclose a stamped-addressed envelope . . .' Hanisch took from his pocket an envelope with a stamp on it. He extracted from the envelope a sheet of paper. He had bought both, earlier in the day. Now, he leaned over and put his hand into Adolf's tin-can of pencils and crayons. He selected a sharp one and put it into Adolf's hand.

'Write to her now, and I'll take it out and post it.'

Adolf looked at him a long moment. The expression reminded Hanisch of the way Adolf had looked in the freezing cold under the Rotunda that previous Winter. 'All right,' Adolf said. He looked around the Dormitory at the inmates lying dozing or smoking on their cots. He looked disgusted. To Hanisch's surprise he suddenly sounded alive.

'Tell me what to write to the silly old fool!'

Hanisch was startled, but approving.

He told Adolf.

A week later Adolf sat facing Aunt Johanna Pohl, his spiel all rehearsed and ready. This time, Hanisch had warned him, he would have to press her. There would be no point in going all that way and coming back empty-handed, or without promises of more money to come. This was likely to be his last chance. He had to tell Aunt Johanna Pohl exactly how things stood. The truth would do, Hanisch had said drily, since it was the best story they had. He was starving, near enough. Just tell her that, Hanisch had advised, drawing on his soiled, second-hand cigar. She'll fall for that, how can she not fall for it, she's your old *Tante*, isn't she?'

Maybe, Adolf thought, Hanisch was right.

He had been right about Aunt Johanna Pohl writing back at once. He had even been right in his prophesy that she would send at least fifty kroner. She had sent exactly twice that sum, plus the rail fare. It had paid for drink for Hanisch, food for them both, and the expenses of the journey to Spital, but now there was very little left.

Adolf ate a vanilla cream-slice and washed it down with a draught of excellent coffee. To Aunt Johanna nothing was too good for poor Adolf, he realised, without gratitude.

'So?' Aunt Johanna Pohl leaned forward, disturbing the snuff hidden in the crevices of her black bombazine, the fine tickling dust irritating Adolf's nostrils. 'Things are even worse than last time?'

Adolf began to pitch in a low voice, the way he always began any kind of peroration, political or personal, leaving the meat of the matter until the end. 'I'm afraid so, Aunt Johanna. I had to help out an old friend. He's been trying to sell some paintings for me, but his health is poor and he hasn't sold many. I was a fool to try to help him but, as I say, he is a friend. I haven't even my rent money. That leaves me in a very difficult position.' Adolf placed his coffee cup on the polished table. 'I could, of course, give up my painting and my architectural studies and go to Angi and Raubal and throw myself on their mercy.'

Aunt Johanna Pohl frowned. Adolf knew she deeply disapproved of Raubal's drunkenness. Adolf paused a moment, almost choking in the stuffy warmth of the room. 'I could do that, but I won't. I'd starve first.' That, anyway, was true. 'I could try to get a job but I am not qualified for any office or labouring job.' He took a deep breath. 'I did once work on a Building Site but I found the work too heavy. I would have continued but it was really not for me.'

'Adolf!' exclaimed Aunt Johanna Pohl, scandalised, 'you didn't! A labourer's job? I can't believe it!'

'A man has to live,' said Adolf. 'And even a labourer is worthy of his hire.' Aunt Johanna Pohl shook her head in dismay, but Adolf pressed on, in an unemotional voice. It was, after all, the truth. 'So, there are my choices.'

Aunt Johanna Pohl shook her head vigorously. 'There are others, surely? You cannot give up your architectural studies. What will become of you?'

'I find it hard to study, Aunt Johanna,' he said. 'My paintings, done for a quick sale, take up most of my time and creative energy. However, I read all I can. I am a member of four libraries.'

'I'm not surprised you are tired!' said Aunt Johanna Pohl. 'You work too hard and you don't get enough to eat! I don't know what your dear Mother – God rest her soul! – would say if she was here. Even your Father would be scandalised that a Hitler should work on a Building Site as a daily labourer!'

Adold said nothing to that.

'Adolf, I have a little money. It's in the Savings Bank. I also have a very small pension, which dies with me. It is enough for me to live on, but who knows how long I will live, or any of us will live? What I can do, and what I will do, is send you, by post, every month, fifty kroner. It is not a lot but it will pay your rent, at least, and leave you a little over, maybe? With that, and whatever you make from your paintings, you will be able to exist and continue your studies?'

Adolf said nothing. The room was darkening in the winter twilight, and he could see only Aunt Johanna Pohl's earnest, wrinkled face, and he felt not that he had a friend, but that at least somebody was recognising him and giving him his just desserts. Fifty kroner was not much but he could – just about – live on it, as Aunt Johanna Pohl said, along with whatever came in from the paintings.

Aunt Johanna Pohl was talking on. 'My savings will be yours when I go. Angi has Raubal to help her and Paula. You have nobody. Of course, I may go on a long time. That is in the hands of the Lord. But, every month, fifty kroner. For a start.' The old woman rummaged in the bag with the broken clasp. 'I took some money out today, because I realised you would be needing it urgently. I'll give you enough to pay your immediate rent-arrears and some over.' Aunt Johanna Pohl put the notes and coins in an envelope and pressed it into Adolf's hand. 'There's a hundred kroner there.'

Adolf nodded his thanks. He had sweated all the long night thinking of this meeting. Now it was over and it had all been so easy. He said, 'I will not forget this.'

Aunt Johanna smiled and poured him another cup of strong coffee.

Adolf put the money in his pocket.

He began to work out what he would tell Hanisch.

Whatever it was, it would be somewhat short of the truth.

That much, the Men's Hostel had taught him.

*

After that, things improved for Adolf.

For Hanisch they went, as he had feared, from worse to terrible. The whole scam with regard to Aunt Johanna Pohl had been his idea! All Adolf gave him was a few kroner. Adolf refused to discuss with Hanisch the exact amounts that were being sent every month from Spital. But Hanisch could see that Adolf was eating better than in a long, long time, hurrying into the Hostel kitchen (at times when those inmates who provided for themselves did their own cooking) whistling a snatch of opera-music, boiling up his mixture of fruit and vegetables and rice, or his sick-making globs of hot bread and milk, topped with flaked chocolate. Hanisch envied him none of that. Hanisch needed, and that with a gut-wrenching urgency, money for drink. He had never pretended to the Capo Greiner that he would be anything but a 'winter tourist' in the Men's Hostel. The summer nights, he swore to himself, would find him once again on his favourite bench in the Prater, the canopy of stars twinkling above, instead of the ceiling of the stinking dormitory, which pressed down on him like some vast duvet, threatening to choke him. For Hanisch's old claustrophobia had returned, and he no longer, quite, remembered how near to death he had been in the snows of the previous winter.

Hanisch had spoken to Greiner of Adolf's duplicity, but the Capo had been unhelpful. 'Hanisch, you are two weeks' overdue again with your rent, are you not? If I were you, I wouldn't worry about Adolf. I'd worry about myself.'

Hanisch had felt so shocked he had offered Greiner his best, hardly-smoked cigar stub, picked up that very afternoon from the gutter outside the *Hussar* restaurant in the Herrenstrasse.

Greiner had looked at the soiled tube of stale tobacco, smiled tolerantly, and with a shake of the head, refused it.

Hanisch decided that two courses were open to him. One was to go out to the East Banhof and tout for luggage-carrying custom amongst the travellers arriving in Vienna. He rejected that. He was too old and too slow. The second option involved Adolf. Adolf had money. Adolf had done him down. It was Adolf he had to con.

But how?

Hanisch lay on the bed almost an hour, thinking. When the answer came to him, it was blindingly simple.

'Adolf, I have an idea.'

'Oh yes, what is it?'

Adolf turned the page of a thick, grubby book, but did not look up. *Das Kapital* once again, Hanisch thought. He may say he hates the Marxists, but by God he reads enough about them! Hanisch lowered his voice: 'I think I know why we are not selling so many of your splendid paintings, Adolf.'

'Oh?' Adolf looked up over the rim of the heavy tome. 'Why?'

Hanisch forced an ingratiating smile onto his face.

'Your paintings are splendid, but . . .'

'But, what?'

'They just aren't big enough.'

Adolf looked annoyed. 'Do you mean size? Or subject?'

There was no doubt about it, Adolf had become fucking arrogant, ever since his old Aunt had been sending him a few kroner. Hanisch took a deep breath. 'Both! You should choose a bigger subject, certainly! And you should paint a bigger picture, one I could ask more money for.' Before Adolf could reply, Hanisch pressed home his point: 'Your smaller pictures are fine in their way, but something larger.' Hanisch spread his hands wide, what the *fuck* was he talking about, he wondered. 'Something in a frame possibly, with a glass?'

Adolf shook his head. 'Framing's too expensive.'

'We get Neumann to do it for us? He has a lot of frames in that old junk-shop of his. All he'd need to do is slip your painting in one.' Hanisch wheedled: 'I know I could sell something big, like *that*, if the subject was a good one?'

Adolf looked at him with some suspicion but Hanisch simply smiled and bobbed his head as if delighted. You can never lay it on too thick in a con, he knew.

'Well,' conceded Adolf. 'Neumann wouldn't do it for nothing.'

'We could cut him in on the profit,' said Hanisch, promptly.

'All right.' Adolf looked interested. The blue eyes bored through Hanisch. 'I'll talk to Neumann in the morning.'

'When will you paint it?' asked Hanisch. 'You see, I'd like to have a go with it this weekend. Friday and Saturday are the best days to sell anything. By Sunday most people are broke, counting their kroner.'

'True,' Adolf nodded. 'It's Wednesday today. I'll paint it tomorrow and we can get Neumann to frame it on Friday morning. You can go out with it on Friday lunchtime?'

'Splendid, Adolf,' breathed Hanisch. 'One other little thing?'

'Yes?' Adolf waited, his eyes dropping to the pages of the heavy tome.

Hanisch smiled an especially ingratiating smile. Then he tried the sting. 'Adolf, I need a wet. I'm parched dry. I don't know if you can let me have a few kroner?'

Adolf stared at him as if he had made an indecent suggestion.

'Sorry, I'm not in a position to help.'

A red mist of rage clouded Hanisch's eyes and it was all he could do to stop himself from smashing his fist into Adolf's pallid face. But fighting was strictly forbidden in the Hostel, and anybody caught at it was in the street, toot-sweet.

Hanisch forced a smile from somewhere.

'You see, Adolf, I'm two weeks behind with my rent again? I only wondered if you could help me?'

Adolf was a long time replying to that.

'I have no money to help you.'

Hanisch knew that to be a lie.

'Even one week's rent?'

'Not even that. I simply haven't got it.'

'Then what am I to do?'

Adolf did not smile. 'Sell the big painting I will produce tomorrow. For double our usual price, or more. Then you'll be in the money.'

'Can you paint me something big *and* saleable – with people in it, a nice fat tart maybe?'

Adolf did not bother to reply. He turned onto his side and took a small, greasy, paper-bag from his locker. He extracted a succulent slab of apple-strudel. He commenced to eat, in small bites, with evident enjoyment.

'See you tomorrow then, Adolf,' Hanisch said, and turned away. Adolf made no reply. He was too busy eating.

Hanisch wondered what kind of portrait Adolf would actually paint? Would it contain a girl as he had suggested, perhaps with the wind blowing her skirt above her fat dimply knees, something mildly saleable like that? Hanisch doubted it.

Meanwhile, he could go out into the snow and try to bum the price of one small drink from some mug. That, at least, with cajoling or threatening or whatever it took, Hanisch could – with luck – probably do. He pulled on his tattered overcoat, the worst-worn in the Hostel, and wrapped his long, frayed, woolly scarf tightly around his neck, and got out of the place.

The wind in the Meldelmanstrasse went through him like a knife.

Adolf's large painting was no better and no worse than his smaller ones, Hanisch saw, looking at it with dismay. He knew Adolf had spent the whole of Thursday on it, painting and drawing far into the small hours of the Friday morning.

Neumann told Adolf, 'It's a nice picture, young fellow, one of your best, I'm sure, but why have you done it so *large*? We can't shift your smaller ones – and this is just the same old Rathaus, only bigger, and with an expensive frame around it? How much are you expecting Hanisch to get for it?'

Adolf had stood in the Study Room, looking at the fucking awful thing, Hanisch realised, with pride. There was, naturally, no fat tart in it.

'If Hanisch cannot get fifty kroner for it, then he doesn't sell it,' Adolf stated, arrogantly, handing the pissing thing to Hanisch.

'Fifty kroner?' Neumann the Jew looked at Hanisch quickly, but said nothing. Finally, Neumann threw up his hands and said, 'If Hanisch feels he can get fifty kroner for it, then maybe he can? All I can say is I wish him good luck with it, and I'd like my own ten kroner for the frame as soon as it is sold.'

'Hanisch,' said Adolf, 'Fifty. Not a pfennig less!'

Hanisch took the painting, wordlessly – Adolf seemed almost reluctant to let it go! – and trudged out of the Hostel. He was in desperate need of drink but his pockets were empty. The painting was protected by a strong cardboard-cover, provided by Neumann, and nobody looked twice at Hanisch as he shambled the four miles to the bar at the corner of the Herrenstrasse and the Tienfallstrasse, where he knew the clientele were moneyed and liberal and foolish and – who knows? – might even buy the fucking thing.

The elderly Patron behind the bar-café frowned at his dirty appearance, something he had not done before, but Hanisch avoided his eye, and deftly approached a blonde young woman, wrapped in furs, who was sitting at a table for two, chattering animatedly to a dark, bewhiskered middle-aged man who was old enough to be her father.

'My Good Sir, I wonder if you would care to look at this painting?' Hanisch slipped onto a chair and struggled the large, framed painting out of the cardboard-case. He could feel the Patron's eyes drilling the back of his neck but he had to ignore it. Normally, Hanisch simply held the smaller paintings in view of the mugs, always remaining on his feet and moving on at once in the event of a surly reception. Such an approach was part of the accepted Bohemian style of this place and of others like it. To sit, uninvited, at the table of a customer, was another thing altogether, and a total breach of the rules. Nobody knew that better than Hanisch, but he was past caring one way or the other.

Hanisch finally got Adolf's painting out of its cardboard pack and held it up, triumphantly. 'A splendid painting of the Rathaus,' he intoned, looking now at the girl, who was very pretty and young and had a lot of soft and blooming flesh. 'By a well-known artist, at this time, unfortunately, in very poor health...'

The dark bewhiskered man was looking at him unblinkingly, but Hanisch, conscious of the eyes of the Patron on his neck, rushed on: 'Your young lady will find it a very romantic reminder, Sir, of her visit to Vienna.'

Hanisch got no further.

The dark man said, loudly: 'This young lady is my niece and neither she nor I are interested in your painting. Please go away.'

Hanisch somehow stuffed the painting back into its case, got to his feet and trudged towards the door. The Patron fell in step beside him. 'And don't come back! You know the rules!'

And he was out. It was snowing very persistently now. Hanisch stood in the freezing wind for what seemed a very long time, and then he started to walk, purposefully, towards the East Banhof, two miles away.

Hanisch sold the painting, frame and all, to a second-hand dealer near the East Banhof for twenty kroner.

Then he got drunk, on neat meths, the hardest hooch available in the city.

'You did *what?*'

Greiner was looking at Adolf in astonishment.

'I put the police on him!'

'You can't do that!' Greiner's voice rose. The Study Room was empty, so it did not matter. 'You can't shop another mate! Somebody from the Hostel! You'll get him barred!'

'I mean to get him barred,' said Adolf. 'He sold my painting for ten kroner. Or so he *says*. Anyway, that's all he gave me. So I went to the Municipal Court and swore out a warrant against him!'

'When?' Greiner put down his mop and bucket, wonderingly.

'Yesterday!' Adolf was getting annoyed, in turn. He could not explain to Greiner the hate and rage he had felt for Hanisch, when the tramp had stood in front of him, smelling and shaking of drink, and had tried to make a fool of him, tried to do him down, betray him! Ten kroner indeed!

'The Police came with a warrant for Hanisch first thing this morning.' Greiner spoke weightily. 'Hanisch was still drunk when they took him.' Greiner sighed. 'It's the end for him here, in the Hostel. Herr Director Kanya will never have him back, now the police are involved.'

'He won't be back anyway,' said Adolf. 'He owes rent for one thing. For another, the Magistrate gave him seven days' imprisonment for fraud, unless he paid me, and he couldn't pay, so he's gone to jail.'

'Jail?' Greiner said to Adolf in amazement, a grudging respect creeping into his voice. 'You were in the Court yourself?'

'Of course I was,' said Adolf, impatiently. 'I had to be, I swore out the charge against him. I had a signed affidavit from Neumann the Jew that I had told Hanisch the price for the painting was fifty kroner and under no circumstances to take any less!'

'Neumann gave you a signed affidavit?' asked Greiner, wonderingly. 'Why should he do that?'

'Because I told him that if he didn't I would never give him another painting to sell. With Hanisch out of the way, I will have to rely on you and Neumann to work harder for me, selling whatever you can.'

'Did Hanisch say anything in Court?' asked Greiner, who had, in his time, been in Courts himself, both military and civil, and knew how strangely events could turn out in such places.

'Not much. He was too drunk. The Magistrate didn't like it.' Adolf actually smiled when he said that. Greiner had never seen him smile before. The smile rather frightened him and Greiner was not easily frightened.

'Did it never occur to you that Hanisch could easily have shopped you?'

Adolf's smile disappeared. 'Over what?'

Greiner dropped his voice. You never knew who was listening in this fucking place. 'Not registering for Military Service. All he had to do was tell them. Then you'd have been in the shit, young Adolf.' Greiner shook his head, half-admiringly. 'You haven't registered, have you?'

'Of course I have,' shouted Adolf. 'And let me tell you that is my business and nobody else's!'

'Not arguing with that,' said Greiner, mildly. He took from a pocket a bar of plain Swiss chocolate of the kind that was sold at the Hostel canteen. 'All I'm saying is, did you think about it?'

Adolf had not thought about it, but he wasn't going to tell Greiner that.

'There was nothing to think about!'

Greiner ate a piece of chocolate and drew on a forbidden cigarette. 'If *they* get wind of anybody evading Military Service, they soon ferret them out. A word, that's all they need. They can give you Time for it, Adolf. A lot more than seven days. And you still have your Military Service to do when you come out. They don't piss about.'

Adolf felt the strange sharp fear that turned quickly to black hate. But he said nothing.

'Careful,' intoned Greiner. 'If I were you I'd step a bit fucking careful, I would.' He broke off a block of the black Swiss chocolate and handed it to Adolf. He then placed a long and none-too-clean finger along his bulbous nose. 'No names, no pack-drill, know what I'm saying, young Adolf?'

Adolf said nothing to that, either.

He was not going to tell Greiner his business. Greiner was as likely to turn out to be his enemy as Hanisch had. After all, Hanisch had seemed all right at the beginning. Who could have suspected that he would betray a friend? Hanisch was, by definition, one of Marx's lumpen-proletariat: tramps, prostitutes, pimps, drug-addicts. Marx was right about them! They were the waste-products of Society and they should be given only *one* chance to reform. If they did not take it, they should be eliminated.

Good, decent people – decent Germans! – should not have to pay to charities to feed, house and clothe such people. Hanisch had had his chance, and he had not taken it. That was the end of the matter.

Adolf noticed that Greiner was looking at him strangely. 'Y'know, when I got you in here, young Adolf, I wondered if you'd learn. You have. You've learned well.'

And Greiner was gone, the door clanging behind him.

Adolf sat in the silence of the Study Room and pondered. What had that remark meant? He decided: very little. If Greiner was inferring that he had discovered how to use his brains against the machinations of his Enemies, then that was not news to Adolf. Of course he had, or he would have gone under a long time ago. Hanisch would have had his few personal kroner, or Greiner would, or some other cunning creature elsewhere in the Hostel would. It was Survival of the Fittest here, as everywhere else in the world. Darwin was absolutely right about that.

Adolf took a loaded brushful of royal blue and white watercolour and carefully smoothed it out into a watery, bluey Viennese sky over the Burghof. He smiled to himself. Greiner was not to know how clever he had been in that Court. Greiner was not to know that he had given his name as Heidler, not Hitler. Greiner was not to know that not only had he never registered for Military Service in the Austrian Army, but that he never intended to do any such thing.

Nonetheless, he had been lucky that Hanisch had been so drunk in that Courtroom. He would not take such a risk again, no matter how desperate the provocation. As Greiner had said, careful from now on.

His Enemies would surely not give him another chance.

Adolf sat at a table outside a superior bar-café on the Herringstrasse, far from the haunts of his fellow-inmates at the Hostel. He had just gorged himself on a cream-slice and a small pot of excellent coffee, which had lasted him almost two hours. He had read most of the newspapers, both German and Austrian, that were freely available to customers. They contained nothing for his comfort, for all the talk of War, this hot summer of 1912, was of Mobilisation of Armies, and threats by one Balkan country to another. Europe was in a ferment. The French Army was on Summer manoeuvres in Normandy. The German Army was on Summer manoeuvres on the Saxon plain. The British Navy was sailing up and down the North Sea – which the German High Seas Fleet called the German Ocean. The High Seas Fleet was sailing on it, too, with their steel-decked ships of the latest design. The British, according to the *Berliner Tageblatt* still had wooden decks, as in Nelson's day. How would those decks fare, if one of the Kaiser's new High-Explosive shells was to fall on them? Meantime, the Russian Tsar was with his family on holiday at the Black Sea resort of Yalta, and the Imperial Russian Army, all those millions of uniformed serfs, Adolf supposed, were bivouaced somewhere, on Summer manoeuvres, no doubt in the bleak Steppes of that vast and terrible country. The Austrian Army was prudently taking no major part in this annual European sabre-rattling, Adolf read, but was nonetheless calling to the Colours its conscripts, a month earlier than usual, for, it assured the populace, strictly administrative reasons. Adolf did not believe a word of it, but what concerned him a good deal more was the paragraph that followed: The Austrian Government, said the Military Correspondent of the *Neue Freie Presse*, was extremely concerned about the number of young men who had not registered for the draft and were taking steps to apprehend such dodgers. Some several hundreds of men from the Classes of 1889–90 had not reported yet. These men should have reported for Military Service in 1909 and commenced training the following year. Defaulters who did not report left themselves open to Twelve-months' Imprisonment or a fine of two thousand kroner, or both.

Adolf digested that fact, with some concern. This was persecution indeed.

Adolf began to tremble with rage. The newspaper shook in his hand. He belonged to the Class of 1889, since he had been born on Easter Eve of that year, but what right had these fat dolts, in their warm offices in the Rathaus, sitting on their fat arses drinking coffee, to presume that he, Adolf Hitler, would ever fight for their ramshackle, discredited Empire, would ever deign to wear their foolish out-of-date uniform – of such prominent colours, dating back to the Napoleonic Wars – that every sharp-shooter could pick it out at six hundred yards! Who but a dolt himself would go into War – for War was coming sooner, rather than later, every man in every café in Europe knew that – in such company?

What had Austria ever done for him?

It had denied him access to its architectural schools!

It had denied him employment of any congenial or suitable kind!

It had allowed him to starve in the snow!

Only his own resources had saved him. Only his paintings sold by Neumann the Jew and the Capo Greiner, in the bar-cafés of the Summer city, had prevented his extinction. That, and the legacy of

Aunt Johanna Pohl. The old servant's death had been a boon of immense magnitude, the money all left to him, all four thousand kroner, more than he had ever expected. Now, two years later, it was mostly gone, despite his very slow spending of it. No luxuries. A set of new clothes: a tweed jacket and trousers; stout shoes; some thick wool shirts, and a heavy coat. All second-hand but serviceable and decent. That amount spent, Adolf had doled out the rest to himself in weekly subs of one hundred kroner a time, to go towards food and rent. That way, he had eked out the money until now he had only six hundred kroner left. The sale of his paintings had fallen off in the Winter, as usual, but had done well enough that Summer. Neumann had been a good salesman and an honest one; Greiner had now totally lost interest. Things had gone badly for Neumann and he was now living in the Hostel himself. He did not share Adolf's dormitory but had ensconced himself in another. He avoided political discussions with Adolf. Adolf had not minded. So long as he sold a few of the paintings, that was enough. However, without Aunt Johanna Pohl's legacy, Adolf knew he would have starved these last two years. Even now, he was still very thin, owing to his vegetarian habits and his diet of bread and milk and vegetables and fruit.

Adolf remembered the expression on the lawyer's face at the little office in Linz, where the news of his Aunt's legacy had been broken to him. The pompous, overfed lawyer, pince-nez on nose, and that nose in the air as a sign of superiority, had told Adolf that all of his Aunt Johanna Pohl's estate went to him alone. All he had to do was sign for the sum, and advise as to where he wished it to be transferred?

'I will take it in cash. Now, if possible!' Adolf had said, coldly furious.

'I should think we can manage that,' said the lawyer, calling in his secretary and making the arrangements. As they waited, the lawyer made conversation.

'You are an artist, I believe?'

'Of sorts, yes.'

'Is there a living in it?'

'For me, yes.'

'I see.' The pince-nez took in the state of Adolf's suit and his shoes, which were in dire need of repair. 'And no doubt you'll be going back to the . . . er, Artist's Quarter of Vienna after your Aunt's funeral?'

'I will be going back to Vienna on the train in one hour.'

The lawyer looked startled. 'You mean you will not be at your Aunt's funeral?'

'No.'

Adolf owed this functionary no excuse, so he did not offer one.

'I see,' said the lawyer and did not speak to Adolf again, or even shake hands as he left the office, the money, in a large buff envelope, tucked into the pocket of his worn tweed jacket.

Adolf sat at the table outside the café and wondered what to do next? A plan was forming in his mind. It was daring, but it seemed, sitting there, almost inevitable. He had made little progress in his attempts to promote his career away from the architectural paintings. Only a few other commissions, despite his touting his paintings around one or two high-class stores, had come his way. A poster for '*Teddy Perspiration Powder*' executed for a well-known store, had been the only commission, apart from a hand-painted poster for shoes, where the shop-owner had actually paid him in a new pair of excellent brown boots, slightly shop-soiled! No, there was nothing but humiliation and defeat for him in this wonderful, marvellous city of Hoffmannstahl and Schnitzler and all the rest of the degenerate modernists who made up the current artistic establishment.

What more could this sink of a city give him?

Nothing. Vienna had nothing to give him.

This city from which he had expected so much!

Now, there was no doubt of it, he had to act.

Now, this moment, was the time of decision.

Adolf did not notice the thickset man in the heavy serge suit sitting at a nearby table. If he had, he would not have been impressed, quite the reverse. Doctor Sigmund Freud, to him, would have been merely a statistic, and an uncomfortable one at that. Freud was one of the twenty-five per cent of doctors of Jewish extraction practising in Vienna that year. Adolf would have taken such a statistic as proof of his theories – that too many professional positions were occupied by Jews in the City, and in the State.

It would have given him ammunition to throw at his opponents. It would have been delivered in such a way that, had Doctor Freud heard it, would, rather than upset or terrify him, have given him food for professional thought.

Freud, at that moment, was revising his paper, *Paranoia, as a Defence Mechanism*. He sat in the café, the *Neve Frei Presse* unread on his knee, habitual cigar in his mouth, and pondered the typical case of Paranoia that he had presented in his paper. Freud shifted in his seat. He was always conscious that he had to present these cases to the medical faculty of his peers in a simple – too simple! – way. But there was no other. The Psycho-Analytical Association was in its infancy. Even if it was an art (all Medicine was an Art, surely, except perhaps Surgery?)

it had to be presented in *seemingly* scientific terms, or the medical establishment would never take it seriously.

Such was the case with the description of a neurosis. If only he could show scientifically that *actual toxins* flooded the bodily system during a neurosis then there would be no problems about the acceptance of his theories! As it was, other physicians in other sub-disciplines had to take them on trust, or not at all. For they could not *see* them! Only the trained eye could see the results of the paranoia, and not always then. For sometimes the results were not easy to see. For example, the patient rarely complained in person. To him, the paranoia *was* reality. It was the only reality, and a terrifying reality it was. For the typical paranoid held onto his paranoia (his fear, his terror, his hatred, call it what you will) because he had processed it into reality. He believed in it, and lived by it.

Such self-imposed suffering was terrible, of course. But he had seen it too often to doubt that it was as real as a brick wall. The trouble was, the sufferer would never admit to it. Or only after a prolonged course of treatment, and not always then. Freud sipped his coffee, thinking.

Paranoia was characterised by Distrust and Suspicion and the Idea of being Persecuted by Others. Hence, Distrust of Other People. Leading to fear. Leading to hatred. The Paranoiac would often attack the Others – his family, whoever – as if they were an Enemy. Sometimes verbally, sometimes physically. In the end, all people became Enemies. Freud half-inhaled his cigar smoke. Since the cocaine, it was his only vice, and surely a trivial one?

Freud considered Paranoia in history. The powerful often became paranoid, or were part-paranoid, to start with. All those who disbursed great power seemed to suffer from it, sooner or later. The fear of the dagger in the back. The betrayal by supposed friend or hidden enemy. The urge to kill before you yourself are killed! The history books were stuffed with the details of such killings. A Paranoiac would certainly kill if he felt menaced enough. Without compunction, for he knew the Enemy meant to kill *him*! The plays of Shakespeare were awash with characters who (since Shakespeare knew nothing of clinical psychology and had to rely on historical observation) took raving paranoia as normal behaviour in Kings and all those who wielded absolute power. Did that mean, Freud wondered, that Paranoia could be an illness of condition and circumstance? Brought to the surface, as it were, by power and the fear of that power being taken away by force, or even by assassination itself?

Freud did not know. But Kings had ruled vast dominions, had obviously been profoundly affected by the disease, and nobody had even remarked upon it. Until long after the event.

Then, they had simply called such Kings mad.

Paranoia was difficult to diagnose, and even more difficult to treat, particularly in its milder, controlled forms, when the Patient had moved it into the pattern of his life, so that it seemed to others – and to himself – almost natural behaviour, surfacing maybe as extremely strongly-held opinions and ideas?

And impossible to treat if the Patient needed it to power his life. As he all too often did.

He sighed. Such things, illness without observable, scientifically-provable criteria, were very difficult to explain to the Viennese medical establishment. Mostly, they remained mildly sceptical. It would doubt-less be so for many years yet. Nonetheless, the work had to go on.

Freud folded his *Neve Freie Presse*, placed it back on the rack, and walked out of the café.

Adolf watched him go along the sunlit street and thought nothing of it.

Another Jew walking the streets of Vienna as if he owned them. What was new in that?

A week later Adolf took a train from the West Banhof. He told nobody, not even Greiner, that he was going, and he carried only what was on his back, and what was contained in a cheap cardboard case: two extra shirts, some underclothes and socks in poor repair, a frayed tie, and Pappi's old cut-throat razor. And of course his paints and easel. He had, after he had paid for his Third Class one-way ticket, five hundred and fifty kroner in the world, all that remained of Aunt Johanna Pohl's legacy.

'Where to?' the stiff-necked clerk in the booking-office had asked him brusquely, not deceived by his would-be artistic tweed jacket.

'Munich,' answered Adolf, with finality.

Even the word had a fine ring to it.

For a very good reason.

It was German, not Austrian.

X

MUNICH was a lucky city for Adolf.

He found lodgings, simply by asking a man in the street, at Schleissheimerstrasse 34, with the Popp family. Herr Popp was a tailor, a man of middle-age and liberal attitudes, who admired all artists without qualification. Frau Popp liked Adolf on sight: her maternal instincts were aroused by his bony, fleshless body, obvious even under the frayed tweed jacket, and she decided he needed feeding-up. This she began to do at once although Adolf's vegetarianism, with its emphasis on pulses and starchy foods generally, made it difficult to put meat, rather than fat, on his bones. An omelette, followed by cream cakes of one sort or another, with good coffee to follow, was Adolf's regular supper-fare at the Popps' small flat on the edge of Munich's student and artist's quarter of Schwabing.

Frau Popp was determined he would have one decent meal a day. To Adolf, the Popps were parlour intellectuals, people who enjoyed talking about politics and to whom talk was all. Adolf, with his romantic Viennese background (an artist who had, by reasons of health, fallen on bad times) appeared to them in Frau Popp's own words, as an 'Emancipated and interesting person'.

Herr Popp agreed. He found Adolf's views on Art and Music, both subjects that interested him, elevating and enjoyed listening to Adolf sing for his supper, a daily event, for Adolf's terms at the Popp establishment included breakfast, usually coffee and roll only, plus the evening meal, which Frau Popp had added after a week or two, at little extra cost. Adolf, for the first few weeks anyway, paid his rent on the nail, using up the last of Aunt Johanna Pohl's legacy. He continued to live much as he had lived in the Hostel. He rose late, breakfasted frugally, and went out into the summer sunshine with easel and painting materials, to sketch and paint scenes not very different from those of Vienna. He sold his paintings, when he could, to small art-shops. He would not, personally, tout in the cafés. He would rather starve.

Adolf strolled at ease in the streets of Munich that summer, his head full of hope for a better life, now that he was in his beloved Germany. 'I have sloughed off Austria, like the old whore she is, and found myself a fresh new bride!' he told Herr Popp. In the easy, sunlit streets of Munich, a provincial capital and a truly German city, he felt sure of his destiny.

For one thing, the paranoia was less acute.

It was only rarely, in those first months, that he felt watched and followed, or in any way surrounded by unknown enemies and those who sought his destruction, a common feeling during his last days in Vienna. The Jews were not much in evidence here. That at least was something. The memory of the Jewish man in the Refuge in Vienna especially haunted him. There was no doubt of it, the Jewish Marxists and suchlike were the enemies of a good German like himself. They were everywhere in Vienna, but all that was behind him now. He felt safe in Munich. These easy-going burghers and their clean, tidy children meant him no harm. They moved through their city confident and carefree. Everybody talked German loudly and laughed often. Adolf found that some of their native confidence and high spirits rubbed off on him.

Of course, one had to remain on guard!

One had to expect *anything*, at any time.

The unusual man would not be allowed to flourish in any society.

Nonetheless, Munich was good.

So, Adolf walked and walked, his step light. There was much to see and much to paint and draw. He stood in awe before the Old Town gates, which dated from the Fourteenth Century, and before the Cathedral itself, a Fifteenth-century edifice, a modern building compared to the Peterskirche, the oldest church in the city and one of the oldest in Germany. Adolf set up his easel and found an enthusiasm that he had thought lost. There was a plenitude of his favourite Baroque and Rococo in the Old Town. The Town Hall in the Marienplatz drove him indoors, to sketch quickly, and 'paint-up' in his room (his *own* room!) the vast wooden-barrel vault. The long Summer days went on, and Adolf worked hard, the sheets of paintings piling up, on his wooden dresser.

These paintings were much valued by the Popps.

So much so, they bought examples quite often, deducting the money from Adolf's rent.

It did not occur to Adolf to be grateful to them.

After Vienna, he was never to be grateful to anybody, ever again.

But Munich was lucky for him, in the hot summer of 1913, as it was to be lucky for him, for many years to come. In some strange way he would never have described as Spiritual (not believing in anything of a religious nature), Adolf felt totally at home in the place. For one thing Munich was thankfully free of the foreign invaders who choked the streets of Vienna. No Czechs, Poles, Jews or Hungarians here. German laws towards foreigners were strict. They preserved their national purity, the Germans. Unlike the stupid, slothful Austrians, who would allow anybody to cross their borders.

Everything Austrian was behind him for ever!

He confessed it to the Popps, as he finished the last cream cake on the plate, over supper one evening: 'I know that I am Austrian by birth and my forbears have lived around Spital in the Waldweirtal for many generations, but I feel German, not Austrian! I never felt Austrian, ever!'

'Why,' ventured Frau Popp, pouring Adolf a third cup of coffee, 'was that?'

Adolf reflected. 'As a very small child I lived on the German side of the River Inn, where my Father was a Customs Officer. I went to a German school. The pupils and staff were almost all German, I liked and admired them. It went on from there, you see? The love of every-thing German. Poetry. Music. Art. Even the Science of War.'

Adolf could see by the Popps' faces that this was a wrong note.

The Popps, like all liberals, vaguely disapproved of War.

'The German genius!' Adolf amended. 'It applies to War as to all else. Look at the fact that only the Germanic tribes gained victories over Imperial Rome. Look at our victory against the French in Eighteen-seventy? We are, in truth, a splendid nation, surely the natural leaders of the whole of Europe.'

The Popps stared at him. They were doubtful.

'We are born leaders,' Adolf said. 'We cannot evade the responsibility. It is our destiny.'

The Popps accepted that statement.

All Germans – even liberals like the Popps – knew that to be a fact. Germany was prepared for her destiny, as Adolf rightly said. Whatever form it took. Germany could not be held back for ever by those who envied her, like the French or even their Saxon cousins the English, and certainly not the vast ignorant hordes of peasants of the Holy Russian Empire.

'Adolf puts into words what everbody feels,' said Herr Popp, smiling comfortably at his wife. 'He has a gift for it.'

'Indeed he does,' agreed Frau Popp, picking up and mending one of Herr Popp's old shirts for Adolf. The poor young man. He needed a wife and family, but how was he ever to have them? She knew better than anybody the state of Adolf's underwear and socks, for she washed them and mended them, and every so often replaced them with cast-off items from Herr Popp's drawer. Occasionally, she bought Adolf something new, like a nightshirt, for a special present. It was quite preposterous that a young man of Adolf's breeding and genteel background should not have correct night-attire.

Adolf never referred to any of these gifts and small deeds of affection from Frau Popp. It was as if he did not notice them, or, if he did, he did not appreciate them.

Frau Popp knew better. She knew Adolf was simply too shy to refer to them. She knew also that Adolf sold piteously few of his water-colours or charcoal sketches of Munich scenes. They piled up, in his small but tidy room. Often she would say: 'Please forget the rent this week, Herr Adolf. I know how it is, for an artist. Your ship will come in, and then we will all benefit. I will insist you give us a party on that day, with cakes and wine!'

Adolf walked the streets of Munich in a dream.

He made almost no close friends, but became a regular in the small artists' café-bar in Schwabing, where he took his midday coffee and cake and dallied for at least two hours, reading the local newspapers and the Berlin *Tageblatt*. Other regulars would sit at his table, bringing over their own coffee cups, with a smile. Nobody ever bought anybody else coffee in that café. Nobody had much money. Some people wrote small pieces of journalism, on a freelance basis, for the many newspapers and magazines of the City. Usually for pitiably low rates as their generally shabby (if colourful) clothes testified. Others taught, part-time, clarinet or pianoforte, or said they did. One or two painted, but they were rare. It was well known that most painters in the town made little money, not even enough to live on, however frugally they lived. By that standard, Adolf, who was known to them as a painter, was doing well. He dressed cleanly, his socks were darned, he was close-shaven, and his hair was neatly combed, and only fell over this face when he became excited, when the subject was politics or art. In a very few weeks Adolf became a renowned café-talker, and was accepted as such. He rarely listened.

'The artist should be State-subsidised,' Adolf declared, leaning forward to put his point to a young freelance journalist and his pretty would-be actress girl-friend, Inge, who was dressed colourfully in a tam o'shanter hat and a velour dress that was, daringly, four inches from the ground. She listened to Adolf saying, 'The artist should, in return, show the good side of the State, the fine things Germany has built and designed, and that all good Germans share.'

'Like the Ludwigstrasse?' asked the young journalist, ironically, irritated by his girl-friend's wide eyes, set so intently on Adolf's pale face.

The monstrous Ludwigstrasse was a joke, to the young journalist and his liberal friends. Not so to Adolf.

'The Ludwigstrasse contains the State Library and is much admired by all Germans, and many who are not Germans,' said Adolf. 'It also contains the University.'

'I know it does,' said the young journalist. 'I went there. And I learned very little that is of any use to me.'

'Where were you educated, Adolf?' asked the girl. The way she looked at Adolf irritated the young journalist even more.

'Vienna,' said Adolf, shortly.

The girl waited.

Adolf said no more.

The young journalist, seeing a weakness – or what he thought was a weakness – pressed. 'Studying what?'

'Art,' said Adolf. 'And I starved doing it.'

'Starved?' asked the girl in an amazed voice. 'Actually starved?'

'Actually starved,' replied Adolf, his blue eyes staring past her so that she looked round, thinking Adolf had seen a friend, but there was nobody. This unnerved her, and she looked to the young journalist for help. Neither of them had ever starved and could not conceive of it. The girl was still a student at the University and the journalist would someday get a job on one of the newspapers for which he now free-lanced. He had hopes even now of the *Frei Presse*.

'Coffee?' the young journalist asked. 'Adolf?'

Adolf inclined his head.

'And cakes?' added the girl, with a quick smile.

They were duly ordered.

Adolf ate all three cakes, and drank most of the coffee.

That must be, the girl thought, because he had once starved for his art. It was said that if a man starved, he never forgot it. The young journalist thought that Adolf might have starved, a long time ago, but that he was not too badly off nowadays. Thin, certainly, but always neat, clean, and despite his occasional husky cough and his pallor plainly well-looked after by somebody.

'Where,' he asked, 'do you live?'

'On the Schleissheimerstrasse,' answered Adolf. 'With friends.' He added, 'Who are excellent people. Regrettably, somewhat liberal, like yourself. I imagine, they see Art as something removed from life. I do not. Art must contribute to the State. Art has a function and should be encouraged.'

The young journalist, who did not share Adolf's Pan-German views, but inclined to pacifism and internationalism, rarely argued these political points with Adolf, for he knew the young Viennese would soon be on his hobby-horse (the Jews, the Marxists, the Social Democrats!) and the pleasant artistic chit-chat would quickly turn into a headache and a bore.

The journalist did not want any of that, really.

So why, he wondered, did he reply to Adolf by saying, 'You may be right that the State should subsidise the genuine artist so that he's free to do his best work. But most of your Pan German friends would not agree. They would say that an artist, like everybody else, should be subject to the market economy. If he is any good, people will buy his paintings. If he is not, then he should go off and do something else. Only your enemies, dear Adolf, the Marxists, would give you money, then demand you paint pictures to the greater glory of Marx!'

Adolf looked at the young journalist a long time, his blue eyes wide and unblinking. This made the young man feel uncomfortable. There was an other-worldliness in that strange abstract gaze. It annoyed him that Adolf was now talking on, in his low and vibrant voice, more to the girl than to him. 'A State that helps its people does not necessarily need to be a Marxist State, does it?'

'Since there isn't a Marxist State anywhere in the world, and since no State, Social Democrat, Monarchist or anything else, helps its artists with grants to live on, I can't answer that question, my dear Adolf,' said the young journalist, loftily.

Adolf leaned forward and his voice was lower than ever.

'One day it will happen. In a truly German State.'

'Ruled by which Party?' asked the girl.

'Who knows?' asked Adolf. 'But come it will.' His gaze had switched off. He seemed to have lost interest in the subject. He took the girl's hand and brushed his lips across her fingers. Her friend, the young journalist, looked contemptuously on at this demonstration of Viennese bourgeois manners.

The girl, however, smiled brightly.

'See you again soon, Adolf?'

'Most probably tomorrow, no?' replied Adolf. And, hefting his easel and paintbox, and without further salutation, he was gone.

The girl watched Adolf as he walked the sunlit street, his hair glinting in the light. How thin he was, she thought: how brave and vulnerable.

'What about his Viennese accent?' asked the young journalist, paying the check. 'Isn't it funny?'

'I quite like it,' said the girl briskly, reaching for her pile of books. 'Do you think when he says he lives with friends, he means a woman?'

'A woman?' The young journalist laughed coarsely. 'Adolf wouldn't know what to do with a woman.'

The girl said nothing to that.

'Do we go to my room or yours?' asked the young journalist, easily.

'Neither. I have work to do. A part to learn.'

The young journalist was surprised.

Inge had never refused him before.

The Summer ended and Adolf stayed more and more indoors, reading and painting, painting and reading. He sold fewer paintings than ever and his money dwindled alarmingly.

The bombshell came in the middle of the following January of 1914.

A Summons, delivered by the hand of an Officer of the Munich Police Force.

Adolf stood with it in his hand, as the Officer waited for his signature of receipt.

Herr Popp watched sympathetically. 'What does this mean?'

'As you no doubt know, the States of Germany and Austria have a mutual agreement of extradition, in cases of this sort.'

'Extradition?' said Herr Popp. 'Is that necessary?'

'If the gentleman reads his Summons,' said the Officer, 'he will see that he is charged with not having presented himself for Military Service in Vienna when he should have done so.'

'That is not true,' said Adolf, his face very white, and his hands trembling. 'I did present myself!'

'There is no record of it,' said the Officer disbelievingly. '*If* you did.' No 'Herr' or even his name.

Adolf remembered that the Police were on the side of the people who paid their wages. So, with an effort, he replied, moderately, 'What do I do?'

The Officer's reply was prompt. 'Present yourself at Linz, in Austria, at the address shown on the Summons, in six days' time, under pain of prosecution if you do not.' His tone held some contempt. Adolf was very conscious of it, but he persisted. 'Is there no way that I can be medically examined in Munich?'

The Police Officer shook his head. He knew a dodger when he saw one.

'You are an Austrian national. A letter – maybe – from the Austrian Consul General in Munich might get you that.' He laughed, a short, contemptuous bark. 'I can't see how you'd get it.'

Adolf did not reply or even thank the Police Officer as was protocol. Herr Popp quickly did it for him, ushering the man out with many gestures of respect. The Police Officer, however, had the last word. 'Tell your young friend if he isn't in Linz on that day I'll be here the day after with a warrant for his extradition, and he won't like that, I can assure you.'

'That will not be necessary, I'm sure,' said Herr Popp, closing the front door. He turned to Adolf, solicitously. 'You will have to go, Adolf. There's nothing else for it.'

'Let us see,' said Adolf, thoughtfully.

The Austrian Consul General in Munich – a cultivated, beautifully-tailored man in his middle-years – was intrigued to see the painfully thin young man in the tweed jacket standing on the splendid carpet in front of his desk.

He stared at the paper in his hand. 'Is it Herr Adolf . . . Hitler? Or is it Heidler?'

Adolf said, 'The name is Hitler, Herr Consul General. But the summons is in the name of Heidler. Possibly that fact has led to some confusion in the bureaucracy?'

'Possibly,' said the Consul General, taking in the young man's clean, if poor clothes, and his stiff and respectful bearing, which he thought hardly that of a draft dodger. 'I see you describe yourself as an architectural student and artist? How long have you been doing that work?'

'Since I lived in Vienna.'

'Oh?' The Consul General brightened. 'You were at the Institute of Architectural Art there?'

'Unfortunately, no. I had health problems and could not accept a place. However, I maintained myself in Vienna, as I do here in Munich, on remuneration earned by my work.'

The Consul General looked interested. This was not the usual young rake or rapscallion he confronted, charging him with lack of patriotism to the Empire. 'Do you sell any paintings?'

'Quite a few, Herr Consul General. Not perhaps quite enough.'

The Consul General glanced at a letter clipped by his secretary to the Official Summons to Report for Military Service. 'I see that Herr Popp, with whom you lodge, speaks most highly of you. Also, that he works, from time to time, for my own tailor.'

Adolf nodded, but did not smile.

A very serious young man. And thin. Very thin.

The Consul General felt a small wave of sympathy.

'What was this health trouble you had, Herr Hitler?'

'A persistent cough, Herr Consul General.'

'Tuberculosis?' The Consul General looked alarmed, and shifted back in his chair. The goddamned plague was contagious, after all.

'No, fortunately. Just bronchitis.'

166

'I see. But serious, nonetheless?'

'Well, Herr Consul General, I think so. I regret it. I would very much like to serve in the Army of the Emperor.'

The Consul General looked pleasantly surprised. 'You would?'

'Indeed, yes. That is why I first registered for Military Service in Vienna in February 1910.'

'You did? Four years ago?'

'Yes, I did, Herr Consul General.'

Adolf lied but the Consul General was not to know that.

'You are certain you did?'

'Yes, Herr Consul General, and I never heard any more. I paid a fee of One Kroner, as required.'

The Consul General nodded and looked at Adolf keenly. The blue eyes stared back at him.

'I think all men should be prepared to take up arms to defend the Fatherland.'

An odd bird, thought the Consul General.

Adolf then played his trump card.

'My Father was a Collector in the Customs Service at Innsbruck and later in Vienna. I could not have faced him had I done anything dishonourable.'

'A Collector? Was he? I see.' The Consul General looked even more keenly at Adolf. 'Is he still alive?'

'Regrettably no, but I can furnish you with details of his Service, which was of more than thirty years' duration.'

'Was it?' said the Consul General. '*Was* it? Well!'

He indicated a chair, and Adolf sat down on the edge of it.

'How is your health now?'

'I think better. Frau Popp feeds me well.'

'Hmm.' The Consul General brooded. 'You want to take a Medical Examination, but not in Linz? Why is that?'

'I have an urgent commission. A portrait. It is well-paid and urgent.'

Again, Adolf lied.

'I see.' The Consul General brooded a little more and contemplated his watch. 'I'll tell you what I'll do. Go next door to my Secretary and tell him to give you pen and paper. Write your request to the Military Board on the paper and bring it back to me. All right?'

Adolf stood up, at instant attention. 'I thank the Herr Consul General.'

'Lay it on thick,' said the Consul General, won over, in dismissal.

Adolf came to attention once more, clicked his heels and left the room.

The Empire could live without a starving artist, thought the Consul General, a man of some learning and with a respect for the arts, in the proper place, of course. This starveling did not look as if he would last ten minutes on a forced march, unless the Austrian Army had changed since he, the Consul General, had served in it.

More trouble than he was worth, probably, and too thin altogether.

Besides, there was something odd about the fellow. Something, perhaps, temperamental. Well, artist fellows were all like that, he supposed. To much brooding.

Still, a very odd bird.

In the office of the sniffy and disapproving male secretary, who was attired in his uniform of dark frock-coat and striped trousers, topped by a formal collar, Adolf sat at a small desk and penned the letter. Lay it on thick the old fellow had said. Very well.

Adolf thought for a few moments and then wrote in a shaky and spidery hand:

"To the Chairman, Military Board.
    Sir:
    I beg to respectfully state my case for a Medical Examination in Germany.
    First, may I state my personal circumstances?
    I earn my keep as a freelance artist, being completely without means (my Father was a Civil Servant). I do so merely to be able to complete my studies. I can devote only a fraction of my time to earning a living, as I am not yet past the training stage as an architectural painter. Thus, my income is very small – I can just about make ends meet. Luckily, I have work in hand and need to be here in Munich to do it.
    Normally my income is 100 marks (German) a month.
    This does not mean I earn 100 marks every month. Oh, no! At this moment my income is very poor, as Art Dealing in Munich has its 'Winter Sleep'.
    I registered in Vienna for Military Service in February 1910, but no record appears to have been made of this.
    I excuse myself from not Registering originally on the correct date in 1909. For two years I had no other friend but Care and Want, and no other Companion but Everlasting Insatiable Hunger. I never learned the meaning of that fine word – Youth!
    Today, I have souvenirs of those years – chilblains on my fingers, hands and feet. And yet I am over the worst. And I have some

satisfaction in recalling those days. Despite my utter penury, in the midst of dubious surroundings, I have always preserved my Good Name! I am Untainted Before the Law. I am clear before my own Conscience. Except for my one Omission – not reporting for Military Service on the correct date – which at the time was not even known to me!

With profound apologies and trusting that you, Sirs, may find it possible to grant my request. I am, your Obedient Servant.'

Adolf read it through, signed his name, took a deep breath and asked permission of the Secretary to see the Consul General once more.

The Consul General read through the document with interest. When he had finished he looked up. There was a twinkle of amusement in his eye.

'I think this should do very well, Herr Hitler.'

'Thank you, Herr Consul General.'

'Leave it with me. I will forward it to the Army Authorities with my comments.'

'The Consul General is too kind.'

Adolf came to attention and clicked his heels. The Consul General nodded, and Adolf made to leave the room.

'Hitler!'

Adolf froze at the door, a supplicant's smile on his lips.

What now, the idiot?

'Yes, Herr Consul General?'

'You have a way with words. Has anybody ever told you that?'

'I prefer the paintbrush, Herr Consul General.'

The Consul General regarded him thoughtfully. 'I feel you may be wrong in that, you know?'

'Then I will keep in mind what the Consul General says.'

The Consul General inclined his head and Adolf clicked his heels yet again and closed the large double-door softly behind him.

The Consul General sat at his desk and pondered.

An odd bird, indeed.

Then he smiled, and wrote a short note in his own hand and appended it to the Summons to Report for Military Service.

It read: 'This Young Man seems to me the victim of a bureaucratic mix-up. He is of good family but his health is not of the best, at least to my eyes. He is certainly patriotic, but I doubt if he will be found fit to endure a hard military regime. I suggest he be examined in Saltzburg, and treated with respect. I find him most deserving of considerate treatment.'

With that, the Consul General threw the papers into his 'Out' tray, and promptly forgot all about the case of Adolf Hitler.

The elderly doctor gazed at Adolf with interest.

'One testicle only?'

Adolf, naked behind a screen but conscious of the other young recruits who were healthy and heavily fleshed, nodded tightly. 'Yes, Herr Doctor.'

'Nothing to be ashamed of. The other is not there at all. We call that a monorchism.' He paused. 'I would not reject a recruit for that alone, but . . .' The elderly doctor gazed over his pince-nez at Adolf's thin body, then at the Consul General's note pinned to Adolf's papers. 'I see you say you had bronchitis?'

Adolf nodded. He could smell whiffs of male perspiration on all sides. Bouts of sudden, stifled laughter came from behind other screens. There was a jollity here in this place, a celebration of the normal, fit, healthy young male body.

Adolf did not feel that he belonged here.

The elderly doctor had a stethoscope at his chest.

'Not tuberculosis?' The elderly doctor pressed, but with a smile.

'No.'

'But a bad cough? And a fever? Often?'

'Well, not often, Herr Doctor.'

'From time to time, I'm sure?'

'Yes, Herr Doctor. From time to time.'

The doctor put down his stethoscope. He looked serious. 'Young man! You are severely underweight. You do not eat enough, or anything like enough. Meat. Eggs. Milk puddings. Plenty of nourishing food. That is what you need. See you get it, Herr Hitler, or I do not think you will be fit to hold down a job, never mind go for a soldier.'

Adolf smiled weakly. 'I'm sure the Herr Doctor knows best.'

'I'm sure you'd like to do your duty to the Emperor?'

'Of course, Herr Doctor.'

If he thinks that I want to serve in the Army of that ramshackle Empire, that filthy diseased whore of a country, then he is mad, thought Adolf.

The Herr Doctor sighed, and indicated that Adolf dress-up.

'I should really leave it until you hear officially, but I am not one for formality. I can tell you that I am going to mark your papers "Unfit for Combatant Duty, or Auxiliary Duty in the Austrian Army. Reason: Too weak. Unable to bear Arms.'

Adolf stared at him.

Too weak? After all he'd been through, in the stews and slums of Vienna? A month of that would kill the fleshy, fully-hung young men laughing behind the screens.

Unable to bear arms?

That he would do, when he had to. In the right cause.

Yes, and ruthlessly. In a way that would horrify the young men.

The elderly Herr Doctor was speaking. 'I'm very sorry. But there it is. Take care of yourself, young man.'

Adolf left the hall, walking on air.

Free.

Frau Popp was scandalised when she heard the reason for Adolf's rejection by the Medical Board. She felt that in some way it reflected on her. It would look bad if people knew of it. Frau Popp is not feeding her young lodger at all well, they might say!

As she said to Herr Popp: 'From now on Adolf must eat a good breakfast each day as well as his evening meal. As it is, the poor young man has nothing but coffee and a roll until the evening. It is not enough!'

Herr Popp demurred only slightly. 'Is he in a position to pay for it?'

Frau Popp shook her head. 'I think not. He has sold very few paintings to the dealers lately. I cannot ask him for more money. And it will only be a couple of eggs extra per day, or something of that sort?'

Herr Popp, who liked Adolf, agreed. But he made a proviso. 'If he begins to sell his paintings again, then we reconsider?'

Frau Popp gratefully agreed.

Adolf's reaction, when the suggestion was made to him, at first pained Frau Popp. 'My good Frau,' said Adolf, loftily, 'I do not concern myself unduly with such matters as food. I am healthy and sleep well. That is enough. I do not need charity, however well-meant.'

Frau Popp's heart went out to this proud young man.

'I appreciate that, Adolf, believe me. But the fact is, the Doctors found you underweight and not fit to serve in the Army. You must look after your health. You must!'

Adolf considered that, and at last nodded his head.

'Only if when I am again in a position to pay I can effect restitution in full?'

Frau Popp was delighted. Her husband's words exactly. She would tell him that when he came home from the tailor's shop. What a fine and thoughtful young man Adolf was. So clever and artistic and talented. And all alone in the world.

'I will put some flesh on your bones, you'll see!' Frau Popp's cheeks burned with pleasure. 'You'll be a stone heavier by Summer, I promise.'

Adolf kissed her hand. Frau Popp blushed furiously. These Austrians! From Adolf this was a gesture indeed.

He saw the effect and noted it.

He liked the Popps.

It was not, strictly speaking, a con.

These people approved of him. Of his ideas.

They listened when he talked of art, of music, of politics.

They got something from him.

It was an even exchange, that was all. He educated them, they fed him. It was as simple as that.

To Frau Popp he said, 'I have nothing against food. It is the fuel of Nature. But no meat, if you please, dear Frau. Fish, I will accept on occasion. Milk, in puddings, or cream in cakes, most certainly. But not meat. To eat it would make me sick.'

Frau Popp inclined her head.

What Adolf did not know would not harm him. Into the good borscht and stews that she gave him in the Winter months, there was often a good base of beef-tea or chicken broth, hidden away under the vegetables. Also, there were many fish dishes, sometimes stewed, sometimes steamed. Again, amply covered by the vegetables. In the mornings, she would inevitably give Adolf two boiled eggs with his roll, and she took to putting another roll with a thick wedge of cheese in his knapsack each day, so that he would eat something, at least, at the lunch hour. After a while she made it two rolls and put in an apple as well. Adolf never thanked her, or seemed to notice, but the food was always gone when he returned in the evening. Poor boy, she thought, and felt thrilled at being able to help an artist. Adolf was now a regular at the Sunday lunch of roast meat, even if he ate only the soup and cheese with his potatoes and vegetables. Frau Popp took to making a large, creamy dessert with fruit and pastry on these splendid weekend occasions. Adolf always ate two large helpings.

Even when the Winter faded, and blossoms appeared on the trees in the streets of Munich, Frau Popp went on feeding Adolf – and her husband – the heavy, suety foods of Winter. When the sun was high and hot in the heavens, the plates of steaming food were still set in front of Adolf.

Finally Herr Popp protested. 'I'm sweltering in these clothes, my good wife, and yet you serve us hot borscht?' He looked at Adolf. 'Don't you think we need some cold food now, salads and such?'

Frau Popp shook her head. 'Adolf doesn't complain!'

'No,' said Herr Popp, 'but I do. For me, cold consomme and cold meats and sausage from now on. Adolf too, eh Adolf?'

Adolf inclined his head. 'As you wish, Herr Popp.'

Herr Popp laughed cheerfully. 'Be satisfied, my good woman. Even Adolf has had enough of this hot stodge. The fellow has put on a stone in weight in the last month! Or is it two, Adolf?'

'I have no idea,' said Adolf, seriously. 'But I am having trouble getting my waistband to button-up!'

Herr Popp laughed again. 'There you are. My dear, you have accomplished your mission. Herr Adolf is no longer underweight. Well, not much. He is by nature thin, eh Adolf?'

'Perhaps,' said Adolf.

Frau Popp looked at Adolf searchingly. 'I do think you look much better. You have put on weight and you do not seem to cough so often.'

Adolf inclined his head. It was all true.

He felt well and rested for the first time in years.

'Enough of that!' Herr Popp filled his meerschaum and puffed blue smoke. Adolf did not care for tobacco and found the fumes distasteful, but it was, after all, Herr Popp's table. 'You read the papers, Adolf?' Herr Popp looked seriously at Adolf.

'The Serbs? What do you think?'

Adolf had indeed read the newspapers.

Who had not?

All summer there had been rumours and counter-rumours of War.

War was in the air, as real as the electric blue fumes from Herr Popp's meerschaum.

'If Austria and Serbia fight, then Germany and Russia are in,' said Herr Popp soberly. 'But how can that be, since the politicians and statesmen on all sides say they do not want War?'

'They may well say that,' said Adolf, 'but it is what the people in the streets want.'

Frau Popp was upset by this talk of War. 'I'm sure they don't, Adolf?'

'Oh, but they do!' cried Adolf. 'Germany has been spurned by the English, who now have an Alliance – against Germany – with the French. The so-called *Entente Cordiale*. Germany is England's natural ally – for are we not cousins? – but the French are now the favourites of the English and our interests are forgotten!'

Adolf's dangerous pallor was suddenly evident as it always was when politics were the subject. Herr Popp wished to avoid an argument, but he felt he had to say something. 'The Kaiser has raised an Army. He has built a lot of battleships. The English are probably afraid of us, now.'

'So they should be!' said Adolf harshly.

Herr Popp shook his head. 'The German Trades Unionists will not fight. They are all dedicated to the idea of International Brotherhood. They stand shoulder-to-shoulder with their French and English Trades

Union Brothers and Workers. They will never fight for the Kaiser, Adolf.'

Adolf shook his head.

'They will all join up on the first day.'

Herr Popp stared at him.

'You have a very low opinion of the German workingman, Adolf.'

'Of workingmen everywhere,' said Adolf. 'A war is an excitement for a young man in a dull job. It would be a welcome diversion.'

'For you too?' asked Herr Popp mischievously, re-lighting his pipe.

'Perhaps,' said Adolf.

Adolf had his mind made up for him, in the Odeonplatz, in Munich, on the first day of August that same year.

War had been declared and he was in the vast crowd to hear it.

Crushed together with a thousand other baying and screaming young men, respectably if poorly dressed in soft felt hat and threadbare jacket, his last few marks in the world tucked in the pocket of his neatly-pressed trousers, Adolf heard the declaration of war with nothing but relief. He had hardly sold a painting all Summer. His payment of rent was now academic. To all extents, the Popps were supporting him, but it could not go on forever. For weeks and months, right through that second Summer in Munich, he had worried and wondered what the future held for him, with a dread conviction, amounting to terror, that it held penury and want on the scale he had experienced in Vienna. For if he was forced to leave the Popps, he would again be on the streets. Now, with War declared, all *that* was academic. So he cried and shouted with the other young men – baying at the enemies of the Fatherland!

'*Gott Straffe* Russia! *Gott Straffe* France! *Gott Straffe* England! Germany Uber Alles!' the young men bayed.

'Perfidious Albion!'

Adolf screamed too, although he liked the English, in theory anyway. He did not, in practice, know any Englishmen.

'Vile and decadent France! Holy Russia, down with it and its slaves and serfs! Deutschland Uber Alles!'

He felt at one with the mass of bodies in the vast concourse. Like him, they were caught up in a mystical experience. Germany was in peril. Germany, who had done everything to avoid War, was now being forced into it. But the enemies of Germany had to be defeated, or Germany was in the dust.

That must never happen.

Germany would fight and Germany would win!

Adolf relaxed in the great waves of warmth from the bodies of the young men. As the chorus of chanting went on he began to feel light-headed, euphoric.

This was written!

This was ordained!

'Deutschland Uber Alles!'

Adolf was almost lifted from his feet by a swirling movement of the crowd which was moving with the instinct of an animal, out of the Odeonplatz. Adolf went with it, gratefully. He felt a sudden urge to sink to his knees and thank Heaven that he was alive at such a moment!

He saw the young journalist in the crowd and the man waved, and shouted, 'We are all going to the Bavarian Reserve Infantry Depot, to join up? Are you coming?'

Adolf waved his hat and shouted, 'Yes, yes!'

But at the Depot – a brawling mass of shouting men, officers, non-commissioned officers, and clerks, all was confusion. Nobody seemed to know anything, but lists were taken of the names and addresses of the young volunteers. When the Sergeant-clerk asked Adolf for his place of birth and was told 'Austria', he shook his cropped head.

'No good. You're a foreign national.'

'What can I do?'

'Go home and join the Austrian Army! Next!'

'I would not serve in that disgraceful rabble!' insisted Adolf. 'I wish to serve Germany!'

The NCO looked at him, then at the blue, staring eyes, and said, briefly, 'Write in person to the Military Command of the Emperor of Bavaria, asking for permission to join the Bavarian Regiment. State Father's name, occupation, your own age and occupation. You may be lucky. Next!'

Adolf struggled out of the mass of heaving, sweating bodies.

'Hard luck, Adolf,' said the young journalist, a slip of acceptance in his hand.

Adolf regarded him frostily. 'I thought you disapproved of War?!

The young journalist smiled, sheepishly. 'In theory maybe. But we are being attacked. I cannot stand by.'

'No?' Adolf turned to go.

'What will you do?' asked the young journalist.

'Write to the Emperor,' said Adolf.

Which he did.

To his amazement, a printed reply came within the week. A printed slip declared that King Ludwig of Bavaria had graciously consented to his request.

One week later Adolf passed a cursory medical inspection in Munich, along with hundreds of other young men. No reference was made to

Adolf's lack of a testicle. Everybody was being taken who looked fit, but they were asked to state details of any medical defect. Adolf said nothing of any disability.

One week after that he was drafted.

Report for Training, said the printed message, *at the Headquarters of the Sixteenth Bavarian Reserve Infantry. Bring only those clothes you need. Uniforms will be issued at once. Training will commence immediately.*

Herr Popp and Frau Popp – in common with the Trades Unionists who joined-up on the first day! – had no doubts.

Germany was under attack by her Enemies.

Adolf, by going to fight, was a hero.

Herr Popp shook his hand, emotionally, at the street-door.

'We will keep your room, Adolf. Also, your books and paintings will be safe. There will always be a home for you here. Write when you can. Come to see us when you get leave. God be with you and Auf Wiedersehn!'

Frau Popp said nothing. Her eyes were red from crying.

Adolf kissed her hand (he knew she liked that) and walked off into the early morning. He did not think he would ever go back.

The next ten weeks passed in a whirl.

'March, march, march!' yelled the Drill-instructors to the stumbling recruits, heads shorn to the scalp, rough field-grey uniforms chafing their necks, stiff leather jackboots reducing their feet to raw lumps of meat.

'Left, right, left, right! Keep your dressing! No man falls out, for any reason, or he does double-drill tomorrow!'

Adolf marched and drilled with the rest.

He wondered how he kept it up, sometimes.

But Frau Popp's food-regime had worked. He was as strong as most, and stronger than many. Also, he had the Will. The Will was everything. Adolf determined to make a success in the Army. He liked the life. He liked the comradeship and he even liked the training and the discipline. The young journalist, who was in the same platoon, suffered agonies with his feet (the route-marches were long and brutal and over open country) and complained loudly, as did most of the other men.

Adolf never complained, not even about the food, which was rough but plain. He put his vegetarianism aside. There were simply no provision for it. Beef with split-pea puree, minced meat, roast dumplings, oats, Beef and sternchensoup (the little star-shaped noodles), and pickled beef with sauerkraut were all given the same gluttonous attention. Adolf ate it all and it gave him strength. He hated meat but there was nothing else for it. It was eat or die. Adolf ate and ate and ate.

'Rifles at the slope!' screamed the instructors.

The recruits flung their heavy rifles onto their skinned and aching shoulders.

'At the targets, aim!'

Adolf aimed and fired. The Mausers had a heavy recoil.

Nobody talked to them about machine-guns, although the earliest reports coming back from the West Front said that barbed-wire and machine-guns were in common use. Stick-bombs for close work, and artillery for long, were the order of the day. No instructor mentioned them. The cavalry on both sides had been massacred almost to a man in the early exchanges, and the survivors were now held in reserve. Molke had dug-in outside Paris and the lines were becoming stable, right across Europe, from Scandinavia to the Mediterranean. Both sides, however, British and French on one, German on the other, still attacked fiercely, hoping for a breakthrough, using the infantry methods of the last century.

Casualties were said to be very heavy.

Nonetheless, the young men ran and drilled and ate and slept soundly in their bell-tents, and as the weeks went by they became a disciplined unit, able to drill and fire a rifle and possessed of a lot of parade-ground qualities, none of which were to be of any use to them, once they got to the Front. At long last, the Regiment marched through cheering crowds, to the Banhof at Munich. The trains took them only part of the way. From the railhead where they disembarked it was all marching, fast on good roads, slow on wet and slippy paths, finally a trudge through a sea of mud, for it was now October and the rains had started. The mud clung to everything: boots, uniforms, equipment, even the rifles, which, on pain of discipline, had to be spotless at all times. They were soaked by the rain and their wet uniforms dried on them. Nobody complained. They sang on word of command: 'We March against England!'

Indeed they did, for the Tommis held this sector of the line. From time to time now, as they approached the Front, they would see English prisoners, smaller, normally, than Germans, with sharp features and a jaunty manner. They looked pale and shrunken and were muddied and sometimes bandaged. They wore puttees wrapped around their legs. These useless strips of cloth were said to be relics of service in India and Africa, to protect against the bite of scorpions and snakes and the sharp, cactus-like plants of that hot terrain. They laughed at the stupidity of the Tommies and regarded their own leather jackboots, now worn-in, with pride.

Soon they could hear the guns.

First their own artillery, firing shrapnel far over their heads at the enemy. Then, faintly at first, the chattering of the Maxim guns. Adolf stopped, as they all did.

'God,' said the young journalist, in the ranks next to Adolf, 'that *sound* . . . ? Will we be all right, do you think?'

'His first battle, to a man,' said Adolf, 'is like a woman confronting her first lover. It is the most important event of his life.'

'Do you really think like that?' asked the young journalist. 'Where are we, anyway?'

'A place called Becelaeren. In Flanders.'

'I only hope I don't run,' said the young journalist, in a low voice. 'I'm scared of being scared.'

'Think of Inge,' said Adolf. He had seen her waving them off at the Depot.

'I can't remember her face,' said the young journalist.

Adolf did not reply. It did not occur to him to be frightened.

These soft young men, fully-hung, complete, well-fed, well-educated, from loving families, this was no place for them. This place was for those who had known want and hardship and even death. He noticed that the rougher workingmen seemed less afraid. They were plainly the ones to rely on.

'God, I'm scared,' said the young journalist. 'Aren't you?'

Adolf said nothing and marched forward.

Finally, Sergeant Max Amann gestured them to a halt.

The Platoon filed into trenches and earthworks, past dead bodies, English and German, half-covered in quick-lime, along saps and into a large, open trench. The sickly sweetness of death was in the air. About them machine-gun bullets hissed, and shells struck the ground in front of them, sending up fountains of mud.

Miraculously, nobody had yet been hit.

'We go over the top of the trench,' said Sergeant Amann, crouching, as they all did, 'and we run for the forest. The Tommis are in there in strength, and they have machine-guns. Once we make the trees we take cover and wait for further orders. Right?'

They all nodded. Nobody spoke.

Five minutes later they attacked.

The young journalist was cut down by machine-gun fire in the first fifty yards. All around Adolf men fell screaming into the mud. By the time he got into the woods – and the large trees were being ripped down around them as if they were wheat, by artillery fire from both sides – half the men of the Platoon had fallen.

Adolf threw himself behind a tree, holding his rifle, and waited.

Strangely, he was not afraid. Here, he could *see* the Enemy.

178

That was a blessing not to be underestimated.

Two hours later, under cover of darkness, they crawled back to the trench they had emerged from. The counting began, the names called out, many unanswered.

Most of the Platoon were dead or wounded.

Three weeks later, the Regiment had lost its Commander, Colonel List, and most of its officers. In four days of heavy fighting and accurate shelling by the British Artillery, more than half of the Regiment's 3,500 men were gone. Munition supplies were erratic, rations non-existent. The surviving troops ate vegetables taken from the fields, and meat from animals found still alive on abandoned farms. Late November found them, shattered, regrouping, with new recruits joining them every day, in front of the ridge at Messines. The Headquarters Unit was bivouacked in the village – or what was left of it. The new Commander, Colonel Engelhart, asked his Adjutant, Leutnant Fritz Wiedemann, a good soldier, no longer young, and a regular officer, to recruit some *meldegangers* for Battalion communications. Captain Wiedemann asked Sergeant Max Amann for recommendations. Amann asked Adolf if he wanted the job?

Adolf, hollow-eyed, unshaven and bone-tired, blinked at the N.C.O. 'What does it entail?'

'It entails not getting killed, at least not too soon!'

Adolf swayed. He stood in a foot of watery mud, asleep on his feet. Around him men slept as they stood. Sergeant Amann did not reprimand them. They would wake up when they had to.

'What do I do?' asked Adolf.

'You run with messages from Battalion Headquarters to companies in the line. Or back to Regimental HQ, or wherever you're sent. It has to beat sitting in the line waiting to be killed! At least you are back of the line some of the time.'

Adolf debated. Runners were expected to *run*, even through shellfire.

It was not, as Amann suggested, an easy number.

Nonetheless, it was nearer the seat of power. A Runner had at least some idea of what was going on in the War.

'The responsibility carries a promotion,' Sergeant Amann said. He was a tough, educated, young man, and Adolf liked him. He never panicked. 'You'll be an acting-corporal at once.'

That decided Adolf. He came to a clumsy attention in the mud.

'At your service, Sergeant.'

Sergeant Amann smiled. He knew his man. A bit of a loner. A bit of a non-conformist. A *meldeganger* needed those qualities. A *meldeganger* had to think on his feet, work out alternative routes, decide which one was best, know when to run and when to take cover. Adolf had survived the random butchery of the first weeks of fighting. That, in itself, was a recommendation.

'Report to Battalion Headquarters at once.'

'Who,' asked Adolf, 'is my superior?'

'I am,' said Max Amann. 'You don't think I'm going to stay in these filthy trenches any longer than I can help, do you?'

Adolf almost smiled, but not quite.

Max Amann thought: that's what I like about this young bastard. He talks a lot about a Greater Germany, about the honour of laying down one's life for the Fatherland – Amann had heard him – but he is still here and the men he talked to were mostly dead. A survivor, thought Amann. He liked survivors. They made him feel safe.

'On your way. I'll see you later. Headquarters is in a cellar. The English shell the village a lot. They know we're there. The sooner we get out of the place the better!'

Adolf found the cellar without difficulty. It was signposted and men stood on guard outside. Others crouched nearby, in their shallow trench. They told Adolf: 'The Tommis have bracketed this place. You're safer in the line.'

Adolf went down into the cellar, full of weary, red-eyed officers looking at maps spread out on wooden boxes, or shouting down field-telephones. He reported to the Adjutant, Leutnant Weidemann, who took one look at Adolf's grey face and said, 'Go into that corner with the other runners, and have a sleep. Take off your greatcoat before you run. No rifle either. We'll give you a revolver to carry. It's all speed here. You *can* run?'

Adolf nodded. He went to the corner of the cellar and threw himself down on the earth floor.

When he woke Sergeant Amann was shaking him.

It was morning.

Adolf blinked. 'What time is it?'

'Seven o'clock. Get up, come with me. Leave your rifle and greatcoat.'

Adolf did as he was bid and followed the Sergeant up the steps into a half-destroyed house. Pieces of dark, heavy furniture were still intact. There was even a mirror on a wall. The effect was eerie.

'This used to be the Priest's house,' said Max Amann. 'There's some water in that bowl. It's cold but it'll do to shave. If you don't look smart around this place they'll send you back into the line, no messing!'

Adolf found his razor and stub of soap and shaved.

It was the first time in almost two weeks and the blade tore at his face.

He winced but did not call out in pain or swear. Amann slapped his back.

'We'll make a Sergeant of you yet, Adolf!'

Adolf glowed at the compliment. As Amann had said, this had to be a big improvement on the Line. Here, no matter what a man's rank, he shared in the planning and despatch of events. Even if all he did was deliver messages, it was important that they got through. The War began to take on a different, almost intellectual hue. Back here, men used their brains. They directed action, rather than took part in it. It was, Adolf reflected, brushing the dried mud from his tunic, the right place for him.

Max Amann had a billy-can boiling on a small wood fire in the grate. There was acorn-coffee and smoked sausage and bread. Adolf had had no hot food for two weeks. He felt a lot better once he had eaten it. He wiped his tin plate with his last crust of bread, and swilled the drains of the coffee.

'What now, Sergeant?'

'You go with Leutnant Weidemann on his morning-inspection of the Line. Somebody goes with him every day. If he needs a message sent, you run with it. Got that?'

'Got it!'

Max Amann offered him a cigar but Adolf shook his head.

This easiness between officers and N.C.O.'s and men at the Head-quarters Unit surprised him. But he realised, it had to be so. The standing at attention and arse-licking of the parade-ground or the blind obedience of the trenches was out of place here.

Adolf went down into the cellar and reported to Leutnant Weidermann.

Weidemann looked at him and murmured, 'That's an improvement, Hitler.'

'Herr Leutnant!' yelled Adolf.

'No need for that,' said Weidemann, easily.

Weidemann indicated the steps to the street. 'We'll get off now.'

Adolf waited for Weidemann to speak to the Colonel, and take his farewell orders. Then they set out together for the Line.

Twice Adolf pulled Weidemann, very respectfully, into a shell-hole and once he pushed him flat on his face as an English Whizz-bang hissed over. He apologised profusely, but Weidermann slapped his shoulder.

'Not at all, Corporal! You did right. I too want to live.'

They crept on, cautiously, keeping their heads down, along saps and shallow trenches – there were no dug-outs in the lines yet, that would come later – and finally were met by a young cadet-officer who came to attention and saluted Weidemann.

'Things all right?'

'Nice and quiet, Herr Leutnant!'

'No activity during the night?'

'A few flares and a little rifle fire. I think the Englanders are digging in.'

'As we are?' asked Weidemann, looking at the fresh earthworks in the shattered and waterlogged trench. Men were filling sand-bags and packing them into ramparts.

The young officer flushed. 'It is as well to be ready, Herr Leutnant!'

Weidemann countered this. 'We hope to attack soon, just the same.'

'Naturally, Herr Leutnant.'

Adolf thought: the young man does not believe him. The sort of casualties we have taken in the last month, attack was the last thing on anybody's mind.

No doubt the Tommis felt the same way.

All that could be heard from their position five hundred yards away was the sound of shovelling. They, too, were digging-in.

Weidemann nodded to the young officer, and they passed on, along the Line.

At Adolf's old platoon, he was received with knowing looks and winks. 'Got a nice number, young Adolf?' said one of his former comrades. 'Safe and sound?'

'Not at all,' said Adolf, frostily. 'It is important work.'

The old comrade dug his boot ironically into the six-inch deep morass in which they stood. 'So's this!'

Adolf moved on, without saying more.

When it was over, and Weidemann was taking schnapps with the Company Commander in his shallow dug-out, Adolf was offered hot coffee with a slug of the spirit in it by the Company Sergeant Major. A week before, he had, like every soldier in the Company, been terrified of this man. Now, the fleshy regular spoke pleasantly to him.

'So long as the Tommis sit on their arses and don't start playing silly buggers we're all right here, Corporal.'

Adolf nodded, sagely.

'Of course it won't last. Our Staff or their Staff will want action.'

Adolf nodded sagely again.

'And then we'll be in the shit as usual.'

Adolf nodded, drained his coffee, and politely thanked the Company Sergeant Major. Following Weidemann out of the line, he thought: defeatist talk, and from a responsible N.C.O.! The man ought to be reported!

It was almost noon before they got back to the village.

Sergeant Max Amann met them, with a white face and staring eyes.

Behind him, stretcher-bearers carried dead bodies from the Head-quarters cellar.

'The Tommis dropped one bang on target five minutes after you left with Corporal Hitler,' he told Weidemann. 'The Commanding Officer is dead, everybody in the cellar is dead. I was up top or I'd be dead. They must have known exactly where it was, and had an artillery fix on it.'

'Everybody?' asked Weidemann, swaying slightly.

'Everybody, Herr Leutnant.'

Weidermann turned to Adolf. 'Except you and me, Adolf?'

'Herr Leutnant!' said Adolf.

Weidermann surveyed him, for a long moment.

'You seem to be lucky for me, Corporal.'

'Herr Leutnant!' said Adolf, again.

The War went on.

Adolf ran.

A *meldeganger* had to have his wits about him, and Adolf did. Soon he was regarded as the best runner in the Regiment.

Weidemann would always send him with the most important mess-ages, knowing he would get through if he could, that he would not be found skulking in some shell-hole, the important message tucked use-lessly in his belt-pouch. Adolf would not be deterred, he would run through shellfire if need be.

The other runners thought him cracked.

'You're getting us all a bad name, Adolf,' they reproved him, lying in the dirty, stinking trenches in the village of Fromelles, south of the line at Lille. 'You'd run to the Tommis with a piece of shit, you ignorant bastard!'

Adolf did not laugh, as he was expected to, at this remark.

'It is our duty to Germany to put ourselves at risk. If need be.'

The other runners looked at each other. Three months of war had robbed them of this kind of talk. Nobody except Generals and civilians talked that way any longer.

Christmas was almost here, for God's sake, and how would they all spend it?

In the mud of Flanders.

Hopefully alive, but no guarantee of it.

The casualties in the line were still heavy.

Even runners were getting hit, by a stray shell or a burst of machine-gun fire, over-directed from the enemy . The so-called soft-spot of *meldeganger* was no longer any guarantee of survival.

'Victory must be ours,' said Adolf, seriously. 'It must be so!'

The other runners laughed bitterly, and drew on their damp cigarettes.

The man was fucking cracked. That was the size of it.

Adolf sat in the trench and continued with his letter to Herr and Frau Popp: *Everyone of us here has only one wish. To settle accounts with the Tommis in the trenches opposite! By the sacrifice and agony hundreds of thousands of us endure every day, by the River of Blood that flows daily in this place – by this our Foreign Enemies will be smashed! So will our Enemies at Home! All that is more important than Territory!*

Adolf considered. They would like some local colour. Very well. *I have not told you of one of our early attacks. Four of our Guns were dug-in. We take up our positions and wait. Now the first shrapnel comes storming over us and bursts at the edge of the forest. It rips trees out of the ground. We don't know the danger we are in so we just watch. We are not afraid.* He added, with a small smile, *Now, we know better, but we are still not afraid.*

'Adolf,' asked Sergeant Max Amann. 'What do you write in those long letters home, and who to? Are you married?'

Adolf shook his head. 'To my only friends. In Munich. Mostly gossip.'

'You have no family, then?'

'None I acknowledge, Sergeant.'

'Leave will come up sometime. Where will you go?'

'Nowhere. I will stay here.

The other *meldegangers* laughed but Adolf was serious, Max Amann could see that. He cut through the foolish noise, saying, 'Adolf doesn't mean that. When leave comes up, he'll run all the way to the rear echelons!'

That made it all right. The men nodded their heads and ate their cold sausage and bread. Adolf was odd, and possibly a few phennig short of a mark, but surely not as odd as all *that*?

However, when the first few men were sent home on leave, Adolf's name was on the list. Max Amann had seen it was there. If you were in the Headquarters Unit, it was amazing what you could fix, using the bait of twenty cigarettes and a half-bottle of cognac, with the Sergeant-Clerk in the Battalion Orderly Room.

'Right, young Adolf!' he shouted. 'It's us, for home. Seven days. We go down the line together tonight!'

He proffered Adolf a tin cup of boiling-hot coffee, or what passed for coffee in the line. It was made, mostly, from burnt acorns.

Adolf sipped the scalding liquid and looked embarrassed but firm.

'I can't go, Sergeant.'

Max Amann thought he understood. 'Nobody to go to?'

'Something like that.'

The Sergeant was a kindly young man, and Adolf, although a strange bird, was one of his lads. For Christ's sake, he deserved something, after what the Battalion had been through since October of last year. 'Come home with me. I promise you a bed, grub, beer. You'll have to find your own women!' It was a breaking of Good Order and Discipline, a Non-Commissioned Officer going on leave with a virtual ranker, but for God's sake, this wasn't Potsdam! 'What do you say, young Adolf?'

Adolf said no.

Max Amann was nonplussed.

'I'm sorry. It is kindly meant, I know. But I will stay. There's nothing back there I want.'

Max Amann looked at the strained white face, the staring blue eyes, and thought he understood. A lot of men refused leave, because they knew that once home they relaxed too much. The booze and the women got to them, humanised them. Back in the line they needed to be ani-mals. In a week they might forget that. They would not ritually duck-down on passing an enfiladed position, or leap into a shell-hole when they heard the first faint whine of an approaching whizzbang. Many men died on their first day back in the Line. Max Amann resolved not to be one of them. But he would take his leave and chance that, by Christ he would!

'All right, Adolf. Draw my bread ration while I'm away. I'll fix it with the cook.' He knew Adolf had given up meat-eating and was perma-nently hungry in consequence. 'Be here when I get back. Right?'

Adolf ran and ran with his messages. From Headquarters to the line. From the line to Headquarters. From Battalion Headquarters to Divisional Headquarters and back again. From sap to front-line trench and from front-line trench to sap. He ran over mud and grass and in shallow water and in water a foot deep. He ran over, and on, dead bodies, Tommis as well as Germans. There was no time to bury the dead. They rotted as they lay. Soldiers on both sides looted them. Adolf did not. He disapproved of it. A man's comrades should not do such a thing. Nor to an ememy. The English might be undersized rabble but a dead soldier was still a soldier.

The other *meldegangers* laughed at that, too.

Puffing *Woodbines* looted from a dead Tommi, they offered Adolf a share, but he declined. He did not smoke. 'What *did* he do?' they asked, winking at each other. He didn't go with them to the Regimental Brothel, where the raddled prostitutes from the sweepings of the German red-light districts lay in wait.

Adolf had sneered, 'A man who stands in line for that is a disgusting and immoral creature, no less, and unworthy of the name German!'

The rascally *meldegangers*, who would not be *meldegangers* if they were not cunning and street-smart, winked at each other again and asked

Adolf, innocently, 'So, what do you do instead, young Adolf? Pull your plonker?'

At this Adolf erupted in rage, as they knew he would.

'I do not indulge myself in such filthy practices!'

They gave him a cheer.

Adolf went further along the line, sat down, and wrote another of his letters to Herr and Frau Popp. They had asked him to spend his leave with them but, in truth, he was happier where he was. The Army gave him his needs, food and drink, such as it was, and the only thing he had to worry about was being killed.

Killed? Adolf snorted.

That would suit his Enemies at Home. That degenerate in the Library in Vienna! The Jew who ran the Soup Kitchen! The drunken Rabaul, who had laughed at his every effort to better himself. The other petty officials of the Austrian Empire, who had thwarted him at every turn – the Principal of the Art School, for example. Even his own schoolmasters in Linz. He had no wish to see any of them, ever again, except as some kind of conqueror, some kind of success, somebody they would call 'Herr'. But for now, Adolf ate bread and vegetable soup and lay in wet clothes in shallow trenches and slept dreamlessly. He had, indeed, found a home in the Army.

Soon, at Weidemann's commendation, he was awarded the Iron Cross Second Class. The other *meldegangers* were most impressed. Adolf was the only one amongst them to be so decorated. He was deeply gratified. In Germany, plainly, his merit was being recognised!

Christmas 1915 came. The Adjutant, now Kapitan Weidemann, whose protege Adolf still was, had it drawn to his attention (inevitably by Max Amann) that Adolf never received any food parcels from home. He approached Adolf and handed him ten Deutschmarks.

Adolf stared at the notes. 'What is this?'

'From the Canteen Funds,' said Weidemann brusquely, embarrassed. 'Buy yourself a Christmas gift. Cigars, cigarettes, food? I hear there are eggs and fried potatoes to be had at the farmhouse. Is that not correct, Sergeant?'

Amann nodded. Was this to go wrong too?

It was.

Adolf handed the money back to Kapitan Weidemann, with a respectful salute. 'Herr Kapitan Adjutant, I cannot take this money! I am in no need of charity!'

Weidemann blinked in deeper embarrassment than ever.

By Christ, thought Max Amann, that's the last favour I'll do this silly young sod! He said, hastily, 'I know that Corporal Hitler will find a use for it, Sir!' He took the money and put it quickly in his tunic pocket, with a terrible, warning look at Adolf. Weidemann nodded, relieved, and made to go, asking only one question. 'Anything else, Corporal?'

'One thing, Herr Kapitan.'

Oh, my God, what now? thought Max Amann.

Weidemann closed his eyes in irritation. 'Yes, and what is that?'

'Begging the Herr Kapitan's pardon, I draw his attention to the fact that we lost three *meldegangers* last week, Sir!'

'I know that,' answered Weidemann, briskly. 'What of it?'

'With respect, I think we should send only the most urgent messages by runner during the day. The less urgent could go under cover of darkness?'

Weidemann said nothing. He stared blankly at Adolf.

'All our *meldegangers* were killed running by day. Nobody was killed by night!'

Adolf came to attention and remained there.

Max Amann breathed in, deeply. It was no good. He would have to get Adolf posted back into the line. He was a fucking menace to Good Order and Discipline, even when he was doing nothing! But *this*! Instructing a superior officer – the Adjutant! – on how to do his job!

Max Amann closed his eyes and waited for the explosion.

It did not come.

'I will bear it in mind, Corporal. Dismiss!'

Adolf clicked his heels and left the Headquarters cellar.

Weidemann looked at Max Amann. 'The man's right. It doesn't matter a damn if some of our signals get there at once or six hours late.'

'No, Herr Kapitan,' said Max Amann hollowly. In the fucking Army you never knew how things were going to turn out, that was for sure.

'Is Hitler fit for promotion?' mused Weidemann. 'We're very short of N.C.O.s in the Battalion.'

Max Amann's reply was prompt. 'Doubt it, Sir.'

'A mite unsoldierly, I agree. But, in an emergency, can you see him as a Sergeant?'

Max Amann was horrified. 'No sir!'

'Reason?'

'Men wouldn't take him seriously, Herr Kapitan Adjutant!'

'No?' Weidemann mused further. 'We could make him up to a full Corporal? Keep him on as a *meldeganger*, of course.'

Max Amann considered this. 'Not really in charge of anybody that way, is he?'

'Good,' said Weidemann. 'That's what we'll do. Fellow deserves something, yes?' He shook his head and smiled. 'I do see what you mean. No leadership qualities. Pity, but there you are.'

The Sergeant came to attention. Weidemann returned the salute, and

Max Amann left the cellar, thinking: Christ, that was a near one. Adolf as a Sergeant, the same rank as himself. It was something to think about! No leadership qualities was putting it mildly.

Amann told Adolf he was to be made up to full Corporal and Adolf seemed pleased. Later, the Sergeant took Adolf, as instructed by the Kapitan, far behind the line, to look at a room in a ruined chateau, temporarily taken over as the Regimental Officers' Mess. In the room hung a single painting, of a German soldier lying mortally wounded in a trench. It was a highly romanticised painting, Max Amann knew, since the soldier did not seem to have any wounds and there was no blood around him and his intestines were not hanging out. In short, the soldier in the painting looked like no mortally wounded soldier Max Amann had ever seen, and he had seen many. He told Adolf, 'The Adjutant wants the walls of the place painting to fit in with that picture and he thinks you can do it best.'

Adolf looked affronted. 'I'm not a house painter!'

'He knows that. He's being nice. It's an easy job. You can make it last a week. Take your choice.' He indicated two pots of paint. 'Blue or Red?'

But Adolf was gazing at the painting.

'Is it any good?' asked Max Amann.

'It serves a purpose,' said Adolf, seriously.

'The fellow's supposed to be dying, and he's smiling,' said Max Amann. 'I've never seen that expression on a dying soldier's face.'

'Of course not,' said Adolf. 'It's propaganda-art.'

'What?'

'It isn't for us. It's for public consumption.'

'You mean it's a bloody lie?'

Adolf took up a brush and dripped it in the can of blue paint. 'Not at all. If you show a man dying in agony, who would want to fight? The Tommis understand propaganda. We do not. They told the world we impaled babies on our bayonets during our first march into Belgium in Nineteen Fourteen. You know that's not true and so do I, because we were there.' Adolf laid a smooth egg-shell blue daub on the wall, carefully removing the painting first. 'But the Tommis convinced the world it was true. We have much to learn from them, in that way.'

Max Amann looked at Adolf with respect.

He was half-cracked of course, but people who were half-cracked nonetheless saw things normal men did not. It was to do with their view of the world. They looked at things differently from ordinary men. Adolf did that. It had to be noted.

Max Amann left Adolf to his work and trudged through the mud back to Battalion Headquarters, in the old Notary's house in Fournes. There, he told the *meldegangers* on duty that Adolf had obtained the Herr Kapitan Adjutant's agreement for them to run some of the messages, the least important, under cover of darkness.

The *meldegangers* were impressed.

It was their skins Adolf was saving.

Then Max Amann told them casually of Adolf's promotion to full Corporal.

They did not begrudge him that, as they might have, had he put it the other way round.

Adolf's stock went up.

The *meldegangers* would now do anything for him except listen to his political diatribes, delivered at top speed, in trench and cellar, and mostly about the misdeeds of the aliens who comprised part of the Empires of Germany and Austria, the Slavs and Jews and other mongrel peoples, most of whom were in soft jobs in the rear. They did not take seriously what Adolf had to say, no matter how vehemently he said it, but at least they did not laugh, anyway not openly.

Adolf might be half-mad, was the general opinion. But he was cracked on the right side. Who else would have spoken sense to an officer?

Some were even sorry when he was wounded.

It happened on the Somme, at Le Barque, south of Baupaume, the scene of desperate fighting in the summer of Nineteen Sixteen. A Tommi shellburst took down a whole party of *meldegangers* on a move across open terrain to a new Battalion Headquarters. Adolf was wounded in the thigh. He went back of the lines to Hospital, full of morphine, with almost no memory of how it had happened.

The wound was superficial but painful. The flesh of his thigh was torn open, but no bones were shattered. He had been lucky, the doctors told him, lying in the Casualty Clearing Station, a stinking marquee-tent, with the soldiers lying on the very turf itself. His muddied uniform was cut away by scissors, so the surgeons could get at the wound. All around him men lay dying, crying for water or their Mutti or both. He was given more morphine and lay there for days, breathing in the smell of ether, and human odour and urine and the sweet gangrenous stench of suppurating wounds. Men cried and men died. The male orderlies, sweating and overworked, ignored all but the most urgent calls for help. At last, he was loaded onto an ambulance and taken by road, a bumpy and endless journey, to a railhead, and thence by train to the Military Hospital at Beelitz, near Berlin. Drugged, he slept most of the way.

In Beelitz, he lay, without visitors or letters, alone.

The nurses were sorry for him, and took time out to chat with him. They found him magazines and gave him fruit and chocolates that other wounded men were too ill to eat. Adolf appreciated the gifts but he could have lived without them.

'How soon will I be able to go back to the regiment?' he asked the tired, white-faced old doctor.

The doctor looked at him curiously. 'Do you want to go back?'

'As soon as I can!'

'Delirious,' said the old man, and shuffled away.

Adolf was very angry to hear that. Worse, his leg healed very slowly. It was drained and stitched and bandaged and propped in front of him on the bed. It itched intolerably. Adolf had to listen to a lot of soldiers' talk. Malingerers in the hospital, men who boasted of opening their wounds before they could properly heal, men who were proud of their ability to fool the doctors as to their condition, men intent on one thing and one thing only, discharge from the Army. Such base cowards were all around him in the ward.

'Germany's no damn good to us, Adolf,' said a big blond Bavarian, offering Adolf a draw on a foul cigarette.

'We should go for a Separatist Bavaria once this lot is over.'

'What?' answered Adolf. 'A Bavaria all on its own?'

'Why not?' asked the big blond man. 'We're going to lose this war. The Amis will be in France soon. They'll kick our arses all the way back to Berlin!'

Adolf was so angry he closed his eyes in shame.

As soon as he could Adolf got back onto his feet.

He hobbled on two sticks around the Hospital grounds and even perambulated into the Administration Block, where male clerks in spotless, tailored uniforms buzzed around self-importantly, carrying pieces of paper!

Adolf stared at them and saw what he expected.

Jews! All Jews!

He said as much to the blond Bavarian, who laughed. 'They're not all Jews, Adolf. And if they are, bloody good luck to them! They're where it's safe. Not in the bloody line. Only the Frontswine are there! Fucking idiots like you and me!'

'Every Jew a clerk, every clerk a Jew!' muttered Adolf. 'They're sucking the blood of the *Volk*!'

'Don't talk crap,' said the blond Bavarian. 'Look at Walter Rathenau? He's organised the War Office. He's brilliant. And he's a Jew. Who wrote *Gott Straffe England*? A Jew! Be reasonable Adolf, for Christ's sake!'

Adolf shook his head.

Reason was no use in a situation like this.

Emotion. The gut feeling.

Only *that* counted!

Adolf shivered. He had to get out of this place. Soon! Before one of the Jew-clerks posted him to some strange Regiment where he knew nobody. Soon, it happened. A chit arrived, discharging him from the hospital and giving him two weeks' sick leave effective from the month's end. He was then to report to a new unit.

That night Adolf wrote to Kapitan Adjutant Weidemann:

'I will soon be fit for Active Service again. I have been told that I will have to join the 2nd Infantry Regiment. The Kapitan will understand my fervent desire to rejoin my old Regiment and my old comrades. May I therefore respectfully ask that you arrange to call me back to the 16th Reserve Regiment, which is, indeed, "Home" to me?'

Three weeks later the order came through.

Three weeks after that, Adolf was back in the line.

Max Amann was burning lice out of the seams of his uniform jacket with a stub of candle when Adolf joined him just behind the line at Arras. It was the chill wet March of Nineteen Seventeen and Adolf's leg wound throbbed with the cold.

'Back again, eh?' said the Sergeant. Twenty-six years old, he looked forty, in the grey flickering light of the deep dug-out. Adolf nodded and examined the sandbags and wooden steps he'd come in by. 'This is a well-built place?'

'Has to be. The Tommis are firing Flying Pigs at us now.'

Max Amann swept the candle-flame along the seams a last time. A crackle and sudden pop ended the life of the last few lice. Adolf felt itchy looking at the spectacle. He knew he would be badly bitten that very night, since he was temporarily clean. It was a pity, but it was the price of war and, perhaps, of victory.

'Flying Pigs?'

'Stokes Guns. Small trench howitzers. They blow everything to buggery! Like our minenwerfers. They fire a few, we fire a few. You know how it goes.'

Adolf nodded. Nothing changed for the Frontswine.

'Who's opposite?' he asked.

It was a ritual question. Everybody asked it. It was proper to know who your enemies were. Even if you never saw them.

'The Northumberland Fusiliers. Call themselves the Fighting Fifth. We have a prisoner. They're attacking tonight, apparently.'

Adolf felt a shiver. An attack, on his first night back?

'An offensive?' he asked.

Max Amann shook his head, put on his uniform coat, and buttoned it. Then he put on the coal-scuttle helmet they wore now, that the

Tommies called Jerries or pisspots. 'Local attack. Try to straighten out their lines. We've got machine-gun posts and wire all the way across the ground. Our machine-guns will fire on fixed points. Criss-cross, continuous stream of fire. My money says they won't come. Colonel's starting to fire two minutes before they're due to begin.'

'Why not,' asked Adolf, indignantly, 'let them die?'

Max Amann shook his lead laconically. 'He's trying to put them off. Tell them we know.' He put his finger along his nose. 'Not supposed to, of course. They'd have his arse back at Regiment if they knew.'

'He's wrong,' protested Adolf. 'The more Tommies we kill the better. The nearer Victory becomes!'

'Are we going to win, Adolf?'

Max Amann sounded bone-tired. He'd been too long in the line. That was the reason for defeatist talk like this. Adolf said, 'The Army must stand firm, and fight. The Army is all that stands between Germany and defeat!' Adolf sat down on a small wooden box. Two of the *melde-gangers*, he now saw, were asleep on makeshift wooden bunks. It was dark in the dug-out, with only the candle for illumination.

'I spent a week in Munich with my old landlord.'

'So you do have some friends?' said Max Amann, curiously.

'I had to go somewhere. The medicos gave me a compulsory leave-chit.'

'Were your friends pleased to see you?'

'Very.' Adolf shook his head in despair. 'They are good people. But like all the civilians, they are starving. No sugar. Black bread only, made from potatoes. Vile stuff. No butter for years. No meat, or very little. No milk. They seem to be living entirely on cabbages and beetroot.' Adolf recalled the Popps' delight at seeing him and their equal enthusiasm on seeing his Soldier's leave-card, which entitled him to meat and sausage, far beyond their own meagre rations. The Popps had looked a lot older, and Herr Popp's clothes hung on him. Adolf had given them his meat coupon and Frau Popp had made soup. That soup had lasted a week. In fact, they ate little else all the time Adolf was there. Frau Popp had joked and remembered how they had fed Adolf for the War!

'Like the fatted-calf, eh Adolf?' Herr Popp had joked.

Adolf had not laughed. 'I am proud to serve the Fatherland!'

'You are one of the few, Adolf,' Herr Popp had responded gently, sucking on his fine meerschaum pipe that had no tobacco in it.

'You cannot mean that?' Adolf said, scandalised.

'I don't know where you've been, Adolf,' said Herr Popp, wearily, 'not to know that every family in Germany has lost a son, a brother, or a father. They had have to pass a law to stop some women losing all their sons! One son is allowed to stay at home and work in a factory.

One son in every family. Some people have lost four, five, even six sons. Adolf, it has to stop. It must stop. Or there will be riots.'

'I have been in the line,' Adolf said. 'I have heard nothing of riots. Or of Germany losing the War!'

'Men dying at the Front,' said Herr Popp wearily. 'Women and children starving at home. The British blockade is slowly throttling us. How can we go on?'

'We must go on,' said Adolf.

'No more war talk, please,' interposed Frau Popp. 'Adolf must have a little of this wonderful soup! He's pale and ill. He's been wounded, we must look after him.'

Herr Popp inclined his head. 'Perhaps the Government will sue for Peace?'

'The Government?' Adolf echoed. 'A lot of Social Democrats and Trades Unionists and arse-lickers.' He stopped and apologised. 'Frau Popp, I have been in the line too long, I forget my manners. Please forgive me.'

'Only if you eat your soup,' Frau Popp said, brushing a strand of hair from her eyes. It was grey now where it had once been brown. Times were obviously terrible for people like the Popps, geunine German patriots. They deserved better than this.

But Herr Popp was talking. 'Adolf, now that General Ludendorf is virtual dictator of Germany –'

'A hero!' said Adolf.

'Perhaps. But he should wait until we have a small victory and then sue for Peace. It is our best hope, with the Americans coming into the War.'

'Americans?' Adolf sneered. 'They are not a warlike people.'

'Perhaps not,' said Herr Popp, 'but there are a lot of them, many of good German stock. They will be too many for us.'

'Never!' said Adolf, rising, leaving his soup untouched. He put on his uniform cap. 'The Home Front must stand firm, behind the men in the trenches. That way we must win!'

'If you want to see the Home Front at its best,' called out Herr Popp, ironically, as Adolf left the apartment, 'go to the Pigalle Club.'

'I have never heard of it,' said Adolf, at the door. 'And why does it have a French name?'

'Who knows?' asked Herr Popp with a shrug.

'Where is it?' asked Adolf.

'Ask anybody!'

The Club Pigalle was a dark, damp-looking cellar off the Herrenstrasse.

Adolf was surprised to be asked for ten Deutschmarks as the price of admission, but he paid it, out of curiosity. After all, what would he do with the money, he would be back in the line this time next week? He was rewarded with a drink and given a rickety table for two in a corner next to the whitewashed wall.

The drink tasted vaguely of wood-alcohol and some kind of sweetening agent, possibly blackcurrant juice. He sipped it out of curiosity, grimaced, and set it down. A girl of perhaps sixteen, but heavily painted and with peroxided hair, presented herself.

'Do you require anything, Herr Corporal?'

Her tone was amused. Not many corporals could afford the Pigalle.

'No.'

'Later, perhaps?'

'Perhaps.'

She smiled a practised whore's smile and melted away into the semi-darkness. Adolf strained his eyes to see who else was in the place. He made out several tables, at which well-dressed businessmen, obviously war-profiteers, sat with women like the girl who had searched him out. This girl had joined the nearest table, sitting on the knee of a gross-looking man in a splendid suit. A man, Adolf decided, with the face of a pig. And, although Adolf could not see the man clearly, probably a Jew! The tart's hand strayed between the man's thighs, but he hardly seemed to notice. To Adolf's astonishment, the men at the table were drinking what seemed to be champagne – a silver ice-bucket contained a magnum – and eating plates of roasted meat, the scent of which almost made Adolf retch.

Gusts of obscene laughter emitted from this table.

Adolf averted his eyes from that table and looked at the next one.

To his surprise, it was filled with German officers of field rank, that was to say it contained nobody beneath the rank of major. This table, too, had its complement of champagne and slices of pork and dishes of crisp fried potatoes and various cheeses, including some splendid Emmenthal. Cigars were being smoked, by their aroma, Turkish, or even Havanas, certainly not the sweepings of the packing-floor considered good enough for the Frontswine. Tarts sat on the officers' knees and plied them with drink.

Adolf began to seethe with anger.

This was reinforced by the appearance on what he had not realised was a stage, at the far end of the dark cellar. A sole spotlight played on a man – *was* he a man? – of middle years, dressed in an evening suit of ancient vintage, and heavily made-up in a decidedly effeminate manner.

This artiste affected a lisp, to suggest that he was a homosexual, but Adolf felt that he was no such thing. Adolf felt that he was nothing.

'Did you hear what the Crown Prince said to the Frontswine?' he asked the inattentive crowd in the dark, packed, cellar.

'Sell your arse to the Tommis, it's all we have left,' said the comic.

Nobody seemed to be listening.

The Army officers went on chatting, uniform collars unbuttoned, fondling the tarts absent-mindedly. The businessmen did not seem to have heard at all.

But it was *treason*!

Adolf waited to hear what came next.

'They're sending lunatics from the asylums into the line,' said the comic. 'The idea is to frighten the Tommies to death!'

Nobody laughed. Nobody listened.

A heavy man in a dark suit, with a scar on his face, presented himself to Adolf. 'If you are not ordering, we need the table.'

No Sir. No respect.

'What price is supper?' Adolf asked.

'If you have the pork and potatoes, it's a hundred and fifty Deutschmarks,' said the man. Drink is extra.'

A month's wages to a worker!

Half a year's army pay!

Adolf said, 'I have an appointment.'

The heavy man nodded understandingly and Adolf left the cellar.

He debated calling the police, but realised the police must know about the Club Pigalle. Senior army officers ate there.

The rot had set in, that was plain.

The Front Line was cleaner, anything was cleaner than this shithole. Adolf trembled with rage all the way back to his lodgings.

Next day Adolf took his leave of the Popps and caught the morning train back to the Front. He was two days early. Everybody who examined his pass on the way to the Front thought he was mad.

Now, sitting in the deep dugout, he told Max Amann, 'We have new guns. We can fire twenty-two miles with Big Bertha. We must blow the Tommis and the Frogs out of their trenches with that!'

Max Amann shrugged. 'Perhaps.' He got to his feet, looking at his watch. 'The Tommis should attack any minute. Want to see it?'

Adolf nodded. The sight of a few Tommies being butchered might cheer him up.

Second Lieutenant Percy Prior of the Ninth Battalion of the North-umberland Fusiliers stood on the firestep, opposite to the Chemical

Works at Arras. He was twenty-six years old. He had been told that the object of the attack was to knock out the German machine-guns along the salient, which jutted out into No Man's Land. He was in charge of a platoon of men, twenty-four in number, instead of the sixty he had been taught to expect in the Durham University Officers' Training Corps, and at Oxford, where he had taken the six-week Infantry Officers' Course before being sent to France. He had a stick in one hand and a Webley revolver in the other, and very little idea of what to do. His company captain, nineteen years of age and already sporting the Military Cross, had simply told him jocularly, 'We'll make a hero of you tonight, Prior.' This self-same man, one Captain Black, was now issuing orders to the men, who were sullen and tired but tough, mostly being coal-miners from Durham and Northumberland. His Batman, an old soldier, had whispered the advice: 'Stick by me, Sir, and I'll see you right!'

Nothing happened for a long time, then a machine-gun barrage started from the German lines. The bullets ripped and whipped over the heads of the men, standing two or three deep on the firestep. They visibly wilted. But nobody spoke or protested. A whistle sounded, and Captain Black waved them forward with his revolver. The soldiers blundered, cursing, into the pitch-black night, through the gaps in their own wire (cut earlier in the evening) and trudged into the hail of bullets, towards the enemy lines. Second Lieutenant Prior looked round for his batman, in time to see him leap into a watery shellhole.

'In here, Sir!' he called. The young man looked down at him, uncomprehendingly, and ran on. The British wire was behind him now, and men were falling all around, with small cries, sometimes without a sound. Second Lieutenant Prior ran towards the enemy lines.

A Very light suddenly illuminated the battlefield, brighter than day itself. He could see the light glinting on the helmets of the German machine-gunners, safe behind their emplacements. Nobody else but himself and a few stumbling men seemed to be still alive. He looked foolishly at the thick German barbed-wire and wondered how, if they had got that far, they would ever have cut their way through it while being machine-gunned? He turned and ran back to his own trenches, going in a straight line and not ducking and weaving, as he had been taught. Astonishingly, he was not hit. He jumped the final ten yards, knocking the breath out of his sergeant, who had arrived there a moment earlier.

'What happened?' he asked the sergeant.

'A fuck-up, Sir,' said the man. 'As usual.'

Adolf and Max Amann watched the Tommies attack from a vantage point in the line, a sandbagged observation post next to a gun emplacement. 'No artillery preparation. No Stokes gun. Nothing. A piss-poor effort,' said Max Amann. 'Poor fucking sods.'

'They are our enemy,' said Adolf, sternly.

'Not them, they're like us,' said Max Amann. 'Frontswine, that's all.'

Adolf did not agree but he did not argue.

It had been slaughter and not nice to look at.

However, if that was the best the Tommies could do, perhaps Germany was safe, anyway for a while.

'Let's get back to Headquarters where we belong,' said Max Amann. 'The Front-line gives me the shits.'

Adolf felt this remark unpatriotic but again, he said nothing.

They made their way, cautiously, back through the support trenches to the rear. They passed the machine-gunners, cleaning their red-hot weapons. The men did not speak, or cheer. If anything, they seemed saddened by the carnage.

Adolf wondered: if this was how men felt when they won, how did they feel when they lost?

To lose was unthinkable.

If Germany lost, everything was gone.

The lice found him again that night. He scratched and grumbled and felt at home. By next morning the memory of the Hospital and of Munich and of the profiteers and tarts in the Club Pigalle faded, as did the grey, pinched faces of the Popps.

He began to enjoy the Army again.

The War, however, continued to go badly.

A long, bitter year later General Ludendorf decided on a last Offensive. He threw every available German division against the lightly-defended lines north of Arras. The aim was a breakthrough to the Channel Ports, the tactic a slightly-amended version of the classic Von Scheifflin Plan, beloved of the German High Command and already used in Nineteen-Fourteen. To smash through into Belgium and wheel South, flanking the French and British Armies.

The List Regiment was in the van of the attack and received extra rations and extra ammunition and extra field-guns and extra reserves on account of it. But, as Max Amann said, as they marched ten, fifteen, twenty miles a day, after the first breakthrough, what the High Command did not give out was an extra pair of feet to each man!

Adolf was brutally exhausted. So were all the *meldegangers*.

Nobody had ever run in open country like this.

The Tommies had simply melted in front of them.

The March Offensive was Germany's last chance, Adolf told the *meldegangers*. They must persist in their duty.

The weary *meldegangers* replied that they didn't give a fuck.

Kapitan Adjutant Weidemann gave Adolf the hardest, longest jobs. Weidemann was as weary as any man in his company, for he was no longer young. 'Keep running, Adolf!' he said. 'We can win yet. Ludendorf knows what he's doing. This is the only breakthrough any general of either side has managed, in the whole War. It must win it for us, before the Americans get here in strength. Or we are lost.'

The look on his face shattered Adolf.

But he ran.

And ran.

The middle of April found the Company in a lush green meadow, not a trench in sight. A few dying cattle, caught by high-explosives, lay moaning on their sides in the field. The soldiers were jubilant. Even the *meldegangers* had to admit it all looked very good.

There was no sign whatever of the enemy.

It was a walk-over!

Suddenly, a hail of artillery shells fell on them. Not only on them but to the far right and left of them. Great spouts of earth rose and fell. Men were blown high into the air and came down looking like butcher's meat.

Weidemann grasped Adolf by the sleeve.

'Run to the rear! Now! Get to the nearest field-telephone. That's our own artillery shelling us. Take this map-reference! Run, run!'

Adolf run. Faster than he had ever run in his life.

His legs did not seem to belong to him.

He found a field-telephone with a light-artillery unit two miles back along a deserted road. He gasped out his message to the Signals Major. He was given water and the message delivered. Inside a few minutes the artillery had ceased firing all along the line. There was absolute silence.

'Listen to that,' said the Major. 'We can hear the birds sing again.'

A week later, Ludendorf's attack petered out.

Two months later, in front of Ypres, the Tommies sent over the mustard gas. Adolf and the men with him were caught before they could don their primitive gas-masks.

All he remembered was the choking, retching pain.

Then somebody pulled a mask over his face and he passed out.

Adolf lay, blinded, in the hospital at Pasewalk, in Pomerania, for six weeks. Slowly, the saline washes took effect, and he could see again, dimly at first. His lungs seemed to be unaffected. His throat was dry and sore, and his voice remained, ever afterwards, husky and grating.

Adolf did not feel bitter, as some of the wounded men in the Ward felt bitter. He was alive. He still could continue to fight. They all could.

When he croaked out this sentiment the wounded men did not even reply.

An officer came and pinned an Iron Cross First Class on his tunic, as he lay in bed. Rankers did not usually get the First Class. That was for officers. The men in the ward were impressed. Adolf refused their offer of a party to celebrate.

A week after that, Adolf was sitting, out of his cot, reading, when the aged Hospital Pastor ran in, tears streaming down his cheeks. A round-cheeked old man, he was hardly able to speak, even after he had called urgently for silence. The wounded men looked at him and at each other, smiling, cynical, and curious. 'Is it the Second Coming, or what?' asked one. Finally the old man spoke, in a tremulous and fearful voice.

'The Kaiser has abdicated, and run to Holland!'

The wounded men said nothing.

'A Republic has been proclaimed in Berlin!'

The wounded men still said nothing.

'Tomorrow, an Armistice will be signed at Compiegne, in France. It is a surrender. We are now at the mercy of our enemies!'

Still, the wounded men said nothing.

The Pastor's hands fell to his side. His voice was broken.

'The War is over!'

The wounded men cheered and danced and sang and behaved as if they were drunk, although none of them had seen liquor for many weeks.

Adolf sat in his chair, not moving. Tears ran down his cheeks.

One of the men called, 'Don't be ashamed, comrade. I know how you feel! But it's over! Jesus Christ, it's over!'

But Adolf was ashamed.

Deeply, deeply ashamed.

For a very good and simple reason.

The unthinkable had happened.

Germany had lost.

His enemies and the Enemies of Germany, outside and inside the State, had triumphed.

He took no part in the drunken bacchanal with all the singing, dancing, drinking (mainly hospital-alcohol) that followed. Nor in the desperate sex between patients and nurses. All these people were doing was trying to forget the last four years.

Adolf stood alone out in the hospital grounds and listened to it all.

They all might try to forget.

He would not.

BOOK TWO

XI

ADOLF HITLER stood at attention.

He knew this was an important meeting. Roehn was an important man. Everybody in Germany knew his name.

'Corporal Hitler reporting, as ordered, Herr Kapitan!' he shouted.

Kapitan Ernst Roehm looked at Hitler, and recalled uneasily the words of the degenerate poet and drunkard, Dietrich Eckhart. 'What we need,' Eckhart had said, in that bierkeller two years ago, with the War freshly lost, 'is a fellow who does not mind the sound of machine-gun fire. We can't have an officer to lead us, not even you, Ernst. The people don't respect the Officer-class any more. You lost the War. We need a *worker*! A man who knows how to talk! Politics is the stupidest business in the world so brains are not necessary. Mustn't be married, that way we'll get the women's vote. Most of all, he *must* know how to talk the way they talk in the street!'

Roehm had laughed. 'Where do we find this paragon?'

'Your task,' Eckhart had said, blearily, 'not mine.'

Was it possible, Roehm wondered, staring at the thin, slightly unkempt corporal in front of him, that *this* was the man?

Ernst Roehm straddled his booted legs in front of the stove in his office at the Headquarters of the Freikorps in Munich, and looked again, puzzled, at Adolf Hitler. Roehm only knew what he had been told. That this young man could make speeches. Why, on hearing about Hitler, had Eckhart's words come back to him?

Well, because the words had been spoken two years ago, and still the man had not been found!

'At ease, Hitler,' said Roehm.

Roehm tried to recall what he had been told. It was not a great deal. Hitler had been sent on the Army's Political Officers' Course. The Chief Instructor had told Roehm that Hitler had a 'natural talent' as an orator. Not only that, his Army record was excellent. The Iron Cross, First Class, after all, was not handed out with the rations. Not to a corporal.

Yet Roehm was disappointed with what he saw.

Adolf Hitler was now thirty years old, still thin and somehow unsoldierly-looking, with protuberant, girlish eyes of a strange sharp blueness, and a hesitant, anxious-to-please manner. No doubt existed in Roehm's mind that this young man was wary of him because he was a member of the Officer-class. The sheet of official paper on his desk told Roehm that Hitler was the son of a civil servant, deceased. Yet nothing about Hitler looked bourgeois. He held himself hangdog, like a private soldier, a worker, but the sheet of paper said nothing about any manual job. Roehm would have taken him, if pressed, for a clerk.

Clerks, on the other hand, rarely won the Iron Cross, First Class!

'Tell me about yourself?' he barked. 'Family?'

Hitler came to stiff attention, again. 'In Vienna. I do not see them.'

Roehm nodded, said softly, 'In your own time. Sit down. Cigarette?'

Hitler sat and shook his head nervously. Roehm remained standing, in front of the stove. Hitler's uniform, Roehm saw, was badly pressed, his boots none-too-well cleaned. Something of a bohemian, perhaps? The possibility crossed his mind that Hitler might be homosexual? That possibility always crossed the mind of Kapitan Roehm when he saw an attractive young man. Everybody knew that he was homosexual. Roehm could spot arse-bait at a hundred yards on a dark night, and Hitler, he knew, was not arse-bait, and by God he knew arse-bait when he saw it, had he not pursued it all his adult life, wasted hours and days and nights in the pursuit of it, probably endangered his career in the Army because of it?

Whatever Hitler was, he was not that. Roehm looked again at the Chief Instructor's report. An exceptional political speaker. That was the point. That was what the report said.

Christ knows, that was what the Army and the Freikorps needed. A mouthpiece! Somebody who could get up on a soapbox and put into words something of what they all felt! That Germany had been betrayed by the civilians at home, that the Army had never surrendered, that the 'November Criminals' who had signed the Armistice – the *Surrender*, call the fucking thing what it was! – should be publicly tried, put up against a wall and shot!

Roehm drew on his cigar and stared gloomily at nothing.

Meantime, Adolf was waiting for permission to start talking.

It had already been given but he was still waiting.

Ernst Roehm liked that. It showed a proper attitude.

He liked his young men passive. He was the old, scarred bull. They were the young, unbroken cows. His groin stirred. Ordinary men never realised that an active masculine homosexual like himself was never off-duty. Godammit, he was in the company of men all the time. In the barracks. In the beerhalls. It was the equivalent, to a heterosexual man, of conducting all of one's daily tasks in a brothel.

'So?' Roehm pressed. 'Tell me? What about your life before the Army?'

'Before the Army I had no life,' said Hitler. 'I lived in Vienna as an art student and I starved.'

Roehm was shocked at the vehemence in the voice. 'Do you mean no food? Nothing?'

'That is what I mean.'

'Where did you live?'

'In Men's Hostels. Places like that.'

'So? You know the streets?'

'Yes, I do.'

'But you are not a Socialist? Why?'

'Socialist means Marxism. *I* want German Socialism. National Socialism.'

Roehm breathed in, softly. '*National Socialism?* I see?' He was very still now. 'Tell me what happened to you? After the Surrender?'

Hitler began to speak, very quietly, at first, and Roehm noted that, with a sense of rising excitement. Don't expect too much, he reproved himself.

Hitler was talking freely now: 'After the Surrender I reported to my barracks at Munich for demobilisation. That was in December 1918. I asked to stay in the Army. I was posted to a Prisoner of War Camp at Traustein, doing guard-duties. That ended, and I reported back to my barracks to find . . . Well, Herr Kapitan, you know how things were then?'

Roehm nodded. How well he knew! He laughed aloud, scornfully. 'The Soldiers' Councils! That rabble who thought they could govern Bavaria!' Roehm snorted. 'Then the Jew Eisner! The Social Democrat! Did you ever see him? A little fellow in a beard, with a huge hat. Anyway, young Anton Arco-Valley shot him and that was the end of Social Democracy in Bavaria, thank God! And then?'

'Three of their men tried to arrest me but I fired my carbine at them and escaped.' Hitler seemed to be telling a story he had told many times before. Roehm noted that, and wondered.

'Weren't you arrested by our people, the Freikorps? Weren't you missing?' asked Roehm idly, glancing at the report on his desk to verify the question. The words hung in the warm room, the ice freezing outside on the window-panes, the room smelling of floor-polish and male sweat.

Hitler said, 'It was a mistake. Officers of my own regiment recognised me, and I was freed. I was with the Communists but not of them.'

Roehm said nothing to that. He wondered again.

Hitler went on quickly. 'I convinced the Tribunal. I gave them names.'

'If you hadn't,' said Roehm, again idly, 'they'd have shot you. The Freikorps are true patriots, every man an ex-serviceman. They are illegal but without them the Reds would run Germany!'

'I gave them the names because I do not believe in Marxism!'

'The men you named were shot?'

'Yes.'

Roehm noted that this admission did not trouble Hitler.

'Then what?'

'They sent me on a Course. As a Bildungs-officer. After that ended, I was posted to my old Regiment. My task now is to combat dangerous theories prevalent at this time. Marxism. Pacifism. Socialism. Social Democracy. To keep the soldiers to their duty.'

'And that duty is?' Roehm had lit a new cigarillo and drew on it luxuriously. Sensation, what else was there in life, save duty?

'To serve Germany,' answered Hitler. 'After all, they're lucky to still be soldiers. Most of their comrades had been demobilised and are walking the streets, looking for work that isn't there.'

Roehm nodded. 'What do you want to do now?'

Hitler swallowed then seemed suddenly to find his confidence. 'I want to go on serving Germany!'

'But the German Government in Berlin is Social Democrat,' said Roehm, softly. 'They rule Germany. All we are is a small opposition, down here in the South, one State, Bavaria.' Roehm paused, innocent. 'What are we to do? Is there anything we *can* do?'

Hitler's eyes were unblinking. What an odd shade of blue? Almost beautiful. Ernst Roehm felt a stir of sexual desire, quickly repressed. For now Hitler was talking again. His voice was husky and different from the apologetic worker's whine Roehm had noticed earlier in the interrogation. For, after all, that's what it was. An interrogation to find out if he was the Man?

'Tell me what Germany has done wrong?' Roehm asked.

Adolf Hitler looked at Roehm in a surprised fashion. 'Germany should never have signed the Treaty of Versailles. We should have fought on and died, if necessary.'

'The American General Pershing', interposed Roehm softly, 'has said that the reason we Germans do not accept our defeat is because no battles were fought on our soil? He asked for a week to show us how thoroughly defeated we were? Was he wrong?'

Adolf Hitler seemed not to have heard him.

'The Prussian Guard marched home in perfect order and paraded in full dress at the Brandenburg Tor in Berlin. The whole West Front Army was in similar good order. The Republican politicians signed the Treaty, but the Army was ready to fight on.'

Roehm knew that was not true. But it was a fiction widely believed in Germany. Roehm knew that Hindenberg himself, the Commander-in-Chief, had told Prime Minister Ebert that they were defeated. He also knew Hindenberg would never admit he had ever said it. The Officer Corp's honour depended on his never having said it.

'Go on,' he said. If Hitler believed it all the better.

'Five billion dollars in gold, as reparations,' said Hitler. 'Plus Coal, Ships, Cattle! The Allies are determined to crush Germany, once and for all.'

'Yet,' murmured Roehm, 'they have left our boundaries intact? Apart from the Polish Corridor and Alsace, we stand where we stood in Nineteen-Fourteen. We are still whole?'

'What right have the Poles, an inferior nation, to dismember Germany?' asked Adolf Hitler, referring to the Polish Corridor.

It was, Roehm knew, the way the average German in the street saw it. Adolf Hitler, it seemed to Roehm, spoke and thought exactly as they did. 'What about the Government?'

'The Social Democrats in Berlin are simply arselickers and apologists for the November Criminals!' said Hitler, suddenly and sharply. 'They care nothing for the soldiers who gave their lives for Germany! All they are interested in is keeping up the Reparation Payments to the French! We should not give the French another bucket of coal, never mind the tons of the stuff we send daily across the Rhine! Enough! We starve in our own streets! We send food to the French which should go to our wives and children! What did Clemenceau say at Versailles? "We'll squeeze Germany till the pips squeak!" Very well! I say to Monsieur Clemenceau. Enough! Not another sou!'

Ernst Roehm stood, very still.

Hitler's eyes had not blinked.

Sweat stood out on his forehead.

'I say . . . *Germany Awake!*'

Ernst Roehm stared at him, transfixed.

'Adolf?' said Roehm gently, as if to one of his boys, afterwards.

'Yes, Herr Kapitan?'

Adolf blinked. He was the worker, the shabby clerk again.

'I think . . .' Roehm put his hand on Hitler's shoulder. Hitler flinched. Roehm removed it, regretfully. 'I think, Adolf,' he said, none-theless, 'that I have a job for you. A very important job.'

Hitler said nothing. He seemed almost not to hear. But he had.

The days since the War had been hard ones for Adolf Hitler. Yet he had been lucky to be selected to stay on in the Army. Most of his comrades of the List Regiment, now stood, in broken shoes that took in water, shivering on the street-corners of Munich, their overcoats long since pawned or sold, their children crying with hunger to their thin anxious wives, the rent-collector hammering on the door. These men, the ex-soldiers, stood in large aimless groups all over the city, sharing the same cigarette, smoking it down so low that the last man to smoke it had to use a pin to stop it burning his fingers.

All over Germany it was the same story. No work. No pay. No food. Unemployment was higher than anybody had ever known it to be. One man in three was out of work in Munich.

Adolf ran meetings of the soldiers of the Freikorps – those men who were not selected to stay in the Army but who, illegally, served the Army anyway. The Freikorps were freebooters, on low pay, and they hated the Reds because they were paid to hate the Reds. These men had shot Reds all over Bavaria, all over provincial Germany, even in Berlin itself. Standing in the snow, stamping their feet, they grunted in agreement as Adolf, under the stern eyes of his Instructors, stammered out his first, awkward, propaganda-speeches.

'Don't go Red!'

'Don't go Social Democrat!'

'Believe in the Freikorps!'

'Believe in the Army!'

'Believe in Germany!'

Adolf had parroted these slogans to the Freikorp men and the Army men who grunted and nodded.

Adolf was not bad to listen to.

Not bad at all.

With his errant lock of hair and his barely-concealed hatred for all forms of authority, he could certainly talk. He might be a bit off-plumb, with his cursing at the Jews and the Poles, and the other 'Inferior Races', but he put it all in a simple way they could understand. Adolf insisted to his tutors that short slogans and short words were the only kind soldiers would listen to. The trenches had hardened him. He spoke harshly of Germany's enemies, with the authority of the ribbons that adorned his tunic.

The more Adolf talked, his words sarcastic and bitter – but lightened from time to time with coarse jokes! – the more his tutors looked at each other, impressed.

Finally, the Chief Instructor, an ex-journalist, asked him: 'Have you thought of a career in politics?'

'Possibly . . . One day.'

The Chief Instructor looked at him thoughtfully. 'I may be able to help you there.'

Hence the meeting with Ernst Roehm, now over.

Adolf walked across the parade ground and went into the barracks. Behind him now, he sensed, were the insults and humiliations of his early life. Now, he was a man, with a man's will. Now, he would only need to step forward to find his destiny.

The Chief Instructor and even Major Ernst Roehm were but steps on the way.

Adolf Hitler was, for the first time in his life, sure of his destiny. He was a political animal and politics was the road for him. A thrill of self-awareness powered through him. Now he would show his detractors, his Enemies, those who wished to see him in the dust, just who and what he was.

The Will was All!

Hitler sat, wearing a shabby raincoat, in the Alle Rosenbad Tavern on the Herrenstrasse in Munich, and yawned. Why, he wondered, did Roehm think there was any danger, or even interest, in the bunch of cranks and misfits, perhaps forty in number, who sat, waiting for the main speaker of the evening, billed, he saw from a glance at the badly printed programme (price ten phennigs) as Comrade Anton Drexler, Chairman of the German Workers' Party?

Hitler looked around the place. The men were workers all right. By the sallow-faced look of them, men who had sat the War out in factories and railway workshops. The pamphlet described Comrade Drexler as a locksmith by trade, as if it was an occupation to be proud of. Well, amongst the workers, it was. Drexler was a skilled man. That put him a class above the unskilled mass. Hitler looked up as a desultory round of applause greeted Drexler himself, a thin, consumptive-looking man of forty-five, uneducated and anything but at home on his feet. Hitler waited, expectantly. When anybody began to speak, he had a professional interest. There was always something to learn.

'Since 1919,' Drexler was saying, stolidly, 'I have had the honour to be your Chairman. My aim has been, as it still is, to found a German Workers' Party based on the Working Class. But not Marxist! I left my Union when it went Marxist.' Drexler peered earnestly through his thick, steel-rimmed spectacles. 'I was a member for a time of the Father-land Front but they are too middle-class for me. They don't know the Worker exists. Nor do they care, Comrades!' Drexler peered earnestly over his spectacles at the forty members of the German Workers' Party. 'Comrades, the Social Democrats are a spent force. They may rule in Berlin but here in Bavaria their writ does not run. What I am asking for is a Workers' Party for the German Worker.'

There was a smattering of polite applause. Hitler felt the audience had heard all this before, many times. Yet, in Hitler, there stirred a feeling of kinship. Drexler was a bumbling fool, that was obvious, but he had the right ideas. He was simply the wrong person to sell them.

Why had Roehm sent him here?

To spy, of course, that went without saying. To assess this Workers' Party, to decide if they were serious people, revolutionaries? Adolf smiled to himself and shook his head.

Revolutionaries?

Why, Drexler was calling for the minutes of the last meeting to be approved and accepted. My God, Revolutionaries?

And yet? And yet?

Another speaker was on his feet. Hitler recognised him. His name was Feder. The man had but one idea. Feder insisted that 'interest-free' loans were the only way to bring Germany back to some kind of financial order. It made some sense. Anybody could see that. A 'Herr Professor' in the audience did not. He stood up to argue, polishing his glasses and consulting his notes, which were closely-written on two pages of foolscap.

Hitler got to his feet. He had seen enough.

At the door, Drexler pushed a booklet into his hand.

'You're new? I haven't seen you before?' he said, respectfully.

Hitler noted that. It was because he was wearing a collar and tie. A Revolutionary? What had given Roehm that idea?

'No, my first time.' He glanced at the booklet. It was entitled, *My Political Awakening, by Anton Drexler*.

'Danke,' he said. 'I will read it with interest.'

The fool bowed, and Hitler left.

He thrust the pamphlet into his pocket and thought no more of it.

That night, Hitler lay in his bunk in the barracks and thought about Germany. He crumbled bread and watched the mice eat the crumbs. All was quiet in the room, except for the odd snore. He felt at home in the place. He pondered: what had gone wrong for the Fatherland?

First, the Surrender and the Demobilisation of the Army!

The flight of the Kaiser to Holland and the end of the Monarchy!

Then, the Declaration of the Republic, with Ebert, the Social Democrat, as Prime Minister. Then the deal struck between the Army and Ebert. In return for keeping the Social Democrats in power the Government would leave the Army alone.

Then the Soviet Councils of soldiers and sailors in Berlin, the armed attempt to turn Germany into a Communist Republic. Put down bloodily by the Army, with the backing of the Social Democratic Government. Rosa Luxemburg and Karl Liebknect killed. The Red Menace, for the moment, crushed.

Then, there was Ebert (a saddler by profession, my God, what a man to lead Germany!) in power, but without an absolute majority. A Conservative minority Opposition, and a complicated system of Proportional Representation. What a dog's breakfast!

Plus a ridiculously liberal Constitution.

The Vote at Twenty!

All Germans Equal Before the Law!

All Germans to have the Right of Free Association, complete liberty of Religious Belief and Conscience!

Good and pure and liberal, thought Adolf Hitler contemptuously.

There were two things wrong with it.

One, it had been tried before. In Austria he had seen it fail.

Two, the German Volk did not want it.

They wanted Revenge for Defeat.

They wanted Respect, once again.

The man who would give them those two things, or even promise them those things, could ask any sacrifice of them.

Adolf Hitler lay awake a long time, thinking about that.

'So?' Roehm leaned back in his chair, and stared at Hitler's report, barely a page in length. 'You went to the Workers' Party meeting, I see, and were not impressed?'

'Who could be impressed by a bunch of crackpots?'

Hitler felt much more at home in the man's office nowadays. Roehm had virtually taken him onto his staff, attached to the Political Intelligence Unit. Their job was to investigate everybody who might be against the aims of the Army, who paid Roehm (and Hitler) but could not admit to doing so, since the Army had to seem non-political.

Roehm was staring gloomily at Hitler's report. 'Crackpots? Nothing in what Drexler says?'

'A lot, if somebody else said it.'

Roehm looked at him, thoughtfully.

'If *you* said it?'

'Me?'

'You could join the Party, take it over, run it? Don't say it hasn't already occurred to you?'

It had, but Hitler demurred. 'Perhaps. But there are very few of them.'

'They are a known political party. They probably have a thousand, two, or even three thousand supporters, maybe more? Better than none at all. Any other way you'd have to start at the beginning, I mean, if you wanted a party of your own?' Roehm drew on his cigar. 'Don't tell me you haven't thought of that, either?'

Still, Hitler did not smile.

What, Roehm wondered, would make him smile? 'I'm a member of the Workers' Party myself.'

Hitler did not smile, but he sat up, Roehm noted.

'Since when, Herr Kapitan?'

'Since now. Look, I've just signed my name to the Application Form.' Roehm held it up, ironically. Hitler shook his head. 'What do we want with such people?'

'We want political power, Adolf,' said Roehm. 'And you can get it for us.'

Hitler felt a shiver, all through his body.

Power?

That, of course, had to be the aim. What else mattered? If you had political power, you controlled everything and everybody. The Police. The Military. The Law. You made your own Justice. You owned every man and woman in the State. They did your bidding. Not, of course, if you tried to rule them like a liberal or a so-called democrat. Then they despised you, got annoyed or angry with you, and voted you out of office. No! You *told* them what to do. Used to taking orders all their lives, they did it. That was the way.

'Me?' he said, nonetheless. "How do I take over the German Workers' Party?'

'Quite simple. You go to the next meeting. You offer yourself for election to the Committee. Then when the time is ripe, you make a big speech.'

'What do I say in this speech?' asked Adolf Hitler, slowly.

'Whatever you like. That's up to you. You'll know what to say when you've thought about it a while, my dear Adolf. Won't you?'

Roehm's voice was kindly and his eyes twinkled. Hitler inclined his head.

He would indeed know what to say.

It took three months for Adolf Hitler to take over the German Workers' Party. As Roehm had predicted, it was easy.

He got himself elected Propaganda Officer and persuaded the Committee to agree to insert advertisements in the Munich newspapers announcing the dates and places of future meetings. That brought the regular attendances up to a hundred people, then to two hundred. He proposed a mass-meeting at the Festvaal of the Hofbrauhaus, which would hold a crowd of two thousand. Drexler and the committee thought Hitler mad. They were a little mollified when he told them it would not cost the Party a pfennig. The money to rent the hall came from Roehm and the Political Intelligence Unit. From, in fact, the Army.

There was a full-house at the Hofbrauhaus. Many of them were Roehm's Freikorps, in civilian clothes, who listened in silence to the preliminaries. There were boos and catcalls from the many Reds waiting to disrupt the meeting. Suddenly, Hitler stood at the podium. The houselights had been dimmed, on his orders, but when he stood up, a single spotlight fell on him. He began quietly, as ever. 'Fellow Germans! Let me come at once to my demands – the demands the Workers' Party will make! Like you, I am an old soldier, I have no time for Debating Societies.' The audience stirred.

'First, we demand a Greater Germany! A united Germany! All the Germanic People as one!'

The audience, surprised, applauded warmly.

'Second, we demand Abolition of Incomes not earned by honest toil!'

'Common sense!' called a voice.

'We demand the Abolition of all Speculation, in Property or in Land!'

There was a very long silence. It was respectful.

'We demand the Restoration of the Death Penalty for Traitors and Speculators!'

There was loud applause for that. Hitler's voice rose a pitch, hoarsely. 'We demand an End to the Treaty of Versailles! To hell with the French, the British and the Americans! Not another ton of coal, not another Mark! Nothing!'

There was a roar of applause. A note in it, purely German, noted Roehm, of hysteria and fury. Sitting at the back of the hall, Roehm felt the hair on his neck stand on end. The hoarse-voiced clerk had this crowd by the balls. There he stood, for Christ's sake, sweating in the spotlight, waiting for the noise to end – as if he was at a bus-stop! – so that he could go on. When he did, there was a new, harsh certainty in his voice, something, Roehm had not expected to hear. Cruelty and contempt mixed, as the speaker raised the intensity of his voice, but not the volume.

'The German *Volk* have begun to wonder if the Weimar Republic is a recovery or a heart-attack!' The crowd laughed. Hitler waited: 'At the end of the war Germany owed eight-million Marks – *and* had also to pay massive Reparations! The product of Germany's work now belongs, not to herself, but to her Foreign Creditors!' The voice was suddenly harsh and high. 'It will keep us slaves for another *thirty* years!' The hall was silent. 'Comrades, we have done this to *ourselves*, we have humiliated *ourselves*!' The voice began to rise again. 'We befoul, besmirch, deny everything we used to hold sacred! The so-called Marxist Revolution in Berlin has made the World our Master!'

The crowd waited.

'The Socialists say: "The *Volk* Govern now!"' Hitler put his hands on his hips. 'Really? The *Volk* have liberties, they say? What liberties? To organise Trades Unions who do nothing! Liberty, Comrades, to be out of work and to starve?' Again, the long pause. 'And who, I ask, has profited from all this? . . . I'll *tell* you! The Banks and Stock Exchange have profited! But the *old* Stock Exchanges are destroyed! The Jewish International Stock Exchange is in charge of the Nation's Money!'

Roehm felt the crowd catch its breath. Roehm knew that Anti-Semitism was rife in Weimar Germany. Hitler had struck a nerve.

'Comrades! The million Workers who lived in Berlin at the outbreak of the War are *still* Workers! They are just poorer and worse-clad. But the Jews from the East, who entered Germany during the War – they arrived in poverty! – are now driving around in motor-cars!'

There was a low, animal sound from the audience.

After a long pause, Hitler continued, his voice rising contemptuously. 'The *Right*? What *can* I say about the *Right*? That it still fails to recognise the dangers of Bolshevism? Well, you *know* that!' Hitler laughed harshly. Roehm had never heard a political speaker *laugh* before. 'All these so-called gentlemen believe in is being elected to the Landtag! With fat-arsed secretaries for mistresses!'

There was a rumble of laughter in the hall. Hitler had broken the tension. 'Social Democracy is *not* the answer! It is not a German thing! It is a *Jewish Invention*!'

The speaker – who Roehm hardly recognised by now – slammed his fist on the lectern.

'The *Left*, God Help Us, leads to Bolshevism!'

'The *Right* has lost its spirit and has no Faith in Anything!'

'With us . . . Everyone who is a German has the same Aryan Blood, and speaks the same language!'

After a pause, almost trance-like, it seemed to Roehm, Hitler resumed, in a low, almost caressing, voice:

'Not so the Jews. Their Blood is not Our Blood! Count Lerehenfeld has said in the Landtag, that as a Christian he cannot hate the Jews! . . . *He* calls himself a *Christian*?' Hitler's voice rose. The audience, he knew, felt his hate. 'Jesus Christ – the First Christian! – recognised the Jews for what they were! Our Lord seized the scourge to drive out that brood of adders and vipers! Today, after two thousand years, I recognise more profoundly than ever before, that I too am a fighter for Justice! If Germany collapses, who will come after us?' The voice rose almost to a scream. 'I would be no Christian if I had no pity for our own people.' His voice fell to a whisper. 'Comrades, I alone will *change* all this!'

At that, there was loud shouting and prolonged applause in the hall. Roehm thought: the religious card always played well. Most of his audience were Catholics. They had been taught that the Jews killed Jesus Christ.

The Reds stood up and protested, loudly. Roehm's men began to manhandle them towards the exits. Fights began.

Hitler stood, in the spotlight, quite still, his eyes staring and his shirt soaked in sweat, while the undercover Freikorps men wrestled furiously with the Reds and eventually threw them out.

'Finally . . .' he said, holding up his hand, palm out for silence. He did not look at Drexler, or the committee men, or at anybody else in the hall. 'The name of this party is changed. It is now the National Socialist German Workers' Party!'

A voice in the darkness called out the word, on cue.

'The Nazi Party!'

The cheers in the darkness told him everything.

Hitler bowed his head to the noise. He did not look in the direction of Roehm, whom he knew to be sitting at the back of the hall.

The moment was not Roehm's or the Political Intelligence Unit's, or the Freikorps' moment, or the Army's moment.

This moment was something he had waited for, for thirty years.

The applause washed over him and it felt better than anything he had ever experienced before. A reaching out, a love, a fulfilment.

The moment was his, and his alone.

'What made you put in the bit about the Jews?' Roehm asked him later in the bierkeller, the bottle of schnapps broken open before them.

'It seemed necessary.'

Hitler did not want to talk. He felt euphoric, empty.

'I liked it,' said Roehm, looking at him curiously. 'The people liked it. Keep it in.'

Hitler nodded. He wanted to go home and sleep.

Home was now a two-roomed apartment in a lower-middle-class district in the Theirschstrasse, near the River Isar. He had, that week, with Roehm's blessing, officially left the Army. He now had no obvious means of financial support. But he guessed that Roehm (and the Army) would not let him down. It was not a good idea, Roehm had said, to be seen hanging around the Freikorps Barracks. They would meet, from now on, in civilian settings only.

'After tonight, you are a public figure,' he said, gently.

Hitler nodded. It was only his due.

'You need a new suit,' mused Roehm. 'You look awful, those cardboard shoes, that terrible dirty raincoat, that hat. God, you look like a failed actor!'

Hitler shook his head. 'I must continue to look poor. The people like that.'

'No new suit?' Roehm asked, bemused.

'No. But . . .' Hitler stirred. 'One other thing. We need a group of men, properly organised, to keep order in our meetings, or we will get our ideas over to nobody. We need a tough man to command the group.'

'No problem,' said Roehm lighting a cigar, and eyeing a fair-haired boy of sixteen in lederhosen, sitting at a nearby table. 'Emile Maurice?'

'Hasn't he been in prison?'

'Of course. All my friends have been in prison.' Roehm smiled at the boy, who smiled back. Cheered, Roehm said, 'We'll put Emile in charge. He's perfect for a strong-arm squad. What shall we call them?'

Hitler said, '*Ordnertruppe?*'

Roehm shook his head. 'We need something stronger. After all, we have a thousand workers now. All fully paid-up.'

'Why not call them the *Sturmabteiling?*' said Hitler.

'Storm Squad?' mused Roehm. 'Why not?'

Roehm drank more schnapps. The evening was turning out very well. He gestured towards Dieter Eckhart, who came across and sat with them. 'Dieter, tell Adolf he was good?'

'He was more than good,' shouted Eckhart, his eyes shining. 'He spoke like the saviour of Germany!'

Hitler merely nodded. He expected to hear no less.

Eckhart, after all, was just an intellectual. He had lent Hitler a lot of books and they had talked together a good deal. But the time for talk was over. He said, to Roehm, 'I want the S.A. to have uniforms. With an armband.'

Roehm looked startled. 'Uniforms? That might mean police trouble?'

'Nonetheless.'

Roehm looked at Eckhart, who nodded enthusiastically, and then asked, 'What kind of armband will they wear?'

'I have been doing some drawings. Trying to find the best thing for us.' Hitler took from his pocket – and Roehm noted his shirt was soaked with sweat – some papers with diagrams on them. 'I have decided on a red flag – the colour of blood – with a design in the middle. The same design will be on our armbands. We will use it everywhere. It will be ours forever.'

Roehm looked bewildered. Until now, he had been the one giving the orders. He looked again, at Eckhart, who raised his glass, in an amused way.

What form will this design take?' asked Roehm.

'A *hakenkreuz*. A hooked cross.'

Roehm shook his head. 'What is that?'

Hitler put on his dirty raincoat and stood up.

'A swastika.'

With that he nodded, and walked out of the bierkeller.

Roehm watched him go. He had a feeling something manageable had come to an end.

And something else, darker, different, had begun.

He did not know if he liked it.

All he knew was that he had no choice in the matter.

'You told me what we needed,' he said to Eckhart, 'now we have it.'

'He who rides a tiger,' said Eckhart, amused and as drunk as ever as he slapped Roehm on the back.

No choice, thought Roehm. No choice at all.

Inflation hit Germany like a blizzard.

Fortunes and savings blew away in the mad whirl of it.

The Mark had stood at Four to the Dollar in 1918.

By 1921 it was Seventy-Five to the Dollar.

The Government asked for a halt in the Reparations Programme.

The French refused, and occupied the Rhineland.

The Workers of the Ruhr declared a General Strike.

Not a wheel turned in the Ruhr.

By January 1923 the Mark stood at 18,000 against the Dollar, and by July of that year it was 160,000 Marks to the Dollar.

The German people knew that money didn't matter any more.

The bank account of a well-to-do middle-class man would not buy a bunch of carrots, or a few pounds of potatoes, or one pound of flour.

Germany was bankrupt.

It had to be somebody's fault.

Adolf Hitler said it was the Republic's.

'The Government goes on, calmly printing these slips of useless paper,' he declared in his next public speech in Munich. 'If it stopped that would be the end of the Government! Once the Printing Press stops the swindle will be seen for what it is!' He had held up his hand to quell the angry applause. 'The State has become a swindler of the *Volk!* We will no longer submit to it!'

The audience in the Hofbrauhaus waited.

The thin figure in his shabby blue suit flicked back the lock of hair from his forehead. They were all familiar with the gesture. Adolf Hitler was a known and respected political figure by now. He took no salary for his work. He was an ex-soldier. He was a good German.

'Comrades,' yelled Adolf Hitler, in his harsh, husky voice, 'what we must have is a dictatorship! With one man as Leader!'

They cheered him to the echo.

Wherever Adolf Hitler and his Brownshirts went, by lorry or motor car, the citizens of Munich stood and stared at them. Some in total bewilderment. Many thought that because they wore a full uniform, they were automatically official – such, Hitler knew, was the German reverence for a uniform, any uniform. Why, even ticket-collectors wore uniform. Alois, his old fool of a father, had worn a uniform all his working life. But his Brownshirts were not ticket-collectors or civil servants! They were Storm Squads, old Frontswine like himself, many from his old Regiment, and their duty was to put the fear of God into the Reds and anybody else who thought Germany was either finished or ripe to be handed over to the Commissars of Red Russia! The evening streets of old Munich would rapidly clear of pedestrians when their camions rumbled in, came to a halt on the ancient cobblestones, and the Brownshirts, carrying clubs and staves, leapt down and ran – always at top speed! – into the Marxist cellars and halls. It was bloody mayhem then, as Red and Brown battled to the death, with chairs and glasses overturned and beer-mugs broken and mirrors smashed and chairs flying and no quarter asked or given. Many of the Reds were ex-Frontswine too, and they could fight. Lenin had said, 'Terror is a Weapon of the Revolution!' Very well, thought Adolf Hitler, I will make such a Terror the Reds will be glad to end it!

The vast pitched battle in the Coburg, with thousands battling on each side, finally gave his Brownshirts the city. Stormtroopers with broken heads and arms and smashed noses and teeth sat in the crowded offices on the Sterneckerbrau afterwards, being bandaged, and given schnapps and beer. Their battered, grinning triumphant faces told Adolf Hitler everything.

The Police had not intervened. That was the most important factor of all.

Munich was his.

Roehm and the poet and newspaperman, Dieter Eckhart, sat in the spartan office of Major General Ritter Von Epp, Roehm's commanding officer in the Reichwehr, and pitched for Adolf Hitler. Epp commanded the thirty thousand men of the Freikorp, all ex-servicemen, while retaining his Army position and rank. For once, the shambling Eckhart was properly dressed, clean and sober. When he was sober he was formidable. So Roehm let him talk.

Eckhart came to the point at once and without any special respect. 'Herr General, what the Nazi Party needs is a newspaper. A means of getting our message across in a respectable way.'

Epp looked apprehensive. 'Newspapers cost money, to start. They cost money to run.'

'True,' said Eckhart, languidly. 'But an opportunity has presented itself.'

Epp looked at Roehm. Roehm looked down at his shining boots.

'The *Voelkischer Beobachter* is in trouble. As you know, it is simply a crude Anti-Semitic gossip-sheet. Nobody buys it. It is a weekly, but if we take it over on the cheap – as we can – we could turn it into an influential daily.'

Epp looked surprised. 'What kind of money are we talking about?' he asked.

'Two hundred thousand Marks and it's ours. Peanuts.'

Epp nodded. In today's climate, such a price was, indeed, peanuts. 'Who would edit it?'

'We will find a good man.'

Against his will, Epp was impressed. A Party newspaper sounded serious. As if the Nazi Party meant real business, not just breaking heads. 'Very well. I will find the money from the Army's Special Account. The buying money only. If you need more to run it, you'll have to find it yourselves.'

'We are also hoping for help from elsewhere,' said Eckhart.

'Adolf has a new admirer, Herr General,' said Roehm idly.

'Oh, who?' asked Epp.

'Frau Helene Bechstein. She has taken to inviting him to her famous parties. He has even been, as her guest, to Beyreuth.'

Epp was even more impressed. 'Will she donate money to the Party?'

'Yes, and even better, she'll get her friends to donate, too!'

Epp laughed at the idea of Adolf Hitler at one of Helene Bechstein's parties. 'How does our puritan friend find them?' he asked.

'I understand,' said Roehm, carefully, 'that when artichoke vinaigrette was served, Adolf startled the whole table by saying, "Frau Bechstein, I have no idea how to eat this thing. Will you please show me?"'

Epp laughed louder than ever. 'My God, at least it was a vegetable!'

Dieter Eckhart leaned forward seriously and asked: 'Would there be Army funds available for a new office for Adolf? At the moment he's trying to run the Party from that damp vault in the Sterneckerbrau.'

Epp stopped laughing. 'Where did you have in mind?'

'A place in the Korneliusstrasse. It's bigger and it's light and airy and it's relatively cheap. He also needs office-furniture for it, a desk, chairs, filing-cabinets and a woman to do the typing.'

Roehm intervened. 'Herr General. If the Party is to mean anything, the headquarters can't go on looking like a Red slum. If we are to attract money, we need a place to show to Frau Bechstein's friends and not feel ashamed.'

'Yes,' said Epp. 'I see that.'

'Putzi Hanfstaengl is coming in, did you know?' said Dieter Eckhart, lighting a cigarette without first asking Von Epp's permission.

'Putzi?' The Hanfstaengls were one of the richest and most influential families in Munich.

Eckhart nodded. 'Adolf is making him head of the Foreign Affairs Department. Putzi went to Harvard, you know.'

'Well, that is progress indeed,' said Epp, rubbing his head. 'The Hanfstaengls, well, they are a catch! Will all this not offend Adolf's Socialist principles? All this consorting with rich people?'

Roehm smiled. 'Adolf has got rid of Drexler and all the other so-called workers now. With them have gone a lot of Socialist ideas. Adolf is a realist. He knows we need money to run the Party. He will do whatever needs to be done.'

Epp nodded. 'Good. Very well. Consider the money for the office will be forthcoming.' He paused, puzzled. 'Do we still pay Adolf no salary?'

Roehm shook his head. 'He will not accept one. I arrange that he makes extra speeches to interested groups – businessmen, ex-soldiers' associations, whatever – and that he gets paid by them. Other than that, he will take nothing.'

Epp nodded, not entirely satisfied. 'Is there nothing he wants, nothing we can give him? After all, the fellow is like other men, he needs money to live, to eat, to drink, women.'

Roehm looked at Dieter Eckhart for an answer.

The poet puffed on his Turkish cigarette.

'He needs nothing. He eats rubbish. He does not smoke or drink. He lives in a near-slum. He works, one way and another, twenty-four hours a day.'

Epp looked incredulous. 'Then . . . why?'

'He wants only one thing, Herr General.'

'And what is that?'

'To rule Germany,' said Dieter Eckhart.

Epp stared at him. 'God forbid!' he laughed, looking at Ernst Roehm for support.

But Roehm did not laugh.

'I have a last question,' Epp said, uneasily. 'I don't know if you can answer it for me.' He paused, took out a packet of cigarettes, fitted one into his holder, and allowed his monocle to drop from his eye, a sign that the conversation was now off-the-record.

'Yes, Herr General?' asked Roehm.

'This business of the Jews? Naturally, I approve. Too many of them have got rich at the expense of the German people. Nonetheless, I am uneasy. We are not in the pogrom business.' By 'we' Epp meant the High Command of the German Army. 'I take it that this is merely an election-winning tactic, and that it will all, as it were, be brought into its proper perspective, once the elections are won?'

Neither Dieter Eckhart or Roehm answered at once.

The smoke from Eckhart's cigarette curled in the air.

'I mean,' said Epp, 'this is purely a political thing, no more than that?'

Roehm said, 'I think it is more. Much more.'

'I see,' said Epp. 'You are saying, are you not, that it is . . . something personal?'

Again, there was a silence. Dieter Eckhart broke it, his voice soft and almost awed. 'Whatever it is, it is what drives him. His words, when he talks about the Jews, are harsher than anybody else's. He hates the Poles and the Reds. So do we all. But the Jews . . . ?' Eckhart's voice tailed away. 'His attitude there . . . is pure hatred. Something so deep, that perhaps he doesn't know why, himself?'

Roehm said, 'I believe that to be true, Herr General.'

'Nothing physical is envisaged . . . ?' Epp asked. 'Against the Jews?'

Roehm shrugged. 'Why should it be?'

Epp felt this was as much of an answer as he was going to get. He put out the cigarette and stood up, in dismissal.

'Thank you gentlemen for coming to see me. You may rely on the Army's continuing support. Tell Herr Hitler that. And tell him we congratulate him on the things he is doing for the Fatherland. Auf Wiedersehen, gentlemen.'

When the two men had gone, Major General Ritter Von Epp sat down behind his large desk. He felt uneasy, and somewhat depressed.

Who would have thought it would come to this, that Germany would rely on a penniless ex-corporal to save them from the Marxists and the Social Democrats and all the rabble-politicians who would sell them to the highest bidder?

That, at least, he comforted himself, Adolf Hitler would not do.

Whatever he was in politics for, it was not money.

This business of the Jews bothered him, but, after all, the German people would have the last say in any of that, and he had great faith in the German people.

Properly led, of course.

Hitler sat now, in his new office in the Korneliusstrasse and talked to a stream of visitors, planned speeches and raids on Red political meetings, and dreamed. In the outer-office the typewriters clacked and there was a constant tread of heavy boots on the wooden floors. The uniformed men of the S.A. were part-timers, who came home from work (if they had any), ate their frugal suppers, put on their brown uniforms (tropical remnants from the German East Africa campaign) with the swastika emblem, and came to the Korneliusstrasse for their orders: a high-ranking party-comrade to protect; a meeting of the Reds to disrupt; whatever Rudi Hess, Adolf Hitler's new secretary, had on his list for them to do. Hess was a find. Totally self-denying, he lived for the Movement. An ex-officer – an ex-flyer – he was prepared to subordinate himself entirely to the Will of the Party. Any man other than Adolf Hitler might have been embarrassed by Hess's adoration. Adolf simply saw a man who would never betray him. Adolf felt safer. The old nightmares of death and loss still plagued him. He tried not to dwell on them but sometimes they broke through into his daytime thoughts.

Hitler's mind swung back to his most recent speech. He had, on impulse, mimicked the mincing manner of the Jew. That had been good, he was learning not to be solemn all the time. He had followed it with his denunciation. 'The Jew burrows into the Democracies, sucking the goodwill of the masses. He knows only the majesty of money. We must deprive the Jews of their privileges! They are a foreign Race!' He had suddenly found himself on a high note of anger and emotion. 'The final aim must unquestionably be irrevocable *entfernung* of the Jews!' That was it! The expulsion! The amputation! The word had just come to him. All was clear now. The Jews were his deadly enemies. 'They control everything,' he had shouted. 'They are the manipulators of Western Capitalism – the Bankers, the Rothschilds, the Barings. The Jews are also the *inventors* of Marxism!' Marx, Trotsky! We want none of them!'

The door of the office swung open. 'Yes?' Adolf barked.

Hess stood, apologetic. The man was almost too hangdog. All the fussing with medicines and the belief in the occult. Hypnotists and such. A bit of a health crank, thought Adolf Hitler, but a useful crank.

'I have a list of visitors. First, Herr Alfred Rosenberg,' said Hess.
He stood aside and Rosenberg entered.

Adolf did not rise. He gestured to a chair and Rosenberg sat.

Adolf studied him with some interest. Dark. Thin. Intense. He felt
some respect for Rosenberg. After all, the man was a qualified architect,
even if he did not practise the craft.

'Herr Rosenberg,' said Hitler, looking at a note on his desk. 'You left
Estonia, a German by blood, and took a degree at Moscow University.
You left there to avoid the Red Terror, and now you occupy a respected
position amongst the many thousands of White Russian refugees in
Germany? These are interesting credentials, but how can the Party use
you?'

'You have perhaps seen my articles, *The Tracks of the Jew Throughout
the Ages*? And *Red Plague in Russia*?' asked Rosenberg, hopefully.

Hitler nodded. He had read neither. In reality, the last thing he needed
in the Party was an intellectual. He wanted men of action. Men who
could *do* things. 'What is your philosophy, in a few words, Herr
Rosenberg?'

Rosenberg blinked, and his thin face lit up. 'I believe that the Religion
of the Blood is the only true Religion. It charts the rise and downfall
of whole Peoples, their heroes and thinkers. Their inventors and artists.
Only the blood matters, and it matters entirely. The Blood must not be
adulterated. The purity of the Blood is all!'

Hitler nodded. It was well put. Rosenberg went on, eagerly.

'The Germans are the Master Race – Aryans, the highest representatives of the Nordic Race! Our Destiny is to Rule Europe. We Germans
are against the Semitic-Latin spirit embodied in the Christian churches
and the Jews! Blood and Race is all that counts.'

Hitler said, 'We need the Churches on our side, at least for the time
being. We do not publicly attack them, no matter how we feel privately.
I need general articles for the *Volkischer Beobachter*. Can you do that?
Write a Philosophy of the Party?'

Rosenberg blinked and stared. He seemed to be having difficulty in
finding words. 'Of course. Based on your own Philosophy and words,
naturally.'

'Then see Eckhart. He's editing it. Say I sent you.'

Rosenberg blinked again. He stammered his thanks. Hitler cut them
short. 'Eckhart is responsible for what goes into the paper. Nothing else.
My old Army comrade, Max Amann, is the Business Manager. Go and
see him too, and tell him what I have said.'

Rosenberg left in a daze of gratitude.

*

Putzi Hanfstaengl introduced Hitler to Hermann Goering.

The occasion was social – a supper buffet at the Hanfstaengls' luxurious Munich apartment, the kind of occasion Adolf did not care for. He still felt, despite his new fame, a little overawed by these moneyed supporters and admirers. Goering was, after all, a national hero, the last Commander of Richthofen's Flying Circus, the holder of all kinds of decorations for bravery in the War, including the highest of all, the *Pour la Merité*.

What Hitler saw was a large, overweight but jovial man of his own age, but, unlike himself, totally at home in this or any other social gathering, profoundly confident of his prestige and his power. Married to a Swedish noblewoman, he had money of his own, but Hitler guessed, was searching for a role in life. The War had left heroes with very little to do. Hermann Goering would be a catch for the Nazi Party. Hitler had no aristocrats or Junkers in his close retinue. He did not like them. His old resentment of all formally-educated people still stirred in him whenever he heard their confident, braying voices. They were his friends, now, of course. But where had they been when he was starving in Vienna?

Nonetheless, Hermann Goering was worth having. Yes, indeed.

Surprisingly, there was no need to push.

Goering already had in his eye that expression Adolf had learned to recognise at a glance: that of a convert, somebody who had recently heard him speak in public.

Goering was clasping his hand in his own large, soft paws. He wore a dark suit but Hitler knew he loved uniforms and decorations of all kinds. 'My dear fellow!' Goering was saying, still holding onto his hands, 'this is a meeting I have longed for, ever since I first heard you speak . . .' He gestured to the tall, lanky form of Hanfstaengl, who was playing popular American music on, inevitably, a Bechstein. 'Putzi tells me you are looking for people who can be of use? Consider me an applicant.'

Hitler smiled and quickly removed his hand. He hated fleshy contact with anybody.

'I need every German who will give his heart to the Movement, Herr Major Goering.'

Hitler always spoke of the Movement or the Party, never of himself.

'And his money?' asked Goering with a smile. The smile transformed the massive face, the great hook-nose and formidable brow and chin. The man was huge and potent, thought Hitler, but he must learn who is the Boss. He said, 'Yes, that too. But any man who joins must realise that I am not running a debating society. You would, Herr Major, have to rub shoulders not only with the great number of decent German ex-soldiers in my ranks but with such people as Julius Streicher? Would that distress you?'

Goering laughed loudly. 'With his whips and his pornography? Well, I suppose I'd rather have him on my side than against me, but I am in no hurry to sleep with him!'

Plainly, Goering expected a laugh or at least a smile at that.

He got neither.

Hitler said, coldly, 'Streicher would be of no use to me in normal times. Too rough, too crude. Too rowdy. But these are not normal times, Herr Major Goering. Fifty intellectuals are not worth one Julius Streicher! Like most of my men, he is an ex-soldier, used to the bayonet and the rifle-butt. I need such men. Middle-class softies would bitch up everything, Herr Major.'

The use of the 'Herr Major' was sarcastic and Goering looked hurt.

'My dear Comrade,' he said, 'I have no quarrel with that! Find me a job and I will show you.'

Hitler looked around the soft, rich room with the soft, rich lights and the soft, rich people. He would rather be sitting in his poor room on the Thierschstrasse (bare lino, a few rugs, a table, a hard cot) organising the next attack on a Red meeting, than standing here. How dare they be so happy and talkative and comfortable while out-of-work ex-soldiers begged in the streets?

'I need a good organiser. Somebody ruthless, who does not have middle-class scruples. It will be rough work but I need a good, hard, military man to lead my Brownshirts.'

Goering looked startled. 'How much power would I have?'

'You will only hear from me when something goes wrong.'

Goering did not hesitate. 'You are the Boss. I have taken orders from people I respected a good deal less than I respect you.'

Hitler nodded. 'Good. Let us meet soon and talk details. Now I must go.'

Hermann Goering looked surprised. 'But the evening is in your honour and it has hardly started. Frau Hanfstaengl –'

'I have work.' Hitler turned away abruptly, spoke a few words of thanks to his startled hostess, kissed her hand, and left the room, not looking back or saluting anybody, not even Putzi, who had stopped playing the piano and was looking concerned that his honoured guest was leaving so soon. He unfolded his six-foot-four frame from the piano, and came hurriedly across the room.

'Adolf, please stay. There are people who wish to meet you!'

'Even so, I have work to do. We meet again soon, Putzi.'

Hitler bowed stiffly and left at once with his minder, the ex-wrestler Ulrich Graf.

Goering laid a fat, beringed hand on Putzi Hanfstaengl's arm. 'It seems he has a job for me, Putzi.'

Putzi smiled.

Ludendorf stood in front of the famous oil-painting of himself and Hindenberg, poring over war maps in the glory days of the Great War. He offered cigars and schnapps to Hitler, who declined both. The journey had not taken long. The party had a motor-car now, for Hitler's personal use, provided by a rich supporter. He even had a driver.

Ludendorf lived in a splendid villa at Ludwigshoehe, outside Munich. Tall stone-walls surrounded the building and its gardens. Hitler had the feeling that somewhere, a small guard of men, probably ex-soldiers, were hidden. Ludendorf had many enemies in Germany and had fled to Sweden at the Surrender? Now he was back. Hitler looked at the face of the victor of Tannenburg, Supreme Commander of the German and Austrian Armies in the Great War. Tall, blue-eyed, powerful, calm. 'It is good to meet. Tell me what I can do?' said Ludendorf.

'Herr General, you were once my Commander,' said Hitler. 'I hardly know what to say!'

Ludendorf smiled and lit his cigar. 'I am a Prussian officer but I have lost all faith in the ability of Officer Class to do anything at all. They simply sit in barracks and wait on events. Like you, I believe the Army was betrayed. I charge the Church, the Financiers, the Jews, with complicity in our defeat!'

'Then,' said Hitler, 'there is little I can tell you. Except one thing. The true enemy of the State are the Marxists. To crush them I need the Army. Not just the Bavarian Army. The whole of the German Army. You can get me that.'

'No,' said Ludendorf, slowly, 'but I can try. Perhaps.'

'Second,' added Hitler, 'we must break the Treaty of Versailles. For that, we need friends in International Circles. At least one country to support us. Mussolini, in Italy, I admire. He is doing for his country what we will one day do for ours. I believe you know him, Herr General? I wish to send an envoy called Luderke to talk to him. May we use your name?'

It was an innocent request, but Adolf Hitler knew that if Ludendorf gave his assent, he was hooked.

Ludendorf knew it, too. For a very long moment he regarded Adolf Hitler. 'Use my name, by all means. For all purposes.'

Hitler stood transfixed. For once he showed emotion. He grasped Ludendorf's hand and shook it.

Ludendorf smiled tolerantly. This man in a tail-coat with striped trousers and a ridiculous moustache and a Bavarian accent – could this be the man he had heard spellbinding the multitude in the Burgerbrauhaus?

Life was strange indeed.

But when only one horse was running, a wise man backed that horse.

He shook Adolf Hitler's hand, in farewell.

At Hitler's order Dieter Eckhart, in the columns of the *Volkischer Beobachter*, stepped up attacks against the Social Democratic Government in Berlin. The Government had declared a State of Emergency, and the Army had put down an abortive Red rising in Berlin. The Government now told the Bavarian Landtag to close down Hitler's newspaper and fall into line. The Social Democrats had the Army behind them in this. 'The Army in Berlin did not give a damn,' said Hitler, to his close associates, 'about the Army or the Freikorps in Bavaria. They had simply done a deal with the Government, to keep out the Reds! Very well! But *we* have done no deal! We must ignore Berlin.' Hitler walked around his office as he talked. Everybody else sat. 'Three men govern Bavaria. Kahr, the State Commissioner. General Otto Von Lossow, Commander of the Army. Colonel Hans Von Seisser, Head of the Secret Police.' He paused. 'To them, all three, the Army in Berlin has said: no more trouble or else!'

Goering, Hess, Rosenberg, Eckhart and Putzi all waited.

'They will obey Berlin?' hazarded Goering.

Hitler inclined his head. 'Naturally. They are order-takers and arse-kissers! But . . .' He smiled, contemptuously. 'Not content with privately kissing arse, they are now going to do it in public!' He held up a give-away handbill. 'They will, all three, be at a meeting at the Burgerbraukeller here in Munich, on the evening of 8 November.'

'So?' asked Goering.

'We will be there also,' said Adolf Hitler.

'All of us?' asked Goering.

'All of us, Gentlemen.'

He looked at each man in turn. Slowly, everybody nodded.

The Burgerbraukeller was crowded. Three thousand sweaty citizens of Munich crowded the hall. They were mostly of the lower-middle-class. None of Hitler's men were present.

For a very good reason.

A party was outside the Hall, some of them mounting a machine-gun at the entrance to the cellar.

Another armed party surrounded the cellar, barring all exits and entrances.

A third party, led by Adolf Hitler, broke into the cellar.

Hitler was wearing a frock-coat and striped trousers and he carried a revolver. His bodyguard, Ulrich Graf, pushed policemen out of his path as if they were children. Hess, also armed, guarded Hitler's back.

A Police Major stepped into Hitler's path.

Hitler pointed the revolver at his face.

The Police Major stood aside.

On the platform Kahr had stopped talking.

Hitler bounded up onto the platform and climbed swiftly onto a table, sending a water-carafe and glasses splintering to the floor.

He fired two shots from the revolver into the ceiling.

A shower of white plaster fell onto his black morning-coat.

There was instant silence.

Hitler broke it. 'This building is occupied! The National Revolution has begun!'

There was a loud muttering of voices followed by some shouted protests and many people stood up. But none made to leave, for now SA men in their brown, tropical-weight uniforms patrolled the gangways.

'No man may leave this Hall!' Hitler shouted. 'Absolute silence or I will machine-gun the gallery!' He paused. The hall was still. 'The Bavarian and Berlin Governments have been removed and a Provisional National Government has been formed! The Police Barracks is occupied! The Army Barracks is occupied! Both Police and Army march under the Swastika banner!'

Hitler waited for the Police Major to give a signal to his men. The fellow looked this way and that but did nothing.

Hitler flushed with triumph. He got down from the table and turned his revolver on Kahr, Von Lussow and Seisser. 'This way, gentlemen. We have work.'

As the bewildered but angry men went into an ante-room, the door held open by Hess, Hermann Goering climbed ponderously onto the platform, and held up his hand.

'Comrades,' he shouted, genially. 'Sit down and stop grumbling and drink your beer! Surely this is more interesting than listening to poor old Kahr?'

There were some laughs. The crowd knew and liked Hermann Goering.

'Drink up, I'll buy the next round. Yes, I *will*!' Goering shouted. 'And don't worry, there's nothing to be afraid of! Bavaria – and Germany – is just going to get a decent government for a change, that's all!'

'What is the meaning of this outrage,' Kahr demanded, as Hess closed the door of the ante-room.

'Don't talk to him,' said Lussow, staring coldly at Hitler. 'He is nobody.'

Hitler felt the blood mount in his temple. 'All three of you are promised excellent posts in the Government.'

'Government?' asked Kahr. 'We *are* the Government of Bavaria.'

'No. I am, and General Ludendorf is.'

'Ludendorf?' asked Lahr, 'how does he come into this mess?'

'I have told you,' said Lussow to Kahr, 'do not talk to him.'

Hitler yelled, 'Gentlemen, this is a revolver. It has four bullets in it. One for each of you . . .'

Kahr looked at the revolver. The fool was trembling.

'And,' said Hitler, 'the last one for me.'

'Shoot me,' said Kahr. 'Shoot yourself! I will do nothing.'

Hitler signalled to Hess to stand guard over the three men. Then he went back into the hall. He stood on the platform and gestured for silence. He still had the revolver in his hand. Ulrich Graf stood close by. Hitler shouted, 'The Bavarian Government is hereby dissolved! A new National Government is hereby declared! I myself will take over the direction of the Government. General *Ludendorf*. . .' He paused to allow the name to sink in and to let the surprised murmurs that greeted it subside. 'General Ludendorf will take over the leadership of all Bavarian Army units at once! He will then take over leadership of the entire German Army and organise a forced-march on that sink of Babel, Berlin!' Hitler took a deep breath, and lied. 'I need hardly add that Colonel Kahr and the others are now with us . . . As I am sure, you are!' He paused. 'Tomorrow my men and I will lead a National Government or we will all be dead!'

There was a long silence and then a burst of spontaneous cheering, led by the Brownshirts. Bavarians had had enough of effete Berliners. It was about time the boot was on the other foot. The cheering was loud and long. Hitler bowed and left the stage, ignoring a raised eyebrow from Goering, who stood at the side of the stage. He gestured, and Goering began in his easy, jocular manner to talk to the crowd, repeating what Hitler had just said. So far, so good.

In the ante-room he was surprised to find Ludendorf. The General looked flushed and angry. The man Hitler had sent to bring him from his house out at Ludwigshoeoe, was a Doctor Scheubner-Richter. Hitler could see from Richter's warning look that all was not well. Ludendorf hardly looked at Hitler, but Hitler did not care about that. Presumably, he had heard the cheering, at the mention of his own name?

Hitler said, 'You have no objection, Herr General Ludendorf, to taking over the Army Command?'

Ludendorf breathed in, deeply. He ignored Hitler.

'Gentlemen,' Ludendorf said to Kahr and Lussow and Seisser. 'Like you, I have been overtaken by events. Quite simply, it is a Great National cause we are all engaged upon. I ask you to co-operate with me.'

The three men looked at each other. Lussow, as an officer, came to attention, clicked his heels and nodded. So did Seisser. Kahr was a reluctant third. But how could any German deny a man like Ludendorf, the victor of Tannenberg, a national hero? He, too, nodded.

'Very well!' said Ludendorf. 'If you will all come with me onto the platform, we will tell the nation we are all together in this!'

'Very well,' said Kahr. 'But I am under protest at this way of doing things.'

The typical remark, Hitler thought, of a bourgeois politician. 'Your protest is noted,' he said. 'Now, let us go out and talk to them.'

The crowd cheered Adolf when he returned to the stage and introduced Ludendorf. They were less ecstatic about the other three men. Kahr and the others made non-committal statements of support which were drowned by impatient cheers. The audience was going wild now. Men jumped on tables and shouted. Others danced in the aisles. Only Hitler managed, in the total pandemonium, to silence them, and then only for a moment. He spoke with total belief: 'Comrades! I now fulfil the vow I made to myself five years ago, when I was a blind cripple in a military hospital. That was: not to rest until the November Criminals in Berlin had been overthrown! On the ruins of Germany as she is today a New Germany, a Germany of power and greatness, of freedom and splendour, will be born!'

The cheers and applause lasted for fifteen long minutes.

Hitler and Ludendorf stood there and accepted it all.

When it was over Hitler hurried back into the ante-room. All seemed to be going well. The big lie had worked. He was soaked in sweat and euphoric.

'Chief?' Hess was at his side.

'Yes?'

'There is fighting between Brownshirts and Army at the Engineer's Barracks. Shall I send men to quell it?'

Hitler debated. 'No. I'll go myself. He added, 'Nobody important leaves the Hall. Understand?'

Hess nodded.

Two hours later Hitler returned. By the time he got to the Barracks the fighting had stopped anyway, but he had stayed to talk to the men, Brownshirts and regular soldiers both, to assure them that he, Adolf Hitler, knew of their worries and their wishes, and would see that their children – and they themselves – lived in a better Germany than ever before! Until then, all Germans must work together! The soldiers had cheered him, and he had left in the Mercedes and driven back to the Burgerbraukeller. Storming in, and finding the crowd dispersed and the place empty of all but Brownshirts, he demanded, 'Where are Kahr and the others?'

'Gone,' said Richter, not meeting his eye.

'Gone?' asked Hitler, the blood rushing to his face.

Was it possible people were such fools!

'Herr General Ludendorf gave his permission,' explained Richter. 'I could not over-rule him. He is here if you wish to speak to him?'

Hitler sat in the ante-room for a long time, his head in his hands.

All that long night, he waited to hear good news.

When it came it was not very good.

Only the dependable Roehm had done his job, with his contingent of Brownshirts, hand-picked, rough and ready ex-soldiers: they had occupied the Bavarian War Ministry in the Schoenfeldstrasse. But the Telegraph Offices had not been occupied, and the word was that the Army Commander in Berlin had news of the Putsch and had sent orders to General Von Dammer, in charge of the Munich Garrison, to surround the War Ministry and arrest Roehm at once. And to arrest all others involved in the Putsch.

'I will go over to Roehm,' said Ludendorf, 'and see what I can do.'

Without looking at Hitler, he left the hall, accompanied by his aide, Major Streek. Then came news that Kahr and the others had gone back on their word, saying they had been blackmailed.

Hitler began to feel increasingly agitated, sitting impatiently in the Buergerbrau. He railed at Hess: 'Am I surrounded by fools? Why wasn't the Telegraph Office taken? We may have lost the day because of that! Do I have to do everything myself!'

Hess was used to Hitler's occasional murderous rages, but even he blanched. 'There is still time.'

'There is not time! Now we have lost the Army! And the Police will not be with us unless we have the Army! They will not fight one another. I wanted a Putsch, not a Civil War!'

Hess fell silent. There was nothing to say.

Hitler was still sitting, staring at nothing, when Ludendorf returned. It was now dawn. 'The Army have a ring of steel around the city,' he said. 'We have to act.'

'I do not want my Brownshirts to fight the Army and the Police, Herr General,' said Hitler. 'We all of us agree on one thing – that the Government in Berlin should be abolished!'

'Exactly,' said Ludendorf, unbuttoning his uniform collar. '*Herr*

Hitler, I do not think that the Army or the Police will fire on *me*!'

Hitler nodded, slowly, 'So?'

'I propose you and I march, as soon as it is possible, with all your Stormtroopers to the Centre of Munich, and take over the city.'

'But if the Police or the Army do open fire on us?' asked Hitler, hardly breathing.

Ludendorf shrugged. 'Then we are dead.'

At ten o'clock the following morning, under a swastika-flag, a column of three thousand Brownshirts in perfect step and good order, marched out of their rallying point, the gardens of the Buergerbraukeller, towards the centre of the city. Hitler and Ludendorf and Ludendorf's aide, Major Streek, were in the front rank. With them, swaggered Goering, as if this sort of thing happened every day, and Rosenberg, white-faced but determined. Doctor Richter strode on one side of Adolf Hitler, who held a revolver in his hand, Ulrich Graf, the minder, on the other. Behind them came the mass of men, many armed with carbines from Roehm's contraband arms-dumps. There were machine-guns on a truck, from the same source, complete with crews, bringing up the rear.

Hitler thought: better than nothing but not much against the Army.

A Brownshirt runner brought news that the Army had surrounded Roehm's forces in the War Ministry, but had not attacked, and seemed reluctant to do so.

So, Hitler reasoned: the Army were undecided. There was still hope.

The Police were certainly undecided. At the Ludwig Bridge they gave way when Goering told them he would shoot hostages if they didn't. There were no hostages, everybody knew that, but it gave them an excuse. They stood aside and the Brownshirts marched across the River Isar into the city.

By noon they were at the War Ministry, facing the Army.

Roehm was trapped in the building.

Troops and Brownshirts faced each other, silently.

What to do now, Hitler wondered.

Ludendorf solved the problem. Pointing, he said: 'We turn down here, into the Residenzstrasse! It takes us to the Feldherrnhalle! We will open the doors and let Roehm out!'

'It's narrow,' Hitler said. 'We'll be trapped in there if anything goes wrong!'

'We can't stand here doing nothing!' said Ludendorf, curtly. 'Forward!'

They were halfway down the narrow alley when the first shots were fired. Hitler had heard the cries of his supporters to the Police Detachment at the end of the alley – he himself had cried *'Surrender!'* Instead, the Police Inspector fired again: his men followed suit.

Richter, whose arm was linked in Hitler's, gasped and fell, taking Hitler down with him. All through the ranks of the Brownshirts men were falling, as the Police fired again and again. Trapped in the narrow alley, the Brownshirts were an unmoving target. Hitler, as he fell heavily onto the cobblestones, felt a terrible sharp pain in his shoulder and knew it was dislocated. Next to him, Richter lay in a pool of his own blood. Nearby, Goering was sitting, holding his side. Blood poured through his fingers. He looked indignant and surprised.

As Hitler lay, he saw Ludendorf, with his aide, Major Streek, walk, in a military fashion, straight towards the Police. The firing stopped. The Inspector raised his pistol, but he did not shoot. Looking neither to the left nor the right, Ludendorf walked on past him.

Hitler did not remember anything else after that.

He was hustled through the ranks of the Brownshirts and into a side-street by Max Amann and Dieter Eckhart. In the side-street a motor-car waited, with its engine running. Hitler and Amann got into the car. Walter Schultz, a physician to the Brownshirts, was in the car. Hitler sat, silently, and Amann looked at him. They were driven out of Munich at breakneck speed, through narrow lanes, to Putzi Hanfstaengl's country house at Uffing. Putzi had escaped. Nobody yet knew where or how.

It had all taken less than an hour since the Brownshirts entered the city.

Helene, Putzi's wife, three months pregnant, admitted Hitler, and asked no questions. Hitler's shoulder was hastily re-set by Schultz. He gave Hitler laudanum for the pain, and left at once.

Helene Hanfstaengl was solicitous, and pressed food and coffee on Hitler, but he drank sparingly and talked not at all. She said the Army were sure to look for Putzi here. Hitler made no reply. He sat in a black haze of hate and fury. Betrayed! The radio soon had a bulletin: the news was all bad. Ludendorf, after his foolish bravado, had been arrested and was now in police custody.

Hitler spent the long sleepless night hiding in the attic. It was bitterly cold.

All he thought about was betrayal. And the fact that he would be snuffed out, finished, his life over.

If necessary, so be it! He would die, fighting. He still had his Luger.

The following morning he heard a knock on the door. He listened for Helene. She walked through the hall downstairs and called out, 'Yes? What is it?'

Hitler waited for the heavy Army jack-boots to run up the stairs.

It did not happen.

He could hear Helene talking, but not the words. She did not seem too troubled and soon closed the door. A few minutes later she came upstairs with coffee and a roll.

'Who was that?' Hitler demanded.

Helene Hanfstaengl said, 'Drink this! Only that gardener fellow who works for Goering. He's a Party-member, I think.'

'What did he want?' asked Hitler.

'To warn Putzi that the Army had been to his employer.'

'Why should he do that?'

'Putzi has done him one or two favours. Got him the job. He's all right.'

Hitler put four teaspoons of sugar in the black coffee and sipped it. 'Any news of Putzi?'

'The fellow said Putzi escaped and the Army are looking for him. Also that Ludendorf has sworn never to wear his uniform again, or speak to any Army officer, after the Army's desertion of our cause.'

'Why?' asked Hitler, astonished. 'Isn't he in prison?'

'Yes, but apparently he's told newspaper reporters that, somehow.' Helene added, 'Adolf, you should run.'

Hitler shook his head. This was all nonsense. 'Frau Bechstein is to send a car for me tonight.'

'Where will you go? Austria? Vienna?'

Adolf stared at her. 'Vienna?'

'Why not? You're Austrian. They'd never send you back?'

Vienna, the place of his humiliation? To run back to *that*, like a rat? Never!

No,' he said. 'I will not run to Vienna.'

Helene looked hesitant, but said: 'I do not care about my own safety. I don't think they'll harm me. But I think that man is right. It is only a matter of time before they come here looking for Putzi. If they do, they'll find you. And what then?'

'Let us wait and see,' said Hitler, bitterly.

Helene told him that according to the radio, Goering had escaped, his wounds attended to, ironically, by a Jewish doctor in a nearby surgery. He was now in hiding, over the border, as was Hess, in Austria. Roehm, brave, pock-marked Roehm, had been taken. None of the Generals behind the Putsch had been touched.

Late that afternoon, they came for him.

The lorry containing a contingent of *Feldgendarmarie* with four Reichswehr officers in charge fumbled into the Hanfstaengl drive. The Leutnant hammered on the door. He greeted Helene courteously and said he understood she had a certain Adolf Hitler in the house? Helene told him to wait and slammed the door. She ran into the kitchen, to find Hitler.

He had the Luger in his hand and his blue eyes stared. 'Those swine out there will not take me. I'll shoot myself first!'

Helene grabbed the Luger out of Hitler's hand and threw it into a flour-barrel. As Hitler moved forward to retrieve it, she put herself in his way and cried out, 'Adolf! No! If you die the Party is finished. Germany is finished! There'll be a trial, but who knows what will happen there?'

The officer began to hammer on the front door again. Helene saw that he was shaking with fury. He did not seem afraid. 'Tell them that Rosenberg leads the Party in my absence. Max Amann is his deputy. Now, go and let them in.' As she moved, he added, 'Wait! If they kill me, and they may, thank you for helping me. You are one of the few.'

Helene wondered why the Army officers would want to kill him? They were Bavarians. They all hated the Republic in Berlin as much as he did.

The officers were, indeed, apologetic.

The Leutnent came to attention and apologised to Hitler for having to arrest him. His eyes did not leave the Iron Cross on Hitler's lapel.

Hitler stopped shaking and shouted at the young officer, 'You break your Oath! You connive at the defeat and despair of Germany!'

The young officer looked down at his polished jackboots and said nothing.

Hitler walked out, without looking back, and climbed onto the back of the lorry, refusing the offer of help from another, even younger officer.

Helene watched the lorry rumble out of the driveway.

Hitler did not look back.

XII

ADOLF HITLER stood in the dock.

He was dressed, as ever, shabbily but soberly, in his dark suit and unkempt collar and tie, his hair slicked across his pale face, the ribbon of his Iron Cross twisted into the buttonhole of his jacket. He neither looked at the President of the Court or at his fellow-conspirators.

All eyes were on him and he knew it.

The Special Court was sitting at the Old Munich Infantry School in the Blutenburgstrasse. It was 26 February 1924 and the court-room was packed. There was not a seat in the public-galleries, and the lawyers were crowded onto a few tables immediately below the dock.

Beside Hitler in the dock sat nine men, Ludendorf and Roehm the only really important ones.

There was a frightening level of noise in the courtroom.

Every newspaper in Germany had made the trial front-page news for weeks now. Every one of those newspapers had a representative in the courtroom. The *Frankfurter Zeitung* and the *Berliner Tagleblatt* men sat, frosty and disapproving, in high white collars and rimless spectacles. Journalists were here from every European newspaper of note. *The Times* of London man was here, bored and superior, in a splendid Savile Row suit. The *Washington Post*, *New York Times* and the *Herald Tribune* men were fretful and busy, in the American way. The London *News Chronicle* man, earnest and liberal, the *Figaro* man, hostile to anything German. The bald, fat man from Rome's *Observetta*, Mussolini's paper, looked approvingly at Hitler over his spectacles. The Austrian *Weiner Tageblatt* man was interested because Adolf Hitler was an Austrian. The man from the *Sydney Morning Herald* was wondering why the hell he was here anyway? Somewhere in the jumble of sweaty journalists, horn-rim glasses on the end of their noses, notebooks open, pencils poised, Adolf

236

knew, was the man from *Pravda*. Well, he would be given something to write home about. So would they all.

The charge against the Accused was High Treason.

A man could be shot for that.

Hitler knew that was unlikely. Possible, but unlikely.

For a very good reason: his accusers, Kahr, Von Lussow and Seisser had been, to everybody's knowledge, in the Putsch with him, until the last moment, when their nerve failed them! True or false, people knew that for fact. The Army, who ran this Court in real terms, had stood by, but had not fired on Hitler and his Brownshirts. Only the police had done that.

'Your opening address, Herr Hitler?' murmured the Prosecuting Officer. He did not seem hostile, merely curious.

The high level of noise dropped, at once. Adolf Hitler could not recall when he had ever spoken to so attentive an audience. 'Herr President of the Court, one thing has to be said first. Lussow, Kahr, and Seisser – who are witnesses for the Prosecution – had the same goal that we all had – to get rid of the Berlin Government. If our enterprise was actually High Treason, then they must be guilty along with the rest of us.'

There was a buzz in the courtroom. The foreign journalists had their heads bowed, writing furiously in their notebooks. 'I alone bear the responsibility, but I am not a criminal because of that! If today I stand here as a revolutionary, it is only as a revolutionary against the Republic in Berlin! There is no such thing as High Treason against the real November Criminals of 1918, who surrendered to the Allies and stabbed Germany in the back!'

Hitler sat down abruptly, to an approving buzz.

It was now Von Lussow's turn, as a Chief Prosecution Witness.

Hitler's speech had put him on the defensive.

He defended himself on the grounds that he would never have seriously associated himself with a corporal, and a badly-educated corporal at that. 'I was no unemployed drifter,' protested Lussow. 'I occupy a high position in the State! I should never have dreamed of trying to get myself a better position by means of a putsch!'

The Chief Prosecuting Officer looked pained. 'What were Herr Hitler's ambitions and *why* were you a part of them, if only for . . . a very short time? You *did* give him support at the Buergerbraukeller?'

Lussow went red, then white. 'We all did! But then we discovered that Hitler thought himself a German Mussolini and his followers thought he was the Messiah.' Lussow stood even straighter, a ramrod army fool thought Hitler, cutting his own throat in public. 'I looked upon Hitler as merely a Drummer, nothing more.'

The Court stirred, amused.

The Prosecuting Officer asked gently, 'A Drummer? A spieler? A talker?'

Lussow was grateful for the translation. 'Exactly! The more I heard him, the more I realised that his speeches are always about the *same* thing. I repeat, he is merely a Drummer.' Lussow looked at the Court, decided he had said enough, possibly too much, came to attention, and sat down.

The other defendants, even Roehm, made their defence low-key. Obviously, they thought that was the way to get a light sentence, possibly no sentence at all. Hitler sat, bored and silent, as the farce dragged on, day after day. Finally, the Chief Prosecutor, off-handedly and with obvious contempt, summed-up. 'At first it seems that Hitler did not want power, or said he did not. Later, he went beyond the position allotted to him.'

Allotted to him? Hitler sat up, a fury burning in him. He had taken full responsibility for the whole business! Now, the Officers' Trades Union was reducing him to an NCO, a spieler, a talker, a *Drummer*! He stood up and spoke, refusing to fall silent at the annoyed gesture from the President of the Court.

'Ambition?' he shouted, above the hubbub. 'For what? To be a *Minister* in some ridiculous State Government?' He laughed contemptuously, hand on hip. 'I do not think a Minister's portfolio is worth striving for. I do not wish to go down in history as a Minister. I might be in danger of being buried beside other Ministers.' The courtroom was shaken by a sudden gale of laughter. Hitler let it subside. Then, low, and with intensity: 'I will become the destroyer of Marxism. Believe me, I am going to achieve that task, and if I do, the title of *Minister* will be an absurdity!'

The courtroom was now absolutely still, hanging on his words. He leaned forward, his voice still low. 'A Dictator *wills* it! He is not ordered forward, he drives himself forward! The March to the Feldherrnstrasse was an act of history! The hour will come when the masses, who today stand in the street with our swastika banner, will unite with those who fired upon them. Not the Army, please note. The Army stands untarnished as before. The hour will come when the Army will stand at *our* side, officers and men alike.'

At this there was sudden loud applause in the Courtroom.

The President of the Court shouted furiously: 'Herr Hitler, I will countenance no rebuke of the Police!' But Hitler was talking again, as if at a public meeting, leaning forward, his tie awry, a dark stain of sweat showing on his shirt, his hair falling across his face. 'The Brownshirt army *we* have formed is growing. It will grow to battalions, to regiments, to divisions! The old German cockade will be taken from the mud, the old German flags will wave again!' Hitler paused, then lowered his voice, and pointed his finger at the President of the Court and his officials. 'It is not *you*, gentlemen, who pass judgment on *me*! It is History. That will judge us as Germans who wanted only the good of the Fatherland! History will tear to tatters the brief of the State Prosecutor and the sentence of this Court! *History will acquit us!*'

There was open cheering in the Court and pandemonium reigned. Men shouted at each other, journalists rushed for telephones in the hall behind the Court, the President banged his gavel, and Hitler stood there, no smile on his pale face.

And everybody in the Court looked at him.

Kurt Ludecke visited Adolf Hitler in the Landsberg a month after his successful meeting with Mussolini in Rome. He travelled an hour by train from Munich to reach the little city on the banks of the River Lech. The soft, rolling hills around the city were garlanded with flowers and trees. The ancient, mellow-stoned fortress, where Hitler was beginning his five-year 'Garrison Detention', looked more like a sanitorium than a prison. Indeed, he had heard that the regime was relaxed. Prisoners could walk around the town and the guards were not soldiers but wardens.

Ludecke, a convert to the Nazi Party, brooded on the ill-luck that had put that great German, Adolf Hitler, into confinement. A genial old warden took his name, checked the Visitors' Book and bade him follow into a wing set apart from the others. There-suddenly-Adolf Hitler stood, his hand outstretched in greeting. He was wearing leather shorts and a Tyrolean jacket, with an open-necked shirt. His cheeks were healthy and his blue eyes clear-looking. Ludecke, who remembered Hitler only as the nervous, twitchy, pallid-faced young orator in a rain-soaked mackintosh, took stock of him afresh. Hitler had put on a stone in weight and looked rested and relaxed. Surprised, Ludecke said as much.

'Yes, I am well. This is the first real holiday I've ever had in my life.' Hitler gestured Ludecke into a large and airy room, which looked out onto the soft country around the Landsberg. A bed, a table, books, flowers, a pile of letters on a side-table. Ludecke had a feeling of ease and relaxation. He shook hands with Rudi Hess, who excused himself and left the two of them together.

'Five years!' exclaimed Ludecke, as soon as they were alone. 'How did they have the nerve to give you that!'

'They think I am finished. But I have reason to believe that I may well be released very soon. Parole is possible for me, anytime after six months, and I have served four already.'

Ludecke hesitated. 'Things on the outside are not good. Rosenberg and Streicher disagree. Ludendorf is disaffected. Nothing gets done!'

Hitler said, with steel in his voice, 'I do not want anything to get done! When I get out of here we will have to rethink our whole strategy. Then I will have need of you, Kurt. Until then, I am grateful for your reports.'

'Mussolini is, I think, our ally, whenever we need him.' Ludecke knew that Hitler, as yet, did not see beyond Germany. Someday, he would have to. Ludecke had travelled, he was middle-class and his family had been moneyed, he knew there was a world beyond Germany. He also knew that Hitler did not, as yet, see himself as a European politician. One day he might have to.

Hitler ruminated. 'Germany's natural ally is England. Somehow, Germany must detach England from France.' He sat, and gestured to Ludecke to do the same. 'At present, the British Cabinet is anti-Hitler. Fortunately Mussolini is not. So, he must be cultivated. He is, after all, the first European Fascist ruler.'

Kurt Ludecke said, gloomily, 'If the Putsch had gone well, the Nazi Party could be ruling in Berlin by now.'

Hitler shook his head. 'We needed the Army and we did not have it. Now we must get into the Reichstag.'

'That could take a long time?'

'Perhaps. But it is the only way. The German People must be made to see that we are the only answer. We must get them to *vote* us into power!'

'We would need all kinds of people on our side? Industrialists, the Army, the Church even?' ventured Ludecke.

'Then we will convince them all.'

Ludecke nodded, but could not see it ever happening.

When Ludecke had gone, with a promise of further visits and reports, Hitler called Rudi Hess back into the room. Hess was the most faithful of all his staff. Had he not voluntarily returned from Austria where he had fled after the Putsch, to give himself up and share Hitler's captivity? In the sixteen weeks that they had all been imprisoned in the Landsberg, Hess had taken down dozens of hours of dictation from Adolf – most of it in the hours just before midnight when Hitler's thoughts ran clearest. He had been given the special privilege of staying up until midnight. The Governor had been very understanding, indeed deferential. He had, Adolf guessed, his orders, probably from the Army.

Now, Hess was waiting.

Hitler glanced at the last typewritten pages, picked up from the table.

Hess had taken down a quotation from Nietzsche, one Adolf Hitler particularly liked.

'The Strong Men, the Masters, have the Conscience of a Beast of Prey! Monsters filled with joy, they can return from a fearful succession of murder, arson, rape and torture, with the same joy in their hearts, the same contentment in their souls as if they had indulged in some student's rag. When a man is capable of commanding, when he is by nature a Master, when he is violent in act and gesture, of what importance are political treaties to him? . . . To judge Morality properly, it must be replaced by two concepts borrowed from Zoology: the *taming* of a Beast and the *breeding* of a New Species of Supermen!'

Hitler thought: how well put! The Leader is above the Mass – he has to be, to lead them at all! Morality was irrelevant, Virtue was irrelevant, to a great ruler, a Man of Destiny. To achieve that destiny, anything was possible, nothing was forbidden, *nothing*!

Alexander, Caesar, Napoleon – all were thinkers, politicians, *and* generals too. Why not himself?

'From millions of men, *One* Man must step forward, who, with Apolyptic Force will create commands written in stone for the Masses to Obey!' said Adolf.

Hess scribbled. Hitler looked out of the window.

'Some Event brings the Political Genius onto the scene. The World never wants, at first, to believe in this Political Genius . . . But he forces himself upon it! His Genius is not easily understood. The Leader works for aims only the few can see. His life is torn between the Present, which does not understand him, and Posterity, which will!'

Hess scribbled. Hitler paused, then: 'The German *Weltanschauung* – the German view of life! – must be *this*! One day Germany will be Greater than she has ever been before! Our Place in the Sun will be built on the superiority of our Aryan Race – the Caucasian Blood which has survived in its most perfect form in Germany and Northern Europe. We Germans must create a caste system or our pure blood will be diluted with that of the Mongrel Races – the Slavs, the Siberians, the Gypsies and the Jews!'

Hess bent over the paper. His pencil flew across it. Tomorrow, early, he would type it all up. Hitler took a deep breath. 'Germany *must* expand. But in which direction?' Hess waited. Hitler gazed out of the window. The Landsberg gardens were peaceful and full of spring flowers. This respite was a time out of War. Soon he would return to it. 'France is the mortal enemy of the German people.' he dictated. 'The French want a dismembered and shattered Germany. There must be a final reckoning with France! But a defeat of France would not give Germany *lebensraum*!'

Hitler brooded a long moment.

'Germany cannot be fobbed-off by such ludicrous things as African colonies! It must be fulfilled in Europe! Nature has not reserved Europe for any *particular* Nation! The soil exists for the people who have the Force – have the *Fist*! – to *take* it! Germany must expand to the East! . . . Against our Enemy, Russia!' He turned from the window. Hess was staring at him, eyes wide.

'Yes.' Hitler repeated in a whisper, 'Russia!'

Hess stared at Hitler for a long time, then wrote the word down.

The days in the Landsberg passed easily enough, with Hitler dictating each evening and the typewritten pages piling up on the table, annotated and corrected by Rudi Hess. Hitler felt that he had given the best possible account of his aims. It had not been necessary, strictly speaking, to tell the whole truth about his own life, if such a thing were ever possible anyway. For example, the German people would rather hear that his Father was a good, if strict, German, than that he was a drunken bully, who beat his sons without mercy. The German people would be impressed to hear that in his darkest days in Vienna he had laboured for his daily bread on a building-site. (Well, he had, if not for long!) He also referred often to God and to Religion, both of which he held in contempt. When Rudi Hess raised his eyebrows from time to time at something just dictated Hitler would reprove him. 'What I am writing *here*, Rudi, is not the Gospel Truth as some of our religiously-inclined comrades might call it, but a Sales Prospectus for the German People!'

Rudi Hess nodded, smiled admiringly, and wrote on.

Hitler read the German newspapers with growing gloom. The Nazi Press was banned, their offices closed. Rosenberg and Streicher and Ludendorf were arguing *publicly* about which way the Nazi Party should go. Adolf's name was not always mentioned in these reports. The worst news of all was that the Republic was weathering the storm. Inflation had virtually ceased. Reparations had been eased and American capital was flowing into the country. The French were leaving the Ruhr and no longer would there be any foreign troops on German soil. The so-called League of Nations was ready to accept the German Government as a member-country. The Nazi Party, without Hitler at their head, had lost a million votes at the recent election.

On his very last night in the Landsberg, Adolf Hitler went around his group shaking hands, with a word for each man, and then he packed his small case, containing a few old shirts and underclothes and the bulk of the typewritten pages of what would become *Mein Kampf*.

The title had been suggested by Max Amann, the manager of the

Nazi press, the same old Max, minus an arm! 'My Struggle?' thought Hitler. Well, it would suffice.

Hitler left the Landsberg four days before the Christmas of 1924. At Thierschstrasse 41, in Munich, everything was as before. The cold lino, the rugs, even his alsatian, Wolf. At first there was only Julius Streicher the Jew-baiter and his old comrade Hermann Esser. Then Rosenberg arrived, complaining quietly about Streicher. Ludecke came next carrying bottles of wine. He had good wishes from Mussolini. More comrades arrived, but there were gaps. Dieter Eckhart had died of drink. Goering was still recovering from his wounds, being pumped full of morphine in some expensive Swiss sanatorium, paid for by his rich wife. Ludendorf was not present. Nor was Roehm, who had resigned his Army commission and was said by Ludecke to be disenchanted with politics and looking for a military instructor's post in, of all places, Bolivia!

Hitler laughed at that. 'It is to escape more jail for his special weakness, I imagine!' But he was sorry to hear it. Roehm had been a dear comrade. One day he would be needed, again.

'The Party is in trouble, Adolf,' said Max Amann. 'We are scattered, disbelieved, laughed at! The Brownshirts are banned. Is there still hope?'

Adolf Hitler drank calomile tea and told them all there was a lot more than hope, there was certainty! The others listened eargerly, anxious to believe. There was much to be done, Hitler said. 'But from now on, no street-fights, not until we are ready. If it takes longer to outvote the Social Democrats and the Reds than it does to outshoot them, then so be it. As I have told Kurt Ludecke, we will hold our noses and get into the Reichstag!' Hitler felt strong and alive again. Words were over, it was time for Action! There was no midnight restriction here, as there had been in the Landsberg. He talked on and on, the firelight falling on the loving faces of his disciples.

Hitler's first public port-of-call after his release, was to see Dr Heinrich Held, now Prime Minister of Bavaria and the Leader of the Catholic Bavarian People's Party.

The jocular Held asked Hitler one question, sitting behind his vast desk in the Presidential Office. 'Do I have your promise of good behaviour? Remember, you are still on parole?'

Hitler was prepared to promise anything to such fools!

'Naturally, Prime Minister.'

Held nodded. 'Good.'

Hitler hesitated. 'There is one thing, Herr Held?'

'Yes?'

'I am interested in getting into the Reichstag by legal means.'

'That,' said Held, genially, 'is anyway an improvement.'

Like most Germans, he now thought of Hitler as a spent force and something of a crank, possibly a harmless one.

'In that event,' said Hitler, smoothly, 'you would not object to the *Volkischer Beobachter* starting publication again?'

The Prime Minister frowned. 'I'm not sure of that.'

'You are a Democrat. All voices must be heard? Even ones you don't like?' Hitler waited: 'Even mine?'

Held was a long time answering.

'Very well. But at the first sign of trouble . . .'

Hitler stood up. He had got what he wanted. It was time to leave. Pious, stupid, priest-ridden bigot, he thought.

'Of course, Your Excellency,' he said.

The next day Hitler wrote a front page 'leader' in the newly published *Volkischer Beobachter*. It was set under an announcement that read: HITLER SPEAKS AT THE BURGERBRAUKELLER TOMORROW NIGHT! In the article, he wrote: *Comrades, the Republic is still our Enemy! What are those gentlemen in Berlin doing? Why are they so prosperous? Why has every street-corner got a new Medical Centre? Why is Welfare money paid to almost any wastrel and shirker who goes to a Government office and asks for it? Why is public-housing in Berlin available at low rent for those in the right Trades Unions or members of the Social Democratic Party? Why do the so-called 'Social Services' of the Republic build theatres, sports-stadiums and fancy swimming pools and still have money to spare?*

Simple, Comrades!

All this money is borrowed! A billion dollars this year, a billion dollars next year – a billion dollars for ever!

Where does it all come from? From America!

How will it ever be paid back?

It won't be paid back!

How will the American loans to Germany Industry be paid back?

They won't be paid back!

This is not a loan to this Socialist Republic of ours, Comrades!

It's a Gift! It's a Charity!

What happens when the Americans grow poor, or don't give us money any more? Poverty! Worse than ever before!

'Those words,' Hitler had told his old comrade-in-arms Max Amann as they pored over the copy, lying on the desk in the newspaper office, 'will set the scene for the meeting at the Burgenbraukeller! Every seat is taken, Max! The old Party Faithful will be there!'

Max Amann looked at Hitler with concern. 'Adolf, remember, they can still close us down or shut you up. This Bavarian Government – Held himself – has it in its power to do just *that*!'

Hitler said, 'He'd never dare!'

Max Amann sighed. 'I think he would, Adolf.'

Max wondered at life. Who could have expected the young Army *meldeganger* to rise to this? Still, Adolf had given him a job. 'I wish you'd rewrite bits of *Mein Kampf*! Adolf, it's dull, a lot of it! I'd hoped you'd give us the story of the Putsch – that's what readers want to know about, not . . .' Max Amann hesitated, then, what the hell, he'd once been Adolf's Sergeant, for Christ's sake! – 'Not quite so much philoso-phising?'

'Max,' Hitler said, gently, 'sell the book! That's your job!'

Max Amann thought: I really wonder how many people will buy the bloody thing!

He was right that Prime Minister Held would not close down the *Volkischer Beobachter*.

He didn't.

But when Hitler spoke to the Alte Kampfers in the Burgenbraukeller that night, Max Amann's heart sank.

Sweat glistening on his forehead, on the high plane of ecstasy and word-drunkenness that he always attained, quite suddenly, after he had been speaking for fifteen or twenty minutes, Hitler cried, 'Comrades, the last time I stood here I had a Luger in my hand and I went out of that door not knowing whether I would be alive at the end of the day! My dear Comrades were wounded in the Battle for the Streets – and you must listen to me when I say that it could happen again! But not yet. For now, we must concentrate our energy against our greatest Enemies – Marxism and the Jew! It is a War to the Death! Either we step over their bodies or they step over ours!'

A roar of angry approval answered that remark, but Hitler held up his hand.

'But I am not going to be *illegal* . . . You know *me*!'

The audience roared and laughed . . . 'I would not *dream* of being illegal . . . I would not dream of fighting against the Republic, now I have given my word on the matter, *would* I?'

The Alte Kampfers slapped each other on the back, and choked over

245

their beer. Hitler spoke, in a low vibrant tone. 'Comrades, in this struggle there are only two possible outcomes. Either the enemy pass over our bodies or we pass over theirs! If in the struggle I should fall, the Swastika banner shall be my winding-sheet!'

The Alte Kampfer rose, roaring and applauding. Hitler stood drenched in sweat in the spotlight.

Max Anamm sighed.

There was no talking to Adolf. None at all.

The next day Adolf Hitler was banned, by Presidential decree, from public-speaking anywhere in Bavaria.

Max Amann was only relieved that the ban did not extend to his newspaper.

That, at least, was something to be grateful for.

In 1925, Ebert, President of the German Republic, died.

The General Election let in the Nationalists and their nominee, General Hindenburg.

Adolf Hitler was downcast. 'The doddering old fool is a Conservative, a Nationalist, the greatest General – some say! – of the War. But he is no use to us. The Socialists we can fight. The Reds we can fight. This old gentleman we can't fight! For the time being we must wait, build up the Party and be prepared.'

Hitler, prohibited from public speaking, sat in his room and wrote articles in the *Volkischer Beobachter*. Max Amann called and told him that *Mein Kampf* had sold 10,000 copies in the first year. Hitler said, drily, 'I now describe myself on my Income Tax Returns as a "political writer"!'

Hitler was reorganising the structure of the Party. 'I'm going to split Germany into *Gaus* and put one prominent Party member – a *Gauleiter* – in charge of each, with full power of action, answerable only to the Leader. I have learned from the Marxists: keep your power by giving it away. We must also form a Youth Section of the Party, the *Hitler Jugend*. It is important to get the young people into the Party!'

Hitler worked long hours in the hot room over the next few months, the days punctuated by visits from his lieutenants, each one more anxious to please than the last.

'Some think only of themselves. Strasser for one,' said Max Amann.

Gregor Strasser was a member of the North German branch of the Party, the section with Berlin as its centre, an ex-officer with an Iron Cross First Class and had a seat as a Nationalist in the Reichstag. Hitler knew that Strasser's ideas were half-socialist, that he wanted the Nationalisation of German factories and promoted other left-wing

246

idiocies, but Adolf was conciliatory when they met, because he needed Strasser in Berlin. The man was a good speaker, and a first-rate organiser. He even ran a newspaper in the capital, the *Berliner Arbeitzeitung.* Strasser was, he reflected, his only rival for power in the Party.

What did Gregor Strasser have that made him a threat? The answer came to mind at once: Josef Goebbels!

Goebbels had masterminded one of Hitler's few defeats within the Party. The point at issue was whether the Nazi Party should vote in the Reichstag that the Royal Families of Germany – and there were many princes and princelings still around – should have their properties and riches taken away from them.

Hitler, who was being subsidised by many such nobles, voted that 'No Action' be taken against the Royal Princes.

Strasser and Goebbels, who were hotly socialistic, voted 'For' and swung the Party Conference, and the vote. Goebbels, a small, dark, agitated clubfoot, waved his order-paper excitedly and yelled, 'I demand that the petty bourgeois Adolf Hitler be expelled from the Nazi Party!'

Hitler did nothing in a hurry.

Six months later, he summoned a Party Conference in Blumberg, in the south of the country, on a weekday, when he knew that the Berlin and Rhineland delegates who supported Goebbels and Strasser would find it impossible to attend, being wedded to jobs and professions. In the event, only Strasser and Goebbels represented the Socialist wing of the Party. They were alone in a sea of Hitler's own supporters, Gauleiters who were full-time servants of the Party. Hitler argued almost all day, to the rapturous applause of his supporters, that Strasser was wrong to think of the Party as some kind of Marxist movement – with banks and businesses Nationalised, like the Reds would do it! Hitler told the Conference that what he envisaged was: 'Two Germanies! One, the Germany we all know – with the Big Industrialists in place, going about their business as they always have. With the Army defending Germany's frontiers, exactly as it always has. That is the State. As we have always known it . . . But!' . . . And here Hitler was looking straight into the fanatical face of Josef Goebbels, as he spoke . . . 'What I *will* create will be a State within a State! There will be a Nazi Army, only it will be called the Brownshirts. There will be Nazi education for the young, only it will be called the *Jungvolk.* There will be a Nazi Political Office, a Nazi Bank, Nazi newspapers and magazines, and a Nazi propaganda machine. We will let the Army and the Church and the Industrialists keep their power, why not? But we will have *our* power too, and one day, our State will take over *their* State. Until that day, Strasser's talk of Socialism is nonsense. We need all Germany on our side – even the

Workers who now belong to the Communist Party! Recruit them when you can, they are disciplined and can serve us well. *That* is as far as I am ready to go, Comrade Strasser, down the Socialist road *you* are so eager to tread.'

Hitler sat down, soaked in sweat as usual, to thunderous applause and a standing ovation. Amazingly, one of those standing, with eyes shining, was Josef Goebbels himself. When the din had subsided, Goebbels shouted in a clear, cold and penetrating voice, 'I renounce my previous position! I am now totally for the policies of Adolf Hitler!'

Hitler promptly shook his hand, and at once tried to conciliate Strasser. 'The Party needs you as a full-time agitator. Your talents are too many for us to neglect you!' At this Strasser gave way too, and Hitler sat next to him for the rest of the day. He could afford to be magnanimous. He had got what he wanted, and even more important, he had got Josef Goebbels. The man called him *Fuhrer* now!

Hitler pondered, back in Munich, sitting in his office. How to consolidate the loyalty of the brilliant, bitter, young university-educated intellectual?

He made him Nazi Gauleiter of Berlin.

Goebbels, sated with power, confided his thoughts that day to his latest girl-friend, Anke Helhorn, in their luxurious bedroom at the Adlon Hotel. Lying on the heavy silk eiderdown of the massive bed, the intense little man said, 'I bow to the greater man, the political Genius! I bow to Hitler, with the manly, unbroken pride of the Ancient Norseman to his Lord! He is greater than all of us! He is the instrument of the Divine Will that alone shapes History...' He was so carried away, Anke reflected, that for once, he forgot about sex – and she had put on her new black silk underwear for him, too. 'I don't think you love me,' she told Goebbels, sulkily, more than half-serious.

'No?' He looked at her, irritated.

'You're in love with Adolf Hitler?'

Goebbels smiled. He did not deny it.

XIII

ADOLF stood and admired Geli's room.
Why not, he had furnished it himself?
Geli stood next to him, in her dirndl skirt and white silk blouse and cried out, ecstatically, 'A room all to *myself*! With a writing desk! And such lovely objets d'art!' She laughed, mock-roguishly. '*And* embroidered bed-sheets! Uncle Adi, you're a rascal!' She gazed round the room with huge delight. 'Oh! You're so good to me!'

Adolf smiled, feeling pleasure at her pleasure. Although he was only her half-uncle she was, now, also his ward, by deed of Law. Her well-being was his responsibility. It was his duty to do such things, provide this room for her. Adolf looked at Geli and thought that he had never seen any young girl so perfect in form or face. So fresh and young and German! So unaffected and enthusiastic and open. So *pure*! So unlike the sophisticated ladies who flocked around him at his villas on the Obersaltzberg, to whom he was pleasant and courteous, naturally. So different from the strumpets at Nuremberg, who brazenly opened their blouses so that, passing by in the Mercedes, the Fuhrer could see their beautiful breasts.

Adolf supposed it was only to be expected, this sexual lure of a Leader-figure. A *Fuhrer* had to be unattainable! As poor, dead Dieter Eckhart had so truthfully predicted, a leader who was not married would attract the women. A man who lived without a wife also gave a signal of total seriousness and commitment to the rank-and-file of the Party. A Fuhrer could never afford to shatter that image. He had to be different from all other men.

They had to need him.

He must have no need of anybody.

'And pastel green walls! And a lovely green quilt!' Geli sat on the bed and bounced and the dirndl skirt rode up and showed her slim, white, beautiful legs, but Adolf knew that it was an accident, an innocent gesture, not a mature woman's sexual display. Geli was eighteen years old and yet life, in Vienna with her mother, Angi, had not spoilt her in any way that he could see.

Now she stood up again and pirouetted around the centre of the room. Then she looked at the wall above her bed. 'There's a painting here? What is it?'

'A Belgian landscape. I did it during the War. It's only a small watercolour.'

'Oh, but it's lovely, Uncle Adi! You should paint much more, you're so talented!'

'I have no time these days. My duties take up all my waking hours.'

It was not strictly true (he knew he was often lazy, his Viennese *Schlamperei* again!) but Adolf liked to think it was.

Geli pouted and threw her arms around him, in a completely natural and unselfconscious way. Her firm young breasts pressed into his chest but he did not feel, with her, any of the embarrassment such a gesture from a mature woman would have caused him.

'Oh, Uncle Adi, the room's so *wonderful*! Would you believe, it's the first room I've ever had to myself! I've always had to share with Friedl!'

Adolf smiled. 'Well, now you don't. Friedl will be at the villa most of the time. This is all for you!' He detached himself gently from her embrace.

Geli pouted again: 'Don't you like me kissing you?'

'Of course I do. But other people might not understand, you know.'

'What is there to understand? You're my dearest Uncle Adi, and if I want to kiss you, I will, so there!'

And she kissed him again, this time on the lips. It went through him like an electric charge, but she was laughing.

'What is so amusing?' he asked, stung by his sharp physical reaction to her.

'Your moustache. It tickles!'

Adolf laughed, and recovered his poise. 'Soon everybody in Germany will wear one just like this, I sometimes think. Most of my Brownshirts seem to cultivate one!'

'Not like yours, though. Yours is special.'

Adolf moved away towards the window. He was trembling and he did not want her to see that. His own feelings were in danger of getting out of control. That would not do. No hint of scandal was permitted a man who one day hoped to be Leader of the whole of the German Reich!

He took a deep breath and looked down into the sunlit Printzregent-strasse. It was certainly a splendid thoroughfare, one of the finest in

Munich. Below, the long, black Mercedes stood, a gift of the makers. Emil Maurice leaned stockily against the shining bonnet, in his chauffeur's uniform, smoking a cigarette. Emil, an ordinary man, had freedoms he could never have. Emil had his beer, his cigarettes, his women. Adolf had advised Emil to regulate his life, marry and have sons for Germany, but Emil had just laughed. Dear Emil, they had driven many thousands of miles together, to rallies and meetings, all over Germany. Never any trouble. Emil was conscientious and did his job well. If he was an ex-convict, what did it matter? He was an ex-prisoner himself. Emil would work all the harder for the Party that gave him a chance in life.

'Uncle Adi, what are you thinking about?'

He said, 'What will you do with your life, now you are here in Munich?'

'Oh, I don't know.' Geli threw herself sulkily on the bed, and the dirndl skirt rode up again. Adolf averted his eyes, painfully. He could not easily identify his feelings towards Geli, but they were, he knew, not unlike those he had felt for the girl Mitzi Reiter, six years before. Mitzi had been sixteen. Mitzi had wanted to make it something it wasn't, love and sex and eventually – so she had tearfully confessed – marriage. Again, this wish to *own*, to bind a man to her, that all women seemed to hide, behind their hot sexual rut! They had once taken off their clothes, he and Mitzi. She had been the instigator, but it had been a foolish, unconsummated business and he had decided that there must be no more of it. What if it got out?

Sixteen years of age, that was all Mitzi had been.

But all woman, breasts, arse, parted-lips and legs.

It had sickened Adolf Hitler. Mitzi had reminded him too vividly of the young village girls his father, Alois, had flouted and bedded, all those years ago in the Waldviertal. The thought that he might, in that way, be anything like his father had been was more than he could bear. He had finally told Mitzi that there must be no more secret meetings, no more kisses and embraces, no more of *this* nonsense!

They would not meet again.

A week later Mitzi had been found with a clothesline round her neck, attached to a high, brass door-hanger. An attempt (but botched) at strangulation and suicide. She was alive when her brother-in-law found her. It was providential that it was not some stranger who might have gone to the newspapers with the story. That would have looked fine in one of the liberals rags like the *Frankfurter Zeitung*! What a field-day the pro-Marxist journalists would have had with *that*!

Max Amann had arranged for private medical treatment for Mitzi, and had – most thoughtfully – obtained her tearful confession, before a sympathetic Notary, that nothing of any scandalous nature had ever transpired between Adolf Hitler and herself.

He had not seen Mitzi Reiter from that day to this.

Geli, on the other hand, who lived under his roof, was his ward, and who was the very personification of innocence, there was no possibility of any kind of scandal. He was her Uncle – well, her half-uncle.

His Father, Alois, had after all, married his half-cousin!

The thought just popped into his head.

Horrified, he shook it away.

'Is anything wrong?' Geli was lying back on the bed. It was a hot day. The Fohn, the hot summer wind that blew through the city and was supposed to make women rabid and men murderous, was stirring the lace curtain of the bedroom. Adolf sighed for the cold December day on which he had first seen Geli, had first experienced the lurch in his stomach at the very sight of her, had discovered his sister Angela's eyes on him – wide, and he thought, knowledgeable – as she looked from one to the other.

'You quite like your little niece, Adolf?' Angela had asked, gently, later. 'She's quite grown-up, you know! You can treat her as . . . a woman? She's no longer a child.'

Adolf had answered, shortly, 'She's unspoilt, let her stay that way. Keep her away from youths, who have only one thing on their minds. She's too good to throw herself away on some callow hobbledehoy.'

Angi had laughed. 'Don't worry, Geli won't do anything like that. She's far too smart.' She had looked up from her sewing. 'She is very fond of you, you know, Adolf?'

'Well, so am I fond of her.'

Angela had smiled and looked directly into his eyes. 'Yes, I know you are, Adolf.'

It was not a warning, Adolf thought, uneasily.

It had seemed more like some kind of an invitation.

Geli was looking at him with wide, dark eyes: 'Uncle Adi, I do have a good voice, you know?'

'You have a pleasant voice, certainly.'

Adolf knew what was coming. He hardened his heart.

'I really think I ought to have my voice trained?' Geli was now at her most cajoling and he had to refuse to be cajoled. It was hard, but he had to do it. 'I'm not going to get anywhere as a singer, unless I do!'

Adolf looked at her, miserably. Didn't she understand that, if she started a career in Music she would be lost to him? Such an undertaking would send her away, sooner rather than later, to Vienna and Berlin. The life of a professional singer was that of an artistic nomad. Of course, being young and beautiful, Geli imagined that her youth and loveliness would open all kinds of doors.

'Oh, don't be so stuffy and tiresome,' said Geli, stretching out on the bed, her long beautiful legs – like some Staatsoper prima-ballerina! – stretched across the quilt. 'Who do you think?'

'I will have some enquiries made,' said Adolf, thinking: well, at least I have promised the girl nothing.

'Oh, I do love you, Uncle Adi,' whispered Geli, lying back on the bed, her eyes wide. 'You are so good to me.'

'It is my duty,' said Adolf, stiffly.

'Oh, don't say it's just duty,' laughed Geli. 'Say it's . . . love!'

Love?

The word hung in the room like a threat.

What did his life, as he had lived it until now, as he expected to live it for ever, have to do with that emotion?

Damn little!

He had not loved anybody since his mother had died.

He was forty years old now.

Geli was eighteen.

Adolf shifted his ground. 'You are very dear to me, Geli. You know that. You have brought youth and happiness and beauty into my life, when I thought it had all but gone.'

Instantly, her approach rebuffed, Geli was flighty, mischievous: 'What about Pola Negri then? Didn't she make you happy?'

'She was a famous actress. I admired her work, that is all.'

'Emil tells me you were . . . fond of her?'

Adolf shook his head. 'Emil tells the truth. She was just a friend. That is all.'

'Emil hinted . . . more?'

'There was no more.'

Adolf felt a surge of anger. What was Emil Maurice thinking about, talking this way to the girl? No doubt just innocent chat, as he took her to shop for clothes in Munich, but really, Emil should know better.

Perhaps, Adolf thought, he should stop giving Geli money?

Geli shopped for clothes around the expensive stores of Munich. Geli loved clothes, and Adolf paid for them. He could not refuse her that. Besides, Geli would say, tossing her thick black hair, 'I'm your special girl, aren't I? I have to look good, don't I? People will notice!'

'You're my half-niece,' Adolf had said. 'But it is true, you need to be well-dressed or people will indeed notice.'

They had noticed already, some of them, as he well knew.

Max Amann had even remarked on it: 'I trust we don't have another little incident like Mitzi on our hands, Adolf?' Adolf had flown into one of his rages about it and Max had gone pale and apologised and said that all he had in his mind was what was best for Adolf and for the Party, and for Germany.

Hitler had retorted that he, the Fuhrer, knew what was best for Germany.

Geli was looking at him, a shade apprehensively. 'Uncle Adi, Emil didn't mean anything. We were only talking.'

Adolf nodded. 'Emil is very loyal. A good Party man.' Nonetheless, he reflected, Emil had not shown proper caution in discussing his private affairs. He would need to reprimand Emil about that.

Can I go to Herr Vogel for music lessons, Uncle Adi?' asked Geli. 'Vogel is a Party member.'

'That does not make him a good music teacher,' said Geli sulkily.

'I'd rather go to Warburg! Everybody's going to *him*!' Geli was impatient, she had tired of the game. 'Really, I'm sure *he'd* do wonders for my voice.'

'Warburg?' Adolf frowned. 'Is he a Jew?'

'I've no idea,' answered Geli. 'Does it matter?'

'Of course it matters!'

Geli shrugged and turned away, sulkily, on the bed. The silk of her blouse tightened around her breasts with the movement. Adolf felt something akin to pain.

'I'm sure Vogel is fine. You must go to nobody Jewish. I forbid it.'

'Oh, Uncle Adi, don't be such a stuffy-boots!'

Adolf Hitler shook his head. Geli didn't care about politics.

Geli cared about life.

It was then that Adolf found himself saying something he did not intend to say.

'Well, make enquiries and find out what Vogel's charges are, and what kind of tuition he proposes, and then we'll see.'

Instantly, Geli was off the bed and in his arms.

'Oh, Uncle Adi, you are the kindest, *sweetest* person!'

Adolf was used to this demonstrative behaviour – it happened every time he did anything for her – but the effect was always the same. He melted. Geli, like himself, had a Viennese accent, but on her it sounded sweet, cute, not husky and provincial, as his own did. But it did sound familiar, which was reassuring: Geli was, like Angi, family. He had been away from his family a long time, but it was prudent to be distant with blood-relations. Families were often untrustworthy, wanted favours (look at Napoleon's family!), but his half-sister, Angi, was not like that, thank God.

Adolf took Geli's hand (so soft, so *young*!) and said, 'Come! Your Mother will be wondering where we are!'

'Mutti knows where we are,' said Geli, rather crossly. 'She's all right!'

'We should go and have some coffee and cakes!'

Geli laughed, indulgently. 'Oh, you and your cakes! They'll make you fat, Uncle Adi!' And she tugged at his waistband.

Adolf regarded his slightly swelling stomach with concern. 'I must not look fat, when good Germans are still thin, not from choice but from lack of food! We still have far too many unemployed men in our midst.'

'What?' asked Geli, coolly, 'about the unemployed women?'

'They should find themselves husbands,' said Adolf, leading the way out of the bedroom. 'Preferably ones who have a job.'

'Honestly,' protested Geli, 'I think you really believe that!'

'Of course I do,' said Adolf.

Angela Raubal rose to her feet as they came into the lounge. She took her spectacles from her nose. That was the trouble with being over fifty years of age, the looks started to go. One's bargaining power as a woman went. Not that it had ever meant all that much in her marriage to Raubal. Raubal had loved drink and what drink could do for him, which sex or love seemingly could not do.

'Here we are,' Adolf said. 'Where are the cakes?'

Angi had watched Adolf's rise from afar, and wondered at it. Adolf was obviously a great and glorious success – *how had he done it?* –and he was, like a good brother, well, *half*-brother, generously allowing them to share in it. Surely, God was good. Angela crossed herself, in her mind (Adolf did not care for overt religious gestures) and offered up a quick prayer that nothing would ever happen to send them back to the near-poverty, scrimping and saving and the watching of every pfennig, that they had endured in Vienna, before Adolf had sent for them.

Angela looked at the room with love. If only she could spend all her time here. The Obersaltzberg was lonely even with Friedl for company and sometimes a bit frightening, with the heavy cloud hanging motionless above the mountains. Angela, a city person, missed the bustle of street and shop. The whole apartment was a dream of riches. Deep, plush armchairs; sofas; lounge-chairs; a pedestal-table; an antique writing-desk; Ormolu chiming-clocks in gilt and gold-leaf and porcclain; Oriental carpets; heavy, velvet curtains at all the windows; many Greek and Roman marble statuettes, some of nymphs and rather 'advanced' for her personal taste. Angela had not selected any of these items. Adolf had done it all, even the furnishing of Geli's room.

Particularly Geli's room.

Angela looked around the room and felt gratitude.

They were all three of them so grateful to Adolf.

And Geli was not grateful for many things.

Here, magically, in this beautiful apartment that Adolf had provided for them, Geli could, if she played her cards right, have almost anything her heart desired. Angela nursed a hope in her heart that this happy life she now so much enjoyed (as the Fuhrer's beloved Sister, she was acknowledged everywhere) would go on for ever.

That could happen. If Geli wanted it.

If Geli got even closer to her Uncle?

If, dare she say it, one day, when Geli was a little older and Adolf more relaxed (and with, hopefully, still no woman in his life, despite all sorts of avid women, society-bitches mainly, throwing themselves at him all the time!) then maybe, who knows, she could hardly dare *breathe* it . . . But a woman knew her own brother and she knew Adolf. She knew things about him that he probably didn't even know about himself. She knew, had always known, his *feeling* for innocence, for youth, for vulnerability. Again, she hardly dared to breathe it, Geli had *all* these qualities. Or *looked* as though she had. Geli was also wayward and capricious, as any young girl with her looks was likely to be. There was no final accounting for Geli's behaviour. So Angela could only continue to hope and pray nothing would go wrong. To pray, if only silently, and to herself!

Geli sat down on the sofa and patted it for Adolf to sit next to her. Angela poured good, strong coffee into shallow china cups, and placed the large, silver cakestand in front of Adolf, and wondered: was Adolf really *so* different a man from the boy she remembered in Leonding? Adolf sipped his awful tea. He was quite bulky-looking, in the Brownshirt uniform he so often wore, at Party rallies and on most public occasions nowadays. His closets housed formal suits of thick blue serge that he rarely wore. He seemed happier in his Brown-shirt and breeches and boots: more manly, confident, harder. She could not deny it, he did have a hard streak now. The rages that had always been there – that came from nowhere – were still in his character. Angela excused that, in view of his responsibilities. A politician, a leader, no doubt of it, had to be ruthless! As a woman, she knew nothing of politics. Adolf needed feminine company to relax in, from time to time, and along with Geli she tried to provide it. Yet, looking at him as he smiled and joked with Geli, she decided he *was*, in some profound way, different from the boy who wanted only to paint and draw and be a famous architect. Something had happened to him, she felt sure, in the years he had spent in those terrible Men's Hostels in Vienna. She still felt guilty about those years. During the War she had wondered, and perused the long casualty lists in the newspapers. But nothing. Then there had been the news in the *Weiner Tagleblatt* that he was in the Landsberg Prison! But not as a common criminal, as a famous politician!

Of course, Adolf paid the price. He seemed nervous and slept badly. He went to bed late, as he always had, often coming home from meetings at one or two o'clock in the morning. All that talking and thinking! Poor Adolf. Small wonder he slept badly.

But the thing that worried her most was that Adolf feared for his life. There were two loaded pistols permanently housed in the apartment. A small Walther .22 in Geli's room, in the cabinet next to her bed. A Luger automatic in Adolf's own room, in the drawer of his desk. When she had, nervously, asked him about these weapons, Adolf had replied: 'A politician, these days, dear Angi, never knows when the enemy may come for him. Perhaps in the middle of the night!'

Angela was stunned. 'People really want to kill you?'

'Of course they do!'

'Who?'

'My enemies.'

'Your . . . political opponents, you mean?'

Adolf had stiffened, blue eyes ablaze. 'The Reds! The Social Democrats! All of them! Also, a politician has to accept the fact that his Enemies are not always known to him!'

For a long moment, she was silent. His face was white and his violent tone shocked her.

'You really fear . . . assassination, Adolf?'

'I do more than fear it. I expect it!'

Adolf's features had a strange stillness. She had seen the expression on his face before, a long time ago. In the middle of a terrible row with Alois, their joint-father, in the old days at Leonding.

'I'm sure you are well-protected by your men, your Brownshirts.' she had said, apprehensively.

'No!' Adolf had replied. 'They are more interested in battling in beerhalls and in the streets. Soon I will need to form a special contingent to protect me. Once I am in power. But until then we must protect ourselves, you and I and darling Geli!'

So Angela Raubal had said no more. It was hard to believe. The whole business frightened her, so she tried to put it from her mind. She did not entirely succeed. The weapons stayed locked in Adolf's and Geli's bedrooms. She did not wish to understand anything about firearms, they were too frightening. Adolf, knowing that, did not press her, but he gave Geli lessons in how to use the Walther, should she need to. What a bizarre idea, thought Angi, but said nothing.

Geli learned well, as Adolf, his arm around her, taught her how to load and point the Walther at a target and how to fire it, slowly and gently squeezing the barrel and the trigger. Like, as Adolf said, a man squeezing a tennis ball! 'Or a beautiful young woman . . . squeezing . . . ?' And Geli had whispered two words into Adolf's ear, and he had looked shocked, and slapped her bottom quite hard, and Geli had looked pleased, as if it was a declaration of love.

Angela worried about Geli.

Surely, she would play it sensibly, so she got what Angela wanted, what surely they all wanted?

Happiness, naturally.

And security, to live in this wonderful place for the rest of their days. Especially that.

Adolf sat and ate his cream cakes and drank his camomile tea. His eyes were never off Geli, and they shone, Angela was sure, with admiration.

Why not? Everybody admired Geli.

'Geli is the only girl I have ever seen,' Adolf said, 'who laughs with her eyes!'

Angela thought that was a good omen.

Emil had another view of things.

Driving Geli around Munich, when Adolf was too busy at his new Headquarters to accompany her, he made sly servant's sexy talk to the young girl.

'The Chief hates to go to the shops with anybody!' He tooled the long, black Mercedes into the heart of the shopping centre and stopped outside the best stores in the city. 'Even you.'

'What do you mean, even me?' asked Geli, annoyed.

'Well, you're his favourite girl, aren't you?'

'I'm his niece!'

'Half-niece,' corrected Emil. 'He could marry you if he wanted to. You're not on the Church's prohibited list, are you?'

'I don't know what you're talking about, Emil.'

'I think you do.'

'No, I don't.'

'Well, let's say I would if I was in his place.'

'What?'

'Marry you.'

Geli laughed. She enjoyed this kind of play, with any man, and Emil, with his dark eyes and knowing servant's smile, was quite attractive, in his way. 'Ah, but would I marry you?'

'You might if you saw the size of my . . . ?' He smiled, disarmingly. 'My Bank balance?'

Geli laughed loudly, throwing back her head, the black hair cascading over her white neck. The loins of Emil stirred, by Christ they did! If the Chief wasn't doing it to her he was a fool and if he was he was a swine!

'I think your Bank balance would be very . . . *small*!' Geli was saying, her lips parted, teasing. 'Very, very small.'

'You behave yourself,' said Emil, 'and maybe some day I'll show it to you!'

'Some chance!'

Geli, still smiling, flounced out of the Mercedes, as the uniformed and top-hatted store flunkey opened the car door for her.

'Danke,' she said, and turned to Emil. 'Park the car and come and help me with my parcels, my man! I'll be on the fifth floor! The Ladies Dress Department.'

With that, and a cheeky grin, she walked across the hot, sunlit pavement, into the dark cool of the store, the top-hatted flunkey scurrying forward to hold the huge brass-and-glass door open for her.

Asking for it, thought the cunning and lecherous Emil, bloody begging for it!

He put the Mercedes into gear and parked it in the store's car-park. Then he went into the store.

Geli was, as she had said she would be, on the Fifth Floor.

Women's Dresses, said the elevator indicator-board. And Emil saw that Geli Raubal seemed to have most of the stock lying on chairs in the fitting-rooms, or over the arms of sweating salesladies, too prim and terrified of losing their jobs to complain. Geli was in the middle of it all, pouting at her reflection in a tall mirror. She was wearing a long evening-dress, in a black chiffon, with a buttoned cleavage she had not bothered to fasten. The shape of her breasts was plain to see, to the hungry eyes of the roused but cautious Emil, who slid into a cushioned chair at one end of the fitting-room, his eyes darting around in the semi-darkness. It was stuffy and hot in the fitting-room and the salesladies (in their black dresses, with lace collars) seemed hot and bothered. The 'Fohn', Emil supposed, was affecting them. The soft and stifling south wind was used as an explanation for all kinds of strange womanly behaviour, usually of a sexual nature. The 'Fohn' was an excuse, like the bandage factory-women wore around their ankle, to show male overseers that they were in their period. The difference was that the 'Fohn', far from putting men off, inclined to incite them. Certainly, Emil felt randy, just sitting there watching Geli, in the warm darkness of the fitting-room.

It seemed to him that he did very little else these days, but watch Geli Raubal.

She knew he was doing it, of course.

The trouble was, Emil warned himself, she meant nothing by it.

Nothing or not, Geli turned to him, the half-open dress showing her white, silk chemise, and called, 'Emil? Do you *like* it?'

The prick-teaser!

'Can't see it properly,' said Emil, brutally. 'You'll have to come a bit nearer.' He added, daring, 'Fraulein Geli.'

The salesladies sniffed and looked as disapproving as they dared.

They were used to the famous Herr Hitler coming with his lovely young niece. A chauffeur, and not a very well-mannered one at that, was not at all to their liking.

The chief saleslady stepped forward, coughed, and opened a small cubicle, so that Geli should have privacy from the eyes of men whether she liked it or not.

Even when Geli went into the cubicle she left the door open.

So that Emil could see her?

Emil watched, but he had not been around all the women in his life without knowing the rules they individually laid down. He decided that, as the Chinaman said, with Geli it was a case of: lookee lookee but no touchee touchee! Or just possibly, eventually, of touchee touchee but no puttee in!

He lit a cigarette and told himself to stop farting about.

Geli was the Chief's bit of crumpet.

Nobody else's. Certainly not his.

Had he not seen enough evidence of that, this past year and more? Had he not, for the first time since the Chief had given him the job, when they were spluttering around in the battered old Selve, the first Party motor, been supplanted by another passenger, to wit, the lovely Geli, smelling of perfume, her long hair flying in the slipstream, the Chief sitting in the back, not, as usual, at the front with Emil. Goodbye, if Geli was in the motor, to the Chief's talk of Party doings and the aberrant behaviour of some of the Party high-ups. Gossip like that gave Emil status in his bierkeller. An admiring group of cronies, mostly, like himself, Party members of low rank, hung on his every word, and were eager to bring Emil, a slow man with a ten-mark note, a large, free drink.

Not that he was jealous of Geli, oh dear me no.

Women were, all of them, slags.

There were no exceptions.

That was every convict's belief. All convicts knew it to be true. Most had experience of it. Running women of the streets for money. Or conning widows. Or being deserted, once in the Nick, by women. All slags, no doubt of it.

Geli was just a more attractive slag than the rest.

Of course, the Chief didn't see her like that.

Oh dear me no.

Emil sighed, as he recalled the times he had taken the Chief and Geli up the mountain-roads to the Obersaltzberg, to the villa (now much extended and decorated), where the Chief had set aside a room of her own for the spicy little tart, as he had also done in the apartment on the Prinzregentstrasse. Emil had sat in the Mercedes, or washed it when it did not need washing, or maintained it when it was in perfect condition, as the Chief took the girl on one of his walks up the mountain, and wondered at the sight.

What did they talk about?

Certainly not sex, the only topic, outside food and drink, Emil ever personally discussed with a woman, any woman. Sex, after all, was all they were interested in, and, at the last, all they were good for. The Chief, if past records were anything to go by, would not push far in matters of sex. Or would he? Did he ask for more than they wanted? Something special maybe?

Bondage?

Emil tasted the idea – an eye on the half-clad Geli in the mirror of the cubicle – and did not discard it.

It was certainly a possibility. One he had debated before.

Yes, indeed.

Had not Suzi Liptauer, the Viennese blonde that the Chief had romanced for a while, with his typical fancy Viennese manners, all bowing and hand-kissing and pissing about, tried to hang herself when he stopped seeing her? She had, it was said, used a rope. That figured, thought Emil.

Little Mitzi Reiter? Only sixteen years old. It had been a *clothes-line* with her!

It made you fucking think. A lot of petting. A lot of play, with ropes. Then nothing? Could *that* be the way of it?

Of course, the Chief hadn't tried that with such as Erna Hanfstaengl, sister of the cadaverous Putzi. Or Winifred Wagner, the tall and stately daughter of Richard Wagner, whom the Chief had met at Beyreuth. To such ladies, the Chief was all good Viennese manners. Also, Adolf liked the Opera. Hours and hours of it. It gave him a charge. All it gave Emil was a rotten headache! Wagner, *Gotterdammerung*! All that. You could keep it, for Emil.

Those kind of women at Beyreuth – Winifred Wagner and Erna Hanfstaengl – were strictly decorative. Emil knew that much. The Chief looked up to them. Admired them. All that guff.

But Geli?

Geli, Emil thought, was somewhere between the two, the poor little tarts like busty Mitzi and the 'musical' hostesses, like Winifred Wagner.

Geli even got to go to the Opera with the Chief.

What she saw in all that fucking noise Emil couldn't think.

Geli sat there, with the Chief, and consulted her programme, and discussed the music with the Chief as if she had been doing it all her life! Women were chameleons, no doubt of it. And as for the Chief, he'd seen it all before, *The Ring, Faust*, he was actually sitting through it for the umpteenth bloody time! Emil knew this to be so because the Chief had told him. Madness, but maybe the Chief needed all that to get into the mood, as another man, a man like Emil himself, for example, needed the stimulus of strong drink.

Not, he thought, catching sight of Geli's trim little arse in the mirror of the changing-room, that he would need any stimulation to put it up little Geli.

But chance would be a bloody fine thing!

Face it, it could never happen.

Lookee lookee but no touchee touchee.

That was about the size of it.

He gave up and closed his eyes. No sense in torturing himself.

'Emil? Are you asleep?'

Suddenly, the little tart was standing in front of him, showing off her trim arse in the new frock. The frosty-faced chief saleslady was holding out a load of parcels for him to carry.

'Sorry, Fraulein!' Emil got to his feet and gathered the parcels.

Geli's eyes were large and amused, in the semi-darkness. She turned away imperiously, and he followed her towards the elevator.

The Princess, everybody called her.

By God, he fancied her.

He would settle, if he had to, for touchee touchee but no puttee in.

By Christ he would.

In the Mercedes, driving Geli back to the apartment, Emil kept his eyes on the road. Geli had plumped down in the seat next to him, something she had never done before. The silk skirt rode up above the silken knees. The white bones of the knees shone through the silk of the stockings and Emil felt an insane desire to stretch his hand out and put it between those soft legs, and then to run it up the stocking to the top, to the garter, and then . . .

Emil kept his hands on the wheel, but he sweated.

A prick teaser! He had known it from the first.

Or possibly it was simply the Fohn?

Whatever, he could do with less of it.

'Do you want to go for a country drive, Fraulein?'

The words were out before he knew it.

Geli's dark eyes were on him, he knew, but he stared straight ahead. There was not too much traffic in Munich in the middle of the afternoon. Most people used the trams.

'What a nice idea, Emil.'

'Where would you like to go, Fraulein?'

'Oh, just back in the apartment, it's so hot, isn't it?' said Geli, lazily. 'All I want is to take my clothes off and have a nice cool bath.'

Emil did not trust himself to reply.

In the Party Headquarters Putzi Hanfstaengl had managed to get Hitler to listen to him. Hitler was always late for appointments with such liberal or uncommitted foreign journalists as Putzi had got interested in him. They had just returned from a disastrous meeting with a man from the *New York Times*. The appointment had been for three o'clock. It had been exactly three-forty when Hitler had walked into the Cafe Nervaier on the corner of Petersplat and the Viktalien Markt. He had his alsatian, Wolf, with him, carried a dogwhip as usual, and called for tea, ignoring the journalist. The proprietor brought the selection of cream-cakes over, personally. Several people, at other tables, brought their chairs over as well, and, uninvited, sat down at the table. Putzi apologised, in a low voice to the liberal journalist, who was American, and a man Putzi had known at Harvard. A piece on Hitler in the *New York Times* would be useful to Adolf. Putzi had been in this situation before. Adolf was not interested in what anybody outside Germany thought about him, one way or the other. Not yet. The time, Putzi thought, would come.

Meanwhile, Hitler remained implacably Continental.

Like Napoleon. Like Blucher. Like Clauswitz.

All he thought of was Europe.

The books in his old apartment on the Thierschstrasse had shown Putzi that. *A History of Frederick the Great.* A biography of Wagner by Houston Stewart Chamberlain – an American turned German, like Putzi himself. Ludendorf's *History of the War.* A Collection of *Heroic Myths* by Von Wartenburg. Nothing surprising there. Until Putzi had come to *A History of Erotic Art*, tucked away on the lowest shelf! The title had given Putzi hope that Adolf was normal after all.

'The Fuhrer is so popular,' he had muttered to the *Times* man. 'But he lived until recently in a tiny flat. He had a piano. He loves music.'

Putzi's American friend smiled. 'You played for him?' Putzi nodded. Hitler leaned across the table for the first time.

'I heard Putzi play often at Harvard,' said the journalist.

'Ah, Harvard,' said Hitler. 'A military college, I believe?'

'I think you are thinking of West Point?'

Hitler frowned (nobody ever, *ever*, contradicted him) and, hastily, Putzi cut in: 'West Point is based on Potsdam, Adolf. But Harvard has an excellent military band. Cheer-leaders orchestrate the crowds at football games. To Sousa or whatever.'

Hitler nodded, impressed. 'Very clever!'

'Very infantile,' said the American.

'Not if it gets the desired effect,' corrected Hitler.

'You think effect is everything?' asked the journalist.

'Yes, I do.'

'What about political content?'

'What do the Masses know about that?'

Putzi intervened, with a quick smile, gently closing the journalist's notebook with a huge hand. 'The Volk cannot readily understand an involved political argument. It is sometimes necessary to put quite complicated points in a simple way. After all, Teddy Roosevelt did exactly that, didn't he?'

The *Times* man looked at Hitler. 'Are we talking about Catch Phrases here?'

'Call them that if you like,' said Hitler rudely. 'It is a matter of indifference to me what you do in America. I have enough on my plate here in Germany.' With that Hitler turned to his other lunch companions and talked to them about the Jews.

The *Times* man looked surprised and offended, and put his notebook away.

Putzi tried one last shot. 'You have heard Herr Hitler speak?'

The *Times* man nodded. 'Who hasn't by now?'

'You do not have to agree with everything that is in the speeches, my dear Tom,' said Putzi desperately, 'to see the Wagnerian quality of the structure? The interweaving of lietmotifs, counterpoint, contrasts? The Fuhrer's speeches are symphonic in construction, you see, and always end in a great climax. Like the blare of Wagner's trombones, wouldn't you say?'

'Possibly.' The *New York Times* man got to his feet. 'But I don't happen to like Wagner much.' He added, 'I'm surprised you do, Putzi. I'll say auf wiedersehen.'

'Yes,' said Putzi. 'Of course. Some other time, Tom.'

Putzi watched the young journalist leave and resolved to try to promote Adolf no more. Let him see, in his own good time, how important it was to have international allies, see that Europe was not the entire World.

Yet back at the Headquarters he said: 'Adolf, you gave me this job.

264

I get you the *New York Times*. You turn up late. You don't apologise. You give no interview. That man won't come again.'

'He will,' said Adolf Hitler, 'when he needs to.' He called out to Hess. 'Rudi, close the door and no appointments!'

'I have two on the list,' said Hess. 'Rosenberg and . . .'

'Nobody,' said Hitler. 'I am with Putzi.' He signalled to Putzi to sit.

'Adolf,' said Putzi. 'Consider. America is a huge country. Its grain harvest is as big as all of Europe's. It is rich and will get richer. Look to her as an ally. There are huge German populations all over the United States. Think about that.'

Adolf shook his head. 'Too far away to influence anything, Putzi. But what you said about Catch Phrases and Bands – *that* I found interesting! I will get the Brownshirt bands to see what can be done along those lines. Using German music, of course.'

Once again, Putzi thought, Hitler had taken from a situation what he needed there and then and nothing else. No forward-planning, no forward-thinking, just opportunism.

Hitler said, 'Did I tell you I had an apartment full of cakes in the form of swastikas for my birthday last week?'

'No?' said Putzi, mystified.

He could think of nothing more vulgar.

'Have you eaten them all?' Putzi asked.

Adolf Hitler shook his head. 'I have eaten none of them. Nor will I.'

'Why not?' asked Putzi, still mystified.

'How do I know none of them are poisoned?' asked Hitler.

Putzi knew that he was serious.

Adolf Hitler never joked. About anything.

The clock struck midnight and its chimes rang out through the open casement into the Alpine air. Adolf Hitler stretched his booted legs, and eased himself, comfortably loosening the waist-band of his breeches. He often did not bother to dress for dinner up here at the Berghof. If there were ladies it was a different thing. One had to follow the conventions. But tonight the company was exclusively male, apart from Angi and Friedl and Geli, all of whom had gone to bed soon after eleven o'clock, on his instructions.

He had stern business to discuss.

That was why he had Goering and Goebbels in the same room for once, much as they hated each other. Jealousy, of course. Hitler didn't mind that. Divide and rule. It always worked.

Rosenberg was here. Still intense, silent, until he spoke, with hatred and spite, of his enemies, the Bolsheviks, who had expelled him from his home in the East. Rosenberg was a German Balt, and the Balts hated the Bolsheviks for a very good reason. They knew them.

Max Amann was there, to give commonsense to it all.

Putzi was there. Huge but essentially lightweight, still he had his uses. He knew the top industrialists. Like Goering, he was an aristocrat. The Party needed one or two of them. They could open doors.

Finally, here was the newly-promoted man, Himmler, the failed chicken-farmer from Waltrudering, a small village near Munich. Putzi had told Hitler the fellow's father had been a headmaster at some superior school Putzi had attended in his youth. Putzi found Himmler somewhat funny, with his rimless spectacles and his tiny, shaven head, but Hitler had a feeling about the fellow. What qualities had he seen in the thin, schoolmasterly creature? Total and complete loyalty to himself, for a start! Not love, like Goebbels. Not cautious respect, like Goering. Not plain self-interest, like Max Amann. Just a rather mad, implacable loyalty. Whatever Hitler told Himmler to do, however strange or odious, Himmler would do it.

Whatever it was.

No questions asked.

Such a man the Party had need of.

Himmler sat amongst them by right, for Hitler had made him the Commander of a new military unit – his own Bodyguard. Max Amann, surprised, had asked Adolf why he needed such a unit? There were the Brownshirts, after all, were they not loyal, were they not the *Alte Kampfer*?

'Yes,' Adolf had replied. 'But can I any longer trust them? They get into fights, in the streets and in the beerhalls, when I expressly forbid it! While I try to make the Party respectable, acceptable to the Industrialists and the aristocrats and even the bourgeoisie, they insist on getting *arrested*! They insist on getting drunk and battling with the Reds. They even threaten to strike if their pay is reduced because of the shortage of party funds!'

'But they are loyal to the end, Adolf!' Max Amman protested.

'I do not doubt it, but my personal safety is paramount! I do not feel I can trust them all. Strasser, in Berlin, controls *his* own Brownshirts. They would do his bidding, whatever it was.'

'Surely you're not accusing Strasser of anything?' Max Amann asked, shocked. 'It is true he still takes the word Socialist in our Party title seriously. Many people still do. But . . .'

'I trust nobody,' said Hitler. 'Which is why I am forming my own *Shultz-Staffel* and putting Himmler in charge of it. I have also sent a cable to Ernst Roehm in Bolivia, asking him to come back and take complete charge of the Brownshirt units. Get some fresh discipline into them!'

Max Amann said, 'Well, that's a good idea, anyway. But – why this new Bodyguard, this SS?'

Hitler exploded. 'Max, I have just told you! If I die, National Socialism in Germany is finished! People have tried to kill me and will try again! A lot of people want my death!'

'Who?' insisted Max Amann despite Putzi's sudden warning gesture.

'The Jews! The Reds! My Enemies!'

Max Amann sighed. It could be true. Or there was every reason to suppose that it could be true. No proof, but that did not mean anything, did it?

Hitler could well be right. He often was.

So now they all sat, the new man Himmler amongst them, dying for sleep, sated on the mountain air, and Adolf Hitler talked.

'We have had the years of waiting. I believe they might be at an end.'

The comrades straightened up, in their low, velvet-cushioned chairs. Goering rubbed his eyes, Goebbels, whose nights were often given to sex, and was always tired in consequence, yawned widely. Rosenberg looked eager. Max Amann waited. Himmler took off his rimless spectacles and polished them, and put them on again.

'Germany has had a defeat in War. Then Inflation.' Hitler's voice was low, detached, as it usually was at the beginning of his speeches, thought Putzi Hanfstaengl. 'A few years of comparative well-being, from the Weimar Republic, owing to the open-handed loans from the Americans. Now, since the Wall Street crash, all that is *over*!' Hitler leaned forward. 'The Republic will be getting no more American handouts. The factories are closing down all over Germany, the workers are unemployed and Germany, like the rest of Europe, is going down into the most terrible and long-lasting industrial and financial slump of the century. It is our chance! It is a Gift to Us! It will put us in power, at last!'

There was a long silence.

'How?' said Himmler.

Hitler held up his hand. He felt uplifted. 'You ask, my dear Himmler, how can we take power? We have only twelve Nazi Party Deputies in the Reichstag?'

Himmler nodded.

'The Nationalists have over a hundred members. We need their members, but not their leader, Hugenberg – that fat, drunken old sot!'

'Then why . . . ?' stammered Himmler, 'did you sign a pact of mutual political assistance with him?'

Hitler's voice was suddenly a whisper.

267

'My dear Himmler, *he* has signed a pact with me, not I with him! And it is a pact I do not intend to keep a moment longer than necessary! Believe me, our friend Hugenberg, will not be around much longer.'

Goering stirred his mountainous bulk, and smiled, a large, dangerous animal-hunter. 'We *kill* him?'

'Worse,' said Hitler. 'We send him into a happy retirement!'

They all laughed except Himmler, who never laughed.

Hitler said, 'Gentlemen. We grow stronger by the day! The Party had 120,000 members in 1929. Now it stands at over 200,000.' He nodded benevolently towards Himmler. 'And all these converts come from the Nationalist Party! You see, my dear Himmler?'

Hitler lowered his voice. 'I have, from a secret source in the Government, obtained the latest figures. There are three million unemployed breadwinners in the land. The official prediction is that there will be another million by the end of the year.'

The six men in the room stared at him, in silent shock.

'Bad years for Germany,' said Adolf Hitler, softly. 'But years of opportunity for us!'

Nobody, not even Himmler, spoke.

'Now, I have to clean stables before I move forward to a full programme designed to get us, at least, a good showing in the Reichstag at the next election, which, with unemployment figures like this, must be soon.'

'Clean stables?'

Inevitably, it was Himmler who was asking.

'Who, exactly, Fuhrer, are we talking about?'

Adolf Hitler almost sighed. 'I mean Strasser.'

Nobody spoke.

Then finally, once again, Himmler: 'Are we this time talking of . . . a dramatic solution?'

'No,' came the soft reply. 'Not this time. Not yet.'

Putzi Hanfstaengl shivered and it was not cold in the room.

Geli was glad to be back in Munich.

The city pleased her, despite the sudden, shocking influx of ragged and starving men on the streets, begging in the gutters and sometimes blatantly accosting passers-by. Mutti said it was like a return to the 'Inflation Days' just after the War. But Geli could do nothing but give the best-looking beggars a coin and walk on. What could she do about it? Oh, it was so good to be back! Just to look around the rich shops delighted her. Even Uncle Adi's long, discursive suppers at the Cafe

Heck did not bore her as much as usual. The Depression was taking hold and there had been a lot of excited talk about it that evening. Such discussion made her head ache. Walking away from the place, into the cool night air, was the best part of it. These evenings followed the same old pattern: heavy food; thick tobacco smoke; hoarse arguments, stilled when Hitler spoke. As usual, Geli had drunk too much wine. Adi never drank alcohol, and rarely thought to order more for the table. She supposed it was because of his drunken old father. Adi ate only salad and soup and sweets. She'd heard Putzi tell an amusing story of Uncle Adi putting spoonfuls of *sugar* into his best Rhine-wine, to sweeten it, when he thought Putzi wasn't looking!

Now, Putzi and his toffee-nosed American wife, Hèlene, walked with Geli along the cool, night streets of Munich, and Uncle Adi loped along behind them, with Wolf, allowing the dog the full length of his chain and, in consequence, taking over the entire sidewalk. Geli found Hélène Hanfstaengl too mature, too knowledgeable, too well-dressed, too aristocratic (or she *thought* she was, as if an *American* ever could be!) for her own taste. Hélène, she thought, deliberately made her feel young and silly and foolish, and used French words for the food, or to illustrate a point of conversation, knowing well that Gell did not understand any of it. Wasn't German good enough for her or her silly, lanky husband, who was an even bigger snob than she was?

The trouble was Uncle Adi fancied Helène. In his way.

Adi, she knew, was often attracted to these grand society women. Putzi even told some story of Uncle Adi going down on his hands and knees to Helène and telling her how much he adored her. Geli did not believe Uncle Adi would ever do that. She believed he'd kissa-da-hand, like the Italians did. But on his hands and knees? Never. Only for her, for his Geli! He was down on his hands and knees to Geli often enough, now that they were alone in the apartment, except for Frau Winter, in the basement. But not to tell her he *adored* her, no indeed! Geli was thoroughly fed up with the Hanfstaengls. The evening had been a bore and she had felt a know-nothing fool too often to enjoy it.

Wolf stopped to inspect a lamp-post and Adolf stopped with him. The Hanfstaengls lingered, then walked on to Geli, who had not broken her pace.

'Aren't you waiting for your Uncle Adi?' asked Helène, Geli thought mischievously.

'I do enough for him without waiting on that dog!'

'Oh? and what *do* you do for him, Geli?' asked Helène Hanfstaengl, smiling. Geli thought, in a contemptuous way.

'Things you'd be surprised by! Things *you* couldn't do!'

The idea! Uncle Adi down on his knees to this American tart!

'What kind of things, Geli?'

It was the soft, sniggering note in the voice that upset Geli.

'I know you think he's not interested in sex?'

'How do you know *that*?' Helène sounded shocked. And why not, thought Geli, with satisfaction.

'Your husband talks a lot. And he has a loud voice.'

'Putzi jokes a lot, you know, Geli.' Helène sounded somewhat shaken, which was how Geli liked it. 'But I'm sure you're mistaken.'

'No, I'm not, but I don't care. You can think what you like.' Geli turned to her and smiled, in the lamplight. 'The fact is, you don't know, do you?'

With that, Geli walked on, swinging her hips in the way she sometimes swung them to tantalize Emil, the chauffeur. At least Emil appreciated her tight little arse, which was more than Putzi – what a stupid name for a man, it meant *small* – ever seemed to do. He never even looked at her. Plainly, he thought she was just a young lower-class slut. Now, having heard a little of the conversation, she had his full attention for once. For Putzi was staring after her, in some concern.

It was reflected in his voice when Adolf caught them up, Wolf at last having come to heel. By this time they had arrived at Putzi's motor-car, parked nearby. 'An excellent evening, Adolf. Geli is such excellent company, too,' said Putzi, who seemed to be having trouble with his voice. 'We must do it again very soon.'

Adolf shook hands with Putzi and, very correctly, with Helène, bowing and clicking his heels.

Geli watched the tableau with scorn, but did not speak. She simply waved as the car drove away, and turned, teetering on her high heels, for home.

Uncle Adi called out, 'Geli! Wait! We're coming!'

The plural meant him and the smelly dog.

Geli was afraid of Wolf. The animal did not seem to like her, either. Wicked Emil had told her what such dogs did with society-ladies in need of a husband! She had pretended not to understand, but Emil's hot, dark eyes had found hers and they had both laughed. What about Helène Hanfstangael and Wolf? She'd have to tell Emil about that possibility. How they would laugh! God knows, she had few people around her she could ever laugh with, about anything.

Uncle Adi put his hand on her arm.

She squeezed it, as if in deep affection.

Wolf objected to that, and tugged at his leash.

Uncle Adi cracked his dogwhip and Wolf cowered.

Me, thought Geli, with a sudden sympathy for the brute, and Wolf, both!

They walked on, all three, down the dark, quiet Munich street.

Hitler, as always, did the unexpected.

He went to Berlin, a city he hated. Was it not full of Marxist theatres performing the work of Brecht and Kurt Weill and other Jewish degenerates? Did not the capital's newspapers carry contemptuous articles about him, and even worse, cartoons showing him to be some kind of Bavarian hobbledehoy? Pornography was on sale at every tobacco-kiosk. Satirical magazines full of filth were on sale everywhere. Probably written by the Jews. Adolf felt a rage burn in him at the very thought of the capital of Germany being in the hands of such people! They degraded the Race. One day, he promised himself, there would be a clearing-out of these dirty stables. In the meantime, he had business to do.

Hitler was accompanied by Hess and several members of his bodyguard. They stayed at the Kaiserhof, and took two suites of rooms. Hitler sent a message to Gregor Strasser to come and meet him there as soon as possible. If he wished, he could bring his brother, Otto. For himself, Hitler said in his note, he wanted this to be a purely private meeting, to mend fences, and he was ready to talk freely and frankly for as long as it took.

Gregor Strasser and his brother Otto were there within the hour. Gregor was the taller, good-looking one, a true rival. Otto was merely a journalist, but all the more dangerous for that.

Hitler greeted them warmly, offered them coffee, and came straight to the point. 'Gregor, I have to say I'm disappointed in the stand Otto's newspaper, the *Sachister Beobachter*, has taken over this Union strike in Saxony?'

'Why?' asked Gregor Strasser. 'Those workers look to us for support. We've given it, unconditionally.'

'In a Party newspaper? Without discussion?'

'There hasn't been time for discussion, Adolf.'

'No, well, I can see that,' said Hitler. 'But what are the people I'm trying to get behind us going to think about it?'

Otto Strasser rudely interrupted. 'You mean the industrialists and financiers?'

Hitler looked at him, as if surprised. 'Well, of course I do, Otto.' He paused, it was important to be calm. 'In a recent article in your newspaper, you say the Party is eternal, the Fuhrer merely its servant. Gregor, *that* is an attack on me.' Neither of the brothers denied it. Hitler waited, his anger barely held in. 'With us the Fuhrer and the Idea are one!

Every Party member has to do what the Fuhrer orders. The Fuhrer incorporates the Idea and he alone knows its ultimate goal! Gregor! You were a soldier yourself. I ask you: are you prepared to submit to Party discipline or not?'

Gregor stared at Hitler but did not reply.

Otto Strasser asked sharply, 'You want to strangle our Revolution, for the sake of collaboration with the bourgeois parties of the Right?'

Hitler stood up. '*I* was once an ordinary working-man! *I* do not allow my chauffeur to eat worse than I eat myself! What *you* understand by Socialism is nothing but middle-class Marxism!' He paused. 'The great mass of workingmen have no understanding of Ideals – Socialist or otherwise! We can never hope to win the workers by so-called Socialist Ideals! By the ethic of *Pity*!'

Gregor Strasser said, in a more conciliatory tone: 'Adolf! We *do* have the word Socialist and the word Worker in our title.'

'You want some Works Council, which has no notion of *anything*, to have the last say in Industry? Are you quite, quite mad?'

'What then would you do with Krupps of Essen if you came to power?' Gregor asked, ironically.

'Leave it alone. You cannot give the Workers the right to have a voice in the conduct of Business. We need a strong *State*. That my Party will provide, believe me.'

The brothers started to speak, both together, hotly, in their defence. Hitler stopped them with raised hand. There were, Otto saw, tears in his eyes.

'In the name of the Party, *submit*!' Hitler suddenly shouted. 'If you do not, I will drive you both *out* of the Party!'

Hitler turned abruptly.

'Guten Tag, gentlemen.'

Slowly, the brothers left the room.

Geli looked around Emil's room with curiosity, sharpened by a sense of danger. What if Uncle Adi ever found out she had been here?

Who would tell him?

Certainly not Emil, now putting a kettle on his primitive gas-ring, having already broken open a packet of biscuits.

Geli felt at home.

Then she saw the photograph of the two people copulating. It was pinned to the wall above Emil's head. What was so shocking about it was that the man was white and the woman black. What was even more shocking was that the man was Emil.

'What do you think of the way I live, then?' he asked, not turning round. Geli hastily averted her eyes from the photograph and looked round at the room again. What a mess! A single brass bedstead in one corner, covered by a quilt. A small wooden table, pushed against the wall, a couple of wooden kitchen chairs that had seen better days; brown lino on the floor; a wooden easy-chair with rockers, carpet-covered. A sink with a gas-ring. The whole lit by an unshaded bulb. My God, it reminded her so vividly, in its poverty, of the last years in Vienna, after her Father died, when she and Friedl and Mutti had lived as best they could on her Father's tiny pension. This sharp and painful memory should surely have made her change her mind and dash out of this low-class place, never to come back again!

Why didn't she feel like that?

'Won't be long with this,' Emil said. 'Make yourself at home.'

Geli looked at Emil's broad back. He seemed even more powerful in his shirt and braces than he looked in his chauffeur's jacket. He had taken off the peaked-cap and the jacket and thrown them on the rocking-chair, quickly, as they came in, an actor changing roles in a hurry. Geli supposed it was rather like that. Emil was now, in his own living-room, a man in his own right, and no longer Uncle Adi's servant. He was making that plain. Geli felt a delicious tremor run over her body. Delicious but frightening. But what sort of foolishness was this?

If Uncle Adi ever found out?

But, again, why should he?

Geli sat on the bed, since there was no comfortable chair, and swung her silken legs.

What the hell, she was bored, bored, bored.

What was wrong with a little devilment?

Nothing was going to happen.

Emil knew that. She knew that.

She had come into the place when he had invited her, out of plain curiosity, Geli told herself. Uncle Adi had gone to Berlin with Hess. Why not, at the end of a long, hot day, with the dreaded 'Fohn' here again, take Emil up on his offer of cold beer and hot coffee?

What else did she have to do?

Only old Frau Winter in the flat, the nosy old thing, all right in her way but a spy to Uncle Adi or Mutti, however you looked at it. She must not be late back, or something might be said by the old lady. Frau Winter had worked for Uncle Adi for a long time now. She must be careful, even if the visit was an innocent one.

Well, of course it was innocent, any other thought was ridiculous.

Emil turned from the gas-ring with a large white jug in his hand. 'You see, Geli, the only way to make coffee is *this*. You put the coffee grounds in. *So!*' He heaped spoonfuls of coffee into the jug. 'And then pour the boiling water on. *So!*' And he did *that* too. 'And then you pour the whole lot into a second jug! So!' And he did that with dexterity, and Geli noticed something she had never realised before, that his whole body was covered with black hair, or anyway his chest was, for his collarless shirt was open to the waist. The sight sent a shiver through her. 'And *then*,' cried Emil, the magician, 'a pinch of salt! So! And then you allow it to settle.' He set the jug down next to two large pot mugs. 'That's all there is to it. Sugar if you must. Otherwise, perfect. A chef taught me that.'

He sat down on the bed. Oddly, she did not feel menaced. 'When did you ever know any chefs?' she asked, with a laugh. Her laugh sounded higher than usual, she thought. Surely, she was not nervous of Emil? He knew his place, of course he did.

'In the Prison,' replied Emil. 'This chef was in for cutting up his girl-friend. That's what you get for working with sharp knives all the time. You use them without thinking.'

'Did he kill her?' asked Geli, fascinated.

'Of course.' Emil poured the thick, black coffee into the cups. 'But he was a *famous* chef and nobody believed he would do that unless he'd gone mad. So the Court reduced the charge from murder to man-slaughter, and he only got ten years. Lucky old chef.'

'Yes, he was.' Geli believed in an eye for an eye in these matters, as everybody she knew did. 'He should have been beheaded!'

'Why?'

'That poor girl!'

'That poor girl had lovers, while he was keeping her. She asked for it.'

'Do you believe that?'

Emil's reply was instant. 'Of course I do. The old chef really was a bit lucky, but with the Republic not many get the Axe any more. Sentences are easier, as well.'

'Is that good?' Geli averted her eyes from the photograph. It showed every scandalous *detail*, even the texture of skin. It was, if anything, ruder than Uncle Adi's paintings, but somehow more honest, she felt, because Emil was actually *doing* it, not just *looking* at it. Nonetheless, she felt herself becoming wet, and squirmed uncomfortably and averted her eyes from the photograph. Who had taken it, there had to be a third person in the room when it was taken? Was it, then, taken by another woman? Or another man?

'Good? Nothing about prison's good,' Emil was answering her question. 'But you get used to it. And I was only in for embezzlement.'

'Did the Chief know you'd been a convict?'

Geli felt she had to recapture the initiative somehow.

But Emil was not embarrassed. 'Of course he did. That's why he gave me a job in the first place. I used to lead gangs of Brownshirts to smash up the Reds. I was his first squad-leader. Then he put me in the car as his personal driver and bodyguard. Why not? He couldn't look after himself in a fight, could he?'

'He has the Iron Cross!' objected Geli.

'Not talking about that kind of thing. I mean against people who want to hurt you. Beat you up, all that.' Emil sipped his coffee and drew in his breath sharply, as he did so. Nobody in Geli's current circle drank coffee like *that*. It was a purely working-class reaction to a rare treat. The way people who needed it drank coffee at the end of a long, hard physical day.

'You were in the early battles then?' asked Geli, impressed. Uncle Adi was always talking about the wonderful Old Fighters. Obviously, Emil was one of them.

'I was at the Coburg, I was everywhere with the Chief. Now, of course, he wants everybody to behave like gentlemen so he can get respectable people on his side.' Emil rolled a cigarette with odd-looking, coarse tobacco taken from a tin he kept in his back-pocket. He lit it with a match struck on his thumbnail, drew on it deeply, held it in, then exhaled the smoke in a thin, grey stream. He passed the cigarette, wordlessly, to her.

Geli looked at the thick tube, the end wet with Emil's saliva. Then she closed her eyes, put it in her mouth and inhaled. The sweet, acrid, smoke choked her and she coughed hoarsely. She set down her cup and coughed again. Tears came to her eyes. Emil just sat and watched her. He didn't offer a handkerchief. If anything, he seemed faintly amused.

Geli found herself apologising: 'I'm sorry. It's so *strong*.'

'Yes. It's not the usual tobacco, *liebschen*.'

She noted the word but let it go.

'What *is* it, then?'

'Something special the Arabs smoke. Are you dizzy?'

'A bit.' She was, and also slightly, well, out of herself.

'Try again. Suck it in. Hold it. Then let it out. Very slow.'

Geli did that. The sensation was even better.

'What *is* it?'

'It has all sorts of names. I got this from a sailor on shore leave. We used to smoke it in the prison sometimes. It varies in quality. This is good stuff.'

Geli felt slightly dizzy and refused a further drag. Emil again drew deeply on the weed. Sexy, Geli thought, I feel really sexy.

It was a sensation she rarely felt with Uncle Adi.

Mainly, of course, because *he* didn't.

Or if he did, he felt it in a different way from, say, Emil.

Emil, whatever else he was, was normal. A man with a man's appetites. The photograph proved that, if nothing else.

Emil turned his head and looked at it. Oh, God, he'd noticed her gaze. But he was laughing. 'You like it?'

'Who took the photograph?' asked Geli, boldly, her voice seeming to come from outside herself.

Emil continued to laugh. 'Her sister.'

'Was she a swartzer as well?'

'Of course she was! They were professionals. Lesbians as well. With each other.' Emil took a bottle of cheap cognac from a cupboard under the gas-ring and poured a measure into his own coffee, and then into Geli's.

'They made love to each other? Sisters?'

'I told you, they were pros. They have to do something different don't they, to get a kick?'

'You *paid* them? The two swartzers?'

Emil shook his head. 'It's free, first night out of prison. The girls don't charge you if you've just done your porridge.' Emil drank his coffee and cognac and gestured to Geli to drink, too. She did, a good deep swallow. What the hell, she was enjoying herself! More than for a very long time. All she ever felt in the apartment were a lot of tensions. Waiting for Uncle Adi to lose his temper, about something trivial. He'd started to do that lately. She guessed he was losing interest in her. Or anyway, he seemed preoccupied with his work and any interruption of it for whatever reason, irked him. To want to be Fuhrer of the whole of Germany was a wonderful thing but it did not seem to make for happiness. Not that Geli expected happiness, exactly. She would settle for excitement, anytime.

Well, she was getting that, here and now.

But of course it had to end.

Soon. But not yet.

'What was it like in prison?' asked Geli. 'I mean, no women?'

Emil shrugged. 'You do without. Or you take a boy. If you can find one. If you have the tobacco to buy him.'

'You did that?'

'Everybody does it. You take what you can.'

'How terrible!'

Geli was scandalised but somehow not censorious. Poor man, locked away for years in one of those awful places, any kind of love must seem all right, she reasoned, taking the curious-smelling cigarette from him, and drawing deeply on it again. The sensation was delightful, starting between her legs and spreading all over her body.

'You know what they say,' Emil remarked, leaning back on the bed, his back against the wall, and kicking off his shoes. 'He who once eats out of the Tin Bowl will eat from it again and again.'

'Who says that?' Geli took off her shoes. It was so hot in the little room.

'All convicts say it,' said Emil, 'because it's true.'

The Fohn, she thought, it is all the fault of the Fohn. The night was hot and oppressive and the wind off the mountains seemed, as usual, to offer no relief at all.

Emil reached forward and took her foot in his hand, gently, and massaged it.

How nice, Geli thought. What a sweet thing to do.

'That tobacco is so nice,' said Geli. 'I could like it, very much, y'know?'   'Just enough, that's the thing,' said Emil, taking the curious cigarette from her, inhaling, dragging the smoke down into his lungs. 'Too much and you go to sleep, my little liebchen, and you aren't quite ready for sleep yet, are you?'

'Yes . . . I think I am,' lied Geli. 'Maybe I should go, Emil?'

But Emil had unfastened her blouse, in one deft movement.

'Really, I *should*! Uncle Adi –'

'Never mind him. He doesn't do this to you, does he?'

Emil was kissing her breasts now. Gently.

It was nice. But . . . it was nice. Let it happen. It's all the Fohn.

Now his fingers had pulled up her skirt and in a swift movement, slipped off the french-knickers she had bought at the last trip to the shops. Emil had seen her buy them. She had, she realised, *let* him see her buy them but she had not meant *this*, oh no, she had not meant *this*, it could not be allowed to happen to her, she could not allow Emil, who was only a chauffeur and an ex-convict and who did awful things to boys and swartzers, Emil with the black hair all over him, could not be allowed to do this to her, Geli Raubal, who belonged to Uncle Adi now, oh no, no, even if it was so full of delight, delight, delight, so hard and rough and no kisses in it, just male want and strength and *aaaah* . . .

Geli cried out, and Emil put his hand across her mouth so that the neighbours would not hear.

The Fohn, she whispered to herself, it's all the fault of the Fohn.

Fritz Thyssen held out his hand as Hitler came into the room.

'Adolf, how good to see you, my friend. Sit down, sit down.'

Adolf sat. He was wearing his blue serge suit and felt uncomfortable, ordinary. But a Brownshirt uniform would not have done, here in Fritz Thyssen's private office in the lavish United Steel Building. Hitler felt like a supplicant.

It was a feeling he did not care for.

But Fritz Thyssen was trying to make it as easy as possible for him. He poured Adolf coffee from a percolator. 'My dear friend, how long it seems since we first met in Berlin? wasn't it?'

Adolf Hitler knew that Fritz Thyssen knew exactly when he had given the Party his first donation. A Hundred Thousand Marks!

My God, it had meant a lot to them then.

Fritz Thyssen was not letting Adolf forget it.

Well, he would not forget it.

Thyssen was the biggest fish the Party had landed. 'I have to thank you, dear Fritz, on behalf of the Party, for your help, and that of your friends in industry, in the last years. Without that help, the Party could well have gone under.'

Thyssen nodded. 'Two million Marks to the Nationalists in these past three years. A lot of money, Adolf.'

'I agree,' said Hitler, swallowing. 'The problem is, my Party gets very little of it! The Nationalist Party has been giving *us* a mere fraction of that amount! I would wish that it *all* came to us, then you and your friends would see what we could really do!'

Fritz Thyssen shrugged uncomfortably. 'This Depression will make things more difficult. I'm not sure there will be much from anybody in the coming years.'

Hitler said nothing for a moment. Then, he made an impatient gesture and stood up. 'Fritz! I want you to arrange for me to talk to the Industry Club. As soon as you can.'

Fritz Thyssen was shocked. 'That would be very risky.'

'Why?'

'Most of the members are supporters of the Nationalist Party. Conservative. Middle-of-the-road. I can't guarantee you a friendly reception, Adolf. Really, I would be against it –'

'Because I am not their kind?'

'No, not at all, it's not *that*!'

'Then please arrange it. If they don't like me they can always show me the door. It won't be anything new for me. My skin is quite thick, my dear Fritz.'

It took Fritz Thyssen a long time – and a lot of wire-pulling – to arrange for an invitation to be extended to Herr Hitler to address a meeting of the influential Industry Club in Dusseldorf. Everybody who mattered, in German industry, was a member. They ran to short Prussian haircuts, London suits, and fine Swiss-cotton shirts. The meeting was held at the Park Hotel and it was, to Fritz Thyssen's dubious surprise, crowded. German industrialists were feeling the dramatic effects of the Depression on world trade. They seemed to be prepared to give this ex-Army corporal a hearing. The air of relaxed self-confidence and smugness that usually characterised these kind of meetings was not present as Hitler stood up to speak. These people were shocked by the Depression, the layoffs and short-time working at their factories. They were looking for answers.

Hitler came at once to the point, and, to Fritz Thyssen's relief, he seemed in a quiet, reflective, and responsible frame of mind. He spoke quietly and reasonably, without histrionics or rabble-rousing. Fritz Thyssen, who had heard him speak so wilfully and wildly wondered at this low-key oration.

'Economic life is about achievement. It is about *authority* – your authority, gentlemen! You all run your concerns in the way you know to be best.'

A rumble of approval, Thyssen noted. 'You lead. Your workers follow. That is as it should be. Unlike Communism. Communism would sweep all that aside, as it already has in Bolshevik Russia.'

At the mention of Communism, the emotional temperature in the room rose. But Adolf Hitler kept his voice steady, his tone reasonable. 'Communism is more than a mob storming about in our German streets! It has subjugated Russia! Unless it is halted it will take over the whole world. An Economic Crisis, gentlemen, is what the Communists pray for and work for. This latest wave of unemployment is driving millions of Germans to look to Communism as a Saviour!'

The industrialists looked at each other uncomfortably. All this was self-evidently true. The fellow was not just a rabble-rouser, that was plain to see.

Fritz Thyssen began to relax. He lit a cigar.

'The *State* must create the *conditions* for prosperity.' Hitler stopped and let his point sink home. 'There can be no flourishing Industry in Germany if it's without a powerful State to protect it.' He paused and raised his voice. 'Ready to strike for *Germany!*' There were some rumblings of assent. 'Some of our Volk want to smash the State! They have hoisted another flag – a Red Flag!'

This was greeted with a total, awed silence.

'Gentlemen. Either we throw out, root and branch, this Marxist nonsense of Class War amongst ourselves! *Or we go down!*'

There were approving voices raised in the room, for the first time. Hitler held up his hand. 'This very day thousands of Brownshirts will be out in the streets all over Germany. They will fight the Reds!' His voice was suddenly harsh. 'These men come back home, in the grey dawn, to go on to their daily work – *if* they have a job. These fine men buy their own uniforms, their shirts, their badges. Yes, they even pay their own tram-fares! If only the entire German nation had the same

Faith as these men Germany would stand tall once again, proud in the eyes of the world. You must, gentlemen, I beg you, help Germany to do that. It is your Duty!'

Hitler sat down suddenly, white and exhausted, to a standing ovation. Fritz Thyssen could hardly believe it. With that speech, Adolf Hitler had made sure of considerable financial support from the major industrial concerns of the Reich. More than that, these men now *believed* in Adolf Hitler.

After a moment, Hitler stood up, nodded, turned and left the room. A loud, final, cheer saw him out. Then the Party Treasurer, bespectacled old Franz Xaver Schwarz, sat down at a side-table and began to note the sums the Industrialists pledged in a large ledger.

Putzi Hanfstaengl looked at the new Brown House in Munich with some distaste. It was not exactly the kind of architecture he admired. Palatial, showy, mock-Baroque, with Swastika flags flying in the hot summer wind.

However, it was an architecture of the kind Adolf Hitler admired and that was all that mattered. Hitler had designed the interior himself. Paul Ludwig Troost, his favourite architect, had built it. Putzi did not care for Troost, a thin, reserved Westphalian, almost as tall as himself.

Putzi strode past the flapping Nazi flags and acknowledged the sentry's salute with a nod. Putzi hated uniforms and never wore the Brownshirt drab, pleading the necessity of looking like a neutral member of the Press Corps. His grey Brooks Brothers suit, button-down shirt and soft Fedora hat were hardly Bavarian streetwear. He made his way through the echoing, marbled hall and took the stairs to the third floor.

He wondered what Franz Xaver Schwarz could want with him? More money? Well, if so, he would be unlucky. Putzi had given and given and given again. No more, for the very good reason that there was not a lot left to give. Also, if the rumours of money coming into the Party from other – Industrial – sources were true (and such rumours usually were) then the Party's days of real penury were over.

It would be good to be in funds again. Putzi scraped along on very little these days. All he took from the Party were his expenses and a clerk's salary. Without his private income from the family business (and his wife's money) Putzi would have been in trouble. Now, seemingly, things were better. In fact, Putzi resolved to ask for a salary-rise first, from old Schwarz, before any other business got under way!

It was about time. Had he not put up much of the money to buy the Party's newspaper, the *Volkische Beobachter*, after the Army had chickened out of buying it, because it could look faintly treasonable?

Putzi knocked on Schwarz's private door and walked in.

Schwarz was sitting at his desk, poring over a large ledger. He had been, Putzi knew, a sort of clerk all his life, finally ending up as a municipal officer in the city. Now, Franz Xaver had reached the pinnacle – Treasurer of the Nazi Party! He greeted Putzi but not with his usual calm authority. He rose from behind his desk, called to his secretary that he had to go out for half an hour, and took Putzi by the arm before he even could sit down.

'Tell you all about it,' said Franz Xaver. 'Outside!'

Putzi was not best pleased and even less so when, after traipsing the hot streets of the city for ten minutes, Franz Xaver found them a small café with tables outside, in the hot sun. Franz ordered coffee and Putzi ordered beer. Putzi was damn thirsty after all this nonsense. 'What *is* all this mystery?'

Franz Xaver peered at Putzi over his spectacles. Then, he looked anxiously around the tables. There was nobody foolish enough to be sitting in the hot sun except them. That seemed to reassure Franz Xaver. He took from his pocket a large buff envelope.

He put it away again when the waiter brought their order.

Thoroughly put out, Putzi sipped a mouthful of cold beer and exploded: 'For God's sake, Franz, what have you got in that envelope? Pornography?'

Franz Xaver went quite pale. 'Why do you say that?'

'The way you're behaving.'

'You said . . . pornography?'

'No. I said *was* it pornography?'

Franz Xaver sat in silence a long time.

Putzi drank his beer and stood up.

'Franz, I'm busy. I have things to do, in my office.'

Franz Xaver became agitated, and waved Putzi to his seat.

'Sit down, Putzi, and listen.'

Putzi sat. 'Go on.'

'I want you to look at these!' Franz Xaver took out the buff envelope again, and passed it to Putzi. Putzi began to open it.

'Under the table, for God's sake, Putzi!' said Franz Xaver, in anguish.

Putzi said, with a grin, 'So it *is* porn?' Except he expected it to be money, a scandal, some minor official lining his pockets, maybe? Well, why not, a lot of the Party bosses did it, on the quiet, he felt sure. Goering, for one.

He opened the envelope and was surprised at what he saw: drawings and paintings of a dark-haired young girl.

In the nude.

In very clear detail.

A lot of pubic hair, a whole bush, Putzi noted.

He had no objection to that.

He held them up to get a better view.

'Put them away!' cried Franz Xaver. 'Give them here!'

Putzi handed the drawings over, with a grin. Franz Xaver stuffed them back in the envelope.

Putzi signalled for another cold beer. 'Who's the artist?'

'Who's the model, Putzi? *Think!*'

Putzi thought.

'Oh, my God!' said Putzi.

'Exactly!' said Franz Xaver, painfully.

'Geli? And done by –?'

'No names!' said Franz Xaver at once. He stuffed the buff envelope into the inner-pocket of his jacket, and was silent until the waiter had put Putzi's second ice-cold beer in front of him.

'I think,' said Putzi, 'I need something stronger than this!' He drank deeply. 'How did you get hold of them?'

'A man – I can't tell you who – wanted to sell them.'

'What did you do?'

'Bought them, of course!'

Putzi sighed. 'That's all right, then. I must say, Adolf's talent improves with age. At least they're a vast improvement on those awful paintings of the Ludwigstrasse he used to do!'

'It's not a joke, Putzi!'

'Yes it is, now you've got them safe.' Putzi mused. 'I must say I envy Adolf. Did you notice her bush?'

Franz Xaver straightened his spectacles. 'That isn't the point.'

'What is then?' asked Putzi lazily. 'Say what you like, Geli has a trim little figure. Wasted on Adolf probably, although the drawing shows promise. Helène always said Adolf was a neuter, but perhaps for once she was wrong?'

'What,' asked Franz Xaver, 'should I do with them?'

'Is that what you brought me here to ask me?'

Franz Xaver snapped: 'Of course, what *else?*'

'I rather hoped we'd be talking about some Party payment for me!' said Putzi. 'But I suppose there's no hope of that, now you've paid a vast sum for these drawings!'

'Don't be frivolous, Putzi, please,' pleaded Franz Xaver. The hot sun was causing him to sweat and his neatly-pinned collar was beginning to soften. 'I have to do something *with* them!'

'How,' asked Putzi idly, signalling for a cognac, 'did this thief get hold of them anyway?'

'He wouldn't tell me,' said Franz Xaver, despairingly. 'But my guess is they were in the Chief's motor-car and he stole them out of it. Not difficult, you know. It's an open tourer.'

Putzi thought instantly of Emil Maurice.

'Did you meet this thief?' he asked, idly.

'No. We did it all by post.'

Emil would, Putzi thought. Once a convict.

'He could have kept some? Not sent them all?'

'He could have, but I don't think so.'

'Why don't you think so?'

'I told him if he kept anything back we'd look for him. And then he'd be dead.'

'That was smart of you, Franz.'

'You seem to forget, Putzi, that I was in the Feldherrnhalle. I am one of the *Alte Kampfers*.'

Putzi shook his head. If it had come to that, Franz Xaver would have asked somebody else to do the dirty work. Another Old Fighter would have tried to arrange a meet with the thief one dark night, and *zip*! The thief, whoever he was, had chosen well in approaching old Franz Xaver.

'Has anybody else seen these things?'

Franz Xaver nodded. 'I have talked to one person.'

Oh, no, thought Putzi! What Party dolt had fingered these erotic treasures? What beery Brownshirt would be talking about them in his favourite Munich beerhall tonight?

'For God's sake, who?' he shouted.

Franz Xaver looked puzzled. 'Father Stempfle, naturally.'

'Why, because he's a priest?' Putzi didn't know whether to laugh or cry. Stempfle was an ex-priest of a strange order, and a violent anti-Semite. 'The man's a total crackpot and a garrulous fool to boot!'

'Well, I only discussed it with him. There is a possibility the house-keeper Winter's son could be the culprit. Father Stempfle might be useful there? Talk to the boy?'

'You're sure it's the boy?'

Franz Xaver shook his head. 'I'm not sure of anything.'

'So nobody else knows?' persisted Putzi.

'Only the Chief himself, naturally.' Seeing the expression on Putzi's face, he added, 'Well, I had to show them to *him*, didn't I?'

Putzi looked at Franz Xaver a long time and then he got to his feet, laughing loudly. The waiter came out of the café to see what was wrong. Putzi said, 'Franz, I always knew you were a stupid arsehole. But this confirms it.'

'He had to know,' Franz Xaver shouted, fear temporarily replaced by rage. 'They're his *property*!'

'You silly old fool, you!' said Putzi. 'And what did he say when you showed them to him?'

Franz Xaver slumped back in his seat. 'Well. He went very quiet and thoughtful; Then he said, "If you've paid the man, that's the end of the matter."'

Putzi shook his head. 'And then he said tear them up?'

'What?' Franz Xaver was trying to pay the bill and get away from the waiter's curious gaze.

'Tear them up,' said Putzi. 'That's my advice.'

'He told me to keep them!'

'What?'

'To put them in a safe in the Brown House!'

'He did?'

'Yes! He seemed, well, fond of them.' Franz Xaver ran a fat, trembling forefinger round his wilting collar and put on his grey Homburg hat. 'What worries me, Putzi, is what if something happens to him, and they're found by people who aren't understanding or sympathetic?'

'If you are hoping I'll say I'll keep them, the answer is no,' said Putzi, making to go. 'I must get along, I'm late.'

Franz Xaver was still counting out the exact tip – a very small one – as Putzi walked away, still laughing to himself.

He never did learn what happened to the things.

But he always thought he knew who had taken them from the motor-car.

It was late when Adolf and Geli got back to the apartment, and Mutti (on one of her rare visits to Munich) had gone to bed. They had been to one of Adolf's favourite Munich restaurants, the Osteria Bavaria.

To Geli's surprise, Uncle Adi sat down on the couch and said, 'Geli, I have to talk to you, seriously.'

Well, thought Geli, that would make a nice change, normally he talked *at* her, almost always about things she didn't understand, politics and such.

'Yes,' said Geli, 'what is it?'

Uncle Adi looked very odd, suddenly, she thought: tense and quiet.

She wondered if it had anything to do with the fact that the blond young SS man had called to him, very respectfully, as they came to the door of the apartment, and kept him in low conversation for a few minutes? Geli had gone upstairs, taking care not to slam doors or awaken Frau Winter in the basement flat. She guessed the blond young SS man had told Uncle Adi that it really wasn't too safe, walking through the dark city streets so late at night, or something of that sort.

It turned out to be a lot more than that.

'I hear, Geli, that a couple of weeks ago you went to Emil Maurice's room in Swabling.'

The room reeled.

Geli said, fast, 'Who *said* that?'

Uncle Adi asked, 'Did you?'

'Of course I did!' Geli said. 'And why not?'

'Because,' said Uncle Adi, who was sitting as still as stone on the sofa, 'Emil Maurice is a servant. He is a driver. He is not a family friend. He is also a young man. He is also a man with a criminal record.'

It was all said so matter-of-fact it shocked her to silence.

But one thing was certain: Uncle Adi was not going to throw her out!

Geli, always sharp and intuitive on a personal level, knew that as surely as she knew that only denial and fury would help her now. Being contrite, evasive, admitting to *anything*, would be fatal! Deny, deny, deny – that was the only way. How did she know Uncle Adi wouldn't throw her out? He was not angry enough! He seemed sad, rather than angry. Geli thought hard: and fastened on a possibility. Emil was, with all his faults, his criminal-record, all that, *normal*. He had everything, he was complete. Somehow, in the ensuing torrent of talk that she knew must come, that one *fact* would never be mentioned by either of them, but it would hang in the air, as real as the glass chandelier hanging above them both. She must play on that.

'Emil may have a criminal record,' shouted Geli, 'but it doesn't stop you employing him, does it?'

'I need his special talents. It isn't the same thing.'

'What special talents, breaking people's necks?'

Hitler looked alarmed. Geli had never spoken to him like this before. Also, what Geli said was true. Emil would harm the Fuhrer's enemies, if he was asked to. He had done it, often.

'Leaving his character, which we know about, aside, brings us to your reasons for going to his rooms. What were they?'

'Rooms? The man only has one, and it's a slum!'

'All the more reason for not going there.'

Geli was still shouting, throwing off her short coat, and kicking off her shoes and slumping in a chair: 'You were away. I had only Frau Winter in this place. Mutti was at the Obersaltzburg. Emil had taken me to see a film. He stayed outside, with the car.' Geli looked Uncle Adi straight in the eyes. 'Yes! He sat in the car for two hours! He couldn't leave it because it's an open-tourer. So when I came out it was late, and I didn't want to go to the Cafe Heck alone, and I felt he deserved a drink or a coffee, so I suggested I buy him one somewhere!' Geli took a deep breath. All that was true. It had happened like that.

Except: both she and Emil had been conscious of a desired excitement, a desired risk. They had taken it. Obviously, they had been fools, both of them, to think that Uncle Adi would not have them watched.

The idea of being *watched* inflamed Geli even more.

'Your SS man may probably have told you I stayed at Emil's room for hours!'

'He said two and a half hours, Geli.'

Again, amazingly, Uncle Adi did not shout.

So *she* did.

'What the hell had it to do with him if I stayed six hours! I was lonely and I needed company! You're around people all the time, it's different for you! But when you go away I'm cooped up in this place, on my own! Oh, I know Mutti or Friedl sometimes come here when you're away but this time they didn't! Now Friedl is in Vienna studying piano but I have to sit around here, twiddling my thumbs!'

Adi winced and Feli saw a weakness there, and thrust: 'I have to go to Vienna! I've told you I want to go, but you ignore it or fly into one of your rages and say I can't go – why can't I go, you say you care about me, you say you *love* me, but you don't feel you have to do anything to prove it!'

Uncle Adi held up his hand. 'I have always cared about you. I have always wanted to protect you. To see that you were all right.'

'I'm twenty-two years old, I can protect myself!' shouted Geli. 'I don't need some *Uncle* looking after me all the time!'

Uncle Adi continued to look at her steadily but said nothing.

Incensed, Geli went for the jugular. 'If you think I've been unfaithful with Emil, say so! Go on! *Say* it!'

Uncle Adi hesitated: 'I didn't say that.'

'No, and you better hadn't! Emil is only a chauffeur and he smells!'

Uncle Adi looked startled. 'Smells?'

'Yes, like all your Party friends! They never wash or bathe or use cologne! They smell!'

It was true. What Geli didn't say was that she liked Emil Maurice's smell.

Uncle Adi looked shocked and a little mollified. 'I'm not saying you . . .'

'. . . Went to bed with your chauffeur, go on, *say* it!'

'I'm not saying it.'

'Well, then, if you're not saying it, what the hell is all the fuss about?' Geli stood up. 'I'm going to Vienna for voice training. If you don't want to pay for me to go, you needn't pay. But I'm going, just as soon as I can arrange it!' Geli walked to the door and turned. 'From now on, Uncle Adi, no accusations! My life is my own. You've shown me how

286

little you care, how you believe your *spies*, before you believe me!'

And she slammed the door hard.

She waited for him to come to her and say he was sorry.

He did not come. Finally, she fell asleep.

Uncle Adi was not in the house when she went, late to breakfast. Mutti seemed nervous (obviously she had heard everything) but she did not offer her normal warnings or platitudinous advice. If she does, Geli thought, I'll bite her head off!

'Where's he gone?' she asked, over her coffee.

'I don't know, liebchen, he left early.' Mutti's eyes were on her plate.

Yes, Geli thought, she'd heard the row. Not every word of it, but enough to frighten her. Well, it had frightened Geli too, but, all in all, she felt she had handled the situation well enough. She had got out of trouble, if only just. There were, of course, some things on her side. For instance, only she, Geli knew, could make Adi as other men (like Emil) were. Hard with want. And then not always, or often. Sometimes, though.

Who else would he find to do *that* for him? Those snobby bitches, the society women he was always fawning over? They wouldn't know how to start! It was work, yes, but it was her salvation, this trick she had for Adi.

If she wanted it. Wanted him and all that went with him?

She was not sure she did.

What she really wanted was to go to Vienna and study and become a great, popular singer!

So that was, Geli decided, what she would do. To hell with Uncle Adi and his shouting and non-stop talking about things she would never understand. To hell with smelly old Wolf and all!

Emil listened to the Chief's words but he did not take them in. He was watching the Chief's eyes.

They frightened Emil and he was not easily frightened.

The hard men of the Prisons had not frightened him.

He, too, knew the Prison rules: straight for the other man's testicles! Here, there was no such simple solution.

If I get out of this with *my* balls intact, I'll be fucking lucky, thought Emil.

Some of those S.S. boys were very hard. All it took was a word from the pale, unfit, moustached man sitting next to him.

So Emil sat in the Mercedes, in its allotted parking-place outside the

Brown House, and watched the Party members walking officiously inside, and waited for a sign, as to his fate.

The Chief was saying: 'You have been a good servant, Emil. A good comrade. I have always had complete faith in you. But you have let me down. You have let Geli down. You have let yourself down. You have let the Party down.'

Fuck the bastard shiteing Party, thought Emil, what had the stupid little cunt *told* him?

The Chief said, not looking at Emil: 'You know what I'm referring to. Fraulein Raubal is my Ward. I am responsible for her conduct and safety. I'm very sorry, Emil . . .' The Chief seemed to be choking on the words and Emil felt a sudden elation, a release, a hope.

Nothing!

He was going to do nothing.

Sack him, yes. Naturally.

But no fuss. No stink.

No trouble.

And he still had his balls.

So long as he had those he could *live*!

'Chief,' he said, looking straight ahead. 'I've been thinking about going to sea. I have a friend who might get me a seaman's ticket. I've been thinking about it for a long while. So . . .'

'Well, there is no job here for you any more,' said the Chief softly. 'Not as my driver, anyway.'

'No?' said Emil, not caring a fuck.

'No,' said Hitler. 'Do you have all your things?'

'I don't carry anything in the car.'

'Then we say good-bye here. Now.'

Emil thought: say nothing. Get out. Go.

He did just that. He opened the car door and got out. He stood, in the sun. 'Shall I turn in my badge, leave the Brownshirts, Chief?'

'No need,' said Hitler, looking straight ahead. 'Some job will be found for you somewhere, I expect.'

What he was saying, Emil realised, was: no fuss. No talk. There was perhaps hope.

But the silly little tart *had* told him?

Even if she hadn't, he knew. He fucking *knew*.

Emil felt a chill at that thought but he simply said, 'Thank you, Chief,' and walked away, from the Brown House, the Mercedes, Hitler, the whole fucking boiling of it. Good riddance to the whole pissing lot of it! If they wanted him for some rotten, dirty, dangerous job they could send for him – if they could find him! Emil walked, out of the Square, passing the stationary, waiting figure of Schreck, an S.A. driver he

288

knew, slightly. Schreck was in uniform and looked nervous. Schreck said nothing and nor did he.

At the far end of the Square, Emil looked back.

The Mercedes was tooling away from the Brown House, towards the apartment. He was going back there to tell Geli what he had done, Emil hazarded. Well, fucking good luck to the lot of them! For himself he had been a fool, a mug, but in the last analysis he'd been lucky not to wind up in the hands of the S.S. Those blond boys were bastards, worse even than Emil's old friends, the Kriminalpolitzi! They were pros who knew how the game should be played. These S.S. butchers of Himmler's were something different.

Emil took a deep breath and walked on, feeling a sense of deep relief. For, after all, he still had his balls.

Geli found the letter from Eva Braun on Uncle Adi's dressing-table. The thought occurred to her it had been left there so she could find it.

Geli was alone with Uncle Adi, in the place. Mutti was at the Obersaltzberg. Apart, of course, from Frau Winter, the housekeeper, downstairs in the basement.

Uncle Adi was in his uniform shirt and breeches, and in a hurry to leave. He was late, as usual. She had never known him to be on time for anything, not even a Party-meeting. People just had to wait for him, that was all.

Moodily, Geli bathed and put on a dressing-gown.

Things had been different between them since the row over Emil. Uncle Adi had started to go out alone at night. To the Opera. To the Residenz Theatre – he'd been there only three nights ago, to see some Bavarian drama by Ludwig Thoma. He'd come back, with Putzi and his smirking wife, still arguing about the ridiculous play. Uncle Adi saying it did not matter if the actors had Berlin and not Bavarian accents. Putzi saying it did.

Helène Hanfstaengl said nothing, she just looked at Geli and smiled: 'We all had supper at the *Schwautzwalder* afterwards,' Helène had said. All? Uncle Adi? Putzi and Helène? And somebody else?

Eva Braun?

Eva worked, if Geli had it right, for Heinrich Hoffmann, Hitler's photographer. Uncle Adi had spoken of her. She was young, even younger than Geli. Other than that, Geli knew almost nothing of her. Until now. Until this morning. Geli looked again at the note. Written in a schoolgirl's hand, it merely said, *'Thank you for a wonderful evening. I enjoyed it so much. I look forward to many other such evenings. Yours, Eva Braun.'*

It was addressed to *Herr Adolf Hitler* and dated the previous day. A bread-and-butter letter, that was all. Or was it? This Eva Braun was no society-girl, from what little Geli knew of her. She worked in Hoffmann's photography shop, a job for an ordinary girl. Geli felt a sudden panic. An ordinary girl, like herself? Innocent, uncorrupted, knowing nothing of sex? Except *she* had, quite a bit, or she'd never have held Uncle Adi as she did. This nincompoop wouldn't have that special ability, of that Geli was sure. The only person who knew she had that ability was Uncle Adi himself. Would he turn away from her for this nobody, this shop-assistant with, from what she'd heard, strict religious parents?

He might.

With his stupid ideas of the Volk and German Innocence and Beauty and all that crap, he just might, thought Geli, feeling cold and desperate, but still hopeful. For, there was something else in the equation, something she hadn't told Uncle Adi yet and didn't know if she could. Yet, what choice was there but to play the card, the only one she had, and see what happened?

But, first, Geli threw the letter down on the dressing-table in front of Uncle Adi.

'What's all this about?'

Adi was putting on his tunic and did not even look at the letter. He looked in the mirror, at his favourite sight, himself. So he *had* left it there, on purpose, she thought? All the absences from the apartment (and, therefore, from sex) had been deliberate, part of a plan to gradually exclude her from his life.

A hopelessness such as she had never known before spread over Geli.

Perhaps she didn't know Uncle Adi, had never known him?

Perhaps his pride came in front of everything.

In front of sex. In front of love.

'Who is this creature?' she nonetheless asked, with only a slight tremor in her voice.

Uncle Adi merely shrugged and put on his peaked cap, exactly square to his brow. He disapproved of jaunty caps.

'I must hurry. Schreck is waiting downstairs.'

Did he put an emphasis on the word 'Schreck'? Not Emil?

Yes, of course he did! Perhaps the thing to do was keep control, say nothing, wait? But the way she felt now, the possibility of losing everything, her whole way of life, the beautiful rooms of her own, both here in the Prinzregentstrasse and at the Obersaltzberg, she could not wait, play cautious, she had to know his intentions! Look what was at stake for her: quite simply, losing it *all*. The money, the dress-allowance, the music-tuition, even Mutti's job at the Berghof would go, Friedl's career as well!

Geli took a deep, shuddering breath. She knew Uncle Adi well enough to know that when he made up his mind he was ruthless. She had bet everything on him not doing anything about Emil. And he seemingly had not. No scandal. No shock. No talk. He had waited, that was all. He had waited, as he so often did. And now this.

'Who is she, this Eva Braun?'

'She works for Hoffmann.'

'You took her to the play?'

'She was there, yes.'

'You *took* her to the play!' Geli was shouting now.

'She is very fond of music.'

'And of other things, no doubt?' screamed Geli, terrified and past caring.

'No doubt. I do not know.'

Uncle Adi picked up his leather briefcase and made to go.

Deliberation, thought Geli.

Planned.

Down to the last detail.

'I'm pregnant,' she said.

There. The last card played!

Uncle Adi stood quite still, it was almost as if he had not heard. Then he crossed the room and closed one of the windows to the street, forgetting the other, larger one. He put down his brief-case and took off his peaked cap. It left a sharp dent in his forehead.

'How can that be?' he asked, in a low voice, his luminous blue eyes searching for hers.

'You're the one to ask?' answered the defiant Geli.

'You are saying, you and I?'

'Yes!'

'I can't believe it, Geli.'

'Believe what you like, it is so!'

The only card she had and she had to play it, to the bitter end.

'I don't think so,' said Uncle Adi, slowly. 'No, I don't think so.'

'Then who, if not you?'

Slowly, Uncle Adi shook his head. 'No, Geli. No.'

'I tell you yes!'

'No.' It was final, sad: the one word that decided her life.

'You say No to everything, don't you!' screamed Geli. 'You say No to me going to Vienna to study – don't you!'

'Yes, I do!'

'I can't do *anything*! I have to sit here and wait for you, and then you're surprised if I want to talk to people, anybody, a servant, just for company!'

Geli knew her words were spewing out into the Prinzregentstrasse and that any neighbour out there might hear, but it wouldn't be the first time she and Uncle Adi had yelled at each other. More often, of course, he had yelled at her. She shouted again, trying to broaden the scope of her argument, to deflect it away from the last desperate card she had just played. True, the thing was true, of course true, but how did that help? Well, *almost* true. Was it Uncle Adi's child? Did it *matter*? Her very life had stopped, here in this room, that was all she knew.

It was enough, by God, the card was enough.

It was always enough with a man.

It demanded action from him.

It brought him to you. Or he ran away.

Geli waited to know which one it would be.

Uncle Adi, smart as he was, however, had fallen into the trap of replying to her subordinate accusations. 'I do *not* restrict your movements. You do as you wish. Your music teacher tells me you are never there. You do no home study. Any idea of Vienna is preposterous.'

Geli felt some hope. Just a twinge of it.

She let her bathrobe slip, revealing her breasts, but of course it didn't work. Adi looked disgusted and averted his eyes.

Geli felt pure panic, then.

She waited. There was nothing else to do. It was all up to him, now.

Adi seemed so calm. So ruthless? Untouched? His voice was very low now: 'This child, if there is one?' He did not look at her as he said the words. 'There is no possibility you can bear such a child. Even if it was not mine, the scandal would be too great. You would inevitably be linked with me.' At that he looked her right into the eyes, and she felt the mesmeric thing everybody talked about, when they talked about Adolf Hitler. Geli moved forward to embrace him. She loved him, she always had, didn't he *see* that, these things she did for him, would she do them unless she *loved* him?

Uncle Adi shrugged back from her embrace and she was left there, her hands pawing the air. They fell to her side, as he spoke, again, very softly: 'You must see a doctor. I will arrange for one to come here, a Party doctor. It will all be quite secret. Then, if you are, as you say, positive, we must take steps.'

Geli knew then it was all finished, all of it, but she still cried out, from the very depth of her body: 'No! We can't! It – it's against the Church's teaching, for one thing! I couldn't, don't make me, Uncle Adi, please!'

'That is all irrelevant nonsense,' said Uncle Adi, briefly. 'I can't allow this child to go on. If the child is there. You are my niece –'

'Half-niece!'

'Just the same.' He stood up and put on his cap again and picked up his briefcase, with an air of total finality. 'I'm sorry, Geli.'

Then he was gone.

XIV

No other motor vehicle was ever allowed to pass the Mercedes. Schreck knew that the Fuhrer incessantly feared for his life. Who amongst Hitler's close associates was unaware of it? And what easier way to kill him than from the passenger-seat of an overtaking automobile?

Schreck drove on, out of Nuremberg, at his customary fifty miles an hour, and noticed in his rear view mirror, a car following. Schreck's impulse was to accelerate until he realised that one of the occupants of the car was dressed in the uniform of a page-boy. He slowed down and said to Hoffmann, 'Tell me, am I wrong or is that a page-boy from the hotel?'

Hoffmann, a small, stocky bonhomous character, well liked because he took photographs and gave them away free, turned round in his seat. He stared back. 'Yes, it is. I think you should pull over, Schreck.'

Hitler, who was wearing his leather flying-helmet, as he normally did when riding in the open-top Mercedes, had not heard anything. He looked enquiringly at Schreck.

'Permission to stop, Fuhrer? The car behind? It's from the Hotel.'

Instantly, Hitler was alert.

'Are you *sure* it is?'

'That young page-boy is in it.' Hoffmann was still staring in his mirror, back at the other car. 'With a chauffeur driving.'

Hitler himself turned, and he too stared. 'Very well, Schreck. Pull over.'

Schreck did as he was bid and the other car came to a halt behind them.

The page-boy jumped out and ran towards them. He was only about fourteen years old. 'Herr Hitler!' he called, 'there is an urgent telephone call for you, back at the Hotel. From Herr Hess. He is keeping the line open!'

Hoffmann stood watching Hitler, in the office of the Hotel Manager.

Hitler called into the telephone, 'Hess! Tell me! Is Geli alive? On your word as an officer, is she still *alive?*'

If Hess made a reply, Hoffmann did not hear any of it.

Hitler turned slowly from the telephone, his face ashen. 'We drive back to Munich, now! There has been an accident with a revolver.'

All the way back Hitler sat, quite still.

Hoffmann felt pity for Adolf.

The man, after all, was Germany's only hope! In a way, Hoffmann's own story crystallized that hope. Hoffmann had been beggared by the War, in which he had served as a military-photographer with a Bavarian Regiment. Photography was in his blood. The Kaiser and many members of the Royal Family had posed for his father. The end of hostilities had found Hoffmann looking for humble wedding-photographs and portrait jobs from his Munich shop. Only after he had become Adolf Hitler's 'official photographer' had he prospered. He was the only one allowed to take pictures of the Fuhrer. The first photograph he'd taken of Hitler (in his Mercedes, coming out of the printing-works of the *Voelkischer Beobachter*, situated opposite from his own shop in the Shellingstrasse) had been promptly grabbed by a Brownshirt and the film roughly exposed to the light.

Adolf Hitler had not even looked at Hoffmann.

The old green Selve had driven away, fast, the Brownshirts grinning on the running-board.

Hoffmann had expected to earn one hundred American dollars – a fortune in 1922 – for that shot. An American news-agency had cabled him offering that sum for any photograph of Adolf Hitler with world-wide copyright.

There was something about the face that fascinated Hoffmann. Not many faces did that. Not after you had photographed a few thousand of them. But soon, he had proven himself at least a supporter. His Nazi Party Membership Card was No. 427. He had put the point to Adolf Hitler when next they met, unexpectedly, at the wedding of Hermann Esser, an aide of Hitler's and a senior Nazi Party-member. Hoffmann promoted the wedding-reception at his house on the Schnorrstrasse, a pleasant, roomy, family-home. When, to his surprise, he learned Adolf Hitler was to be amongst the guests, Hoffmann went round to the confectioners providing the wedding-cake and asked for a sugar model of the Fuhrer to be placed on top of the cake.

It had been a great success with everybody, except Hitler himself, who had merely frowned and stared at it blankly. He even refused to make a speech. 'I'm no good at speaking to a few people. I need a crowd.'

Nobody seemed to understand that. Quickly, Hoffmann invited Hitler into his office and showed him his favourite portraits and diplomas: his King Gustav of Sweden Medal, not many German photographers had *that*. And his portrait of Caruso, the famous tenor, the most popular singer in the world.

Adolf Hitler was impressed. He inspected everything Hoffmann showed him with evident interest. 'I envy you, Hoffmann. You are doing something artistic and fulfilling. Like you, I wished to do something of the sort. I always wanted to be an architect.'

'Why did you give it up?' asked Hoffmann.

'I have been too busy building the Nazi Party. But I find time, now and again, to talk art or architecture with old friends.'

Heinrich Hoffmann decided he would try to become one of those friends.

Now, as Schreck drove silently through the night towards Munich, Hoffmann glanced sideways at Adolf (who sat absolutely still, staring at the road ahead) and wondered uneasily if any of this trouble was connected with his shop-assistant, Eva Braun?

He had introduced them.

Adolf had shown an interest in Eva, had taken to calling in the photographer's shop just to talk to her, had only recently escorted her to the Opera and, more intimately and secretly, to the cinema, which Eva liked better than the Opera anyway. He had advised her not to press too hard, where Adolf Hitler was concerned, but he realised that his words were not even heard by the besotted young girl, who could only see that an important and exciting man was taking an interest in her. Well, Adolf did that with girls. There had been episodes with other attractive young women Hoffmann had introduced to him at various mildly 'Bohemian' parties. Adolf liked young, fresh girls. Or anyway, he liked talking to them.

Hoffmann had met Geli often, and had grown to like her. He had long assumed that there was something between the girl and her Uncle Adi. Heinrich Hoffmann was not born yesterday. What the something was, he neither knew nor wanted to know. All he did know was that there had been a cooling-off in relations between the two of them, lately. Otherwise, why would Adolf have wanted to meet Eva Braun? Why would he have squired her about, obviously and openly, in the very places that, only days and weeks before, he had squired Geli Raubal?

So, something *had* gone wrong between Adolf and Geli?

Heinrich Hoffmann shifted uneasily in his seat.

He hoped that anything Eva had done would not rebound on him. Adolf Hitler was his patron and the best patron a man ever had. Had he not said to Hoffmann, at their very first meeting at that wedding, almost ten years ago: 'My dear Hoffmann, the Americans offer you one hundred dollars! It is an insult. I have turned down 20,000 dollars and will demand more when I rule!'

Certainly, the way Adolf Hitler looked at the moment, slumped back in his seat, staring blankly at the road, ahead, no photo-editor in London, Berlin, Paris or New York would see him as a World Leader: the white face, the wide, staring eyes, the trembling hands gripping his knees. This was no Superman. This was an ordinary man struck down by sorrow or guilt or remorse.

Hoffmann wanted to ask questions but did not dare. He took a deep breath, as the car tooled into the outskirts of the city.

One thing was certain. They would soon know.

Hess met them at the door of the apartment on the Prinzregentstrasse.

His face told them everything.

Hoffmann held back, staying in the Mercedes until he judged Adolf had heard the worst. That it was the worst, it was easy to see: the slump of the body, the head falling forward, Hess's arm on Adolf's shoulder, only of course for a moment, for Adolf hated to be touched by another man, expressly forbid it, told the whole sad story.

Hitler took a deep breath and went inside, Hess following him.

There was a uniformed man of the Munich Police Department standing at the door. He saluted Hitler respectfully, and Hoffmann, too, as he entered, after a respectful wait of ten minutes or so.

The housekeeper, Frau Winter, her middle-aged face white with shock, her workworn hands plucking at her blouse, stood on the first landing. She greeted Hoffmann with gratitude, he was somebody she could tell her story to, once again. 'Herr Hoffmann, what a terrible business! When Fraulein Geli didn't come to breakfast, I went to her room and called out to her. I called and called to Fraulein Geli but she didn't reply. Not at all! So, then, in the end I asked my husband to break the lock – and there she was on the floor, poor girl, in a pool of blood!'

'Dead?' asked Hoffmann, softly.

Frau Winter nodded. 'Of course.'

'You didn't hear the shot?'

Frau Winter shook her head. 'She'd put a face-towel round the revolver. We heard nothing.'

'A terrible shock,' said Hoffmann.

'She loved him,' replied Frau Winter, sternly. 'No doubt of that, Herr Hoffmann. But she did say to me, only the other day, "I don't know what Uncle Adi and I have in common!"'

Hoffmann nodded, looking up and down to see if anybody might be listening. Frau Winter talked on: 'She wrote a letter. To a girl, a friend of hers. It's upstairs. She didn't post it. It's just an ordinary letter, saying she was hoping to go to Vienna to study. Her voice, you know, Herr Hoffmann?'

'Yes,' said Hoffmann. 'Don't talk about this to anybody, Frau Winter. There may be an Inquest?'

Frau Winter sniffed. 'The Police President was here, Herr Gurtner.'

Hoffmann was surprised. 'In person?'

'Only for a few minutes. His men took poor Geli's body out the back way. In one of those special bags they have.'

'I see.' Hoffmann did see. Gurtner was a close personal friend of Goering and a long-time supporter of Adolf Hitler. No Nazi, but a member of the Nationalist Party, he had expedited Hitler's early release from the Landsberg. Again, obviously, he had proved helpful.

'I have cleaned up everything,' Frau Winter said. 'They told me it was all right to do that.' Her eyes filled with tears. 'It is a terrible business. Poor Herr Hitler.'

'Yes,' said Heinrich Hoffmann, going on past her, up the stairs. Thank God it did not seem as if Eva Braun was in any way connected with the whole rotten business. He knew Adolf well enough by now to hazard that in a matter of this sort, there was no way of predicting how he might react. Rage, fury and hate was certain to follow the pain and sorrow.

In the large living-room Hitler sat, his head in his hands.

Hess stood, his back to them all, his cadaverous face sorrowful, a telephone in his hand. 'Muller will come at once!' Hess put the telephone down and turned to the Party Treasurer Schwartz, who, to Hoffmann's surprise, was also present. 'He must get away at once. The newspapers will get onto it and when they do they'll go to the obvious places. Here And the Obersaltzberg.'

'What then?' asked Schwartz. 'Is Muller going to help?'

'Of course.' Hess turned away from Schwartz and sat next to Adolf Hitler on the sofa. Very softly, he said, 'Adolf, I don't think it would be wise to go to Geli's mother at the Obersaltzberg?'

Adolf Hitler straightened up. His eyes were terrible to see.

'No, I would not go there anyway.'

Hoffmann wished he had a camera to record all this, my God, it was History! But he put the thought away, quickly.

'Anything I can do?' Hoffmann asked. 'Anything at all?'

Hitler looked at him, then: 'Will you come with me to the Turgensee? To Muller, the printer's house?'

'Of course I will,' said Hoffmann, promptly.

'What are the arrangements?' asked Hitler in a low voice.

Hess replied: 'Muller is sending his servants home. He will wait there with the keys. The house is yours as long as you need it.'

Hitler nodded. 'Very well.' He looked at Hess. 'Rudi. Nobody is to go into that room. Nobody!'

Hess nodded. 'The police won't be back. That is all taken care of.'

'Nobody, Rudi!'

'As you say!'

Adolf Hitler very slowly got to his feet. 'Find out what the funeral arrangements are. I expect her mother will make them. Let me know as soon as you know. Run the Party office while I'm . . . not able to. Talk about all this to nobody.' He swayed as if he might fall.

Hess did not put out his hand to help. He knew better.

'Very well, Fuhrer.'

Hitler took a deep breath. 'I will go downstairs and talk to Frau Winter.'

'I will follow you down in a few minutes,' Hoffmann said.

Hitler walked, rather unsteadily, out of the room.

Hess looked at Hoffmann, dubiously. 'I would come with him but I'm needed here, to clean up this mess!'

'Will there be an inquest?'

Hess nodded. 'Gurtner has promised it will be a formality.' He closed his eyes. 'What bad luck, when he has such a busy calendar of events, important meetings, coming up in the next weeks.'

Hoffmann replied, 'I'm not sure he'll be fit for anything like that for some time. You may have to do a few things without him.'

'That is impossible,' said Hess, sharply. 'There is only one Fuhrer. You know that. See that he gets some rest and food.'

Hoffmann went downstairs and found Hitler with Frau Winter.

Frau Winter was saying, 'Rely on me, Herr Hitler, I will keep the key to the dear girl's room to myself, on my own person, all the time, every hour, until I see you again. I will put a bunch of fresh chrysanthemums in the room every day, never fear. Oh, Herr Hitler, I am *so* sorry . . .

Adolf Hitler pressed her arm, went out into the street, and got into the Mercedes. The policeman saluted him. The street was unusually quiet for that time of day, but Hoffmann imagined that the inhabitants were watching from behind their curtains.

It was late morning when they arrived at Muller's splendid house near the lake. Adolf Hitler had not spoken all the way there. When the

Mercedes turned into the drive, he stayed in the back of the car. Hoffmann got out and took the keys from Muller, who was waiting in the drive.

'There's food in the kitchen. Anything you need, help yourself. I've sent everybody away and I'm going off myself, now.' Muller indicated his own car standing in the drive.

'I know he will be grateful,' said Hoffmann.

'Shall I say anything?' asked Muller, a heavy man with prominent teeth. 'Offer my condolences?'

'I think not, he's upset,' said Hoffmann.

Muller nodded and walked to his car. He got into it and drove away. Hoffmann opened the front door of the house, and turned to find Adolf Hitler standing behind him, looking paler than ever.

'If you would like to go in?' Hoffmann said.

Hitler walked in without speaking. His hands shook as he opened the vestibule door.

Hoffmann looked round to see Schreck, holding Hitler's leather overnight bag. 'If you'd like to take this, Herr Hoffmann? I'll find myself a room in the servants' place at the back?'

'That would be best, Schreck,' said Hoffmann.

'Oh, and I took the liberty of taking *this* . . .' Schreck held out a Luger automatic. 'It's the Chief's. He keeps it in the glove compartment of the car. I thought you'd better have it?'

Hoffmann nodded wordlessly, and put the weapon in the inside pocket of his overcoat. Then he followed Hitler into the house.

Adolf Hitler did not sleep that night.

Hoffmann lay wearily in the room below and listened to Hitler pacing the floor above, six steps forward and six steps back, until at last Hoffmann fell asleep. Schreck, who had transformed himself into a butler, brought coffee at seven-thirty.

'Herr Hoffmann? Shall I take tea to the Chief?'

Hoffmann sipped the hot liquid and shook his head. 'Better if I do, I think. You stay out of sight for the time being.'

Schreck clicked to attention. Then raised his eyes to the ceiling. 'Has he slept at all?'

'Not much.'

Schreck clicked his heels and disappeared to the servants' quarters at the back of the house. Hoffmann hardly saw Schreck for the next three or four days but somehow the stoves that heated the large and sumptuous house were refuelled and the dishes in the vast roomy kitchen were washed and placed ready for re-use. Not that Hitler could be got to eat anything very much. Hoffmann took tea each morning. He accepted it, hollow-eyed and unshaven. Hitler stayed in his bedroom all day long, looking out over the woods around the Turgensee. It was October and the winds were keen and easterly, but the house was warm. Hoffmann did not dare leave it in case of telephone calls from Hess. These were at irregular intervals of three to four hours and were anything but reassuring. The liberal press, Hess said briefly (using no names at all, a proper caution, in Hoffmann's view) had written about 'the case' a great deal and attempted to link the Chief to it in a disgraceful way, hinting at sexual irregularities. The law of libel had prevented them going too far, but they had given reports of the Chief's alleged rift with his half-niece full coverage. Hopefully that was all behind them now the Coroner had declared Death by Misadventure. Hoffmann asked how much of this he should report to Hitler. 'Only the general outlines, nothing specific or upsetting, you do understand?' Hess said.

'Is there any . . . news?' Hoffmann asked. 'Of the . . . formalities?'

Hess hesitated. 'Is he fit to travel?'

Hoffmann said, 'It has been four days now. I imagine the shock is wearing off?'

'There was a quiet burial at the City Cemetery in Vienna today. It was the family's decision.'

'What should I tell him?' Hoffmann asked, thinking: all that was very quick.

'Just what I have said. Plus, I have a certificate for him to use should he wish to. It gives him special permission to cross the border into Austria, incognito. I am sending the certificate out to you by messenger at once.'

Hoffmann saw Gurtner's hand in that. The portly Bavarian police-chief would have been able to fix such a thing with one telephone call.

'You will come yourself?'

'I might be noticed, and followed.'

'Of course. What should I do?'

'Tell him what I have told you. Telephone me with his decision once you know it.'

Hoffmann put down the telephone, thoughtfully. Then he went upstairs to tell Hitler.

The next day Schreck drove them to Vienna. Hoffmann was so exhausted by the broken nights and empty days that he fell into a doze and wakened only when the Mercedes drove into the vast City Cemetery. Hitler was dressed in a dark blue suit with a black knitted tie, clean-shaven and pale. Hoffmann shook himself awake, got out of the Mercedes, and inquired of the Cemetery office-keeper the location of the grave. He thanked the clerk and told Adolf where it was.

Hitler nodded and got out of the car. He carried a bunch of flowers.

He stared around at the acres of dark tombstones, many of them huge, ornate family vaults, others vast effigies of angels with outspread wings, all in darkened stone, without expression. There was a keen wind and Hoffmann asked if Hitler would like to borrow his coat, but Hitler made no reply.

'Shall I come with you?' Hoffmann asked.

Hitler shook his head and walked, abruptly, in the direction Hoffmann had indicated.

Hoffmann watched him go, shivered, and got back into the car.

He accepted a swig of cognac offered by the ubiquitous Schreck.

It went down very well.

Forty minutes later, Adolf Hitler returned to the car.

Hoffmann, who was expecting a desolate and grieving man, was surprised to see that Hitler had no moisture in his eyes and that he was no longer trembling. Hitler ordered Schreck to drive, not back to Munich as expected, but to the Obersalzberg, at full speed. Hitler's voice was almost normal, husky and harsh. Schreck swung the Mercedes out of the Cemetery. Hitler seemed to Hoffmann – who found it difficult to understand, but then he found many things about Adolf Hitler difficult to understand – somehow rejuvenated, made more hopeful by that dismal place of death.

Hitler does not fear death, Hoffmann thought, wishing devoutly for a camera and permission to *use* it. He feels at home with it, death is a friend, death lies in wait for us all, but it is, in some way, to Hitler, a sort of ally. Was that possible or was it just fancy?

Heinrich Hoffmann did not know.

Hitler settled back in his corner of the car.

'So, Hoffmann, the Struggle is *resumed*. The Struggle we *must* win!'

Somehow, all Hoffmann could think about during the long journey home was the death of Geli Raubal, the sad, inexplicable fact of it. Her face haunted him, all the way.

Later that week Hoffmann witnessed a quite amazing turnaround: Adolf Hitler, seemingly untouched, back to his most effective form at a meeting of the students at the Berlin University School of Technology. Hitler arrived in a suit, and spoke earnestly, in a low voice, despite roars of encouragement from his many student supporters. Here, he was talking mostly to the unconverted, and to them (as the young, newly-qualified architect Albert Speer in his audience, noted) he seemed reserved, almost shy. In that bierkeller Hitler was talking to learned professors as well as the bulk of the student body, persuasively and patiently outlining the Nazi Party programme, Hitler led the Herr Professors and their students into a Germany without unemployment or want. There would be jobs for all, not just the workingman, but the professional man as well. Every German had something to give to the country and would have the opportunity to serve. The business of the Jews was hardly mentioned and if it was, this audience disregarded it. After all, this was a new party. Everything would be ironed out when it came to power. The Herr Professors, monocled and spectacled, high of shining collar and broad of belly and watchchain, stood, at the end, with every shabby student in the bierkeller, and applauded furiously. There were loud salutes of 'Heil Hitler' but the speaker simply shook his head, gathered up his shabby raincoat and hat and, with the same shy smile, left almost immediately after his speech ended. Hoffmann got his pictures. Albert Speer joined the Nazi Party the next day.

The Nazi Party was short of funds.

The Brownshirts did not get their pay.

Hitler appealed to them, personally. 'Stay with us! Tighten your belts! Soon, we will be victorious!'

Strasser and many others were doubtful.

Hitler reassured them. 'Six million Unemployed! One Breadwinner in Three on the Starvation-line!'

'There must be Elections,' he shouted, in smoking-rooms and beer-halls and at Party meetings.

'Give us Elections and see who the Volk want!'

Chancellor Bruning gave the Germans Elections.

Five in Nine Months.

The 'Alte Herr' did not like Adolf Hitler on sight.

Hindenberg liked Roehm, the famous Army homosexual even less. Why had the Bavarian corporal brought the fellow? Drummed out of the Army, this scarred and portly pederast had the nerve to propose to talk to Field-Marshal Paul Von Hindenberg, President of the Republic, on matters of State?

Very well! He had to talk to these two gutter upstarts. There was no way out of that. The Nazi Party had, amazingly, got eleven million votes in the latest election (five million more than Thaelmann, the Communist leader, whom Hindenberg liked even less than these two unsavoury fellows) and only four million less than Bruning himself. He had to talk to them, so he would. It was his duty. It could not be worse than talking to Bruning.

Bruning was useless! The country no longer believed in him, or his Centre Party. They blamed Bruning for the six million unemployed men walking the streets. There was nothing anybody could do about that, the *Alte Herr* knew. If you were in charge, you took the shot and shell. Bruning and the Social Democrats, too, had had their chance. The voters did not believe in anything they had to say, not any more. If they stayed in power, the Volk might begin to think the *Alte Herr* – himself! – had something to do with the total mess in which Germany now found herself.

And that would never do.

The Old Man, they called him. Very well, he *was* old. Eighty-four years old, a soldier since his eleventh birthday, the day he had enrolled as a boy-cadet in the Prussian military-school. The Iron Cross against the French in 1870, twenty-two years of age. Then the Victor of Tannenberg, although some cheeky young officers on the Staff had hinted Ludendorf had done it all.

Nobody had called out, 'Hoch Ludendorf', had they?

No, they had not.

'*Hindenberg! Hoch! Hoch! Hoch!*'

That had been the toast, throughout Germany, in that heady year of 1915, when all had looked won. At the end the Kaiser himself had thanked him personally, shaking his hand for the last time: a shrunken figure in civilian clothes, the withered hand shoved into the pocket of the tweed Norfolk jacket. There had been tears in both their eyes when the All Highest had stepped onto the train for Holland and exile. Hindenberg had said, 'I know my duty, All Highest, I will not rest until you are back. I give my oath on it!'

And yet this fellow Bruning – this business-manager of the German Trades Unions – had asked him, pleaded with him, to run as Chancellor against this Bohemian corporal! Break his word to the All Highest? Forget his duty to Germany, get down into the mire of day-to-day politics where such creatures as Hitler and Roehm lived and had their being? In the gutter? Gutter-press, gutter-war, gutter-politics, gutter-everything?

Bruning was losing his nerve and when a Comrade lost his nerve there was only one thing for it. He would have to go.

Resign? Sacked? It did not matter how it would be put. Such men as Bruning were not of the Prussian caste.

The *Alte Herr* looked at Adolf Hitler and Ernest Roehm with distaste. 'Yes, what can I do for you?'

They were not even gentlemen, so he did not ask them to sit down.

'Your Excellency,' said Hitler. 'We, the National Socialist Party, have met recently with Bruning, the Chancellor –'

'I know,' Hindenberg interrupted, rudely. 'Bruning tried the Nationalists first. For me to run for Chancellor? The Nationalists said No! So Bruning then tried you. You also said no. Only Bruning wants me as Chancellor, it seems.' He looked at the shocked faces of Hitler and Roehm. 'Bruning and, no doubt, the German People!'

Roehm said, coming to attention, 'Of that there can be no doubt, Herr Field Marshal!'

Hindenberg ignored that. He spoke directly to Hitler.

'Bruning even suggested that, for my co-operation, he would propose the Restoration of the Monarchy? With me as Chancellor, if you please!'

Roehm was scarlet with humiliation but he remained at attention.

'I do not want to be Chancellor of Germany. I am a soldier, not a politician, thank God. I am President of this Republic, and when the Reichstag votes for a Restoration of the Monarchy nobody will be happier than I!'

Hitler said, 'Herr Field Marshal, there have been two elections already this year. A third is likely. Do you wish a Government of the Right or of the Left?'

Hindenberg looked at him and then away. 'The Communists stand alone. They lose votes every election.'

'And who,' asked Adolf Hitler, gently, respectable in his dark blue suit and stiff white collar, 'do you think wins the votes from them? Bruning and his Centre Party? The Nationalists?' As Hindenberg was about to reply, Hitler lifted his hand, palm outwards, and Hindenberg, to his surprise, did not interrupt. 'Herr Field Marshal, *we* win those Communist votes.'

The *Alte Herr* was having none of that. 'Your terms are ridiculous. Your man here' – he would not even mention Roehm by name – 'wants his Brownshirts absorbed into the Army. Don't deny it!'

'I do not deny Kapitan Roehm wants that,' Hitler said, evenly. 'But Herr Field Marshal, all these points are open to debate.'

'Your Brownshirts are a menace to public order. Bruning wants them disbanded, did you know?'

'I guessed,' said Adolf Hitler. He was much quieter than Hindenberg had expected him to be, much more respectful, much less bombastic and foolish than his reported utterances, and his occasional radio broadcasts, would suggest. Now he was saying, in his respectful voice, 'If my Brownshirts are to be banned, and Herr Field Marshal, I would not do that, I cannot promise what would happen then . . .'

'You threaten?' asked Hindenberg, mildly.

'Not at all! My men are old soldiers. They will obey my orders. But they are tired of having to listen to the insults of the Communists. That is why they fight and brawl. But it is in a good cause. The cause of Germany!'

'So you say,' grunted the *Alte Herr*. 'But you will be relieved to hear that I said no. If one organisation is to be banned, all must be banned. That would include the *Stahlhelm*, the ex-Servicemen's Association. So, you see, Herr Hitler, I am even-handed in these things?'

'Yes, indeed, Herr Field Marshal,' said Adolf Hitler. 'But I must ask, is not a Coalition of Bruning's Centre Party and ourselves agreeable to you?'

'No,' said Hindenberg with brutal relish. He was getting tired of all this, and wanted his afternoon coffee.

'We would not be asking for more than a few seats in the Cabinet,' persisted Hitler. 'But we would need to have one appointment guaranteed!'

'Oh yes?' said Hindenberg. 'And what would that be?'

'The Office of Chancellor would need to be ours.'

'Yours?' exploded Hindenberg.

Hitler's blue eyes bored into his. Extraordinary fellow, thought the *Alte Herr*, odd, not the usual thing at all.

'I would assume office, naturally,' said Hitler.

'You?' Hindenberg turned his surprised laugh, his first reaction, into a heavy cough.

'Herr Field Marshal, it will come to that in the end. We will go on making inroads into the Nationalist and Centre Party votes. Why wait?'

It sounded very reasonable, put like that.

It was even possible the jumped-up fellow was right.

After all, the blasted Reichstag was a babel of conflicting and warring voices these days, the main note being one of panic. Bruning had no mandate to run the place, unless the Nationalists or the Nazis ran with him. Which neither would agree to do, not with Bruning remaining as Chancellor. Bruning seemed afraid of Hitler but the *Alte Herr*, looking at him across the polished oak table of the President's airy and untouchable room, did not share his feelings. This man was just a Drummer, a magnificent gutter orator, but no statesman, how could he be, he had no education, no training? Why, the accent alone was common, plebeian, *Austrian*.

'Herr Hitler, I cannot offer you anything!' said Hindenberg, gruffly. 'But by the rules of my office as President, once you get a majority in the Reichstag I will have to.' Hindenberg smiled, the huge, square head shaking with inner mirth, the bull neck chafing against the tight collar, the cropped Russian haircut. Adolf Hitler thought: this wooden Colossus is the very idol of the old Germany but one good push will topple him over! But he found a smile. Legality, first. Votes, first. Then Power. That was the way.

'Herr Field Marshal, I am sorry if we cannot agree. But I do not feel this is our last meeting. I wish you Guten Tag!'

And to Hindenberg's amazement, Adolf Hitler came to attention, and turned, in a correct military fashion, and left the room. Roehm, surprised, followed him.

Without permission, by God!

Hindenberg half-collapsed into his gilt chair. State-Secretary Meissner coughed discreetly, behind him.

'That guttersnipe!' said Hindenberg. 'Chancellor of Germany? I'll make him Postmaster General and he can lick my stamps – with my arse on them!'

He was rewarded by a suppressed low chuckle, the nearest thing Otto Meissner could ever muster to a laugh.

In the street outside the Chancellery, Adolf Hitler and Roehm got into the Mercedes. Frick, Hitler's Senior Civil-Servant-designate, joined them. He lifted his eyebrows and waited.

'The *Alte Herr*,' said Roehm, 'had us for breakfast. I felt like a lousy cadet at officer-school. When we get power I'll show him, the stupid old fool! Him and the whole god-damned Army!'

'No, no, Ernst,' Hitler said, placatingly. 'We need him. He'll open the door for us.' Hitler waved Schreck to drive away. 'We step up our pressure on the masses. We promise them work and bread.'

'I would promise them bullets and bayonets, myself!' said Roehm, still smarting from Hindenberg's contempt. Roehm was not very subtle, indeed he was disrespectful. Roehm never called Adolf 'Fuhrer', which everybody else, even Goering, now did. Ernst called him Adolf, even when other people were present. It was true Roehm had put him on the road in politics, had been the first to recognise his talent. But there had to be an end to gratitude. Adolf Hitler made a decision. If he went to talk to Hindenberg again (and he had no doubt that he would) Roehm would not be in the party.

Every man had his uses. It was possible, Hitler thought, that Ernst Roehm had outlived his.

When Hindenberg, three weeks later, faced Bruning his words were short and brutal, like an unpleasant but necessary order.

'Bruning, it's no good. You'll have to go!'

Bruning stood there as if poleaxed. 'Herr Field Marshal! Another Election! Now?'

That was the trouble with these damn civilians, even a stern, scholarly creature like Bruning. They couldn't understand an order. He, Hindenberg, was President of the damned Republic, was he not? Did Bruning want to sit down and discuss it all over again? Act! That was the soldier's way. Talk, talk, talk! It was all these politicians ever wanted to *do*!

'Herr Field Marshal! I cut government expenditure, I cut official salaries, I cut wages, I cut unemployment benefits. I've done everything I could to keep inflation down! Inflation is the prime enemy, we saw that in nineteen-eighteen.'

'Water under the bridge, I'm afraid, Heinrich,' Hindenberg said.

The use of his first name sobered Bruning.

'I'm going to give Papen a chance.'

Bruning looked amazed. 'But nobody knows him, in the street.'

'You dislike him personally?'

'No. He's a gentleman. But he's a socialite, he *hunts*! What will your six million unemployed make of that'

Hindenberg shrugged. 'He's somebody I can talk to.'

'Herr Field Marshal,' said Bruning gently, 'if you give Von Papen the job you will have another Election, and a riotous one, on your hands inside a month.' Bruning sighed. 'My resignation is in your hands, Herr President.'

Hindenberg nodded and let him go. Fellow meant well, but no good. No good at all.

Adolf Hitler faced Von Papen across the room.

'It was good of you to come to see me in Munich, Herr Kanzler.'

Hitler and Papen were alone in the official ante-chamber. Somewhere a typewriter clacked. Papen was dressed in English tweeds and wore an expression of regretful disdain at having to deal with such as Adolf Hitler. The man's taste in clothes was execrable. That *suit*. That *tie*. That *haircut*. It would not have done for the Herrenklub. Or indeed any of the circles in which the lean, horsey Papen moved. A quick mind was there, he had not been in Intelligence for nothing, Hitler reasoned, happier pulling the strings than dancing on the end of them?

Papen poured coffee, black and strong, with enormous courtesy. 'You know of my admiration for you, Herr Hitler? I don't need to tell you, I have leaned over backwards to show it.' Hitler nodded and waited. 'I know I have your support. Or I hope I do?' Still, Hitler did not speak. 'I have the Army and Big Business behind me, but I do not have a majority in the Reichstag. With your support, I would.'

'Herr Von Papen, what would you offer me?'

Franz Von Papen studied his cigarette, which was English, a Player's Perfecto. 'I think I could run to yourself as Vice Chancellor and two other cabinet posts?'

Adolf Hitler's reaction surprised, nay, alarmed him. The man went white in the face and his eyes widened. 'I have thirteen million votes,' said Hitler, crudely. 'I have only one thing to say and it is this: I demand the Chancellorship!'

Papen smiled, very, very politely. 'I can't see that happening, but if you got it – just for my own information – what would you do with it?'

Adolf Hitler stared at him, and Papen had a feeling he saw contempt – of all unlikely emotions – in that strange, mad, face. 'I would give my Brownshirts three days to clean up Germany!'

'Would you?' breathed Papen. 'Would you *really*?'

He rose languidly to go through the motions of a polite leave-taking, but too late.

Adolf Hitler was gone.

Papen sat down again, somewhat deflated.

He had been relying on Adolf Hitler. Maybe he should have offered more? Three or four Cabinet posts perhaps? But the Chancellorship?

Hitler?

Papen laughed aloud.

Another month. Another Election. Another Chancellor.

Papen, hurt and offended, resigned.

Hindenberg, still vacillating, appointed Kurt Von Schleicher.

Schleicher had served in Hindenberg's old Regiment, the Third Foot Guards. He was a brilliant diplomat but not much else.

And no diplomat on earth could get rid of Papen without making a lifelong enemy of him!

And Schleicher could not hold the Reichstag together, at all. Despite secret meetings with Roehm and Strasser, meetings so secret that Adolf Hitler knew all about them but held his fire.

Roehm and Strasser were proven traitors now. Their time would come.

Meanwhile, the Brownshirts fought the Reds hand-to-hand in the night-streets of Berlin and Frankfurt and Munich and Hamburg, and mainly they won.

And the workless starved.

Hitler and Papen met a second time, in a far more serious and secret vein, a meeting *nobody* knew about, at the lavish house of a Cologne banker, Kurt Von Schroder. Franz Von Papen was much more respectful towards Adolf Hitler this time. Wearing a Savile Row suit and smoking yet another Player's Perfecto, he came, almost at once, to the point.

'Confidentially, the *Alte Herr* is already fed up with Von Schleicher, who, as you know, is a dandy and a fool.'

Hitler thought Papen a dandy but not a fool, despite his expensive education.

'If you and I join forces,' Papen said, 'I have the Industrialists and the Army, you have your own people and just possibly the Nationalists. Together I think we have a winning hand.' He smiled. 'I can talk the *Alte Herr* into considering us, as a team.'

'You know my terms,' said Hitler. 'Chancellor or nothing.'

'With myself,' asked Papen, idly, 'as your Vice-Chancellor?'

'Naturally.' Hitler stared at him, not moving, hardly breathing.

'But of course.' Papen allowed himself an ironic smile. 'Always provided you can convince the *Alte Herr* you are his only option?'

Adolf Hitler still did not move, blink, or even seem to breathe.

He really was, thought Papen, somewhat uneasily, a most curious fellow.

Hindenberg's reception-room at the Presidential Palace was as grand, and as spacious, as ever: all polished wood and gilt and soft carpet and high-curtained windows.

This time, Hitler took Hermann Goering with him.

Even the *Alte Herr* could not ignore the *Pour la Merité*.

This time, Hindenberg asked them to sit down. But his voice was gruff, if weary. Hitler felt a sudden, triumphal ecstasy. The Old Man knows already, Hitler thought, about the vast, cheering crowds at the Kaiserhof (so superbly organised by Goebbels) and the mobs who had cheered the car all the way to the Palace. 'Herr President, I place my Movement at your disposal only if I am to be *Kanzler*.'

'Once more, Herr Hitler, when your Party has a majority in the Reichstag, not before!'

Adolf Hitler saw a red mist before his eyes. But he managed to say, 'Herr President, talk to Von Papen. Call me again when you must.'

And again Hitler is gone, again without asking permission!

The *Alte Herr* could hear, outside the Palace, the roar of the crowd that greeted Adolf Hitler as he stepped out, got into his car and was driven out of the courtyard. It was a deep, ominous sound and, thought Hindenberg, boded ill for Germany. He sat down suddenly, feeling his years.

*

Outside Adolf Hitler stood in the open tourer and saluted the crowds, but he was not happy in Berlin. The city was a Marxist stronghold, and it was full of intellectuals and liberals and all kinds of enemies. Now, he was smarting from the *Alte Herr's* rejection, witnessed only by his secretary Meissner but no doubt all over the Wilhelmstrasse by tomorrow.

Hess asked: 'Back to the Kaiserhof?'

'No. To Munich.'

'But Von Papen will be calling on the telephone?'

'Let him call me in Munich.'

Hess nodded and gave instructions to the driver, Schreck. Hoffmann, who had accompanied Hitler but had taken no photographs, was glad of that. Rarely had he seen Hitler look so outraged.

Hitler did not speak at all, all the way to Munich.

In the Brown House in Munich a group of Hitler's henchmen awaited him.

He strode into the Senate Hall, followed by Hess, Goering and Hoffmann, and his S.S. bodyguards. A gigantic Swastika stood above the huge brass-bound interior-door. Colour standards, in red, were furled at the entrance, where two more S.S. guards, helmeted and with pipe-clayed belts, stood at attention, smacking their rifle-butts as Hitler entered the Conference Room. Busts of Bismarck and of Dieter Eckhart loomed, and were gone, as Adolf Hitler threw down his jacket and the hat he had never bothered to wear and called to his white-jacketed major-domo, 'Tea! And whatever these gentlemen want!'

His wave encompassed Goebbels and Hans Frank, Hitler's personal lawyer, who both rose as he entered. Frank had been in courts all over Germany for the last six months, day in, day out, defending members of the Brownshirts accused by the Civil Police of crimes of Assault and Disturbing the Peace and Insulting Behaviour and, in some cases, Serious Bodily Harm and Murder. Frank had been telling Goebbels about the problems of convincing judges that all the Brownshirts were doing was protecting their speakers, on some occasions Goebbels himself. The intense little man was listening with interest but jumped to his feet the moment Hitler entered, the love of his Fuhrer showing (Frank thought) a little too obviously. And yet Frank accepted that Goebbels was sincere. Nobody had worked harder in the war of words of the endless Elections.

Hans Frank also stood up, hailed Hitler and blinked hard to prevent himself from yawning. Nobody in the room, Goering, Goebbels,

Himmler, Frank himself, had slept more than an average of five hours in the last fourteen nights. Hitler never went to bed at all some nights, after a big speech, being unable to unwind until dawn. He just cat-napped whenever he could.

He looked more harrowed and angry than exhausted.

Hans Frank thought: now starts the talk that will go on until the early hours. It was a routine with which they were all familiar, but it got no easier to bear.

Mind, this time Adolf had plenty to distress him.

Papen had promised him virtually promised, the Chancellorship. What an insult the *Alte Herr* had given him. The old fool! He would learn, he would bend the knee yet. Hitler felt rage and more rage. Nobody spoke. Hitler sat, brooding, in one of the large leather chairs.

Goering was talking about Hindenberg. As the man who had masterminded, in a strictly practical way, Adolf Hitler's road to the top, through his contacts in Big Business and the Army, Goering could go further than any other man in Hitler's company. 'You know, Fuhrer, we should not worry too much about poor old Hindenberg. He is going to give us what we want sooner or later.' 'It has been said that Ludendorf won his battles and Hindenberg betrayed Ludendorf. The Kaiser made him a Field Marshal and he betrayed the Kaiser. The Right elected him President in 1925 and he betrayed the Right. The Left elected him in 1932 and he betrayed the Left!'

Everybody laughed except Hitler, who remained sober and brooding.

Goering said, 'Fuhrer! He is a clockwork figure-head, no more!'

At that moment, Hess entered. 'Fuhrer, I have Von Papen on the telephone. He wishes to speak?'

Hitler stared at Hess a long moment, then waved his hand dismissively.

'Tell him, tomorrow!'

Hess hesitated, then clicked his heels. 'As you say, Fuhrer.'

There was a silence in the Conference Room.

'Let him stew!' shouted Hitler, suddenly. He got to his feet and walked to the window, and stared out.

'The only way we can win, Fuhrer,' said Goebbels quietly, 'is to get the Nationalists on our side!'

'We cannot do that,' said Hitler wearily, without turning round. 'Hugenberg would never come in with us.'

Goebbels said, 'He might, if we tell him he can have some cabinet posts?'

Hitler shook his head, still without turning round. 'I doubt it, Josef.'

Hess re-entered, walked quickly across to Hitler, and whispered in his ear. Hitler nodded, looking a little more cheerful, and sat down. Kannenberg, Hitler's major-domo, supervised a string of assistants with trays, on which were meat and cheese open sandwiches, Swedish-style, coffee and more wine. Hans Frank relaxed as he ate. It was still possible that they might all get away early, and get some sleep before Hitler began his almost inevitable nightly diatribe.

It was, of course, not to be.

'Von Papen says he's trying to do exactly what you referred to a few moments ago,' said Hitler. 'You must have second sight, Josef. That is probably why he telephoned. If so, let him do it, he doesn't need my permission!'

Goebbels smiled, as a child might, at some small praise.

Goering snorted and drank a large mouthful of Liebfraumilch.

There was a general loosening of tension.

Hitler was talking about Berlin and his sudden decision to drive to Munich that night. 'Maybe I am just a poor provincial, but I sometimes hate that City! A den of Marxists and degenerates of all kinds, of musicians like Hindemuth who cannot compose a tune, of artists who think the German Race is lower than ordure! *These are German artists?* Gentlemen, Berlin is a sink! A sink of Jewry amongst other things – in Berlin the Jews have penetrated Law, Medicine, Property, the so-called Arts, the Theatre! I could not remain another minute there! When I next go, it will be as German *Kanzler* – and then we will see what we will see!'

Everybody in the Conference Room applauded.

Hitler sat back, pleased at the reaction.

But Hans Frank remembered another Adolf Hitler.

A worried one.

Nobody else in that Conference Room, not the bumptious Goering, or the little Doctor, or Himmler blinking behind his thick glasses, or even the ever-trusted Hess himself, had seen Adolf Hitler as worried as he had, that day.

Even now, Hans Frank rarely thought of the occasion without awe. And another feeling: horror.

Awe, because of the content of the trust Adolf Hitler had placed in him.

Horror because he had to keep the secret, no matter what.

Even if it was not a secret worth keeping.

Even that.

Adolf Hitler had entrusted him with it.

And that was enough.

Frank had worried about the secret every single day since. That was part of his temperamental weakness no doubt, the weakness the other, hearty, ruthless men in the Conference Room would have laughed at: but they would not have laughed if they had seen, as he had, Adolf Hitler standing alone – in the drawing-room in his apartment at the Prinzregentstrasse, taking from his pocket a letter written in a sprawling and ignorant hand and bearing a Berlin postmark. 'Frank! You are my personal lawyer.' Frank had nodded. 'I can rely on absolute confidence, yes?' Frank had smiled and nodded again.

Hitler looked him straight in the face: the Fuhrer was angry, and to Frank's surprise, anxious and pale, and possibly uncertain.

'It is a repulsive attempt at blackmail by one of my disgusting relatives! It concerns my own parentage! Read it!'

Hans Frank had read the letter. He recalled the first phrase even now, every word fired into his memory. The spidery, slum-school hand, the cheap notepaper: '*There is certainly an interest in the Press with regard to some very peculiar circumstances of our family history.*' The rest was ill-written innuendo, nothing at all specific, hinting merely that Adolf Hitler knew what the writer was talking about.

'Who has sent this letter?' Hans Frank had asked, looking up.

'William Patrick Hitler. The son of my step-brother, Alois.'

'Is it money he wants?'

'Without any doubt. He is a chip off the old block, obviously. Alois is no good, either.'

All Frank knew about Alois Hitler was that he kept a bar-restaurant in a not very fashionable quarter of Berlin. Adolf Hitler rarely talked about his relatives, except to say that it was important not to 'play favourites', as Napoleon had done.

This seemed a different business. *Blackmail?* What could this William Patrick Hitler hope to gain? Well, money obviously, as Hitler said, but asking for it was a risk surely, unless there was some truth in it all?

Hans Frank knew that some of the anti-Nazi gutter-press had continually accused Hitler of being part-*Jewish*! What an insane idea! He had dismissed these articles as muck-raking by Hitler's political enemies.

'Find out,' said Hitler, 'what the truth is, if any, behind these accusations.'

Frank started. 'You are asking me to investigate your own family?'

'The truth must be known. But only to the two of us, and in the strictest confidence.'

Frank had reported in a matter of weeks: he had not found it an easy task but he made his report as businesslike and unemotional as he could. He gave Adolf Hitler a single copy of his report, on one sheet of paper. Hans Frank had laboured long and alone over the wording. It read:

"All in all, I have found out the following from all kinds of sources: Adolf Hitler's father Alois was the illegitimate child of a cook named Schickelgruber from Leonding, near Linz. She was employed in a household in Graz. According to the law which states that an illegitimate child has to bear the mother's family name, Alois, he was called Schickelgruber, until his fourteenth birthday when his mother (your grandmother) married Herr Hitler. With that action, the illegitimate child, your father, became the legitimate child of the marriage 'per matrimonium subsequens'. *I must stress that this is all logical and not really unusual. The cook Maria Schickelgruber, had been recently employed in a Jewish household, the Frankenbergers of Graz, when she gave birth to her child Alois. And Herr Frankenberger paid agreed alimony on behalf of his nineteen-year-old son to Maria Schickelgruber, from the child's birth until his fourteenth year. (All this happened in the 1830's.) There is existing some correspondence between the Frankenbergers and your grandmother underlining the fact that both parties knew of, but kept quiet about, the circumstances in which this child was conceived and which made it necessary for Frankenberger to pay Maria Schickelgruber alimony, according to law. This correspondence was in the possession of a lady, related to Alois Hitler through the Raubal Family, living in Wetzesdor, near Graz."*

The document had stated facts. It was a lawyer's epistle.

'I know about all *this*!' said Adolf. 'My Father was not the son of the Jew from Graz! I have heard this story from my Grandmother and from my Father! I also know about my Grandmother's premarital sexual relationship with the man she later married. You must understand these two people were poor. I have been told how the Jew was prevailed upon to pay alimony – a highly desirable contribution to a poor household. Doubtless, he dreaded any publicity about the matter.'

Frank wanted to ask: are you saying your Grandmother told you she had intercourse with this Frankenberger but was *not* made pregnant by him yet nonetheless claimed maintenance-benefit for her son from him, saying the son was *his*? If Hitler's Grandmother had told him *that*, Frank reflected, then it was a miracle! For he had discovered in the course of his investigations, that Hitler's Grandmother had died forty years before Adolf Hitler was born. Of course, his father, Alois, could well have told him. It could all be just as Adolf Hitler said.

The whole story was no doubt embarrassing.

But who could burden a Grandchild with his Grandmother's Sin? Who could abuse him because of that? It seemed to Frank unlikely that Adolf Hitler had Jewish blood in his veins. It was of course not completely out of the question that Hitler's father was a half-Jew! If that were so, then obviously, his feeling towards all Jews would be hatred. Or would it? The question was very far-fetched. It had all happened so very long ago. Who was to analyse it all?

Certainly not Hans Frank.

For him, it was finished. He never expected to allude to it again.

Frank was jerked back to the present by a sudden stir in the now darkening room. Hess, heavy-booted, had just come in with a message: Herr Von Papen was on the telephone yet again and absolutely must talk with the Fuhrer. Hitler rose from his chair and was ushered out by Hess, to take the call in a private office.

Frank sneaked a look at his watch: one-fifteen, in the morning.

To Hitler, it was still early.

Frank looked round. Goering was drinking from a large wine-glass, at his elbow a bottle of Liebfraumilch, in a silver ice-bucket. Goebbels was already asleep. Himmler got to his feet and stretched his skinny limbs, encased in the black-and-silver uniform of the S.S. He was just about the least-military figure Frank could imagine, although he was said to impose impossibly high standards (of family, education, but particularly of Blood) on his recruits. Blue-eyed, golden-haired youths were favourites to get into the select body of men guarding the Fuhrer. The major-domo took the opportunity to serve black coffee to everybody.

They all got to their feet as Adolf Hitler came back into the room.

His face had an expression on it that Hans Frank was never to forget.

'Gentlemen!' said Adolf Hitler, 'I think this time the *Alte Herr* will *do* it! I see him next week in Berlin.'

Everybody stood and shouted.

My God, thought Frank, perhaps . . . ?

And I'm part of it! His knees felt weak and he sat down, abruptly. Everybody laughed.

The *Alte Herr* was in a heavy black frock-coat and his grey moustache curled upwards in the Prussian manner. This time, he will have to ask me to sit down, thought Hitler. Politely, he enquired as to the President's health and got a gruff grunt in reply. Hindenberg knew it was all settled and the resigned set of his shoulders told Hitler that he had accepted Papen's ultimatum – for that, in a sense, was what it was. He had told Papen: 'Chancellor or nothing! Plus the War Ministry, plus the Prussian Ministry!' Papen had replied, with good grace, 'But of course, and the Vice Chancellorship for me?' Hitler had smiled. 'Naturally.' Papen had regarded his English cigarette. 'I also need an Enabling Bill, signed by

Hindenberg, that means I can make changes in the way the Reichstag is run.'

Papen smiled, thinly. 'Not yet, I think.' He had puffed on his cigarette and smiled through the blue smoke, which irritated Hitler. 'As I said to the *Alte Herr*, with the Right in the saddle . . .'

Hitler had interrupted: 'And Hitler the prisoner of the Nationalists?'

Papen looked startled. 'Did I say that?'

'I expect so,' Hitler had said.

'No, I'm sure I didn't . . .' Papen had looked disconcerted. 'What I did say was I thought the time might soon be right for a restoration of the Monarchy.'

'I trust he didn't believe you.'

It was not a question. Papen had begun to smile, then saw the eyes of the man facing him. He had had a sudden, terrible feeling that what he had done was somehow irreversible. Von Papen felt that Adolf Hitler would make a mess of things, once he was in power, that the Nationalists and the Centre Parties would, sooner rather than later, vote him out.

That, anyway, had been the theory.

'Hitler can be handled, Franz,' Goering had told him.

But could he?

Now in the Presidential Palace Hitler settled comfortably in the chair that Hindenberg had indicated.

The *Alte Herr* creaked down into his, on the opposite side of his vast, polished desk.

'No need for talk,' said Hindenberg. 'We know what is agreed.' What was it Papen had said about the fellow? A Prisoner of the Nationalists? Well, time would tell.

'Herr Hitler,' said the *Alte Herr*, tonelessly, 'you have a following in the country – I have seen the crowds outside – and now, you lead a majority coalition, by two votes, in the Reichstag. I cannot withhold any longer from you what you have in the past asked of me. I hereby offer you the Chancellorship of the German Republic.'

Adolf Hitler did not reply for a very long moment. An odd, glazed expression was on his face.

Slowly he rose to his feet.

He extended his hand and reluctantly the *Alte Herr* took it.

Adolf Hitler held onto it as if he would never let it go.

'Your supporters await you,' said Hindenberg, brusquely.

Adolf Hitler came to attention, and left the room quickly.

The silence that followed was a blessing. Hindenberg sat down again, heavily. Meissner put a cup of strong coffee and a glass of cognac in front of him.

Outside, there was a sudden roar.

Hindenberg had never heard such a noise.

'My God!' he said to Meissner, 'just listen to *that?*'

'*Heil Hitler,*' came the chorus, through the open casements, the reverberations ruffling the long drapes.

The Palace itself seemed to rock with the sound.

'My God,' said Hindenberg, 'you'd think he was Caesar!'

The Old Man watched the Brownshirt procession (some said, ten thousand strong) march through the streets of Berlin, from behind the windows of the Presidential Palace. The windows were kept closed, for his doctor said night air did not agree with his chest condition. Hindenberg had been acknowledged by the Stalhelm, as they passed by in perfect formation. Well, they would, they were his own men, were they not, the ex-Servicemen of the last War, loyal as loyal, if nowadays a bit longer in the tooth. In contrast, the Brownshirts marched badly, but some of them were mere boys and had no barrack-square training. No doubt that would come, it would have to. Some of them were singing, some were shouting, some were laughing, and many held blazing torches, waving them about, rather than simply holding them aloft. Plenty of room for discipline there, as he had told the silent, awed Meissner.

Well, it was a great spectacle, say what you like.

A torchlight procession four hours long, all the way to the Brandenburger Tor.

Berlin had never seen anything like it.

Nor, for that matter, had the *Alte Herr* himself.

It was said that if you lived long enough you saw everything. Well, it certainly seemed that he had.

Who could have prophesied it?

A corporal?

Inside the Chancellery there was amazement and joy.

None of them could believe it had really happened!

Not even Goebbels, who had stage-managed the whole march.

Not even Goering, who had manipulated Von Papen.

Not even Von Papen who had tried to manipulate Hitler.

Certainly not Hans Frank, who wondered what changes the Fuhrer's victory would bring, in his own life?

Or Hess, who had tears in his eyes.

Or even Himmler, who was, typically, out marching at the head of his S.S. detachment.

They all stood there, as the sound of triumph beat through the room, each one called, in the order of precedence (as Hitler turned, eyes blazing), to join him for a few minutes, on the balcony.

Frank manoeuvered himself, so that he could see Adolf Hitler's back: the white uniform coat and black trousers, the flick of the head to throw back the lank wisp of hair from his forehead, the right arm held straight-out in the Nazi salute, the whole tableau against the smoke and flame of the hundreds of torches.

Outside the voices sang and cheered, the *Horst Wessel* roaring from a thousand throats. This was what they had all worked for, this was a sweet and victorious moment none of them would ever forget.

'*Heil Hitler . . .!*'

'*Heil Hitler . . .!*'

Hans Frank, in the midst of all the noise and the triumph, the darkness and the flame of the torches, suddenly felt a premonition of disaster: he shivered, then reproved himself: be brave, fearless, ruthless!

They were on their way.

XV

ADOLF HITLER stood, at attention, in the Garrison Church at Potsdam and looked around him: it was, indeed, a sight to remember, a personal triumph to savour!

A Dedication Service before the opening of the new session of the Reichstag – what a spectacle for the Volk! To see the Old Germany and the New in such amity and splendour!

The Brownshirts down one side of the Church.

The Stalhelm – the ex-servicemen of 1918 – down the other.

The Army, in field-grey, at the front of the Chapel, at strict attention.

In the front pews the Crown Prince himself, eldest son of the Kaiser, with the old commander Von Mackensen at his side, both attired in the magnificent dress-uniform of the Death's Head Hussars. With the creator of the small but lean modern Army, Von Seeckt, and the senior naval-officer, Admiral Raeder, both in uniform and full medals, standing stiffly next to them.

The Cabinet – most of them Hitler's men now, Goebbels, Goering, Papen, Hugenberg – in civilian clothes, were almost at the font.

What a Victory, in sheer propaganda-terms, to get them all here, before the eyes of the whole nation! The Service was being broadcast on the radio (excellent work by Goebbels) and photographers had been taking discreet pictures for what seemed like hours, Heinrich Hoffmann, inevitably, foremost amongst them.

Yes, indeed, all of Germany was here.

United. At one. For the first time in many years.

There were no Communists and no members of the Social Democratic Party.

The voice of the *Alte Herr* was booming through the most famous military chapel in the land. Hindenberg, in his grand, bemedalled uniform of the Prussian Guard, loomed over the tomb of Frederick the Great.

'I remember well the day in 1886 when I stood, at this very spot, a young Leutnant in the Guard! Four years later we were at War with France! We won that War because we were United!' The *Alte Herr* coughed, the congregation shuffled. The priests had long ago had their say and were relegated to the sidelines. This was the important part of the Dedication, the *Alte Herr*'s words to the Nation. He paused and Adolf Hitler waited.

'We now have a truly National Government,' intoned Hindenberg. 'I urge you all, each and every one of you, soldier, sailor or civilian, to stand behind this Government! Do anything, anything at all that is asked of you, to support this *National* Government in its most difficult work!'

A low approving buzz came from the congregation.

The Brownshirts, Stalhelm and Army men looked steadily to their front.

Adolf Hitler, now German *Kanzler*, in dress-suit and striped trousers, crosses the dais and grasped the *Alte Herr*'s hand.

He holds it firm, as the cameras click and the magnesium flares pop.

Then, he turns to the congregation. As usual, he waits for absolute silence.

'Neither the Kaiser, nor his Government nor the German people willed the War! Yet weak and foolish politicians accepted *our* War Guilt!' He pauses. 'Now, national honour has been restored!' He turns to Hindenberg. 'Thanks to your understanding, Herr General Feldmarschal, a marriage has been consummated between Germany's old greatness and her new strength!' He lowers his voice and bows low, but all hear the words and see the gesture. 'We pay you Homage! A protective Providence has put you at the Head of Our Nation!'

Again, Adolf Hitler takes the *Alte Herr*'s hand.

Again, the cameras click and the magnesium flares pop.

The organ booms.

A brass-band strikes up *'Deutschland Uber Alles.'*

Adolf Hitler stands erect and still, at the sound.

So does the entire congregation.

Deutschland, indeed, Adolf Hitler thought, *Uber Alles.*

Hitler, supremely confident and ecstatic with glee, strides around the Chancellery with a spring in his step. The eyes not only of Germany but of the whole world are upon him. This is what he has worked for, this triumph of the Will! Comfortable in his cream jacket, his boots clip-clopping along the corridors of the building, blond sentries coming to attention at every door, Adolf Hitler rubs his hands together and feels a sudden *rightness*. This is where he belongs: here, in the very seat of power. 'All of Germany is mine,' he told Eva Braun, on a brief visit. 'I am master of the greatest nation in Europe. Unbelievable, but true, my dear!'

Eva nodded and said nothing. She, like Germany, was over-awed. 'I can do anything I like. Anything at all!' Hitler's eyes bulged and gleamed. Eva turned away. There was something very odd about Adolf, at such moments.

Hitler called new elections.

The Nazi Party won Seventeen Million votes.

Von Papen was voted out and lost his place as Vice-Chancellor.

The Stalhelm mounted the Swastika on their armbands.

It did not save them: they were amalgamated into the Brownshirts.

Goering got his reward. He became the Prime Minister of Prussia.

But the *Volk* said to themselves: while the *Alte Herr* is there, everything will be all right.

Even Eva Braun's father was reconciled to Adolf Hitler.

Had not the man shaken hands with Hindenberg?

Hitler spoke to the Nation over the radio. Everybody in Germany hears him. 'Fourteen years have passed since the day when, blinded by promises of Peace, the German *Volk* lost their freedom! Fourteen years of neo-Marxism has all but ruined the country! The venerable Leader of the War years has called on us – as before at the Front – to fight once again for the salvation of the Reich!'

Almost nobody in Germany disagrees with those sentiments.

Or if they do, they say nothing.

Then Adolf Hitler bans the Communist Party.

Papers found in a raid on the *Karl Liebknecht Haus*, Communist Head-quarters in Berlin, is the excuse, not that one is needed.

A Coup is planned, Hitler says. The captured papers prove it.

All over Germany, Communists run for cover.

So do many others: anybody who had ever declared himself against Hitler is in danger.

Bruning himself never sleeps in the same room two nights running.

Finally, he gets to Switzerland, and then to America. To talk. And talk.

Many are not so lucky.

The Brownshirt Squads are everywhere. Hammering on doors, kicking them open. Dragging men out, throwing them onto lorries.

The Camps at Dachau and Oranienburg are full to overflowing with Communists, Social Democrats and Jews.

In the Camps, there are beatings and rough treatment, sometimes of elderly, unfit men, by young uniformed thugs, but, as yet, no open or deliberate killings. Press photographs show the inmates of these Camps doing hard labour, and the text points out that it is a new experience for them.

The killings are, however, taking place, in cellars and empty warehouses. Old debts are paid off.

To wear the Brownshirt is to be King.

There is a list. Every *Gauleiter* has one.

If you are on it, God help you. Nobody else will.

The Reichstag is burned down.

A halfwit called Van der Lubbe is found guilty.

The Police (now accompanied everywhere by Brownshirts) arrest him and he is summarily tried and hung. A Communist, Dimitrov, makes a fool of Goering at the trial and is acquitted.

The Judges are not yet trained in their duty to the Third Reich.

They soon will be.

No Communist deputy turns up at the next meeting of the Reichstag, which takes place in a theatre, since the Reichstag building is a mass of rubble. Adolf Hitler now has his 'Enabling Bill' and can pass any law he likes.

Hindenberg has said, 'The *Kanzler* has told me he will not use the Act without first consulting me!'

But Hitler's Brownshirts still allege a Communist Plot. Goering has shouted: 'Everyone of those Communist Deputies is a traitor and must be strung up!'

The *Alte Herr* sends Hitler a telegram.

It reads: *You have, by your brave personal actions, nipped Treason in the bud. You have saved Germany. For this, I express my most profound thanks.*

Hitler whoops with pleasure when he reads it.

The *Alte Herr* is Eighty-six years old, now.

But Eva Braun's Father is impressed.

So is Germany.

Fritz Braun has written a letter to Adolf Hitler, in fact.

Your Excellency,
I find myself in the extremely unpleasant position of having to write to you with a problem of a private nature, and to convey my distress as a Paterfamilias.

My family is at present divided, my two daughters Eva and Gretl are living in an apartment you have put at their disposal. I was presented with this as an accomplished fact.

I am old-fashioned enough to believe that a child should live at home until she is married. Quite apart from this I miss my daughters enormously.

I should therefore be grateful, your Excellency, if you would grant me your help? I end this letter with the plea that you will not encourage this thirst for liberty in my daughter Eva, despite the fact that she is over 21.

Please advise her to return to the bosom of her Family.

Yours very Respectfully,

Fritz Braun.

Fritz Braun handed the letter to Heinrich Hoffmann.

He did not see how he could put it in the post to the man!

Hoffmann, of course, handed it, unopened, to Eva.

Eva read it through, silently.

Then handed it to Hoffmann to read.

Then she tore it up.

My God, Hoffmann thought, standing in his Munich shop, times do change, they do indeed.

Heinrich Hoffmann recalled Eva, then eighteen, ringing the doorbell of his house on the Shnorrerstrasse, fresh from her years at the Kloster on the River Inn. The Convent had not made her too submissive, Hoffmann had thought: the neat, brown-tweed costume, topped with a jaunty brown beret on the newly-cut blondish hair was fashionable, even daring. The girl was certainly attractive: large eyes, athletic figure, a ready smile. She was looking for a job in Hoffmann's shop. Her credentials were good: a Catholic family, father a teacher, the middle one of three sisters. Hoffmann had sat her down in his living-room and asked a few questions.

'How was the Kloster?'

'I hated it. Too many girls. Too much discipline.'

Hoffmann laughed. He had seen a couple of other girls. None had this frankness. Or the basic sweetness of her smile, a trifle melancholy maybe, thought Hoffmann the professional photographer, underneath the modest manner.

'Did you have any special gifts?'

'I was in all the plays. Mostly I played leads.'

A dramatic nature under the modesty? Hoffmann became interested.

'Your father is a teacher? Your mother is also from Munich? I seem to know the name?'

'You may well, Herr Hoffmann. She was Bavarian ski-champion, a long time ago, of course. And something of a swimmer, too.'

Heinrich Hoffmann nodded. 'And what do you do in that line?'

'I have climbed rocks.' Eva smiled. Yes, he was right, there was a sadness in the smile. 'And I like ice-skating. And, of course, dancing.'

'Was that allowed at the Kloster?'

'Mother Superior did not mind so long as the girls did not dance too close together.'

Heinrich Hoffmann nodded again, amused, and despite the hour – it was only four in the afternoon, poured himself a drink, a brandy. He was drinking too much, but what the hell, these were exciting times. It did not occur to him to offer Eva anything. 'Look, the job is waiting-on in the shop. Also, filing negatives, and so on. There may be some opportunity to do some dark-room and developing work. Would you be interested in that, at all?'

'Very much so,' said Eva. 'I like technical things.'

'Excellent.' Hoffmann nodded. 'Then the position is yours, you can begin on Monday next. We start work at eight-thirty.'

Eva smiled, collected her gloves, and took her leave.

His daughter, Henny, came in, after she had gone.

'Who was that? Have you given her the job?'

'Yes. She seemed the right sort. She was at the Kloster on the Inn.'

Henny snorted. 'Keep her away from the customers. Convent girls get so man-hungry!'

Heinrich Hoffmann had laughed tolerantly. He loved his daughter and hoped for big things for her. The way the Party was going (that was 1931) he felt optimistic. Business was good again, mostly due to his Party connections. And his sole right to publish photographs of Hitler, as his own copyright, was making him, slowly, prosperous.

That had been a strange business, the meeting of Adolf and Eva.

It was only a month or so before the death of Geli Raubal.

To this day, two years later, Heinrich Hoffmann did not know if the two events were connected. All he knew was that Adolf Hitler had been smitten by Eva Braun the first moment he saw her. That he had shown it by the way his eyes ran up and down her almost perfect figure as he slumped into a seat in Hoffmann's shop, throwing down his felt hat and inevitable raincoat, and said, 'I see you have a new assistant, Hoffmann. You must introduce me?'

Hoffmann, knowing Adolf's liking for fresh young women, did so at once (calling Adolf 'Herr Wolf', his cover-name as always) but Eva seemed unimpressed. Plainly, she had no idea who Adolf Hitler was Hadn't she noticed his photographs, there were enough of them around? She went off promptly to the dark-room to finish some developing work for Hoffmann. He could not grumble at Eva's application. She was keen and made herself useful. Also, the girl was friendly with his daughter, Henny.

'Who is she?' asked Adolf Hitler, seeing her, in Hoffmann's shop, that first time.

'Eva Braun. Her father is a teacher, just promoted to Professor. I think he's also had a little luck with an inheritance. He'll need it, with three girls to marry-off. They seem comfortable, they have a maid and a small car.' Hoffmann waited, to see if Adolf would bite. He did.

'Very vivacious, Hoffmann. Most attractive.'

Hoffmann waited until Eva came out of the dark-room (talking with Hitler about his speaking-engagements and arranging to accompany him to the biggest ones) and then he asked Eva if she would mind, as she was working rather late, going out for sausage and beer for all three of them?

Eva looked surprised but complied. When she returned, Hoffmann poured her a glass of beer but she only sipped it. She refused the sausages, as she was trying to lose weight. Hoffmann knew this because she had told him so. Adolf talked to her in his usual Viennese way, paying her compliments, saying what a lovely skin she had, hadn't Hoffmann thought of taking portraits of her, and then sounding her out about music, and discovering that she only really liked jazz, which Hitler hated, thinking it negroid in origin and therefore decadent. To Hoffmann's secret amusement, he showed none of this, and finally offered her a lift home in his motor-car, waiting outside, with his new driver Schreck at the wheel.

Eva refused promptly, politely, but without much explanation.

'I have a call to make on my way, I wouldn't trouble you, Herr Wolf.'

Adolf Hitler nodded, got abruptly to his feet, kissed her hand, and left. All in a moment, in his usual way. The shop-door slammed, the Mercedes revved up outside, and he was gone.

Hoffmann laughed at Eva's surprised expression.

'Don't you know who that is?'

'You called him Herr Wolf?'

'It's Adolf Hitler.'

'Who?'

'He's the most famous politician in Germany!'

Still, Eva did not look impressed. She put on her beret and wished him *Guten Abend* and left the shop. Hoffmann thought: this is probably one who will get away.

*

326

Eva, however, asked Vadi about Adolf Hitler.

'Hitler?' Fritz Braun looked up from his supper. 'How did you meet him?'

Eva sensed disapproval and said, quickly, 'He was in the shop.'

'Yes, Hoffmann seems to be his favourite photographer.'

'But who is he, Vadi?'

Fritz Braun took a deep breath. 'He's an imbecile who wants to reform the world.'

Her sister Ilse looked up, amused. 'He's very important, obviously?'

Eva said nothing to that and concentrated on her borscht, which was, of course, fattening. She decided she would turn up her skirt-hem a couple of inches. That would take men's eyes off her waist.

'What is he like?' asked Ilse, pressing. 'Adolf Hitler?'

'He has a funny moustache and a big felt hat, and he's forty or more,' said Eva, discouragingly.

Adolf *Hitler*?

Not really.

The next day at the shop Eva looked up the files under 'H' and that was when she suddenly realised – so *that's* who he was! For Hitler's face was in Hoffmann's pictures everywhere: at rallies in Nuremberg, surrounded by the Brownshirts: holding the Romanesque banners that Heinrich Hoffmann told her Adolf Hitler had himself designed. Hitler, looking somewhat middle-aged, to Eva's eyes, his cross-over belt rounding an incipient belly, his black hair falling across his forehead as he punched the air with his fist. All very impressive, she was sure: but it was the *women* she noticed, in the adoring crowds. The strange expressions of love and desire on their faces, how very odd. Adolf Hitler had seemed anything but physically attractive, sitting in the shop.

Of course, she hadn't been thinking of him that way, then?

Was she now?

Well, not really, was she?

He was far too old for her – she could imagine Vadi's face.

Nonetheless, every time Adolf Hitler came into the shop, he sought her out, bringing little gifts of sweets and chocolates. Eva was intrigued, and waited for the invitation that never came – supper, the Opera, whatever? Nothing. All she heard from Heinrich Hoffmann was the name of somebody called Geli Raubal. Apparently, this girl was living in Adolf Hitler's apartment, was some kind of distant relative, and went everywhere with him.

Eva told Henny Hoffmann all this and Henny, who was a direct and cheerful girl, simply said, 'Forget him, Eva, there are plenty of men in the world.' Not, thought Eva, important men like Adolf Hitler. But why should such an important man want her, Eva Braun? No possible reason, was there?

'Let's go dancing,' suggested Henny.

So that is what they did.

Dancing, and swimming on Sundays in the Starnberg Lake.

The time passed, and Eva hardly ever thought of Adolf Hitler.

Of course, his name was in the newspapers and his voice was on the radio. It had a strange, husky quality that made Eva shiver a little. It sounded savage, not at all like that of the soft, gently-teasing, middle-aged man who had pretended to drink beer with her in the shop.

Plainly, this very important Herr Adolf Hitler had better things to do than pursue a mere shopgirl. She was as clever and as attractive as Henny and they would go out dancing at least one night of the week. The two girls made up a foursome and 'paid their end'. No young man, in the Depression, could afford to pay for a girl to go dancing and dining.

Adolf Hitler, of course, was another matter. He was older: and richer.

Then suddenly, the death of Geli Raubal! Whom she had never met or even seen. *Suicide*, her father said. 'Any person Adolf Hitler is connected with will go wrong, anybody can see that.'

Eva kept her tongue between her teeth: for a very good reason. Adolf was already seeing her once or twice a month, in secret. He had taken her on a couple of picnics, then to cinemas in the Schwabing or Schauburg districts. To tea, at the Carlton Cafe. At none of these places had they seen any of Hitler's Party comrades. At none of these places had Adolf been anything but pleasant and avuncular and complimentary. And very, very polite. No sexual innuendos or any suggestion of impropriety. Usually Brueckner, his aide, was with them, and a couple of bodyguards in mufti, at a distance. Adolf told her, 'Eva, I have to keep my movements secret. I travel a good deal, as you know, but what you do not know is that my life is in constant danger.'

Eva was thrilled but a little taken aback by this statement.

It seemed unlikely to her that anybody might want to kill him. Yet, plainly, he believed it. Suddenly, too, Hitler's calls for Eva's company grew less frequent. Henny Hoffmann told her: 'It means nothing. The Fuhrer is all over Germany, talking to the people. My father is with him, so I know. And you think of marriage?' For Eva had been foolish enough to speculate, idly, to her friend. 'Eva, Hitler will never marry anybody, ever!'

Henny seemed to like to tease Eva. She'd noticed that.

Eva thought: maybe Henny fancies Adolf herself, every woman seems to, that's what it is.

After all, Henny saw him often, always had. He was always at the

Hoffmann house, when he was in Munich. He didn't find time, apparently, to call her, Eva Braun, shopgirl, but why *should* he, that seemed to be what Henny Hoffmann was saying!

'He says women ruin politicians,' remarked Henny, a girl, with a lot of airs, but, of course, a useful friend.

Just the same Eva could not help riposting, 'He has his Achilles' heel, like all men! He'll marry me, sooner or later, you'll see!'

She was furious when Henny Hoffmann laughed out loud.

But she joined in to show that really she was only joking.

Except that she wasn't.

The thing Eva hated most was hearing how wonderful Geli was.

Adolf, when they did meet, seemed to talk of little else.

So Eva determined to be like her, in all ways.

To be attractive, for a start. That meant new shoes and dresses and, finally, of course, french-style silk underwear. She raised the hemlines of her skirts again, and Henny Hoffmann's eyebrows were raised with them, with amusement. Eva told nobody at home, not even her sisters, anything of her relationship with Adolf Hitler, but she knew her sister Ilse guessed, and did not approve. Ilse had a Jewish boyfriend, a doctor, and could not be expected to like what Adolf Hitler stood for. But Ilse knew how headstrong Eva could be, and warned her once or twice, in a tangential way, against 'unusual' relationships with older men. By this time Eva was past caring. The ghost of Geli Raubal had to be laid and there was only one certain way to do it.

Sex.

The problem was where and when?

Eva, although a virgin, was not afraid of the prospect of the sex act, unlike so many of her fellow-students at the Kloster. To her, it seemed a natural business. She was good at all things physical (skating, dancing, swimming, calesthenics) so why should she be anything but excellent at yet another physical exercise?

Well, boiled down to basics, that was what it *was*, wasn't it?

And from one or two hints Adolf had let drop Eva had gathered that the wondrous, beloved Geli was not exactly the fairest, most fragrant maiden in Bavaria when it came to sex. For sex, of a sort, there had plainly been between Adolf Hitler and Geli Raubal. What sort, she could only guess at, but whatever it was, any sex between *herself* and Adolf Hitler was going to be robust and healthy and natural, with Adolf Hitler the aggressor and herself the submissive, pliant, loving, lubricious partner.

Oh yes, Eva Braun knew exactly what she wanted out of the relationship with Adolf Hitler. If you could call it a relationship, the amount of time she saw of him! An evening here, an afternoon there, with great yawning gaps between!

Of course, she had her job and that filled her days. Boringly.

She had Vadi, who loved her so much and had once taken six months of his spare-time to build her a doll's house, complete with furniture, bedding and kitchen utensils.

What would he say if he saw me *now*?

Those were her thoughts as she fell back on the velvet sofa in Adolf Hitler's apartment on the Prinzregentstrasse, and gently, sweetly urged him to become her lover, to use his body to pleasure hers, to become his, forever.

And to blot out the ever-present memory of Geli Raubal, whose portrait hung in the locked bedroom, along with the daily chrysan-themums, arranged by Frau Winter: and everything as it had been the day she died in there, only nine months before.

The sex was good, and she guessed normal, and quickly over, and Adolf Hitler looked somehow relieved and satisfied. Her guess was that the kinky sex-stuff with Geli was something he didn't need with her and it gave her a sudden feeling of power, and of hope.

It was not to last long.

She did not hear from Adolf Hitler for four weeks.

When she did, it was an urgent summons to the apartment, sex, a few hours together, more sex, and then, a whole lot of loneliness. No talk of love, of marriage, of a future of some sort, any sort, together. Just the ceaseless ringing of the telephones, and the waiting Mercedes and the insistent hurry, hurry of his life.

There was something desperate and brutal about it all (Adolf shouted down telephones a lot) but that did not worry Eva. A man's world was different from a woman's. Politics were brutal and people got excited and sometimes hurt. Maybe Adolf was right when he said his enemies wanted to kill him? Her heart went out to him when she thought that. He was a great man and he loved her, didn't he?

Of course he did. That much was obvious.

She even told Henny Hoffmann some details of the closeness of their relationship. She pointed to a photograph of Adolf and said, 'I bet nobody knows how close he is to me?'

'*That* close?' asked Henny Hoffmann, curiously.

'*That* close,' said Eva, triumphantly. Well, why not? 'I could even be . . . you *know*?'

'Not pregnant! Eva!'

'Well!' Eva pouted. 'I could be, for all I know. Would he mind if I was, do you think?'

In reply, Henny, wordlessly, held out a recent set of Heinrich Hoffmann's photographs, part of a collection to be called *The Hitler Nobody Knew*. Eva looked, with a sinking heart. Almost every photograph showed Adolf Hitler surrounded by beautiful young women. Some of them, Eva saw, were dressed in the height of fashion. Henny was watching with some sympathy, as Eva's eyes narrowed. 'He has to be nice to these women – it's his duty. He hates it!'

Eva left soon afterwards, dry-eyed and silent.

That evening Eva Braun was alone in the Braun apartment.

Her sister Ilse was out with her boyfriend, the Jewish doctor.

Vadi and Mutti were visiting relatives.

Eva took from her father's bedside-table his Army revolver. She aimed it, clumsily, at her heart and pressed the trigger but the 6.35 Walther bucked in her hand, and the bullet lodged in the artery of her neck.

Blood spurted everywhere: onto the embroidered sheets of her bed, onto the pink scatter-cushions lying across the coverlet, and onto the floor, in bright little pools.

Before she pulled the trigger, Eva had telephoned Doctor Platte, Heinrich Hoffmann's brother-in-law.

She had also sent Adolf Hitler a bouquet of flowers and a farewell letter.

The Doctor responded first, and in great haste. He got to the Braun apartment to find Ilse Braun already there, having just come in. Deftly, Platte took out the bullet from Eva's neck and found that not too much damage had been done. He consulted his brother-in-law, Heinrich Hoffmann, by telephone, and arranged for Eva to go at once to a private clinic in Munich. He took her there himself. He did not report the accident to the police but he reassured Eva's parents that it *was* an accident, and that Eva – after a few days' rest – would be fully recovered.

Well, Hoffmann had said: absolute discretion and secrecy!

So that is what he had got.

Eva woke up to find Adolf Hitler, holding a bunch of flowers, sitting at the bedside. He grasped her hand and asked her if she knew what she had done? Eva was dreamy, made no reply, and feigned sleep. Adolf left, gently. His flowers stood in the vase all the time she was in the clinic.

Adolf Hitler did not need to swear the Doctor to silence.

It had already been arranged by Heinrich Hoffmann.

331

'They saved her just in time,' reported Hoffmann. 'She aimed at the heart, apparently.'

Adolf Hitler paced around Hoffmann's living-room.

'She did it for love of me. It must not happen again.'

Hoffmann knew he was thinking about Geli Raubal.

'You don't owe her anything,' he replied. 'My brother-in-law says her wound will heal. It should leave no trace.'

Hitler stopped pacing. 'I must look after her. I must at least do *that*!'

It was at that moment that Heinrich Hoffmann realised the date.

It was All Saint's Eve, November the First, 1932.

Almost exactly twelve months after Geli Raubal had shot herself.

A replay, Hoffmann thought. Extremely dangerous.

But it had worked.

Adolf Hitler had taken her on.

Now, almost two years later, Adolf Hitler was *Kanzler* of Germany and Eva Braun was known, to a very few people, as to all extents and purposes, his mistress. He had set her up in a small villa at Bogenhausen, in Munich, along with a maid, chaperoned by her younger sister, Gretl. Hoffmann knew all this because he paid the rent on Adolf Hitler's behalf. The little shopgirl in the brown beret, Eva Braun, was now the kept woman of one of the most powerful men in the world.

Times, thought Heinrich Hoffmann wryly, do indeed change.

Adolf Hitler has told the Army: with 100,000 men you cannot wage War. But you can change Germany!

The Young Officers were with Hitler, the Old were not.

But Hitler has three million Brownshirts.

Or has he?

Do they not belong to their Commanding Officer, Kapitan Ernst Roehm?

And what will Roehm do with them?

Nobody, not even Hitler, knows the answer to that.

The Army had stayed in Barracks while the Brownshirts rampaged. Reichenau had seen to that.

Young, ambitious, cunning, he had proposed to his somewhat doddering old boss, the War Minister Blomberg, to alter the Officer's Oath (once dedicated to the Kaiser) to now read: *'I swear loyalty to the Fuhrer of the German Reich, Supreme Commander of the Wehrmacht!'*

It was an Oath to the Death.

*

'The Left is destroyed, the Marxists, Communists, Social Democrats, all gone!' said Roehm, chewing on his cigar in Josef Goebbels' palatial family house in Berlin. 'Very well, Josef! What now? The Industrialists? Big Business? The Financiers? The Aristocracy? The Junker Land-lords? The Army Generals?' He took a swig of his schnapps. 'Do *they* get off, free? Do *they* run the Germany we have liberated for them?'

The blackhaired, intense little man shook his head.

'The revolution must not be halted, Ernst, I agree.'

'I knew you would,' said Roehm, the red, scarred face cracking into a brief smile. 'What we need is a Second Revolution! We are the genuine Workers' Party, after all! That is the Party you and I joined, Josef. I have a big speech coming and this is what I will say – I'd like your thoughts, my dear Comrade?'

Goebbels sat and listened. He was still, somewhere in his deepest being, a sort of idealistic socialist. He did not like the idea of the bankers and industrialists eating the fruit of his own efforts, and those of the Party.

Roehm said, still warming his arse to the fire: 'We have won one victory! We have set the Revolution rolling. But it is at the half-way mark, that is all. Josef, I will not allow it to be betrayed at *this* point. The Revolution must be a National Socialist one! Some people in top positions will not accept that. I tell you this – they will be ruthlessly eliminated if they deny the forward march of the Revolut-ion!'

Goebbels listened, and nodded, but he was worried.

Of course, a slab of Socialism was already imbedded into the victory. Now, any man, any Party Member anyway, could climb the Party ladder. No longer did he need to have the proper background or education. To be an *Alte Kampfer* was enough. 'Ernst, I agree, but what will the Fuhrer say to all this?'

'Adolf, you mean?' asked Roehm, rudely.

Goebbels nodded, warily. Sometimes Roehm was too abrasive, too scornful of others. But he had 300,000 men at his back and that had to mean something.

'I'll tell you, Josef, what Adolf will think,' said Roehm, gazing at the glowing tip of his cigar. 'He'll think that he needs time to consolidate. The Left is broken, or in prison. That is enough for him. Now, the Right, the Army, Hindenberg, Big Business, must be given way to! In short, back to Business as Usual!'

Goebbels did not like the scornful way that Roehm spoke about his beloved Fuhrer, but he had to admit that he agreed with the words and sentiments of the stocky, balding ex-officer.

'Adolf will never move until he's *sure!*' Roehm added, derisively. 'By that time it could be too late. The Army? A hundred thousand men and they are well-disciplined and well-armed, but how loyal are they? I have three times that number. But we have no cannon or artillery or airplanes!' Roehm threw the butt of his cigar into the fire. 'I say we must incorporate the Brownshirts into the Army, now. While we can!'

'It needs thinking about, certainly,' Goebbels again temporised.

'It doesn't need thinking about, Josef, it needs *doing!* Or else the Army will run Germany once again!'

Goebbels thought: Roehm and Hitler had been together from the first day. Only Roehm could talk to Adolf Hitler as he had just talked to Goebbels. Even Goering had said: 'Beside the Fuhrer we are all nothing, we mean no more than the ground on which we stand!' It was a time to be prudent, thought Josef Goebbels. Socialism was all very well, so was idealism.

But against the Will of Adolf Hitler?

Goebbels was relieved when his new wife, Magda, came in to say that dinner was ready.

Goebbels knew that the Reichstag was passing laws purging the Civil Service, removing any official of Jewish descent or anyone who had ever shown Left-wing or Republican sympathies; that lawyer's entry to their profession was now regulated. All journalistic, musical, theatrical and radio work was brought under the control of Goebbels himself, by the establishment of a Reich Chamber of Culture. Nazi Party-members were now mayors of most cities, or Reichstag or Landtag deputies, or minor government officials. The Professions of medicine and the law were now denied to all Jews.

Into the gaps, Goebbels knew, were rushing the *Alte Kampfers*, who had been Party members since 1922. God knows they deserved the jobs, they had fought for them!

Of course, the *Marzgefallene*, the hoppers-onto-the-bandwagon, who had only joined the Party when it was safe to do so, were ready and eager to grasp a share of the spoils.

Hitler had won. Everybody wanted a piece of him.

And there were still six million unemployed.

The Election had not changed that.

Not even the banning of all the Independent Trades Unions had affected that. All workers were now members of one Nazi Union, the Workers' Front.

Certainly, Ernst Roehm had a point. The workers must not lose out!

Goebbels ate and drank and laughed with Roehms that evening in the comfort and security of his own home, but was uneasily aware

334

that they were – almost – talking treason here. Treason, to Adolf Hitler, was anything he didn't personally endorse. It was punishable by death.

That had to be remembered.

Roehm, however, was not to be denied.

To all who would listen, he insisted, 'I have three million men in uniform. Amalgamate them into the German Army! That would lift the world off its hinges!'

Roehm was conscious of the Brownshirts' growing unpopularity now the Revolution was won. Reports of their severe handling of their enemies had caused some alarm amongst the lily-livered. Many of the *Alte Kampfers* were still volubly out of work, still waiting for their reward. To them, at the Berlin Sportspalast, Roehm shouted: 'And what of those who think the Brownshirts have outlived their usefulness? I have news for these *gentlemen*! We are still here! And we mean to collect our dues!'

He was cheered to the echo by the belligerent Brownshirts, many of whom were still workless and wanted to know why.

Hitler had tried to placate the Army about the Brownshirts, two months before: 'We have no wish to take the place of the Army, or to enter into competition with it!' And, to further show the Army he was on their side, Hitler had spoken for two hours to Generals (and Admirals of the Navy) assuring them that his first priority was to *re-arm*, and fast. To make Germany a World Power again. He felt a sense of history as he talked, easy, on his feet in uniform and jackboots. These men were *his* now.

Ernst Roehm riposted to Goebbels: 'Adolf puts me off with *words*. He'll do a deal with the Army first, if we let him, and try to make National Socialists of them afterwards. Some hope of that! Why does he respect these Prussian dolts? They're the idiots who lost us the last War, and they'd certainly lose us the next!'

Hitler, however, temporised and conciliated all round. The Army. The Navy. The Civil Service. He even went so far as to make Roehm a member of the Cabinet. Roehm was mollified but not much. Hitler after deep thought then wrote him a friendly, open letter, published in the *Volkischer Beobachter* and beginning:

> *Dear Chief of Staff,*
> *When I summoned you to your present position we were passing through a serious crisis. It is primarily due to your efforts that you and your Brownshirts helped me to lay low the Marxist enemy!*

At the close of the first year of the National Socialist Revolution, therefore, I feel compelled to thank you, my dear Ernst Roehm, for the imperishable services which you have rendered to the National Socialist movement and the German people, and to assure you how very grateful I am to Fate, that I am able to call such men as you my friends and fellow combatants.

In true friendship and grateful regard,
Adolf Hitler.

Roehm should have been silenced by such gratitude, but he wasn't. Rumours of Hitler's conciliatory offer to the Allied Powers – the French and the British diplomats were showing signs of restiveness at such dramatic developments in Germany – of cutting down the numbers of the Brownshirts, now standing at almost three million men, reached his ears. He talked to Josef Goebbels, of betrayal, of action, forgetting that Goebbels had left Gregor Strasser at the last moment to side with Hitler. Goebbels had become aware that Goering (who hated Roehm) and Himmler were telling Adolf Hitler that he must move decisively against Roehm, and soon. Goebbels could not afford to be left out of that coalition. Adolf Hitler was the Fuhrer, as Hess rightly said, and the Fuhrer was Germany!

Adolf Hitler sent for Roehm.

They met in the Chancellery, which put Roehm on the defensive, as it was intended to. Hitler made sure he was friendly and conciliatory. Under constant pressure from Goering and Himmler, and from the Army, to show Roehm that he did not run the Party, Hitler nonetheless remembered the 'Dear old Ernst' of their days of struggle together. Adolf drank tea and ate cake, and Roehm drank schnapps and smoked, as the evening drew in. Adolf, as usual, did most of the talking, and Roehm was reminded of their first meeting, when the shabby corporal had turned into a radical orator before his eyes. Where would Adolf be, without him? The answer was nowhere. He became irritated as Adolf told him, 'My dear Ernst, you must listen to what I say to you. You must, you really must, stop this mad talk about taking over the Army, for that is what it is, *mad*. You know very well I have never agreed with you on that . . .'

'You haven't agreed,' cut in Roehm rudely, 'because all you do is try to keep the Army Generals happy. Hindenberg, too. Is he dead yet, by the way?' Roehm laughed, crudely, and Adolf felt a sudden, cold rage. Roehm had not changed. He still thought the boot and the fist right for all occasions. If he were *Kanzler* – which God forbid! – he would know

336

that some situations needed diplomacy, not blood. There was always room for blood if diplomacy didn't work.

'Hindenberg is ill, but not dead,' said Hitler stiffly.

'The next thing I'll be hearing,' said Roehm, 'is that once he's dead, you'll be bringing the Kaiser back to the throne!' Again, he laughed rudely and Adolf recalled how he always felt in Roehm's presence these days. Uneasy and at a disadvantage. It was, he supposed, partly to do with Roehm's sexual weakness. He never saw a problem from an ordinary man's point of view. If only Roehm knew how often Adolf had defended him against the tittle-tattle of his enemies, inside and outside the Party.

'Ernst,' he said. 'I have no intention of dissolving the Brownshirts. I give you my word on that.'

'I'm very grateful to hear it!' replied Roehm, laughing disbelievingly.

'You are making things very difficult for me, just the same.'

'I'm weeping salt tears about that, Adolf.'

'I'm talking about when Hindenberg dies. Decisions must be taken then.'

'So it's to be you, and not the Kaiser, well, well, well, you surprise me!'

Adolf Hitler felt quite ill with rage. Nobody talked like this to him any more.

Except Ernst Roehm.

He drank tea and looked over the top of his cup at the stocky, scarred, buccaneer. He would kill me, thought Adolf, he would press the trigger or push in the knife and he would sleep soundly the same night. We have both seen men die and we both nowadays command men who have seen men die. Life means as little to him as it does to me. But I have a Destiny, which he does not, and I must protect that Destiny.

It was as simple and as complicated as that.

'So,' Roehm was saying, with an air of heavy finality, 'you will not, under any circumstances, find room in the Army for my Brownshirts, preferring to trust the Revolution to the Generals?'

'I do not put it like that . . .'

'I know you don't, but I do.'

Adolf Hitler set down his coffee cup in silence. The clock ticked. The coals fell in the fire. The room was warm but a freeze was in the air.

Hitler said, 'I have one last item that may offend you, Ernst. So I apologise in advance.'

'Don't bother, what is it?'

'The Nazi Party is now the party of Government. It cannot afford scandal. Do I need to say more?'

'Scandal?' The blood surged to Roehm's scarred face. 'You didn't use to care what I did?'

Roehm's leather boots creaked as he leaned forward in his chair, the khaki shirt stretching round his belly. Unlike Hitler, who wore a plain white uniform jacket and dark trousers, Roehm was always dressed for war.

'No, I didn't,' said Adolf, 'because times were different. We had only to please ourselves. Now, we have to win over those Germans who are still not sure about us.'

'You mean the middle-class who never voted for us in their lives?'

'Amongst others. They are still Germans.'

'But you've abolished all the other parties,' said Roehm, brutally. 'They couldn't vote for anybody else if they wanted to.'

'It might be as well for you to remember that, Ernst,' said Hitler.

There was a silence. Coal fell in the grate.

Ernst Roehm rose to his feet.

'I don't think it matters two pfennigs' worth of dogshit to them or to you or to anybody else that I'm an arse-bandit,' said Roehm, brutally. Adolf Hitler winced. Roehm knew he did not care for that kind of barrack-room talk, but that was the rub of it. Roehm had never left the barrack-room and never would.

Hitler stood up. 'I have supper, then other meetings. This has been very helpful, Ernst. I know you will think about what I have said. We have not come this far together to fall out now!'

Silently, they shook hands.

The non-offer of supper was, Hitler knew, a snub, but he had had enough of Ernst Roehm for today.

'Bon Appetit, Adolf,' Roehm said, and left.

No *Heil Hitler*.

No clicking of heels.

No salute of any kind.

Adolf Hitler sat in the opulent, darkening room of his Chancellery and thought: I did not give anything away, did I?

On the whole, he couldn't think that he had.

Behind him, in the heavy metal ashtray on the table, one of Ernst Roehm's foul cigar-butts continued to fume, the smoke hanging blue in the air.

The buccaneer Roehm did not know, Hitler thought, as he sat at table and smile genially at his pretty secretaries and at Rudi Hess, how very difficult the current situation was for *him*: that Von Papen was shooting off his mouth to Hindenberg and even about to publish in the *Frankfurter Zeitung* (always a thorn in his side) an appeal to the German people for a return to 'reason and reasonable behaviour'. This, from his

338

own Vice Chancellor, that idiotic tailor's-dummy! And now, there was the Army, through Blomberg, half-agreeing with Papen. Truly, he had to decide, and soon. Was it Roehm? Or was it the Army?

It could not be both.

At their usual morning meeting, Dietrich, the diminutive Press Officer, showed Hitler a copy of the *Volkischer Beobachter*.

'Blomberg *did* it!' said Dietrich.

'No!' shouted Hitler, in triumph.

Dietrich beamed in pleasure, and nodded his head, several times.

Hitler, who had put on his hated spectacles, was reading aloud:

"The Army stands, loyal and disciplined, behind the President, Field Marshal Von Hindenberg, its supreme Commander, and behind the Fuhrer of the Reich, Adolf Hitler, who came from its ranks and remains, as always, one of our own."

Hitler took off the spectacles and put them away in his case.

'A good start to the day, Dietrich!'

The German Officers' League officially expelled Ernst Roehm from membership that very afternoon. It made all the evening papers. The two items could not be unconnected, to anybody with eyes to see. Dietrich had the early-evening editions ready for Hitler, who dismissed him, then sat thinking for quite a long time. It was inevitable. Nothing was gained by indecision. Adolf Hitler sent for, and received in audience, Hermann Goering, Josef Goebbels and Heinrich Himmler. They sat in conclave at the Chancellery for many hours, going home only as dawn broke grey along the Wilhemstrasse, the long official cars droning away like black beetles into the watery morning light.

Adolf Hitler did not go to bed for another two hours after that. So much had been talked about.

So much had been agreed on.

So much hung on the decision being the right one.

Ernst Roehm was still asleep when he heard Hitler's voice.

Adolf was shouting something in the corridor of the hotel and at first Roehm thought it was a dream. He mumbled, still half-asleep.

'Adolf? Is that *you*? What the hell are you doing here, at this hour?'

His voice echoed down the corridors of the Hanslbauer Hotel, in the small town of Weisee, outside Munich. Roehm had booked an entire wing to house his Brownshirt officers, for conference and discussions, a regular occurrence. He was expecting Adolf Hitler later that day, had in fact booked tables for his expected party at the famous Four Seasons restaurant in Munich. For Hitler, he had ordered a vegetarian meal. He also had an oak commemoration-plaque, especially made, which he was to present to Adolf after the meal, complete with a speech of amity and comradeship. Adolf had written to him recently, offering the hand of friendship.

'Adolf?' Roehm called again.

The answer was a loud slamming at his bedroom door, as if somebody was striking it with a fist. 'All right, coming, coming,' bawled Roehm, an old soldier, used to being woken for duty at ungodly hours.

Suddenly, the door of the bedroom opposite was thrown open by uniformed and well-armed men of Himmler's S.S. They hauled Roehm's brawny second-in-command, Heines, out of bed, along with the naked young Brownshirt trooper sleeping with him. Heines had no time or opportunity to reach for his revolver, tucked into the holster of his uniform, folded neatly on a bedside chair. Four uniformed S.S. men held each naked man and pressed them towards Adolf Hitler, who stood, dog-whip in hand, in the corridor of the hotel.

'What do we do with them, Fuhrer?'

Adolf Hitler looked into the face of Edmund Heines, Obergruppen-fuhrer of Silesia, convicted murderer, a suspected and now proven homosexual. Hitler's face was working with rage and fear.

'Shoot them both!'

Then he turned and slammed his fist again and again on Roehm's bedroom door.

By the time Roehm had opened the door, having pulled on his uniform-trousers and his boots, the first shots had rung out from the grounds of the still-sleeping hotel. As Roehm, bemused, opened the door he saw, at Hitler's side, the battered, grinning face of Sepp Diet-rich, one-time butcher of Munich and head of Adolf Hitler's killing-squad. Roehm's sleep-haze cleared and he suddenly felt very cold.

'What is going on?' he demanded. The hotel was full of armed S.S. men in their black and silver uniforms. An entire commando was here. His men had been surprised, and it was all over, he guessed, already. His stomach turned but he showed nothing.

'Hello, Ernst? Sleeping all alone?' asked Sepp Dietrich, softly.

Roehm ignored him. He looked at Hitler for a very long moment, in silence.

'So, Adolf? It has come to this?'

'Get back inside, you!' said Sepp Dietrich, savagely, gesturing with the Luger in his meaty hand. Roehm could smell his offensive sweat. He swallowed hard, but backed inside. He had a revolver under his pillow. Why had he not reached for it? One grew old, one grew careless.

Hitler and Sepp Dietrich followed him into the room and Sepp Dietrich kicked the door shut. He looked at Roehm. 'Don't try anything, shit!'

Roehm knew there was no hope, from that moment. But he said: 'Adolf, I talk to you alone. Not with the pig present.'

Sepp Dietrich surged forward but Hitler raised his hand.

'Leave us, Sepp. For a few minutes.'

Sepp Dietrich glowered, his huge body still thrust aggressively towards Roehm.

'Only a few minutes,' said Hitler, insistently.

Sepp Dietrich nodded, his eyes not leaving Roehm's. 'I'll leave the door open.'

He did that: Roehm could see the glint of the grey dawn light on the squat barrel of the Luger. Roehm could also hear the harsh cries of his men as they were driven with blows and kicks from their rooms to the lorries drawn up, he supposed from the engine-noise, in the forecourt of the hotel.

Adolf was *here*, that was what surprised Roehm.

My God, the frowsty little Corporal had found the guts to do something himself!

'Normally, Adolf,' Roehm said, as easily as he could, and mustering from somewhere a smile, 'you leave business like this to other people. Why not let Sepp Dietrich just shoot me? He'd enjoy that.'

Adolf Hitler's face was chalk-white. He was, Roehm thought, no man for this moment. He had won his medals in the War, but that was an impersonal business. Adolf's shaking hands and his fury told the whole story. He was no professional, like himself or even Sepp Dietrich. Adolf could order executions, but when it came to doing them, he would be absent. He was a student, a theorist, a mad scholar, not a man of action. A coward, in the last analysis.

But Adolf Hitler was answering his question in a high, forced voice: 'I'm here, Chief of Staff, because I had to confront you face-to-face with your treachery! You and your conspirators, all of you wreckers and well-poisoners!'

Roehm shouted: 'Treachery? To whom?'

'Me! Germany! Don't you say you did *not* mean to have a Putsch! You're known – don't deny it! – to have talked to the French, to Papen, to dissident Army Officers – even to Goebbels!'

Roehm shook his head. 'So the little cripple's run to Uncle Adi? I can't say I'm surprised.' He knew it was no use saying any more. The forces around Adolf had propelled him this far. He would not, he could not, back away now. Besides, he had started shooting people already. When that began who knew when it would end?

Nonetheless, Roehm persevered. 'Adolf, ask yourself *this*! If I meant to kill you, would I be sleeping here, in this hotel, without a guard? My guards are on leave, at their homes. I planned no Putsch, as you can see by just looking round you!'

'Your fellow-conspirators in Munich are arrested!' Spittle appeared on Hitler's lips. 'I have torn the epaulettes from their shoulders myself!' The mania that always affected Hitler when he felt his life was in danger was plain to see. Roehm had, of course, seen it before – at the Feldherrnstrasse and, later, in the cellars of Munich. Roehm, who had always expected a violent death (what other kind was there for a soldier?) asked, in a tone of contemptuous enquiry: 'Are you proposing to *shoot* my Brownshirt officers in Munich? They're loyal Germans! Are you quite mad?'

Hitler shouted, 'No, you are, to think that you might kill me and take over Germany!'

'Adolf, you are destroying the Revolution, can't you see that much, with your schoolboy fears. If I'd wanted to kill you I could have done it a dozen times, any year! My Brownshirts love *me*, not *you*, you neutered fool!'

Adolf Hitler's face went totally blank at that. He stared into Roehm's face and his mouth worked, but no words came.

Sepp Dietrich stepped quickly into the room. 'I'll take over now, Mein Fuhrer!'

Adolf looked at Roehm, for a long time, without speaking. Then, he turned on his heel and walked out.

Roehm knew he would never see Adolf Hitler again.

That was Adolf's way, and always had been. To decree a thing, however unpleasant, menial, desperate or horrific, and leave others to *do* it!

'Shoot me, Sepp,' said Roehm. 'Get it over with!'

'Put your shirt on, pansy-boy,' said Sepp Dietrich. 'And get on the lorry outside. You get the same treatment as your boyfriends, no better and no worse.'

Slowly, Roehm put on his shirt and boots.

Then he went outside.

Four lorries were packed with half-dressed officers and men. Some wore tunics and breeches and no boots. Others had on boots and shirts only. All were bareheaded, their short, golden hair mussed and uncombed. Many had badly bruised and swollen faces and some had bleeding head-wounds, inflicted, Roehm knew, having seen it before, by the butts of rifles. Roehm was himself flanked by four huge S.S. men of Hitler's own Bodyguard, who pushed him roughly onto the tailboard of the last truck. His men called to him but Roehm was not allowed to answer. His arms were pinioned and he was forced up into the Army

lorry which had, he realised ironically, Reichswehr regimental markings.
He caught sight of two long black Mercedes, one of which he recognised
as Adolf Hitler's own, driving snakily away from the hotel. Trust to
Adolf, to order the deed and run away.

Leave it to the butchers, Sepp Dietrich and the others.

He saw, without surprise, the armoured-car standing at the entrance
to the hotel. It was crewed by uniformed Reichswehr gunners; he could
see their badges. So the Army, too, were in on the action. He shook his
head in an effort to clear it. Not just on it, but behind it! Adolf had
obviously taken their side, egged on by Goering and Himmler. Where
was Goering, he wondered? Where was Himmler?

Sepp Dietrich grinned up at him.

'Take your last breath of freedom, schwul!'

Roehm spat at him and missed. Sepp Dietrich grinned again.

Then the tailboard swung up and was fastened by one of the horde
of black-uniformed S.S. men.

What, wondered Roehm, had happened in Berlin?

If it had gone wrong for Adolf there, there was still hope.

Next to his own arrest, Berlin was the key.

Ernst Roehm tried to think positively as the lorries bumped their way
along the country road, the cocks crowing in the farmyards, the dust
billowing up after them, as they skirted the glinting waters of the
Turgensee on the long, last road to Munich.

In Berlin, Roehm thought, I have a hundred Brownshirt officers.
They will not be taken so easily, surely?

In Berlin, Goering and Himmler ran the operation, with brutality and
again, surprise. The S.S. men stormed into the Brownshirt Headquarters, brandishing their Lugers. Goering walked through the offices,
pointing out men at random. These bewildered officers were taken at
gunpoint to the Lichterfelde Cadet School, outside Berlin.

There they were shot, the following day, by men of Himmler's S.S.,
now running the *Night of the Long Knives*, as they had started to call it.

Not all were given warning of their deaths.

General Von Schleicher was shot, on his own doorstep, his wife with
him. His killers were thought to be Emil Maurice and Christian Weber,
both old comrades of the Fuhrer himself.

Gregor Strasser, bon-vivant, woman-lover, gambler and sometime
Socialist, was arrested at noon on that Saturday without a chance to
offer resistance, and executed next day in the courtyard of the Prinz
Albrechtstrasse Prison, in Berlin, by an S.S. firing-squad, on the orders
of Heinrich Himmler.

His teenage son, asked what he felt about his Father's murder, replied woodenly: 'Adolf Hitler is still our Fuhrer.'

In a wood near Munich, Gustard Von Kahr, one-time Prime Minister of Bavaria, is hacked to death by assassins using axes. Nobody saw it happen.

Father Bernhard Stampfle, the Nazi Priest who knew more than anybody the details of the death of Geli Raubal, and the so-called pornographic drawings of Geli, by Adolf Hitler, and who had never been discreet about any of it, is found with three bullets in his heart, in a country-road, outside Munich.

Papen's chief-assistant is shot and Papen himself arrested. Goering intercedes on his behalf with Adolf Hitler and he is released, after four long, terrifying days that were to shake his nerve for ever.

Nobody knows how many others died.

In the Stadelheim Prison at Munich, the dazed and dishevelled Brownshirts are taken, in threes, out of their cells, put up against a wall, and shot by squads of Himmler's S.S. Those who wait to be executed can see it happening from their cells. They call out encouragement to be brave.

Walter Buch, an *Alte Stampfer* and Party Member since 1922, is in charge of the executions.

He shouts, '*The Fuhrer Wills It! Heil Hitler! Fire!*'

Many of the Brownshirts call '*Heil Hitler!*' as they are shot.

Dead are August Schneidhuber, Chief of Police in Munich. Fritz Von Kramm, War Hero. Pete Von Heydebreck, a one-armed, much-decorated soldier, so brave he had a town in Poland named after him. And many, many more, all of them long-service supporters of Adolf Hitler.

Roehm will not face a firing squad.

Adolf Hitler has sent a message.

'Give him a revolver. Let him take the honourable way out.'

Roehm laughs when the butcher Sepp Dietrich gives him the message and the Luger. He is dressed only in breeches and boots and is unshaven.

'If Adolf wants to kill me, why doesn't he do it himself?' he asked Dietrich, contemptuously. 'Let him do his own dirty work!'

In reply, Dietrich shoots him three times with his service revolver.

Roehm falls backwards across his cot, blood pulsing from his wounds.

Adolf Hitler's oldest ally and benefactor is dead.

Late that night, Hitler lands at Tempelhof Airfield in Berlin. He is met by Goering and Himmler, both in uniform. Hitler is dressed in a brown leather jacket and boots. It has been, as always, chilly on the aeroplane. He looks tired and haggard but he shakes hands with the crew and only then turns to greet Goering and Himmler. The three men stand alone on the deserted airfield, guards and police watching from a respectful distance. Himmler takes from his uniform breast-pocket a long, tattered piece of paper. It contains the names on the Berlin execution-lists. Hitler reads through it slowly, nodding his head. Then all three get into the waiting Mercedes. It drives away, swiftly, out of the Tempelhof, towards the city.

The next day Adolf Hitler announces, by radio, to a stunned nation: 'We had to clear up the sexual lewdness. We had to exterminate the pestilence and cut the tumour. We had to stop the Treason!'

Hindenberg sends a telegram to Hitler: *'Again, you have acted to fore-stall Treason. The deeds of June 30th were totally justified in self-defence. Hindenberg.'*

The nation is used to sudden brutalities, by now. The newspapers all print the same story. There is no more to say, nothing to discuss. The death-list is put at sixty by Hitler, for public consumption. Nobody knows what the real figure is.

Hitler flew alone from Berlin to Munich.

He went directly to the Brown House, by car from the airfield.

He stayed fifteen minutes.

His bodyguards could not guess what his thoughts were, alone in the vast, echoing rooms, full of the memorabilia of the old Brownshirt Days of Struggle, the stone wall-memorial bearing the names of those who fell at his side at the Feldherrnstrasse; the bust of Dieter Eckhart along-side flags that were carried and the paintings of those who carried them on that day. Standards, designed by Hitler, flanked the doors. It was a shrine to the *Alte Stampfer*, who Adolf Hitler decides will be disbanded the next day. He stood shivering in the vast chilly room, full of unexpec-ted remorse. What did any of them know about the awfulness of the decisions a leader had to take? Yet this decision, painful as it was, must stand. The Brownshirts belonged, all of them, dead or alive, to the Past. Today, and Tomorrow, belonged to Himmler's S.S., the officers and men who ran the killing-squads, whose loyalty had been demonstrated in their ex-comrades' blood.

Hitler called for his car and was driven back to the Airfield, en route to Berlin and the Chancellery.

It is over.

It had to be done.

And now it is over.

XVI

ADOLF HITLER and Adolf Hitler alone ran German foreign policy. 'The Age of Versailles is over,' he told the world. 'We make our own decisions now!' he shouted to the German Volk.

Everywhere in Germany he was applauded and feted.

Not just at Nuremberg, where Goebbels arranged and Leni Riefenstahl filmed the machine-like men-at-arms in that vast amphitheatre, the setting for his great speeches, to which not only Germany but the whole of Europe listened in awe. Wherever he went in Germany now, standing arm outstretched in his Mercedes, long lines of men standing at attention greeted him. Women pressed from behind them, adoring, beseeching him for a word, a glance.

The idea of the searchlights pointing upwards to the dark night sky at Nuremberg was that of Albert Speer, Hitler's young architect, who was helping him to redesign the Chancellery building. Speer blocked off the bolt-hole to the Adlon Hotel, a passage-way along the eaves, that all previous *Kanzlers* had known about, even if they never used it. Hitler told Speer, 'We will not be needing *that*! We are here to stay!'

The Brownshirts had a final and tearful march-and-reunion party, nationwide, before they handed-in their arms and the Romanesque standards Adolf Hitler had designed for them, fifteen years before. Those who could, joined the S.S., now second only to the Army itself in status and independence, and responsible only to the Fuhrer. Heinrich Himmler had a new assistant, Reinhard Heydrich, an ex-navy-cadet, tall, handsome, blond, homosexual and a quarter-Jewish. On being told this last fact, Hitler brooded and asked Himmler how it had happened?

Himmler, a food-and-health faddist, was a total zealot where the 'blood' of his S.S. men were concerned, but all he could mumble to Adolf Hitler, as he stood in the *Kanzler*'s office, was: 'Reinhard is from

346

a good German family and he served in the Navy.' He did not tell Hitler that Heydrich's fellow-cadets had called him 'Ikey!' or that Heydrich had left the Navy under a cloud. All he knew was that Reinhard Heydrich had joined him early, had worked indefatigably during the Roehm Purge and before, and was totally ruthless, dedicated, and efficient. 'I know his family-line says a quarter Jewish but just *look* at him! Six feet tall, blue eyes, blond! I think some Swede slept with his grandmother!'

Himmler said nothing to Adolf Hitler about the homosexuality. He had warned Reinhard personally, and that surely was enough? After all, they were putting sodomists in the Camps and the offence carried the Death Penalty. Reinhard would curb it and all would be well. But the Jewish thing was different. This the Fuhrer had to know. His obsession about the Jews was total, his hatred more personal than Himmler's own, which was almost scholarly, academic.

If Reinhard had to be sacrificed, then so be it.

After all, Jews were scrubbing the pavements in front of their shops, in the big towns. They were running out of Germany – the ones who had the wit and the money to do it! – as fast as they could! Granted, Goering had Jews for friends and so did a lot of Government officials and even highup Party members. They often came to Himmler with requests for help or leniency in such matters. If it was worth his while, Himmler sometimes helped them. Not often, and never if Adolf Hitler was in any way involved or knew about the case. Just now and again, if the suppliant Party-member or Government-official merely wished an exit visa or some such for his Jew. That was sometimes possible, provided always the Jew in question left the Reich almost penniless, as per the Nuremberg decrees. Friends in high places (and Himmler was always surprised at the foolish sentimentality of some senior Army officers and diplomats towards their Jews) could always come in useful, if one was building a 'State within a State', as Himmler was.

To build a 'State within a State', Himmler needed Reinhard Heydrich. Heydrich was ruthless, tireless and a killer, seemingly without conscience, and he worked twenty-four hours a day. He was admired by his S.S. rank-and-file for his good looks, soldierly bearing, and courage.

Himmler, with his pince-nez and prominent adam's-apple and his older, domineering wife, had none of these qualities. The idea of execution or torture was, to Himmler personally, rather nauseating. Of course, he covered *that* up. Like the Fuhrer, he was interested in the history and future of the great Nordic German Race, as personified by his beloved S.S. men. 'Blond and Beautiful', that fat-arsed fool Goering called them.

Well, one day Heinrich Himmler would show them all, Goering included.

The S.S., now the Brownshirts had gone, were all that stood between Adolf Hitler and the Army. One day, Heinrich Himmler hoped, they would stand equal to the Army itself. To that end, Heinrich Himmler needed an immense organisation, properly run, by somebody who took practical decisions without referring every single one of them up to him. Somebody to *run* the S.S., arrange the dirty jobs, see they got done.

That man was Reinhard Heydrich: which was why he had said more than he had intended to, on his behalf.

'Unfortunate,' Adolf Hitler was saying, frowning. 'Were not the usual credentials demanded of Heydrich? Proof of pure Aryan ancestry and so on, as laid down?'

Heinrich Himmler shook his head. 'They were not laid down when he joined. I had nobody, if you remember, Fuhrer? You said, get me a bodyguard, men I can trust to keep the assassins at bay, men who will die for me? Your own words, Fuhrer.' Himmler took off and polished his pince-nez. He did not sit down. Hitler was, as always these days, at his desk, and his manner was brusque and businesslike. Meissner, his State Secretary, effortlessly carrying out his duties as he had for Hindenberg, was somewhere in the outer-office. The Fuhrer always sent him out when they talked Party business.

'Reinhard is prepared to die for Germany. To kill for Germany. And, of course, any dismissal of such a high officer could look bad.' Himmler hesitated, wondering how far to go. 'Also, I do not actually believe he has any Jewish blood, *but* . . .'

He waited. It was all in the Fuhrer's hands.

After a long moment, Hitler surprised Heinrich Himmler.

'Destroy any records that prove, or seek to prove, Heydrich a Jew, or part-Jewish. He is working well for us and if we leave him alone he will work even better.'

'As you say, Fuhrer,' purred Heinrich Himmler. 'I am sure that is a wise decision.'

Himmler, of course, intended to destroy nothing.

He had a secret file on Reinhard Heydrich an inch thick.

He had a secret file on almost everybody.

Including Adolf Hitler himself.

But all he said was, in a different voice, 'The Foreign Press are still making a fuss about the Camps, Fuhrer. It is not as if we are killing people there. They are simply corrective institutions. I wish our Propaganda people would say so more often.'

Hitler looked up. The eyes were amazingly blue and Nordic, thought Heinrich Himmler, despite the dark, non-Aryan hair and suspect sallow skin of the South. 'Soon I will give them something else to think about, Heinrich,' said Adolf Hitler.

'War?' asked Himmler.

'Peace.'

Hitler made one of his most important speeches to the Reichstag in that fateful year of 1933. The Nazi Press called it his *Friedensrede*, or Peace-Speech.

Hitler shouted: 'It is in the interests of everybody that problems should be solved in a reasonable and peaceful manner! The use of violence in Europe would not help the political or economic situation, or reduce unemployment!'

The applause was vigorous and heartfelt. Hitler thought: they don't want War. Even the Party Members. They must get used to the idea. 'A Great People like Germany cannot be permanently kept from her place amongst the Nations!' More applause. 'Germany demands the disarmament of the *other* European nations! We have carried out the Treaty. Well, then! So must they!'

Hitler said later, to a British journalist, 'Nobody here wants war. Almost all the leaders of the National Socialist Movement, including myself, were combatants in 1914. I have yet to meet the combatant who desires to see again the horrors of those four-and-a-half years. Our Youth is our hope for the future. Do you imagine that we are bringing them up to be shot down on the battlefield?'

Hitler made these statements for world consumption and the world consumed them, as he knew it would. What fools they were! The British *Daily Mail* printed his words on Page One. In the French *Le Matin*, their correspondent confessed he was impressed by Hitler, who insisted that – once the 'Saar Question' was settled – he had no quarrel with France on any points whatsoever.

The middle-aged, middle-class politicians of the British and French Governments breathed a deep sigh of relief, and went back to worrying about Unemployment. Hitler was invited to a Disarmament Conference at Geneva.

'Will you go?' asked Goebbels, as they walked on the Obersaltzberg.

Hitler tugged at Wolf. He looked up towards the mountains: 'No. They will only tell me to behave myself.'

'What, then?'

'I will sign a Non-Aggression pact with Poland.'

'Will the Poles agree? They have French protection.'

Hitler smiled. 'Poland has a frontier with Germany. France is half-a-continent away.'

Two weeks later the Poles signed. To them, it made sense. Hitler never meant to keep the terms of the pact with Poland, but the Poles did not know that.

The French protested, but did nothing. Adolf Hitler was beginning to see that the British and the French really did not want war. *At almost any cost, they meant to avoid it!* It was an immense and joyous truth and one he hugged to himself as he proceeded, very slowly, and almost without risk, to get his way in Europe.

Adolf Hitler, who had never held office anywhere.

Who had no formal education at all.

Who had never been outside of Germany and Austria in his life.

Meissner, his State Secretary, portly, grave and be-sashed in his dark dress-uniform, hovering ever at Hitler's side, had served Hindenberg, Von Schleicher, Von Papen, Bruning. They all had education, culture, learning, breeding, background. They had all listened respectfully to Meissner and the monocled, superior, highly-educated Civil Servants of the Wilhelmstrasse.

Adolf Hitler listened to nobody. If any Civil Servant waved a 'paper' in front of him, he tore it up! He issued a string of orders and waited impatiently for them to be taken-down in writing and acted on. The field of German foreign policy he continued to make his own. The other fiefdoms he left to Goering or Goebbels or Himmler or Ley or Schacht. They got on with the business of 'getting things right'. As Hitler put it, 'Come to me only if you have problems!'

Nobody did.

Suddenly there was a set-back. Sitting in the Chancellery, he agonised aloud over his decision to encourage the Austrian Nazis to attempt a take-over in Vienna and kill Dollfuss, the 'Little Chancellor'. This they did, very bloodily, by shooting him. He took hours to die, while newspaper editors all over Europe wrote leading-articles about the shame of it.

'I have told them what to do!' Hitler shouted at the startled Meissner. 'I have given them advice, weapons, everything, and they have bungled it!'

Meissner, hesitant, held out to him the latest despatch. Kurt Von Schuschnigg, the new Austrian Chancellor, had used regular troops to capture the Nazis. They had been arrested, were to be summarily tried, and if convicted, would be hung.

'Schuschnigg?' shouted Hitler. 'We will deal with him!'

Meissner nodded. It was not safe to comment, on such occasions.

A ceaseless stream of generals, admirals, party-members flowed through Meissner's office. But these were not the worried men of the Hindenberg days. Meissner took notes as Hitler told General Beck, chief of the Army General Staff, that he would introduce military conscription within a year and treble the Army. Beck was astonished and not a little afraid of world reaction, but he was also gratified. More soldiers, to a Prussian career-officer like Ludwig Beck, could be only a good thing. Beck did not think of war. He thought of the Army, which he loved.

To Admiral Erich Raeder, who loved the German Navy, Hitler presented two new battle-cruisers of 26,000 tons (far larger than Versailles allowed) to be named *Scharnhorst* and *Gneisenau*, after those great German heroes. He also promised submarines, in due time. When Raeder asked about money, he said, 'Don't worry. We'll find it.'

What he meant was, as he said to Meissner, 'We'll *print* it!'

Goering – on Hitler's orders – started to build an Air Force. Contracts were placed with aircraft firms. 'The first bombers will be disguised as Lufthansa airline passenger planes,' he reported to Hitler. 'They can be converted to bombers in a week! The pilots will be trained at one of the new glider-clubs!'

Krupps, gunmakers to the world, laid down designs and began the manufacture of tanks and weapons that were vastly in advance, in technique and armament, of anything the Democracies had. Hitler told his tankmen: tell Krupp what you want! The director of I. G. Farben, the great Chemical Trust, was told by Hitler: 'We are not the British, we have no Malaysian rubber plantations. We have no oil. Give me synthetic gasoline and rubber!'

A quarter of a million factories across the Reich were put on a war-footing. There was no hiding that.

The British Government, represented by grave, old-school diplomat Sir John Simon, took fright at this confident display of strength and hastily offered Hitler a place at the Disarmament Talks table. 'Why don't we *all* have equality of arms?' asked Hitler, guilelessly, in his written reply. The French didn't agree. They mistrusted Hitler because they mistrusted everybody. But the British persisted, and the French capitulated. Hitler instantly pushed it further: he officially brought in military-service, calling half a million young Germans to the colours.

He waited, alone at the Berghof, for the Allies to act.

They did not act.

The German generals were intoxicated with delight. So was the German Volk. A public rally was staged in Berlin. Everybody who was anybody went. Everybody present wore his uniform, old or new. The old songs were sung. Speeches were made. It was good to be German that night.

The Democracies finally did something. They held yet another Disarmament Conference, at Stresa. Hitler did not go.

But he did make another Peace Speech. 'Germany declares herself ready to agree to any limitation on artillery, battleships, cruisers and torpedo-boats so long as other governments do the same! Whoever lights the torch of war in Europe will bring nothing but chaos! We in Germany want the Renaissance of the West, not its decline! Germany will make a huge contribution to this if she is allowed to! That is our proud hope!'

Dietrich read out to Hitler an article from the London *Times*. The editor, Geoffrey Dawson, boasted he kept out of that most influential newspaper anything that might offend German sensibilities. Dietrich read: "*No one with an impartial mind can doubt that the points of policy laid down by Herr Hitler may fairly constitute the basis of a complete settlement with Germany – a free, equal and strong Germany instead of the prostrate Germany upon whom Peace was imposed sixteen years ago!*"

'Wonderful,' breathed Hitler.

Dietrich beamed.

The French sniffed disbelievingly at Hitler's speeches, but *they* had a common-border with Germany. The British did not. The French had five million unemployed men – every one a breadwinner – standing, ragged, hungry, and ill-shod on their street corners. The British had four million.

The Germans had six million workless in 1933. By the time Adolf Hitler had been *Kanzler* for three years, the figure was two million and falling fast. Even the death of Hindenberg caused little comment, merely sadness amongst the German people. Hitler was now the sole hero of the Volk. 'Everybody in Germany,' boasted Adolf Hitler, 'has a job and a full dinner-pail!' He did not add that it was his Rearmament programme that was causing the factories of the Ruhr to work double-shifts. Nobody cared. They were working again. That was what mattered.

One by one, the Ministers of State came to the Chancellery office to hear from Hitler, booted and endlessly walking, their orders: Walther Darré, an agricultural expert, had written *Um Blut und Boden*, a Nazi hymn to blood and the soil, that had impressed Hitler. To him, Hitler said, 'The farmers – and Germany is still an agricultural country – have been in dire straits since the War. Most of them are in debt. We abolish – now! – all interest payable on farm-loans! We will stop this obscene speculation by city financiers in German land! A new law from today will keep every farm in the hands of the family currently owning it. Farms will not be sold or mortgaged! On the owner's death, the farm goes to the eldest son. Only Germans of pure Aryan stock, dating back to 1800, will own a farm!'

'Fuhrer, no farmer in the land will object to any of this.' breathed Darré.

'We must become self-sufficient in food, and soon!' said Hitler. 'Tell them that.'

Hitler remembered the financial wizard of the Weimer Republic, the stern, forbidding Doctor Hjalmar Schacht. An expatriate, brought up in the United States, Schacht declared to his hesitant friends in Big Business: 'I desire a great and strong Germany and to achieve it I would enter into an alliance with the Devil!' He adroitly kept Big Business out of direct Nazi Party control. Hitler said to him: 'Do what is best for us!' So Schacht brilliantly negotiated a huge series of highly-profitable 'barter' deals for Germany, a nation with no capital or financial reserves, with almost every country in the world.

Barter was all he had, so he bartered, and bartered.

'Basically,' Schacht told Hitler, 'what Germany can produce, it can wear or it can eat. What it can't, it must do without! Nothing – but *nothing* – can be bought with cash from any other country.'

'Single-handed,' said Hitler, 'you have made Rearmament possible for Germany!'

Schacht expanded all Public Works, including the construction of the Autobahns, massive motorways striking from Berlin to the borders of the Reich. This labour force sopped up the remainder of the workless. The Nazi juggernaut ran on and Hjalmar Schacht provided the fuel. Some of it was money taken from dispossessed Jews, who mostly fled Germany with a pittance. Schacht had no conscience about that.

Once again, Adolf Hitler had found himself the right man.

For the German Workers Hitler produced Robert Ley. An ex-pilot of the Great War, Ley had been a qualified chemist with I. G. Farben, but had been dismissed for drunkenness. He joined the Nazi Party early, and became a close personal friend of Adolf Hitler. He ran the Labour Front, to which every German worker had to belong. Pay was low, hours were long, and morale slumped.

'We must give them circuses, Fuhrer,' declared Ley, a large glass of schnapps in hand. 'It's more important to fill their emotions than their bellies!'

Hitler looked at the cunning, obese man in front of him. 'What do you propose?'

'Strength Through Joy. A new Idea. Sport. Exercise. All Free.'

'Will they join it?' asked Hitler, doubtfully.

'I'm certain of it, Fuhrer,' said Ley, who knew his workers. Strength Through Joy sounded like sex to them at first but it wasn't, except possibly as a by-product. Ley took over the workforce's leisure hours. Later, he told Hitler, 'Fuhrer, I have organised many clubs of all kinds – everything from football to weight-lifting to athletics. Seven million are now members of Strength Through Joy. The Olympic Games of 1936 will be our message to the world that we exist as a great sporting nation!'

'I am not making German youth fit just to win athletic events!' said Adolf Hitler. But the foreign tourists who brought their hard-earned dollars and francs and pounds-sterling into the Third Reich – to visit the Olympics, to sail the Rhine, to hike in the Black Forest – were impressed. The Third Reich was glad to take their money.

Meissner did not care for Ley: but he was careful not to say so.

Baldur von Schirach, Meissner approved of! Son of a Junker father and a rich American mother, with the signatures of two ancestors of the American Declaration of Independence, Schirach was a Nazi Party member from the age of seventeen. A rebel against both his Junker and American family traditions, he totally renounced Christianity. 'The Remembrance Memorial to the fallen Nazis of the Beerhall Putsch is more holy than any Church Altar! Adolf Hitler is a genius, his greatness touches the very stars!'

Hitler found such utterances pleasing. He made Schirach, then twenty-six, leader of the Hitler Youth. 'Give me a Race of Supermen! Do it any way you can. You are responsible to nobody but me!'

Von Schirach looked more like an American college-boy than a typical young Nazi. He had Hitler's writ and he used it boldly. Every German child of either sex, from the age of six, was organised into a junior section of the Hitler Youth. At ten, after tests in athletics, camping and Nazi history, he graduated into the *Jungfolk*. At this point, he swore an oath: "*In the presence of this blood banner, which represents our Fuhrer, I swear to devote all my energies and my strength to the saviour of our Country, Adolf Hitler. I am ready and willing to give up my life for him, so help me God.*"

At fourteen, the boys entered the Hitler Youth proper, with its uniforms, rifle and pack, camps, marches and indoctrination into Nazi Party lore and soldiering itself. At eighteen they went into the Army to serve their hitch. After that, they went into a job through the Labour Front.

Hitler attended many ceremonies. He told Schirach, 'This is great work. Our future is here, with these young people! Wonderful!' He was applauded and worshipped by the young Germans.

German girls conscripted into the *Jung-maedel.* They marched and sang and they had a uniform of white blouse and black skirt and thick-soled black shoes. At 18, they did their *Land Jahr* – a year's work on a farm. They helped in farm-houses and fields, and some got pregnant, to the silent fury of their parents, by the young men of the Hitler Youth. No parent had any power of protest. No parent could hinder his child's progress in Nazification. The girls, after all, had been taught that the role of a young woman in the Third Reich was to be a healthy mother of healthy children.

By the late 'Thirties there were eight million members of the Hitler Youth. It was an even greater honour to have a boy at one of the *Adolf Hitler Schools*, where selected pupils went at twelve years of age, for six years' training, to become the leaders, military and administrative, of the future Reich. Himmler's S.S. ran these schools with iron discipline. Competition to get in was fierce.

Hitler told Von Schirach, 'We have the imagination of Germany's youth!'

To those upper-class parents who sometimes grumbled to him about their children's almost total absence from home, Baldur Von Schirach replied, tartly: 'Go and ask them if they're happy? You'll find they say yes. If you object to the idea that all Germans, the farmworker's son as well as the son of a Prussian landlord, are not as one in Hitler's eyes, then you are a blind fool! What harm does it do a boy or girl to be fit and strong? The Democracies *talk* about equal opportunities – but we *have* it, here in our Youth Camps! Look at our fit, bronzed, eager young people! Then go to Paris or London and look at *their* unemployed! Thin, undersized, teeth gone at twenty, hanging about, half-starved, on the street-corners, and tell me – tell Adolf Hitler himself! – that we are wrong!'

Meissner, going home in his state car, on an evening in the May of 1933, witnessed a torchlight procession along the Unter den Linden. Hitler's Brownshirts were burning books written by, amongst others, Erich Maria Remarque, Thomas Mann, Ludwig Renn, Stefan Zweig and other anti-Nazi German authors, including Heinrich Mann, Jacob Wassermann and Arnold Zweig. The psycho-analytical works of Freud, Havelock Ellis, the political essays of H. G. Wells, and those of Upton Sinclair, Jack London, Zola, Gide and Proust were also thrown onto the blaze. So were hundreds of others, all of them on Josef Goebbels'

'*Verboten*' list. Shouted the little man: 'These flames light up a New Era!'

Meissner wasn't too sure about that. He somewhat disliked Goebbels, who was even more working-class in origin than Hitler himself. He had heard Goebbels outline his plans to Hitler. 'The Reich Chamber of Culture will cover Music, Theatre, the Press, Literature, Radio and Film, and the Fine Arts. Fuhrer, any artist working in any field has to join by law. Anybody suspected of political unreliability is out.' Hitler nodded, sitting down for once, in respect for Goebbels' limp. 'All Jews, so heavily represented in all the arts under Weimar, are out. They are no longer recognised as German citizens. All books to be submitted to the Propaganda Ministry before publication!'

Hitler signalled his approval with a nod. Meissner took notes, as usual. He knew that many artists had already left Germany, almost the first being Thomas Mann, who wore the ribbon of his Iron Cross and yelled in fine Prussian fashion at the Customs Officers examining his improper exit-visa. They hastily stamped it and let him go, to safety in Switzerland. The music of Mendelssohn was banned: he was a Jew. Some musicians remained and made their peace with Nazism. Furtwaengler stayed. Richard Strauss, too. The Berlin Philharmonic and the Berlin State Opera companies flourished, although purged of their Jewish musicians. Max Reinhardt had left. So had Lotte Lenya and Kurt Weill and Berthold Brecht and anybody else who had offended the Nazis.

As for Art, well, Adolf Hitler knew about *that*. 'Modern Art is a degenerate mess,' he declared. 'Get rid of Van Gogh, Matisse, Chagall, Picasso, Cezanne, Grosz and Kokoschka, and their ilk!' It was done. Around 6,000 paintings were taken down from the walls of German Museums. Hitler said, 'Works that cannot be understood without a set of instructions will no longer reach the German nation! Artistic lunacy and pollution is at an end!' He set up a *House of German Art* in Munich, pseudo-classical, in a building designed by himself and Troost, the senior architect of the Reich. Only German Art was to be accepted. Mainly representational, these paintings and sculptures took an optimistic and patriotic view of their subjects, often young men and women in the nude, with the accent on strength and purity, at work in field or farm. Hundreds of paintings of the Fuhrer himself were submitted but only one per year was hung, on Hitler's orders. He took a great interest in the yearly Exhibition and took part in the final selection process. He was so offended by some 'modern' work foolishly submitted that he kicked holes in the canvasses with his own boots.

Goebbels reported to Hitler at the Chancellery office on the state of the Press. 'Fuhrer,' he told him, 'I have instituted a meeting every morning of the editors of the Berlin daily newspapers and representatives of all provincial papers and magazines. Besides a spoken "Briefing", each newspaperman will be issued with a typewritten aide-memoire. Smaller newspapers will be sent these written directives by mail or telegram. So the *Frankfurter Zeitung* will carry the same headlines as the weekly-journal of some small town in Bavaria! Our point of view will be put by everybody!'

Hitler sat up. 'Brilliant, Josef!'

'No editor of a German newspaper can be a Jew or married to a Jew,' said Goebbels. 'The *Frankfurter Zeitung* only continues to publish because its Jewish board-members are out.' Goebbels sat back, smiling at the other occupant of the large, airy room. Max Amann, Adolf Hitler's old sergeant from the List Regiment, had become Reich Leader for the Press. He could close any newspaper or magazine he wanted to. He could also buy it again, cheap. In a good year, Goebbels knew, he made a million marks. Adolf Hitler also became a millionaire, from the royalties of *Mein Kampf* – every household had a copy. Hitler, Goebbels knew, never carried money in his pocket, and had to borrow small-change from his aides, if he needed it, sometimes from another old army comrade, Kapitan Weidermann, for whom he had found a job on his personal staff.

Goebbels told Hitler: 'Fuhrer, the films and radio are Germanised. Our new Nazi films are not as popular with audiences as American trash, but they are all there is. Radio is, in my view, the most effective propaganda instrument for us in time of crisis or war.' He had talked Adolf Hitler into using radio more and more, although Hitler did not like it as much as haranguing and amusing an audience in a large hall. Radio speeches had to be spoken to a time-limit and the whole thing lacked the buzz he got from impromptu speaking. Still, he took Goebbels' point and worked at microphone-technique. It paid off. All Germany stood still, in utter silence, when he spoke on the radio.

In these speeches, Hitler often invoked God.

Hitler said to the glowering Bormann, whom he had grown to totally trust: 'I know your views on religion, Martin. But the Christian churches are essential to safeguard the soul of the German Volk. Von Papen has signed a concordat with the Vatican, guaranteeing the freedom of the Catholic religion. But we have banned the Catholic Youth Movement, and many Catholic publications, too. Pope Pius XI has protested against these so-called violations of the Concordat. But,' said Adolf Hitler, born and raised a Catholic, and once a choirboy in Leonding, 'I think we can ignore that.'

Bormann, simian and hairy (and he knew described by Goering as a sedulous ape) said, 'The Protestants have four voices. Lutheran, Reformed, Methodist, Baptist! Martin Luther, the founder of the Protestant religion in Europe, was anti-Semitic. He said Jews should be robbed of their jewels and banished from Germany! The Catholics are different'

Said Hitler, 'But they too are putty in our hands. But do what must be done.'

A month later Bormann reported, 'Objectors to Nazism have been sent to serve a term in a concentration-camp. We have arrested four hundred Protestant pastors, and Catholic priests to date!'

'That many?' Hitler frowned, crossed his booted legs. Martin Bormann was like Streicher, a zealot: but he needed such men. 'Fortunately the German people do not object to their priests and pastors being told what to do. The Churches in Germany, Protestant and Catholic alike, have a tradition of obedience to the Government in power. We need not fear them.'

Martin Bormann wiped his sweaty brow, and smiled. 'Yet National Socialism, and Christianity are irreconcilable, Fuhrer.'

Hitler reflected that he had always believed *that*, ever since his days haunting the libraries of Vienna. Those times had given him his political world-views and he had *never* changed them. He could say nothing as outright as that in public. It took the son of a Prussian regimental sergeant-major who had grown up in a household where his father's shouted word was law, to do it. Bormann was low on the Nazi Party totem-pole, but Hitler found him useful. Bormann, who had murdered his elementary-school teacher as an act of revenge, and served a prison-term for it, was a man-of-action, somebody to admire! A model secretary, he was solicitously at Hitler's elbow, literally twenty-four hours a day. The Churchmen, the Generals and the educated middle-class who ran the Civil Service, thought Martin Bormann coarse, ill-educated and boorish. His appearance did not help. He did not even look Aryan. But the Party functionary beavered away, to make himself indispensable to Adolf Hitler. Nobody else in the Party hierarchy, save Hess, could stand more than a short time in the Fuhrer's company. The sudden swings of temper, of praise and passion, of calm and rage, were too much for them. Bormann, an Army brat, was impervious to it all.

So when Bormann attacked the Churches, Hitler simply smiled and reproved him; but gently.

*

'Hitler is the only law in Germany,' said Hans Frank, Chief Law Officer of the Reich, to his underlings. 'The law and the will of the Fuhrer are one.' He lectured the judges and jurists: 'The National Socialist ideology is the foundation of all our basic German laws, as explained in the Party-programme, and in the speeches of the Fuhrer. Say to yourselves: '*How would the Fuhrer decide, in my place?*'

One thing Hans Frank knew: behind the Law stood the Gestapo and the Camps.

Goering had used the Gestapo, originally a mixture of Secret Police and Military Policeman, to arrest and murder opponents when he was Prime Minister of Prussia. Frank brooded: he had always disliked Goering. When Goering became 'Second Man to Hitler in All Germany', he had relinquished the post of Gestapo Chief to Himmler, who took over and amalgamated it with his S.S. This plain-clothes squad was named the Gestapo, and Himmler put Heinrich Muller in charge. Frank stared out of his window. 'Gestapo' Muller was only thirty-three, a Bavarian of course, a short, stocky, impassive man, a thinking thug. He did what was asked of him and Heydrich made him an S.S. Brigadier, a very high rank indeed, for a man who was not an old Party Member. Meantime, all Muller needed to do was to remember Hitler's dictat: 'As long as the police carry out the will of the Fuhrer they are behaving legally.' Muller did that, a simple task, and look where he was, only thirty-three years of age, and well thought of by the Fuhrer! While he, Frank, what was he, a Minister Without Portfolio? It was not to be borne! Even the thugs who ran the Camps were better regarded than he was and he had been with the Fuhrer from the beginning. Look at Heydrich, beloved golden-haired boy of the Fuhrer and Himmler, now barely thirty years old and unassailable! In contrast Frank had lately been sacked from his job as Minister of Justice. Why? As President of the Academy of German Law, had he not spent many hours in his office planning his dream of resurrecting 'Popular German Law', a combination of Volkish myth and Nazi *realpolitik*, and putting it in place of the Roman Law? He knew many of the top Nazis thought this a foolish notion. Very well! He had made some possibly foolish 'legal' points about the murder of Roehm and his men. These men had just been murdered. There had been no trial. That was wrong, surely? Hitler lost patience with him at that, and made him a 'Minister Without Portfolio': which meant, in effect, as Goering guffawed, 'Minister for Nothing Whatever!'

So, Frank sat in the long aimless afternoons in the Wilhelmstrasse, irresolute about the things he might influence and resolute about those he could not influence, and cursed his own pedantic, lawyer's weaknesses. The time would come, he promised himself, as he sat, dark, weak and handsome, and still only thirty-five years old, when the Fuhrer would need him for some monumental task, one needing resolution and bravery and perhaps, if absolutely necessary, brutality. Well, why not? He had not yet been brutal because it had not yet been asked of him! The Party until now had needed only his brains, his legal judgement and his courtroom experience! Frank brooded: he had marched with Adolf Hitler on the Feldherrnstrasse, let nobody forget *that*!

Still, he knew Hitler thought of him as 'merely a lawyer'.

And, for some personal reason, Hitler despised all lawyers.

Obviously, a hangover from his youthful days in Vienna. Perhaps he had appeared in some dingy court, been badly treated, harshly questioned even, by some busy advocate? It would not take much. Adolf Hitler never, ever, forgot a personal slight. Everything, Frank knew — everything! — with Adolf Hitler was *personal*.

Dressed up, of course, as policy. As Party policy. As an intellectual idea. As a profound thought for the moment, or for eternity! All Adolf Hitler's speeches, or even his late-night diatribes and musings, however lofty or abstract, seemed to Frank the trained lawyer, to flow from a *personal* spring of hurt or prejudice. Taught to 'see both sides', conditioned to present a case for either the defence or for the prosecution with total lack of prejudice, and used life-long to looking *behind* the accusing or protesting word, Frank thought he could trace almost all of Adolf Hitler's holy tenets of National Socialism to *some incident, or series of incidents, in Adolf Hitler's early life*!

To begin with: Hitler's hatred of the Versailles Treaty and the Nations that had imposed it?

Well, Germany had lost the War and yet she *hadn't*, she'd been *betrayed*! How could she *lose* the War, if Germany (and *Adolf Hitler*!) had fought for the Cause?

Then there was Adolf Hitler's almost insanely powerful desire to topple those at the top, to usurp them, cast them down from their seats of power? What about that?

Well, Hitler had been an Underdog, a bright, envious, starving youth in Vienna. What more natural than to say: it's my turn now, you bastards! Out with all your Laws and your *entire* way of running things.

Let's try *mine*!

Frank had defended the top Nazis, Hitler included, in many a Weimar courtroom. He had always put up the sort of defence a Judge would accept. Never, ever, the reality: *that Adolf Hitler intended to own that Judge — and his courtroom*!

Yes, well, Frank thought, drawing on the cigarette he would never dare smoke in the Fuhrer's presence: what about this love of all things *German*? Well, Adolf Hitler was an Austrian and incomers always took the extreme stance as far as 'patriotism' was concerned.

All right. This Purity of *Blood* then, this Nordic Race theory, this rock on which the whole edifice of National Socialism rested? Frank lit a new cigarette from the butt of his old one, and inhaled.

Everybody said they *believed* in it, except possibly Goering, who as a Prussian aristocrat only believed in the Prussian way of doing anything. But why did *Adolf Hitler* believe so madly in it, why was this *blood* business – plainly a lot of unscientific nonsense really, if one thought about it for a moment – so fixed in Adolf Hitler's mind that he would talk so hotly about it, for hours on end? That it upset him, drove him, burned within him, day and night?

Hitler laughed, privately, at some of Himmler's cranky excesses, like measuring the craniums of the prospective brides of his S.S. men, to ensure none were Jewish or Slav? As if one ever *could*. But it was a teasing, approving kind of scorn. For was not Himmler simply carrying out, in humourless detail, what Hitler had laid down in his speeches, and in *Mein Kampf* itself? Like the rest of Hitler's henchmen, was not Himmler, in the best way he knew how, simply promoting the wishes of the Fuhrer? In Hans Frank's private opinion – which could get him hung for heresy! – the very *personal prejudices* of Adolf Hitler?

Frank stared out of the window across the tree-lined avenues and mused. Of course, it could be argued that *all* ideas, political or social, came originally from a basis of personal prejudice? The human animal being the human animal, it could not be otherwise, surely? Few Prussian landowners became Marxists but many dockworkers did, because, like Hitler, they had been underdogs and were *looking* for a system that gave them the chance to be topdogs.

Very well. But most people used such ideas as an intellectual or emotional sled to take them to where they wanted to go. A safe job. Money. Women. Fame. Having got what they wanted, they relaxed and enjoyed the fruits of victory. A great many of the Nazi leaders had done just that. Goebbels had a splendid house, a loving wife, blonde children, and a string of young, pliant mistresses. Goering had a vast house, Karinhall (named after his first wife), in which he housed his second wife, the statuesque actress Emmy Sonnemann, and a great many art treasures, stolen from rich Jews. Goering also shot huge quantities of game and gave vast, vulgar parties afterwards. He was getting something tangible out of it all. Much the same thing applied across the whole spectrum of those who had done well out of the Nazi revolution. Even Himmler was happy with his 'Bloodline' charts (did he, as Goering sneered, really think people were *horses*?) and his dictats about the kind of food his S.S. recruits should eat.

But Adolf Hitler never changed, or reconsidered or forgot, not one iota. Where the Purity of Blood was concerned, Hitler's Will was unchanging and iron.

Where the Jews were concerned!

A key phrase from the Nuremberg Laws had lodged in Hans Frank's mind: *No Jew may employ a female Aryan servant under thirty-five years of age.*

Female?

How many Jews, by 1935, employed servants, anyway?

How many Jews, by 1935, if they had money or sense, had not fled from Germany?

Female? Under Thirty-Five Years of Age?

A bureaucrat's fine distinction, maybe?

But Hans Frank did not think so.

Frank's lawyer's mind kept going back to Hitler's passage in *Mein Kampf,* which in its ferocity still made his (possibly too sensitive?) mind whirl. He took down from his bookshelf his own personally-autographed copy, inscribed *'The Fuhrer Greets His Comrade in Arms, Hans Frank,'* and thumbed it open.

There the words lay

"The black-haired Jewish youth lies in wait for hours on end, satanically glaring at and spying on the unsuspecting girl he plans to seduce, adulterating her blood and removing her from her own people. The Jew uses every possible means to undermine the racial foundations of the Volk. In his systematic efforts to ruin girls and women, he breaks down the last barriers of discrimination between himself and the Volk."

To gain maximum effect, Hans Frank spoke the words very slowly to himself: then repeated . . . *In his systematic efforts to ruin girls and women?* If everything Adolf Hitler ever said or wrote was personal, which girl or woman was he talking about?

Frank's mind went back inexorably to those hectic and horrifying days he had spent, at Adolf Hitler's *personal* request, investigating the parentage of Hitler's father, Alois Schickelgruber, also known as Alois Heidler, finally known as Alois Hitler.

The same man, whatever he was called, with the same father.

Was *that* father the man the records at Linz had stated him to be, namely Johan Nepomuk Heidler, as, at the age of eighty-four the old man had declared him to be? Nobody locally had believed he was the father of Alois. He had not married Anna Maria Schickelgruber until Alois was fourteen years old. Locally, some people had thought that Alois' father was really the man's brother, Georg, a married farmer of some standing, a good Catholic who could never marry Anna Maria Schickelgruber.

But Anna Maria Schickelgruber had *never* said who the father was.

Drifting unannounced, a whispering, unwanted memory, there came the single-page report he had given to Adolf Hitler, those years before: *Alois Hitler, father of Adolf Hitler, was the illegitimate son of a cook named Schickelgruber from Leonding, near Linz . . . She was working for a Jewish family named Frankenberger, when she became pregnant . . . Frankenberger paid Schickelgruber, on behalf of his son, aged nineteen . . .*

And then Hans Frank looked again at the open page of *Mein Kampf.*

The black-haired Jewish youth lies in wait for hours on end, satanically glaring and spying on the unsuspecting girl he plans to seduce, adulterating her blood and removing her from her own people . . .

Hans Frank took a deep breath, and thought, again, of the one-page report.

A Paternity allowance from the time of her child's birth until his fourteenth year . . .

Hans Frank stood up and shut *Mein Kampf* abruptly.

He was a lawyer and a lawyer needed evidence.

What evidence he had was not the kind that could stand up in any court of law, Napoleonic, or Roman, or even German *Volk*. The evidence, as he well knew, was lost. Gone. Destroyed.

Unbidden, Hans Frank had done Adolf Hitler's will.

After Hitler had derided his report, protesting that he knew all about the Jew of Graz, that all his grandmother had done was, well, resort to mild blackmail, that it was all nonsense, Hans Frank had done one more thing. He had gone to Graz, to the Registry of Births, Marriages and Deaths, and taken out of the archives all references to Adolf Hitler's ancestry that still remained there. He had not considered the action. He had simply done it. Better safe, he had decided at the time, than sorry.

Adolf Hitler did not know, and could never know, what his Minister Without Portfolio, Hans Frank, had done for him. If he had, then possibly he would consider giving the said Hans Frank his due: some post of real distinction and power in the Reich, where he could display *openly* his loyalty to Adolf Hitler, and if necessary, his courage and fortitude and even, yes, even – if demanded of him! – his brutality.

If ruthlessness was called for, yes, why not?

He was not just a lawyer, was he?

Like Adolf Hitler, he, Hans Frank, son of a struck-off lawyer, a man with no silver spoon in his mouth, had helped to turn Germany on its head, to make black white and ill well and horror acceptable. They had shared in all that together. Who cared which loins Adolf Hitler sprang from, or what engine powered his political genius?

Hans Frank, very slowly, put his copy of *Mein Kampf* back on the bookshelf and stared down into the quiet, sunny street. Civil-servants hurried, carrying thick cardboard files, across from one building to another. The Wilhelmstrasse was a hive of industry these days. Everybody had an important job to do. Everybody, it seemed, except himself.

Hans Frank stubbed out his cigarette on his huge cast-iron ashtray, fashioned in the shape of a swastika, and gazed at the portrait of Adolf Hitler looking down sternly from the wall behind his desk.

Someday soon, the Fuhrer would send for him. Nothing, all things considered, was more certain.

XVII

Hitler, as supreme Dictator of Nazi Germany, preached spartan routine to his followers. He ran his own life, as ever, on bohemian lines: I have not struggled all my life, he thought, to dance to everybody else's time. I am the Fuhrer and I make my own time. Who cared what hours he kept? The way his people loved him, that was the important thing. He had wooed them and they had submitted to his Will, like a woman to a conqueror. Nowadays, he often stood, in awe before them, the whole nation, as they clapped and applauded him, with tears in his eyes. They loved him and he loved them in return. To think he had come this far, in so short a time! Sometimes, he could hardly believe it himself: but here he was, beginning another day for Germany.

Dietrich, as always, had brought him all the newspapers, domestic and foreign. That was, on waking, at ten o'clock. If there were cartoons of Hitler in the foreign newspapers, particularly by the artist Low in the London *Daily Express*, Dietrich tried not to show them to Hitler too soon. When he saw them Hitler's good mood fell away (his enemies were indeed everywhere) and he became very angry and abusive. To the leading articles in *The Times* of London, or *Figaro*, he paid less attention. 'People don't read all that print! But they see Low's cartoons, and they make me look a fool!'

After bathing, which he always did alone, and dressing, with the aid of his valet Linge, who forever complained that the Fuhrer liked uniforms better than formal suits (of which he had only five), Hitler took a frugal breakfast of cold milk and cake and chocolate, and applied himself to his first conference of the day.

The young Army and Navy officers who were his adjutants at the Chancellery in Berlin found his hours hard to bear. His old Party assistants, Hess and Bormann, were used to them and did not complain. For these were, after all, halcyon days. Enormous decisions were being taken by the Fuhrer. What did a few hours of sleep matter?

After the Night of the Long Knives and at the very beginning of his Rearmament programme, Hitler had told his generals and admirals, in a secret speech: 'We must prepare for War against the East. We must be ready, sooner or later, to tread the Path of the old Teutonic Knights! We need *Lebensraum* and the East is where we will – we *must*! – expand!'

On a visit to the Fuhrer, Grand-Admiral Raeder, sitting stiffly in full uniform in the stateroom at the Chancellery, cautiously reminded Hitler that the Democracies were unlikely to sit still for ever and allow Germany to become a great Power again. When did he think they would come into the reckoning?

Hitler's answer had been dismissive. 'They will get their nerve back around 1943.'

Raeder – tentatively – it was the way everybody spoke to Adolf Hitler – said, 'Fuhrer, all I am saying is, we must never risk a war on two fronts, must we?'

That was the first tenet in the catechism of German naval and military belief. They had won in 1870 fighting the French, and *only* the French. In 1914, they had lost to a War on two fronts, Russia to the East, France and Britain to the West. The real point was: would the British and French go to Russia's aid if Germany attacked?

Hitler, relaxing in his chair at the Chancellery, said no. 'These old gentlemen want peace at any price. They do not realise that the only sure and permanent peace is to be found in the grave.' Adolf Hitler was talking of Chamberlain and Daladier, Prime Ministers of Great Britain and France, respectively.

Grand-Admiral Raeder did not care for these airy statements of the Fuhrer's. Death happened, or could happen, to any sailor of any navy, while doing his duty. That was an unspoken but understood fact. One did not theorise about it. Hitler added: 'Let England keep her colonies and the Royal Navy so long as it is at parity with ours.' He paused. 'To that end, I have offered the British a Naval Treaty. I think they may well sign it.'

Erich Raeder's impression of the British, having fought them at sea, was that they were unlikely to sit still and watch while Adolf Hitler conquered Soviet Russia and then France. 'How can England and France, with a written Treaty of co-operation, be parted?' he asked.

'Both are terrified of Communism,' said Hitler. 'What did that old drunk, Churchill say? "Better to crush the Bolshevik egg in the nest, than have Bolshevik chickens running all over the world!" Well, they all think that.'

Raeder was forced to smile. Hitler made all his opponents seem to

366

be bumbling incompetents. Just the same, Admiral Raeder felt he had to say one thing: 'I wonder about Soviet Russia? Napoleon failed there. Stalin seems a capable leader.'

'Admiral,' said Hitler, 'You are only saying that because there is no glory for the Navy in a huge land campaign! Don't fear, the Navy will get its turn. I have commissioned a fleet of U-boats.'

Taking his respectful leave, with a Nazi rather than a naval salute, dignified, conservative Erich Raeder could not but wonder: was Adolf Hitler really the political genius and schemer everybody said he was? Or was he an opportunist, who acted when he saw a chink in the other man's armour, and not before? Who drove, as the saying went, by the seat of his pants?

Getting into his staff-car with the swastika-pennants flying alongside the ancient Naval emblems, Erich Raeder leaned back in the leather seats and brooded: Adolf Hitler had better be right, or the German High Seas Fleet would go down for the second time in twenty-five years.

One thing was certain. If that happened, it would be the end for Germany.

Raeder was glad to get out of the motor-car and sample the biting east wind of Keil, to see the newly-commissioned destroyers riding at anchor, to cast his practiced eye over the orderly shipshape bustle of it all. Keil was his place. He understood this, he'd lived his life in the salt air ever since he was a boy-cadet.

Just the same: a war on two fronts?

Unthinkable!

Erich Raeder sighed. The title of Grand Admiral was all very well. But the spectre of those great warships of the old Imperial German High Seas Fleet, going stern down into the icy waters of Scapa Flow, still huanted him.

Unthinkable!

In the February of 1936 Hitler occupied the Rhineland.

The scene was set for him by Mussolini. Said Hitler, 'It is his turn to get something for himself. So he has invaded Ethiopia, using poison-gas on the native population, who have nothing but spears to fight with!'

Hitler called in Von Blomberg: 'The British and French and the entire League of Nations, have condemned Mussolini. Their so-called "Sanctions" against the Italians will get nowhere. While the Democracies are in confusion we put three battalions of German Infantry into Aachen, Trier and Sarrbrucken.' Von Blomberg, terrified of the massive superiority of the French Army, quavered, 'Fuhrer, they'll make mince-meat of us!'

Said Hitler, contemptuously, 'They'll do nothing.'

The German Army marched over the Rhine bridges in the grey dawn hours. It was in place before anybody moved. Neither the French nor the British moved a single soldier.

That very night, Hitler stood on the stage at the Kroll Opera House in Berlin and feeling the untouchability that he *knew* was uniquely his, told a roaring, ecstatic audience: 'Germany no longer feels bound by any treaty! We have re-established the sovereignty of the Reich in the Rhineland! We will yield to no force!' He had held up his hand for silence. 'We pledge however to strive for an understanding with our Western neighbours! We have no further territorial demands to make in Europe!'

Said Grand Admiral Raeder grudgingly to General Von Blomberg, 'One thing is plain, Werner. In Foreign-affairs, the Fuhrer's judgement is superior to ours.' A shaken, vastly-relieved Von Bomberg agreed. 'Nobody can argue with success, Erich.'

Behind them, in the Opera House and in the streets, the celebrations went on. Hitler left for the Chancellery, slept fitfully (his insomnia was worse than ever) and after a full day's work at his desk, decided to take the week-end away from Berlin. He elected to go, as usual, by motor-car to the Obersaltzberg. He called Eva Braun in Munich. She was surprised and delighted. He had not seen her for some weeks. He knew she felt neglected, and no doubt with good cause. Eva was something of a problem but he did not, on balance, regret adding her to his life, since the German public knew nothing about her, or that she even existed. He shuddered at what the hostile International press would make of it.

It had been a strange business between them, and he still felt somewhat manipulated by Eva. He had not wanted a woman in his life and now he had one. Very well. Eva had got what she wanted, but on his terms. No marriage. No children. No appearances on public occasions. It was a hard bargain for Eva, but to her credit she did not seem to hold it against him. She was everything a German woman should be: quiet, discreet, loving and tender, ministering to the man as the prime being in her life.

Adolf Hitler sighed and looked out at the autobahn along which they drove, the back-up bodyguard's motor a car-length behind. The autobahn was by no means completed, but progress was being made. Gangs of Hitler Youth and skilled-labourers and engineers had toiled together to build the magnificent three-lane highway, the first of its kind in Europe. Soon, hundreds of Opel Volkswagens – Hitler's 'People's Car' – would speed along it. Many Germans had put down cash deposits on cars not yet made. That response had heartened him. It showed how the people trusted in him and his policies. No doubt, many of the buyers would have to wait some time for their motor-cars, because few were being made: the demands of Rearmament were too strong.

Hitler leaned back and thought about Eva waiting for him at the Berghof. What was there between them other than sex? Sex with Eva inclined to be loving, almost domestic. He thought of Geli and their sexual games, which he had so foolishly illustrated! It seemed to Hitler that his life with Geli had happened in another time. Yet it was less than five years ago. He sighed. Soon, far too soon, he would be fifty years old, and after fifty, time for a man was short. That was what Eva did not seem to realise. A man had to accomplish his mission while he was young enough and fit enough to do it. Democratic politicians went on until they were seventy years of age, but people like himself and Mussolini had only the years of vitality Nature had given to them. Once a man grew old, his nerve started to go. If he was to strike East against the Soviet Union, he would have to do it before he was fifty-five! And that was not such a long way off. Yet there was much to do before then. Eva had to realise that he was leaving her alone in the Berghof or in the apartment on the Prinzregentstrasse, not because he did not wish her company but because he had his life's work to do.

Eva, he knew, did not see it like that.

That business of her diaries, for instance. He felt irritable, even thinking about the business. There they had lain, on the bedroom dressing-table in the Prinzregentstrasse apartment, deliberately left open so that he would read them. As who would not? Eva's written words were still imprinted in his mind:

I have taken more sleeping tablets than I should. All I want to do is fall ill. I have waited outside the Carlton and watched Adolf buy flowers for Anny Ondra – and she is married to Max Schmelling, the boxer! Why does he do this sort of thing?

Another entry, Hitler recalled, uneasily, had read:

I have written Adolf a decisive letter.
Will he take it seriously?
If I don't get a reply I'll take twenty five sleeping tablets!
Is this the mad love he promised me?
Of course he's busy! He's always busy!
If I don't hear by tomorrow, I'll take the tablets.
I'll make it Thirty Five!

He sighed, again. Eva had left those diaries around so he would read them and feel guilty about her. He did not intend to feel guilty. He had said it before: first, the woman attracted the man. Once he was in her sexual power, she began to pull in the strings. Why should Eva be any different? It was her nature, that was all! He brooded: she was giving up children and marriage for him, he must remember that. Yet he was determined not to feel grateful. He would have to remind her, when he saw her, how important it was that she did not attempt to worry him or use women's wiles on him. There was the inescapable fact that Eva did somewhat smother and embarrass him, with her semi-public touchings of his hand or arm. He supposed it was the lack of children: all the affection went in his direction. He could not recall his own dear mother being unduly smothering towards his father. But where his mother had the children, Eva had only himself. One of his secretaries had said, greatly daring, how very like his mother (whose portrait hung on the wall of his study) Eva was?

There was no doubt a resemblance.

Yet, Eva remained a constant, if small, worry to him. There was always something, with Eva. Possibly, with her love of dancing and music, Eva would have been better-off with a younger man, one of the dozens of eligible Army officers who stalked importantly around his Headquarters? He has even put the thought to her. But she had cried (Eva was always ready to cry if it helped her cause) and he had desisted. He hadn't meant it, anyway. He was used to her by now and she was a loving bedmate and an undemanding partner, on the whole. She knew her role.

Nonetheless, this business with Geli's mother, his half-sister Angi, was getting somewhat out of hand. All because he had relented and taken Eva to the last Nuremberg Rally. Angi had much resented that. She did not like Eva. It was easy to understand why that would be. Still, there must be less open hostility from his half-sister towards the girl. Eva was his choice and Angi must accept that. It was not as if he had taken Eva to Nuremberg as his consort. She had gone as a member of the Party entourage, settled down innocently at the Party hotel amongst his lady-secretaries. But Angi had tried to cause trouble over that, with, he had heard, a lot of silly talk. That sort of thing had to stop. Fortunately, the secretaries were sensible girls, and ignored Angi's outbursts. Or so Bormann assured him.

Bormann had also instigated an enquiry as to how many people knew Eva was resident with him in the Prinzregentstrasse. He had reported: only his Army and Navy adjutants and a few senior Party-members: Goering, Goebbels, Himmler and Hans Frank, for example. Almost none of the high-up officers of the Reichwehr, Luftwaffe or Kreigsmarine had any idea of Eva Braun's existence. When Hitler invited such officers to the Berghof, Eva did not sit to supper with them. Whereas his half-sister Angi sometimes did, as his hostess and housekeeper.

That was, he supposed, the root of the trouble.

Angi had been with him a long time.

She had never got over the death of poor dear Geli. Well, nor had he, as far as that went. He tried to see the situation from Angi's viewpoint. All was going as well as maybe, then onto the scene had come this interloper, Eva Braun: that was how she must see it.

Well, obviously there would be friction.

Why should one expect anything else?

The Mercedes ate up the miles, speeding along the autobahn. Hoffmann, his photographer, did not speak. He never initiated conversations although he often rode as a passenger. They would drop him off in Munich, on their way to the Berghof. Hoffmann belonged to the old days, but unlike many of the *Alte Kampfer* he was still of use. Hoffmann remained Hitler's answer to the scurrilous cartoonists of the French and British newspapers. One photograph of Hitler dominating a vast audience at Nuremberg or the Sportspalast from Hoffmann's magic lens, was a harsh and salutary antidote to the vitriol those hirelings of their Jewish masters poured over his image in their liberal rags! Sometimes (it was natural) he yearned for the old free-and-easy days, when he had driven the length of Germany without fear, with Schreck and Hoffmann in the open Mercedes, sitting in the front, the wind in his face, wearing his long silk-scarf and the old leather flying-helmet. Nowadays, he did not drive in an open tourer unless the weather was very hot, or at a very important State occasion. In an open car he was an easier target: any mad political idealist could take it into his head to shoot the Fuhrer. He took a deep breath, to steady his nerves. When it happened, it would be violent. He had always known that: but until then, he had his mission and he must take every precaution.

That old leather-helmet, my God! The memory made him smile. No longer did he wear it except when he actually flew, which was more often than he liked. At Goebbels' suggestion, he had taken to arriving at the venues of his big provincial speeches by aeroplane. The vast, waiting crowds looking up to see the winking lights of the Junkers roaring above them in the black night-sky, about to deliver a German God! Well, that was what Goebbels said, in his warm-up speeches. Hitler would get out of the aircraft wearing the old leather flying-helmet, a scarf and a long leather coat, whisk them off to show his Brownshirt uniform underneath, and be driven at speed to his speaking-engagement.

It was a very heady and tiring business, but it worked.

The *Volk* loved it. The torches, the warm-up speeches by Hess or Goebbels. But it was Adolf Hitler they waited for.

The *Volk* loved *him*. As simple as that.

Adolf Hitler yawned.

He felt the sudden pull of a stomach cramp, possibly due to the motion of the car. Since 1935, he had been troubled by the disabling complaint that rarely kept him from his desk, but struck without seeming pattern or cause, often in moments of rest or relaxation, like now. He recalled telling the symptoms to his doctor, Brandt, who had wanted him to undergo a series of tests at the top Berlin hospitals, minutely scrutinised by the most eminent specialists in the country. He had refused. My God, he told Brandt it would be all over the capital, and then the country, before he could sign himself in at the hospital. The Fuhrer could not be seen to be ill, it was as simple as that. He did not like Army doctors anyway.

Heinrich Hoffmann had come up with Doctor Theodor Morell.

Hoffmann had confessed he had consulted Morell himself, on 'a delicate and personal matter', and knew the man to be totally discreet. When Hitler first saw the doctor he was not impressed. The fellow seemed grubby, almost dirty, and did not seem to care about his clothes or his appearance or even wash very often. Yet there was something about him, an odd, rebellious manner. Morrell's genial but open contempt for conventional physicians like Brandt struck a chord in Adolf. He warmed to Morell, and when the doctor left his card (at a private party in Hoffmann's house) Adolf had sat looking at it thoughtfully. The card, expensive and gold-blocked, read: *Dr Theodor Morell: Skin and Venereal Diseases*. The address was at the smartest end of the Kurfurstendamm. Obviously, Dr Theodor Morell was a success.

'The Crown Prince is a patient,' said Heinrich Hoffmann, softly.

'I am not surprised,' Adolf Hitler had replied.

A week later, Morell came to the Chancellery to see Hitler in private. The examination took place in Hitler's bedroom. Adolf had sat on the hard bed and with some reluctance told the sweaty, unkempt doctor about his stomach cramps; his flatulence; his insomnia. Normally, he would never put himself in that situation of weakness with any man, physician or not. With Morell, somehow, it did not seem to matter, simply because it did not seem to matter to Morell. He could have been anybody. As Hoffmann so rightly said, Morell worked at the end of the trade where discretion was all. Morell merely grunted sympathetically and undid Adolf's trousers without asking permission, pressed his stomach with long, nicotine-stained fingers, grunted often in a mildly curious tone and said, 'I note the monarchism, only the *one*, we don't see it too often!' Hitler said, 'I was told the testicle had not dropped.'

'That was wrong' Morell had said. 'It was never there. Happens. Nothing to worry about. No trouble with it, I take it? Everything *works*?'

Hitler looked angrily into the man's face and saw to his surprise no insolence, only the same mild curiosity. He suddenly laughed aloud. 'I don't advertise the condition!'

'Naturally. But some ladies I know would be entranced!'

Hitler laughed again, with unexpected relief. He was feeling better already. He began to understand why the Crown Prince patronised Dr Theodor Morell, and guessed what physical affliction took him there.

The overweight, dishevelled fellow sat on the bed next to Hitler and said: 'Look here, I think what is wrong – the cramps – is partly due to an overburdening of the nervous system. The thing is, what do we do? My diagnosis is a complete exhaustion of the intestinal flora. If I can cure that, the other symptoms will lessen and finally go. I want you to go on a diet, just to rest the system. And I want to give you a restorative regimen of vitamins, hormones, phosphorus and dextrose, all of which I propose to inject. The full treatment will take twelve months. We should see an improvement long before that, but I promise nothing for a year.'

Hitler was very impressed. But asked, 'Is this injection treatment usual?'

Morell shrugged. 'If it was usual, I wouldn't be me! Other doctors fool about. I get people well.'

Hitler made his decision about Morell as he had made it about many men he had given top jobs. On the instant. 'Excellent! When can I have the first injection?'

Morell tapped his medical case. 'Now.'

'Did you know I would agree?'

'I hoped you would, yes.'

Hitler was at once under the spell of this strange, quack-like, shambling figure in the crumpled suit. He felt the man didn't give a damn about anybody, and was also totally discreet. He braced himself. 'Let us do it, then.'

As Morell prepared the substances for injection, and it took some time, Adolf Hitler did something that astonished him. He said, 'I have one other problem – or I *had* one other problem – many years ago.'

Hitler stopped. There was a long silence.

Morell, whose back was to Hitler, murmured, 'Yes, and what was that?'

Hitler said, 'I don't know if you have read *Mein Kampf*?'

Morell replied, casually, 'Enough to know that you must have been unlucky with a lady yourself many years ago?' He went on filling the syringes and laying them carefully in a kidney-shaped enamel dish. 'Tell me, what sort of treatment did they give you, and how long ago was it?'

Hitler laughed again. Why did he worry about such things? It was all so easy with this man. If you told him you had just strangled your mother he would just ask: how?

'I was twenty-four. In Munich. She was a young prostitute. It was only the one time.'

'It always is,' said Morell, working on, but his voice was neutral. 'That is all it takes!'

'I was very poor. I just went to an ordinary clinic. I was lucky in that a young doctor was trying out Salvarsan.'

'You were lucky,' said Morell. 'I'm glad it wasn't the mercury. Did you get many treatments?'

'Only the one injection,' said Hitler, sombrely. 'It was all he could do, or so he said. He said Salvarsan was new and many people needed it, he had very few supplies and had to ration them.'

'Did the symptoms go?'

'Yes, almost at once.'

'They do, with Salvarsan. But you should have had back-up treatments, one a year at least, to make sure?'

'Inside a year I was in the Army. Nothing was said there.'

Morell squinted at his latest syringe. The liquid in it was yellow. 'Nothing we can do now.'

'Is there any possibility of any kind of recurrence?'

Morell looked mildly surprised, blinking over his spectacles, which needed wiping. 'You mean you have never checked it since, no blood tests, nothing?'

'No. I cannot afford to be ill. Certainly not with *that*!'

Morell nodded, unsurprised. 'Nobody can, actually. But I see the point. The thing is this. The disease shows itself at first, as a chancre, a sort of boil. Untreated, it goes away. Most patients do nothing about it. If they are lucky, nothing else happens ever. Two in three are lucky.'

Hitler said, after a moment, 'And the unlucky one?'

'Nervous system goes. Or heart-attacks. Or paralysis. Death, one way or another, a little earlier than would otherwise happen to them.'

'My God,' said Hitler, abashed. 'I read it all up at the time. But I *did* have the Salvarsan!'

'Not as much as you should, but probably enough, I'd say. If you are worrying it might be connected to these cramps, I'd say no, almost certainly not.'

A sweat broke out along Hitler's forehead. 'Thank God for that.'

Morell gave him his first injection, in the arm. It did not hurt, only a prick. Morell was musing on, talking, as if to himself. 'Might get trouble, if you get really ill with something else, later in life. You'll have to watch it. Not too much desperate stress, but that, I know, would be difficult for you.'

Hitler smiled, warily. 'Later in life?' How long did somebody like him, running a *country*, responsible for everybody in it, how did he ever 'Take it easy'? he said, 'I have a mission, my health is secondary. And anyway, how did you know I'd had the foul thing?'

Morell put down the syringe mildly. 'You spend pages and pages going on about what a plague it is, in *Mein Kampf.* If I may quote? "The struggle against Syphilis, and Prostitution which prepares the way for it, is one of the gigantic tasks of Humanity." Have I got that right? Nobody would write that way unless he'd had a dose himself once, would he?'

Hitler was silent, and aghast. At last he said, 'Do you think other people can have guessed?'

Dr Theodor Morell held up a new syringe, and squinted at it.

'Hardly. I am a bit of an expert in these things, after all, mon ami!'

Hitler stared at him. Then he laughed, aloud.

A chambermaid, passing along outside in the corridor, wondered: 'I've never heard the Fuhrer laugh like *that* before!'

Eva recalled her surprise, mixed with terror when Adolf had told her to move from home into the house at Bogenhausen. It had happened three years ago, in the Osteria. She had stammered, 'I can't, what will Vadi say?'

'You're twenty-one now, Eva,' Adolf had replied, sternly. 'You can do as you like. I've rented the place, all you have to do is move in. Take your sister Gretl with you, if she'll go. It'll look better.' He had glanced at his watch. 'I'll come to see you when you get settled.'

'But what shall I tell Vadi?'

'Nothing. Tell your mother. Then go. Both of you. See you very soon!'

With that, he had gone out of the restaurant, got into his long black Mercedes, made a sign to the driver and zoomed away, once again, out of her life.

Eva never knew what Mutti had told Vadi but Vadi never talked to her about Adolf Hitler again. He rarely talked to her at all, but sat uncomfortably behind his *Munchner Neveste Nachrichtar* and smoked his pipe. When she visited the old house, he said little, and nothing that was personal. That made her sad. She so wanted Vadi and Adolf to be friends, but it seemed such a thing was impossible.

Her sister Gretl went with her to the villa in Bogenhausen. They had an Hungarian maid to do the housework. She was in love with an Army sergeant and his long woollen underpants fluttered on the clothes-line more often than any of the girls' silken underthings.

The two sisters hilariously-laughed at that.

They laughed at a lot of things that long summer and the ones that followed. Eva continued to work at Hoffmann's shop, which she increasingly grew to hate (was that how Adolf thought of her, as a *shopgirl?*)

and then she went back to the house in Bogenhausen to her supper.

And waited for Adolf to call on the telephone.

And waited.

As far as the Berghof was concerned, Angela Rabaul was the problem. She always said to Adolf: 'I need notice of how many people are coming, and when, and who?'

Adolf merely replied: 'Good God, the place is big enough, surely?'

So Eva had always been shoved into some small room at the back of the house.

With the result that Adolf did not come to her.

Which was exactly what Angi intended.

Eva went out onto the balcony, putting a coat over her shoulders, and looked up at the stars. She shivered: there was a moon and the Obersaltzberg looked like a frozen icecake. The snow glinted silver on the mountain slopes and lay crisp in the gardens surrounding the Berghof. Light blazed in the Signals-room half-hidden from view, but up here it was almost possible to feel, for a moment anyway, that she was alone in the still, cold night, waiting for a lover.

Well, what else was she?

Certainly not a mistress, in the ordinary, practical sense.

Frau Winter was a considerable pain in the neck at the Prinz-regentstrasse apartment. At first she resented Eva but had to acknowledge her orders and authority in the end, albeit grudgingly. Frau Winter made reference, often, to the lost and beloved Geli and made a big show of putting flowers in the locked bedroom each and every day.

Gruesome, Eva thought it all, very creepy.

But she was not going to let Frau Winter or anybody else drive her out of the Prinzregentstrasse. She had worked too hard, endured too much, to get into it in the first place.

For the house in Bogenhausen had not worked out.

She had stuck it for three years. Adolf could not say she hadn't tried. Of course, her sister Gretl had been a brick, and stood by her during Adolf's long absences. Gretl would say, 'He's Fuhrer of Germany now, Eva. He can't do what he likes. He's got such important duties to perform. Each day his card must be full. Just look in the Newspapers if you don't believe me!' And Gretl would put the *Munchner Neveste Nachrichtar* in front of her, and there would be Adolf opening some new Hitler Youth hostel, his hand resting paternally on the head of some blond schoolboy; or a dramatic Hoffmann photograph of an Adolf she hardly knew, ranting on at a mass-meeting about *Lebensraum* or the Jews or somesuch.

Eva did not know this ranting Adolf.

He had a short temper at times, that was accepted, but never before women did these rumoured rages show themselves. Even the secretaries rarely heard the Fuhrer's voice raised, for he was politeness itself with them. Eva thought: they're all smitten with him but Adolf is mine. It was the wild guesses of the Press that irked her – the newspaper photographs, and rumours of the Fuhrer dallying with such luminaries as Leni Riefenstahl, the film-director, and Hanna Reitsch, the daredevil woman-pilot. What arrant nonsense that was! Eva knew her Adolf. He did not want these bright, driving women. Talkative, intellectual females irritated him. When she had told him her favourite book was *Gone With The Wind*, he had nodded approvingly. When she said she loved Pearl Buck's novels, he had smiled. He never read fiction. Facts were his business: his memory for them was quite amazing. The Press Chief, Dietrich, said that the Fuhrer knew the tonnage and firepower of every ship in the German Navy, as well as the basic specifications of all armament and aircraft in current service. Eva was not impressed. Surely those facts could be looked-up in a matter of moments. Why bother to learn them?

Men, however, were impressed by such things. They were like little boys in their competition with each other for the Fuhrer's acclaim. The way they hovered around him, vying for a good word or a nod! She would not be surprised if some of them were ready to kill for him. That was why they wore his uniform and had taken their famous Oath of Loyalty to him. It was all crass maleness and she didn't even try to understand it.

Eva shivered, looked at her watch (Adolf would not be here for almost another hour) and went back into the warmth of the vast living-room. She rang for coffee she didn't want, and when the new maid (what was her name, Voller?) brought it she sipped it and grimaced with distaste.

Well, Goering had said: 'Guns Before Butter!' Now – undrinkable coffee. It was astonishing. Alone, amongst all the leaders of Germany, the Fuhrer of them all would not drink anything that was not available to the ordinary man-in-the-street. What a fuss Adolf had made, for example, over that god-damned caviar. He'd been eating it for months, quite cheerfully, until somebody told him how pricey it was. He had stopped eating it that very day. When Eva, who thought his diet far too plain and tasteless (there was no meat in it at all, or fish) had protested: 'Adolf, you *like* caviar, why not give yourself a tiny treat?' he had replied: 'I cannot have it getting about that I eat something that is so expensive. It is all right for Goering to do that. Everybody in Germany knows his appetites and likes him for them. My case is different. I am the Fuhrer and must eat what my people eat.'

'You don't eat meat and they do. All they can get!'

Eva did not say: steaks are good for sex!

Adolf would not have laughed and he would not have eaten the steaks either. So Eva sighed and said no more. Once she was in charge of Adolf's catering, she would see a few changes. Even if she couldn't get him off a diet of vegetables and sweet puddings, she could augment it with soups with a meat-base he'd never know about, and other small protein supplements. It could be done. If Angi could be got out of the way.

That would not be easy.

It would take some working on.

But then her key to the Prinzregentstrasse apartment taken some working also. A lot of misery, too. All that loneliness, night after night, after Adolf had become *Kanzler*. She had not realised that as soon as he *did* win those elections he would have no privacy at all, just a body-guard of half-a-dozen men everywhere he went.

He had solved the problem in his usual way, by not coming to see her as regularly. Something had got to be done about that and she had done it.

For Eva knew about one thing. She knew about men.

Adolf Hitler might have his own fleet of cars and everybody kissing arse all the time and a train at his disposal twenty-four hours a day, but in the end he was the only one man.

Pressure. That was what counted.

So she applied it, but with great tact and discretion.

It had not been easy. It had taken guile.

It had taken, well, more of the same.

She could not repeat the 'overdose' ploy.

So she simply went drip, drip, drip, on the loneliness theme.

It was true, after all, it wasn't as if it wasn't *true*!

It would be so much easier if she was in his apartment in Munich, wouldn't it? she had whispered to him, not in bed, because he would never go to the bedroom at the Bogenhausen place, even when the girls had been ushered out, preferring to make love on the old sofa in the living room. Sometime, she guessed, he had learned that sex was only a perfunctory thing. Well, if that was what he liked, then she would not try to change it, anyway not yet. Beds and warm bedrooms and eider-downs and pillows and bedside-tables with glasses of water standing on them were the stuff of domesticity, and he did not, obviously, want *that*! Also, he was always in a great hurry, the black Mercedes standing discreetly in some side-road, the men in long leather coats waiting on the corner of the streets that approached the villa. Their love-making was always hasty in the Bogenhausen villa.

'Wouldn't it be easier if I was at the apartment?' asked Eva, her arms around his neck. 'You have good security there. Nobody would know any more than those who know now, need they?'

At first he had demurred.

It had taken months of work and of whining.

Eva was not usually a whiner. Vadi hated whiners.

But she felt, on this occasion, that she was justified.

So, at last, Adolf Hitler had installed her in the Prinzregentstrasse: that was after she had taken the overdose of sleeping pills, wakened up in a nursing-home, and waited for Adolf to do something about it!

What choice had he had? Not much, she thought, with quiet satisfaction. Despite the dark side of his nature, which she never saw (but knew was there) he had begun to look at her as his responsibility, as his sick mother had been his responsibility. That was all she asked for, that he take care of her. Marriage? Children? She'd given up on all that. One day maybe. 'Till then, she lived a day at a time.

All that had happened in this year of our Lord, Nineteen Thirty-Six.

From that moment on, she had seen more of him.

Not a lot more, but certainly more.

Then, and then only, had she asked him about the Berghof. She had been there a few times, always frostily received by Angi Raubal. Never called by her name. Always 'Fraulien'. Never allowed to talk, for long, with Adolf. Always interrupted by his hostile half-sister.

But now she was here, at the Berghof and Adolf had, on occasion, invited her up the twisty iron staircase that even Angi was not allowed to ascend. Up there were the Fuhrer's private quarters, where his own valet, Heinz Klinge, had his own room, and where Erich Kempka, his Army driver, also lived. Unobtrusively, at the end of the long corridor that had no windows to the outside world, and was lined with oil-paintings of Adolf's choosing, all of them extremely valuable, and every one a favourite work of the Fuhrer's, were his rooms. She would spend tonight *there*, with Adolf.

A sudden roar of powerful car engines in the driveway of the Berghof brought Eva to her feet.

Him! It was *him*!

But when Adolf Hitler came into the room, he merely kissed her hand. After that perfunctory greeting, he promptly sat down on one of the huge sofas and called for food. The fleshy Angi – of course, *she* was there as soon as Adolf entered – flashed her dark eyes in triumph at Eva: but Eva refused to acknowledge the glance, and nestled down on the sofa next to Adolf.

'*Liebchen*, you look tired,' she whispered, pressing his hand.

'I am, but once I eat I'll be fine.'

Hitler glanced up as Bormann entered: another prompt supplicant! If there was anybody in the world Eva Braun hated more than Angi it was Martin Bormann. The hairy, simian body was encased in a white uniform jacket and dark dress-trousers, an exact replica of the Fuhrer's. Was there anything in which Bormann did not ape Adolf Hitler? Ape was indeed the right word, for that was what Bormann looked like, some heavy, shaven monkey. The cropped head, lowering brow, and dark, beady eyes bored into a person. Bormann presented Adolf with a batch of official papers for signing.

'Adolf, you're tired, do you need to work already?' Eva asked, protectively.

'Only signatures, that's all.'

Hitler took from his tunic-pocket the gold-rimmed spectacles he never wore in public and looked quickly at the documents. Then, he initialled them, saying, 'Martin, you will join us for a bit of supper? And, of course, Rudi if he's arrived?'

'He has not arrived as yet, Fuhrer,' said Bormann, his lips tightening. Bormann disliked Hess, who was his immediate superior and not likely to be easily displaced in Adolf Hitler's affections.

'Fuhrer, if I may speak on another matter?' Bormann took the official papers, now signed, from Adolf Hitler's hand and slipped them into a leather-folder. Everything neat and swift, like, Eva thought, an executioner. Well, that's what the whispers said, about his early days in the Party: a killer, if need be.

Adolf Hitler folded his spectacles and put them away. 'Yes, Martin, what?'

'Nothing of importance, Fuhrer.'

'Then why mention it?'

Hitler's voice was irritable and he sounded, to Eva's practiced ear, very tired. His blood-sugar was apt to get low, if he did not eat. Doctor Morell, Hitler's newest physician, that obese and grubby man, had told her. 'The Fuhrer's diet is healthy enough, but he doesn't get enough protein to give him energy. Also, he doesn't eat enough carbohydrates. So when he runs out of energy and his blood-sugar is low, he eats chocolate or cakes, anything sweet, rather like a diabetic, to raise his blood-sugar level. It is fattening, and not a perfect way to do things.'

Eva had thought how nice of Dr Morell to tell her that as if she was the Fuhrer's wife and might be able to do something about it. Of course, they both knew that she couldn't.

For some reason Bormann suddenly looked at Eva, as if for help. Eva looked back at him, toying innocently with her tourmaline ear-rings and finger ring, a matching-set, the first jewellery Adolf Hitler had ever bought her, and worn tonight in honour of the occasion. A meal with Bormann and Hess and almost certainly Angi, it wasn't exactly what she had hoped for. Eva sighed. She so rarely got what she hoped for, with Adolf. It was part of the game, if it was a game. Eva said gently: 'After we eat, then you can talk important matters, Adolf?'

But Hitler had held up his hand, palm outward, as he so often did. It was a typical, emotional gesture of rejection, in public or private.

Martin Bormann went slightly pale, then said, very quietly: 'My Fuhrer, it is simply that I have effected all the buy-outs of private houses on the Obersaltzberg, as we discussed, and nobody now overlooks the Berghof in any way. Also, I have taken the liberty of putting in place a detachment of S.S. – with of course Reichsfuhrer Himmler's approval – as extra guards around the house. Also, I have approved the erection of barbed-wire fences, which if need be, can be electrified.'

But Adolf Hitler had cut him short. 'I do not wish to hear of these attempts to safeguard my life, Bormann.' The 'Martin' had been dropped. 'I take it for granted that my adjutants will do what has to be done, to ensure that some idealist does not shoot me with a telescopic rifle, one fine day, as I take my exercise in the grounds.' His voice rose, hoarsely, sarcastic. 'It should not be beyond the military expertise of my highly-rewarded staff, to see that we do not get a repetition of that incident last Summer.'

Martin Bormann was at attention now, the clipboard at his side.

Eva noticed the fingers that held it were trembling.

My God, Adolf had the power to make this ape *tremble*?

'That will not happen again, Fuhrer!'

Hitler closed his eyes as if in pain. Eva could never be sure, on these occasions, if we was acting or if it was all for real. She said nothing and sat quite still. Unexpectedly, Hitler turned to her and said, quite gently, 'A soldier. One of my own men, can you believe it? He had a revolver in his knapsack, when the Gestapo arrested him, here, just outside the Berghof! Imagine *that*! If I had gone out for a walk with the dog Blondi, the madman could have shot me!'

Eva Braun was shocked. Adolf spoke incessantly of the people who wanted to *kill* him – Reds, Foreign Agents, Jews, anybody at all, the list seemed endless – but the idea that somebody had actually *tried* to do it amazed her. The Fuhrer was surrounded by his own uniformed S.S. Bodyguard, or his plain-clothes men, everywhere he went. She said as much, soothingly: 'The man was discovered, so no harm was done. How could he hope to do that and get away?'

Adolf Hitler turned on her, his blue eyes wide. 'We are not talking of rational people here, Fraulein!' The *Fraulein* hurt, as Adolf had doubtless meant it to. Bormann looked relieved, the fire was going, thank God, in another direction. 'That soldier was prepared, no doubt, to sell his life for mine!' Hitler's voice rose. 'I do not fear those assassins who want to kill me and make their escape. They will always fail. But the man who does not care, who will die to do it, that man I *do* fear!'

Eva did not know what to say to that, so she said, as usual on these supercharged, emotional occasions, nothing.

Martin Bormann came to a military attention and excused himself, hastily: 'Fuhrer, I thank you for your supper invitation, which of course I accept with gratitude. I will just go and complete an outstanding task.' With that, he exited, his boots clip-clopping on the parquet floor of the vast room.

'Eva, I tell you, one day one of these maniacs will get me.'

To Eva's consternation, Adolf's voice held self-pity. It was a rare note for him and showed only how tired he was. 'Why don't we have some food on a tray upstairs, just the two of us?' she whispered, putting her soft hand on his. He jerked his hand away, irritably. 'How can I do that, you just heard me ask Bormann to supper, and Hess too, when he gets here? Do you want me to deny them that?'

'Of course not. It was just a thought.'

If Eva knew anything, they would be glad to miss supper, the temper Adolf was in: but then, to Bormann and Hess this electric atmosphere was quite usual. For herself, she rarely experienced it and when she did, it always shocked her. This *hating* had an element of hitting-back in it. *Anybody* would do, when Adolf was in a near-frenzy. This emotion was stronger when he felt menaced, or in danger. *That* was when he struck back. That was when he was most ruthless.

Well, she thought, he had not become the Fuhrer of Germany by being a milksop. The country was full of ex-soldiers and all kinds of tough, able men, who thought they had the qualifications to run Germany – but only Adolf Hitler *did*. He was entitled to lose his temper, sometimes.

Calm, Eva told herself, keep very calm. Don't do anything or say anything ro upset him further. Let him rest, until after the food comes.

At that moment, Angi came in to say that the table was laid and ready in the Great Hall, and that Herr Hess had arrived and was delighted to join the Fuhrer for supper. Did the Fuhrer wish anybody else, asked Angi, her malicious eye on Eva. Anyway, Eva thought it malicious, and Eva was rarely wrong when pure, raw emotion was in the air. Angi had known the time Hitler would arrive, to the minute, and that he would require supper instantly, had known the fact for hours but had not bothered to tell Eva Braun, had delighted in the fact that Eva would not have Adolf all to herself, as she expected.

Hitler got to his feet, and yawned. He was almost paunchy now, and had bags beneath his eyes.

The poor man, thought Eva, he works so hard.

Hitler said, 'We'll come at once! Eva.'

He had actually smiled, showing the dentures at the side of his mouth. Eva had been astonished at the state of his teeth (the fillings he had!) but he had explained that he had had a very poor diet as a young man in Vienna, and his teeth had suffered. Now, too late, he had good dentists. Poor, dear Adolf, he had so much to contend with, all the enemies who devoutly wished his death, and the constant nag of his entire entourage – male and female alike – for his attention and approval. Eva Braun slipped her slim arm in his, and held it there a long sensual moment (to remind him she was a *woman*) and then took it away again, and went before him, into the dining-room he liked to eat in, when the party was small.

Eva was irritated to see that not only was Angi at table, but was acting as hostess, a role she always took upon herself, as if it were her right. Well, plainly Adolf liked it that way, or did not object, so there was nothing to be done about it. For now. There were three men, Hitler, Bormann and the lugubrious, lanky Hess, also in uniform and also a vegetarian.

'Good barley soup with dumplings and vegetables to start,' said Angi, spooning out large helpings, to everybody. Rye bread was already on the table, and a bottle of Liebfraumilch. Bormann, Eva knew, would drink sparingly. Hitler did not care for the smell of alcohol.

There was absolute silence while the Fuhrer ate.

Hitler had two bowls of the formidable soup and two slices of bread. Eva managed one and felt waterlogged. Hitler and Hess (who did not drink alcohol) refused the middle-course of cold cuts of chicken and ham, to which everybody else helped themselves. Bormann ate half of the chicken on offer. Hitler had two large helpings of apple-torte, with whipped cream and chocolate-flake dressing. He drank fruit-juice.

After the food, when conversation was limited to an odd mumble, nobody smoked. Eva knew Bormann was dying for a cigarette and was amused at his discomfort. Eventually, Bormann excused himself and went, she guessed, to the lavatory for a quick inhale! Like a little boy, she thought. When he returned, Bormann smelled slightly of peppermint.

The awful herb tea, which Hitler insisted on taking, was served to him in the Hall and they all sprawled around an open fire on the velveteen cushions of the huge wooden armchairs. The new servant-girl, Kohler, brought in the so-called coffee. Hitler drank his well-sweetened herb tea very hot. The colour, Eva saw, had returned to his face, which had been putty-looking when he came in. His eyes too had regained a little of their manic gleam, and he seemed, generally, to have been re-charged by the food in a way the others were not. Eva stole a quick look at her wrist-watch. It was almost eleven o'clock.

Eva made a quick guess. If they were all in bed by one o'clock they would be lucky.

Hess, as eager as ever, waited until Angi, pleading housewifely duties, had excused herself, and asked: 'So, Fuhrer, it was a great victory in the Rhineland after all the Generals' funk about it?'

Hitler smiled and nodded. He was now ready to talk. 'In its way. But there are bigger things to come. It is only a beginning, Rudi.'

Eva stifled a deep yawn. She had been up at seven o'clock that morning, in the apartment at the Prinzregentstrasse. Adolf had telephoned her at two in the afternoon and the official motor-car from the Berghof had collected her at three. An hours of worrying what to wear, and deciding at last on a demure brown dress, with the sentimental jewels. Eva had packed a tweed skirt and blouse for the next day – having no idea if Adolf would be there or would depart at ten or eleven o'clock the following morning, back to the Chancellery in Berlin. It had been a long day. She had hung around the Berghof for hours, waiting for him to arrive. Now that he had, she was bone-tired and her eyelids were heavy.

Still, it was nothing new. She would get her second wind in about an hour. She usually did.

'Do you have anything . . . else in mind, Fuhrer?' asked the credulous Bormann, softly.

'Austria,' said Hitler, after a long pause. 'But not quite yet.'

Oh, God, thought Eva Braun. Not *Austria*.

'There are two ways to restore Austria to its Germanic heritage,' said Hitler, settling to his theme. 'One is to invade her and take the country by force. Which, of course, we could easily do.' He paused, looking at Bormann and Hess in turn. Both knew better than to speak. 'The other is to get what we want by political means.'

Hess said, 'Schuschnigg is a curious fellow. At one time I thought he was one of us.'

'He ought to be one of us.' Hitler was away on the subjects nearest to his heart, politics and chicanery. 'He is a Catholic of the Right. He believes in Austria as I believe in Germany. But he wants to be dictator of Austria, as I am dictator of Germany.'

They went on talking about Schuschnigg for what seemed like hours. At last Eva Braun could keep her eyes open no longer; her head fell back on the velvet cushions and she slept.

It was now one o'clock in the morning.

At almost one-thirty Angi said, 'Perhaps we ladies should retire now?'

Adolf had looked up briefly, in full diatribe, to say to Eva that he had to discuss important business with Bormann and Hess. As if he had been doing nothing else for hours. All about *Schuschnigg* and *Austria* until Eva's head reeled with it!

But she managed a sleepy smile – somehow – and got to her feet.

All for nothing, said Eva bitterly to herself. All the preparations, the dressing-up, the waiting.

Not for the first time, of course.

Eva's anger fastened on Angi. It would have been very simple for Angi to have said nothing, done nothing, arranged nothing, to have allowed Adolf and herself to slip away to his room upstairs, whenever he had finished talking. The public announcement she had made, coming into the room, 'Fraulein, your room is ready, if you'd like me to show you?' had ruined any possibility of that.

Eva stood for a full minute, waiting for Adolf to say something: but he didn't.

She pressed Adolf's arm and said, 'Adi, I'm going to bed.'

Adolf looked round blankly. 'Are you? Yes, you said so.'

Angi jumped in: 'I've put the Fraulein in the new wing.'

Adolf looked irritated at the interruption. 'Yes, yes, whatever.' And returned to the discussion, or rather diatribe. 'I tell you, we must have Mussolini on our side. Do you know the last thing the *Alte Herr* said to me before he died?' Hess and Bormann shook their heads. 'He said, never trust the Italians!' Bormann and Hess nodded. 'But he was wrong,' said Hitler. 'Mussolini is a fascist, not the usual, weak-kneed democratic politician. He gave me a fine reception, in Rome, last year. It is a great, ancient city, worthy of its ruler. If we march against Austria, he'll support us, I'm sure of it.'

Still, Eva waited.

Still, Angi stood and watched her wait, contemptuously.

At last Eva said, 'Well I'll say Guten Nacht, Adolf?'

Hitler stopped talking and looked round irritably. 'Yes, yes, see you in the morning.'

He turned back to Bormann and Hess: 'Yet if I have to choose between Italy and England as an ally I'd have to say England. I hope for a future alliance with the British.'

'Is that really possible?' asked Hess.

'It has to be. Our interests are the land. England's is the sea. We complement each other.'

Bormann shook his head. 'The British will side with France, surely? If it comes to War?'

'Not with Edward on the throne! He's for us. The English would have moved against us in the Rhineland, but for him.'

'Will he *ever* be crowned King?' asked Hess. 'Canaris has a lot of information about this Mrs Simpson. It seems he'll marry her, whether his Parliament approves or not.'

Eva would have liked to hear more about that. She had a certain fellow-feeling towards Wallis Simpson. That woman's problems were not unlike her own. But Adolf was looking at her, suddenly. 'You look tired, liebchen. I'll see you in the morning.'

'You'll be here a day or two?'

'At least.'

And with that he turned back to Bormann and Hess.

Eva followed the triumphant Angi out of the room.

She's getting fat, Eva thought, maliciously. It's the soft and easy life she leads here, in this place. As the Fuhrer's sister, there's nothing she wants for: money, food, clothes, company, prestige. Angela Raubal had succeeded beyond her most ambitious day-dreams. But it would have to stop.

In the chilly bedroom Angi said, 'I hope you rest well, Fraulein.'

'Oh, I'm sure I shall. Guten Nacht.'

'Guten Nacht, Fraulein.'

At the door Angi turned back. 'I'm sure the fraulein knows the rules here?'

Eva slipped off her skirt: her long slim legs were her best feature. Let the cow see what she was up against. 'Oh, what rules are those?'

'The Fuhrer sleeps late. No noise at all, no radio, no singing, no gramophone music, or anything of that sort, until noon. And not very much then. The Fuhrer sleeps until ten or eleven and must not be wakened earlier. He has many worries and does not fall asleep until dawn sometimes, poor man.'

The 'poor man' was just permissible because, Fuhrer or not, Adolf Hitler was her half-brother. But Eva was tired and irritable and her customary caution deserted her. 'I think I know as much as anybody about the Fuhrer's sleeping habits, Frau Raubal,' she said, sweetly. 'And in the future, before you make arrangements to put me alone in an ice-box like *this*, I wish you would confer with him and see what his wishes are.'

Angi coloured with anger. Her dark, heavy face was suddenly very like her half-brother. 'I do not think he would be interested where the *Fraulein* sleeps.'

'Oh, but he would. Very interested.' Eva kept her voice sugar-sweet. 'If I weren't so tired I'd tell you *how* interested, Frau Raubal!'

In reply, Angi shut the bedroom door with a slam, with herself on the other side of it. Not before Eva had seen the effect of the words, however.

That went home, didn't it, you rotten old cow, thought Eva.

Eva took off her white silk blouse and her jewellery, all very slowly, because she was bone-tired; peeled off her long black stockings, first flinging off the ruched garters (which she had made sure Angi had seen, and why not, serve her right, probably a bit incestuous about Adolf anyway) and drew her slip over her head. She stepped out of the black French-knickers (Eva spent more thought and money on her underclothes than her dresses) and slipped, nude, between the icy sheets.

One thing was for certain.

That cow would have to go. One way or another.

Eva Braun closed her eyes, and slept at once.

In the corridor Angi Raubal, in her lisle stockings, elastic-trimmed bloomers and tight cotton bodice under her plain blue woollen dress, stood stock-still, shaking with anger.

The cheeky young tart, who did she think she was?

Did she suppose she could take the place of her lovely Geli?

Did she think Adolf would fall for her because she had long slim legs all the way up to her arse?

That game had been tried on Adolf Hitler already, by the most beautiful women in Germany. All kinds of women had thrown themselves at him. Movie stars, like Hilde Krahl and Olga Tschechowa – he could have them with a snap of his fingers! Society women of all kinds, from the highest families in the Reich, fluttered their eyelids at him. Why would he want Heinrich Hoffmann's shop-girl?

Of course, it had to be admitted, he had slept with Eva Braun once or twice, even at the Berghof.

That was to be expected. She was available, the little slut, and he was a man with a man's weakness: and, of course, Angi thought, she was young, and probably, to Adolf, seemed unspoilt.

Unspoilt?

That was a joke. She had the soft, pliant manner of a top-class courtesan.

Angi moved off, almost wearily, along the corridor, towards her own room on the first-floor-front of the Berghof. The stairs seemed extra steep tonight. She was getting heavy. It was the good rich food she ate. The cook Schliesan (from the *Adlon* in Berlin) would always be glad to make a special delicacy for the Fuhrer's sister: a pan of *Crepes Suzettes* maybe, in the middle of a long afternoon? Or a freshly-baked apfel-strudel, with rich, clotted cream? Angi ate well when Adolf was not in residence at the Berghof. True, her hips were heavy these days, and she was almost fifty years old. But what the devil, after Raubal, she had no desire for a man. Raubal's years of drinking and debt had cured her of any romantic illusions about marriage. The desperate loss of Geli had marked the end of many things for Angi Raubal.

Even now she wondered why Adolf had not come to her immediately after Geli died? She wondered what had been the truth of it all? The *real* reason Geli had the accident with Adolf's revolver?

For, good Catholic that she was, Angela Raubal could not admit that the accident might have been anything but an accident. Adolf had told her it was so (as had Hess, who broke the news to her first, driving out to the Obersaltzberg to do it) and Angi had been only too glad to take it as the truth.

Even now, she could hardly believe poor, dear, lovely Geli was dead.

Slowly, she trudged along the interminable corridors of the Berghof. Life was hard for Angi, only the Madonna herself knew how hard.

Back in the comfortable bedroom, Angi rang for a glass of hot milk. It helped her to sleep and tonight she needed her rest, with Adolf at the Berghof for two or three days at least, by the sound of it. It was good to see Adolf but even better to see him go back to Berlin. It was all work while he was in the place.

Angi sat on the bed and kicked off her soft, comfortable shoes. She looked around the room with love: chintz-cushions on the basketwork bedroom chairs, her own selection of pattern, to go with the embossed wallpaper: the small, oak occasional-table, for the bedside-snacks she often fancied, last thing at night, as now, when the work of the house was done. The big brass-knobbed bed, with the deep, soft, goosedown quilts: the solid oak wardrobe, packed with the kind of clothes that she had never thought she'd ever wear; excellent tweed-suits from the best stores in Munich. Shoes and stockings and good white cotton underwear galore, much of it either not charged-for by the stores, or priced at a 'special rate'. Being the Fuhrer's housekeeper (as well as his half-sister) had its advantages. Salesladies in the select boutiques of the city left titled clients and crossed the floor to greet her, if she as much as looked into their establishments.

Not that she ever bought anything expensive.

Angi's purchases were modest. They had to be. Adolf frowned on any kind of excess. Not that he ever enquired, about anything. Martin Bormann ran the Berghof, from the books to the kitchen, from the new, modernised cowsheds to the guardroom. That man's influence with the Fuhrer was a constant source of wonder, to Angi. She cultivated the swarthy, bandy-legged little ex-state manager for all she was worth. With such as Eva Braun around, she needed all the allies she could get.

The new maid brought her hot milk and no biscuits, which she had forgotten to ask for, but a slice of cold strudel, just what she fancied, fattening or not.

'Danke!' It was not necessary to thank the maids but Angi always did. Adolf, too, although he hardly noticed them. The domestic workforce at the Berghof was large and for security reasons (Bormann, again) none of the servants stayed more than a few months. Except, of course, the senior-employees like Adolf's personal valet, Linge, and his major-domo, Kannenberg, and the head cook Otto Schliesan, and naturally, since she held the keys to the establishment, herself.

The maid was new, and young, fair-haired and pretty, but with dark rings under her eyes.

'What's your name?' asked Angi idly, sipping her milk. 'You're new, aren't you?'

The maid bobbed. 'Only two weeks here, Frau Raubal.'

'You speak well? You're German?'

'Yes, I am, Frau Raubal. From Berlin.'

Angi was impressed by the girl's voice. 'You don't sound like a maid. Have you done a lot of this work?'

'No, Frau Raubal. Well . . .' The girl hesitated, looking a little frightened, Angi could not think why. 'I was a maid with Herr Walther, and he recommended me to Herr Bormann, you see.'

'Herr Walther, the Industrialist?'

'That is correct, Frau Raubal.'

'Are you nervous? Why are you trembling, girl?'

'I don't know, Frau Raubal. I think perhaps I'm a little tired.'

Angi was interested now. Anything, to put her mind at peace, help her to forget the long dangerous legs of Eva Braun and her black stockings with the frilly garters at the top.

'What did you do before you worked for Herr Walther?'

'I – I worked in an office.'

'How did you lose that job? I take it you lost it?'

'Yes, I did, Frau Raubal.'

'But why? Were you –' Angi thought she knew, 'Pregnant or something?'

The girl went white and red in turn, so it *had* to be that.

'Well, something like that, Frau Raubal.'

'I see. I'm sorry. But you have a good job here and you'll learn from your mistakes in life, as we all have to do.'

The girl bobbed her head again, not meeting Angi's eyes.

'Yes, I'm sure, thank you, Frau Raubal.'

Suddenly, Angi was tired of the girl.

'Yes, very well, about your business!'

'Yes, *Guten Nacht*, Frau Raubal.'

'*Guten Nacht* . . . What's your name again, girl?'

'Voller, Frau Raubal.'

And the girl had slipped quietly out of the bedroom.

Angi took off her sensible white cotton underclothes, and put on her long winceyette night-gown (clean every night, believe it or not, Raubal, if you are watching up there in Heaven, you old rascal, did you ever think to *see* such a thing!) and slid under the warmed goose-down covers: a stone hot-water-bottle was waiting for her cold feet. Her circulation was no longer good.

Angi Raubal switched off the rosy, fringed lamp at the bedside. She closed her eyes and said her brief nightly prayer, thanking the Madonna for the blessings of the day.

Such as they had been!

The face of Eva Braun came into her mind at once.

That young tart, with her long legs! No tits to speak of, at least that was something. Realistically, what chance did she have of an important relationship with her dear brother Adi?

None at all.

She was just a quick poke.

Nothing would come of it.

She, Angi Raubal, would see to that.

Adi would soon tire of her, as he'd tired of all the others. A nice pair of legs was an attraction for him, as to any man, as was Eva's youth (he certainly liked the soft, young ones) but there was nothing else to hold him but the sex, as far as Angi could see. He had installed Eva in the Prinzregentstrasse, of course, and that was bad news: that was an insult to her dear, darling Geli, as well as to herself. Angi never went to the Munich apartment these days. She was never invited.

Yes, it was an insult, say what you like.

Here she was, at an hour when, normally, she had been asleep for four hours (ten o'clock as a rule) thanking the Blessed Madonna for her blessings, and she was still thinking about that little shop-girl.

Angi Raubal closed her eyes and tried to sleep.

That little whore! All *she* knew about was how to open her legs to poor dear Adi! First, the Prinzregentstrasse, now the Berghof.

Angi could see her little game: to slowly but surely make herself emotionally and sexually indispensable to the Fuhrer.

It would have to stop! She owed it to poor dear dead Geli to see it *did* stop!

It was a long time before Angi Raubal slept.

*

390

Voller the maid walked slowly back towards the kitchens, situated at the rear ground-floor of the Berghof. Her legs were leaden but she had food in her belly today and would sleep six hours, uninterrupted, tonight. That was, indeed, something to be grateful for. Suddenly, she stopped and looked around. She had wandered from her usual corridors and felt uneasy. It was so simple to get lost in the vast labyrinth of rooms and passages of the Berghof. Its origin, as a simple farmhouse, had meant that the new extensions created a maze. Everything was new and perplexing to Voller. The whole set-up backstairs was scarifying, there were so many people giving orders, not least the bitter, barking Head Maid, the sour and wizened old cow, called simply 'Frau'. This vindictive creature terrified Voller: a look from her sent Kohler into an instant panic, which she covered-up by becoming bovine and expressionless, and accepting whatever came. Not that it was much, after what she had seen. After that, this was Paradise.

Voller, hurrying now, and taking what she was sure was another wrong turn, suddenly found herself facing the Great Hall of the Berghof, with its vast panoramic window running down one whole side of the room. She had been in the Hall with the cleaning-squads in the early mornings, but that was all. The place had frightened Voller, at first. She had thought the window a vast painting, until she saw her own reflection in it. The male-servants (bucolic, army-type batmen, in white bum-freezers and starched wing-collars) had laughed coarsely at her naivete, and later, in the servants' hall, had patted her bottom, and allowed their fingers to linger on the fabric of her thin black dress. They wanted sex from her (all men she had even *talked* to for the last two years had wanted sex from her, and many had got it) but they dared not try for it, not while they were locked into the bitter backstairs discipline of the Berghof. It was said the men were S.S. but Voller did not think so, and she knew her S.S. men, by God yes.

Voller stood, wondering how she could by-pass the Great Hall. It was, of course, unthinkable to walk through it, even if nobody was there.

Then she heard the Fuhrer's voice.

She stood very still and listened, terrified.

The Voice boomed huskily out of the semi-darkness of the Great Hall where, straining her eyes, Voller now saw three figures sitting around a table at the far end of the vast room. Hess, she recognised, and then Bormann. Bormann was always in the place, walking around, criticising, bellowing orders. Bormann ran the Berghof: the servants knew only too well that he was the master here. He could have people dismissed or worse, as the other women servants had whispered to her, on her arrival: his power was absolute. Even *Frau* (who only came from behind the scenes at the ritual of early-morning dusting and cleaning, all in total silence because the Fuhrer still slept) was in terror of him.

The *Voice* – Voller had heard it many times on the radio – spoke huskily, with passion: 'I talked to the Generals at Hossbach six months ago. I told them then, to their faces, of my secret plans. I said to them: I mean to launch a Lebensraum War inside five or six years. I said to them: we cannot feed ourselves, and we never quite will! I talked to those cowards for six whole hours! I said to them: I might have to take Czechoslovakia too, after Austria! All I got from Blomberg and the rest was: "Fuhrer! Please! No war on two fronts! What if the French and the British come in!"' The husky voice rose: it sent tremors down Kohler's spine. 'What did Goering say to that? Goering said, Fuhrer, let's get out of Spain. Franco's adventure is not our business. We need our troops on call in the Fatherland, if your plans are to go to schedule.'

There was a pause while the other men mumbled. Kohler could not hear what they said. The Fuhrer continued. 'I told Goering, Spain will grow into a big local war but nobody wants it to spread and it won't. We'll train our Luftwaffe there, it will be a rehearsal for the big event.'

There was a little more mumbling and some subdued laughter from the table and Voller recalled that she had heard in a snatched moment of listening to the radio that a Civil War raged in Spain. She was sorry to hear that the War would not spread to Germany. Anything that could harm, in any way, the malevolent devil sitting, talking, at the far end of the Great Hall, was to be wished for, worked for, prayed for. Not that Voller believed in prayer any longer. She still tried it but it altered nothing. The Reds were right. To fight Adolf Hitler you needed what he had: guns.

Guns?

Voller almost laughed out loud at the idea of anybody in Germany having a gun that did not belong to Adolf Hitler, except that she had not laughed for two years and did not think she would ever laugh again.

The Voice rose again, remorseless, hectoring: 'Both Frisch and Blomberg are hopeless. I need Generals who *want* to fight, not nannies who think armies need mollycoddling. What are armies for, if not for fighting? My S.S. men are ready, even if the Reichswehr is not!'

At the words 'S.S.' Kohler started to shake.

Keep still. Don't move. It will go, she told herself.

It usually did, with time: it was just a couple of *words*, after all. Schutz-Staffel! What was so awful about that?

Well, everything. Everything evil in the world.

The S.S. guard occupied the barracks at the back of the Berghof but Voller saw nothing of them and was immensely grateful for that. It was rumoured that whores were brought in from the red-light district of Munich, very discreetly, when Hitler was away, in S.S. trucks, driven right up to the back-door of the barracks. Other servants (there were almost fifty of them in the place, all told) whispered this information to her, but she said nothing in reply and behaved as if she had not heard. Some of them had not been where she had been and didn't know enough to keep their teeth (and their legs!) together.

Voller did. She had learned in a hard school.

'Teeth-and-legs-together!' the other women-prisoners had hissed in her ear, the first day in the prison-block in Ravensbruk.

'If you can,' they had added, mirthlessly. Voller had been shocked, just looking at them. They all seemed so old, these women, in their filthy, ragged prison-smocks, with teeth missing or broken and incipient black eyes and short matted hair and multiple bruises (which they ignored) all over their bodies and legs. She had supposed the bruises to be caused by the hard work but had soon been disabused of that.

The S.S. had soon shown her the facts of life in a Work Camp. Lolling behind his desk, in his beautiful uniform (she had never known his name) in his clean and shining office, the S.S. Major had greeted her that first day (there had been no trial, just a Committal Order signed by an unseen Sturmbannfuhrer) with a crooked smile and the one word, 'Attention!'

Voller was still in her civilian clothes, but feeling dirty and grubby, for it had been seventy-two hours since her arrest. She felt anything but alluring. But the S.S. Major had seen her in a sexual light, as his first question showed.

'Nice tits, Voller.'

Voller had said nothing, tried to feel nothing.

'Voller? Daughter of a known Red?' He examined a file lying open on his desk. '*Two* Reds, the *Mutti* as well? You are a Red whelp then, *liebschen?*'

Voller, remembering what the women prisoners had said to her, did not reply.

'Nineteen, I see? Still a virgin, are you?'

Voller had not replied to that either.

'No little Red boyfriend? I thought all you Reds believed in free love?'

She was still a virgin, yes: and she had a Red boyfriend, yes. He was in hiding and she prayed every night for Franz's safety, even if she had been taught by her Pappi that prayer was useless, that only actions counted.

Still, she said nothing.

'You need a good S.S. man up you, *liebschen.*'

Voller shouted at him, actually shouted – God, what guts she had then! She had known *nothing*. 'You will not talk to me like that. I demand to know why I am here, in this place. What am I charged with?'

393

Demand to *know?* God alive, what a brave little fool she had been!

Standing there, alone in the S.S. Major's office, in her best clothes, the demure blue dress with the white Eton collar that Franz had liked so much, and her court-shoes and a permanent-wave in her hair and her wrist-watch with its trim little elasticated band on her wrist. And still carrying her best little leather handbag, a present on her seventeenth from Mutti and Pappi!

Voller had thought – she had actually *thought* – that all those civilised little things made her invulnerable.

The S.S. Major had laughed loudly, throwing back his sun-reddened face, as if she had said something very funny (which, of course, she had, in *that* place!) and returned his gaze to the file. 'I see your Father is in Dachau and your Mother is . . . well, wherever she is, it doesn't say here. Both in Protective Custody for uttering menaces against the State. Your own offence, too, I see?'

'When am I supposed to have done *that?*'

Her voice had still been strong, she had still believed she had rights here. Even though she had seen them take Pappi in the middle of the night, from his own bed. *Mutti* had disappeared later, had simply not been there when she had returned from work with the sacking notice in her hand. The Office Manager had whispered, looking away from her, 'I'm very sorry, Fraulein Voller, it's company policy.'

Mutti had simply *gone*, and no neighbour was prepared to even speak of it to her, how it had happened, who had *done* it, anything at all! That was, she supposed, when she had failed to keep her teeth together, and spoken the fatal words: 'Who do you think Hitler is, *God?* He is the *Devil*, that's who he is! Are you afraid to even speak his *name!*'

None of the neighbours had answered but they had all heard her.

The next day she was in the police-van, on her way to a work-camp. It amazed her that the police, who had always been fair enough in their own rough way, even to Pappi, the trade-unionist, were now creatures of the Nazi state, and had merely 'booked' her and handed her on to the S.S.

That was when she should have realised how far things had gone: but she had only been seventeen years old, and still spirited: and mad with worry about her parents' fate. She had shouted – yes, actually *shouted* at the S.S. Major in Ravensbruk.

God, to think she'd done such a thing turned her cold.

The S.S. major had finished reading her file and then he had said, quite calmly, 'Take your knickers off. Now.'

At first, she did not think she had heard aright.

'I will do no such thing. I demand to see your senior officer!'

He had laughed even louder, then: 'Liebchen, I am the Senior Officer here. Think yourself lucky I fancy you.'

'You are a disgrace to your mother, you foul-mouthed pig,' she told him, coldly, trembling in every limb, but brave and angry.

He came from behind his desk like a big black cat and, quite calmly, felled her with a terrible blow to the temple. When Voller came to (and was promptly sick into a dirty tin basin) she was in a hut-dormitory of sorts, and her head throbbed terribly: her face was swollen all down one side, and she had difficulty in speaking. She trembled uncontrollably (no man had ever hit her before) and she was, she knew, in deep shock. That was when the women had whispered to her, the camp motto: 'Teeth-and-legs-together! If you can!'

The women-prisoners' long day's work was over and they crowded round her, in their thin, dirty workclothes, asking news of the outside. They seemed to totally ignore her pain and distress and after a while she knew why: everybody was in pain and distress, it was normal in that place. The Nazis called it a Work Camp and their idea (so a lesbian Capo told her, fondling her breasts – she didn't mind – she had given up minding about anything) was to administer a short-sharp-shock and let you go. Sometimes, if you were a Jewess, you could bribe your way out, but the rates were high and it was rare. The lesbian Capo said, sliding her fingers between Voller's legs, the only thing to do was keep in with important people like herself and do your time and keep saying how much you loved the Fuhrer.

Voller had said dully, 'I *hate* him!'

'So do we all, liebchen.' The Capo gave up, this girl didn't care, there was no fun in it. She lit a cigarette instead, made from newspapers and fragments of what looked like the pipe-tobacco Pappi used. 'If that S.S. Major asks you again, say yes.'

The S.S. Major did not ask her.

She was a prisoner now, with shorn hair and bruises and a vacant stare. He passed her by at a roll-call four days later and did not even see her, in her coarse, evil-smelling, striped work-clothes.

The next man to ask her had been a guard.

He had offered her food: bread and meat, in a sandwich.

They did it standing-up at the back of the hut and she felt nothing.

The guard did not even unsling his rifle.

But things got a little easier, then.

Another guard came to her. And another. And another.

She didn't care.

The lesbian Capo said, 'Becoming the camp bicycle, aren't you?'

Food. That was what mattered. Food. Nothing else.

She worked in the quarry and in the laundry. She felt nothing but hunger.

The lesbian Capo finally said, 'You're going. To the cook-house. I've recommended you, so behave. It's the next step to the Outside. Don't steal anything. Eat a mouthful of whatever you're cooking now and again, everybody does. It's shit but it'll keep you alive, Anna!'

'How about you?' asked Kohler, who had by now almost forgotten her name was Anna. Nobody ever called her by it.

The lesbian Capo shrugged. 'In here for life, that's why I'm a Capo.'

'What did you do?'

'Killed my girl friend. She was a top Nazi's wife. I was lucky to get life. I've done two years now. All I can pray for, liebchen, is a War and Germany loses it. Short of that I'm here for ever.' She had pressed a piece of cheese and grey bread into Voller's hand. 'But I know the ropes, I work the angles, with any luck I'll still be Capo in ten years' time.' She grimaced. 'At least none of the bastards want to fuck me.'

It took another year for Voller to get out. She shouted *Heil Hitler* incessantly, and told everybody how much she loved the Fuhrer. Nobody believed her. It didn't matter. She *did* it. That was what counted.

They had told her, in the office, a large wooden-hut surrounded by a sea of mud, 'You've done well, Voller, been obedient. There's your Workcard.' The Sergeant-clerk had looked over his glasses. 'Don't lose it. And we've found you a job, aren't we nice to you?'

'Yes, Herr Sergeant!' she yelled.

'Go to that address. They're expecting you.'

'Very good, Herr Sergeant!'

'*Heil Hitler!*' He raised a tired, clerkly hand.

'*Heil Hitler!*' she yelled.

He winced. 'Get out and don't come back!'

Voller walked out of that Camp as if on eggs.

The Walthers, her new employers, had turned out to be Heaven on Earth.

Herr Walther was kindly but stern. He believed in discipline, he told Voller. She should know all about that after where she had been. One half-day a week off. Frau Walther would tell her her duties. That was all. Herr Walther's so-called sternness, after what she had seen and suffered, was a joke.

Frau Walther was silly and merry and had affairs with young officers. So Voller was liked, because she kept her mouth shut about visits in the afternoon and cries of pain and pleasure from the bedroom.

Voller's hair grew and she fattened up a little.

It lasted six glorious months.

Then Martin Bormann came to supper. It was a great occasion. The best silver. The best china service. Voller had behaved well, for she had learned, easily, how to serve at table. Frau Walther had taught her. She was not in the dining-room much but it was plain that Bormann and his wife, Gerda, had enjoyed themselves, for Bormann's laugh was loud, coarse and frequent. She was never to see him behave like that at the Berghof.

The problem came a week later.

A letter from Bormann offering her a job at the Berghof.

As Herr Walther said unhappily, it was impossible to refuse.

So, watched by Frau Walther's sympathetic eye, Voller had packed her few things into the small attache-case, and clutching her train-warrant, had travelled long hours, third-class. Finally, hungry and tired, she reported to the Berghof, which seemed like the top of the Earth, set in high and gloomy mountains. Voller had never been at such an altitude before.

Martin Bormann had seen her himself in his spacious office, accompanied by the Head Maid, *Frau*. 'You will behave well or go back where you came from, and I don't mean Herr Walther's establishment.' His little piggy eyes scared her so much she trembled, as usual. This seemed to satisfy him. 'I can see you're cured of your Marxism, or so your Workcard says?'

'*Heil Hitler,*' Voller yelled, on cue.

'No need to shout. She's all yours, *Frau*.'

One look at *Frau* told Voller it was not like Herr Walther's establishment. Soon, she had proof of it.

The second night she witnessed a servant's beating.

The young girl, whose place she was taking, was flogged with a cane on the bare arse by *Frau*.

'She goes back where she came from,' said *Frau*, deeply satisfied, when it was over and they all stood, the female staff, in obedient lines, showing nothing. 'We will have discipline here, ladies! See you obey the rules or you'll get what she got!'

Voller had obeyed the rules.

'*Voller!*'

She turned, heart pounding. Oh my God!

It was *Frau*! Peering at her in the half-dark. 'Get to your room.'

Voller finally found her way back to the small bedroom she shared with three other maids, all exhausted and asleep. Voller lay down in her chemise, trembling all over. She muttered the words, barely aloud – unless she *said* them they didn't count, did they?

Please God, let lightning strike the Fuhrer and kill him!

Voller mumbled the words over and over again until, exhausted, she slept, to dream of the S.S. Major. In the dream he raped her, then strangled her.

It was a regular dream and did not frighten Voller.
Not any longer.

In the Great Hall Adolf Hitler was winding-up his talk for the night. Even he could see that Hess and Bormann were more than ready to sleep. It was now past two o'clock, but he always felt wound-up for days after a big speech, and the one the previous evening had been big. Tonight, perhaps, he would be lucky and fall asleep at once. Sometimes it happened, but more rarely nowadays. As soon as he lay down on his iron army-cot his mind became alive with the events of the day, as seen through his personal prism. Small, unimportant conversations with Goering or Goebbels, or even Hess and Bormann, assumed large, important status in the dark hours. Diplomatic telegrams from German embassies in London and Paris, hardly glanced at during the day, suddenly become worthy of deep cogitation. Problems existed to be thought-through. Sleep eluded him in these long, dark periods of the night, and his body began to ache, as he turned and twisted on his hard, army mattress. Sometimes, if Eva was with him, he would sleep better (anyway, for a while) relaxed by Eva's adroit sexual wiles and a final sexual release: but, even then, he would wake after two or three hours, almost as if he needed the insomnia so that he could steal a march on all the normal, sleeping people in the world who had only their waking-hours in which to plot against him, or in some way thwart his plans for Germany's future greatness. And his own.

But little Eva had gone to some distant bedroom, so there was nothing to be done about that. Perhaps he should not have let it happen, but it would not have been easy to countermand Angi's arrangements, not to her face.

So all he had, as so often, was a dying fire, and Bormann and Hess. Bormann said, 'Fuhrer, is there news of Blomberg and the woman?'

Adolf was revived, at once. 'You didn't hear the latest on *that* subject?'

Bormann and Hess shook their heads.

'Von Blomberg asked my permission to marry a lady who turns out to have a very colourful past. She is known to the police and has a dossier as a prostitute and as a person who poses for pornographic photographs.' Bormann's eyes gleamed, he enjoyed that. 'Also, she is twenty years younger than he is.' Hitler shook his head, these *generals*. To think he had once stood in awe of them!

To think that only two short years ago, he had been worried enough about the Generals to convene a meeting of them all at the State Opera House on the Unter den Linden, to assure them of his undying loyalty to the Army. To think that he, Adolf Hitler, had had to bend the knee to these Junker gentlemen because they had the guns – if not the will – to depose him. A military putsch was the only way to bring down a dictator, historical events bore that out, from Julius Caesar to any tinpot South American upstart. And a military Putsch in Germany could only start one way, with the death by assassination of the Fuhrer, Adolf Hitler! By disarming and returning his Brownshirts to civilian-life he had, in fact, delivered himself to the Army. He had shouted desperately to them in the Opera House. 'The Army is a pillar of Germany, just as the Nazi Party is a pillar of Germany! Both are vital! Germany is invincible so long as they are united!' He had spoken for two whole hours, hoarse, nervous of an audience for almost the first time in his life. These men could *kill* him, these pompous, scented, shaven-headed popinjays, with their tarty women and their bum-boys and their certainty that Germany belonged to them and always would, that Adolf Hitler was but a passing political phenomenon. If the worst came to the worst and there ever was a Generals' Plot, he still had Himmler and his S.S. It was a small band by comparison with the Army, but if used quickly and ruthlessly, it could defend his life and Germany's future.

Hitler stirred, shivered, and came back to the present.

To think he had worried about these Junker gentlemen. All they cared about was rank and promotion and status and, seemingly, cock! He would not ignore them or the possibilities of their treason, but they were Generals and he was offering them War and Glory. No General ever born would deny that offer.

'The Generals,' he said aloud, but as if to himself, 'are mine. Anyway, for the moment.'

There was another long silence.

Then, gently, after a warning sideways glance at Bormann, Hess asked, 'Fuhrer, what *are* your exact plans for Schuschnigg?'

Smiling suddenly, Adolf Hitler told them. A note of hate and contempt for the man who stood in his way entered his voice. Even Hess and Bormann, who had heard him like this so often, were chilled and overpowered.

They listened, as ever, as long as he spoke, totally mesmerised.

Then, when he had finished, they laughed.

And so did he.

Hitler stood in the Great Hall of the Berghof and waited for Schuschnigg.

He had it all planned, as he had told Hess and Bormann that night, months before, down to the last, ruthless detail. This vain, obnoxious fellow thought he could come here and talk man-to-man with the Fuhrer of all Germany, and win?

For Schuschnigg had boasted of it, actually boasted of it, to his own tame newspapermen, back in Vienna. 'I know that Hitler and I can talk ourselves into a sensible solution. Man-to-man, I know I have nothing to fear from him.'

The pompous, puffed-up idiot.

Nothing to fear? From a politician who had outgunned and out-guessed such as Gregor Strasser and Roehm and Eden and Daladier and even the American Roosevelt? Had he not said to Roosevelt, in one of his earliest public speeches as *Kanzler*: 'You Americans make a fuss about our Jews? Will you not take them off our hands? We will pay their passage to your shores and give every one of them a thousand marks to take with him? What is your answer to that, President Roosevelt, you who is so concerned about the fate of German Jewry? When will I hear that you have taken me up on this offer?'

For answer, there had been a deafening silence.

Von Ribbentrop came in: quietly and slyly as was his way. He was now Hitler's Foreign Secretary. A snobbish fellow, some of the Generals found him. A social-climber, with a bogus 'Von' before his name, now that he had married well. Hitler did not mind any of that. Ribbentrop had influential friends abroad, especially in England, where he was a weekend guest at Cliveden and other country-houses owned by the English aristocracy. The foreign policy of the British Empire was decided in these places, Ribbentrop asserted, not in Parliament, which was just a talking-shop. Hitler was prepared to believe that. He ignored and distrusted his own Foreign Office in the Wilhelmstrasse, who never got anything right. He ran Germany's foreign affairs himself and Ribbentrop was his mouthpiece.

'Fuhrer, Schuschnigg has been met at the station. He is in the Army half-track as you ordered, not in a limousine.' He added, drily, 'And there are a hundred men of our Austrian Legion drawn up outside the Berghof. If that does not impress him, Fuhrer, I don't know what will?'

'When will he arrive?' asked Hitler, dressed at his most military, in brown Party-tunic and black trousers. He wore a swastika armband. He always felt more commanding in uniforms and God knows, he needed to be that today.

'In about ten minutes.' Ribbentrop laughed, discreetly. 'The road is icy. He should have a hair-raising ride!'

Hitler permitted himself a brief smile. 'Then we will see what he is made of. Are Sperrle and Reichenau ready?'

'Standing by, Fuhrer.'

'Good!'

Hitler had picked his two toughest-looking generals to stride next to him down the front steps of the Berghof to greet Von Schuschnigg. When the moment came, in the icy blast of wind that swept off the Obersaltzberg, and Hitler steeled himself for the moment of even icier greeting, he was glad he had done exactly that. Schuschnigg emerged, blinking with cold and visibly shaken from the half-track, the well-wrapped-up crew grinning behind him. Schuschnigg's thin city top-coat had been little protection against the weather, and his hand was icy as it took Hitler's own. He had not shaved that morning, Hitler noted, and the shrill, shouted orders of the officers made him start nervously. He looked wrong-footed and alarmed, not least by Hitler's two burly, scowling generals, and muttered, 'Schuschnigg!' as if Hitler might not know his name.

Hitler merely saluted, did not smile, and led the way inside. Ribbentrop fell into step with Schuschnigg and indicated a small ante-room, where the Austrian diplomats (who had followed in a limousine) should go. Schuschnigg looked surprised at the idea of talking to him absolutely alone, Hitler noted with satisfaction. Well, it was what he had said he wanted, wasn't it?

Brusquely, Hitler indicated a chair at the vast table, giving Schuschnigg no time to comment on the magnificence of the Great Hall or of the panoramic view from the vast window. Everybody who came into the place for the first time remarked on it, and Hitler had a stock answer ready for them: 'I have built a house around a window!' he would joke.

But today, with Schuschnigg, jokes were out.

Hitler nodded to Ribbentrop, who bowed politely to both men and retired.

Alone, in the vast room, the two men sat.

Hitler waited for Schuschnigg to speak.

Schuschnigg said nothing. Tall, bespectacled, still shivering from the bitter cold, he had not, as yet, taken off his top-coat. He looked wan and worried, but stubborn. After two minutes of silence it became clear to Hitler that this meeting was to be no walk-over, despite his preparations. It was possible the ploy had made Schuschnigg more wooden-headed. Very well, he would begin.

'There are 95 million Germans in the world,' Hitler said, in his low, husky voice. 'Only 65 million are in the Reich. The rest are in Austria, the Baltic, and Czechoslovakia.' He paused. 'But most are in my own country, Austria. It is a state of affairs I cannot allow to go on.'

Schuschnigg blinked: 'You cannot, Fuhrer? You are our brothers, I agree. But *you* cannot? What do you mean, *you* cannot allow it to go on? *I* am Kanzler of Austria. Our independence is guaranteed by the Versailles Pact, and underwritten by France, Great Britain, and the United

States of America. I head the Government. I am perfectly prepared to accept that Germany and Austria should be allies – indeed, I want nothing more! – but this talk of annexation, if that is what you are suggesting, I will resist with all my strength!'

So, the creature was showing fight?

Hitler, as always, when violence was in the air, welcomed it.

'Herr Chancellor,' he said, 'You are arresting and harassing my Nazi Party comrades in Austria – that *I* cannot allow!'

'I have documents, Fuhrer' said Schuschnigg, quietly, 'captured documents that prove conclusively that the Austrian Nazi Party will soon attempt another *Putsch*!'

'What is that to do with me?' asked Hitler, mildly, somewhat taken aback.

'I should say everything, Fuhrer,' replied Schuschnigg, steadily.

The arrogance of the fellow!

Hitler stood up, 'I am going to be totally frank with you, Chancellor!'

Schuschnigg sat, still in his top-coat, waiting.

'My Generals advise me, Herr Von Schuschnigg, to invade your country next Saturday, the 26th February. They have everything prepared. Tanks, artillery, infantry. It will happen, my dear Von Schuschnigg, unless I am able to tell them that you and I have reached an accommodation.' Hitler looked out at the snowy mountain-caps. It was indeed a wondrous view. 'What do you have to say to that?'

There was such a long silence that Hitler, finally, turned round. He found a Schuschnigg he hadn't seen before. The man was on his feet, gesticulating. 'That is a threat of War against my country. If you attack us, you start a European War. Have *you* thought of *that*?'

Hitler was impressed. The fellow was putting up a good fight, especially since Adolf Hitler knew, from wire-taps on the French Embassy in Berlin, that the French were ready to fight but the British most certainly were not. Lord Halifax had said to the French that he was not prepared to go to war over Austria. The Americans were too far away to matter and in Adolf Hitler's opinion would never enter a European War again.

'My dear Von Schuschnigg,' said Hitler, 'We both know that the French would – perhaps! – fight over Austria. But only if the British do, and the British *won't*. You are a wilful fellow, I know, but even you must see that you are sitting at this table with a very poor hand?'

'I deny that!'

'I have had enough of talk!' shouted Hitler. 'I will use a couple of pioneer battalions to take control of Austria this very weekend, if you do not show some co-operation with me. I am the Fuhrer of Germany, and I will not be dictated to!'

'I am not attempting to dictate anything,' protested Schuschnigg, alarmed.

'No, and nor will you! *I will dictate!*'

Schuschnigg did not reply. Hitler could hear a hush all over the Berghof. Everybody, including Schuschnigg's civil servants had heard *that*.

'I have this to say, and I only say it because I too am an Austrian,' Hitler went on, lowering his voice. 'I will not allow my Generals to invade Austria. What I will do is give you an Agreement to sign which my Foreign Minister will draw up during lunch.'

Schuschnigg looked astonished but, thought Hitler, vastly relieved. 'Well, I will have to see this Agreement before I can say if I will sign it, won't I?'

'Naturally,' said Hitler, almost jovial. 'And now, lunch! You look rather cold, Herr *Kanzler*? Why not take off your top-coat and let us go in? I think I can assure you of a good, plain, Austrian meal.'

Bemused, Schuschnigg took off his coat, shivered, rubbed his cold hands together, then caressed his unshaven face. Slowly, he followed Adolf Hitler out of the Great Hall.

Hitler excused himself early from the lunch-table, which he had crowded with his Generals, to further depress Schuschnigg with their military talk. They, led by Keitel, that rarity, a professional soldier totally loyal to the Party and the Fuhrer, discoursed on the new German Panzer divisions – tank battalions such as no other European nation possessed. Aircraft, too, to back up the tanks, the infantry to press forward only when tank and bomber had blasted a path for them. Von Schuschnigg listened gloomily to all this, making no comment, not even consulting his anxious aides, and eating almost nothing. Finished, Hitler thought, he has no cards and he knows it.

'Our object today is to soften up Schuschnigg. We have done that. If he signs this paper we have him. He'll just disappear, politically. Then our Austrian Nazis will win any election. Then we'll amalgamate the two nations. Good?'

'Brilliant, my Fuhrer!' said the smiling Ribbentrop.

Schuschnigg did not smile, when he read the agreement, half an hour later: 'I can't sign *this*!'

Hitler, by now, was in his study, and sat alone, once again, with the Austrian leader. 'All I am asking is that you cease to persecute my Nazi brothers in Austria, and appoint as Minister, Seyss-Inquart, who will see the persecution *does* stop! If you cannot see your way to agree to that, I will invade Austria *tomorrow* and have done with it!'

Schuschnigg, to Hitler's satisfaction, was still trembling. To his dissatisfaction, the man stood firm. 'By law, Fuhrer, I cannot appoint Ministers. Only the Austrian President, Miklas, can do that. I will have to report back to him and discuss it.'

'*Discuss* it?' shouted Hitler, angrily, 'I will discuss nothing more! I will act.' He got up from his chair and went to the door of his study. 'Bring me General Keitel at once!'

Schuschnigg blanched but said nothing and walked slowly, along the corridor, to his advisors. General Wilhelm Keitel hurried in, uniformed, beribboned, close-cropped, with a pallor from his severe war-wounds, yet sprightly enough for his fifty-six years: 'Fuhrer, you want me?'

'Just sit down and don't talk!'

Mystified, Keitel did as he was bid.

Two minutes later Ribbentrop appeared. He carried two copies of the document. Both bore Von Schuschnigg's signature.

'Victory, my Fuhrer,' said Ribbentrop, quietly.

'Yes,' said Adolf Hitler, feeling suddenly exhausted. 'Schuschnigg has signed it. But will he keep to it?'

'What choice has he got?' asked Ribbentrop. 'It's all over for him.'

Hitler shook his head. He was not convinced.

Ribbentrop wondered why that was? For himself, he was delighted. He had the Anti-Comintern Pact with Japan under his belt already. This could be his first diplomatic triumph in Europe: and, he thought, with luck, surely not the last.

Ribbentrop, perhaps fortunately for him; was away in London when Adolf Hitler sat in the Chancellery in Berlin and listened to Schuschnigg on the radio, telling Austria and the world that he was declaring a *Plebiscite*: The Austrians themselves must decide whether they wished a close union with Nazi Germany. Neither himself nor President Miklas could decide such an irrevocable step on behalf of the nation. The nation itself must decide. *Yes or No?* The voting-papers would ask only that.

Hitler banged his fist on the Chancellery table. 'I knew it! After I had tried to be friendly, tried to conciliate – let nobody deny it! Very well, Herr Von Schuschnigg! We *march*!'

Goering and Goebbels hastily advised: 'Let us set up some kind of insurrection inside Austria first. Let us have an excuse!'

'An excuse?' thundered Hitler.

'Something to tell the world,' said Goering.

'Something they might believe,' said Goebbels.

Hitler said, 'Very well. Do what you can.'

Goering and Goebbels exchanged glances and went off to make threatening telephone calls to their agents in Vienna, and to the Austrian government itself. Goering demanded the immediate resignation of Schuschnigg. The Austrian President, Miklas, refused. Hitler thought: Schuschnigg must be confident of help. Hitler spoke to Ribbentrop in London. His question was simple: 'If we invade, will the English march?'

He listened to Ribbentrop's studied reply. 'Not this time. They are not ready. Halifax is not Eden. He will do nothing.'

Hitler digested that. 'And the French?'

'As before, they hate and fear us and would fight. But not without the English at their side.'

'And Mussolini?'

Ribbentrop coughed, delicately. 'My Fuhrer, you know more of the Duce's intentions that I do. Or any man perhaps, except the Duce himself?'

Hitler's call to Mussolini in Rome was very brief. After exchanging personal greetings, Hitler said, 'Duce, I march into Austria. My information is that the Democracies will do nothing. I know Austria is in your sphere of influence so I ask for your help. If you do nothing, my success is certain. Do I have your assistance in this bid to unite my people?'

There was a silence at the other end of the line.

Quickly, he added, 'Should you throw in with me, Duce, I will never forget it. I will be at your side always.'

There was an even longer silence.

Then Mussolini said: 'I am with you. Von Schuschnigg is in the wrong. He signed an agreement and he's trying to get out of it, anyhow he can. Rely on me.'

Adolf Hitler said, with emotion, 'I know you have borne the brunt of the Franco business in Spain. I will do more to help you there. Whenever you call on me, no matter what the circumstances, I will be at your side. I promise that.'

He was not to know, at that moment, how dear that promise was to cost him.

After he had put down the telephone, Hitler sat thinking for five minutes. Then he nodded to State Secretary Meissner to admit General Ludwig Beck, Chief of the General Staff. Like Keitel, Beck was too old, in

Hitler's opinion, for hard soldiering. Fifty-eight years of age, in Hitler's view he had left his balls on the Western Front, like most of the older Generals. He knew Beck instinctively for a conciliator. A Prussian Christian, for God's sake, full of high moral scruples and, so Himmler's spies told him, about the only senior Army officer capable of mounting a putsch against him. Was he a possible sometime-traitor or just a coward? Adolf Hitler didn't know, but brilliant planner though Beck was supposed to be, he'd prefer Keitel a dozen times over, because at least Keitel was loyal. Just the same, he put the proposal to Beck, with respect, as befitted Beck's position. It was necessary to go through the form, where the Army was concerned.

'Herr General, you are in charge of Army Planning. I intend to invade Austria very soon. What is your reaction, and what plans do you have to present to me?'

Beck looked stupified. 'We have no plans prepared for the invasion of Austria, Fuhrer.'

'Then what forces can you mobilise?' asked Hitler impatiently.

'Two Panzer, some reserve infantry – most of the Army is on manoeuvres, as you know, Fuhrer!' Beck added, 'I can take no responsibility –'

'I can!' said Hitler, brutally. 'If necessary, I'll use S.S. troops only.'

Beck protested: 'My Fuhrer, can this not be done another way?'

'No,' said Adolf Hitler, in curt dismissal. 'It can not. Guten-tag, Herr General.'

A bemused Heinrich Hoffmann found himself in Hitler's Mercedes on the stroke of noon, March 12th, 1938. He had been summoned by a functionary of Hitler's own staff, which was not unusual. The functionary had seemed overawed by whatever the occasion was (what *was* it, anyway?) and merely repeated, when Hoffmann asked for more details: 'It is the personal order of the Fuhrer. Be at the place and time stated. You will be away for an indefinite period, so please bring plenty of film.'

'I always bring plenty of film!' retorted Heinrich Hoffmann, who hated being wakened early, especially by a shrill telephone, especially when he had had a little too much to drink the night before. He promptly went back to sleep again.

Nonetheless, here they were, Erich Kempka driving and himself sitting in the rear with Hitler and the General, Fritz Halder who, it was rumoured, was to replace Beck as Chief of Staff of the Army, sitting in front. Hoffmann raised his eyebrows in enquiry and looked long at Halder, a laconic old professional, and received only a quizzical smile in reply. When Hoffmann had reported to the Brown House as instructed, it was only to learn that Hitler had just flown in from Berlin. They were now driving very fast out of Munich on the road towards the Austrian border. It was one o'clock in the afternoon, and they were accompanied by two Army staff-cars, full of officers and armed troops.

'You have plenty of film, Heinrich?' enquired Hitler, who seemed to be in a jovial mood. It was a crisp day in early spring, but cold in the open tourer.

'A full-camera, naturally, Fuhrer,' replied Hoffmann, mystified. 'But what am I to use it on?'

'You will find many subjects today,' said Hitler, mysteriously. 'You will photograph a great historical event, before the day is out. That I promise you.'

'But Fuhrer, where do we go?'

Adolf Hitler smiled, a rare event, and Hoffmann itched to use his camera *then*: but knew Hitler would forbid it: The Fuhrer only smiled when he was photographed with children. At the Berghof their parents were allowed to walk by, with a respectful nod towards the Fuhrer, but were not allowed to speak or make conversation. S.S. men always checked such crowds for possible assassins.

Hitler said, 'I have a yen to visit my birthplace.'

Hoffmann was even more mystified. 'But isn't that Braunau, across the River Inn? In Austria?'

'Exactly right, my dear Hoffmann.'

'But?' Hoffmann looked for help to Halder. The General looked at Hitler, who nodded. 'German troops crossed the Frontier this morning. They have been received by cheering crowds everywhere. Schuschnigg has resigned. It has been on the radio,' said Halder.

'Not yet,' said Hitler. 'It will be announced in two hours. Goebbels was most insistent we said nothing to the world until we had a fait accompli, with myself on Austrian soil.'

'No resistance anywhere?' asked Heinrich Hoffmann, incredulously.

'None whatever,' said Halder, 'from the Austrians.'

'Halder is a German General,' said Hitler, a trifle sharply. 'He is still afraid of what the French and the English might do!'

'Not afraid, my Fuhrer,' said Halder, easily. 'Curious, perhaps.'

'Nothing,' said Hitler. 'They will do nothing.'

An historic occasion *indeed*, thought Heinrich Hoffmann, awed.

Simbach, the last German town in their path, was festive with flowers, crowds, and massive swastikas hanging from every public building. Huge, blown-up photographs of Hitler, all of them taken by Heinrich Hoffmann himself, were everywhere. Hitler stood up in the Mercedes, and Heinrich Hoffman, in a sweat of flurry and excitement, was snap-snap-snapping away, now inside the car, now hanging with one hand on the running-board of the Mercedes, his Leica in the other, still snap-ping, as they crossed into Austria.

Braunau was a replay of Simbach. Crowds. Children. Men wearing their war medals. Women throwing flowers. Hoffmann snapped and snapped.

The late afternoon found them in Linz, the city Hitler called his own. Almost a million Austrians were in the town, waving and cheering.

Hitler speaks from the balcony of the Municipal Hall. He is overjoyed, this is where he started out from, this is where he dreamed his earliest dreams, a lifetime ago, with Gustl: these are the streets he walked, as a lost youth, after the death of his beloved mother. At first, he is overcome, as he looks down from the balcony at the vast crush of people in the Square below. Then, to a tumultuous roar, he steps forward, a lone, still, uniformed figure. He allows the roar to go on and on and finally he raises his hand for silence; and gets it.

The crowd wait, totally passive. The whole of Linz is silent.

Then he says, and they can hear every word clearly: 'If Providence sent me out from this city and called upon me to lead the Reich, then surely it must have had another mission in mind for me? And that can only have been to return my native country to the German Reich!'

They would not let him continue. They cheered and danced in Linz, as they were to cheer and dance in Vienna later that night, when Hitler, the one-time starveling student watched them from the opulent Imperial Hotel. But *this* was the moment that mattered most, this moment in Linz. Hitler looked down on them all, crushed in a vast mass in this town he had grown up in and knew so well. It was a sweet moment, one of the sweetest of his life. To come back a hero, the dream of every man who ever left home.

Anschluss!

XVIII

'**H**E who has Czechoslovakia has Europe!'
How often throughout 1938 had Eva Braun heard those words?

It seemed sometimes that they were the only words Adolf Hitler said, as he sat, in the new Tea Pavilion on the Berghof, sunning himself in the long, lazy days. There was a constant procession of homage to the Fuhrer through those weeks. The supplicants all had one thing in common. After the great triumph of the *Anschluss*, they wanted to rest on their laurels for a while and savour the fruits of that astonishing, bloodless victory.

All of them, except Adolf Hitler.

Slowly, one by one, they bent to his iron will.

Eva, the little woman, quiet and unassuming at the Fuhrer's side, sat and watched Hess and Bormann, who never opposed Adolf Hitler on any issue, capitulate first. Then Goering and Goebbels, who both seemed hesitant, especially Goering, about any further 'adventures' that year. Finally, the Generals.

After all, the Fuhrer had been right about Austria.

The Democracies had done nothing.

Ribbentrop reported from London that the British were not over-concerned; they regarded Austria as a German nation and the obvious delight of the Austrian population at the union of the two countries had surprised and, in their own phrase, 'rather stumped' them!

Ribbentrop said, 'The attitude in London is: if the Austrians want Hitler, it's their business, not ours.'

Of course, not all the Austrians had wanted Adolf Hitler.

Eva knew, from the foreign newspapers that Hitler's aides spread across the long table in the Great Hall each morning, that terrible things were happening in Austria. If these newspapers were to be believed.

Eva heard the aides talking. The Reds and the Social Democrats and the Jews had all been 'restricted'. The Jews, in particular, who had considered themselves safe in Austria, had 'a very nasty shock when they found themselves scrubbing the pavements in front of their Viennese shops!' smiled the aides. It was fashionable in military circles to find the Jews funny.

Eva tried not to think of these unpleasant things. They were the men's business and no concern of hers.

Hitler, on the other hand, listened keenly to all reports from Vienna. 'An *Office for Jewish Emigration* has been set up in Vienna, Fuhrer,' said his military aide. 'It is the only place from which any Jew wishing to emigrate can obtain an exit visa. The officer in charge of the *Office for Jewish Emigration* is Karl Eichmann. He is from Linz, the Fuhrer's home-town,' added the aide. Hitler nodded absently. He held in his hand a document, a report that said in plain policeman's language that a certain Reinhold Hanisch, of no fixed address, had been taken into protective custody because of many derogatory articles about the Fuhrer in the Viennese press, inspired by the said Hanisch, who had given gross and disrespectful information to scurrilous journalists, for money. Regrettably Hanisch, whose health had not been good, had died while in police custody. The document was not signed and was marked *Extremely Confidential*. It bore the imprint of the Commandant of the Gestapo Central Office in Vienna.

'Von Schuschnigg,' said the aide, 'has been given no diplomatic quarter, as the Fuhrer instructed. He has been put to cleaning out the lavatories of the Gestapo Headquarters at the commandeered Hotel Metropole in Vienna!' Hitler laughed, a short, sharp bark. The aide was startled but remained at attention. He ventured, 'A great personal satisfaction for the Fuhrer? Such a return to Vienna?'

Adolf Hitler nodded, slowly, tore up the Gestapo's memorandum and dropped it into the waste-paper basket. He felt nothing, why should he, nobody was allowed to piss on the good name of Germany, nobody!

The aide said, anxiously, 'Many of the Fuhrer's old friends no doubt enjoyed the festivities?'

Hitler said nothing to that. There had doubtless been men standing in those crowds who had known him in another time: and almost, it seemed to him, another life. He thought of his old schoolmasters and his fellow-pupils at the Realschule and of the inmates of the Men's Home, Greiner the Capo, and Herr Director Kanya. He thought of the homosexual Herr Senior Librarian, and of the bespectacled Herr Professors who had refused him admission to the College of Fine Arts. Had they been (those who were still alive) somewhere in the vast, excited, almost hysterical city, gazing wonderingly into their beer or their schnapps, musing at the amazing things that can happen in life, when such a pitiable down-and-out as young Adolf Hitler can become *Kanzler* of Germany, and now of Austria?

It was no wonder they would find such a thing hard to believe. Sometimes he did himself.

That evening of the great takeover, as the city still noisily celebrated long into the late hours, Adolf Hitler had stood alone in the dark Square before the Hofburg, filled with lingering, bitter memories of Vienna: of the failed examination at the Academy of Fine Arts; of the awful room on the Stumpergasse he had shared with Gustl; of the stink of unwashed feet in the dormitory of the Men's Home. As all these memories returned to Adolf Hitler, the triumphant elation, the ecstasy almost, that had sustained him all the way from the hysteria of Linz to the grand pomposity of Vienna, suddenly evaporated. He had looked up at the vast looming bulk of the Hofburg (how many times had he set up his easel in this place, hoping to make a few marks?) and felt a sudden, violent distaste for the very stones of the Citadel.

What did he owe this sink of a city that had so rejected and humiliated him?

Nothing!

The bloodless victory in Austria, Eva Braun thought later, as she studied the Fuhrer's daily itinerary at the Berghof, the better to assess which lunches and suppers she should attend and which not (depending on whether the guests knew of her relationship with Adolf) seemed to have unsettled the Fuhrer, rather than calmed him. The constant flow of Generals with this plan or that, for Hitler's proposed (but only talked-about-in-whispers) occupation of Czechoslovakia, was a symptom of it. Although he never discussed matters of state or policy with Eva, she *was* with him a great deal of the time and could pick up on his intentions in a way that was denied to even his closest aides.

Well, what was so unusual about that? She slept with him, didn't she?

Eva recalled many things Adolf had said to her, things nobody else would ever hear. Had he not said, in one of their private moments: 'I am fifty years old. It is the crown and apex of a man's life. But from now on the road must be downhill, physically and mentally!'

Eva had joshed him gently, encouraging and woman-like, and remarked coyly on the fact that his sex-drive was undiminished, although she knew that it *was* somewhat, and little wonder, the energy he expanded on everything else, including *talk*. Adolf had brushed that aside. 'If I am to do the great things for Germany that are within my power, I must do them soon, while I have the energy for it.'

Eva recognised that this glorious Summer at the Berghof might be the last spent in a comparatively peaceful atmosphere and so she determined to make it memorable for both herself and Adolf. She had her own victory to celebrate.

The victory over Adolf's half-sister, Angela Raubal! It had, when it happened, been so very easy. Hitler had again and again invited Eva to the Berghof. Again and again, Angi had housed her in the small bedroom in the new wing.

Finally, Hitler had noticed the ploy. 'Why are you always put in this ridiculous situation?' he asked her, as they lay on the hard, horsehair mattress of his own bed, in his bleak bedroom on the top-floor of the Berghof. Sex was over and they were simply lying there, talking. There was never anything romantic about Adolf's small talk.

'I don't mind the room,' Eva said, easily, gathering her silken dressing-gown around her. 'It's no trouble to me, really.'

'No, but it's a trouble to me,' said Adolf, the lines in his face hardening, in a way she recognised. 'You should not be walking around the corridors of the Berghof – that is all wrong. Anybody might see you, and talk will begin.'

'Angi always puts me there,' said Eva. She smiled. 'I think she feels you shouldn't sleep with me or have anything to do with me, since I am nobody very much, just a little shop-girl from Munich?'

When she said the words she laughed out loud, dismissing the whole idea. But Adolf said, angrily: 'Tonight is the last night you do this! From now on you have a room up here with me, on a permanent basis, as you have at the Prinzregentstrasse.'

'Well, if you think it wise' said Eva. 'What about all your old Generals? They're very stuffy, you know.'

Adolf Hitler did not laugh, as she intended him to do. He frowned and conceded her point was a good one. 'All we do is exercise care and discretion. We do not want our relationship in the German newspapers, do we?'

Eva would have liked nothing better, but she shook her head.

'If a word got out, my enemies in France and England would have a heyday with the story. I have always said I will never marry because I am married to the *Volk*, and I must, to the world anyway, remain so.'

Eva, with a sinking heart and a ready smile, nodded.

'Go now, *liebschen*,' he had said. 'We will talk all this over in the morning.'

Eva Braun left the bare, chill room (if anything, worse than the one she was going to) thinking: well, if I am to have a room of my own, one thing is certain, it's going to look a lot different from this soldier's billet.

With light step and clad only in her silken underthings and her dressing-gown, she made her way back to her room.

She had met nobody except the maid, Kohler, carrying a glass of hot milk to Angi Raubal's room, and all the girl said was 'Guten Nacht, fraulein.'

Eva smiled mischievously at her, one young girl to another.

She slept soundly that night, as ever.

The following morning Angi was gone, bag and baggage.

Just like that.

While Adolf breakfasted – and Eva sat, waiting – Dietrich said, quoting from a newspaper: 'Chamberlain said in the House of Commons yesterday that nothing could have stopped what happened in Austria unless force was used. We were not prepared to use it. Soviet Russia has asked for a meeting with the British and the French to decide what to do about Germany ... Chamberlain says such a meeting would be against the interests of peace!'

'I *love* this old man!' Adolf cried, delightedly. 'He is worth two whole armies to me!' He slapped Dietrich on the back and walked across to Eva's table, with a sudden, jaunty step.

'Adolf? Have you breakfasted well, or can I get something for you?'

'Possibly a slice of gateau. I feel like celebrating!'

'Why is that?' Eva signalled for cakes.

'Because I know – I *know*! – I can go into Czechoslovakia and the British will do nothing!'

'That sounds wonderful,' said Eva, her stock reply to any political remark from Adolf. She added, 'I believe Angi has gone?'

'Yes,' Adolf's face darkened, 'and she won't be coming back.'

Eva sat, thrilled with triumph. 'What happened?'

'I asked her why she resented your being here with me, and she was quite personal and insulting. She is my half-sister, but she has no special rights to comment on my personal affairs. I told her to pack her bags and leave this morning, before I rose. She will be taken care of but not too lavishly. I will provide here with a flat and a small pension. It is my own fault for taking care of my relatives in a special way. The Fuhrer of Germany must not do that. I told Angi that, and bade her *Auf Wiedersehn*.'

How long, Eva wondered, had Angi *been* here? Five or six years?

'Will you see her at all, in the future?' she asked, still shocked.

'I cannot see why I should. There will be no reason ...'

The cakes arrived and Adolf selected the slice of gateau that Eva offered him, and ate it with appetite, unfolding one of the bunch of German newspapers he had carried over to the table.

Watching him, awed, Eva resolved never, ever, no matter what the reason, to criticise Adolf Hitler in any way, personal, political or emotional.

Plainly, it did not pay.

'Czechoslovakia,' said Adolf Hitler to his aides, as they pored over military-reports at their daily conference at the Berghof, 'is a mish-mash, created by Versailles! It has ten million citizens – but not even half of them are Czechs. Two million are Slovaks, a million are Hungarians. Three million are Germans, or anyway Austrians.'

Bormann said, 'Fuhrer, the Czechs have a Treaty with France. I cannot see France deserting them, if we march.' Bormann hesitated, his dark eyes troubled, his heavy face solemn. The Fuhrer was always right, but sometimes it was wise to put to him the Generals' way of thinking. If it did nothing else it aired the problems. It was of course a risky tactic. The Fuhrer could explode: he often did. 'The Czechs have a good army and one of the largest munition-works in the world, the Skoda plant at Posen. The Generals –'

'Those shit-lickers! The Czechs are helpless against us. We can walk in any time we like.' The Fuhrer was on his feet, shouting. The Naval and Army aides, whose business it was to repeat nothing to *any* General or Admiral that Hitler did not want repeated, looked away, confused. Young men with their careers to make, they knew the Fuhrer's sarcastic words were an insult to the uniforms they wore. Yet they had to pretend they had not heard. It was hard. They prayed for transfers that never came.

The Czechs, to the astonishment of Hitler and everybody else in Europe, mobilised their Army and stood on their heavily-fortified borders, ready to fight. Hitler heard the news in the Berghof and it sent him into a new paroxysm of fury. 'Who are these Slavs who threaten the German nation?' he shouted. Later, as he walked the woody paths of the Berghof, alone (Eva knew when to let him be) he thought: if the Czechs do fight, then the French will be forced into it and then maybe the British also, no matter what their reservations. Raging with hate inside, but ever the strategist, Adolf Hitler gave ground. He sent a message to the Czechs saying he had no intention of attacking them. He had no troops on their borders. His aides looked, astonished, at each other, as they processed the messages through the Signals Unit at the Berghof. They were well aware Hitler had twelve divisions (ten infantry, one artillery, one mountain) on the Czech borders.

To them, Adolf Hitler, conscious that this looked like a set-back and a climb-down, merely looked up from his map of Central Europe, spread out over the vast table in the Great Hall of the Berghof, and laying down his large magnifying-glass, said: 'Nonetheless, gentlemen, we march by

2 October. No matter what happens. No matter what England or France or anybody else does!'

Hitler ordered his troops back from the border. He sent them on manoeuvres, to keep them ready for action. To the warnings of the Generals (particularly Beck) that Germany was not yet ready, in terms of material or men, to fight a full-scale European War on two Fronts, he tartly responded, 'I will only take action against Czechoslovakia if I know for sure that neither France nor England will move against us!'

With that, the Generals, mutinous, grumbling and fearful, had to rest content. Only Beck felt that they owed on allegiance higher than the Oath sworn to Adolf Hitler. He proposed to his fellow-generals that they try to talk Hitler out of all further adventures, for three years at least. The Generals listened respectfully: Beck, after all, was still the Chief of Staff. They pondered long. They then fell back upon the Oath of Loyalty to the Fuhrer, and did nothing. Hitler demoted Beck and appointed Halder in his place. He allowed Beck, whom he suspected of considering a *putsch* against him to officially 'retire'. Beck acquiesced.

A few days later, at his daily conference, Hitler suddenly shouted, 'Have you seen *this*? Chamberlain, in an interview with American newspapermen at Lady Astor's country house, has said neither France nor Russia nor Britain would come to the aid of Czechslovakia if she was attacked. Britain thinks the answer is to give the German Sudetenland to Hitler!'

Adolf Hitler stood, flushed with incredulity and disbelief. 'Good God, he's telling the Czechs to capitulate! He's telling them, don't rely on *us*!' Hitler could not believe it. 'The old gentleman with the umbrella is terrified! He's given in! Don't you see, we can have everything *without* war, if only we play our cards right!'

His military advisers Keitel and Jodl, the young Naval and Army aides, and the inevitable Bormann stared at him, the newspaper in his hands. Standing with his back to the vast panoramic window of the Great Hall, Adolf Hitler seemed to Keitel at that moment, a truly heroic figure of history, a man whose enemies melted away when he challenged them. He was untouchable.

'Fuhrer, our congratulations!'

'Too early for that,' replied Hitler. 'Much to be done, yet.'

But he could not contain his elation. The old Englishman with the umbrella, unasked, in those few words, had given him what he had been waiting for.

That evening, Adolf Hitler was good company.

Eva Braun had never known him so elated. Not even after the Austrian victory. At supper Adolf declared: 'Chamberlain is sending his Minister, Runciman, to tell the Czechs to give up the Sudentenland. It doesn't matter a damn what my Generals think or do. We will get Czechoslovakia – and with it all of Central Europe – on a plate! And for nothing!'

Eva Braun relaxed in her luxurious bathroom that evening, confident that Adolf would come to her in a good mood.

Obviously, all was going as well for Germany: as it was for Eva Braun. As she soaped herself liberally, Eva turned off one of the gold taps with her toes. It was a trick she had. Not her *only* trick, by no means, she smiled to herself. She had drunk half-a-bottle of champagne at supper, and come up to her suite on the top-floor early, and slightly tipsy, in the hope that Adolf would not talk forever downstairs. It was now past midnight and she had let him know by a coquettish glance that she would be waiting for him. Nobody else had seen it and what did it matter, anyway, if they did? She was the mistress of the Berghof now, in everything but name.

Eva brooded. Name? Well, *that* hadn't changed.

The lack of a name, of respectability, had prevented her meeting some of Adolf's most famous visitors to the Berghof. The Indian potentate, the massive Aga Khan. The Welsh wizard, the tiny, twinkly-eyed, white-haired Lloyd George, whio had told the photographer Hoffmann on parting, 'Germany is lucky to have such a leader at this time.' Such important foreign visitors were off-limits to Eva, in case word about her was transmitted by them to the Foreign Press. Adolf was very touchy about the Foreign Press. His image was of paramount importance, as he had explained to her: 'I do not wage open warfare. I wage psychological warfare. How they *see* me is all that matters. I must be somebody unknown that they fear, not some ordinary man with a wife!'

Eva sighed and soaped her small breasts. Small but perfect, Adolf said. Well, he was the only man who'd ever seen them or ever would. If he was satisfied, only that mattered. Eva looked round the square bathroom: both bath and surrounds were of magnificent Dolomite marble and the towels were Turkish and huge. Adolf had spared nothing. An unusual feature about the bathroom was that it had two doors.

Eva got out of the bath, dried herself, slipped into a silk robe and went out of the door that led into her own suite. After Angi's sudden departure, Adolf had personally re-designed the entire top-floor of the Berghof, giving Eva a suite, with a living room and bedroom of her own. The bathroom with two doors had one that led to Adolf's own bedroom, which was martial and unchanged. The living-room which Eva entered was luxurious and had walls covered with silk drapes. Adolf may have

416

designed the place but she had the furnished of it. Adolf had said, laughing, 'It looks like a Franz Lehar operetta!' Eva didn't care what he said. It was *her* room, she had to spend a lot of time in it, on her own, whole evenings sometimes, if Adolf had important foreign guests downstairs. There was an immense sofa, with velveteen cushions; a splendid oak radiogram; a low, inlaid table; various statuettes selected by Adolf; fringed lampshades that discreetly lit the room. On the wall opposite from the sofa, there hung a flattering oil-portrait of Adolf Hitler, one of the many entries submitted each year to the Festival of German Art. This one showed Adolf in Brownshirt and breeches, wearing a severe expression that amused Eva, who, whatever else, was not the slightest bit afraid of Adolf Hitler. Across the room, above the sofa and facing the portrait of Adolf, was an excellent full-length oil of a reclining, nude: a woman.

That woman was Eva Braun.

Eva looked at her watch. Twelve fifteen.

Adolf surely would not be long now?

She went into her bedroom, which contained a very large bed, weighed down with a huge, silk eiderdown and a magnificent dressing-table covered with expensive French perfumes and beauty-aids brought to the Berghof for her by the secretaries, from shopping-trips in Berlin. Adolf would not have bought them for her, left to himself. Anyway, it was better he did not know the source of the sexual mystery she still seemed to exert over him – when she got the chance!

Eva propped up the huge, soft pillows and stretched out on the bed. She lit a Turkish cigarette, taken from a cedarwood box, with a gold lighter, and thought of telephoning somebody, to pass the time. But who? Her sister, Gretl, was a possibility? Eva glanced at her watch and sighed. Gretl would have been in bed for an hour, by now. Henny Hoffman? She was in Berlin these days and they had remained friendly, despite Henny's busy marriage to Baldur Von Schirach, the young half-American who was head of the Hitler Youth Movement. It had been a good marriage for Henny but it meant the two girls met only rarely these days. Henny Hoffmann was one of the few people with whom Eva could be utterly frank. She had known Adolf as 'Uncle Adi' since she was a little girl. But Henny would be out, at some dinner-party in some fashionable Berlin salon. Henny had done well: Baldur Von Schirach was a catch, so handsome and young and well-mannered, and a gentleman, unlike most of Adolf's retinue of Ministers. Most of them, far from marrying anybody, were divorcing their working-class wives as fast as they could and going in for new, younger, educated models. Some Army wit had called Hitler's Cabinet Office 'the Ante-Chamber to the Divorce Courts!'

They were not all like Martin Bormann, who had no less than ten children! Of course, Eva giggled to herself (she *had* had rather a lot of champagne) with ten children it was impossible to divorce his stolid wife, Gerda. It would have made him look silly and Bormann would never look silly.

Eva got up and turned on the 'midget' radio she kept in the bedroom. It was portable with a bakelite cabinet, one of the newest productions by Telefunken, part of the revitalised German telecommunications industry. After a fiddle with the knobs, she got a British station, the BBC in London. The announcer said, 'Henry Hall speaking . . .'

Eva poured herself a small brandy from the decanter, housed in a discreet oak-cabinet, and lay back on the silk pillows. The music soothed her. She liked Henry Hall. The important thing was: Adolf must not come in and find her listening! He disliked any kind of jazz, calling it negroid rubbish.

Not that Henry Hall was jazz exactly. More, dance-music.

One of the things Eva missed was dancing.

She closed her eyes, picturing herself and Henny Hoffmann on the floor of the old dance-hall in Munich. Even when she was staying at the Prinzregentstrasse apartment, it never occurred to her to go dancing any more, much as she loved it. Who would she go with? Adolf never danced. Never had, as far as she could make out.

Occasionally, greatly daring, she would beg a foxtrot or a quickstep from one of Adolf's young military-aides (they had a gramophone, being young) and cavort around with them gleefully. She had to be careful. If Adolf saw her he would certainly disapprove. She sighed: Adolf disapproved of so many things.

Well, no doubt Henny Hoffmann danced as much as she liked at the Adlon in Berlin or wherever she went with her young husband, Baldur Von Schirach.

But Henny Hoffmann was not the Fuhrer's woman. She did not share the highest aspirations of the Fuhrer.

She was simply married to a man who took the Fuhrer's orders.

Eva thought: what amazing things have happened this last eighteen months, since she had come to live at the Berghof! The job with Hoffmann had gone, of course. She was a shopgirl no longer. She had sat quietly and watched some wonderful things happen, in the last twelve months.

Like the Fuhrer's incredulity at the defection of Putzi Hanfstaengl!

The tall, gangling aristocrat had been the victim of one of Goering's practical jokes. He had taken it that an order from the Fuhrer to fly across the Red lines in Spain (where the Civil War still raged) and parachute over enemy territory, was genuine and not just a made-up nonsense of Goering's!

Putzi had got out of that airplane at the first opportunity and promptly fled to Switzerland. He was said, now, to be in London.

Adolf had not believed it, at first. He had been very angry with Goering about it. Putzi had been an old friend, one of the *Alte Kampfers*. The fat man's jokes sometimes went wrong. That time, disastrously so. Still, Eva preferred Goering to Himmler, who made her flesh creep. Not that she saw much of either of them. Adolf mostly met his Cabinet at the Chancellery, in Berlin. This year, however, he had spent almost the entire Summer at the Berghof. Eva felt it was a good sign. The Berghof was his home, as much as he had one. And she was there.

Eva lay on the bed, drowsily, and listened to Henry Hall playing late-night dance-music from London. Currently, he was playing a tango, *South of the Border*. Eva giggled. The English sang a popular song about the *Mexican* border, while Adolf Hitler's troops faced the Czech one! What silly people they were, with their heads stuck into the sand. Adolf was right. They were not to be feared.

The tango was quite jaunty, just the same. Nice beat.

It would be pleasant to dance to, if she had a partner.

Of course, Adolf was fifty years old now: his dancing days were over, not that they had ever begun.

Eva drained her brandy glass and poured herself another measure.

Yes, it had been a great year, the year of Adolf's 'Fiftieth.'

Germany was 'going mad' for it. A public holiday had been declared. Adolf had stood for four hours at the saluting-point as his tanks and soldiers paraded past and his Luftwaffe flew overhead – four whole hours with his arm outstretched in the Nazi salute at least half of the time! Not many men of fifty years of age could boast that kind of fanatical fitness.

And the Birthday Presents. From all over Germany.

Gifts of silver, of gold, of rare glassware, of rarer paintings, from the Nazi heirachy alone. From Goering and Goebbels and Ley and Von Schirach, from everybody at the top, such priceless art. Some, Eva guessed, looted from rich Jews, but many had been specially made for the occasion. Adolf, typically, made little of it, except for the paintings, a source of great pleasure to him.

Not so the hundreds of home-knitted pullovers! The dozens of bicycles! The scores of motor-cars! The hundreds of bad paintings of the Fuhrer! The crates and crates of Moselle! The thousands of home-baked cakes!

Not that Adolf ever ate or drank anything that was sent as a gift.

In case it was poisoned.

Well, Eva knew by now, it was a very real possibility.

Adolf, like all great men, had many enemies.

Many admirers too, a great number of them female. They had sent him *thousands* of hand-embroidered cushions, such beautiful, patient workmanship, crafted lovingly over many hours.

And hundreds of pairs of *knickers*, used and unused!

Harlots, thought Eva, grinning tipsily to herself.

It was said that women all over Germany cried the Fuhrer's name as they went into anaesthetic on the surgeon's table; at times of crisis; and, it was also said, at their sexual climax.

They all *wanted* him, all those loose, avid women.

Only she, Eva Braun, *had* him.

With that comforting thought, the empty brandy-glass slipped from Eva's fingers, her head turned into the silken pillow, her eyes closed and she slept.

Adolf found her like that when he came into the room an hour later.

He looked down at her a long moment, then he covered her with the eiderdown, and quietly left the bedroom, switching off the lights behind him.

Neville Chamberlain, Prime Minister of Great Britain, came to the Berghof in September.

'The old gentleman is sixty-nine years of age' said Adolf Hitler, incredulously. 'He has never flown in an aeroplane before in his life. He speaks no German, as far as I know, nor a word of any other European language!' Hitler paused, shaking his head at Ribbentrop, as they sat in Hitler's study at the Berghof. 'It's a flight of – how long, London to Munich?'

'Seven hours and extremely uncomfortable,' said Ribbentrop, idly. 'I have done it all too often.'

Hitler looked at Chamberlain's telegram. He knew it by heart but he still found it difficult to believe the old gentleman had ever sent it!

IN VIEW OF THE INCREASINGLY CRITICAL SITUATION I PROPOSE TO COME OVER AT ONCE TO SEE YOU WITH A VIEW TO TRYING TO FIND A PEACEFUL SOLUTION. I PROPOSE TO COME ACROSS BY AIR AND AM READY TO START TOMORROW.

'What do you think is behind it all?' he asked Ribbentrop.

Ribbentrop crossed his elegant legs. 'Fear. The English don't want war with Germany under any circumstances, Fuhrer, as I have so often told you.'

Hitler frowned. 'I cannot believe the British Empire, that rules over one third of the globe, will not defend itself under *any* circumstances?'

Ribbentrop knew Hitler had made up his mind the British would not fight but needed reassurance. He gave it to him: 'The British people think Chamberlain is coming to see you, as possibly Asquith should have gone to see the Kaiser in 1914, to stop a world war. They are totally behind his efforts. Their Poet Laureate, John Masefield, has even written a poem in the *Times* extolling Chamberlain's peace attempt, in coming to see you.'

'They are as afraid as that?' Hitler mused.

'Their leaders are. The people, who knows? Only Churchill, as ever, stands against it.'

Hitler nodded. 'So? I can take it – as *I* have said all along – that Chamberlain will accept our proposals?'

Ribbentrop shifted uncomfortably in his chair. 'Our Embassy in London has told me that Mr Chamberlain is in a frame of mind to take any sensible German proposals about Czechoslovakia very seriously indeed.'

Hitler sat quite still for a long moment, wondering.

'You know, Ribbentrop, I begin, as time goes on, to like old Mister Neville Chamberlain more and more!'

They met on the steps of the Berghof at four o'clock in the afternoon. Adolf Hitler, fifty years old, uniformed, booted, clad in military cap, rested and alert. Mr Chamberlain, a year off seventy, in black city overcoat and homburg hat, had been on the road since dawn: seven hours on the aircraft; another hour (part of the time in an open car) from Munich Airport to the Banhof; three hours on the train from the Banhof to Berchtesgaden; then by motor-car to the Berghof.

Mr Chamberlain was exhausted and looked it. Even his young aides and Ambassador Henderson looked weary. Hitler could easily have halved Mr Chamberlain's journey by meeting him in the Rhineland, but such a thought had not occurred to him.

As Mr Chamberlain climbed the steep steps of the Berghof and shook Hitler's hand, the Fuhrer was reminded of the weariness in the face of Von Schuschnigg, as *he* had come up those same steps, seven months before. These bourgeois politicians, Hitler thought, lead unfit lives and they are too tired and too old for the work they do. Mr Chamberlain's hair was flecked with grey, his moustache the same, and his wing-collar and dark jacket with pinstripe trousers were the garb of a dusty small-town lawyer, not the uniform of a man who presided over the Empire of Wellington and Nelson and Drake and Raleigh. For if Neville Chamberlain had no working knowledge of German history, it was certain Adolf Hitler knew the main events in the five hundred years of English domination of the globe.

But this old man was here – if Hitler had it right? – to bargain away that glorious five hundred years. Adolf Hitler felt euphoric. He had always respected and admired the British. They were – or had been – ruthless and determined and a model to emulate. Now, guiding the old gentleman – and he had indeed brought his umbrella! – into the Great Hall to take tea, he felt convinced the British were on the slippery slope all great Empires must, inevitably tread on their last journey to oblivion, crushed by a stronger Race. If so, it was almost sad, but of course inevitable.

At tea no politics were talked. Mr Chamberlain ate his cakes with relish and drank tea with milk and sugar, the English way, and seemed restored. Afterwards, Hitler decided to put his case vigorously. 'Herr Prime Minister, I must ask you if you would tolerate for your own people a situation like the one in Czecho-Slovakia for the German minority there?'

Mr Chamberlain heard this translated (only Hitler's translator was with them) and nodded vigorously, but Hitler held up his hand. 'I am enormously hopeful for Peace between our two nations. But in Czecho-Slovakia I have three million Germans, subject to harassment and injustice. I am determined to bring them back inside the borders of Germany, where they belong!' Mr Chamberlain nodded, again most vigorously, and once more attempted to speak. Again Adolf Hitler held up his hand. 'I am absolutely determined, Herr Prime Minister, not to tolerate any longer a small, second-rate country like the Czechs treating Germany as an inferior! I am no longer young but I am still young enough to lead Germany in a World War if it comes to that!' As Mr Chamberlain looked alarmed, Hitler added, 'Herr Prime Minister, do not think, I beg you, that I want war. I do not. But I cannot step back.' As he paused for breath, Mr Chamberlain took his chance. 'If the Fuhrer has determined to settle the matter without discussion between us, why did he let me come here to Germany? Have I wasted my time?'

Hitler was shocked at the old gentleman's intervention. He asked, abruptly, the question he had prepared all day long and had not expected to put until much further along in the talks, the question on which everything hung.

'Will Great Britain agree to giving Germany the German-occupied zones of the Czechoslovak Republic, or will she not?'

Mr Chamberlain smoothed his pepper-and-salt moustache with a careful forefinger, mused a moment, and said pedantically, 'I cannot give that undertaking on behalf of His Majesty's Government. What I can do is state, here and now, that personally I recognise the rightness and justice of your request.' He paused. The bulbous, watery, innocent eyes blinked at Hitler. 'I will, of course, have to return to England,

and report to my Government and secure their approval of this . . .' –
Chamberlain coughed delicately – '. . . for the moment, personal
position.'

Then Mr Chamberlain sat calmly waiting for Adolf Hitler to approve.

Adolf Hitler nodded and turned involuntarily away to hide the
expression on his face. Cut it up anyhow you like, the old gentleman's
words meant only one thing.

Surrender.

Mr Chamberlain met Adolf Hitler again, this time at the picturesque
town of Bad Godesberg, on the Rhine.

It was a meeting the Fuhrer did not want.

Ribbentrop had warned him: 'There is some opposition to Chamberlain's obvious surrender, in the British Parliament. Not much, but it
would be politic to meet and reassure the old gentleman.'

So here Hitler was, in the last balmy days of September, sitting in
the soft morning light of the old town, on the terrace of the Hotel
Dresden, waiting once again to greet the British Prime Minister. Mr
Chamberlain wanted only to work out the details of the Czech surrender
(or so Hitler had been told) but Hitler felt a suspicion that this might
be a cunning delaying-tactic. 'Is it agreed that Germany has the Sudentenland? By *your* Cabinet? By the French Government?'

'Yes,' said Mr Chamberlain, with a smile. 'Certainly, it is.' Hitler was
at a loss. 'Then what do we need to talk about?' Mr Chamberlain
coughed, delicately. 'We suggest a Council, composed of German,
Czech and neutral observers, to agree the take-over in detail?' Mr
Chamberlain smiled. 'You get what you asked for, Herr Hitler. It will
simply take a little time.'

Hitler suddenly erupted: all was agreed and now this quibbling! 'I'm
sorry, Herr Prime Minister, but your plan is no longer of any use to
me!'

Mr Chamberlain sat up at that, at the tone and the contempt in it,
looking flushed and nonplussed. He waited for more but Hitler cut the
meeting short, and at once Chamberlain left, much put-out, for his
hotel. He telephoned London, to report that war looked certain and that
the French and British government should advise the Czechs to mobilise. Meantime, he would stay a little longer, and see what happened.

Mr Chamberlain saw Hitler the next day with the excuse of slightly-
amended proposals, but the Fuhrer was not listening. 'The Czechs are
mobilising!' said Hitler. 'Herr Prime Minister, I tell you my terms. If
they do not evacuate the Sudentenland in forty-eight hours, I invade!'

Mr Chamberlain was shattered. All his work had been for nothing, he told Hitler. He sat blinking, in his wicker-chair, in the late September sunshine, looking lost. 'Then it is War?'

Hitler demurred. 'I would not say that.' After a moment he added, 'I never change my mind, Mr Chamberlain, but for you I will hold back until October the First. Six more days? What do you say to that?'

Mr Chamberlain, instantly heartened, flew back to London.

A diplomatic letter to Hitler was next. Mr Chamberlain had to communicate to Germany that the French and the British would support the Czechs, if it came to War.

'The German nation are being treated like *niggers*!' Hitler shouted. 'On October the First, I march! Let the British and the French do as they like.' So great was his fury that Franz Halder did not dare to direct his attention to the fact that, if the French Army attacked in the West, he had only four divisions available to face them. The French had ninety divisions, ready or in reserve.

Hitler gave a speech at the Berlin Sportspalast that evening. In a frenzy of rage and hatred, more terrible than any he had ever given, thought Goebbels, Hitler told a riotous, cheering audience: 'It is up to Herr Benes, the President of Czechoslovakia. If he wants Peace, fine! If not, *War*!' Goebbels leapt to his feet as Hitler sat down. 'We will have no repeat of 1918 if we *do* go to War! This time we will win!'

Two days before Hitler's start-date for War, Mr Chamberlain flew to Munich, once again. He had suggested, with Mussolini's backing, a meeting of Italian, German, French and British representatives, plus of course the Czechs, to 'discuss the whole situation and effect a solution agreeable to everybody.'

Hitler refused to have Czech representatives present.

A compromise was reached: Czech delegates would be at Munich but would not be allowed to take part in the discussions about their future. They would stay in an ante-room.

Hitler met Mussolini at Kufstein on the Italian-German frontier. He greeted the Duce with the words, 'If the talks are not successful, I will wipe Czecho-Slovakia off the map! Whatever happens, you and I know that the time will come when we will have to fight side-by-side against the French and the British.'

Mussolini sighed, and nodded. 'Agreed,' he said.

Hitler then gave Mussolini a piece of paper. It had been drawn up by Hitler's aides and roughly outlined his 'Peace Terms'. Mussolini agreed to present it as his own.

Prime Minister Chamberlain and Premier Daladier did not meet or plan any joint action. They were surprised when Mussolini listed his suggested Peace Terms. These were in fact Hitler's own plans for the dismemberment of Czecho-Slovakia. They did not differ, in any important way, from his original demands.

Mr Chamberlain listened to them gravely, as if they were new, and said, 'I value the Duce's proposals, made in an objective and realistic way. I can see a solution along these lines.' He and Premier Daladier of France meekly signed the Munich Agreement, allowing the German Army to march into Czecho-Slovakia on 1 October, Adolf Hitler's deadline for that event.

The Czech diplomats in the ante-room were told that their fate had been decided. Mr Chamberlain and Premier Daladier had little to say, and the betrayed Czechs even less.

Mr Chamberlain flew home. But not before he had obtained from the triumphant but incredulous Adolf Hitler, his signature on another, totally irrelevant and non-legal document, one he was to wave at the airfield at Hendon when, tired but triumphant, he told a huge and vastly-relieved crowd (and the rest of the British nation through the film-newsreels) that there would be No War!

Holding up the single piece of paper in a high wind, he declared, 'This is a document which bears the signature of Herr Hitler as well as my own . . .' Later, at Downing Street, he called out from the window: 'It is Peace with Honour! It is Peace in Our Time!'

In the House of Commons Chamberlain's triumph was complete.

Riotous scenes of acclamation greeted him.

Only Winston Churchill spoke to the contrary.

'It has been a total, unmitigated defeat,' he said.

He was shouted down.

Hitler's forces occupied Czecho-Slovakia without a shot being fired. The Czech Army of men was disbanded. The Czech President, Benes, flew to London, a refugee, to try to form a 'Czech Government in Exile.'

The vast Skoda arms works began at once to make weapons for the Germany Army.

Doctor Hacha, a small, fat, unknown man went to Germany to sign the takeover papers. Adolf Hitler gave him the Schuschnigg treatment. He raved and shouted so much that Hacha had a heart-attack. Hitler's doctor, Morell, gave him an injection and Hacha recovered enough to sign the papers. The Republic was dismantled.

The Slovaks were given a slab of the nation and set up as a pro-Nazi puppet state under German control. The Poles, Hungarians and Rumanians were all given a small slice of the dismembered Republic, by Hitler's gift. As Allies of France, who had spent years making those alliances, they would almost certainly have fought against Hitler, if France and England had moved. Now, they were Adolf Hitler's allies.

Now, France had no allies by Treaty in Europe. Britain had only Poland.

'Brilliant, Fuhrer,' breathed Ribbentrop. 'But —'

'No buts! They will do nothing,' said Adolf Hitler, sprawling in his chair at the Cabinet table in the Chancellery. 'Until they are attacked themselves, and very possibly, not even then!'

Everybody laughed, including those Generals present. They did so uneasily, for some of them had contemplated in the last weeks and months of the year a bloody putsch against Adolf Hitler.

The surrender at Munich had changed their minds, abruptly.

For one thing was obvious.

Adolf Hitler was untouchable.

In the May of the following year, 1939, fourteen curious and somewhat apprehensive senior Generals of the Third Reich assembled in the Chancellery in Berlin to face an ebullient and confident Adolf Hitler. The day was warm and the Generals sweated in their thick woollen uniforms and leather belts. Amongst them were Goering, Keitel, Halder and, from the *Kriegsmarine*, Grand Admiral Raeder.

As they stood in the ante-room waiting for Hitler, they conferred with one another, considering that Hitler was perhaps learning at last to be a statesman, not just a politician. 'He is threatening the Poles over Danzig, of course,' said one to another. 'All he is asking for is an open port for German shipping and a road-link from Germany.' 'He's offered the Poles a Non-Aggression Pact!' a third added.

'They have a Pact with Great Britain,' interrupted Halder, grimly.

'What can the British do to help them? They're not even in Europe! No, tbe Poles will sign with us.' They turned to Halder. 'Don't you agree, Franz?'

Halder hesitated. 'You know the Poles. They are stupid enough to think England can help them, and if England can't — and she can't, she's too far away — that they can beat us themselves anyway.'

'What, with all their cavalry and rifle-companies?' the Generals smiled at one another. Franz Halder was very dry. It was one of his jokes. Naturally, the Poles being the Poles, they would go in for a great deal of sabre-rattling, but Germany wasn't asking them to give up Warsaw! It was only Danzig, after all. The Poles were not liked by the Prussian Junker Generals, most of whom had lost ancestral lands to them at Versailles. The Bavarian Halder rather liked the Poles. He did not have to live with them just across the Vistula. The Generals smoked Turkish cigarettes in the vast reception-hall, fingered the Heidelberg sabre-scars on their faces and rubbed their hands over their cropped and balding heads. The room smelled of expensive tobacco, male sweat and good cologne. The Generals laughed with one another (almost everybody in the room had been to Potsdam or Heidelberg or Kiel together) and agreed that, say what you will, times were good for Germany again, at long last.

Even the Civil War in Spain – a possible scene for the start of a European war – was virtually over. Goering's Luftwaffe had learned a lot there, about the bombing of troops and of cities. Franco had Spain secure now, and he was a friend. Hitler, with his recent Treaties with the Romanians and Hungarians and, soon, no doubt, the Poles, was dominating Europe without having to fight a war to do it. The massive French Army was still in the so-called Maginot Line, and did not seem ready to move out of it. The English, as usual, behaved as if they still owned the globe. Well, Adolf Hitler had shown them they did not, and about time, too.

The young military-aides coughed discreetly.

The Generals and Admirals fell silent.

Goering came out of the vast doorway that led into the Committee Room. He was wearing a uniform of his own design, in a light blue shade of cotton and carried his Field Marshal's baton. 'Gentlemen, if you would please step this way?'

The Generals put out their cigars and cigarettes in the ashtrays provided, after taking a last lingering puff. There was no certainty they would get another opportunity for a smoke before lunch. It was, of course, eleven o'clock already. The Fuhrer kept his own hours.

The Generals bustled into the Conference Room, guided to their seats by the young military-aides. They fastened their uniform collars and opened their leather briefcases and took out their notebooks and fountain-pens. Goering said, in a loud voice, 'Gentlemen! The Fuhrer wishes no notes to be taken today.' The Generals put away their pens and, arms folded, waited in silence for the Fuhrer to arrive.

Hitler came in five minutes later. The Generals stood at once to rigid attention.

Hitler raised his hands in a flapping gesture, and Goering nodded for them to sit.

Hitler wore his uniform of plain white, double-breasted jacket and dark trousers. The only decoration was the ribbon of his Iron Cross, First Class, and a swastika armband. His dark hair, showing a fleck of grey, was freshly combed and his dark moustache trimmed and sharp.

'Gentlemen.' Hitler looked intently at the fourteen men present: men who would have to fight his War for him, if it came to that. Nobody knew what Hitler was going to say. As Hitler himself often said: 'There is that which I tell my Enemies. There is that which I tell my friends and associates. And there is that which I decide, myself. The last, I tell to nobody.'

He stood against a table. He had some notes, but he did not refer to them. It was as if this speech had been thought about and rehearsed many times. As usual, he started low-key, outlining facts everybody in the room knew. As he talked only his adjutant, Colonel Schmundt, took notes.

'Germany,' said Adolf Hitler, 'still faces its greatest problem. *Lebensraum*. We have an expanding birthrate, the only one in Europe, and nowhere to put our children. Our children's children will face even worse overcrowding, if we allow it. So where do our young people go?' He paused. 'To our old colonies in Africa? The British might give them back to us. But do we want them?'

The Generals waited to be told. Hitler surprised them by suddenly, coarsely, laughing. 'I think not! A few thousand square miles of jungle will do nothing for us!' The Generals permitted themselves a low titter of amusement. 'If – and gentlemen, by if I mean *when*! – we move, it has to be to the East. We go East and have our own Colonial Empire, on our own borders!' The Generals, who had heard this all before, glanced at each other, wondering what was coming. They were not long kept in doubt.

'To do that, to expand East, is to face one fact!'

Hitler slapped the table. It rang like a pistol shot.

'*War is inevitable!*'

The Generals were suddenly very still indeed.

'I am not talking about Russia! Not yet!'

The Generals hardly breathed.

'I am talking about Poland!'

The Generals breathed, but only just.

'If we fight the British, as eventually we may have to, it will be a battle to the death, and it will last a long time. Britain is old and tired but very, very strong.' Hitler waited. The Generals sighed. 'To that end, if it comes to War, let me outline my fears and hopes. If we fight in the West – and we may have to! – then the Army's task is to take Holland and Belgium and then France, at once, in a Blitz! The French Army is very large, I grant you, but its morale is low. The French Generals do not want to fight. They are old men who were brave in the last War, men who have seen death as young boys and not been terrified. But such men are often terrified in later life – at the memory of it all!' Adolf Hitler was taunting the Generals. He was talking not only about the French, but also about *them*!

The Generals allowed themselves a buzz of low conversation, rapidly brought to a halt by Hitler's familiar swiftly-raised hand. 'Let me then turn to our own military position.' He paused. 'When I became *Kanzler*, we had *seven* infantry and three cavalry divisions!'

The Generals laughed comfortably, awed at the recollection. Had they ever really been as weak as that?

'Now,' said Hitler, 'We have *thirty* infantry divisions!' He brought his hand down – *slap*! – sharply, on the table. 'We have four motorised and three Mountain divisions!' *Slap!* 'We have five new Panzer divisions!' *Slap!* 'Four light divisions!' *Slap!* 'Twenty-four Machine-gun battalions!' *Slap!* 'The Navy has two new Battlecruisers!' *Slap!* 'Two new Armoured Cruisers!' *Slap!* 'Seventeen Destroyers!' *Slap!* 'Forty-seven U-boats!' *Slap!* 'We have two Battleships, four cruisers, an aircraft-carrier, five Destroyers and seven U-boats under construction!' *Slap!* 'The Luftwaffe has a quarter of a million men and twenty-one Squadrons of aircraft!' *Slap!* 'We have, also, three hundred Anti-Aircraft Batteries to protect the Homeland!'

Hitler's hand slapped down for the last time. His voice rose, hoarsely: 'Will Poland stand against *that*? Will France? Will England?'

The Generals shuffled and stared. Sweat broke out on many foreheads. Handkerchiefs were reached for and noses blown. Glances were shot at neighbours. No word of protest, however, was spoken.

Halder, who had, more or less expected something of the sort, found himself breathing very quickly. There was no doubt, when Adolf Hitler spoke, the very air was charged with emotion. There he stood, eyes staring, quite still, a shine of sweat on his face, the lock of hair fallen over his temple, as he uttered the final words of his address.

'September First is the day, gentlemen!'

The Generals stopped their small movements and froze.

'September the First! The day we attack Poland!'

The hot Summer of 1939 wore on, with Halder and his Army Staff working long feverish hours on plans to attack both Poland and France, Grand Admiral Raeder's *Kriegsmarine* planners redoubling their efforts to build a submarine fleet big enough to choke Great Britain. Everything, until now, was on paper only. Nothing was certain, except that the Fuhrer had declared a date for the invasion of Poland, and the Fuhrer never changed his mind. Or had never done so, yet.

The General Staff was excited by the promise of war. Great careers were in the making. Greatly daring, Halder stood in the study at the Chancellery: 'Germany is in a vastly stronger military position than she has ever been, since the War. But so are the Allies; the French and the

English are rearming. Our Army is nothing like as big as the French, the *Kriegsmarine* is nowhere near the surface strength of the Royal Navy.'

Hitler merely smiled. 'We are not talking about numbers. We are talking about men, and tactics, and the Will to Win!'

'I do not deny it, Fuhrer. But we don't have the industry or material, or even the men, to fight a long one. And you yourself have said that any war against the British Empire will be a long one?'

'The English seed has gone bad,' said Hitler. 'They will fight if they have to, long and sourly. That goes without saying. They are Germanic in origin, unlike the Latin French who will capitulate if things go badly for them, which, with our new Panzer divisions, tanks supported by infantry, and our new Stuka dive-bombers, it will, my dear Halder, it *will*!'

Halder sighed and went back to his drawing-board and his staff of young planners and tried to forget the fact that Hitler's operation, if it went wrong, could involve fighting virtually the whole of Europe, with Soviet Russia unlikely to remain a bystander for long!

Halder worked and smoked and drank and worked again, and tried not to think about any of that. He was a soldier and a soldier did what the politicians told him. Especially if he had sworn an Oath of Loyalty to the Fuhrer.

Hitler went to the Berghof for the hot months of Summer. He did not like Berlin in the heat, finding it stuffy and oppressive. Speer's new Chancellery was splendid: had Hitler not designed it himself, in all essentials? What a pity that Speer and himself were finding it hard to meet to plan the great buildings of the Thousand Year Reich. The New Berlin. The Motorways. Even a new Linz. Speer was getting on with the drawings and models but Hitler was, for now, unable to see them. The loss irked him. The Chancellery, with its vast marble floors and reception-rooms and black-uniformed S.S. guards crashing to attention every few yards, was a splendid place to bring those people he wished to impress: foreign dignitaries: his own Generals: but he needed to think hard, this long hot Summer, and the place to do it, ideally, was, as ever, the Berghof.

Eva was overjoyed to see him 'home' so early, but she soon saw that he was even more introverted than usual. She went out of her way to accommodate his moods, which veered from wild optimism to silent gloom. Ribbentrop's name came up often. That meant Foreign Affairs. To Eva, that meant War. Even to Eva, the most non-political of women, War was something to fear. Like all her generation, she had grown up listening to her parents' tales of the death of half the young men of

Germany, of starvation-rations for the civilian population, of the loss of the easy, secure life of the lower middle-class to which her parents had belonged. Until now, Adolf had kept Germany out of war. Now he would say to her, in their few hours together, 'This may be our last Summer of Peace, Evie. We must make the most of it.'

He was sleeping badly, too, and the stomach cramps that the grubby Doctor Morell had successfully treated with his injections (vitamins, or whatever they were) were troubling him again. Usually, at the Berghof, Adolf could relax, some of the time.

At the Berghof that Summer he was besieged by urgent telegrams and diplomatic letters, and there was an endless tramp of Generals, notably Halder and Brauschwitz, through the Great Hall, to sit later with Adolf, locked in his study for hours at a stretch, from which meetings he would emerge over-wrought and excited and irritable, even with her. Eva felt hatred for the Poles. They had taken German territory in 1918, gifted to them by the Allies, and had done nothing to earn it. Now Germany was asking for some of it back. That, she knew, was how most Germans felt, that was how Vadi felt. Adolf had offered the Poles a deal. They had refused it. If war came, Adolf said, it was all the fault of the Poles.

Eva agreed with that, taking his arm (walking Blondi, Hitler's alsatian and her own two Scotch terriers) as they promenaded along the wooded lanes of the Berghof after lunch, to take tea in the Pavilion. Fortunately, nothing, not even the worry of war, seriously disturbed Adolf's routine. Late-to-rise; breakfast; a conference with his aides about the Foreign newspapers; discussions and orders despatched about 'secret matters' (dealt with in Adolf's study) and then a late lunch. Finally, tea and a pause (for Eva) until supper. After tea Adolf usually worked in his study, and Bormann usually visited one of the secretaries, for sex. Or so it was rumoured. Eva told Adolf nothing about that.

'Everything I do,' Hitler had told a neutral diplomat at the Berlin Chancellery earlier that year, 'is directed against the Soviet Union. My current Polish problem is part of my long-term plan. If the West do not see this, or are too blinkered to see it, that is their problem!'

That statement sent a shiver around the Embassies of every country in Europe, as Hitler knew it would. The truth was, as he told his late-night guest, Ribbentrop, at the Berghof: 'If I go into Poland and the British do declare War, they'll never fight it!' He looked at Ribbentrop acutely. 'Herr Ambassador, is that *your* reading of the situation?'

Ribbentrop knew better than to argue, though in fact he was detecting a new stubbornness in London. Members of Parliament and journalists and others were demanding that Hitler must be stopped.

'You know my opinion, Fuhrer. The British are rearming, but very slowly. Their heart isn't in it.'

Hitler brooded on Ribbentrop's words. He needed to do something new, and shocking. He had to take the initiative. After all, success was what mattered. After the event, nobody questioned how it had been obtained. 'Ribbentrop, I'm going to send you to Moscow to talk to Stalin.'

If he had thrown a bucket of ice-water over Ribbentrop he could not have had a greater effect. He smiled sourly, as he watched Ribbentrop trying to recover his wits. It was late at night, Eva had gone to bed an hour ago, and Ribbentrop had no doubt been half-dozing in his large armchair. 'Shall I send for more coffee?' asked Hitler, sardonically.

Ribbentrop shook his head and sat bolt upright. 'To Moscow? To talk to Stalin. *What* about?'

'Stalin has two Four Year Plans in the works. If our intelligence reports are anywhere near right, he'll soon be very strong, in a military way.'

Ribbentrop snorted disbelievingly at this. German intelligence on things Russian was notoriously unsafe. 'The German Ambassador in Moscow, who probably knows as much as anybody, tells me Stalin is afraid of a war because it would bury the Bolshevik Revolution – entrusted to him by Lenin! – if he lost!'

Hitler said, 'I have sent a cable asking Stalin to receive you.'

Ribbentrop looked astonished. 'Will you accompany me, Fuhrer?'

Hitler shook his head. 'For the same reason Stalin won't come here.'

'And what is that?' asked Ribbentrop faintly, obviously still getting over his astonishment.

'An assassin's bullet,' said Hitler, sombrely.

Ribbentrop's mind raced. 'What is the object of this mission?'

Hitler smiled, thinly. 'To conclude a Non-Aggression Pact with Stalin.'

Ribbentrop said nothing for almost a minute. When he spoke his voice was low and grave and profoundly shocked. Perhaps he thinks I am going mad, thought Hitler, amused.

'That, Fuhrer, is to deny all you have ever said, all that National Socialism has stood for. We have always told our people that Bolshevism is the arch-enemy?' He paused, his face pale with shock. 'Fuhrer, you will have thought deeply about all this?'

Hitler did not bother to reply. He looked impassively into the dancing flames of the huge open fire. Their light flitted across his face, seeming, to Ribbentrop, to give it a quite different expression: to turn him into a

Mephisto, or an actor playing Mephisto. Ribbentrop shook his head and put away such thoughts. Moscow? Stalin? A *Pact*?

My God, what next?

Heinrich Hoffmann was surprised by the call to the Berghof. He was even more surprised to hear what the Fuhrer had in store for him.

Ribbentrop, looking extremely worried, was present, as was Bormann, naturally, and Hitler's military aides. Everybody had a slightly dazed look, thought the professional photographer as he wondered what might be the cause of it. He accepted a glass of champagne from Kannenberg, Hitler's butler. 'Why champagne?' he asked, lightly. 'What are we celebrating?'

Hitler sipped a fruit juice, holding it up to his aides as they sipped their champagne and toasted, to Hoffmann's surprise, Ribbentrop.

'Congratulations, Herr Ambassador,' said the Fuhrer.

'Congratulations!' the young aides echoed.

'For what, for what?' asked Hoffman, grinning, turning his head this way and that, wondering if he'd missed something.

'Shall we put Hoffmann out of his misery?' asked the Fuhrer.

The young aides smiled.

'Stalin has agreed to meet and talk to us.' Hitler slapped his knee. 'Ribbentrop flies to Moscow tomorrow to sign a Pact with him.' He took the photographer's arm and walked him out of earshot of the others. 'Well?'

Hoffmann said, after a thoughtful moment, 'I'm wondering what the Party will make of it, Fuhrer?'

'Hoffmann, the Party knows me and trusts me. I agree they'll be astonished! But they will know that behind this gambit lies my Ultimate Aim – a Unification of All Europe!'

Hoffmann sipped his champagne and said nothing.

'Hoffmann, I have a commission for you.' He began to pace, six steps forward, six back, along the Great Hall. 'You will go to Moscow with Von Ribbentrop. I want you to convey my greetings and good wishes to Stalin. Do your photographs and all that.' He paused. 'Hoffmann, I want to use your trained eye, as an observer of people, I want you to come back here and tell me what kind of man Josef Stalin is! What am I dealing with here, what kind of ruler is he? Is he strong, weak, well or ill, quick-witted, slow, what?' Hitler looked at Hoffmann, his eyes wide and staring. 'I want to know *who* he is? You understand me, Heinrich?'

Very soberly Heinrich Hoffmann sipped his champagne and nodded.

*

433

Heinrich Hoffmann flew with Ribbentrop and several German Foreign Office officials from Konigsburg to Moscow, a journey of five hours' duration. Hoffmann slept all the way. He was tired most of the time these days. He now had a string of photographic shops in most European capitals, and running them filled his life. But he had no grumbles. He was in line to become a millionaire, from his Fuhrer royalties alone. As soon as he got out of the aircraft, the first thing he saw was the Swastika and the Hammer and Sickle, flying side-by-side above the airport building.

All he could do was stare at them, in awe. He had never thought he would live to see the day!

The German Ambassador to Moscow, Graf Von Schulenberg, met the party, along with General Koestring, the Military Attache, who told Hoffmann that the Lucullan cold buffet at the Embassy was all flown in from Sweden. 'They starve here!'

Hoffmann, remembering his mission, asked, 'What do you think are Stalin's real feelings towards Germany?'

Koestring looked thoughtful. 'Stalin says he sees no reason why we should not exist side-by-side?' Koestring looked at Hoffmann closely. 'Of course, any arrangement would be a sort of *Mariage du Convenance*, would it not?'

The following morning Hoffmann was taken by Koestring on a lightning-tour of Red Square and the Kremlin. He took many photographs. Of people. Of interiors. His impression was: Poverty. Barbaric. Strong. Unknowable.

'What do we want from this meeting?' Hoffmann asked Ribbentrop as they sat in his quarters, back at the Embassy. 'At least tell me that, Herr Ambassador, or I have no idea what I'm looking for!'

Ribbentrop glanced at his watch. They were due to meet Stalin at his office in the Kremlin in an hour. 'It is the Fuhrer's intention to attack Poland very soon. When he does so, the Soviet Union – if they sign this Pact – will then move their own troops, once we have taken Warsaw, into Poland. They will take about one half of Poland. We will take the other half. We will have Trade Agreements with the Soviets. Coal. Cattle. Lead. Zinc. Grain. Things we need. But most important, the West will be deprived of Societ Russia as an ally, probably for ever. They will regard the Russians as every bit as bad as Germany, if not worse. Brilliant, don't you think?'

Hoffmann nodded, amazed.

Two days later, Hoffmann reported to Hitler at the Berghof.

They sat alone in the Fuhrer's study.

'Tell me, what is he *like*?'

Hoffmann had made notes, to which he intended to refer, but found he had no need of them. He opened a file containing the photographs he had taken at the Moscow talks and spread them carefully across Hitler's desk.

'Until the Agreement was signed, Stalin did nothing. He simply stood behind Molotov and smiled and nodded in a friendly way.' Hoffmann chose his words with care. 'As you can see from these pictures.'

The photographs showed Stalin wearing a white jacket buttoned to the neck in the Russian way, smoking a thick, cardboard cigarette, wrinkling his nose against the smoke, as he watched Molotov sign the Agreement.

'Why is he smoking? It looks disreputable,' said Hitler. 'If you use these photographs for propaganda purposes, can you erase the cigarette?'

'No problem,' said Hoffmann easily. He spread out the next set of photographs. 'Here, this is after the signing. Molotov opens the champagne. It was Crimean and quite drinkable.' Hitler nodded. 'Yes, what else?'

'Well,' said Hoffmann. 'A curious thing. Everybody drank from a champagne-glass. Except Stalin. He had an ordinary glass tumbler. I suppose, because it holds more? He's a good, heavy drinker.'

'No! It is so that his glass cannot be switched. He fears poison. Assassination.'

'Only Molotov and the servants were there,' protested Hoffmann, surprised. 'And ourselves?'

'All the more reason.'

'I think perhaps Stalin understood more German and English – which I talked to Molotov – than he showed. Molotov's German is good, he was a young student in Berlin. Molotov?' Hoffman pushed a photograph of the Soviet Foreign minister, balding, rimless-glasses po-face. 'Molotov, I see as a functionary. He turns to Stalin all the time, to see if he is doing things right.'

'You said Stalin drank?'

'General Koestring says he drinks people under the table. Deliberately.'

'Did he say why?'

Hoffmann shrugged. 'Obviously Stalin will use any advantage. Fortunately,' Hoffmann smiled, 'with me it had no effect!'

It was a joke but Hitler, as usual, did not see it.

'But what did *you* think of him?'

'I was impressed, Fuhrer. He is strong, squat in build. Powerful. Deep voice. My impression was of intelligence, shrewdness, bonhomie.'

To underline his point, Hoffmann rapidly pushed forward other photographs of Stalin, for Hitler to see.

'Did he seem to give orders?'

'Not at all. Molotov is his mouthpiece. He says little himself.'

'Does he keep control of events?'

'Absolutely. We all waited for his nod. All of us.'

'You were impressed, Heinrich! You'll be voting Communist next!'

'Hardly, Fuhrer. But he is redoubtable, certainly.'

'But . . . possibly a drunkard?'

'Sometimes men drink a lot and it makes little difference to how they function.'

'Nonetheless,' said Hitler, who hated drunkards.

'And you'll paint out the cigarettes, in the photographs?'

'Naturally.'

'Excellent, Heinrich. Most interesting.'

Hoffmann felt he could say much more, but the Fuhrer was standing. The interview was at an end. Hoffmann left at once.

Driving back to Munich he thought, well, well, he got his Pact, but what will the Party think of it?

Hoffmann had his answer next morning. The garden at the Brown House was full of the discarded badges of hundreds of local Party members. A general air of incredulity swept through Germany. Why had the Fuhrer done this? A Pact with *Stalin*?

But the anger ended there.

Nobody important resigned from the Party.

The newspapers, especially the *Volkischer Beobachter*, were quick to point out that Germany's defences to the East were now secure and if the Western Democracies wanted a showdown with Germany, they would face the full might of the Fuhrer's new armies!

In London and Paris, and Washington even, there was incredulity. Many British, American and French Communists resigned from the Party. After the defeat in Spain, *this*! It was too much.

The British Foreign Office sent Sir Neville Henderson, British Ambassador to Berlin, to the Obersaltzberg with a proposal from Chamberlain. Hitler met him with ill-grace. He did not want complications at this stage. Henderson, red carnation in buttonhole as always, said, 'We have to live up to our guarantee to Poland, no matter what. Mr Chamberlain's proposal is: we ask the Polish Government to talk directly to you.'

'What will that accomplish?' asked Hitler, harshly.

But he was shaken. Surely Chamberlain realised the implications of the Soviet-Nazi Pact? England could not move now! He said to Henderson, 'If you want to hand out blank cheques to people like the Poles, and honour them no matter what they write on them, then you must take the consequences.'

Henderson was shaken. 'I will convey your message to Mr Chamberlain. I would have thought it proof of Mr Chamberlain's good intentions that Churchill is still not in his Cabinet, despite strong pressure for it in London.'

'You know my Pact with Stalin is mainly a trading agreement. The Soviet Union is no longer the brutal Bolshevik tyranny it used to be!'

Henderson did not comment but looked disbelieving.

'Very well, I'll make a last concession,' said Hitler quickly, his nerve almost failing. 'My lowest demand is: Danzig and a Rail Corridor! There? Could I ask for less?'

Stonily, Henderson said he would report to London. And with that he took his leave.

'The British,' said Hitler to Goering, 'will never fight! Chamberlain will never fight, it isn't in him!'

Goering said, cautiously, 'I think Chamberlain may have no choice?'

'In that case, give me time to try for a better political solution?' said Hitler, thoughtfully. 'What if we go on the first of September, our original start-date?'

'That is better,' said Goering. 'If we do go, we will need full mobilisation. One hundred divisions.' He went away to make the necessary telephone-calls, without enthusiasm. He knew Goering had hopes of a Peace, through his Swiss diplomatic connections.

Adolf Hitler sat alone on the balcony of the Berghof, for a very long time, a lone figure in the warm afternoon sunshine.

'The blind fools, the idiots, did they think I was bluffing?' Hitler asked his aides, twenty-four hours later. The British Government's reply to his generous offer to Ambassador Henderson was simply a foolish reiteration of their position. They had guaranteed Poland and would stand by that guarantee!

'They *do* think I'm bluffing!' Hitler shouted. 'But I think *they*'re the ones who are bluffing!'

Hitler sat alone in his study all day, refusing to answer telephone calls, even from Goering or Goebbels. He ate in his study. Finally, at one o'clock in the morning, he went to his bleak bedroom, lay down on his army cot, and fell asleep at once.

Eva Braun wakened instantly he touched her arm. Drowsy, befogged with sleep, she sat up and switched on the bedside lamp. A rosy glow filled her bedroom. Adolf, in his shirt and trousers and looking very tired, perched on the edge of her bed.

'What time is it? Are you all right?'

'It's four o'clock. I hoped you might be awake.'

'Well,' she smiled wryly, 'I am now. What is it?'

'I have decided. About Poland. You know how things come to me. I worried all day. I worried when I went to bed, I slept, then I wakened and it was all clear to me, what I must do!'

Eva felt a sudden, cold fear, but she just nodded. Adolf talked on: 'I must follow my intuition. My Duty. I was tempted to settle for less. I was very tired, I almost gave way.'

Eva said nothing. A feeling of utter helplessness came over her. There was nothing she could do. Adolf had made his decision. It was pointless to question it.

'I just thought I would tell you.' He kissed her on the cheek, and stood up. 'I'm sorry to have wakened you. Go back to sleep.'

'You *know* what you must do?' she whispered. 'You're *sure*?'

'Yes.' He nodded his head, and without looking back, he crossed to the door and softly closed it behind him.

It was a long time before Eva Braun slept. She cried first, for a very long time, but quietly, so that he did not hear her.

Hitler, after he left Eva Braun, gave the signal, by telephone from the Berghof, for the 'preparatory' attack on Poland to begin. Various S.S. Squads had been stationed on the German side of the Border, to stage 'incidents' that looked like Polish military excursions against the Germans. For example: since 10th August one of Heydrich's trusted S.S. officers, Naujocks, had been waiting at Gleiwitz, near the Polish frontier, in order to stage a faked Polish attack on the German radio-station there. Muller, the head of the Gestapo, had ready thirteen condemned criminals, dressed in Polish uniforms, and arranged them, lying dead on the ground, in a field on the German side of the Border. They had already been given a fatal injection of cyanide by an S.S. doctor. They were then shot, with small-arms fire. Members of the German Press and some friendly foreign-correspondents were taken to the scene of the incident to inspect the corpses. They all expressed horror at the scene.

Fighting began, soon afterwards, all along the German-Polish border.

Hitler received an ultimatum from Mr Chamberlain late that night. It was to the effect that if the British Government did not hear from

Germany by 11 a.m. the following day, the British Empire was at war with Germany. Goering had been right. Chamberlain had no choice. The British Parliament and influential rivals like Churchill had forced his hand. The common people knew only what they read in their newspapers, but it was to be war, all right.

By that time German armoured-columns were pouring into Eastern Poland.

And Adolf Hitler, dressed in field-grey, was in his special train, *Amerika*, heading away from a blacked-out Berlin, and the deserted *Anhalt* Railway Station, towards the War Zone.

BOOK THREE

XIX

'AMERIKA' sped at sixty miles an hour through Prussia towards Poland, Adolf Hitler aboard. He sat in the rosewood-panelled dining-car of his 'Headquarters' train, sipped coffee and listened to his short, stocky, crippled Chief-adjutant, Colonel Schmundt listing the earliest successes of the Campaign: 'There has been resistance, Fuhrer, but you will not believe *this*! Our tanks have been attacked by Polish cavalry! *Cavalry?*'

Hitler was both astonished and cheered by such news. It bore out his most strong belief! all his enemies were fools, dumkopfs!

Schmundt laughed, coarsely. 'One could almost feel sorry for the Poles if they were not so goddammed proud! What kind of fool sends horses against tanks? And what kind of bigger fool rides them?'

'No,' said Hitler, soberly. 'I salute the horsemen. It is the Polish nobles and generals I spit on!'

Schmundt said no more about the horses. It was never possible to predict how the Fuhrer would react to anything. 'If the Fuhrer would like to come along to the Command Coach, the latest field-reports await him? We have broken through and the enemy are in flight.'

'In a moment,' said Hitler. 'I will be along in a moment.'

Schmundt, stood up, clicked his heels and went out of the dining-car. It would, Hitler knew, take him all of five minutes to get to the Command Coach. Emotion coursed through him: everything was going to plan. He composed himself and stared out of the window at the country spinning by. What a train *Amerika* was! Fifteen coaches long with two locomotives to pull her. Armoured-wagons with flak-guns were at the front and rear. The Fuhrer's personal quarters, a drawing-room and separate sleeping-accommodation were in the middle. Hitler's adjutants, and Dietrich's Press Office were behind: bringing up the rear was a signals-unit, with telephone and radio-links and teletype machines with connections to Berlin, and to the Front. There was a squad of Bodyguards on board with their own quarters. Finally, this splendid dining-room. It was, indeed, going to war in style.

Hitler sat, gazing at the rolling countryside, thinking: now it is real war, not walkovers like Austria and Czecho-Slovakia, certainly not the ultimate conflagration Russia would be: but the real thing, just the same. He attempted to curb his optimism. It was beginning well, but there were risks. If France got her soldiers to put down their copies of *La Vie Parisienne* and got their arses out of their warm, comfortable bunkers, half-a-mile inside their so-called impregnable Maginot Line, and decide to attack the West Wall, what then? What *if* the British used their long-distance bombers and attacked German cities?

What *if* . . . ?

Hitler thought: If? If the Allies were bold? Ruthless? Hitler smiled to himself. He associated Mr Chamberlain with neither of those qualities. He rested his head against the velvet headrest and closed his eyes. He'd had no real sleep at all for days, just lying in the dark, fretting over a War to fight. The Poles were badly led and would pay dearly for it. As an Austrian, he didn't hate the Poles as the Prussians did, but they had had their chance. A sudden feeling of power surged through Hitler. This was, after all, what he had planned and prayed for all his political life. The realisation of a dream of greatness. He did not come as a wet-arsed careerist, some respectable Minister of War in some soppy Social Democracy or Royalist State, bending the knee to some cross-bred Monarch. No, he came as a conqueror, as a Charlemagne or an Atilla the Hun! Well, why not, that was what he was! Great Men made Great Empires and those Empires only perished long after the Great Men who founded them had gone. A time came for all great conquerors, an hour when they were unstoppable. Atilla's time had come when he plundered Europe and Rome, the greatest Empire of all, had staggered under his attack. Well, the Romans had adopted the Jewish religion, worshipped the Jewish Christ, and finally gone down before the Barbarians! All the scholars and historians thought that was a terrible thing but it wasn't, it was a natural thing. The strongest Race ruled, the weak went to the wall, the fire, the torture-chamber, the execution block.

The British Empire, like the Roman, had also come to an end. India, the Jewel in their Crown, was far away and in a state of ferment and revolt. Their other colonies, dotted around the globe, were too remote to give much help to the Mother Country. Britain, the last of the great naval powers, had been master of the sea, and therefore of the world, for almost four hundred years. Their time was up. This war would be won on land, by the new iron-ship of the plains and the Steppes, the tank! Were not German panzer-corps smashing their way now, unhindered, towards Warsaw?

The British Empire was virtually finished. There was room in the world for another great power. A *land* power, holding sway over all of Europe and Asia. There was only the French but after their losses in 1914, had they any blood left to shed? They had a huge army, bigger than Hitler's, but did it want to fight? That left only one other Power to contest Germany's claim to straddle all of Europe and Asia, to establish her armies from the Rhine to the Ural Mountains!

Soviet Russia.

Hitler opened his eyes. The sun was beginning to set, rays of gold filtering and flickering through the green pine branches. Soon, they would be at their destination and the stern business of War would engage him again, for the first time since he had run, as a *meldeganger*, with the messages for Herr Kapitan Weidemann How times changed!

Now he was indeed Atilla the Hun.

And like Atilla, he would change the world.

Hitler rose to his feet and walked along the compartment towards the Command Coach.

Adolf Hitler counted the days.

Standing in the Command Coach of the train, he listened and watched as his generals waged the battle, interfering only occasionally, conscious all the time that if the French and British meant to attack in the West, it would take the Allies at least three weeks to mount an artillery offensive. This was the estimate of the shrewd Colonel Jodl, whom Keitel had brought in as his assistant.

Hitler considered the situation. The battle for Poland, run by Brauchitsch, was basically a classic encirclement by German tanks of vast concentrations of Polish infantry. The Poles had deployed most of their Army too far to the West, expecting to defeat the Germans and press forward onto German soil. What foolish nonsense! Had they known the strength of the Panzers they would have grouped at the Vistula river. However, it would not have helped them much. The Panzers had cut through their infantry like cheese-wire through good Gruyere.

Hitler soon became impatient with the physical inactivity of the Command Coach. Nothing but arrows on maps and field-telephone calls and chess-board manoeuvres. 'Let us go out and see the real war,' he told Schmundt. The Chief-adjutant was apprehensive, but an order was an order. The Mercedes and Kempka were made available, with two back-up trucks filled with members of Hitler's Bodyguard, the *Liebstandarte S.S.* Hoffmann, the photographer, was alerted, clambered in beside

Kempka, and the convoy started off down the blazingly hot farm-tracks of the country, stirring up clouds of yellow dust so thick they could feel it on their skin, in their eyes, and in their hair. Hoffmann cleaned the lens of his Leica, continually. The problem was to find something to photograph.

Suddenly, a sweet, sickly stench filled the air and Hoffmann knew he was on a battlefield. A wide road opened in front of them, and on it lay a confused mass of broken and abandoned field-guns. Rifles of Polish make were thrown down everywhere; machine-guns on rickety legs, their muzzles at strange angles; uniformed bodies rigid in the road and in the ditches and hedgerows. Horses, already bloated by gas, lay in their dozens, quite still, their spindly legs sticking up into the air. Everything was quite still in this bosky place, the silence broken only by the buzzing of a million huge, black flies.

This was war at its saddest, thought Hoffmann.

There was nothing here to show the *Volk*.

They drove on. Nobody spoke.

Soon, Hoffmann had a better subject: the total admiration of the back-of-the-line soldiers for the Fuhrer. Hoffmann snapped and snapped and snapped again, as the men pressed forward, trying to get a glimpse of Hitler. Hoffmann soon had their brown, adoring faces in his sights, their crease-worn eyes and reddened necks, the sweat that soaked their thick uniforms. It was hot weather to fight a war, but they seemed more like boys on a picnic. Apart from the danger and the noise, it was probably not very different from their Strength Through Joy years in the Hitler Youth. Hitler bore their adoration with pleasure, and Hoffmann got some good shots, just what was needed for the magazines back in Berlin. But Polish artillery shells began to fall nearby and Schmundt persuaded Hitler to order the convoy back to the *Amerika*, which was hidden away from spotter-planes in a tree-protected siding.

Hitler heard of Polish atrocities against his soldiers, and told Commanding Officers: 'Guerillas operating behind German lines will be court-martialled by military-law and shot at once!' Sometimes he flew, using one of the three Junkers at his disposal, and was met by Staff-Officers and taken to a forward observation-point. He met ordinary soldiers and officers, men bone-tired but smiling, and men bloodily wounded and groaning. He laughed and talked a lot to officers and men alike and was in high spirits throughout. Hoffmann thought: he likes war, he feels at home in it, he isn't afraid, he doesn't think he'll be killed on a battlefield, the risk exhilarates him. It was curious, Hoffmann thought, snapping Hitler and the adoring soldiers, that he worries so much about assassination, but here he feels safe.

Inside two weeks, Warsaw was surrounded by German armour and artillery.

The Poles were offered surrender, but refused it. The civilian population of Warsaw was prepared to shed its blood. Men tore up tramlines and made anti-tank traps. They filled sandbags and put up barbed-wire and dug anti-tank ditches. They built barricades across the main streets. The Poles were trying to emulate Madrid, Hitler realised. They wanted house-to-house fighting, of the kind that had gained the admiration of the world for the Reds when they had defied Franco. Remembering his own time-table (the War was to last no longer than four weeks!) Hitler ordered: 'We attack by air. Every aircraft at our command. Every gun.'

The unopposed air attacks terrified the civilian population. The artillery did great damage. The tanks rolled in, to only sporadic, if brave, resistance. The Polish Government fled to Romania. Thirty-five Polish divisions disappeared off the military-map in twenty days, and with them the name of Poland itself. 'Let the world shudder and marvel at the success of German arms,' said Hitler, to his bone-weary generals. 'Let the Soviets occupy their half of Poland. If Stalin wants to say he's doing it to protect Russian civilians in Poland, let him!'

Himmler formed an *Einsatzgruppen*. These murder squads shot Jews in family-groups – men, women and children, young and old, in Polish towns in the early days of the War. *Wehrmacht* officers who saw these happenings were horrified, and many protests found their way back to the Base. They were ignored. Hitler told Himmler, 'I want a purge of all Jews, and of all intellectuals, aristocrats, and upper-class Poles. Put them all together somewhere, if that is possible. I leave the details to you.' Himmler was used to those sort of orders. He simply passed them on to Heydrich, who did all that was necessary. The Poles shuddered and averted their eyes from the Jewish massacres.

'Stalin has done well out of the War,' said Hitler. 'He has half of Poland and it has not cost him the life of a single Russian soldier. He still has the vast granary of the Ukraine – which we need! He has oil-wells in the Caucasus, and we have none at all!' Sitting in the returning *Amerika*, en route for Berlin, gazing at the Pomeranian sky of eggshell-blue, broken only by the green fronds of the pines, Hitler considered what he had seen in the East and was *disgusted* by it!

The Poles and their Jews lived in hovels!

Their villages were insanitary and derelict, even the towns were dirty and had little industry. Sloth and poverty were everywhere. These were an inferior Eastern people and it showed. From now on they would work for the Reich! That would be their fate, as bondage and slavery had been the lot of the tribes Atilla the Hun had crushed in battle, almost 2,000 years before! As for the Jews, had he not told them where they stood. Their leader, Chaim Weizmann, had assured Chamberlain that Jews everywhere were behind him in the fight against Hitler. What else could Hitler expect from his enemies? He had told the Reichstag: 'If International-Finance-Jewry, inside and outside Europe, manages to propel the world into War, the outcome will be, not the Bolshevisation of the earth and the consequent triumph of Jewry, but *the annihilation of the Jewish Race in Europe!*'

Hitler had stood, trembling with rage and hate, as the crowd roared. *These people meant his death*, let there be no doubt of it! Very well! The world would see who triumphed in the end!

From along the train came the sound of revelry, of raised voices and the clinking of glasses. The celebrants of victory were drinking good German beer. Let them enjoy it while they could. Soon, they would be fighting again. Against harsher opponents than the Poles.

Great deeds were afoot. Soon he would go along the car and compliment the men.

Amerika rushed on into the bright day. Pondering on the fate of the Jews, Hitler thought of Hans Frank, his Minister without Portfolio who was burning to show how good a Nazi he was, how ruthless he was. Frank had been privy, to details of the meeting of Hitler and his half-nephew William Patrick Hitler. The boy's mother, Bridgit Hitler, wife of Hitler's step-brother Alois had been there along with Adolf's half-sister Angi. Hitler had told them all: 'The family cannot expect a free ride to fame, just because *I* am famous!' Angela and Alois had nodded sensibly to that. 'There are details of my ancestry that must never be known! The *Volk* must not know *who* I am!' The family had stared at him as if they had never seen him before. Hitler had paid money to William Patrick and sent him and his mother Bridgit out of Germany, back to England. So, disaster had been avoided, if only just. Frank had then made his investigations and come up with nothing that proved dangerous, so long as it was hushed-up. The idea of any Jewish taint was an obscenity, of course, and could be dismissed: but his enemies would make a very great deal of it, *they could destroy him with it*! And nobody except the pernickety Hans Frank (what a soft fool he was!) knew any details at all.

Now Frank wanted to show what a good German he was? Very well!

Let Frank prove himself in the dark, frozen forests of Poland. Let him show how ruthless he is!

Let him be Governor-General of Poland!

Hitler laughed aloud, delighted with the thought.

Let him have the stinking place!

In the West nothing happened.

The small British Expeditionary Force and the huge French Army stayed put behind the Maginot Line. The Germans waited behind their West Wall. They had only twenty-four divisions to thirty-six French, but September and October went by and the two Armies faced each other without firing a shot.

The British, using an American word, called it the 'phoney' war. The Germans called it the '*Sitzkrieg*' after Goebbels' propaganda film *Blitzkrieg*, which terrified the neutrals. Hitler made a Peace Speech in October. 'To France I say this. It is my desire to bury forever our ancient enmity and bring together our two nations!' he told the Reichstag, with enormous insincerity. The Reichstag was mystified but applauded, on cue. 'I believe today that there can only be real peace if Germany and England come to an understanding. Why should this war in the West be fought?' His hands were on his hips, he was smiling. 'For the restoration of Poland?' The Reichstag laughed and applauded. 'The question of Poland will be solved by Russia and Germany. It would be senseless to annihilate millions of men to reconstruct it.' The Reichstag cheered. 'Let those who want war reject my outstretched hand! If the opinions of Churchill and his followers should prevail, this appeal will have been my last!'

The audience cheered him. The offer sounded fair.

Hitler's Spymaster, Canaris, told him that the old French hero, Petain, and the politician Bonnet wanted Peace Talks with Germany, but from London, Chamberlain had said, No. Or rather he asked for continuing proof that Hitler meant peace. Hitler, suddenly exultant, asked his generals if an attack on the French was possible now, that very winter? Brauchitsch, huge and commanding, another wooden colossus, much as Hindenberg had been, was alarmed at the idea. He stood in Hitler's Chancellery and pleaded: 'Fuhrer, we need months to repair and refit our tanks. Our ammunition is exhausted. We have enough for fourteen days of battle, that is all!'

'I want plans made for an offensive! We will attack through Belgium and Holland!'

Brauchitsch swallowed: 'Neutral countries?'

Hitler barked, testily, 'They are the only undefended part of the

Franco-British front. Would you rather we attacked the Maginot Line full-face?' Really, these Generals were idiots! They wanted to fight Total War with clean hands. 'A *Blitzkrieg*, as in Poland. Stukas, Stukas, Stukas! Tanks, tanks, and more tanks!'

Brauchitsch swallowed again, and hoped that he would be able to report good news of progress and a Battle Plan soon. The General left, to grumble to his staff, but also to prepare for the Battle of France.

As Hitler told Albert Speer, his architect, and a constant supper-companion at the Chancellery, 'After a victory like Poland, they still plot and plan against another victory!' With the handsome young Speer he went off to view the latest cardboard-models of Linz and Berlin, designed by the two of them in the years of peace. Little had been actually built but there were hundreds of architectural-drawings and models in work. Speer was besotted by Hitler and felt he was the luckiest young man in Germany to have the opportunity to plan and built Art Galleries and Autobahns and Amphitheatres for the new Thousand Year Reich. He was a long-time veteran of Hitler's dinner and supper parties, both at the Chancellery and at the Obersaltzberg. He had designed the new Chancellery and seen that work actually completed. But all the rest was merely dreams and now the War had begun Speer wondered how much time the Fuhrer would be able to give to these visions of future splendour. 'We will build roads like the Romans' and cities like the Greeks'!' declared Hitler. Certainly, the models looked good. Speer said, 'The War goes on, Fuhrer?' Hitler nodded. 'We will pursue it with the utmost vigour.'

Speer was silent as he brought out and unrolled new plans for Adolf's home city of Linz, which was to be almost totally rebuilt. The whole thing seemed irrelevant now. Speer wondered what he should do? Join the Army, he supposed. 'Do we go on with our autobahns?' he asked tentatively.

Hitler looked surprised. 'Of course we do! The War will not last long. It must not! A long War would ruin us!'

Speer, who knew little of Hitler's War-aims and had no desire to learn more said: 'But Fuhrer, you will not have time to work on these things?'

'Always,' said Hitler. 'I will always find time. It relaxes me.'

Hitler looked at the models of Linz. Once he had stood with his friend Gustl and explained what he would do with the City. Gustl had not believed him then: perhaps he did now. He had seen Gustl once only since those days: at the Festival at Bayreuth, two years ago. Gustl was now a professional musician, and they had talked of the old days and taken supper with Winifred Wagner, the composer's daughter, a great moment in Gustl's life. Hitler had asked Gustl as they shook hands, if there was anything he wanted? Normally, it was not a thing he ever asked anybody, but Gustl was special, Gustl was his youth. Gustl said, 'Nothing, Adolf. It is enough to see you again, in person.' Hitler felt warmth, recalling that moment. Truly, there were some people who simply wished him well, people like Gustl, and the *Alte Kampfer* to whom he would soon speak, as he did on the yearly anniversary of the March on the Feldherrnstrasse. The War would not interfere with *that*.

'Very well, Fuhrer,' Speer said. 'As always I am at your disposal.'

'We build for a thousand years. No man since Charlemagne has held unlimited power in his own land, as I do . . . I will use it for Germany in this War, but if it is not won, then I will know that Germany has not stood the test. In that case she will be doomed, and deserve it!'

Speer felt suddenly cold and horrified; but he went on showing Hitler his plans for the Linz of the future.

A bomb exploded in the Braubergerkeller in Munich, ten minutes after Adolf Hitler left the place, having given his yearly speech to the *Alte Kampfer*. Some people were slightly injured and the cellar was wrecked. Photographs appeared in the German Press and the *Volk* were horrified. The British Secret Service were implicated by an ex-Communist carpenter called Elser, who had been arrested by the Gestapo. He was now in Dachau, but had yet to be executed. Hitler said, 'There is nothing the English cannot bungle!'

Hitler's aides recalled his fear of assassination. When he entered Warsaw in an open car, any Pole standing at a window had been automatically sentenced to death. They were puzzled about Elser.

Hitler again addressed his fighting generals assembled uneasily in the conference-room at the Chancellery. He allowed them to sit, and launched at once into his speech. He was tense and angry. 'Meinherren, the purpose of this conference is to tell you my decisions!'

Hitler stood at his table, hand raised.

'I am irreplaceable! Neither a military man nor a civilian could take my place, in case any such a thing has occurred to you!' Hitler paused and looked at each officer in turn. 'Assassination attempts may be repeated, of course. I have led the German people to the heights – even if the world hates us now! The fate of the Reich depends on me! We must be more ruthless than our enemy if we do not want to go under! The only solution is the sword!'

Hitler stood quite still.

'We must be harsh. We do not have a two-front war to fight but nobody can know how long for. We have the Treaty with the Soviets.' Hitler snorted, it was almost a laugh, he would soon show those Bolsheviks! 'Treaties are fine as long as they serve a purpose. We can attack Russia only when we have won in the West!'

The Generals were silent and looked studiously at their highly-polished boots. Angrily, Hitler raised his voice: 'I shall attack France and England first. Breach of the neutrality of Belgium and Holland is of no importance! Nobody will question that when we have won!'

The Generals looked sullen and wooden, like reproved schoolboys. Hitler, shaking with a sudden fury, shouted, his voice echoing off the panelled-walls of the huge room. 'We are at War! Fate demands from us what it demanded from the great men of German history! As long as I live I shall think only of the victory of my people! I shall shrink from nothing! I will *annihilate* everyone who is opposed to me!'

He stood there, shaking, his hand on the table to steady himself, his face shiny with sweat, eyes staring. There was a long silence. Nobody moved. Halder stood up, quickly. 'Gentlemen! The Fuhrer thanks you! Attention and Dismiss!'

The Generals dispersed, sober-faced and shocked. Bruachitsch thought: Good God, the man is mad, he is a megalomaniac, what more can we do for him, for Germany, that we are not already doing? He wondered uneasily how much, if anything, Hitler knew of the secret and no doubt treasonable discussions the generals held about him, from time to time. He fervently hoped nothing.

Hitler motioned for Brauchitsch and Halder to stay behind. Then he launched into Brauchitsch. 'The Army High Command and most of *your* Generals are defeatists!' To Halder, he shouted, 'And *your* General Staff has a stiff-necked attitude towards me and my orders!'

Both Generals volubly protested their loyalty, but Hitler would not be silenced. 'I want your deeds! Not your words!'

Brauchitsch ventured, 'If you want my resignation, Fuhrer, it is yours!'

'No!' shouted Hitler. 'You stay and do your duty! Both of you!'

Abashed, the two Generals came to attention, saluted and left the room, white-faced and shaken. Outside, in the huge ante-room, Brauchitsch turned to the quieter, normally laconic Halder. 'He is unstoppable, Franz. Nothing will hold him now. He will run events his way from now on.'

'Yes,' said Halder, solemnly. 'We must go along with him. It would be dangerous to think of anything else.' He was talking about a possible *putsch*, and they both knew it.

They saluted one another and went their separate ways to prepare the final plans for the attack on France.

Hitler went to the Obersaltzberg from Berlin, in the Mercedes. He sat, in a cold rage. The Generals! Cowards! At least the Navy *did* something! A U-Boat Commander had just sunk the unarmed British ship *Athenia* in the Atlantic, with a loss of over 2,000 civilian lives. What was wrong with *that*? But the Navy wished to state publicly that the U-Boat Commander had made a mistake, thinking her a merchantman. 'No,' Hitler had said. 'Let the British tremble.'

At the Berghof, Martin Bormann was waiting. He was full of arrangements for the War-planning conferences and had secretaries and code-and-cypher staffs all ready. Thank God for men like Bormann and, of course, Himmler, men who would follow his orders unconditionally and without question. On arrival he sent a message to Himmler, demanding an urgent meeting. A fury burned in him: he would not be denied any longer! It was time to release the fires that had been banked down in him for so long, fires of revenge and denial. Soon, he would talk to Himmler again: the Jews were being ignored in the heat of battle. That would not do.

Eva Braun saw the change in him. She put it down to his war experiences in Poland. 'It is a sink of poverty and stagnation,' Hitler told her. 'We will clean it up, make it fit for good Germans to live in. We will turn Poland into a dairyland for the victorious soldiers of the Reich, once this War is over.'

Eva saw to it that his valet, Linge, had laid out his tweed suit but Linge advised her: 'The Fuhrer will not wear it. He has told me he will wear field-grey and nothing else until the War is over.'

'Surely not here?' protested Eva, dismayed. She had been so looking forward to their having some time together, giving Adolf a chance to recover from the bloodiness of the fighting in Poland. She knew how awful it had been because she had visited a hospital near Munich, full to overflowing with wounded Wehrmacht men. The women of Munich had flocked to help, taking food and flowers and little gifts. But the men had looked so young, to be so badly hurt. Many had lost legs and arms. They lay silently, in rows, doped against the pain, she supposed. It was said that they had lost only thirty thousand men, but that was thirty thousand mothers and wives without a son, or husband. The wounded were many times that number, and yet they had *won*? The women in the hospital were full of stories that there were not enough beds in the ordinary hospitals to accommodate the wounded, or doctors and staff to nurse them. Many of the Insane Asylums had been taken over. What had happened to the Insane people, Eva Braun had asked innocently.

All she had got was an uneasy look, and silence.

She even mentioned it to Adolf, in a wondering kind of way.

To her surprise, he reacted angrily. 'I need doctors and nurses and beds for my gallant young men! Of what use are these mad people?

They occupy good space and eat good food and they produce nothing. They are useless, to themselves and to Germany. It would be a kindness to them if they were all done away with!'

Eva, with her strict Catholic teaching about the sanctity of life, felt like protesting, but did not. Adolf was back from the War, upset and angry by the things he had seen. It was understandable. And yet, there was a sudden hardness in him, a new harshness, or maybe one that had always been there. He had always talked of his enemies with hatred (well, they were trying to kill him, weren't they, look at that Bomb in the Burgerbraukeller!) but now he was talking with hatred of Germans – even if they were sick or ill they were still Germans, weren't they?

These thoughts upset and worried Eva, so she did what she always did with anything that worried or upset her. She put it out of her mind and concentrated on trying to calm Adolf down, getting him to watch her latest calesthenic exercises: she had taken them up again, feeling she was getting a little plump here and there. A few spells on bars and ladders soon helped to tone up her muscles. Adolf was impressed. 'You look good, Eva. Anybody can see your mother was a champion.'

Eva was pleased by that. Adolf rarely referred to her family. She took the opportunity of saying that Vadi was looking for a way of serving Germany. He was little older than Adolf himself, and had much to give. Eva knew Hitler's aversion to appearing to help relatives: but since nobody knew of her, nobody knew of any reason why Vadi should be found a job, did they?

To Eva's delight and astonishment, Adolf later, without alluding to it again, found Vadi a desk-job, in the Army, with the rank of Colonel, well out of danger's way, at a supply-base not too far from Munich, so he could get home from time to time. Vadi, by now, was like most Germans, a total supporter of Adolf Hitler and everything he was doing for Germany. 'The world knows we will not be put upon!' declared Vadi, resplendent in his stiff new uniform, the belt tugging at his gut, as he stood in their Munich house. 'Adolf has his shortcomings, as we all know too well in this family. But the man is a leader such as Germany has needed and longed for!' Vadi glowered. He could not accept any reason why Adolf Hitler did not marry his daughter, and the suspicion crossed his mind that the uniform and the rank of Colonel was a sop, a bribe, because the *Kanzler* had not married Eva and never intended to.

'Vadi! Adolf does what he must! He is not an ordinary man who must have a wife and children and a home. He sacrifices all that for Germany. He sacrifices himself for Germany. If you only knew his worries, you would not be so critical of him!'

The words hung in the room, and neither of the old people replied.

They looked stricken at her words, and yet she knew they wanted to say more, to criticise and upbraid her. They felt they had failed; that their daughter should not live with a man to whom she was not married, whoever he was! That, she knew was what they felt: but were afraid to say so. Afraid of her man, of Adolf Hitler.

When Eva left the family home she felt two emotions, both of them very strong. First, shame and bitterness that she appeared to them like that, a scarlet woman. And the determination not to go back home again, for a very long time. Let them see if she cared!

That led, as she stood in the windy suburban street to a blind emotion, one that was almost a constant with her: loneliness.

Himmler and the Fuhrer sat down in the study at the Berghof for one of their secret meetings.

No minutes were ever kept of these occasions.

Hitler, nowadays, often issued orders to his Staff, his adjutants, even his Generals, by word of mouth only. Orders that might, if put to paper, offend the sensibilities of his charming secretaries. The Army officers, used to written orders all their lives, were often put out by these rapid verbal instructions which the Fuhrer would quickly call out. Coming to attention, they would leave the room at once and write down what they recalled of it, as near as they could. To distinguish these orders from all others, they called them '*Fuhrer Orders*', and they came to have more power than the written ones. It was as if Hitler had actually spoken to the recipients. In total confidence and secrecy.

Which was, Heinrich Himmler reflected, as he sat in his black and silver S.S. uniform, blinking through his thick spectacles at Hitler, all too true. Himmler was tired but exhilarated. These were great and shining times: history was being made. Fortunately, he had a great staff behind him. Reinhard Heydrich for one, his deputy. Without Reinhard and his drive for success, much would still be undone.

Hitler seemed, to Heinrich Himmler, to be more manic than usual. He did not sit down, but then he rarely sat down. His eyes found Himmler's. 'The incurables?'

Himmler glanced at the slip of paper in his hand. 'We are carrying out the Euthanasia Programme against mental-defectives all over Poland, and in Germany itself. I can give you figures, Fuhrer?'

'No, no. Just, how is it proceeding?'

'We are using rather antiquated methods of disposal, I'm afraid. Carbon-monoxide and so on. I have borne in mind that we must not shoot these people. I have several centres operating, and I have every reason to feel that security is being kept. Only my *Einsatzgruppen* are working in these places.'

'Good!' Hitler turned and paused. 'We can expect trouble from the Churches sooner or later, moaning about their sanctity of life, but we will meet that when we have to. We are stripping down for Total War!'

Heinrich Himmler absolutely agreed. 'My men sometimes feel sympathy for these people, but I have told them the requirement is to be strong.'

Hitler spoke in a different, whispering voice: 'Poland?'

Himmler stared through his thick glasses. 'The nobility, the intelligentsia and the clergy? The cleansing operation against them is proceeding, as to plan. The Army has been a problem. They don't want to be blamed for anything my squads did and still do, particularly the operations against the Jews.'

Adolf Hitler was looking out of the window and said nothing to that. But then, Heinrich Himmler reflected, he never did.

It was almost as if it all had nothing to do with him.

Ah, but it had. It had everything to do with him! Adolf Hitler sat here in the Berghof with his 'family' all around him: Eva Braun, the wife-mistress, the shopgirl with a hundred dresses: her sister Gretl and the women secretaries, all of them like relatives, Hitler's favourite sisters by proxy. Hitler and Eva fussing over their dogs like the children they would never have: Blondi, his alsatian, Eva's two Scotch terriers, for all the world like an old married couple! Here, at the Berghof, Hitler sat, taking these earth-shaking decisions – surely not even the Turks had sat so quietly as they planned to eradicate the Armenians? Himmler was impressed with the calm and certainty of those decisions: no word of doubt ever crossed Hitler's lips. It was ordained. Here he sat, Himmler thought, taking tea with his guests as if he is a country gentleman, going for slow walks in the forests after his daily conferences and his lunch, talking to his guests as if there was no War going on anywhere, certainly no *exterminations* going on anywhere, chattering of small, womanly things: his secretaries' birthdays, endless reminiscences of his childhood, all that cosy, unbelievable domestic nonsense! Eva Braun, moving against his guests, seeing they were in the right places, Hitler falling asleep over his cumin tea, Eva smiling and holding his hand, nobody daring to smoke a cigarette. My God, thought Himmler, he steps away from all that cosiness, that late-night diet of rubbishy American films, and he tells me to order my men to do things that no leader since ancient times has instructed other men to do, not even the infidel Turk! Himmler tugged at his uniform: not that the S.S. would be found wanting in the great enterprise of cleansing Europe of its Jews! Now that there was no hope of sending any more of them out of Germany, now that ideas like Madagascar as a refuge for them had been abandoned, what else was left? Half the Jews in Germany had fled, the rest would be worked to death for Germany, then die. If Hitler attacked Soviet Russia, as he must, to be true to *Mein Kampf,* then millions of Jews would fall into their net and he, Himmler, would be responsible for them. It was an enormous task. Meantime, his men, hardy S.S. troopers, fainted, and were physically sick to their stomachs at what they had to do, for Germany! The one time he had attended a mass-shooting himself he had felt ill. Afterwards, he had told the splendid fellows they were doing this awful task, which he hated as much as they did, for Germany and the Fuhrer! Staring at him, hollow-eyed (drink was freely available to the executioners, all rules were broken in those God-forsaken places of death) the young blond S.S. men had looked unconvinced, but had come to a weary attention when he shouted at them to remember their oath to the Fuhrer! He would not go again, all that could be left to Reinhard Heydrich, who was his right arm in this battle against Jewry. Heinrich Himmler was proud of the monumental task given him by the Fubrer: but part of him pulled in another direction. Hitler had said, 'The Jews began the War but we will end it with their destruction.' Very well. But Himmler recalled the rumours (no doubt only rumours, but one never knew) that Hitler had Jewish blood himself somewhere. It was a heresy to say it, but no heresy to think it. He knew because he had sent Gestapo agents to ferret out the facts about Hitler's illegitimate father, Alois. They had come back with nothing concrete. All was rumour and supposition.

One day, he might need such rumour. Dictators did not live or rule for ever. Who knew when a man like himself, standing so dangerously close to the Fuhrer, might need a card, even a blackmailing card? Himmler pondered uneasily: what if the rumours were not true *but Hitler thought they might be*? That could be the mainspring of so many of his decisions: there had to be a mainspring for the first purpose of a man's life, certainly an extraordinary one, a unique one, like Adolf Hitler's. He sat in the Berghof, drinking his cumin tea and smiling like a fond paterfamilias at the adoring young women and the respectful men? While he sat an hour later in his office, as he was sitting now, and made these decisions, issued these world-shattering orders:

Hitler sat in these *rooms* and never, ever visited the torture-chamber or the killing-grounds! Himmler felt a wave of anger, quickly suppressed. Perhaps the truth, as Roehm had said, was that Hitler was a dreamer who evaded witnessing the realisation of his dreams? He, Heinrich Himmler, could not do that. He was charged with the carrying-out of the most amazing orders ever issued to a commander, orders so secret that they were never put on paper – *Fuhrer Orders!* Himmler swallowed. He must never forget the *other* side of Adolf Hitler: the great orator, master, fate of the German People!

Hitler turned from the window, the blue eyes blazed: 'You are doing great work for Germany, Heinrich.'

Himmler felt a surge of pride. He came to attention. Tears of gratitude started to his eyes. Nothing was too much for this man, for Germany. nothing.

'Yes, My Fuhrer,' he said.

Von Brauchitsch (with a great deal of nerve-straining) finally faced Adolf Hitler with the news that there was no possibility of the Army being ready to invade France before the Summer. 'It is simply not possible to move earlier. Both Halder and myself feel May or June would be a possibility? The tanks need good dry ground to move on.' Hitler was about to launch into another harangue about the Army's defeatism and dilatoriness when his naval aide brought a signal that British Naval forces were landing troops in Norway. The *Altmark*, a German prison-ship with British seamen-prisoners aboard, had been boarded in Norwegian waters by men of a British destroyer and the prisoners released. The British Press were ecstatic. As Dietrich reported to Hitler, 'They have had very little good news to tell their people, so they have made a lot of it!'

Hitler ordered German Army units, some of them mountain-troops, to attack Oslo and Narvik by sea. The Norwegians put up a resistance, quickly quelled. The British troops already ashore were Territorial reserves, badly-prepared, armed, and officered and were almost instantly mopped-up by the battle-hardened *Wehrmacht*. 'The first direct clash between land-forces of the British Army and the *Wehrmacht!*' said Hitler, delighted. 'There is no doubt who has the victory. These bedraggled and freezing British prisoners of war will keep Goebbels and his propaganda-machine busy for weeks!' The Royal Navy launched a desperate attack on Narvik harbour, sinking ten German destroyers, three cruisers, and doing severe damage to three battle-cruisers, including the *Bismarck*. But the day was Hitler's. He danced for joy at the British withdrawal and made Vidkun Quisling, a Norwegian Nazi, the Protector of his country. Most European countries now had Nazi parties. Mosley, in Britain, was interned, but others flourished. Nazism was exportable, especially when it was a success. The name Quisling went into the language, and Norway into the Nazi net.

*

In June 1940, Hitler gave the signal: the German Panzers attacked France and the Low Countries. It was the hottest June in living memory. Days and days of sunlight, baking the ground so hard that almost no tank was ever bogged down in the entire six-week campaign. Belgium and Holland fell first; the Belgian government had promised to make stronger defences at Louvain and other points: but the insane truth was that the Maginot Line did not *go on* across the Belgian border but *simply stopped at that border*! Adolf Hitler could hardly believe such a blunder! The generals of the British Expeditionary Force did not mind it, since they thought it gave them a chance to get at the Germans – the British Army was living in the past, Hitler knew that. It was still fighting 1918-style, whereas his own Panzers had a *mobility* neither French nor British armies could ever begin to match. 'Their class-system makes the British an army of upper-class boobies commanding underweight and underfed conscripts and reservists armed with rifles and Lewis guns!' Hitler's generals exulted. 'The French have as many tanks as us, but they've spread them around in sixes and sevens!'

The Order of Battle the Generals had given Hitler was a version of the old Von Schliefflen Plan. He had all but accepted it, when General Von Manstien, an extremely gifted, but not a senior officer, made a suggestion to Hitler personally: 'Strike through the Ardennes Forest, at the French Centre, where the opposition is weak, with only over-age reservists.' Hitler accepted Manstien's plan and claimed it as his own.

Hitler, in a high state of excitement, observed the first stages of the Battle from *Amerika*. Then, to Hoffmann's surprise, from a Command Post in a bunker. Hitler had a room with a bed and a table and chair. It was hot and cramped and briefings took place in the open air. Goering reported that his Luftwaffe had attacked seventy enemy airfields. The tanks were moving smoothly through the Ardennes. The British Expeditionary Force, under Lord Gort, blundered forward into Belgium to engage the Germans. Hitler was happy and smiling. It was all going to plan. German sappers, landing by glider, immobilised the huge fort of Eban Emael by dropping explosive charges down the air-vents. The Belgian soldiers inside surrendered. Hitler claimed credit for planning the raid. The Dutch put up some resistance but the bombing of Rotterdam, with a thousand civilians dead, brought them to heel. They too, surrendered.

General Von Kliest's army crossed the River Meuse and established a bridgehead. These Panzers rolled West towards the English Channel. Von Rundstedt's armour cut-off the British Army in Belgium, which had been bloodily repulsed in St Valery and was beginning to retreat. Von Kliest's tanks were moving so fast (refuelling with gasoline from roadside garages as they went!) that Adolf Hitler got anxious and agitated, and ordered them to slow down, so that the infantry could catch up! He told Rundstedt: 'Our Southern flank is in danger!' He need not have worried. By the third week in May twenty British and French divisions were trapped north of the Somme. The signal came, 'We are at Abbeville!'

Hitler stood in his Command Post, in his field-grey uniform and visored cap, and executed a dance of triumph. To Keitel and Jodl, red-eyed with fatigue from poring hour-by-hour over maps, in artificial light, minds blurred from lack of sleep, Hitler shouted, 'We have it won, gentlemen! We have split them in two! They can't recover now!'

Keitel looked up, tears in his eyes. He was shaking with emotion. 'Fuhrer! You are the greatest captain of all time!'

Even Jodl, much more phlegmatic, was bemused by such success. Much of it was due to Hitler's planning or, anyway, his selection of the plans put to him. The man was uneducated and of common origin and often without what Jodl would call good manners. He knew little of the tactics of war (how could he, he wasn't a trained soldier?) but he had bold and original ideas – sometimes frighteningly so! – and Jodl was, somewhat against the grain, extremely impressed. The man had waged war on the old enemy, France, and virtually defeated her in less than a month! Who could deny this kind of success? Suddenly, a fateful decision was taken by Hitler, that, later, Jodl was to worry about. Von Runstedt had asked that his battalions halt on a prominent ridge outside Dunkirk, and wait for the British forces to be swept westward by the rapid German advance. Rundstedt's tanks were also in urgent need of repair. Hitler agreed. The tanks halted on the ridge.

For two days they stayed there.

In that time the British began to embark their defeated Army onto anything that floated, from destroyers to Thames river-barges. Hitler said to a General who urged immediate attack, before the English got away: 'Don't worry, the Luftwaffe will mop them up on the beaches and on the roads to the beaches.'

It did not happen.

The RAF Spitfires were in action for the first time and they commanded the air over the beaches. For the first time, also, the German bombers found they did not have an easy task. The Stukas were sitting ducks and the Messerschmitts found that the Spitfire could turn inside them. Meanwhile, the British rearguard, fighting well by now, protected the patient crowds on the beaches.

Goering was furious: 'They'll have to swim home!' he shouted.

That didn't happen, either.

The British got 300,000 men off at Dunkirk.

Two-thirds of their Army, most without weapons, were away by 20 June.

It was a humbling and savage defeat but they were home. And soon they would fight again.

Hitler was upset by the British escape-act but thought it no more than that. Touring the battlefields by car, surrounded by ecstatic Party members and his personal Staff, he told his senior Generals at Brussels: 'I stopped the armour at Dunkirk because I was worried about the French. If they had attacked while we were refitting, we had nothing to fight them with.' He waved his hand dismissively to the question: 'But what about England now?' He smiled. 'We can do a deal with England, later. But France must be stamped into the ground!'

Soldiers cheered him wherever he went.

Bruly-de-Peche was a mosquito-ridden village in a forest in North Belgium. It was built by Dr Todt, Minister for Munitions, as Hitler's new Headquarters. He did not care for it, but cheered himself with late talk-fest suppers for his Senior Officers, and stayed awake until dawn.

The fighting still raged north of Paris, was being lost catastrophically by the French Army, which had neither the material or morale to withstand the Stukas and Panzers. 'Winston Churchill,' said Hitler, derisively, 'has flown to Paris. He has offered complete union with Great Britain!' He laughed when General Weygand, the wiry, hesitant French Commander – 'Ten years too old, nerve gone' said Hitler – declared the battle for Paris lost and suggested suing for peace, at once. Premier Reynaud and others protested, but it was no use. The Cabinet resigned and Marshal Pétain took over the Government of France. He wrote to Hitler asking for terms of surrender.

When Adolf Hitler heard the news tears came to his eyes. Now, he was the Ruler of Europe! The greatest victor since Napoleon. The blood rushed to his face and he brushed the moisture away from his eyes. There was no God, he knew that, but if there had been one he would have offered up thanks to Him! A feeling of great gratitude coursed through him: he was the chosen instrument. That must now be obvious to anybody, even to his enemies. He sat down in silence, watched by his staff officers, and then, slowly dictated the terms he would offer Pétain. They were harsh but not like the ones he had imposed on Poland. Paris would not be a battleground, blasted to pieces like Warsaw. That, Adolf Hitler knew, was what terrified the French. He felt a cold contempt for them. Soldiers should go down fighting. To the last man.

Adolf Hitler sat in his speeding Mercedes, in a small military convoy, on the hot, dusty road to Compiègne. It was noon, 21 June. He felt

461

rested and free of anxiety, for the first time in many months. 'The greatest Victory of all Time!' he had told the ecstatic German *Volk* on the radio. Mussolini, to the disgust of the German generals, had invaded Southern France in the last days of the campaign. Hitler had reassured his Staff: 'All they will get is the town hall of Nice.' The generals had laughed at that. The Fuhrer was in great form these days. 'Also,' Hitler had reminded them, 'we need allies in Europe. These are great days to come and the Duce will be at our side.' Overtures and fervent congratulations had come from the Romanians and the Hungarians. Everybody wanted to touch the sleeve of the victor.

The Mercedes turned into the shady, wooded clearing, in which stood the French General Foch's train. The shameful Armistice had been signed there in 1918. The sun beat down, dappled, on the victorious Germans, as they got out of their motorcars. First, Hitler himself, then General Von Brauchitsch and Keitel, in new uniforms. Then, Admiral Raeder, incongruous in his *Kriegsmarine* formal-dress with white wing-collar; Ribbentrop and Hess, also in full uniform. Finally, Goering, holding his Field-Marshal's baton, grimacing at the scene. Hitler accepted the salute of the German officers already in place. He did not need to ask if his orders regarding Foch's train had been obeyed. Sappers were demolishing the protective wall around the old *wagon-lit* and exposing it to full view. The signing would take place exactly as twenty-two years before. Only this time Germany dictated the terms.

Hitler walked forward followed by his entourage. He gazed at the French statue of victory. It was now swathed in the Swastika flag of the Third Reich. A feeling of joy and revenge, so profound he could hardly contain it, swept through his body.

Revenge was sweet indeed!

And with the revenge went scorn and contempt for the losers.

Hitler stopped before a huge granite block in the middle of the bosky clearing. His retinue paused with him. Although Hitler had no command of French, he knew by heart the words engraved on the inscription: *Here on the Eleventh of November 1918 succumbed the Criminal Pride of the German Empire, vanquished by the Free People it attempted to enslave.*

Criminal Pride?

Was that the way to talk of his friends who had died so bravely in the trenches and on the barbed wire?

The French would learn from him what was criminal and what was not!

He turned to his entourage, hand on hip, and foot on the barrier around the hated stone.

'Somebody! Blow up this monstrosity!'

*

462

Hitler sat in Marshal Foch's chair, in Marshal Foch's train.

Five minutes later the French delegation arrived, shocked by the place they had come to – only hours before had they learned where the meeting was to be. General Huntziger led the group, with an admiral and airforce general and a diplomat in tow.

Nobody of importance, Hitler knew, ever attended surrenders.

Hitler sat only until the German terms had been read out and then left the *wagon-lit* without a glance at the Frenchmen. General Keitel remained, to go through the document with Huntziger: but he had no instructions to vary it, in any way. The French, Keitel explained, had to take it or leave it. They would have an 'Unoccupied Zone' in the South, which it could govern as it wished. Germany would occupy Paris and the industrial towns of the North. All anti-Nazi escapees in France to be handed back to the Germans. The French, with their long tradition of sanctuary, cavilled at that, but Keitel shouted them down. The French Navy was to be demobilised and kept in French ports. All French Prisoners of War would remain in Germany until complete hostilities ended. The French generals agreed that. They did not expect England to hold out long: 'She will have her neck wrung like a chicken's,' said one of them.

The negotiators dickered and bickered on other points, but the so-called French Government sitting in Bordeaux was composed of beaten men: Pétain (who was almost eighty, and had not fought) and Weygand, whose disastrously-botched campaign had lost France the War. The swarthy, moustachioed Pierre Laval, once a Socialist, now an eager collaborator, was hoping to ease the German terms anyhow he could: and the many other French defeatists and collaborators, in high and low places, felt the same way.

Their attitude was: 'Say what you like, Hitler is against Bolshevism!' And, 'Whatever happens, we must not let Hitler turn France into Poland!'

'We must at least be grateful for that!' they told each other.

The French signed, on Adolf Hitler's terms.

The Fuhrer took a holiday. He went to Paris.

Goebbels and Hoffmann made sure the world saw him, dancing a jig on the apron of the Eiffel Tower, gazing down at Napoleon's tomb, zooming in a long, well-armed motorcade along the Champs Elysees.

Not a single Parisian saw him.

For the simple reason that it all took place at five o'clock in the morning, before the great city was astir.

The Fuhrer did not mean to be assassinated at the time of his greatest triumph.

Winston Churchill was now Prime Minister of Great Britain.

He commanded a nation in chaos.

The survivors from Dunkirk had brought nothing back but their rifles and themselves.

They were tired, dispirited, and defeated.

The British people waited to be told what to do.

Churchill told them: 'I can promise you nothing but blood, sweat, toil and tears.' 'Let us so brace ourselves,' he said, 'to our duties that, if the British Empire lasts for a thousand years, men will still say, "*This* was their Finest Hour"'

He also taunted Hitler with the words, 'We are waiting for you. So are the fishes.'

They were good words, great words, but only words.

Everybody knew that. Including Hitler and Churchill himself.

But Churchill still had the Royal Air Force pretty much intact. Air Marshal Dowding had refused to send it to France to be lost piecemeal, despite Churchill's threats and pleas. Churchill did not like him for it.

There was also the Royal Navy.

And there was twenty-two miles of water.

Estimates varied as to what it would cost Hitler to take England.

British Staff-Officers said, languidly, 'Half the German Navy and two armoured Corps and untold infantry?'

The German Army was even less enthusiastic. Admiral Raeder could not guarantee to put the *Wehrmacht* ashore on the 'Broad Front' they asked for: from Dover to the Isle of Wight. 'Perhaps Dover to Sheerness?' the Navy suggested. The Army said, 'No good, the English could defend in depth on such a narrow front!'

The German Army was a continental army and did not like water.

The German Navy had an inferiority complex where the Royal Navy was concerned. They collected Invasion barges at Brest and Calais and the RAF bombed them by day and night. The tides began to flow and the English Channel became heavy with the mountainous swells of autumn. There was little time for delay.

In Washington, Isolationists in high places worked to keep the United States out of the War. They had powerful allies. Ambassador Joe Kennedy told Roosevelt the British had no hope of holding out. Colonel Lindberg, the idol fly-boy, said the same.

In the Wilhelmstrasse, civil-servants played with files in the hot airless rooms, wondering how long it would take England to see sense and come to table. They telephoned their mistresses, suggesting supper at the restaurant owned by Hitler's half-brother Alois, to whom Hitler never spoke.

In Whitehall, civil-servants worked day and night turning Britain into a tightly-controlled War-economy. They telephoned their wives in Bexley or Surbiton to say they would be sleeping at the office again, and did.

In the Chancellery, Hitler lost patience. He told Von Brauchitsch and Grand Admiral Raeder, 'A landing in England can succeed, providing air supremacy can be attained. The date of attack is to be decided. Begin preparations immediately.'

He also made another 'Peace Speech', at the Berlin Sportspalast, heard by all Europe. He stood in front of an ecstatic crowd, flushed with the heady success of the French campaign and had fun at Churchill's expense. 'From Britain I now hear only a single cry! The War must go on! I don't know whether Churchill has any idea what the continuation of this struggle will be like!' His voice held amusement and contempt in equal quantities. Churchill was a drunk and he did not like drunks. Churchill was upper-class and he hated upper-class persons of any stripe. Churchill had the effortless, detested, English superiority that all Germans secretly admired and hated at the same time. 'Churchill declares that even if Great Britain should perish, he would fight on from *Canada*!' Here Hitler waited for the laughs. 'I am not like other politicians. I am not the kind of leader who would run, like the Czechs and the Poles and some of the French leaders have run! To England! Where will they run now?' Hitler laughed out loud. 'Only the politicians will go to Canada! The *people* will have to remain in Britain! Churchill should listen when I say his great Empire will be destroyed – an Empire which it was never my intention to destroy!' Hitler paused for the applause he knew would come. It did. 'I appeal to commonsense in Great Britain. I can do this, I am not the vanquished begging favours, but the victor speaking in the name of Reason.' He paused and spoke the final words, softly: 'I can see no reason why this War must go on. It is up to the British?'

There was more applause than he expected. The German Volk had a great victory: they were in a mood to be charitable.

Churchill's reply came within the hour.

It was no.

Hoffmann the photographer is at a Conference at the Chancellery in Berlin, busily taking pictures of the high-ranking officers present, for that week's editions of Goebbels' newspapers and magazines. He is

465

sure that the captions around them will read: 'PLANS TO INVADE ENGLAND GO INTO FORCE'.

For Hoffmann knows the Invasion is scheduled to start at ten o'clock that very evening. He has been told, in the strictest confidence, by one of the staff-officers, who gloomily adds, 'If we go tonight it will be a disaster. Nobody wants it. It cannot succeed! Drop a word in his ear if you can!'

'Why me?' asked Hoffman, who intended to do no such thing.

'Well, we've been trying all day,' said the despondent officer.

Neither of them knew that Goering was ensconced with Hitler in his study at that very moment. The Field Marshal was leaning forward earnestly. 'Fuhrer, both the Wehrmacht and the *Kriegsmarine* are agreed on one thing. It will be costly to invade by sea, perhaps very costly.'

'We have barges and men and supporting aircraft ready to go,' said Hitler, but there was a note of doubt in his voice. He did not want to lose half his Navy and a quarter of his Army, and gain – what? A pile of rubble that could do him no harm if he left it standing as it was? Britain was out of the War, only they didn't know it. He grudged the English a single German soldier, a single German ship. He was going to need them, elsewhere.

Goering solved the problem for him.

'Fuhrer, I can reduce their cities to ashes by air attack,' he said, eagerly. 'I give you my word. Save your Army and Navy. Let *me* do it!'

Hitler sat frowning, in his stuffy Chancellery study: the blackout blinds were up, since Royal Air Force bombers (carrying bombs, not leaflets) were making tentative raids over the Reich. Not yet in any force. Just pin-pricks, but they irritated Adolf Hitler. He pondered for five whole minutes. Then he said, 'Not quite yet. Unleash the Luftwaffe on British military targets. If we take their forward-airfields, we invade . . .'

Goering smiled.

Some forward-airfields of the Royal Air Force were put out of action, but not enough. All those long summer weeks the Luftwaffe and the Royal Air Force did battle. It was in fighter-planes almost even, but with heavy advantage going to the Royal Air Force, which downed over a thousand bombers. In all, three thousand aircraft to the Luftwaffe's fifteen-hundred. Hitler said, 'I grow disenchanted with Goering's promises of victory.' Goering explained, 'The British have this Radio-direction-finder equipment, which tells their underground Operations Rooms the position of our bombers: their height, their numbers.' Hitler was unimpressed. His mind seemed to be on other things, Goering thought gratefully. The RAF bombed Berlin, in retaliation for a raid on civilian-targets in London. Then, Hitler stood in the Chancellery garden, shaking with anger. 'Very well! If they want to be barbarians, we too can do that!' He wanted action, retaliation. He listened to Goering plead: 'Fuhrer, let me bomb them out of the War? *By night!* My Luftwaffe can do it! I promise!'

It was too late, anyway, for Operation *Sea Lion*. It was almost October, now. No attempt at a sea-crossing could be entertained any longer, and the generals breathed again.

Hitler cancelled the daytime attacks, and gave Goering his head. The Luftwaffe began a nightly *blitz* on London and other big cities.

What Hitler did not know, and what the German General Staff did not know and what no single Senior British Commander knew, was that Winston Churchill had two RAF squadrons standing by, loaded with mustard-gas. If the invading Germans had got as far as the beaches, he would have used it.

XX

ADMIRAL Wilhelm Canaris was fifty-two years old, something of a dandy and extremely pessimistic by nature. Hitler didn't mind that in a spymaster, the last thing he wanted was some optimistic fool! Known as 'the Greek' because of his father's nationality, Canaris was something of a dilettante, Hitler suspected. Too sophisticated by half, Canaris had objected to the S.S. and Gestapo 'murder' tactics in Poland, especially those against the officer-class and the intellectuals, people, Hitler thought sourly, like himself. But the fact that the Generals disliked him did him no harm with Hitler.

'Tell me what the *Abwehr* knows about Soviet Russia?'

Canaris shook his immaculate shirt-cuffs and shrugged. 'Very little, Fuhrer. It is almost impossible for a foreign power to glean any information at all. Foreigners working at the Embassies are spied on. These people spy on themselves. On their own mothers!' Hitler grimaced and Canaris coughed, delicately. As far as he was concerned, Nazi Germany was not so very different. Thank God the *Abwehr* still had some decent standards and was not in the business of beginning interrogations by pulling off a suspect's fingernails with a pair of pliers. He could leave all that to the Gestapo. Canaris had to provide Hitler with information about the enemy. Until now, a much cleaner process. He went on: 'I do not disagree with the figures Halder and the others have given you, Fuhrer. They are based on what I have given them. I do not have a single reliable agent in place in Moscow. Would that I had.'

Hitler studied the slight, silver-haired, foxy little man and recalled that Canaris had always seemed plagued with doubts before his own large decisions (Poland, France) but after he had been proven right had instantly declared the Fuhrer a genius! 'The Hungarians, Romanians, Yugoslavs? Surely some of these people,' he suggested to Canaris, 'know something about Soviet Russia. They are on her borders!'

468

Canaris said, regretfully, no. 'The Soviet Secret Police are very efficient. So much so that millions are purged, dead, or in the camps in the Arctic Circle. They work them to death there. Freezing temperatures, almost no food.'

'That is unproductive,' said Hitler. 'But their General Staff?'

'They have good men,' replied Canaris. 'Or rather they *had* good men. The Show Trials got rid of the old ones about whom we knew something. The younger officers are just names to us.'

'Canaris, your department sounds to me to be inefficient?' said Hitler, quite mildly. It occurred to Canaris that he perhaps preferred no news to bad news.

'Nobody knows any more than we do,' said Canaris, equably.

'Or less, seemingly.' Hitler brooded. 'What of their morale?'

'Fuhrer, I can confidently say it is not good.' Hitler nodded approvingly. It was, Canaris knew, what he thought himself.

Canaris brightened a little. An estimation of enemy morale did not require hard knowledge. He relied on White Russian emigrés to provide him with information, said to come from friends inside Russia. But he did not trust it. The White Russians, ex-nobles and sometimes even minor royalty, were poor now, subsisting as tax-drivers and whores all over the West. They had good educations and, consequently, good imaginations. Canaris knew that. He'd paid them good deutchmarks for unreliable crap. 'The mass of the people are serfs,' he told Hitler, confidently. 'Little different from what they were under the Czar. My sources...' Canaris hesitated. The White Russians were still aristocrats even if they did not have a pot to piss in. 'My sources, Fuhrer, tell me that Stalin and the men at the top are generally hated. The standard of living is bad, far below what we know in the West.'

Hitler said, 'The poorer and more primitive the soldier, the better he fights.'

Canaris thought this shallow and silly but merely replied, 'In a modern war, a man needs to be something of an engineer. The Soviet peasant, used to shovelling shit all day, is hardly up to driving a tank, with all its complicated mechanisms.'

'Von Brauchitsch says we should cut off the heads of the leaders. Halder says we should expect surprises. Nobody tells me what Stalin has *got*?'

Canaris protested: 'Nobody *knows*, Fuhrer! But it cannot be what we have, can it? They have desperately bad harvests. They cannot feed their people! We know that much, from the peasants who flee into Romania and Hungary, and even Poland. They all tell the same story. Hunger. Dirt. Poverty.' Canaris laid it on thick, since he knew so few facts. 'The view, generally held by military experts, all over the West, British and American as well as ourselves, is that Soviet Russia is not so very different from Czarist Russia. She will fold pretty much as she folded at Tannenberg, when Russian soldiers ran into the attack without arms, hoping to pick up a comrade's rifle.'

Hitler looked pensive. 'They lost almost a million men in the first year of the last War. Yet they went on fighting until 1917?'

'That is true, Fuhrer. But they were not fighting against tanks and Stukas. They will go down as the Poles went down.'

'The Poles are Slavs, lazy and dirty.' Hitler was off on one of his history lessons, then suddenly said: 'What do you expect to happen, Admiral Canaris, when *Barbarossa* goes ahead?'

'Like Halder and Von Brauchitsch, I expect almost instant victory.'

'Where would you aim your strongest forces?'

Canaris looked surprised. 'At the capital, Moscow, naturally.'

'Why?'

'It is the railroad centre. It is the supply centre. It is the centre of what they call a Parliament. It is the Civil Service headquarters. And, presumably, Stalin will be there?'

'Is that a question, Canaris?'

'No, Fuhrer. But he stays in the Kremlin most of the time. Unless he's at his dacha, and that isn't far away. Yes, I would go to take the capital.'

'That,' said Hitler, 'is what Napoleon did. He found it burning! Anything new to tell me?'

Canaris smiled. 'Reich Minister Goering sent a delegation to Moscow to visit their aircraft factories. I understand he was impressed.' He was reluctant to mention Goering's name, in any favourable way. Since the failure of the Luftwaffe to either prepare the way to invade England in the Summer or bomb her into submission in the following winter, Goering was thought, generally, to be in decline.

'Anything the Soviets showed us would be the best they had,' sniffed Hitler.

'True,' said Canaris, knowing it would be.

For himself, he was astonished the Reds had any good aircraft at all. He said as much. 'They have all these Five Year Plans, but they starve.' He added, 'Of course, the Japanese calculate their army at 250 divisions. I don't know how much credence we can put on that estimate.'

Said Hitler, thoughtfully: 'That is a lot of men, if true, which I do not believe it is. The quality is what we hear nothing about?'

'The Japanese,' said Canaris, hating to be specific, it could so easily rebound, 'Share a border with Russia in Manchuria. They rate the Soviet Eastern Army highly.' As Hitler's brow knitted, he added, hastily,

'In terms of clothing and equipment and so on. They have not fought them, so they know nothing of their fighting qualities.'

Kannenberg brought in coffee and cakes. Hitler ate three cakes and drank cumin tea. Canaris sipped his own milkless coffee and grimaced, but forced the grimace into a polite smile. The rubbish Hitler ate and drank. Who did he think it helped, eating like a poverty-stricken clerk? Of course, a clerk could not afford the Black Forest gateau Hitler was spearing with his cake-fork.

'The Soviet forces concentrated in front of Moscow concern me,' said Hitler. 'How many are there?' Canaris said it was impossible to know. 'The Italians,' Canaris added, hoping to deflect Hitler, 'Are fairly sure we have the British on the run in the desert?'

Hitler swallowed another mouthful of cake and cream. He felt a surge of energy: the sugar went into his system almost at once. 'The Italians are very lucky to have us. Or rather to have Erwin Rommel! I despair of them, and I feel for Mussolini. What a crowd to have to lead to War! Rommel has had the British running for months. Out of El Agheila, out of Sollum, he is on the doorstep of Tobruk.'

'The Italians are lucky we are in North Africa at all,' said Canaris.

'We have to be there,' said Hitler. 'Churchill knows how important it is. He even sent an army there right after Dunkirk.'

'Talking of Churchill,' Canaris said, quickly, 'I do have a small piece of excellent information. The Bulgarian Ambassador in London has been more than helpful. The Bulgarians still have representatives in London. He tells me the English are standing up well to our bombardments but . . .'

As Canaris feared, Hitler held up his hand for silence. 'The English are a Germanic people. They are not easily cowed. Their ruling class may be effete and decadent, but the ordinary people have good blood in them. Himmler does not admire the English,' added Hitler. 'He says they are Germanic but their blood is too diluted. Indeed, you could always talk to Himmler, or Heydrich, about the Soviets. You know Reinhard very well, am I right?' Hitler's bright blue eyes bore into Canaris'.

Canaris nodded. 'I trained Reinhard Heydrich as a naval cadet. We live close by one another even now, Fuhrer. He has exceeded even my own hopes for him. He has done excellent work.'

Hitler agreed. He knew, of course, that Canaris hated Heydrich these days, that their respective positions demanded it! Reinhard Heydrich was Head of the State Security Office. Canaris had to work with him, whether he liked it or not. The S.S. was the way to the top, for so many ordinary Germans, without serving in the *Wehrmacht* or the *Kriegsmarine*. It was a State within a State. At some time, Hitler suspected, the S.S.

would have to take over the State, become the premier power in Germany. Hitler knew every S.S. man was *his*. He could not say that of the Army. The Army would not soil its hands on very dirty but necessary things that had to be done. The S.S. did those things without complaint. Look at Poland! From his reports, Hitler knew that Heydrich ran it with total ruthlessness. The Jews were in the ghettos, and the thirty thousand German Gypsies with them. The Gypsies had left India a thousand years before, certainly. But they were nomads, like the Jews. They had nothing to do with the blue-eyes Aryans who had left ten thousand years before them. They would not work at a job, belonged to no religion and were parasites. They could share the fate of the Jews. Hitler wondered what Stalin did with the Gypsies? His Jews had an Identity Card stamped 'J', he knew that much. Stalin was no doubt, in his way, a great man. But he stood in the way of history.

'Yes,' Hitler said to Canaris, 'you should speak to Reinhard about the Soviets. He runs Internal State Security after all. There may be things he knows you don't.' Hitler stood up. The audience was over.

'Fuhrer,' said Canaris, rising too, 'I respect and love Reinhard. But I can't think he knows anything about the Soviets that I do not.' He smiled. 'But I will certainly talk to him, in case there is.'

He may know things I do not, thought Canaris, but I know things about Reinhard Heydrich that nobody else knows. I know exactly who he is and what he is: I know about the Jewish thing and I know about the homosexuality. I know it has not stopped! Himmler was said to have a file on everybody in Nazi Germany. He, Wilhelm Canaris, had files on the people Himmler had no files on. Including Himmler himself.

To survive, such deceit was necessary.

The head of the German Secret Service saluted Adolf Hitler, whom he had always seen as an upstart corporal and a nobody, and clicked his heels.

'*Hitler ist Deutschland! Deutschland ist Hitler! Sieg Heil!*'

Poor old Hess had shouted those words often enough at Nuremberg. Even then Canaris had seen that one day somebody might have to try to stop Adolf Hitler, for Germany's sake. Now, it was probably too late.

Canaris turned smartly and left the room.

Hitler sat down, closed his eyes and rubbed them, then carefully fitted on his spectacles, and looked at a paper on his desk. It was weeks old. It told him that Rudi Hess had defected to London. Or anyway, to Scotland. It was old news now, but he still felt deserted. What had possessed Rudi, who had been with him since the beginning, to do such a thing?

The idiot had only flown to England to arrange a 'Peace Pact' with Churchill! Hitler could still not believe it had ever happened. But it had: Hess' adjutants had been imprisoned for not looking after him better. His wife Ilse was spared, but his children were rechristened. He had taken Rudi's name off the Party rolls. Of course, Rudi had always had a screw loose, everybody knew that. He was dead, or as good as. Churchill would squeeze him dry, like an orange. It was possible he'd tell them about *Barbarossa*. Hitler sighed. What did it matter now, if he did? It was too late for Churchill or anybody else to stop *Barbarossa* now.

Late in that hot Summer of 1941, Adolf came to the Berghof.

He wore his field-grey uniform the few days he was there and Eva Braun knew that when he went away she would not see him again for a long time. Eva knew great plans were afoot. She had sat, hardly breathing, at the news on the German radio that Mussolini's adventure against the Greeks had become bogged down. Adolf had sent German troops to his aid, chasing the British, first out of Greece, then off the island of Crete. Paratroopers and glider-squads led by General Karl Student had taken it by storm. It had been thrilling to hear the victory of German arms proclaimed loudly over the radio, after the cymbal-crashing *Radetsky March* had identified the station. It seemed in those halcyon days that to hear that piece of stirring martial music was to hear nothing but good news, and to thrill to the fact that one was a German and that Germany, under Adolf Hitler, was in the right, and unbeatable.

Eva Braun always felt that when she heard the *Radetsky March*.

All summer the Berghof was a hive of excitement, activity and optimism. Bormann had installed deep air-raid shelters and the signals-section was greatly extended. Everywhere stalked officers in field-grey, sometimes huge booted creatures like Otto Gunsche, Commanding Officer of Hitler's *Leibstandarte*, sometimes the diminutive Dietrich, forever holding a bunch of newspapers or marked-up press-releases for the Fuhrer's approval. Dietrich had once half-suggested to Eva that she try to get Adolf to rise earlier ('Only an hour earlier, my dear Frau') so that he could prepare statements for the German evening newspapers and the Foreign Press. Eva had laughed at him. As if she or anybody else could persuade Adolf to get up in the morning! He worked and worried all night, she reprimanded Dietrich, while everybody else was sleeping. 'His insomnia is worse than ever. He rarely sleeps before dawn. His stomach cramps are improved, thanks to Doctor Morell, but he never takes off any real time. Who does more for Germany?' Abashed, Dietrich retreated.

Still, Adolf was not as well as he should have been and there was nothing Eva or anybody else could do about it. The fat and grubby Morell (his body odour was so repugnant Eva could hardly bear to be near him) was giving Adolf too many injections, in Eva's opinion. God alone knew what was in them. She objected about this to Adolf but was put in her place as quickly as she'd put Dietrich in his. 'My dear Eva,' said Hitler, 'It doesn't matter at all if I live a shorter life, in the end, because I do not rest properly or take holidays like a bank-manager. In the end all that matters is, have I completed my mission?'

Eva had looked past him to see the eyes of Morell on them both, as he sat, a fixture now at the Berghof, or wherever Adolf was to be found. The venerealogist was now the Fuhrer's personal physician. Eva expected that he would go with Adolf to Russia or wherever, once the War started in the East. She knew it must be soon, and trembled with excitement and anxiety at the idea. Russia was not like Poland or France, was it? The place was unknown, unknowable. But Adolf said the Bolsheviks were the ultimate enemy, and on things like that he was never wrong.

Also, this time he was not alone, was he?

The Romanians, the Hungarians and the Finns had all promised to be with him, in the attack, when it came. They had no idea when it would be. Eva knew this because Adolf had flatteringly and thrillingly, taken her into his confidence, late on his last night, as they sat over his tea (and, in Eva's case, cognac) in Eva's living-room on the top floor of the Berghof. In woollen shirt and his braces, collar undone and shoes off, Adolf sat opposite with Eva. She had on her high heels, silk stockings with garters, French-knickers, silk evening dress from Paris, brought as a gift by Bormann (who, now Hess was gone, was running the Reich while the Fuhrer concentrated all his energies on the War). Eva even had some scent behind her ears and in the crook of her elbow and behind her knees, on the insides of her thighs. She was trying too hard, she knew: but with Adolf that was usually necessary. Often, he simply became too weary for sex. His ration of daily stress did not help the sexual urge. She was sure Doctor Morell's injections had something to do with the fact that Adolf seemed to desire her sexually less and less these days. On one thing she was determined: they would make love on this last night at the Berghof.

'Well, at least the Americans stay out,' murmured Eva. With the defection of Hess and the sinking of the battleship *Bismarck* in the Atlantic, there was not a lot of good news on tap and she tried always to talk good news to Adolf. Rudi's defection had been a terrible blow and Adolf had raged about the Navy's incompetence in sending the *Bismarck* to operate, virtually alone, against the Royal Navy. All those young cadets, only sixteen years old, lost, 400 of them. Germany had wept for those boys.

'We must win in Russia,' said Hitler. 'Then England will have to throw her hand in. She'll have no alternative.'

'That's good, surely,' sympathised Eva, kicking off her expensive shoes and tucking her feet up on the sofa, being careful to show the silk-clad legs as she did so, and to carelessly leave them on view. 'What about the Italians?' asked Eva, covering her legs only by lifting her skirt high in the first place.

'Mussolini will send some divisions. Not many. He had his hands full in North Africa.'

'You did well to rescue him in Greece,' ventured Eva.

'I had no choice. Otherwise the British would have struck north and taken the oil-fields at Ploesti, or sabotaged them. We need that oil desperately. Without it we will lose the war. We also need Romania's army. And Hungary's. They'll be in, come the day. The Finns – what a brave people they are! – have given their pledge already.' Hitler shook his head. 'I intended to go on the attack in Russia in early May, or even before. I have lost five whole weeks rescuing Mussolini from his Greek folly. I have to wait for those troops to regroup. It all takes time.'

'Will it matter, those five weeks?'

'It should not. But how can one tell, in a War?'

He sounded, suddenly, apprehensive and sad. Eva's heart went out to him. What a lonely figure he was! Everybody wanted a piece of him. They crowded round him, Bormann particularly with his new tactic of putting long propositions to the Fuhrer which, on approval, would instantly turn into Fuhrer-Orders. Then there were the Generals, jostling for notice and promotion, vainly kept off by Keitel and Jodl.

The fact that Adolf was talking to Eva about the attack on Soviet Russia was, she knew, some kind of farewell. Adolf had all this to worry about and all she wanted to do was get him to bed this last night together. It was a silly wish and yet it seemed to matter to her a great deal. She knew that Adolf was more thoughtful when he was away than when he was at the Berghof. He telephoned each day, usually in the late afternoon, from the Chancellery in Berlin. Sometimes he stayed on the telephone a full half-hour. In the Berghof he seemed to relax and fall asleep whenever he was not stimulated by talk, usually his own. Tomorrow, she thought, he will be gone.

Now, he was drifting into a weary sleep on her sofa and there was nothing she could do about it. Adolf's eyes were closed and he was breathing gently and rhythmically. To wake him now would be an unkindness. He would almost certainly be jumpy and either talk for a long time or go into his own room to try to sleep. Tears came to her eyes as she sat opposite from him, scented and dressed in her finery, and realised that *this* really was her farewell to the rather unhealthy-looking middle-aged man who meant life itself to her. His head had slumped back, his mouth was open showing his ill-fitting dentures, and the lank strand of black hair had fallen across his face.

Eva sipped her cognac until it was all gone. Then, very quietly, she switched off the central chandelier, leaving only one table-lamp burning. She sat once more on the sofa and looked at Adolf quite steadily, trying to fix him in her mind permanently. But after a while she tired of this, her own eyes closed, and she, too, slept.

Next day Hitler was back in Berlin, at the Chancellery.

The latest news from Russia was that vast Soviet armies were now grouping along their own borders. 'They know we are going to attack but don't want to admit it,' Halder said. 'What I can't understand is why they just wait like a fat sow at the butcher's. They should strike first, if they are ready!'

Hitler was cheered by Halder's irritation. 'They have seen us in Poland and France. Stalin is terrified of us.'

Halder pursed his lips. 'Stalin has taken over the chairmanship of the Council of People's Commissars. That must mean a crisis that only he can deal with. I think when they fight they'll fight hard. The Commissars run their army. I'm not sure it's wise to execute them on sight. Their professional soldiers are likely to know more than any Commissar about how to fight a war.'

'Commissars! *Jews*, you mean!'

Hitler was restless, manic, unable to keep still. The time was so near. All that had to happen was for the whistle to blow! What did Franz Halder mean by not executing the Red Commissars? Had he not made himself plain to the Generals a month before? Had he not made an effort to put some spunk into their pathetic, gentlemanly loins? 'The war against Russia will be such that it cannot be conducted in a chivalrous fashion! This struggle is one of ideologies and racial differences and will have to be conducted with unprecedented, merciless and unrelenting harshness! All officers will have to rid themselves of obsolete ideologies! My orders must be executed without contradiction. The Commissars are in a death struggle with National Socialism! Therefore, the Commissars will be liquidated!' Halder, self-contained, uniformed, bathed, barbered, shaved and ready – to him this *Der Tag* was simply *work*! – was silent. 'The Generals have their orders,' continued Hitler. 'Himmler will seal off vast tracts of captured territory and there the S.S. will take control.' Had Halder not read the *Most Secret* Memorandum? Hitler almost knew it by heart: 'There may be famine in the wake of our success. Any attempt to save the Russian population from death by starvation by importing food from Germany is forbidden'.

Jodl came in the room carrying a file for Hitler's signature. It was something unimportant. Hitler waved it away. Jodl and Halder were calm. It was as if they had been doing this every day of their lives, whereas to him it was the culmination of everything else he had ever done! He was Atilla the Hun, he had even destroyed his own brother (well, what else was Roehm?) as Atilla had. Like Atilla, he lived simply and ate sparingly. Had not the Roman Pricius, who had seen Atilla in his camp, been intrigued by the man: short, squat, with deep-set, magnetic eyes – and what, pray, did people say about *his* eyes? Atilla, Pricius had observed, sat at a rude table, eating a simple meal from a wooden platter, while his lieutenants picked at delicacies on silver plate robbed from the Romans? Had not Pricius been impressed (and what a thing it was to impress a Roman like Pricius!) that Atilla was also not entirely a Barbarian, but could, on occasion, be kindly and considerate? What did the Volk say of *him*, Adolf Hitler? They said that, like Atilla, he had the interests of the Tribe at heart. And to whom did a leader owe everything, his very being, his reason for living, the reason his heart beat and his pulse throbbed? Why, to his Tribe of course, as Atilla the Hun had known, all those centuries ago, when the shaven and perfumed Pricius had come to him with a false treaty and a plea: please don't attack Rome and her minions, show them mercy, become a Jewish Christian like us, turn the other cheek, be *circumcised*! And what had Atilla's answer been? The sword, the axe, the rope, the torch!

That too would be his, Adolf Hitler's, reply to his enemies.

He was conscious, suddenly, that Jodl must have said something, by the way the two men were looking at each other, puzzled and amused. Jodl repeated his question: 'Well, Fuhrer, all is done. We can do no more. What do you think will happen when we attack?'

'We have only to kick in the door and the whole building will fall down!'

The two generals laughed, the rough, male sound echoing in the huge, panelled room. Hitler did not join them: they seemed removed from him by time and place. The sun shone hot through the long windows of the Reich Chancellery. Outside, the limes swayed gently in the summer breeze; the heat and fecundity of the earth itself drifted into the room, through the wide-open windows. It did not seem possible, in that ripe moment, that there was such a season as winter.

'Let the world hold its breath,' Hitler said. He sat at a table, uniformed, motionless, for twelve hours as the terrifying events unfolded: 'I have waited all my life for this, the end of Marxism,' he whispered.

In the early morning of Monday, June 21st. 1941, along the German frontier from the Black Sea in the South to the Arctic in the North, three million soldiers of the Wehrmacht (soon to be supported by Romanian and Finish divisions) with a total of three thousand tanks and two thousand bombers and fighter planes, attacked the Soviet Union. The German Ambassador in Moscow had just handed Molotov, the Soviet Foreign Minister, Hitler's formal Declaration of War. The taciturn Molotov, who had earlier made to an annoyed Fuhrer the famous remark: 'If the English are finished, why are we having this conversation in an air-raid shelter?' had nothing witty or insolent to say now. He stared at the paper in his hand, in disbelief, and then looked up at the German Ambassador and asked, 'But what have we done to deserve *this?*'

Ribbentrop had finally told the Soviet Ambassador in Berlin – at four o'clock in the morning, the news of the attack. Then he had broken it to the Italian, Hungarian, French, Japanese and Romanian representatives. They were as surprised as Molotov had been. They knew it was coming and yet, and yet . . . ? The world did indeed hold its breath, but not for long. By the end of the following day all those countries (Hungary apart) had pledged support for Adolf Hitler and Nazi Germany in their fight against Bolshevism! Romanian troops were in action at once. The Luftwaffe attacked Kiev, Krovno, Odessa, Sevastapol and Murmansk. Hundreds of Soviet aircraft were set ablaze on their own airfields. The first reports over the German radio announced that many thousands of Russian prisoners had already been taken.

Hitler bathed, shaved, put on his field-grey uniform and joined his heavily-protected motorcade for the Front.

The *Radetsky march* crashed out on the German radio, one month later.

Every man, woman and child in Europe listened.

'Smolensk is in our hands!' cried the announcer.

Smolensk was 400 miles inside the Soviet Union.

A week later, the *Radetsky March* again.

'German tank-forces are at the gates of Kiev!'

Bock's Centre Army was at Smolensk: Moscow was only 200 miles away. The Northern Army under Von Leeb was pressing towards Leningrad. The Southern Army commanded by Von Runstedt was almost at the Dnieper.

They took 350,000 Soviet prisoners.

The Germans had nowhere to put them.

They marched in long winding columns, peasant boys glad to be out of the War, in dirty, ragged uniforms and cardboard shoes, to Prisoner of War Camps that had food for only a few hundred men, not the tens of starving thousands that besieged them. One third died of starvation before they even got to the Camps. Many more died, once they arrived, of dysentery and typhus. Any man who fell out on the march, for whatever reason, was shot. Hitler sent an order: 'The Russians stay in Poland! I don't want them inside the Reich, spreading their disease of Communism!'

Hitler's *Kommissar Order*: 'Identify and shoot all Political Officers', was obeyed to the letter. S.S. murder squads scoured the camps looking for them. Military Officers of field-rank went to Camps in Germany and Poland and got some food, a little bread and some thin soup. Amongst them was Stalin's eldest son, Jacob Djugashvili, a Soviet tank-commander. He was kept alive: but later he deliberately walked into a *verboten* area and was shot by guards who neither knew nor cared who he was. German prisoners, in Soviet hands, as yet were few.

To the surprise of the German victors, whirling along on a thousand-mile front, from the frozen plains of the Baltic to the hot, sultry roads to the Black Sea, a few units of the Soviet Army fought and died where they stood. But in the main they operated as huge masses of infantry, badly led, blundering into the encirclements the Panzers laid for them.

'Get me Leningrad!' Hitler told his generals. 'To cut off the Bolshevik head. I need the Ukraine for the grain harvest!'

'Moscow?' queried Bock, on his field-telephone, covered in dust and dirt, travel-weary from a month or more, no longer young and no longer feeling it. 'What about Moscow?'

'Never mind Moscow,' was Hitler's message. 'I want the *armies* destroyed, not their capital occupied!'

Bock thought about that: but pressed on for Moscow just the same.

At his Headquarters, the Wolf's Lair, in East Prussia, Hitler was ecstatic. Even Atilla could not have been happier when the Romans broke and ran before him! Even the phlegmatic Jodl was smiling. The staff-officers laughed and slapped each other on the back, when they weren't swiping at the mosquitos with specially-made metal swatters. The camouflaged wooden complex was hidden in a thick forest, not far from the town of Rastenburg, close to the General Staff Headquarters at Angerberg. A collection of wooden huts and concrete block-houses, Hitler's quarters were stuffy by day and cold by night. The ventilation-system was noisy, and sleep was difficult, not just for Hitler but for everybody: his staff and his two girl-secretaries.

Hitler's day was to his usual pattern. He rose at nine, bathed and shaved, went to the Map Room to hear the latest positions of the armies sent over from the Staff Headquarters. He breakfasted frugally, on orange juice and toast. Then to the daily 'Conference' in the Map Room where Hitler would gladly hear from his adjutants of massive enemy losses: aircraft, tanks, men. There seems to be an inexhaustible supply of them. Then lunch, in the small, communal dining-room, a meat stew for most of his staff, for himself a vegetable hot-pot. Later, in the broiling heat, everybody sleeps for an hour or two. Then, for Hitler, more briefings by his adjutants: details of victories and holdups, the small-change of War. On a map, Jodl thinks, it looks very clean and clear, arrows pointing here and there to signify an advance. The dead bodies and the blood don't show. The dead horses don't show. The smashed and burning tanks don't show, with the crews burned black as cinders. Here, it is all clean and clear.

In the evening Hitler has supper, more hot-pot for those who want it. He has cakes and tea with Morell, his adjutants, Gunsche and his secretaries. They listen to the radio as they eat their cakes and drink their tea, having given up on the hot suppers sent by the cooks. Hitler insists that they eat army-rations and no more. 'Victory is as good as won! The Russians retreat to no plan!' What else should we expect? They are a peasant army, no organisation anywhere but at company-level and not much there. No commissariat, no ammunition supply-line, no battalion or divisional back-up worth talking about.' He sipped his cumin tea, a lecturer. 'The higher the echelon, the worse the performance! At company-level, occasionally disconcertingly good. Excellent use of ground, stubborn, primitive, brave. If well-led, could prove difficult to dislodge. But like the British at the Marne and the Somme, they are led by donkeys!'

The scented, monocled colonels and majors of the *Wehrmacht*, schooled at Potsdam and at Heidelberg and in Poland, Norway and France, found it in the main almost too easy. Russian soldiers, in their dirty grey-serge blouses, subsided on bits of stale bread shoved into their pouches. Once taken prisoner, a great many of the tattered horde attached themselves to German units in the guise of cooks, mechanics, horse-copers, handymen of all kinds, in return for food. Hitler, on hearing about this, angrily forbade his units to harbour these men, who should be sent to the rear at once. The forward-units never got the order. Or if they did, they disobeyed it. Bone-tired and choking on dust, with very little sleep for six weeks now, the Panzer crews were in no mood to refuse free help. It only showed, they said to each other, that these peasants didn't know what the War was about, probably didn't even know *who* they were fighting! They knew enough, however, to keep out of the death-camps at the rear.

Hitler, gazing at the maps of Russia on the wall of the Bunker, gave his opinion: 'We'll be in Moscow by the middle of August!' Word came that the Russian Government in Moscow was burning its files and getting ready to evacuate the city. Where would they go, Hitler asked. 'East beyond the Urals,' he decided, answering his own question. 'The War,' he asserted at one of his late supper talks, 'will be over by the end of September and we can all go home.'

They all blinked sleepily and smiled. It would be good to be home again.

'All of Europe supports us! That is something the British and the Americans will never admit to, not now, and probably not ever! Hungary and Bulgaria and Finland and Romania are with us to the end! The new state of Slovakia is with us. Thousands of Frenchmen have rallied to us, we have the best bomber-pilots in the French Air Force in our ranks. Norway, Denmark, Belgium, Spain, all these countries are raising volunteer-divisions to defend Europe from Bolshevism! They don't have to do it, nobody's forcing them to do it! They are Europeans and see where their duty lies!'

Only Japan stayed aloof. 'She's playing her own game,' said Hitler, laughing at the radio-news of Churchill's offer of help to the Soviet Union. 'He hates Communism as much as I do! And what help can *he* give anybody?'

Hitler said, 'By instinct, the Russian does not incline towards a higher form of society. The Germanic people are active. A man works from morning to night. To the Russian peasant, civilisation is vodka! He always does as little work as he can. Our dedication to work is beyond him.' He went on talking his thoughts aloud, to the company. 'Can anything be done in Russia without the help of the Orthodox priest? Only the priest has ever been able to get the Russian to work – by promising him happiness in the next world!' As he spoke, Hitler noticed an officer making notes, and recalled that he had given Bormann permission for his 'random thoughts' to be collected for posterity. It gave his mind a rest from the hammering it received during the working day: logistics and decisions, decisions and logistics.

One logistic worried him very much.

The size of the Soviet tanks!

To Canaris, who was foolish enough to venture forward into the Command Bunker, Hitler put with brutal directness the questions that worried him. 'The enemy has built, in the last year or two, massive concrete fortifications in front of almost every town or object of strategic value! He has built fifty airfields we know absolutely nothing about and presumably he has the aircraft and the pilots to man them?' His voice rose and Canaris shivered. 'Now, we discover he has a tank weighing fifty tons – fifteen tons heavier than our Tiger! – with armour plate inches thicker than anything we have! We are using our 88-millimetre artillery-pieces on it because our ordinary anti-tank shells bounce off!' Hitler leaned forward. 'How many of them are there? Even more important, why did we know nothing of any of this? Why did the *Abwehr* know nothing?'

'Fuhrer, as I explained, we know so little because they are a secret people. Churchill has called them a riddle inside an enigma!' said Canaris, sweating uncomfortably, trying to keep a level tone. 'But surely our advance could hardly go faster?'

'We have slowed down in the last two weeks. Due partly to the depth of resistance put up by their tankmen, partly to the fact that their infantry have started to fight to the last man. Stalin has told the Russians to fight behind the lines, to turn themselves into partisans.' Hitler rubbed a hand across his face.

'Fuhrer, what can unarmed peasants do?'

Hitler erupted savagely. 'They can blow up bridges, burn crops, burn trees and forests, destroy rolling stock, arms-dumps, attack us by night! Stalin has instituted a Scorched Earthy policy, as the Russians did to Napoleon in 1812! He has found a new slogan: *Death to the German Invader*! The Soviet radio pumps it out all day and all night!'

Canaris wished to God he was back at sea. At least that was a clean place to fight, just yourself and the enemy and that enemy of all sailors, the water. Here, the way the Corporal was putting it, the German Army was about to fight a whole people, men, women and children. Would the Russian peasants do what Stalin ordered? Well, who could guess as to that? Rosenberg was saying openly that they should have treated the Ukranians and others as anti-Stalin, made them allies. Hitler had said no. 'Your *Abwehr* have let me down, Canaris. If I had known of the existence of these huge tanks I might not have attacked this year.'

Canaris went ashen and stammered a reply. 'Fuhrer, how was anybody to know about these tanks? They are a secret people.'

Hitler said nothing to that, but simply nodded, in a tired way. One of the aides had told Canaris he was not going to bed until five o'clock in the morning, and rarely went out for air. Did he expect to keep well, in an unhealthy place like this, with a regime like that?

Outside, in the haze, tiny drops of moisture collected on the herbs and grass at the side of the road. It did not, as yet, freeze.

That evening, after supper, Hitler strove to ease his mind of the worry of the monster tanks and the slowing down of the Panzers. After coffee and cakes he addressed his heavy-eyed audience. 'The heaviest blow that ever struck humanity was the coming of Christianity. Bolshevism is

Christianity's illegitimate-child. Both are inventions of the Jew! The deliberate lie of the Next World came from Christianity! Bolshevism tells a lie of the same kind, when it claims to bring Liberty to All Men! In reality, it seeks only to enslave them!'

Hitler leaned back in his chair. 'Without Christianity, we would not have had Islam. The Roman Empire, under Germanic influence, would have developed in the direction of World Domination. Let it not be said that Christianity brought man the life of the soul! That evolution was in the natural order of things!' A final thought struck him. 'You know, Stalin is one of the most extraordinary figures in world history! He began as a small cleric and he has never stopped being a cleric! Stalin governs from his office, by a bureaucracy that obeys his every word. When Stalin loses Moscow, he is finished! We will turn Russia into our India! Every German soldier will have his farm and his plot of land. We will educate the Russians just enough to read the signs on our Autobahns!'

He yawned again and got to his feet. The officer in the corner stopped writing. '*Guten Nacht* everybody,' Hitler said, and left the room.

It was almost two o'clock in the morning.

Eva Braun decided to go back to work.

The Berghof seemed so empty without Adolf.

Besides, Munich was home: Vadi and Mutti were there, and her sisters, and Adolf did not seem likely to be home for months. She telephoned Heinrich Hoffmann's shop and volunteered to come in two days a week? Hoffmann, just back from the Russian front, was delighted. She called in, as soon as she got to Munich, before she even went to the apartment on the Prinzregentstrasse.

Hoffmann was, as ever, genial and he had what she wanted most, news of Adolf. He poured them both some cognac and showed her his latest photographs, taken only a few days before: of tanks crashing through the Russian countryside, raising vast clouds of dust, the begoggled S.S. tank commanders in their black uniforms, peering out of their turrets. Withered, uncomprehending old peasant-women shading their eyes at the amazing sight: the German infantry in shirtsleeves, caps set jauntily on their heads, gas-mask containers and haversacks slung behind their backs, out of the way of their machine-guns. Aircrews, sprinting to their Messerschmitts and Dorniers, ready to fly another sortie against the enemy, and many, many other photographs of this astonishing war.

Eva looked closely at pictures of Adolf, standing in the dust-covered Mercedes, master of all he surveyed. She thrilled to the sight of victory.

The *sound* of victory she heard every day on the radio but this was proof indeed.

'Tell me, how *is* he?'

'Tired,' said Hoffmann. 'Mosquitos, heat and all that, the whole country is a shit-house, if you'll pardon my French.'

Poor Adolf, she thought, how awful a place to be cooped-up in.

'Has he been forward with the troops, then?'

'Yes, but don't worry. Ivan is running backwards so fast he'll be in Moscow this time tomorrow!'

'Things are going that well?'

Hoffmann pursed his lips. He seemed oddly hesitant. Then he said, with a great enthusiasm that was somehow bogus: 'We are almost in sight of their twin capitals, Moscow and Leningrad. Adolf has issued orders, so I was told on highest authority, that they are both to be levelled to the ground, once we take them!'

Eva frowned. 'Leningrad? Hasn't it got a lot of palaces and things?'

Hoffmann grinned, and put a finger along his nose. 'And a lot of priceless paintings and works of art! Don't worry, they won't get destroyed. We'll bring them home to the Reich.'

'Yes,' said Eva. 'Of course.' She didn't care about the works of art. She wanted Adolf home, alive, as soon as possible.

'What news of home?' asked Hoffmann. 'I got back only yesterday but hear the *Terrorflugers* were over the Ruhr again last night.'

Eva shook her head. 'We are told very little on the radio. Only that the English are not bombing military targets or even trying to! They are swine!'

Hoffmann shrugged. 'We have to expect that. Churchill is being advised that if you bomb the workers' homes there'll be no workers! Let us hope they don't bring their calling-cards to Munich one dark night.'

Eva stared. 'Is that possible?'

'Likely, I'd say,' said Hoffmann. 'But not yet. It's a much longer flight, all the way from England and then back again. They'll stick to the Ruhr for now.'

He suddenly brightened and poured some cognac. 'At least the War has brought us some of life's luxuries. I have some silk unmentionables for you. From Paris.' He passed her a beautifully-wrapped parcel marked *Worth*. Eva made to open it, excitedly. 'No. Let no man see them but the Fuhrer.'

Eva blushed a little, and laughed. 'Not much hope of that, Heinrich. He won't be home until the War in Russia is won.'

'Oh, I don't know about that,' said Hoffmann. 'I think he'll be back well before that, Evie.'

Something in the way he said it made Eva look up quickly from her *Worth* parcel. His face, however, was expressionless.

Hitler was in a fury: but he held his tongue.

Before him stood Halder and Jodl and his own po-faced aides. Halder was explaining, in his professional, laid-back way, why more progress was not being made. 'Fuhrer, they are simply learning how to fight us. We have made enormous gains. We cannot expect that, in the very nature of things, to go on for ever.'

Why not, Hitler wanted to ask, to scream, but still he waited.

Halder, his bearing erect and soldierly, his uniform impeccable, his shave very close and every hair in place on his cropped head, held a stick and pointed to the map on the wall of the General Staff Map Room. Hitler, with Jodl, had come by motorcar and created something of a sensation. Normally, he waited in his own Headquarters to be appraised of events. Now, it seemed, he was too impatient to wait. The stolidity of the long-suffering Jodl told Halder that, but war was war and had to be conducted a certain way. Commanding Generals had to take decisions in the light of all they had learned in years of fighting wars and studying the great generals of the past. Soldiering, like all professions, had its rules. God knows, they existed to be broken, but not every day. The Fuhrer had a fine, bold grasp of aggressive war and until now it had served Germany well. Nobody could deny that. But attack was not the answer in every situation, even if you had the seemingly-inexhaustible man-power of the Russians. He said as much, drily and with a relaxed air that infuriated Hitler.

'Fuhrer,' said Halder, 'the element of surprise has gone. They are standing and fighting, even when they are encircled and have no hope. They did that against Blumentritt at Minsk. He was surprised but perhaps he should not have been. The enemy has more men and far better equipment than we ever expected and regrettably we have to face that fact.' Halder paused. 'It is obvious that we underestimated all round. They have more transport than we imagined, thousands of lorries and trucks, not just horses, as we'd been told. Our official estimate of 200 Russian divisions in the field was a long way out. We have identified 350 already and there may even be more.

Hitler thought: this *defeatist*! I will have him *shot*!

But still he said nothing.

'I must tell you, Fuhrer, the moment I engaged the enemy I realised that everything written about Soviet Russia is nonsense. They have a modern army, in many ways. Plus they have millions of men, and don't even count their losses!'

'And our losses?' asked Hitler, in a strangled voice.

Jodl shot a warning glance at Halder but the tall, dandified general ignored it. 'Our front is three thousand miles long and therefore inevitably *thin* in places. We are vulnerable to counter-attacks. The enemy has realised this. He is now making those counter-attacks. Not heavy ones. Yet. But this tactic is slowing us up, all along the Front.'

'Thank you, General,' said Hitler, icily, 'for the lecture. I am not interested in lectures. What I want to know is what you are doing about all this?'

Halder laid down his stick, and steepled his fingers. 'Fuhrer, I know you feel we should strike for Leningrad to the North and Stalingrad to the South, rather than directly at Moscow?'

'Feel?' said Hitler. 'I *order* it!'

'Von Brauchitsch feels as I do.' Halder refused to look at Jodl. 'We should go for Moscow. As the main source of armament production, the centre of the transportation and communication systems, and the capital of the nation.'

Hitler was silent a long moment. He had begun to tremble with impotent rage. How many times did he have to tell these idiots what was important and what was not?

'I want the oil in the Caucuses. I want the granary of the Ukraine. I want Leningrad, the home of the Revolution! I have been saying that for weeks, General Halder!' Hitler pointed a dramatic finger at the map. 'I demand you send divisions from Army Group Centre to Army Groups North and South – and at once!' He shouted: 'We need to capture not Moscow but Stalingrad to the South and Leningrad to the North – the two holy cities of Bolshevism! That way the War is won! And we must do it before the Winter sets in!'

Halder was stoic. 'Fuhrer, that is an order?'

'Yes, it is,' said Hitler. 'And so you will feel happier about it, General – since I know Generals like written orders! – I will send you a memorandum, copy to Von Brauchitsch in Berlin. You will have it in an hour!'

And Hitler marched out of the Headquarters, leaving a stunned silence behind him. Hastily, Jodl, and his aides – Jodl with another warning glance at Halder – followed him out.

Halder put down his stick. Nobody spoke to him. He had said what everybody thought. That had been his mistake.

Hitler dictated his memorandum from the Wolf's Lair, when they returned by motorcade. Jodl noticed but did not comment on Hitler's furtive gripping of his stomach and facial grimaces of pain. He knew that the Fuhrer had been ill for days and suspected dysentery. Not to be wondered at in a marshy, low-lying place like this. The wonder was that they all did not have it. After Hitler had gasped out the order and instructed it be sent to Halder at once, by despatch-rider, with a copy over the teleprinter to Von Brauchitsch in Berlin, he retired to his room and sent for Morell.

The portly doctor found the Fuhrer doubled up on his bed, pale and sweating. He took Hitler's pulse. 'Diarrhoea? Stomach pain? Nausea? High temperature?' To all these, Hitler nodded. 'Dysentery,' said Morell. 'Inevitable. Also, you seem very agitated Fuhrer.'

'So would you be,' said Hitler, 'If you had to deal with my Generals!'

Morell knew better than to prescribe bed-rest and sedative medicines to Hitler. He would not have accepted them. He prescribed Kaolin and codeine and a very bland diet and, if possible, longer hours of rest. Hitler said, 'I cannot rest, there is too much to be done!'

Doctor Theodor Morell did not like the look of Hitler or his general physical condition, even when the worst of the dysentery had gone. He took an electro-cardiogram of Hitler's heart and sent it, anonymously, to Berlin for analysis. The consultant's confidential opinion was that the patient had a rapidly progressive coronary sclerosis. Morell considered that a diagnosis not to be wondered at and not necessarily fatal. But there was always the danger of angina pectoris: a heart attack.

Doctor Theodor Morell was a past-master, as a lifelong venerealogist, in how much or how little to tell any given patient at any time.

He told the Fuhrer of Germany nothing.

Hitler was still in pain and very weak when Brauchitsch later paid him a rare visit. A coward at heart, Hitler thought. At least Halder faces me out. This ancient monument will go as soon as I can get rid of him. For his part, Brauchitsch, who was indignant at the insulting tone of Hitler's memorandum recognised that this shaky, pasty-faced man sitting on his bed, doubled-up with stomach-cramps, was possessed of the will to inflict himself on the Generals.

'Attack Kiev now!' Hitler ordered. 'It is the gateway to the South!'

Brauchitsch made his excuses, saluted and left. In his staff-car his fury erupted. He swore grossly. To be ordered about by a corporal. It was insufferable.

In September, Kiev fell. Cried Hitler, thin but recovered from the dysentary, 'Four Soviet armies destroyed! Tanks, guns, men! Over half-a-million prisoners!'

The *Radestsky March* played joyously again and again, on the German radio. In the Wolf's Lair Adolf Hitler celebrated. 'If I had not *told* these Generals to do it, they never *would* have done it!'

Everybody, even Von Brauchitsch (who had already himself suffered a mild heart attack) and Halder (who was made, Von Brauchitsch thought, of steel wire) had to agree. The route to the Caucasus was now open.

Moscow came next. Moscow had to be taken, before winter set in. Said Hitler, furiously, 'Timoshenko has been given far too much precious time! He has used it to dig line-upon-line of defensive trenches in front of Moscow!' He gave the Army a message: 'One last, mighty heave and smash the enemy before the winter sets in!' He knew that Russian winters normally began in late October, but that it rarely snowed until November. There seemed to be time enough. By the end of the first week in October Jodl told him, 'Von Leeb has struck to cut the sole railway-line between Moscow and Leningrad. In Moscow, the government and diplomatic corps has gone. Only the soldiers in the trenches remain. There is a smell of ash everywhere, from the burning of official papers. Nobody knows if Stalin is still in the city. It is like a ghost-town, waiting for the end.'

Hitler slept well that night.

The next day it rained. Cold, ceaseless downpours twenty-four hours a day. The tanks and men of the besieging army sank down into the mud and slush. Lorries were buried up to their axles. Cranes were used to try to winch them out. Hitler sat in the Wolf's Lair, listening intently to the reports coming in: the tank-commanders were sitting on their vehicles, soaked to the skin and unable to move, the report said. The infantry had found any kind of improvised cover they would, wrapping themselves in greatcoats (if they had them), capes (if they had them), and scarves (if they had them). The rain fell unceasingly upon them all: a massive army of a million men, quite still, in a huge silence, for the first time in almost seven months. Still, and wetter than they had ever been in their lives. Forty miles from Moscow, where there were houses and fires and protection from the weather.

It began, suddenly, to get a lot colder, especially at night.

The Army shivered, and the shiver went back a long, long way, through the rear-echelons, through the communications-centres, all the way back to Germany itself.

In the Wolf's Lair, Adolf Hitler sat alone and silent. No telephones rang. No teletypes clattered. No voices were raised.

Soon, even the steps outside the Wolf's Lair were muffled.

The snow had come.

XXI

ADOLF HITLER sat in his stuffy, chilly map-room at the Wolf's Lair, paralysed, as the German Army froze unto death in the snow. He listened unbelievingly to the reports, whispered by his nervous aides, as Keitel, sweating and tremulous, nerved himself to say the unsayable: 'Fuhrer, the plight of our men is terrible. Field-hospitals are amputating feet, hands, ears, even legs. Snow-blindness is common. Fuhrer, we are equipped for a summer-campaign and have no warm clothing. No man has more than his greatcoat. Oil and petroleum are freezing solid in the gas-tanks of vehicles, bullets freeze in rifle-breeches, fingers freeze trying to get them out, the icy winds from the steppes freeze everything, flesh and metal, together.' Hitler showed no sign of having heard Keitel. Jodl took over, softer: 'Fuhrer, horses die by the hundred and are cooked and eaten, railway-points are frozen, trains cannot move, roads to the rear are impassable marshes.' Hitler did not seem to hear that, either. He merely sighed and switched on the German radio, to hear Goebbels asking for every fur-coat in Germany, every scarf, sweater, every pair of high, fur-lined boots, men or women's, it didn't matter. 'There! That is the spirit I need!'

'Fuhrer. We are stalled,' said Keitel.

'No.' Hitler's voice was weary and barely audible. 'I hereby order a total offensive against Moscow.'

'But Fuhrer, we are stopped solid –'

'No. It can be done. Make every commander responsible for it, personally!'

'If it goes badly . . . ?'

'Do it,' said Hitler, for once not shouting.

Somehow it was done. A triumph of will and organisation. No other Army in the world, Jodl thought, could have moved forward in that snow. It was the biggest concentration of armour the world had ever seen. Every regiment, battalion, platoon that could move was pushed forward towards the Capital. The Soviets brought workers out of their factories to serve in the lines of trenches outside Moscow. The fighting was heavy, no quarter asked or given. The tank-traps, the ditches, and the snow finally proved too much. Von Bock, himself ill with dysentery, reported to Hitler that his troops were exhausted and that he had no more to give.

He used a word never before spoken in the entire campaign.

Defence.

Guderian, in the South, reported a temperature of thirty-one degrees below Zero. 'My tanks,' he told Hitler, 'are immobilised. I must pull my men back or lose them.'

From Army Headquarters North, Bock signalled, 'The attack is finished. I have failed. I send in my resignation to the Fuhrer.'

Hitler asked Jodl, 'What else can we do?'

'Fuhrer, we are stopped everywhere. The weather has beaten us, as it beat Napoleon. We can dig-in and wait for Spring. It will be a desperate winter and counter-attacks are certain, but if we start to prepare our fortifications now, we have a chance!'

'A chance!' Hitler shouted. Jodl noted that his face had changed colour. It was almost yellow. 'Go to trench-warfare, like 1914?'

'It is better than a defeat,' said Jodl, quietly turning away. The expression of Hitler's face was terrible to see. They all felt bad, desperate, suicidal, the whole staff: Halder, himself, the aides. But they were soldiers. Reverses happened. You expected that, in war. A war was a series of battles. The enemy won some, you won some. That was the way it went.

The Soviets were a strong enemy. Stronger than anybody had dreamed. It was therefore obvious what should be done. Fall back. Dig in. Let him attack. Sap his strength. Counter-attack, when you can. Make him pay for every foot of ground.

General Georgi Zhukov, a new name to Hitler, and to Jodl, had replaced Timoshenko a few weeks before. Now, he threw in, across a two-hundred mile front, one hundred new divisions. These were made up of his Siberian Army, plus new infantry and artillery units the German General Staff did not know existed. They were backed by hundreds of airplanes and tanks, including the feared, lumbering T 34's. The German Army, totally unprepared for an assault of this size and ferocity, fell back. The crack Siberian divisions, warmly-clothed and, seemingly, well-fed, attacked in waves, leaving a carpet of dead men lying in the snow. They over-ran the *Wehrmacht* forward positions all along the front.

At General Staff Headquarters there would have been panic if Halder had not been in charge. The map changed from being predominantly Blue (for the Germany Army) to being predominantly Red (for the Soviets). Hitler came hastily to the Headquarters, accompanied only by Jodl. To Halder, he said, after he had looked a long time at the map: 'So, we are beginning to run. It will be a rout!'

'We must fall back and regroup, Fuhrer. They are in massive strength.'

'Even so,' said Hitler. 'Once we start to go back, where do we stop? Germany?'

There was a sudden hush in the frenetic operations-room.

Halder looked at the shaking, ill, implacable man in front of him.

'Fuhrer,' he said, gently. 'Sometimes an army must retreat.'

'No,' shouted Hitler. 'Every unit holds fast. No retreat. Never!'

'But Fuhrer –' began Halder.

'Napoleon retreated,' shouted Hitler, hoarsely. 'Look what happened to him!'

Halder said nothing. It was true enough: but in the military manual, if you were in the position the Germany Army was in, you retreated, you tried to do it sensibly, but you retreated. What else *was* there to do?

Hitler stabbed his finger at a position marked blue on the map. 'Get me the General in charge of this position! He wants to retreat?' Halder nodded. One of his aides nervously manipulated a field-telephone. Hitler, not speaking, waited. Telephones rang and teletypes chattered, in other parts of the Operations room. Nobody moved. All eyes were on Hitler.

'Fuhrer, the General is on the line.' The young aide held out the receiver towards Hitler. He took it.

'General?'

'Yes?' A tired voice whispered to Hitler across hundreds of miles of snow.

'This is the Fuhrer.'

There was a silence at the other end of the whispering line.

'*Ja, Mein Fuhrer?*'

The voice had brightened, if only in surprise, Hitler noted. 'I understand you wish to retreat from your present position?'

'I do,' said the weary, faraway voice.

'How far back do you wish to go?'

'Fuhrer, I don't know.'

'Do you plan to retreat ten miles? Twenty? Thirty?'

'Fuhrer, I cannot hold out here.'

'General, if you retreat thirty miles, do you think it will be any warmer? Do you think your transport and supply problems will be any better? If you retreat will you take your heavy weapons with you?'

'No, Fuhrer. I won't be able to do that.'

'So you intend to leave your heavy weapons for the Bolsheviks?'

'Mein Fuhrer, save the Army, to hell with the weapons!'

'Do you intend to retreat, General, all the way back to Germany?'

There was another silence at the other end of the line.

'General! The eyes of the German *Volk* are on you!'

A long, whispering silence. 'Very well, Fuhrer, we fight and win or we fight and die. Heil Hitler!'

Slowly, Hitler replaced the receiver.

He turned to Halder. 'You heard that?'

Halder, who had been listening-in on another line, nodded.

Hitler said, 'I stay here until the crisis is over. Every divisional commander who wants to pull back, I talk to him personally. Any hour of the day or night.'

He then talked to his Chief of Replacements, General Fromm in Berlin. 'I must have a few divisions of riflemen, with ten days' canned-rations. How soon can they be at the Front? Take them from anywhere! But I must have them now! I'm not talking about tanks or airplanes or guns. Just men, men, and more men! Telephone me back in two hours!'

Fromm telephoned in ninety minutes. He had, ready to move, four-and-a-half-divisions of men from all over Germany, equipped with winter-clothing. They would be on their way to the Moscow Front in twenty-four hours.

'You see,' said Hitler. 'It can be done!'

Halder nodded. Hitler did not understand that it could only be done by *him*. He was the Fuhrer. Everybody listened to him and jumped to obey. It was a totally different thing for Hitler to tell Guderian or Bock to do something than it was for Halder to tell them. Most of his time was spent arguing with the Front-line generals, all of whom he knew personally and all of whom felt he knew nothing because he wasn't on the spot and they were. Hitler did not understand that a Headquarters-unit issued orders and was damn lucky if the generals in the field accepted and acted on half of them! If they refused to do what Halder ordered them to do, what then? *He* could not dimiss the generals. Many of them had seniority over himself. Also, he knew them all personally, for God's sake. Hitler however, could sack them, and did. To Brauchitsch he said, 'I want your resignation. My orders to stand and fight are still not getting through to your battalion commanders!' The old man went off to his country-estate and sat out the War there. The *Wehrmacht* gasped at such a peremptory dismissal of a senior officer. To Von Bock, Commander of Army Group North, Hitler said, 'You go!' The *Wehrmacht* were astounded when Guderian, tank-commander extraordinary, victor of France, was *cashiered* for retreating without permission. 'I will not have cowards in positions of command,' said Hitler. The other generals fell silent.

General Hans Von Sponek had the highest decoration, the *Ritterkreux*, for his part in the airborne-landings at the Hague in June 1940. Sponek pulled his troops back when he found Soviet seaborne infantry had landed *behind* him, in the Crimea. Adolf Hitler, without interviewing him, stripped him of his rank, put him before a court-martial, and had him sentenced to death! Halder pleaded for Sponek's life and Hitler sent him to prison instead.

The *Wehrmacht* was silent now: and afraid.

Bock, Guderian, Sponek?

Who was next? What was next?

Hitler declared, 'I now command the Army!'

He kept Halder, and together they ran the campaign, from the General Staff Headquarters in East Prussia, their joint efforts broken only by Hitler's occasional trips to Berlin to attend to vital developments in other areas of the War. The Italians in retreat; the growing strength of the British in North Africa; the success of the U-Boat campaign, run at operation-level by the brilliant Doenitz. The British were losing merchant-ships faster than they could build them. All these things were important.

But the Winter War held priority.

By the end of December, the German Army was one hundred miles back from Moscow but their line was not broken. They had retreated but they were not routed. Casualties had been very heavy. Hitler asked Halder for the figures for the entire Russian campaign. Halder took up a single sheet of paper and read them out. 'Total losses, Fuhrer, are a million men killed, wounded or missing. One third of what we began with!'

'A third?'

'Roughly. But we have three-quarters-of-a-million wounded. Some may rejoin the fray.'

Hitler said, slowly, 'And we do not have Leningrad, Stalingrad or Moscow?'

'No. We do not.'

It is beginning to look, Hitler thought, what Germany needed was a miracle. To his astonishment, he got one, or thought he got one, the next day. His Signals-officers told him that an American radio-station had reported that the Japanese Air Force had attacked the American Fleet moored in Pearl Harbour, and had sunk five battleships and damaged three more. Casualties were heavy. Hitler jumped to his feet and shouted, 'We are saved!' He told Keitel and Jodl, 'It is now impossible

493

for us to lose the War! The Japanese have not been defeated in a thousand years.'

Hitler at once declared War on the United States, and promised an alliance to-the-death with the Japanese. The benefits, Ribbentrop considered, were obvious: the Japanese attacks on Singapore and India and Australia would stretch the British Empire to the limit. Certainly, after Singapore fell and the Royal Navy battleships, *Prince of Wales* and *Repulse* were sunk by torpedo-bombers, the Japanese did seem a worthwhile ally. The sound of the tiny bespectacled Japanese general slapping the burly English Governor of Singapore across the face, in the lounge of the Raffles Hotel was, Hitler said delightedly: 'the thunderclap destroying British power in the East.' Hitler declared to Ribbentrop, 'Things are going our way at last! We have promises from the Hungarians and the Romanians that they will help with more men. All of Europe is behind us! Nobody wants the Bolsheviks!'

Ribbentrop demured. 'Fuhrer, American industrial-potential is enormous. We must get the Japanese to attack the Russians in the East. Take their port of Vladivostok! Shut Murmansk to American and British arm-supplies. We have a year, in my opinion. Unless we do those things, the man-power of the Russians plus the industrial-power of America will be extremely formidable.'

Hitler said, 'I will persuade the Japanese to do that. And we will attack all convoys to Murmansk.' The Luftwaffe did, but the Japanese High Command ignored Hitler's request to attack Vladivostok. They didn't even declare war on the Russians. Their troops and aircraft carrier-fleet pressed on south, towards Australia and India.

As the terrible retreat of the *Wehrmacht* began to slow, Hitler, at the Wolf's Lair, tried to get some semblance of order into his life again: but it proved impossible. His working-hours became ever more erratic. He now rarely ate his main meal until six in the evening. Jodl looked on in alarm but refused most invitations to a light supper. Nowadays, *that* ended at two o'clock in the morning, with the secretaries sound asleep in their chairs and the aides fighting to keep their eyes open. Hitler told them, after they had listened to records of Richard Strauss or Wagner, how awful things had been for the ordinary soldier in the retreat, which now had an epic quality for everybody. They realised how close Germany had come to utter ruin, and most of them felt that only the iron will of the Fuhrer had avoided catastrophe. No ordinary general, no ordinary commanding-officer could have done what Adolf Hitler had done. He had inspired defeated troops to stand and fight, to stop worrying about Soviet capture and the likelihood of instant death. The Soviets were killing wounded men in the military hospitals. They hung some upside-down and burned them with gasoline, so Jodl had been told. My

God, they were fighting savages! Against these people anything held. At one desperate point, poison-gas had been suggested. Hitler was against it, saying, 'I have myself suffered from it. However, one day it could happen.' Now at last the line had stabilised all over the East Front. For once, Adolf Hitler had nothing to say. The Army had been saved. That was enough.

Two weeks later, Doctor Fritz Todt, Reich Armaments Minister, flew in a visit to Hitler, at the Wolf's Lair. 'I never interfere with my Minister,' Hitler told Todt at supper that evening, 'unless something goes very wrong.' Todt had built Hitler's autobahns and his West Wall. He had now begun work on the Atlantic Wall, a defensive-system against an impending invasion by the British and eventually the Americans. To do all this, he used hundreds of thousands of slave or semi-slave labourers, Poles, French, Russians, anybody the S.S. forced-labour-squads could lay their hands on. Todt was an unqualified success, as far as Adolf Hitler was concerned. He did not know that Todt was deeply pessimistic about the War. Only that day he had told his assistant, the architect, Albert Speer, who had accompanied him to Hitler's Headquarters: 'I fear this is a struggle in which the primitive Bolshevik people will prove the stronger.'

The next morning he was dead in the wreckage of his aircraft, stalled on take-off from nearby Rastenberg airfield. Hitler was profoundly shaken by the news, and was left alone to get over the shock. When he recovered, he called the handsome, dark-haired young architect Speer. 'I want you to take over Todt's job.'

Speer protested he was not up to it, but Hitler held up his hand. 'There is nobody else.' Speer said no more. Now, anyway, he would be doing a real job, not planning cities that would never be built.

That night Adolf Hitler lay awake, in his room in the bunker. If only his mind would stop working! If only he could get some real rest, some real, natural sleep! His hair was greying now. He had frequent bouts of giddiness. The injections that Morell gave him would help, he was sure. Now, he took a heart-tonic, and a stimulant for his circulatory-system. The range and dosage of Morell's medicines steadily increased, but Hitler saw no other doctors. The fat man's brash, bright manner towards Hitler was acceptable because Hitler always felt cheered when Morell had examined him. Morell kept him going, Morell made it possible for him to run the War.

He had given his life to Germany and what had he got in return?

The death of so many old friends, ending with Todt, who would not be the last. Hess, his old comrade and *Alte Kampfer* had gone mad and deserted him. Roehm, his earliest comrade-in-arms, had betrayed him and paid the price. The Generals, who hated and despised him for being

495

of lowly origins, might one day depose him. The Army, despite the growing size of the S.S., still held the real power in Germany. One day some of the people he had disgraced and demoted might turn on him.

His enemies were everywhere.

They still plotted his death, on every side.

It had been the same, all the way from the streets of Vienna.

The black nameless fear of the bullet or the knife or the bomb.

One day it would happen. He knew it would.

The Jews were behind it all, of course. For obvious reasons they wanted him to die, to lie in his grave disgraced and anonymous! Whether disguised as Bolsheviks or bankers, they remained his enemies, as they had plainly been his family's enemies!

At some point, a decision had to be taken about the Jews.

A Final Solution.

Certainly, much was being done.

But Himmler must get on with it!

If his other enemies – the Bolsheviks, the English, the Americans won the War, they would not find their allies, the Jews, waiting for them!

That was certain.

Still twitching and unable to sleep, Adolf Hitler lay on his horsehair cot, the blast of the hot air-conditioning in his face.

In Warsaw Hans Frank reigned supreme.

His quarters in the old Royal Palace at Cracow were lavish. He occupied, for public business, a huge throne-room, with royal hangings and valuable oil-paintings around the walls. He ate off gold-plate, while Poland starved. He had a large secretariat and a long title: Governor-General of Poland! The son of the struck-off lawyer had come a long way: but two things rankled. First, he had seen the Fuhrer only once since the war started. It seemed as if Adolf Hitler had pushed him out of the way, out of his sight, wanted to forget him! Cracow, this ancient city of Poland, was to Frank a detested exile. Much as he loved the pomp and circumstance of his title and the power of life or death he held over every man, woman and child in the vast territory of the General-Government, it remained a backwater of the War. Goering was in Berlin, running the Luftwaffe, with access to the Fuhrer whenever he liked. Goebbels was everywhere, working like a maniac, often seen in close consultation with the Fuhrer. Bormann was rarely far from Hitler's side, when he was in Berlin or at the Berghof. Even the architect Speer now had his ear and his approval. And where was he, Hans Frank, who had been at the Feldherrnstrasse with Adolf Hitler?

In Cracow, in stinking Poland, with its death-camps, epidemics of typhus and typhoid, and all its human *filth*, surely the worse plague-spot in the Greater Reich. The General-Government of Poland was nothing, cut it up anyway you like, but a killing-ground, an abattoir: and nobody knew anything about it. All eyes were on Russia, Singapore, Malaya, the Philippines, the Atlantic Wall! Poland was a dirty, twilit, forgotten place. Nobody important came here, and if they did they went away hurriedly, sickened by what they saw.

Yet, it was the Fuhrer's Will, no doubt of that.

Had not Hoess, the fussy, stern bureaucrat, now Commandant of Auschwitz, whispered to him: 'Himmler has told me the Fuhrer means to be rid of the Jews once and for all. A final solution.'

'Do you mean extermination?' Frank had asked, shocked.

Hoess had nodded his thin, functionary's head. It was difficult to believe he'd won the Iron Cross as a young man. 'Of course, what else? Our old system of shooting won't do. My squads are sick of it. They drink too much. They get ill. They don't report for duty. They ask to be transferred. They know they work for Germany's future, and they should be brave and harsh, but there is a limit to everything. Don't you agree, Hans?'

Frank had nodded, not a little disturbed. What would be the end of all this? Who would stand up at the end and say, *I did all this*?

Certainly, Hoess, a cradle-Catholic like himself but from a stern lower-middle-class household, did not seem worried about any of that, but Hoess had been selected by Himmler and Heydrich for the work, and was quite simply a petty-bureaucrat. It occurred once again to Frank that there would, sometime, be a reckoning, and then who would say *what*, admit to *what*, say I did that but I didn't do that, and who, anyway, would listen?

'The Fuhrer wills it!' Hoess repeated, as if it was a prayer. It was, Frank recalled, the phrase shouted out at the shooting of Roehm and the others.

He shivered. 'A whole race? Gone from the earth?'

Hoess nodded. 'And the Gypsies. And a lot of Slavs. All peoples classed as Racial Undesirables.'

'But there are only a hundred thousand Jews left in Germany?' said Frank.

'Millions in Poland, Hungary, Romania, Bulgaria, Russia.'

Frank stared at the clerkly, meek-looking man, sitting in the wondrous medieval room, eating rich food from Royal gold-plate, drinking the finest Rhine wines, and talking as if this were nothing!

'All of those people? To go?'

Hoess swallowed a crumb of cheese. 'Every one.'

'Not possible!'

'It is. We are not going to shoot any more of them. Or poison them, as we did the mental-cases – before that goddam Bishop Galen of Cologne stopped it! – with carbon-monoxide. Too messy. Too slow.'

'What, then?'

Hoess looked slightly shocked at such directness. Hans Frank knew that Hoess did not attend executions or floggings or 'selections' of any sort, but kept himself aloof from all that. Why, did he really think it was just another job, did he think that explanation would save him, come the day?

'I have had I. G. Farben create a new gas for me. It is odourless and it works fast. We call it Zyclon B.' said Hoess, primly.

'Zyclon B?' Frank felt sick.

'We'll use camp detainees to do the work. Spare my *Einsatzgruppen*. They can do the administrating. Or go off to fight. We have it all planned out.'

'Nor Work Camps any more?' asked Frank. 'Extermination Camps?'

'I wouldn't talk about it,' said Hoess, 'But the S.S. and Gestapo are picking up Jews in every Occupied country. France, Belgium, Holland, Norway, and of course, Germany itself.'

'This will take years!' Frank protested, his head reeling.

Hoess nodded, affably, chewing on a hazelnut and gulping his wine. He nodded, a zealot. 'It is the Fuhrer's will.'

'Have you ever,' Hans Frank, greatly daring, but he felt lightheaded, somehow out of kilter: nobody had told him anything about this: of course he knew the intention but the reality was different. 'Have you ever thought why the Fuhrer feels as he does towards the Jews?'

Hoess pondered, moving creakily in his leather-belt and cross-strap. 'Only what I've always been told. The Jews are the enemies of Germany.'

'The enemies of the Fuhrer?'

'Naturally.' Hoess chewed, looked curious, as far as he ever looked anything. 'Why, what are you trying to tell me?'

'Nothing,' said Hans Frank.

But I could tell you a very great deal, he thought. I could tell you something that would blow your tiny clerk's head off your narrow shoulders: I know something nobody else in the entire Reich knows, and what do I get for keeping my teeth together?

I get Poland. I get dirt, typhoid, typhus, starvation – in the shape of the whole lousy population of her ruined cities. I get death.

Death, he reflected, drinking his Rhine wine not for taste but to get drunk the faster, was another name for Poland.

Hans Frank began to change his tune. If the Fuhrer wills it, very well. He boasted to a Nazi newspaperman, 'If I put up a poster for every seven Poles shot, the forests of Poland would not be enough to manufacture the paper!'

Hans Frank said: 'I ask nothing of the Jews except that they disappear! They will have to go. We must destroy the Jews wherever we meet them and when opportunity offers. We must do this to maintain the Reich. We cannot shoot them all, can we? We can't poison them, can we? But we can take other steps!'

There, Adolf Hitler would hear *those* words, how could he not, and surely approve?

No word of approval came from Adolf Hitler.

Frank, hurt and bewildered — what *more* could he do? — then complained, directly to Hitler, that the extermination-policy (which, of course, he approved of in principle) denied him labour-power to run Poland! The S.S. were responsible. It was foolish to simply kill people? Surely they could be *worked*? It made more sense.

There was no reply from Adolf Hitler.

Hans Frank fretted, in his lonely palace, wondering about the legality of everything Himmler and Heydrich were doing! Did the Fuhrer really *will* it? Was it not a total S.S. plot, all of it?

Frank did a daring thing. He went on a tour of the German universities in his capacity as *Reichkommisar of Justice*. In his speeches, he pleaded for a return to legality and constitutional rule. His audiences at these law schools were horrified, and left his lectures in droves. Most of his lawyer-friends thought his insane behaviour was due to the execution of an old friend for *fraud*! Well, fraud was a capital offence now, under the Third Reich. Hans Frank should have known that. Or was it something else that explained this madness, this criticism (for that was what it was!) of the Fuhrer!

Hans Frank was stripped by Adolf Hitler of his office as *Reichkommisar for Justice*, and told to go back to Poland and attend to his duties there: and consider himself extremely lucky that he was an old personal friend of the Fuhrer's!

This news was conveyed to him by Himmler.

'You *are* an old friend of the Fuhrer's, aren't you, Hans?' Himmler had said, thick goggle-glasses glistening on his thin schoolmaster's face. What a man to lead a racial crusade, Hans Frank thought, he looks more like a pox-doctor's clerk!

'Yes, I am a friend of the Fuhrer's and always will be,' said Hans Frank. 'Let no man question my loyalty!'

'Then you will leave the S.S. to get on with its work and make no more complaints, I am sure? You have been very foolish, Hans.'

Hans Frank nodded, and smiled insincerely at the raving crank.

He knew what he knew and for once it was something Himmler, who knew everything, did not know. Not even Himmler, for all his Gestapo files! Hans Frank sipped his brandy, back on his throne in the Royal Palace at Cracow and ate his venison from gold-plate and did nothing about saving the Jews because the Fuhrer willed it so.

How strange it was, he wondered tipsily, how passing strange that a very human action between a young Jewish boy and a fat German cook of forty years of age, a hundred and fifty years ago, should somehow lead to *this*? To all that was happening here, in Poland.

Was he being fanciful and foolish?

Hans Frank sat in the large, cold and draughty room into which the smell of death, an ashy, dry taste that hung in the very air of the place, settled over him like a shroud, and thought not.

Not at all.

One day he would talk. Tell all. One day.

The Final Solution was devised and promulgated, at a conference at the Wannsee, near Berlin, in January 1941. Hitler was not present, nor was Himmler. Reinhard Heydrich prepared the agenda and the words murder, extermination, gassing, were not used. Words like resettlement, living-space, movement-of-peoples were used. Civil-servants wrote the words down, knowing full well what they meant. No document was to be promulgated, with reference to the Final Solution, that bore the name of the Fuhrer.

Heydrich, the 'Blond Beast', a first-class fencer, an excellent horse-man, a skilled pilot, and an able technician of power, was also arrogant, neurotic and exhibitionist. Head of the Nazi Security Police, he wove a web of intelligence over the Third Reich. He had extensive dossiers on friend and foe alike. He had been an instigator of the *Kristalnacht* action against Jewish houses and places of worship. After the conquest of Poland, he ordered Polish Jews into ghettos and appointed so-called Jewish councils. With the help of Eichmann, he organised the mass deportation of Jews from Poland, Germany and Austria to Hans Frank's General-Government in Poland. Ghettos and the stealing of Jewish wealth were only the beginning. On Goering's direct order, to carry out an *Endlosang*, Heydrich took over all duties of organisation, adminis-tration and finances of the Final Solution. His *Einsatzgruppen* which had murdered tens of thousands of Poles and Jews, were to murder, in all, a million Polish and Russian Jews and many Soviet Kommissars and officers. At Wannsee, Heydrich had laid down the rules. 'All Jews cap-able of work to be taken to the Occupied Areas in the East and 'employed in road building', in which no doubt eventually many will naturally pass away, as is usual in life. The survivors would be given 'appropriate treatment', since they must not be allowed to go free, to spread their Jewish genes. Having arranged it all, and his name having been given to the extermination-programme for Polish Jewry – *Operation Reinhard* – he went to Czecho-Slovakia as Deputy Reich Protector or Bohemia.

The dirty and boring work of carrying out the *Endlosang*, he left to S.S. minions such as Hoess and Eichmann.

Eichmann's office was the headquarters of the *Endlosang*. By 1942 he had developed 'gassing-techniques' and the European-wide system of convoys that were to take European Jewry to its death. Eichmann was a mild-looking bureaucrat who followed orders to the letter, an apparatnik who complained about inefficiency and delay in his task of mass-murder. He was irritated by the lack of cooperation of Hitler's allies, Italians, Hungarians, Romanians, Vichy French, in giving up their Jews. In the August of 1944 he was able to report to Himmler that four million Jews had died in the death-camps, and two million more by mobile extermination units. He was almost unknown in German official circles, which closed its collective mind – the Army, the Navy, the Air Force, the Civil Service – to the *Endlosang*.

In the Reich, the Camps were first whispered about, in 1942.

Slowly, the truth spread into the society: millions were being killed in the East.

Train drivers knew it. They drove the obscene transports.

Industrialists knew it. They used the slave-labour.

Scientists knew it. They invented the Zyclon B gas.

Contractors designed and built the Camps. They knew it best of all.

The Volk knew something of it, however little of it they knew.

They averted their eyes and got on with the War.

One man, however, did act.

Kurt Gerstien was an S.S. Lieutenant, sometime Head of the Waffen S.S. Institute of Hygiene in Berlin. Born in Munster in 1905, he was by profession an engineer and mining assessor. From the age of 20 he was a member of the Protestant Youth Movement. He joined the Nazi Party in 1933 but remained a member of Pastor Niemoller's Confessional Church. This organisation had links with what was later to become the Christian Anti-Nazi Resistance Movement. In 1936 he was arrested by the Gestapo for giving-out religious tracts. In 1938 he was for a time in a Camp, then released, after asking to serve in the S.S's so-called 'Health' Department. Few questions were asked. His reason for joining, he insisted later, was to find out the truth about the *Endlosang* Programmes. He did, and memorised the information. Soon, he was working in a department handling 'poisonous disinfectant gasses'. In the

Summer of 1942, Gerstien was sent, as an assessor, to persuade the Commandant of Belzec death-camp, near Lublin, to switch over from diesel-gas to the new Zyclon B gas, a form of concentrated prussic-acid, thought to be more efficient, by the 'Health Department' of the S.S.

Gerstien left behind a hand-written description of what he saw there. He declared that his real work was not that of an S.S. official but as a 'witness for the Confessional Church'. His desire was 'to gain insight into the whole machinery of the camps and shout it to the world!'

After his visit to the Camp, Gerstien contacted a Swedish diplomat, Baron Von Otter. Gerstien requested that Von Otter report the Final Solution to his government and to the Allies – at once! – as every day's delay costs thousands of lives. The Swedish government never passed on the information to anybody. Gerstien urged friends in the Dutch Resistance to tell their British contacts, and they did so. The British Foreign Office were believed to know the facts already, but Gerstien's report was nonetheless dismissed as 'atrocity propaganda'. Gerstien then tried the Papal Envoy in Berlin. He refused to listen. The Protestant Bishop of Berlin, Otto Dibelius heard him out. As head of the growing Resistance Movement against Hitler he had to be extra careful. In fact, he could do nothing.

Lieutenant Gerstien's touted evidence was in the form of an eye-witness report to the world: *The next day we went to Belsec. A small station had been built especially for this purpose on a hill just north of the Lublin-Lemberg Chaussee in the left corner of the demarcation line. South of the road some houses with the notice 'Sonderkommando der Waffen-SS'. As Polizeihauptmann Wirth, the actual head of the whole Killing installations, was not yet there, Globocnik introduced me to SS-Hauptsturmfuhrer Oberme-yer (from Pirmasens). I did not see any dead that day, but in the hot August weather the whole place smelt like the plague and there were millions of flies everywhere. Right by the small two-track station there was a large shed, the so-called cloakroom, with a large counter where valuables were handed over. There was a room containing about 100 chairs – the barber's room. Then an outdoor path under birch-trees, with a double barbed-wire fence on the left and right, with the sign:* To the Inhalation and Bathrooms. *In front of us was a sort of bath-house with geraniums, then a few steps, and then three rooms each on the right and left with wooden doors like garages. In the rear wall, hardly visible in the darkness, large sliding doors. On the roof was the Star of David! In front of the building a notice: Heckenholt Institute. More than that I was not able to see that afternoon.*

Shortly before seven the next morning I was informed: 'The first transport is coming in ten minutes!' The first train from Lemberg did in fact arrive in a few minutes. Forty-five wagons containing 6700 people, of whom 1450 were already dead on arrival. Children were looking out from behind the barred windows, their faces dreadfully pale and frightened, their eyes filled with the fear of death. The train came into the station. Two hundred Ukrainians tore open the doors and drove people out of the wagons with their leather whips. A loudspeaker gave further instructions: 'Undress completely, take off artificial limbs, spectacles, and so on. Give up valuables at the counter without credit notes or receipts. Tie shoes together carefully!' Then the women and children went to the barber, who cut off all their hair with two or three chops with the scissors and stuffed it into potato-sacks. 'That is put to some special use in U-boats – for caulking or something like that', the S.S. Corporal on duty told me. Then the procession started to move. With a lovely young girl at the front, they all walked along the path, all naked, men, women and children, some without their artificial limbs. I stood with Hauptmann Wirth up on the ramp between the chambers! An S.S. man stood in the corner and told the wretched people in a clerical tone of voice: 'Nothing at all is going to happen to you! You must take a deep breath in the chambers. That expands the lungs. This inhalation is necessary because of illnesses and infection.' When asked what was going to happen to them, he answered: 'Well, of course, the men must work, building houses and roads, but the women don't have to work. Only if they want to, they can help with the housework or in the kitchen.' This gave some of these poor people a glimmer of hope that lasted long enough for them to take the few steps into the chambers without resisting. The majority realised – the smell told them what their fate was to be! They climbed the steps and then they saw everything. Mothers with babies at the breast, little children, adults, men, women – all naked. They hesitated, but they went into the gas chambers, pushed on by those behind them, or driven in by the leather whips of the S.S. Most of them without saying a word. A Jewess of about 40, with eyes blazing, called down upon the heads of the murderers at the blood being spilt here. Hauptmann Wirth personally gave her five or six lashes in the face with his riding-whip. Then she too disappeared into the chamber . . .

Henny Hoffmann came to the Berghof, as Adolf Hitler's guest.

Now a mother of young children and the wife of Baldur Von Schirach, one of Hitler's favourite Ministers, she had always been a favourite of the Fuhrer's. She had known him since she was a little girl and her father, after all, was Hitler's photographer. Hitler had spent many hours in the Hoffmann house. To her he was Uncle Adi.

Dark and pretty, and dressed in an oatmeal-tweed costume, Henny seemed, to her friend Eva Braun, to be troubled about something. Her eyes were red and she seemed nervous. Eva asked her what the trouble was but Henny would not say. Eva took it to be a tiff with her husband, and thought no more of it.

Later, she wished she had pressed Henny about it.

Adolf was back, for a rest, from the Wolf's Lair. The War in Russia was going badly, a lot worse than the newspapers or the radio were saying. She could not help but overhear low conversations between Martin Bormann and the huge, stolid Gunshe, about conditions on the East Front. The Bolsheviks were human devils, who killed the wounded German soldiers and had no mercy on anybody, including themselves. They were primitive savages and beating them was going to take longer than anybody had ever expected.

Adolf said little. His health was not good, his hands shook. He was sleeping worse than ever, and his face was a very bad colour. A few days rest and recuperation at the Berghof was all she could hope for. Adolf, of course, pressed on with his work, his telegrams, his orders. His study had a ceaseless stream of staff officers passing through it. But at least some of the time he was able to sit in the wintry sunshine, on the patio, looking out at his favourite view, the magnificent Obersaltzberg with the snow on it.

It was as near peace as he could get.

And Henny Hoffmann spoiled it all. She suddenly put down her tea-cup and said, in a shaky and yet indignant voice, 'Uncle Adi! Do you *know* about the deportation of the Jews?'

Hitler said nothing. His face was like stone.

Henny Hoffmann persisted. 'It is the most terrible scene! I saw it myself last month in Vienna. Convoys of Jews, in the most awful condition. Men, women and children, being marched to the trains taking them to the East! I have seen it with my own eyes! Can you know about this? Can we be doing this, as Germans? Do you know about it? Do you approve?'

Hitler got up from his chair. He said, in a faraway voice, 'Stalin killed thousands in the Katyn Forest. My men are dying in their hundreds of thousands in the Russian snows. You should ask them what they think.'

Henny Hoffmann just stared at him, tears of rage and indignation in her eyes.

Adolf left the balcony and went into his study.

He did not come out until much later, when Henny Hoffmann had gone.

All he said to Eva was, 'Do not invite her here again.'

Eva Braun was furious with Henny Hoffmann and did not trouble to hide it.

Didn't she know that nobody – nobody! – talked to Adolf Hitler that way!

His every whim must be taken into account, for without him where would Germany, where would any of us, be?

The Fuhrer wills it!

XXII

B

Y the Spring of 1942 the oil was running out. The way to resolve it, Hitler told his generals, was plain. 'An Offensive, aimed at the Caucasus oil fields! Stalin needs them as much as we do. More, they are his only source of supply! Forget Moscow. Strike south-east along the Don River towards Stalingrad, and capture it sometime in the late Summer!' The *Wehrmacht*, having survived the worst winter in history, plunged forward towards the Kerch peninsula. Manstein commanded Panzers with heavy air-support. The Soviets were taken by surprise. They expected an attack on Moscow. Within days, two hundred thousand Russians were killed or taken prisoner.

'Press on with all speed,' urged Hitler, now Supreme Commander of the *Wehrmacht*, with new administrative duties to match. He read official files before he got up. Jodl said to Keitel, 'It's too much. His freshness of vision will go if he tries to be what he is not: a conventional general-officer.'

Walking in the woods, near the Wolf's Lair, Hitler said, 'Jodl, I am going to ask Raeder to machine-gun British survivors at sea! I am going to shoot these British *Kommandos* who come ashore, to sabotage our armies in the West! The same applies to their so-called Special Operations people, these saboteurs and bombers. 'Set Europe ablaze,' Churchill demands. I will meet that kind of fire with fire of my own!' They walked on through the woods, Blondi frisking beside them. Jodl was sure Raeder would not fire on British sailors struggling in the icy waters of the Atlantic: but the rest seemed likely enough. As an old Wehrmacht-hand, he could not really disapprove of the Fuhrer's *Kommando-order* calling for the deaths of any Allied soldier, in or out of uniform, operating behind German lines. It was, after all, a rule of War that a man behind enemy-lines was a *franc-tireur* and as such would be shot. They were shooting hundreds of Russian partisans every day, so

505

why not Americans and British? Just the same, there *was* a difference, thought Jodl uneasily. The English were, like themselves, Europeans. The Bolsheviks were savages. The Americans, who were surrendering in their thousands to the Japanese at Bataan and Corregidor, had doubtless expected the Geneva Convention to obtain. It had not. The Japanese – savages again! – had used the Americans for bayonet-practice, housed them in starvation-conditions and subjected them to all kinds of cruelty. It was not a way to run an honourable war and that seemed to Jodl important. If a soldier did not have his honour he had nothing. Adolf Hitler was not a professional soldier and could not be expected to understand that, probably due to his harsh, deprived upbringing.

They were interrupted by an ashen-faced aide. 'Fuhrer, an urgent signal. The Protector of Bohemia has been shot by Czech agents of the British Government, in a street in Prague.'

Hitler was sick at the news. Heydrich, the Blond Beast, the favoured successor, dead! 'This is what we face! Assassination! Nobody is safe! It could have been me! We will root out the killers, we will execute their entire families!

On 1 July Von Manstein took Sevastapol. Hitler made him a Field-Marshal, saying: 'The Spring-attack is now a Summer-offensive! The Soviets are reeling at the speed and ferocity of our German advance. The ground is hard, and good for tanks. We Germans are fighting a war we understand, full of mobility and dash!'

Hitler followed the *Wehrmacht*'s triumph. He flew, with his staff, to a new Headquarters at Vinnitsa in the Ukraine, code-named '*Werewolf*'. Vinnitsa was a district of thick scrub, and trees and rustic byways. But, again, Hitler was reminded that he was in a land of primitive sanitation and poverty. The place swarmed with deadly mosquitos. Even the drug Atabrine, which turned everybody yellow, wasn't proof against the insects. Hitler felt ill and out of sorts, but he had other things to think about besides his health. He had a vision of taking the Caucasus and linking up with the German forces under Rommel in North Africa: a giant pincer that would knock both Soviet Russia and Great Britain out of the European War!

The key was Stalingrad.

The problem was nobody knew how many tanks and men Stalin had in reserve! Colonel Gehler, Chief of Army Intelligence, told Hitler, 'Fuhrer, I rate the total Soviet strength at about 600 divisions. Stalin has about 60 new infantry and 60 new armoured divisions available.'

Hitler dismissed the figures. 'Stalin makes a thousand tanks a month and I make only six hundred? Is that what you are telling me?' Gehler fell silent.

As Summer wore on, the German offensive slackened. Hitler and

Halder began to argue over strategy. Hitler accused Halder of being a 'chairbound general in both wars!' and Halder retreated into his *Wehrmacht* officer's stoic reserve. Nothing important had been achieved in the summer that Hitler prayed would go his way, and all the time at his back, the bogey of a Second Front. He knew from intercepted signals that Stalin was demanding it almost daily from Churchill and Roosevelt.

Hitler also fell out with Keitel and Jodl. 'You say yes to my orders, then disobey them! I insist that from now on *all* orders to be taken down by stenographers and records kept!' In the dark watches of the night, as he lay sleepless on his bunk in the wooden hut at *Werewolf*, Hitler decided that he could not trust the generals – any of them! – any longer. They lied to him, they pointed at him when things went wrong, they accepted no responsibility for their own errors, they looked down upon him because he had been a lowly corporal!

They were, in plain fact, his *enemies*!

And yet he was in their hands, for who else could fight the War for him? When it was over, he resolved to do away with them. In the coming days of Peace he would rely entirely on the S.S.

Meantime, Stalingrad!

In mid-September General Von Paulus began his assault on the city. It had been a long fight to get there but the General was confident. He felt the Soviets had few reserves to call on and went for a quick victory. He did not wish to go the way of General Halder, summarily sacked by Hitler. The job had gone to General Zeitzler, known in the messes of the *Wehrmacht* as 'Thunderball'. Zeitzler was an extrovert, an action-man, only forty-seven years old. Von Paulus, on the other hand, was holding his first field-command at fifty-two, and was more than a little apprehensive. Hitler's orders were for all-out attack. But the city was perfect for defensive warfare. The outlying buildings were destroyed by artillery fire and the inhabitants and soldiers fought from the ruins, which were far better protection than any man-made trench. Paulus, with Hitler's voice harrying him over the radio-link, pushed slowly forward.

Adolf Hitler flew back to Berlin and then on to the Berghof, leaving Zeitzler in charge. He had more confidence in this bold young staff-officer than in any other. Had not Zeitzler refused to accept Hitler's angry statement that all generals were chairborne idiots and demanded that Hitler speak with more respect for Senior *Wehrmacht* officers. Hitler had been astonished, then gratified. 'A man of bravery – he even argues with *me*!'

Back at the Berghof the news was not good. Rommel had lost North Africa to the British. Rommel, who had promised Hitler North Africa was safe with him!

'Of course,' Hitler boomed, standing on the balcony at the Berghof, 'By now, the Americans have landed at Oran and Casablanca! They have funked a frontal-attack on Europe! Africa is just a side-show, the Americans showing the British they have a commitment in Europe. Europe?' repeated Hitler. 'What Churchill and Roosevelt will not accept is that one man in two on the Eastern Front is *not* a German but a Hungarian, a Romanian, a Balt, a Norwegian, a Frenchman, an Italian, a Spaniard! Mine is a European Crusade against Bolshevism!'

Bormann nodded his cropped head. He sat glowering because the Fuhrer was glowering, at the bad news from Africa. 'Anyway, Rommel is flying home!'

Only months before, Eva Braun thought, watching, Rommel had been Adolf's darling, his favourite of all the generals. Times did indeed change. Mussolini and his dark, charming son-in-law, Count Ciano, had been welcome guests and allies. Now, seemingly, they too were becoming embarrassing liabilities.

Eva felt strange and uneasy with Adolf, these days. She saw so little of him, even when he was at the Berghof, because he was swallowed up at once in conferences and telephone calls and urgent matters of one sort or another. He still had the awful, yellow skin caused by taking the Atrabine. He had lost weight and seemed much more nervous and agitated than she had ever known him.

'Adolf, I know you have to take these stimulants from Doctor Morell, but now that you are away from the Front, perhaps you can rely more on natural things for a while? Good, wholesome food, and uninterrupted rest?'

Adolf shook his head, his eyes closing. It was two o'clock in the morning and still he was not in bed. 'Morell keeps me going. That is all there is to it, Evie. Tell me what is happening on the Home Front? What are the ordinary people saying?'

Eva wondered what the *Alte Kampfer* had told Adolf at his annual reunion in Munich a few evenings before? It was an occasion he never missed. Presumably, the old Brownshirts saw the War through rose-tinted-spectacles and told the Fuhrer nothing he didn't want to know.

Eva knew what the ordinary people were saying. That their husbands and sons were dying in Russia and that the food rations for each family were now very low. Even at the Berghof, Adolf insisted on eating 'Patriotic Stew', a noxious vegetable collation, at least twice a week. None of the other Nazi leaders did any such thing, excepting Goebbels. Goering feasted on his venison and game, which were not on any ration! They had eaten the 'Patriotic Stew' that very evening, and she could still taste it!

Eva said, carefully, 'Well, the bombing of the cities worries everybody. Of course, we don't see much of it here in Bavaria, but I think it bothers men at the Front too, when they hear about it?'

Adolf opened his eyes and said, sharply, 'A soldier has no business thinking about such things. His duty is to fight and if need be, die. No proper German wife and mother would worry him at such a time!'

'No, I agree,' said Eva, hastily. 'It is simply that these raids seem to get worse and worse.'

Hitler brooded. Speer had told him that, if the Allied air-attacks grew at the speed they had until now, it would not be long before they would be over Germany in very great force – maybe a thousand bombers – every night! Speer had quoted 'Bomber' Harris' reply to some British Army General who said, 'You can't win a war by bombing the enemy.' Harris had replied, apparently, 'It hasn't been tried yet!'

Murderers, Hitler thought! Terror-flyers! If this went on he would order British aircrews who survived by parachuting to be executed! Uneasily, he recalled Speer saying, 'The day will come when we will need half of all our resources to fight the Battle of the Ruhr!'

Before then, the Bolsheviks would have fallen. That must be so.

When they did, he would unleash the Luftwaffe on Churchill!

Eva was tired too, but not too tired for sex. She had dressed discreetly but daringly, and hoped for Adolf's attentions that evening. But it was beginning to look unlikely, now. The silk stockings and Parisian frock and the *Worth Bleu* perfume were, again, obviously wasted. Adolf thought of nothing but the War, talked of nothing else, apart from his after-supper monologues. Eva sighed. She regretted nothing, really. But it was hard, this lack of affection, this hatred for his enemies that ate at Adolf the whole time. She wondered if she should speak totally frankly to him, to suggest that it was burning him up.

Suddenly, the telephone rang.

Adolf picked it up, instantly awake.

It had to be important – Martin Bormann had orders not to disturb him when he was in the apartment, except on the most urgent grounds. General Zeitzler was on the line from his Headquarters in East Prussia. He had alarming news from Stalingrad. 'Fuhrer, an overwhelming Soviet attack, with heavy tanks, has broken the Romanian Third Army North of the city. South of it, another strong Soviet force is attacking the Romanian Fourth Army.' Zeitzler stated, as calmly as he could, the obvious: 'The Soviets are driving from North and South to cut off Stalingrad by a huge pincer-movement. Paulus must retreat to the West, or find himself surrounded!'

Eva looked at Adolf, in alarm. His face, yellowed by the Atrabine, had an other-worldly look in the light of the soft, fringed lamps. But his voice was calm. 'You are suggesting we retreat to the River Don, and reform there?'

Zeitzler said, vastly relieved, 'Yes! It is obvious, Fuhrer.'

Adolf Hitler suddenly shouted, causing Eva to jump almost out of her skin. 'No, it is not obvious! I will not retreat! Hear me when I say this! We will not retreat from Stalingrad! Not one mile! That is my order! Do you *hear* me?'

Eva didn't know what Zeitzler said to that because Adolf slammed the telephone down, very hard.

All she knew was that their evening together was spoilt.

Hitler returned next day to the Front, arriving at the Wolf's Lair four days later. By this time the news was desperate. The Soviet Armies driving South had met the Soviet Armies driving North.

Paulus radioed: *We are surrounded. Orders, please?*

From the Wolf's Lair, Hitler radioed the reply: '*Form hedgehog defence. We will supply you from the air until we can come to your aid.*'

Paulus replied: '*Agreed. Heil Hitler!*'

Hitler asked Goering on the long-distance telephone, 'Can the Luftwaffe do it?'

'Certainly, Fuhrer,' Goering assured him.

The figures they were talking about, Hitler knew, were seven hundred and fifty tons of foodstuffs and ammunition and medical supplies every day. The weather over Stalingrad was becoming heavy and there were blizzards beginning to blow. The Soviets had the air above the city filled with fighter aircraft.

Goering telephoned. He did not dare meet Hitler face to face. 'The Luftwaffe did its best. It has never met the tonnage required on any single day.'

'What now?' replied Hitler.

'My pilots tell me the weather is now impossible.' Goering sounded defeated. His boast was seen by Hitler for what it was: bombast and rhetoric. Hitler called Manstein to his Headquarters. 'Take Army Group Don. Push straight forward to Von Paulus in Stalingrad.'

Manstein looked puzzled. He was aware of his own reputation. He was the most successful tank-commander of the War and a Major-general to boot! He was in the history books for his Ardennes offensive alone. He had a lot to lose, personally, if this went wrong. So he decided to tell Hitler the truth. 'Fuhrer, there is only one way to handle this situation. I fight my way *in*, Von Paulus fights his way *out*! We meet! There is no real chance that I can get to him, if he holds his position. I would be exposed on my flanks all the way, and you would lose two Armies, his and mine.'

Hitler did not agree. 'I will not pull my troops back from the Volga! We are in Stalingrad, and there we stay!'

Manstein looked quickly at Jodl, who looked away.

Then at Zeitzler. The 'Thunderball' smiled broadly and said, 'Fuhrer, Manstein is, I think, correct . . .'

'The General has his orders!' said Hitler sharply. 'He obeys them or I find another General! There are plenty of them standing about doing nothing!'

Manstein flushed and Zeitzler shook his head.

Manstein said, stiffly, 'Fuhrer, I will do all I can.'

'I ask the utmost,' said Hitler, turning away.

Manstein saluted and left to organise his attack-force. It stood seventy-five miles away from Stalingrad. On the day it began to move, the first full fury of the Russian winter struck with blizzards of gale-force, zero temperatures, and heavy snow. After a week of hard fighting in desperate conditions Manstein's army was thirty miles from Paulus' besieged men in the city. They sent up flares to each other. Manstein radioed to Headquarters. *'If Von Paulus moves now, in full strength, we can link up!'*

Zeitzler saw Hitler at once, as he pored over the maps, with his magnifying-glass. 'Fuhrer, we must give Von Paulus permission to break out.'

'Never. He holds firm.'

'But Fuhrer, we *must*!'

Hitler did not look up. 'Only if we hold Stalingrad as well.'

Zeitzler said, despairingly, 'We cannot do that. We haven't enough men.'

'Then Von Paulus stays where he is.'

'Fuhrer! His men are freezing and on starvation rations. And there are two hundred thousand of them! Better they get out and live to fight another day, surely?'

Again, Hitler did not look up. 'We hold Stalingrad.'

Zeitzler felt hope seep out of his boots. He had hoped his cheerful and confident manner would work with the Fuhrer, as it had always worked with everybody else. He was a first-class staff-officer, he knew it. This decision should be his, not Hitler's. He knew that, too. He now saw what Halder and the others had been up against. An ego so monstrous that it would, for a principle – 'I never retreat!' – throw away the lives of two hundred thousand German soldiers!

He tried once more.

'Fuhrer, I beg you. Reconsider.'

Hitler did not even reply.

Manstein's army came to a stop in a blinding snow-storm a little less than thirty miles from Paulus. Manstein disobeyed orders: he radioed Paulus, on his own initiative, advising him to strike out *now*! He would hold firm where he was. *Come now*, he radioed, in a message picked up by Paulus but nobody else.

Paulus was not a brave and confident man and this was his first big command.

Also, he had the Fuhrer's order. 'Don't move!'

Paulus did not move. He stayed in his dug-out, under heavy artillery fire, while his soldiers froze outside in their trenches of bricks and mortar, melting snow for water and drinking it hot, with a piece of rotten sausage chopped up in it, to make a soup. The soldiers knew what was happening: they were angry and afraid. The senior officers were mutinous and urged Paulus to escape, or try to, while he could!

Still Paulus would not move.

Manstein's attack broke down. The Soviets attacked it on the flank and Manstein conducted a fighting retreat of great skill. Soviet troops then attacked an Italian army to the North. A chain-reaction of retreat followed. The German armies pulled back, in self-defence, leaving Stalingrad to its fate.

Stalin sent a message to Paulus: *Your situation is hopeless. We propose you surrender. If you do you'll have normal Soviet rations. All prisoners will keep badges of rank and personal belongings. You have twenty-four hours to reply.*

Paulus radioed Hitler: *Do I have freedom to make the decision?*

Hitler, fidgeting and furious, not having slept properly for six days and nights, pale, and with the dull ache of failure in his chest, radioed back: *No! Fight on!*

Fight on Paulus did, as 5,000 artillery pieces rained shells on his hungry, freezing soldiers. For six days they fought, hand-to-hand, in the icy city and by that time they held only half their original positions. The Soviet Commander asked them to surrender. Again, Paulus radioed Hitler: *Without ammunition. 18,000 wounded. No dressings or drugs. Collapse inevitable. Permission to Surrender.*

Hitler answered: *Surrender is forbidden. You will hold your position to the last man and the last round of ammunition. By your heroic endeavour you will make an unforgettable contribution to the salvation of the Western World against Bolshevism.*

The soldiers, in their dug-outs, now down to a third of their original strength, listened to Field Marshal Goering on their crackly radios: 'A thousand years hence Germans will speak of the Battle for Stalingrad with reverence and awe and will remember that, in spite of everything. Germany's ultimate victory was decided here!'

The soldiers laughed, bitterly: 'What victory?'

Adolf Hitler made Paulus a Field-Marshal over the radio-link. He said, 'There is no record in German military history of a Field Marshal surrendering!'

A German reconnaissance aircraft, flying over Stalingrad, radioed to the ground: *Can see no signs of conflict.*

It was over: 90,000 German soldiers, including Von Paulus and 23 other Generals, were in Russian hands. The rest were dead. There had been 300,000 of them eight weeks before.

Hitler paced around the Headquarters, watched by Zeitzler and Jodl. They looked at the floor as he ranted. 'They have surrendered like cowards! They should have closed ranks and shot themselves with their last bullet! Paulus should have shot himself, just as the old commanders who threw themselves on their swords when they saw the cause was lost! Even Varus gave his slave the order: 'Now kill me!'

Hitler walked round and round the Map Room, gesticulating, staring, wide-eyed. 'What happens now? Paulus will be taken to Moscow! There he will sign anything! He'll make confessions, proclamations – you'll see!'

Hitler was right. Paulus did just that, two weeks later.

'What is life?' asked Hitler, shaking his head at his prophecy. 'Every individual must die! But beyond the life of the individual stands the Nation! Von Paulus could have ascended into Eternity and National Immortality, but he prefers to be a traitor in Moscow! *Generals!*'

Hitler turned away in a gesture of disgust. He issued a proclamation to the German *Volk.*

The battle of Stalingrad has ended. True to their Oath to fight to the last breath, the Sixth Army, under the exemplary leadership of Field-Marshal Paulus, has been overcome by the superiority of the enemy and by the unfavourable circumstances confronting our forces.

He also declared four days of national mourning.

The chill wind from the Steppes blew all the way back into Germany itself. The whole nation shuddered. The loss of North Africa at El Alamein went almost unnoticed.

This was defeat on a grand scale.

Troubles came not singly for the Third Reich that year.

Mussolini was the victim of a coup by his generals.

They felt the War was lost and there was no point in going on.

They arrested Mussolini, contacted the Allies, asked for an armistice, and got it.

But it took six whole weeks, and Hitler had moved by then. He sent armies he could not spare into Italy, seized the initiative and formed a line south of Naples. They disarmed Italian troops they considered to be dubious, and dug-in. The British and Americans came slowly and warily to battle-positions. Italy was held, at least for a while. Hitler breathed easy again. His Southern flank was safe. The S.S. General Otto Skovzeny rescued Mussolini from his mountain-top prison, using airborne troops to do it. It was a brilliant operation and cheered everybody, especially Hitler. Mussolini looked old and was reported by German staff-officers to be already senile, a broken reed. 'He must now savage his betrayers! Kill them!' Hitler ordered. Mussolini duly signed the execution order of his son-in-law, Ciano, who had demanded, along with everybody else, his abdication from power. Ciano was shot and his wife Edna screamed and broke china in horror at this desperate act.

Eva Braun, who loved the man who had demanded Ciano's murder, nonetheless felt for Edda Ciano. What, she wondered, as she worked in Heinrich Hoffmann's darkroom (anything was preferable to sitting in the Berghof, waiting, just waiting, for Adolf to come back) would she do, if she were ever placed in the same circumstances? Would she defend Adolf like a tigress, as Edda Ciano had defended her husband, ranting and shouting at Josef Goebbels when he told her the Fuhrer's decision?

She hoped she would.

But she did not know.

She shivered, and put the possibility from her mind.

Grand Admiral Raeder reported.

'Fuhrer, the Battle of the Atlantic is lost. The British have discovered Asdic and the Americans have bombers that can track U-Boats from the air. The North Atlantic is clear of U-boats.' He waited for the storm. It came. 'You are telling me that the American convoys, full of guns and men, will sail unhampered to Britain?'

Raeder said yes.

514

Hitler, ill and shaking, sat in the Wolf's Lair. Nothing looked good. The Japanese had long lost the decisive naval Battle of Midway, and failed at Imphal to take India, and had been on the retreat ever since. Their usefulness consisted entirely of the fact that they used up American resources! In the East the German Army was executing a skilful retreat. Hitler called Zeitzler, "no braver than the other cowards!" The bouncy, ebullient general, reported 'sick', went home on leave to recover, and never returned, pleading progressive illnesses, accompanied by copious medical certificates. Hitler stripped Zeitzler of his rank and his right to wear uniform and described him as a 'malingerer'. Stalingrad and the terrible tank defeat at Kursk had broken Zeitzler's nerve. Adolf Hitler had to soldier on. He had to save Germany. He was Europe's only hope. One day everybody would see that.

Two months later Hitler was back at the Berghof. Greatly daring, Josef Goebbels approached him. 'Fuhrer, do we try for a Peace Settlement with one side or the other?'

Hitler stood, thinking about what Goebbels had said, not yet raging as Goebbels had feared he might. His left hand was shaking, his right hand gripping it to stop the tremors. Goebbels was shocked at what he saw, but he had been warned. An eminent physician considered that it could be Parkinson's Disease. What was also possible was another cause that Goebbels had long suspected. As a veteran of women's beds Goebbels had always taken strict precautions against infection. He had not just been lucky, he had been experienced. Hitler, in the land of venery, was neither. It would be strange, Goebbels thought, if Hitler, the despiser of women, had become a member of Schnitzler's *La Ronde* syndrome, whereas he, the lover of them, went scot-free!

'Stalin is a realist,' Hitler said. 'It might be possible to come to an accommodation with him, if we could have a victory, even a small one. Otherwise, no.' Did he not still have all of Europe and a slice of Asia? Did he not still have his V1 and V2 terror-weapons in development at Peenamunde? Why should he sue for peace with anybody?

Goebbels was shaking his head at the idea of Stalin. 'Fuhrer, the English can't want a Bolshevik victory! Churchill himself is an old anti-Bolshevik. His alliance with Stalin is simply a case of: my enemy's enemy is my friend! As he said himself!'

Hitler held his shaking hand so tightly the knuckles showed white. 'The English will one day come to their senses. One day they will have to make a choice, the Bolshevik, or us! Historically, Josef –'

Goebbels felt that his desperation was being buried under the

Fuhrer's usual welter of words. 'Fuhrer, allow me to say why I think we must seriously consider an approach?'

Hitler looked surprised and sat down. Goebbels noticed that he was dragging his left foot. That was new. He looked at Hitler in concern. Unlike many of the other Nazis around Hitler, he felt the need to get together a sensible policy. Fight on, certainly. But look for any possibility of a deal! He had talked to Goering and Himmler about such a way forward: but neither had been willing to move. They were both afraid of Adolf Hitler and what he might do. This, from Goering with his *Pour la Merité* pinned on his chest. This, from Himmler, who had actually sent a Gestapo team to Linz, to find out whether there was anything in the rumours, persistent throughout Hitler's time in power and before it, that Hitler had Jewish blood somewhere!

What had Himmler thought he might do, Goebbels wondered, if he did obtain proof of it?

Depose Hitler, on the strength of the allegation and take power?

Goebbels thought: Himmler was mad enough on the subject of Race to try it!

One thing Himmler should know by now. There were no secrets in the Third Reich.

'Fuhrer, we had one thousand bombers over Hamburg the night before last. Let me read you what Gauleiter Kaufman reports?'

Hitler turned away, and gazed out of the long window of the Berghof. He did not reply. Goebbels thought: he will not make any public speeches now. He will not even tour the bombed cities, as I do. If he goes through them on his train, he pulls the blinds down! He coughed and took Kaufman's report from his tunic pocket. 'If I may, Fuhrer, just part of his report?' He coughed and recited: 'This last bombing raid is a catastrophe that staggers the imagination. A city of a million inhabitants has been destroyed, in a manner unparalleled in history. We have problems almost impossible to solve. We have almost a million homeless. They need food, shelter, clothing.'

But Hitler was not listening: he was fondling Blondi's fur and murmuring to the dog. After a long moment, Goebbels, very quietly, folded up the report, put it in his pocket and let himself out of the room.

A bomb was placed on Adolf Hitler's aeroplane, when he flew to Smolensk to review the situation on the Eastern Front. This bomb was British-made, dropped by the RAF with the object of getting foreign nationals to pick it up, see what it was, and use it to sabotage the German war-effort. The prime-motivator of the plot, General Von Tresckow, had two junior officers plant the activated bomb on the aeroplane. It was in the form of a bottle of brandy, being carried to a friend, by an unknown officer on the plane. It failed to go off, and the young officer, a man called Sehlabrendorff, reclaimed the bottle from the officer at his Headquarters. Two other attempts were made by this group. On both occasions the Allied bombs failed to work.

Adolf Hitler had the luck of the devil.

In the Summer of 1944 the long-awaited Allied invasion-forces landed in Normandy. Not, as Hitler and everybody else confidently expected, at the Pas de Calais. Reported the BBC, 'The British, Americans and Canadians are ashore in good order, using a massive floating harbour to supply their forces. They have massive air-cover. Up to now they have encountered little resistance.'

'Eisenhower, not Patton, is in command of the Allied Forces,' said German Intelligence to Hitler. They had noted Patton as a daring tank-man in North Africa. 'Eisenhower, an American general who has never commanded any force in any battle? He's a compromise commander!' said Hitler. But the fact was the Allies had breached the Atlantic Wall. They were back in Europe.

Runstedt and Rommel looked at each other in their West Front Headquarters, and realised that Nazi Germany was now almost certainly finished. They were soldiers, however, and they acted like soldiers. They ignored Hitler's immediate, hysterical demand by field-telephone. 'The Invasion beachheads must be cleared-up at once!' but sent in their 21st. Panzers, the only armoured unit in the invasion area able to contain the Allied thrust, at least for a while. About the continued landing of large enemy forces they could do nothing. Both men felt desperately sure that a vast defeat stared them in the face. Ten days after the Allies landed, Hitler arrived at Margival, near Soissons, at a large underground bunker. Here, Rommel told Hitler bluntly how things stood: 'The struggle is hopeless, Fuhrer. The enemy has superiority, both on land and in the air. We must retreat away from their huge naval artillery, regroup and bring them to battle under better terms.'

Hitler listened no longer. He jumped to his feet, spilling his coloured crayons onto the maps in front of him. 'We do not retreat! I have unleashed on London today a Secret Weapon that will bring them to their knees!'

Rommel and Runstedt stared at him.

'My VI terror-weapon is flying over their capital now!'

'What is it?' they asked, looking at each other.

'A pilotless aircraft, full of explosive!'

Rommel pondered. It sounded helpful, but it did not do anything about the thousands of troops landing in Normandy at that very moment. 'Fuhrer, let us be practical,' he said. 'The Front here may well collapse. A breakthrough into Germany itself will be next. The Eastern Front is also in danger of collapsing, as we all know. Soon the Soviets will be in Germany. In two-or-three weeks, perhaps.' Hitler was staring at his favourite general, the stocky, crop-headed Rommel, with incredulity. 'Fuhrer, we are finished, militarily and politically. We should end the War.'

'Never!' shouted Hitler. 'You do your duty and fight the invasion. Let me worry about the future of Germany!'

He left, at once.

The two generals looked gloomily at each other.

'Now, I have told him. It was his last chance,' said Rommel.

They both knew exactly what Erwin Rommel meant.

On July 20th Adolf Hitler was back at the Wolf's Lair. The Soviets had broken into East Prussia, a huge medieval army on the march. 'First the T 34 tanks, huge lumbering monsters: then the infantry, carrying their weapons; and ammunition. A satchel containing their personal food-ration, vegetables dug out of the ground, or coarse grain to boil in water and eat as a porridge. They live off the land as they march, their horses following behind with carts carrying whatever supplies they have. The horses eat the thatch of the country hovels. Peasant-women march with them: punishment battalions are driven first, into minefields. The whole spectacle is staggering. *A medieval army on the march!*'

The officer recalling the scene, a shaven, scented product of Potsdam – was retailing this story as the Fuhrer walked into his daily conference. He shut up at once, but not before Hitler had heard most of it. 'The Siberian is a peasant but he is a hard fighter. If we are to defeat him we must live on as little as he does, expect as little as he does! Gentlemen, to work!'

Hitler sat at the centre of the long, solidly-built conference table, his back to the door. Generals Heusinger, Korten, and Colonel Brandt sat close to him. Jodl sat, as ever, next to the Fuhrer. All told, eighteen officers sat or stood at the table, as Heusinger began a report on the situation on the Eastern Front. Hitler looked up and nodded as Keitel came in, accompanied by an officer with only one hand, covered by a black glove, and a black eyepatch. This man, Hitler knew as one of German's greatest heroes. His name was Colonel Klaus Von Stauffenberg, and he was here to present a special report to Hitler, at the end of the conference. Hitler nodded to him and Stauffenberg sat down, putting his briefcase under the table. So did Keitel, nearer to Hitler.

Heusinger continued with his report.

After a little time, Stauffenberg left the room.

Hitler concentrated on the words the general was uttering: like all the generals, he seemed to relish defeat. The words were always the same; retreat, retreat, retreat. Hitler found his attention wandering and looked out of the window of the Conference building. The sun was shining and the wooded scene was peaceful.

The explosion blew Adolf Hitler out of his chair.

As he tried to rise, he fumblingly checked himself for damage. He could not hear anything. His hair was smouldering and singed. His back hurt, obviously hit by a fallen wooden-support. The whole room was a wreck of wood-splinters and shards. His right arm would not move, and seemed paralysed; his uniform was blackened and in shreds.

Adolf Hitler stared foggily around him: dead and dying men lay in strange, still, attitudes across or under the vast table: there was blood everywhere.

A bomb, he thought, dully.

His enemies had come for him with a bomb.

Keitel, miraculously, was also uninjured.

Together, they staggered out into the daylight.

His enemies had come for him with a bomb and they had failed.

Now, whoever they were, they would pay.

Hitler, badly shaken, followed the trial of the conspirators with interest. The film of the proceedings was sent to him each day, as he recuperated at the Berghof. Nobody but himself saw them. Eva Braun, to whom he had sent his scorched and torn uniform, was struck mute by the outrage. She moved quietly around the place, attending to his small needs. He had told her only the bare bones of it all. There was no point in upsetting her further, none at all. These *canaille* would pay for their crime. Rudolf Freisler, the Judge, had their measure. After their experiences at the hands of the Gestapo they had him to face, as they stood clad only in rough flannel shirt, shoeless, and holding up their trousers with their trembling hands. 'Stop playing with yourself!' Freisler shouted at Witzbelen, the oldest of them, as he tried vainly to protest that it had all been for Germany!

Who were these traitors, these filth who would deliver Germany into Bolshevik captivity?

Generals, every one!

Stauffenberg, who had left the bomb, under the table in his briefcase, was dead by his own hand.

Beck, the leader, or one of them, had – lucky for him – gone the same way. Rommel – of all people, Erwin Rommel! – was guilty and given the choice: face trial and see your family disgraced, or shoot himself. He shot himself and was buried as a national hero.

Witzbelen, a Field Marshal, sixty-three years old! The man who was to take Hitler's place, as Chancellor of Germany – *look* at him now the Gestapo had done with him, shaking and fiddling with his trousers!

Gordeler was known to have contacts with the Allies. Two diplomats, Schullenberg, former German-ambassador in Moscow, no longer young, and Hassell, former ambassador in Rome, were amongst the *swinehunds*, as was Fromm, who had changed sides far too late.

Canaris even! No real proof, but his senior Abwehr staff had been in the plot and were executed. He escaped trial but was in Sauchenhausen, while Hitler decided what to do with him.

On and on the trials went, all that hot summer as the battles raged, East and West. They had almost ended when a stray Allied bomb killed Judge Freisler, coming out of his court-room.

The executions started. Most of the conspirators were hanged, after lengthy torture, with piano-wire strung on meat-hooks.

Von Witzbelen was at the point of death several times, but released, and hung all over again.

Hitler watched the execution alone, on film, and gloated.

His enemies had tried for his life, yet again but unlike the Duce hanging upside-down with his mistress, Clara Pettaci, in a square in Milan, he was still alive!

Alive and ready to fight on!

'A Winter Offensive in the Ardennes?' The Generals had, at first, gasped, but Hitler had convinced them. Now, he walked around the reserve camp, haranguing and exhorting the men, wearing his long leather coat. The men were a splendid sight, the best fighting army the Reich could put together in the autumn of 'Forty-Four. The General Staff had pulled together all the armour they could find and the best of the remaining Panzer and Infantry divisions. Hitler stayed and watched the first units go forward. In deepest winter, the Wehrmacht struck through the thick forests towards Brussels. Allied troops were celebrating Christmas in the blacked-out Belgain capital. At first, the news was good everywhere. Finally, the Americans held firm at Bastogne, and then Montgomery brought in tanks and infantry reinforcements. The allied line held. The fog, which had protected the Panzers, suddenly cleared. The RAF Typhoon pilots could see their enemy clearly, in the snow. The German tank losses were heavy. The attack fizzled out and the survivors withdrew, in the cold, silent snows of Winter.

Adolf Hitler went back to the Chancellery, in Berlin.

He was cold, ill, and felt, for a desperate moment, defeat. He shook it off at once. His V1 pilotless-planes had fallen on London and killed thousands of civilians. He hadn't enough of them, but he had ordered more. He might yet force Churchill to evacuate his capital with the V2s, the huge rockets against which the RAF had no defence. *Faster than sound itself!* They would bomb London to bits! He was not finished yet, not by a long way.

Hitler sat alone in his study in the Chancellery, and quietly began to plan the Summer campaign of 1945. Morell kept up his injections and Hitler took all the stimulants he was offered. Eva Braun was at the Obersaltzberg, and he did not think he would ever see her again.

Unlike Atilla, he would die alone.

Not, like Atilla, in a wedding-bed, making a nonsense of a great life, no, not *that*!

At the head of his troops, fighting for Germany!

That was how he would fall, come the day.

Which was not yet.

XXIII

E VA BRAUN joined Adolf Hitler in the Berlin Chancellery in the
bleak January of 1945. She had been working with Hoffmann
and living in Munich with her younger sister Gretl, at 12 Wassen-
burgstrasse. Gretl's new husband, SS Sturmbannfuhrer Hermann Fegelin, was at the Chancellery as Himmler's liaison-officer to the Fuhrer.
Eva was concerned about Adolf's health. He had had a polyp removed
from his throat and when she asked how the Fuhrer was, Heinrich
Hoffmann was uncharacteristically evasive. 'The strain is terrible for
him, and, well, frankly, I don't know how he manages to go on!'

Hoffmann seemed strangely fatalistic. He was still taking his photographs, but there were very few newspapers publishing on a regular
basis any longer. The Third Reich was grinding to a halt. Hoffmann
seemed, to Eva, to represent those who had done well out of Adolf
Hitler. Now the party was over. Still, to do him credit, Hoffmann
remained loyal. He said, wryly: 'Two years ago I was a millionaire, from
the royalties on my photographs of the Fuhrer alone.'

Eva retorted fiercely, 'Adolf will be a great man, before history, whatever happens! Your photographs will be in demand for centuries!'

'Possibly, but the German historians will not write the history books.'

'Even so! His name will ring for evermore, Heinrich!'

Hoffmann nodded, and said, gently, 'If all goes wrong, Eva, none of
us will have anything. As I say, my fortune in German marks will be
gone, but I don't care about that.'

'Anyway, I'm going to Berlin tomorrow' said Eva.

Hoffmann looked surprised. His hair was white now and he had lost
his old ebulliance. He was, she supposed, almost sixty years old. All the
men who were anybody in the Reich were of his generation. Adolf
himself was fifty-six in the coming April – where would they all be, by
then? Where would they all be by her own birthday in February?

Hoffmann said, 'I thought the Fuhrer wanted you to stay here in Munich, where it's safer?'

'I won't tell him, I'll just arrive.'

Which is what she did, in the Mercedes that he had put at her disposal, along with a handsome, blond S.S. driver. Eva took with her six pieces of luggage, and wore her magnificent silver-fox coat, plus all the toiletries she would need. Two large bottles, the last, of her favourite *Worth Bleu* perfume, and all her jewels. The journey was uneventful, although the Americans were bombing targets by daylight and the British were bombing by night, so that the skies of Germany were full of danger twenty-four hours a day. Eva had been in Berlin only months before but she was astonished by the state of the city. Buildings were down everywhere, converted by high-explosive into vast piles of rubble. The roads were often impassable and they were re-routed again and again by *Feldgendarmerie* with their distinctive metal breastplates, who were checking everywhere for deserters, and hanging them from the lamp-posts as a warning to others. Huge bomb-craters were everywhere and few shops seemed to be open. There were long queues of dull, dirty, apathetic people at the ones that were. She asked her driver what they were in line for? 'Bread, if they're lucky,' he replied, laconically.

'Where do they live?' she asked, horrified.

'In their cellars, nowhere else is safe any more. Or so I'm told.'

Adolf was astonished to see her.

But it was obvious to her – and to everybody else – that he was delighted. His face lit up in a smile of such joy that she could have cried to see him. It was all she could do not to cry anyway; he was skeletal, a spectre, his uniform hung on him like a shroud. Oh, no, not a shroud, things were not yet at that pass, anything could happen to save them yet! Of course, he did not kiss her when he saw her, in the Chancellery office, but he put his arm around her shoulders and that was as much as he ever did, in public. The secretaries looked on dewy-eyed, and smiled and chattered and welcomed her. They too looked tired and pale. She supposed it was the lack of air in the offices of the *Kanzlerai*: the windows were covered with strips of anti-glass material; many were simply boarded-up. Sandbags were piled around all the entrances to the building. S.S. guards were everywhere, bristling with weapons; sub-machine guns in their hands and hand-grenades in their pouches. She wondered: would they not be more use fighting at the front, now only fifty miles away? But Bormann, ever-present and quickly at her side, told her in a whisper, 'The Fuhrer is afraid of a kidnap attempt. As we took Mussolini, so would the Bolsheviks take him, if they could. That is his opinion.' It was obvious nothing had changed: Bormann was still running things.

There was one good thing about Bormann: he was loyal. He did not think about defeat. Perhaps he did not dare think about defeat. Well, Eva thought, nobody did.

Adolf ushered her into his study. 'Evie! I said don't come here!'

'But you're glad to see me! I can see it in your face!'

'Of course I am! When am I not?'

'Then you can be glad all the time because I'm staying. To the end.'

He was suddenly still. 'The end?'

'I share your fate. Whatever it is. You know that.'

He shook his head. 'I don't want that for you.'

'Then that's a pity, because I'm here.' Eva began to unpack her toilet-case. The air of Berlin was foul: there seemed to be a pall of fine, gritty dust over everything. It got into the very pores of the skin. 'Now, I'm going to wash, and then you can tell me what's happening?'

'I can tell you that in one sentence, Evie. We are holding the Bolsheviks! We will continue to do so until the British and the Americans come to their senses! Soon, they will see what a Bolshevik victory would mean to them. The savages rampage all over Europe. Soon, they will have to confront the savages, face-to-face! Soon, they will realise the only hope is an alliance with us. Then we will all fight as one, in a Western Crusade against the Bolsheviks!'

'You think that can happen, Adi?' she asked, solemnly.

He kissed her on the cheek: her heart turned over at how sallow and ill he looked. The tremor in his hand was worse than before, his left foot dragged behind him. The bomb, she thought, that was what it was all due to, the bomb the cowardly generals had tried to kill him with!

'It can happen,' Adolf said, in a flat, dead voice. 'It must. Or the West is lost and the future belongs to the Siberians.'

Eva hesitated, then asked, softly, 'The Unconditional Surrender the Americans and the English talk about on the radio, do they mean it?'

'They mean it now. In a month, when they see the primitive might of the Bolsheviks ever closer, they may have another view. Also remember the Vatican. Rome has always been with us. The Pope's influence will make itself felt. The Roman Church wants Stalin less than they want me. I would not abolish religion, I have always said I would let it wither on the bough. The Bolsheviks will kill the priests and turn the Cathedrals into museums.'

'Have you thought of a Peace Feeler? To the Americans and the English?'

'Peace Feeler!' Hitler said, sharply. 'I could not do that. Goebbels wanted to do it, still does, I think. But how would it look if I did, and the Allies said no? How could I ask my men to fight on, after that?'

Eva nodded, tears filling her eyes. Poor dear Adi, he looked awful. 'I'll go and wash,' she said. 'Then we'll talk.'

'I have an urgent conference with my generals. But we'll meet for supper, yes?' He smiled ruefully. 'I still have my family suppers, although sometimes they take place in the Bunker.'

Eva stared. 'The Bunker?'

'The Air Raid Bunker, here in the Chancellery garden. We go there to sleep some nights. It's no longer safe up here, if the bombing is heavy.'

'Will it be heavy tonight?'

'We have no way of knowing. At one time, when we had our great radio listening-out posts, we knew when the blow would strike and how heavily, by the sheer weight of the RAF radio-transmissions, to each other. Now, we are denied that.'

Yes, Eva thought, because the vast discs of the radio-listening stations are in Holland and France and they are long over-run. 'I should have asked, how is your throat?' she said.

'My throat?' He looked surprised. 'The operation was quite minor. I'm fully recovered. Don't worry, *Tschespetyl*.'

Eva was touched. He rarely called her by the Bavarian endearment.

But fully recovered? His weight was thirty pounds less than when she had seen him last, two months before! What was Morell thinking about – to allow him to get into this terrible state?

Eva excused herself and found a vast bathroom with gold-plated taps and her maid running a bath for her. What a blessing she was! 'The water is hot, Frau, but how long for, nobody is sure! What a mess!' The maid had laid out a complete new set of silk underclothes and a dress for Eva. 'It might be easier to change in here. I will be back to help you in fifteen minutes, if that is in order, Frau?'

Eva smiled and thanked her. She took off her travel-stained dress and stockings and shoes and threw them down. She stepped into the delicious hot water and liberally dosed it with bath-oil. From Paris, and almost the last of its line, it smelled heavenly. Eva luxuriated in the water, and thought: the way Adi *looked*! What had to be done was to get him well again. She got out of the bath at last, and dried herself on the huge, white bath-towels. Ah, it was good to be cossetted. A girl might as well live as well as possible, while she could. Eva studied herself in the long mirror: she still had a wonderful figure, never mind the thirty-three years! Thirty-four next month. Children, however much she had wanted them, would have spoilt it, by now. Men, and Adi was no exception, would look elsewhere then: they always did. They loved the wife of their children but they went to other, younger women with figures like her own. Adi liked young girls: obviously, he always had: but since she had been with him, he had not strayed. She was as sure of that as any woman could ever be. Adi was, despite his insistence that he was not good husband-or-father material, loyal and loving. That rotten old swine, Alois Hitler again, had put him off marriage for good, there was no doubt of that in Eva's mind, none at all. She admired herself in the mirror: her breasts were small but still well-shaped: her waist and legs reflected, in their firmness, the hours she had spent exercising and swimming and walking. She was her athletic mother's daughter, as Adi was his bullying father's son. It is all decided for us, Eva thought, there is almost nothing we can do about it.

Eva dressed quickly, and sought out Doctor Theodor Morell. She found him in his box-sized office in the Chancellery. He seemed cynically unaffected by what was happening all around him. His suit fitted him no better than it ever had, his chin needed a shave and his body-odour was still strong. His tongue and brain were as sharp as ever.

'Ah, Fraulein Braun. I did not expect to see you here. It is hardly a health resort these days.'

'Nor I you, Doctor Morell.'

'No,' he replied, urging her to a seat, a rickety, dusty-looking chair. Eva sat down, disdainfully. He looked over his spectacles. 'What can I do for you, Fraulein? A glass of wine perhaps?'

'I must say you look well,' the venerealogist replied. 'Wait until you've spent a few nights in the Bunker. You'll lose your girlish complexion, I'm afraid.'

Eva frowned. He seemed to be laughing at her. He was always doing that. 'I want to know what is wrong with the Fuhrer? He looks terrible,' she said.

Morell took off and slowly polished his glasses with a grubby handkerchief. 'He is in a poor state of health. It is not to be wondered at, considering his regime. I do what I can.'

'Which is?' Eva asked, suspiciously.

'You would not be any the wiser if I told you. But dextrose and various stimulants.'

'Could you be more specific?'

Morell yawned, not covering his mouth, revealing irregular, yellowish teeth. 'Certainly, I can. I have given him regular doses of my own specific, to aid his digestion, and to ease his cramps.'

'Adi has had stomach-cramps ever since I have known him!'

'Just so. My treatment always helps, I'm glad to say.' He hesitated. 'You recall that the Fuhrer had injuries from the Bomb?' As if she was likely to forget it! 'The Fuhrer's tympanic membranes were both broken by the explosion. He also suffered irritation in the labrynth of the ears,

526

which affect his power of balance. He had also a subcutaneous haemorrhage in his right arm . . .'

'I know all this,' Eva interrupted. 'He went to bed for almost a month and was better. But he's still unwell. He looks yellow. He drags his left foot. His hand trembles. Is all that due to the bomb they tried to kill him with?'

Morell looked at her studiously, and spread his hands. 'How much do you know of the Fuhrer's medical-history, before you met him?'

'I know he was wounded and gassed in the First War, that is all. He hates to talk about his health. For some silly reason he thinks it a weakness.' Eva looked curiously at Morell. She had an idea he was holding something back. But *what?*'

Morell said, finally, 'He has said nothing? Of any incident in his earlier life? In the time he was alone in the world, in Munich, particularly?'

'No. Did he have consumption or something? I think he had a weak chest as a boy. Is that what you are talking about? Or cancer? He has always feared it. His mother . . .'

'Not consumption. Or cancer.'

'What then?'

'You will have to ask him yourself, Fraulein Braun. I am his doctor and my oath does not permit me to discuss my patient's health.' Morell paused, delicately. 'Even to his . . . nearest . . . friends.'

Wife, Eva thought furiously, *wife* would have been acceptable.

'Are you talking about his own . . . physical disability?' she asked.

Morell said nothing.

'I mean his lack of a testicle,' she said, in an attempt at brutality.

Morell merely smiled. That had been a mistake. Nothing would shock Morell.

'Not quite,' he said.

'Then *what?*' Eva demanded.

He was silent, a long moment. 'You will have to ask him yourself, Fraulein Braun,' he said, in a curiously sympathetic voice. She supposed being a venereologist taught him the manner. After all, that was what he had been, famous for it. Well, plainly she was getting nowhere. She said, 'Are all these injections absolutely necessary to him?'

'The Fuhrer thinks so.' His tone was final.

Morell had profited by the sale of his patented 'Russia' flea-and-lice powder to the Wehrmacht: the contract had made him a millionaire. Like Hoffmann, she thought: rich but with no way of spending the money he had accumulated. She wondered why Morell was still here. It occurred to her that, he had, despite his cynicism, fallen under the spell of the Fuhrer. She did not like the grubby little doctor any the more for knowing it, but at least she understood him. Like herself, he

527

was staying to the bitter end, while others, like Goering and Himmler and Doenitz, remained at their own headquarters, knowing that the Bolsheviks had squads combing the Reich for Hitler. Anybody with him, if he was ever captured, would receive short shrift. Eva shuddered, very slightly, at the thought of it.

'Are you all right?' Morell was regarding her seriously.

'Yes. I'm fine.'

'If there's anything? Nerves or anything? I'm always here.'

Eva did not reply. She left, in search of the other faithful ones, who had been attracted, like moths to a flame, to the bunker.

Ribbentrop was there (as usual, pompous and formal) in his Chancellery office, which was curious because she did not think of him as the most loyal of people. He had been out of the limelight for a long time. If 'Peace Feelers' were in the air, Ribbentrop, as Foreign Minister, would be the obvious one to negotiate with the West, or even the East. After all, he had met Eden and Molotov and all those people. Artur Axmann, Reich *Jugend-fuhrer*, was there, but only from time to time, as the boys of the *Jugend* were manning the bridges across the Spree against the eventual Soviet Attack. Only fourteen, or even thirteen years old, they had been called to the colours that year. The *Volksturm*, men too old for military duty until now, were with them.

God, Eva thought, the children and the old men, is that all we have left?

At supper, which they took early in the antechamber before the light failed and the bombers arrived, the full roll-call was taken soundlessly, by Eva. Generals Bergdorf and Krebs, stern military men whom she hardly knew, and their various young aides, looking strained and yet unconcerned, a curious mixture indeed. She supposed they were all afraid to die, being so young. Well, she was young too, and she wasn't afraid.

Doctor Stumpfegger, the S.S. medico, was present, avuncular and easy, and, naturally, Bormann. People she did not know well, like the aristocratic Klaus Von Below and others, were going busily about their duties, whatever they were. Eva could not think what they might be. She shut her mind to all that and greeted somebody she did know, Hermann Fegelin, her brother-in-law, tall and handsome in his S.S. Gruppenfuhrer's uniform, with his Knight's Cross with Oak Leaves. She had often thought that Fegelin had married her young sister Gretl for personal advancement. It didn't hurt to be married to Eva Braun's sister. He had done well for himself, and was now go-between for Himmler with the Fuhrer himself. Fegelin embraced her cheerfully and she was conscious of his masculinity and strength. She knew his reputation with women – who did not? – but she kissed him back effusively. No point in showing any criticism. He was Gretl's husband and that was that. It occurred to her it might not be a bad idea to bring Gretl to the Chancellery? Plainly, her husband was leading a full sex-life here: but then he led a full sex-life wherever he was. Fegelin was a lucky man, and women can smell out luck on a man, Eva thought, good or bad. Well, she had had the good with Adolf, and the bad, if it came, would be no worse than she had expected, anyway for at least the past year. Before that, she had thought her happiness would go on for ever.

Fegelin said, 'How's Gretl?'

'Fine, when I left this morning.'

'Good. She's best away from here, in her condition.'

For Gretl was four months pregnant.

'She misses you,' said Eva.

'All the women miss me,' said Fegelin, outrageously. 'Then they go off with somebody else!'

Or you do, thought Eva. On impulse, she said, 'Before we eat, a private word?' They went out into the Chancellery garden. It was grievously changed. A huge air-raid shelter was constructed there, lying in the grass like some giant concrete sea-liner, half-sunk into the ground. It was heavily guarded by S.S. men.

'Good Lord, what's that monstrosity?' she asked.

Fegelin laughed. 'The Fuhrer's personal shelter.'

Eva said, 'I suppose I'll go in it tonight?'

'Only if the bombers arrive. They don't come every night. About one in three.'

Eva said in a low voice, 'About the Fuhrer. He looks bad.'

Fegelin hesitated. 'Yes. He does.'

'I think Morell is giving him too many injections.'

Fegelin hesitated again. 'I talked to one of the S.S. doctors. I won't say who. He reckons Morell gives the Fuhrer too many stimulants. Dextrose and hormones are all right but you need more and more every time. And he's been giving him a lot of anti-flatulence pills – his valet Linge just dishes them out to the Fuhrer. He said that it's all right for a while but now the Fuhrer is dependent . . .' Fegelin stopped. 'Eva, don't try to do anything about it. The Fuhrer believes absolutely in Morell.'

'Yes, I know that, too,' said Eva, linking arms with Fegelin. He had been helpful, he was a friend. 'Let's go and eat supper before the bombers come.' As they turned to go back into the Chancellery building she heard a low rumble, like thunder on the far horizon.

'What's that noise?'

Fegelin was silent, for a long moment. 'Russian artillery.'

Eva said nothing.

They walked into the Chancellery building, arm in arm.

Eva's older sister Ilse came up from Munich in early February. She didn't give a reason for her visit, already more dangerous than Eva's own, a month before. The bombing was worse than ever: American aircraft ranged free over Germany by day, bombing and machine-gunning at will. No German fighters went up to contest them. The Luftwaffe was *kaput*, said Fegelin, since the failure of the Ardennes offensive.

Eva arranged for Ilse to stay at the *Adlon*, and went to have lunch with her there, which they took, alone, in the lavish suite. Despite the War and the imminent danger to everyone in the city, the *Adlon* had its standards. For Ilse and Eva there was room-service with Rhinewine of impeccable vintage, various cold meats including goose and ham, following a creamy pea-soup, and with excellent torte to follow, accompanied by real black coffee. 'It must be the last coffee left in Berlin?' said Eva to the Headwaiter, who had himself supervised the serving: he knew who Eva was. It was his business to know things like that.

'Almost, dear Frau, but we hope for better days ahead.'

'Indeed we do. Everybody at the Chancellery is optimistic.'

'I am delighted to hear it, and may I wish you ladies *bon appétit?*' And he bowed and was gone and the two sisters were alone. They instantly burst out laughing and giggling, and were sixteen again.

'Shall we eat first and talk afterwards?' asked Eva, smiling at her sister's wide-open eyes.

'Yes, let's! I haven't seen food like this for years! And this room!'

'Suite!'

'Well! Look at it! A beautiful bedroom, clean sheets, everything like pre-war! Flowers! Where do they get *flowers* from?'

A copper bowl standing on an opulent English oak-sideboard, held a bunch of winter lilies.

'Don't enthuse, Ilse! Enjoy!'

Ilse ate every last crumb of torte. She leaned back, holding her crystal-glass of *Liebfraumilch* in her hand. There was still another bottle in the silver bucket. 'Talk about fiddling while Rome burns, Evie!'

Eva didn't like that remark. After all, *she* wasn't living like this. She was in a room, comfortable enough of course, at the Chancellery, but not quite the *Adlon*: which, downstairs in the lobby showed signs of the times. Officers on wounded-leave were billeted, four to a sumptuous room in the hotel, and to be seen, on crutches and sticks, sitting in the lobby, nervously reading the two-sheet newspapers that were all Goebbels could manage these days. The *Volkischer Beobachter*'s front page exhorted the troops and the entire Reich (what was left of it!) to one last gargantuan effort to repel the Barbarians, to buy breathing-space while the Reich's secret weapons reduced London, while the Fuhrer's large forces in Norway and in Italy, still intact, fought their way back to the Fatherland!

Dreams, Eva thought: we are all living on dreams.

The V2's were no longer falling on London. She knew that. The firing-ramps at Peenemunde had been bombed, and for all she knew, over-run. The last remnants of the Wehrmacht were fighting desperately in an ever-narrowing circle, with Berlin at the centre. It was now only a matter of time. She knew that. Well, *c'est la guerre*. Not to worry. Everybody, as Adi often said, died sometime.

'It was nice of you to come, Ilse,' she said, softly.

Ilse, sturdy and dark and the oldest of the sisters, was the most independent and fearless of them. What, Eva wondered, had happened to her boyfriend, the young Jewish doctor? Had he got away to some neutral country, or what? She had never asked, in case Ilse asked for help. It was no use asking for help. Never had been. Anybody who stayed had been a fool. There were signs to see. Probably the doctor had got away. She hoped so. She had liked him.

Really, Adi was strange about the Jews: it was the one thing she could never understand about him. Once or twice, she had brought up the subject, when they were alone. But he had always evaded any discussion. When she pressed too far he had shouted; 'Enough!' And she felt what Fegelin said about it: that it was *personal* with the Fuhrer. By now everybody knew about the Camps. Wasn't Goering saying it was the one thing that would put the noose around everybody's neck, that anything might be forgiven in war, except *that*?

Well, *that* had happened, for better or worse, and no changing it.

Eva didn't understand Adi's action with regard to the Jews and the Gypsies and the Slavs. But he was her man. Twelve years was a long time.

'Evie!' Ilse's voice was bold and loud. Eva realised she was a little drunk. Well, they both were. 'Evie, Vadi and Mutti are worried about you.'

'Ilse, I'm worried about myself, who wouldn't be, we are at War, or hadn't you heard?'

Eva giggled and poured more wine. It was chilled and quite delicious. Enjoy every single moment like this and no regrets, that was the thing to do. 'Stay a few days, Ilse, why not, who knows when we'll see each other again, yes?'

Ilse drank a large mouthful of wine at a gulp, as if it was water. It was not ladylike to do that, Eva thought, but what the devil, anything went, now. The S.S. detachment in the barracks next to the Chancellery were having street-girls, bribed by food, in the barracks at night. Officers were looking the other way. She knew because Fegelin had told her. Fegelin knew everything.

Fegelin, however, had looked doubtful when she told him Adi was still full of hope that Wencke's Army in the West would drive to Berlin and reinforce the garrison in the city: but he had said nothing.

Nobody did, any more.

'Evie, I'm going back tomorrow.' Ilse's eyes glittered, she seemed to be forcing herself to talk. When Eva protested, 'Why so soon?' she replied, 'No, I must! Who knows what may happen in the next week or two? I want to be in my own house when the worst comes. Whatever it is.'

Eva said, slurring her words, 'That's defeatist talk, Ilse.'

Ilse took a deep breath and her voice was stern and loud. The elder sister, Eva thought, always the elder sister. 'Evie! Wake up! Open your eyes! Breslau is lost! Silesia is lost! Berlin is almost surrounded! Everywhere, people flee, pushing hand-carts even, leaving everything, their homes, their possessions behind them!'

Eva waved her glass, tipsily. 'Nonsense! Wencke's Army is on the way!'

'Even if it is, it's too late to save Germany!'

'What?' Eva put down her glass, unsteadily. This had gone all wrong. She had got Ilse into this suite at the *Adlon* for a last, fond farewell, not for this! 'Ilse, please don't say any more.'

Ilse said, steadily, not seeming to be drunk any longer, 'Hitler's mad, Evie. He's dragged Germany into the abyss.'

Eva stared at her sister, aghast. Such ingratitude! Blood rose to her face. She found herself shouting: 'You are the one who is mad, you stupid, ignorant woman! You don't understand what the Fuhrer is! He's a genius. He's a great man. History will show it!'

'In that case, why are we being bombed and shelled to death?'

Eva felt the palpitations start, in her chest. She'd been having them for three weeks now. They started, it seemed, for almost no reason at all, but in the last week or so they had got dramatically worse, and came, unexpectedly, at any time. It was as if her heart was a fluttering bird, trying to burst out of her rib-cage. She pressed her hand against her breast to try to contain the terrified creature within. *Didn't it know there was no way out?*

Eva shouted, again, her voice ringing round dizzily in her head: 'After all Adi has done for you! You deserve to be put up against a wall and shot!'

To her surprise, the words had an instant effect.

Ilse put down her wine glass, and dropped her eyes.

Eva got unsteadily to her feet. She slammed out of the room, grabbing her silver-fox fur-coat as she went, banging the door behind her. As she walked down the thickly carpeted corridor, in her head still rang the words, *put up against a wall and shot* . . . To her own *sister*, she had said the words to her own *sister*! As she strode towards the stairs that took her to the crowded lobby and the waiting Mercedes, the words went on and on, repeating themselves in her head. Something about the way she had shouted the words reminded her, in their intonation, of something, or of somebody. Suddenly, she knew: Adolf.

Adolf Hitler now spent all his days in the Fuhrer-bunker. It had been hastily erected and the concrete was still wet and seeping, in places. The ventilation-system was noisy and inefficient and the air was foul: but the rooms were under deep concrete slabs that would protect the inhabitants against anything known: American and English bomb-blast or Russian artillery-shell: the Soviets were approaching the city now, fighting for every street and house in the outer-suburbs. Hitler himself ran the tactical defence of Berlin: by now Keitel and Jodl had ceased to argue. The game was up and it did not really matter, Jodl reflected, how the end came. Like everybody else in the Fuhrer's entourage, he felt it was his duty to remain at his post. It was the way he had been trained, all his life, and he could think of nothing else to do. It was Eva Braun he was sorry for. He hoped she would get away, at some point. He was astonished when her younger sister Gretl, heavily pregnant, appeared in the bunker. With these lower-class people, he thought, wonderingly, you could never really tell what they might do next.

Everybody who could, including Fegelin, assembled for General Heinz Guderian's Press Conference at the *Adlon*. A room had been set aside, with plush chairs, and flowers in a vase on a dais. The newspaper-men, shabby and ill-at-ease, stood around with champagne-cocktails in their hands: there was no food for them, but the *Adlon*'s cellars were by no means exhausted. Most of the journalists were German, Goebbels' hacks writing their last bylines. But there were a few Swiss and Swedish neutrals, their passports and travel-warrants in their pockets, for now the city was all but ringed around by Soviet forces. Still, this was a star occasion: Heinz Guderian, in and out of favour with Hitler over the years, had not been implicated in the Bomb Plot, and was now Hitler's senior general, once again. Himself, he would have said he fought for Germany, and was soon to tell Hitler to end the War: and be dismissed, again. Now, with the diminutive figure of Goebbels limping in the background, the great past-master of tank-warfare, author of its very handbook, '*Achtung-Panzer*', victor of the Ardennes, in 1940, stood on a dais in his full Field-Marshal's uniform with his ribbons and Iron Cross, and cleared his throat.

'Gentlemen of the Press,' Guderian spoke stiffly and held a paper in his hand, 'I am a soldier and do not usually talk to journalists.' He made it sound, Fegelin thought, as if he did not frequent brothels. 'However, I feel I must raise my voice in protest at what is happening all over Germany in the wake of the Russian advance, and will, unless the Russian High Command stop it, happen here in Berlin. He paused. 'Gentlemen, I am talking about *rape*.'

The journalists were stunned, and looked at each other, but they took no notes. Guderian went on: 'The Russian soldier is no doubt like any other in a non-Western Army. I liken him to the Chinese or Japanese. He is a peasant at war, and needs discipline.' The Field-Marshal paused. 'He is not getting it. He has plainly been told that German womenfolk of any age are spoils of war. He is raping young girls and their mothers and grandmothers too, in small towns and villages all over Germany, and soon, no doubt in Berlin itself. To their everlasting shame, his officers are doing the same thing.' The Field-Marshal coughed, bleakly. 'There is an orgy of rape going on out there, gentlemen of the Press, connived at, nay encouraged, in my opinion, by the Soviet High Command. I think you should tell the world that fact.'

The journalists waited but Guderian merely nodded his head, clicked his heels and left the room. One of the neutral journalists said, in a low voice, 'Hasn't he heard about the Camps the Allies have found in the West and the state of the people in them?'

'Propaganda! Atrocity stories!' shouted Goebbels. Voices were raised, in accusation and denial.

What were they all arguing about, Fegelin wondered?

In War, there are no rights or wrongs.

If you win, you say what was right and what was wrong.

As Hitler himself said: Success is all.

Fegelin made his way thoughtfully out of the conference room. When generals talked like that it was time for a man to think of himself.

Eva's thirty-fourth Birthday Party was held in the Bunker, to a rumble of distant Soviet artillery. Present were Martin Bormann, Dr Morell and his wife Hanni, the young aides, and Fegelin. 'You are going to have to behave yourself, Hermann?' said Eva, as they danced to the tinny music of the gramophone.

Fegelin grimaced. He knew she was talking about women. Well, sex was in the very air of the Bunker now. In the S.S. barracks, anything went. Drinking was non-stop now. Luckily they still had food. The ordinary Berliners were so hungry they had eaten the swans off the city lake. Horses, lying dead and bloated in the streets, were being hacked-at by hungry housewives, desperate to feed their children. Food distribution had broken down. So had law and order. It was, thought Fegelin, almost time to go. The Fuhrer-bunker was a death-trap.

So Fegelin danced with Eva, who seemed flushed and happy, on her thirty-fourth birthday. He wondered at the blind self-deception women possessed, when they loved a man. In Eva's case, Adolf Hitler. Well, there it was, a fact of nature. If Eva had not been so hell-bent on staying with her beloved Fuhrer, Fegelin would have whispered to his sister-in-law, 'Now, Evie, or very soon, is the time to run! Himmler is trying to talk to the Allies, don't ask me how I know, but he *is*, and Goering is getting in on the game. And don't say they wouldn't do such a thing. They aren't *here*, are they? Only Goebbels is here, the clubfoot little crackpot, but he would be, he loves Adolf Hitler as a man loves a woman! Despite his six blond children and his blond wife – and what's going to happen to *them*, when Ivan gets here, for God's sake?'

But handsome Fegelin smiled and danced and said none of this to Eva Braun, but clapped and applauded when Adolf Hitler presented her with his birthday gift: a pendant of topaz, surrounded by diamonds. What haul had that come from, Fegelin the cynic wondered? Where would Adolf Hitler get such a beautiful piece of jewellery, at this time? There were no jewellery-shops open, anywhere in Berlin. Anybody who had any jewellery had it buried in the earth, by now. Jewellery and precious stones of all kinds kept their value. Fegelin had some of his own and his particular lady-friend-of-the-moment (an employee of the Swiss government) had more. Fegelin had made his preparations, oh dear me, yes: but the jewellery now nestling round Eva's pretty little throat? Fegelin thought he knew where that had come from: some Gestapo haul, here in the city. From the Jews. There were great stocks of loot from the victims hoarded all over Germany. God knows what would happen to it all.

So they all danced on Eva Braun's thirty-fourth birthday.

They danced and got drunk and danced again.

They ate from their inexhaustible stock of excellent food.

They laughed and pretended that life was as it had ever been, in the good times: Hitler, pleading work, left early. As usual, he had not danced, even with Eva.

The others, including Eva, danced and laughed and drank and ate until it was time to go to their makeshift beds in the Bunker, to fall fitfully asleep so as not to hear the subdued roar of the Soviet artillery, louder every night.

Hitler, awake in his room, worked on, poring over his war-maps until dawn.

As always, Hitler kept to his routine. The late-supper now lasted until four in the morning, and took place in the Bunker. Eva was always present. Adolf and herself had quarters at one end of the Bunker: Eva's was nicely-furnished and had a bathroom attached. Her maid was nearby. Hitler slept in his camp-bed next door, in a cheerless room containing only a dresser and a chair. He was there only to sleep, and that badly: the air-conditioner roared all night, only the dead drunk slept through it.

So Hitler stayed-up later than ever, and he talked. Bormann still made sure that his words were recorded for posterity. An officer-stenographer took down every word. Bormann, later, edited them, and sent them, finally, out of the Bunker, by hand of a respected officer, for safe-keeping in a bank-vault in Bavaria. History, Bormann said to Eva, would want to know the Fuhrer's final thoughts on the War and his own life. As she sat, wretched with the desire for sleep, Adolf talked on, the words and thoughts running into one another, as if designed to drown out, in a mad chorus, the persistently louder boom of the Soviet artillery. It seemed to Eva that the whole world was burning and exploding, but Adolf was still talking! Eva wondered at the spectacle. This great orator who had ranted and raved at – and sometimes amused – millions of people, now had only these few bone-tired nerve-wracked, quietly terri-fied men and women: Bormann, Fegelin, the ever-loyal secretaries, the young military-aides, and herself. That Voice, once so magnetic and certain, droned on, regretful now, almost it seemed, resigned. Eva fell asleep, then wakened guiltily and listened again. Her reception of Hitler's thoughts was erratic, jumbled, now clear, now faint, like the short-wave-radio that connected the Bunker with the outside world. She supposed it was lack of sleep.

The Voice said: 'We lost the War by five weeks! The five weeks we lost when I went to Mussolini's aid in Greece! It held me back from attacking Russia *for five weeks*! We lost the opportunity! Moscow was not taken!'

And . . . 'Roosevelt is now *dead*! I had hoped I might be saved by that event, as Frederick the Great was saved by the death of the Tsarina; but it was not to be!'

And . . . 'I offered the Europeans a Crusade against Russia! They failed me!'

And . . . 'I should have thrown my lot in with the Nationalists in Africa! Rooted out Colonialism! Germany was never a Colonial Power!'

And ... 'The West is rotten. The Bourgeoisie are terrified. The Generals are reactionary! Christianity is corroded!'

And ... 'Whatever happens, the British Empire is finished! Churchill could have made Peace with me in 1940, and preserved it! But no! At the behest of International Jewry – and of Roosevelt – he pressed on with his War!'

And ... 'I have always been absolutely fair in my dealings with the Jews – on the Eve of War I gave them one Final Warning! I told them if they started another War I would exterminate them throughout Europe, once and for all!'

And ... 'Marxism is a Religion! It promises the Workers Paradise on Earth – *but not yet*! Lenin couldn't quite do it. Nor could Stalin. But the day will come!' Hitler laughed, sarcastically. 'So they *say*!'

And ... 'The Marxists make the same sort of Promises that Christianity makes! Except Christianity says: In the Hereafter!'

And ... 'I have been Europe's Last Hope! She proved incapable of refashioning herself by means of voluntary reform. She was impervious to charm and persuasion. To take her I had to use violence!'

And ... 'If we are destined to be beaten in this War our defeat will be utter and complete! Our Enemies have declared their Intentions! They will destroy National Socialist Germany, and reduce it to a heap of rubble! In this War, two ideologies confronted each other. Total Destruction of one side or the other: that had to be the outcome. It fills me with horror to think of the Reich hacked to pieces, by the Victors! The *Volk* exposed to the savage executioners of the Bolsheviks and the American Gangsters! But the more we suffer the more Glorious will be the Resurrection of the Eternal Germany! For myself, I cannot bear to live on in this period of defeat. The thought of Germany wallowing in the Mire! *No!*'

As Hitler finished his diatribe, the Soviet artillery seemed suddenly a lot nearer and sharper, the stale air of the Bunker suddenly colder.

Hitler signalled to the stenographer: no more. Then he left the room.

Sleepy and bemused, stretching her aching limbs, Eva followed him.

In the Map-Room at the boarded-up and sand-bagged Chancellery, Adolf Hitler was still, staring through his magnifying glass at the huge maps, moving battalions that no longer existed to positions long over-run. His aides did not correct him any longer: it was futile to try. Far easier to say, 'Mein Fuhrer, the exact position is unclear' than to declare, 'That battalion last called-in by landline fifty-six hours ago. Nothing has since been heard of them!'

Such a remark would only draw fury from the hunched, prematurely-aged figure in the well-creased uniform (his servant, Linge, would never allow the Fuhrer to look anything but spick-and-span) but his stoop and the halting movements were, thought Albert Speer, a late-arrival at the bunker, awful to see, when one recalled the same man at the Nuremberg Rallies a mere six years before. Two hundred thousand uniformed-men, absolutely immobile, hanging on his every word, the night-sky lit with his own brain-child, the anti-aircraft searchlights spaced in a ring, every sixty yards! The singing of the *Horst Wessel* and finally *Deutschland Uber Alles*, roaring from two hundred thousand throats! Heady stuff! It had seduced Speer, as it had seduced them all. Adolf Hitler had been his benefactor, had given him a career and a life. Finally, one of the biggest jobs in the Reich, Armaments Minister. In that task, he had done all he could: dispersed factories: built new ones, underground. Used slave-labour, of course, what alternative was there? Speer had told Hitler, told them all, that the RAF night-raids would take up exactly half of the Reich's manufacturing-effort before it was done! And so it *had*! Could anybody now, looking at the ruins of Cologne, of Essen, of Hamburg, deny that the English had bombed them out of the War in the West? The finest Radar-screens and flak-guns had not stopped them. The Lancasters, piloted by the Grammar-school-boys of England, had laid the Ruhr waste. They had only stopped when Eisenhower had demanded total allocation of all materials and resources to the invading land-armies. And a slow, sorry mess they had made of *that*! They should have been in Berlin months ago!

Yes, the Royal Air Force in the West and the weight of numbers in the East had blasted Germany out of the War. The Americans had supplied the materials and men, when it finally counted. Speer had tried to save what he could. He had given orders to his staff: no more blowing-up of military or civilian installations; or electrical power-stations; or hydro-electric-dams or railway rolling-stock — what was left of it! He had hoped to explain to the Fuhrer, the man to whom he owed so much, that the German *Volk* must be left with something when the fighting stopped. He had told Hitler, a long time ago, that they had no possibility of winning. Hitler had simply shaken his head and said, 'Speer, you are a technocrat, you do not understand military matters.' For old times' sake, they had neither of them said any more. Goebbels — still a leveller, a sort of mad socialist under it all — *still* ranted on the radio that 'The Terror Fliers spare neither the dwellings of the rich nor the poor! The class-war has ended, once and for all! There is no end to Revolution! We welcome the bombs because they blast away much that is old and finished!' Was he mad, were they all mad? 'Now everything is in ruins,' exulted Goebbels. 'We will be forced to rebuild Europe! In the past, such bourgeois ideas as private possessions, wealth, family, held us back! Now the Bombs have smashed the prison-walls! The Enemy has smashed the Past! Everything Old has *gone*! We welcome the New Order in Europe!'

Speer had heard all that before: it was Goebbels' swan-song. That speech, or something like it, had been dinning itself (through the German radio) into his ears for what seemed like weeks. Speer had even toyed, in his despair, with joining a conspiracy against Adolf Hitler, his old benefactor: but nothing had come of it. Nobody was prepared to strike the final blow. In the end, such a move meant killing Hitler. Speer could not do that, and personally knew nobody who would. The Generals had tried it and failed. Besides, history would take care of everything, by the look of it, very soon. Speer didn't really know why he *was* here, at the Bunker, except to say good-bye to the Adolf Hitler he had once known, the enthusiastic amateur-architect, certainly not the mass-murderer and tyrant. Like the others, Speer had ridden the gravy-train, and it had stopped. There was no point in prevaricating. He embraced Eva Braun, who had cried out, on his appearance, 'Look! I told you Albert would come to see you!' Then Hitler had embraced him, in greeting. Now, he did so again in a wordless farewell. Speer had been shocked by what he saw at that first meeting, a shaky old man, with death in his eyes. Speer said nothing directly to Hitler, but approached Goebbels, who was present, and to his surprise found an ally. 'Don't destroy everything, Josef. Leave something for Germany!' Goebbels said, 'The *Volksturm* can fight just as easily outside the city walls as in it.' His tone was conciliatory. He had approved of Speer coming to the Bunker. Speer did not know if any of this would happen: he just hoped. He shook hands all round and left the Bunker. He never saw Adolf Hitler again.

After Speer left, Hitler ordered-up a final onslaught on the Soviet forces ringing the city. This was the *Steiner Attack*, named after its commander, an Obergruppenfuhrer of the S.S. Hitler called every man, tank, artillery-piece remaining on the Wehrmacht's strength, into the attack. 'Any officer who does not supply every man and gun he has, will face a firing-squad!'

The attack never happened: but nobody would tell Hitler directly that it had not. Nobody dared. At the regular mid-day conference, the usual participants sat: Keitel, Jodl, Krebs and Bergdorf, generals all, but not a word to offer between them. Doenitz had gone the day before, to his new headquarters in Schleswig-Holstein. The rats, Jodl thought to himself, were leaving the ship. Finally, the news was muttered part of it by one officer, part by another, until Adolf Hitler, trembling and shaking, was left facing the bald, unspeakable truth.

The *Steiner Attack* had not taken place!

It was never going to take place. The men who should have been in the *Steiner Attack* were dead and the tanks had long foundered, blazing, and the guns were destroyed or in the hands of the enemy. There was no attack, as there was no Wencke's 'phantom' Army to come to the rescue, of either Adolf Hitler or the besieged city or of Germany itself.

To those present, an awesome thing happened.

From somewhere Adolf Hitler found the emotional energy to mount the most terrible rage any of them had ever seen from him: and they had all seen, Jodl thought, plenty. Sitting there, as the white-hot words spurted over him, Jodl thought: the man is simply a street-corner hater, that's all he's *ever* been: we have all thrown our lives away on *this*!

Hitler screamed at them, spittle on his lips. 'So! I have been deserted at the last! You Generals, traitors and scum and lickspittle Junker aristocrats — you have failed and funked all, in the end! Traitors, every one of you! You and your like! I should have hanged or shot every General — every one of *you*!' He pointed his finger at the shocked, silent men. Nobody stirred. Jodl thought for a moment Hitler meant to have them taken outside into the Chancellery garden and actually shot there and then. The S.S. guards would have done it, if ordered to do it. Hitler was, probably, capable of it, in a hysterical frenzy like this. The atmosphere was electric: the smell of death was in the air. But, suddenly, Hitler's voice changed, dropped an octave: as in one of his great speeches, he switched from rage to sadness. 'Gentlemen, the end has come. It is all over. The Siberians are too strong. The Volk have failed me. We bend our knee to the stronger enemy. I will personally take over the final defence of the city. I want a radio announcement to that effect: the Fuhrer is not leaving Berlin. Here, I will remain, fighting at my post, until the end. 'He slumped into his chair and waved his one good hand, signifying the conference had ended.

They all loudly protested, robot-like. There were possibilities of a Peace feeler? Ribbentrop still had high hopes! But Hitler was not listen?-ing. He sat there, a still and silent figure, his back towards them, hunched in his chair.

Slowly, they collected their bulky, useless files and left the room, not looking at each other.

Sturmbannfuhrer Fegelin left the bunker silently and alone. He made his way through the ruined city to an apartment he had rented in a quiet neighbourhood. There, he changed into civilian clothes and waited for the Swiss lady to come and collect him. She had organised passports and papers. Soon, he would be out of the burning wreck of Germany for ever. He lay on the bed and waited. There was a knock at the door and he got up quickly. The Swiss lady was before time, all was well. He opened the door. Four Gestapo men stood there. Hope seeped out of his boots. He pulled rank, demanded their permission to telephone Eva Braun, at the Chancellery, amazingly got through to her (most lines were now down) but she sounded distant. The silly cow was like some Hindu princess, determined on *Suttee*. Fegelin shouted desperately, 'Talk to the Fuhrer! Eva! I was going to take Gretl! It's for the family!'

Then he put on his uniform and went with the Gestapo men to the waiting car.

Eva spoke to Hitler about Fegelin. 'Surely there has been some mistake?' Adolf said, 'My officers are talking to him now,' and walked away. Eva thought, by his tone, all would be well. Surely he realised that the *family* could not go on unless Fegelin was with his wife? Thank God, Gretl was comparatively safe with Vadi and Mutti in Munich. Eva lay on her bed in her silk underwear and tried to sleep. The palpitations had started again. It was now two o'clock in the morning. She must have dozed because when her maid came in with coffee, it was dawn; she looked shocked and her eyes were full of tears. She gulped and said, 'Oh, Frau, they have shot poor Fegelin.'

Slowly, Eva Braun turned her head to the wall.

The palpitations had, astonishingly, stopped.

She felt nothing. Nothing at all.

Later, Adi told her that Fegelin had known of Himmler's treachery. Himmler was negotiating with the Allies. Goering was attempting to take over power. Fegelin's duty had been to tell him that, and he had failed in his duty and paid the price.

'It is all over, Evie,' Adi said, 'Really all over.'

Eva said, 'Yes, I know.'

'If Stalin captures us alive, he will put us in a cage at Moscow Zoo!'

Groups of refugees began to flee the Bunker.

Hitler asked Hoffmann to talk to Eva, persuade her to go South to Munich with him.

Eva refused, saying, 'You know I cannot leave him now.'

Hoffmann goes, by motor-car, south to Bavaria: within hours, Soviet forces close this, the last road out of the city.

Hanna Reich pilots in, to attempt to rescue Hitler. Soviet artillery is pounding the Tiergarten and the Wilhelmstrasse. Hanna Reich asks Hitler to come with her. He refuses, and she flies out, the last aircraft out of the smouldering, burning city.

The next day Eva and Adolf Hitler were married by a notary.

The wedding rings came from a stock of Gestapo-held Jewish loot. Adolf's ring fitted, and he wore it. Eva's slipped off. She gave it to her maid, with instructions to pass it on to the family.

Eva signed the Marriage Certificate: *Eva Hitler*.

At last, she thought, not crying. At last. She felt light-headed and happy and laughed and embraced the guests and, for the very first time in public, Adolf Hitler himself. Everybody applauded this. There was champagne and cakes, as for any other wedding.

Hitler shook hands with everybody present, smiling distantly, then went into the secretaries' room. He dictated his Last Will and Testament. Trudl Junge took it down in her impeccable shorthand, too tired to cry.

Hitler dictated: 'Since our forces are too small to withstand, any longer, the enemy's attacks, and since our own resistance is worn down by a Soviet army of blind automata, I will share the fate of Berlin, and remain here in the city. I will not fall into the hands of an enemy who requires the spectacle of my public humiliation and death to divert his hysterical masses. I have decided to choose death voluntarily at the moment I believe that the Chancellery can no longer be held . . .'

'*Before my death*, I expel from the Party the former Reich-Marshal, Hermann Goering and withdraw from him all the rights conferred upon him by the Decree of 29 June 1941, and by my Reichstag speech of 1 September 1939. In his place I appoint Grand-Admiral Doenitz as Reich-President and Supreme Commander of the Armed Forces.'

'*Before my death* I expel from the Party and from all his offices the former Reichsfuhrer S.S. and Reich Minister of the Interior, Heinrich Himmler.

Goering and Himmler, by their secret negotiations with the enemy, without my knowledge or approval, and by their illegal attempts to seize power, have brought irreparable shame on Germany and the *Volk*.'

Adolf Hitler paused.

'During the Years of Struggle I believed that I could not undertake the responsibility of marriage. Now, at the end of my life, I have decided to take as my wife the woman who, after many years of true friendship, came here to Berlin, already besieged, of her own free-will, in order to share my fate. She will go to her death with me at her own wish, as my wife. This will compensate us for what we both lost through my work in the service of my *Volk*.'

Adolf Hitler went to his bare room and sat down, alone. He no longer heard the Soviet artillery: it was simply a backdrop to his thoughts. So it had all been for *this*? The strivings to make himself an architect, impossible that his Enemies would ever let that happen, why hadn't he seen that? He had to be saved for greater, more terrible sacrifices than that? He had to starve in the snows of Vienna, to eat charity food, to be humiliated by petty bureaucrats, to know poverty and want and, yes, war. All *that* his Enemies had granted him, all those trials and favours, so that he could be ready for his task, to take his tribe, the *Volk*, to the leadership of Europe, and eventually, of the World, and then to dash it from his grasp, to say their final *No* to him! To say to him: the *Volk* are not the Chosen Ones, they are not strong enough, the future belongs, anyway for the foreseeable future, to the Siberians. He would not be here to see it. He would not be a shamed exhibit for his Enemies – who all his life, right back to his father Alois' beginnings, had dogged his footsteps. No, he would die without leaving a trace of himself. He had left orders with Gunsche, captain of his Bodyguard, to burn his body. It would be the last act the survivors would perform before they fell into the hands of the Bolsheviks. His enemies, whose name was legion, would hope that his name would be forgotten, but he knew that would not be. Men still spoke of Atilla. They would speak of him, too, and the sons of his Enemies would spit when they said his name, a thousand years hence. But his name would be *spoken*, that was all that, ultimately, mattered.

He looked up as Eva entered. She looked oddly content and not at all nervous. Women, he thought, I have never understood them: but this one is above rubies, and it is too late to tell her so. He simply asked, 'Is all arranged?'

Eva sat next to him. 'Yes. Blondi is dead. The cyanide is all right.'

Tears came to his eyes. Poor, dear Blondi. She had performed her last task for him, in proving the capsules were still potent. He could not have saved her anyway. Everybody in the Bunker had shot their dogs. The S.S. alsatians were gone. Even our animals have to suffer, he thought.

'Well, *liebschen*, it is all over.'

Eva was very still. 'Yes, Adi.'

They sat, like an old married couple faced with a bereavement, side by side on the horsehair sofa.

'Together, anyway,' she said.

Adolf Hitler made no answer. His eyes were closed and he looked as if he was asleep: but she knew he was not.

The next day, in their apartment in the Fuhrer-bunker, dressed in their best clothes: a spotless cream jacket, dress-trousers, Iron Cross pinned to his lapel, for him: a new dress with the first jewellery Hitler ever bought her pinned to that dress, for her. Eva Braun and Adolf Hitler took their own lives. Eva Braun by cyanide, Adolf Hitler with a pistol-shot to the temple.

It was indeed, over.

XXIV

ALMOST two years later: an officer of Hitler's Bodyguard, a prisoner of the Russians all of that time, was still kept under close-guard and interrogated every single day of his confinement. After all, he had seen Gunsche bury the bodies of the Fuhrer and his woman in the Chancellery garden. He had seen gasoline thrown over them and the torch applied. Then he had run, and run, and been captured by a Soviet patrol. Now, on a day like any other, he had been taken, without explanation, from his prison-cell, thence by jeep to a bosky glade, some ten miles from the prison. The NKVD colonel in charge of the expedition gestured him to get out of the jeep and follow. Together, they approached a wooden hut, outside of which stood a single, armed infantryman, savage and Mongolian-looking, as they mostly were.

The last two years had seemed like twenty. Over and over again, he had doggedly told his story, to a succession of interrogators – some grim, some genial – in a series of dark rooms and cellars. How he had run, like everybody else, from the Fuhrer-bunker; how they had all run: Morell and his wife; the Generals and their aides; the secretaries; Bormann and Axmann; everybody had run. He had told his interrogators, again and again, how he had helped to bury Eva Braun and Adolf Hitler, how he had witnessed the suicide of Goebbels and his wife and their children. Bormann was dead, last seen lying on a pile of rubble near the Banhof. The NKVD did not believe that. Axmann, lucky swine, was said to be now in the West. The officer told the NKVD interrogators it had been every man for himself!

The NKVD interrogator always returned to the same question, put softly or harshly. Was Hitler *really* dead, burned in the Chancellery garden? Or was that somebody else, a blind, a cover? Was Hitler *really* in South America, transported across the oceans in a U-Boat? The officer had lost three stones, answering that question, put in a hundred different ways, and had been deprived of food and maltreated, often. He had always told them the same story: the truth.

Inside the hut it was dark: what light there was filtered in from a cracked and dusty window. There was a sharp smell the officer did not immediately recognise. An oldish man in a dirty white coat, a pathologist, he surmised, stood there. He was the only occupant of the room. Sunlight fell on a cardboard box standing on a rough wooden table. The man in the dirty white coat looked at the NKVD colonel, who nodded.

The man in the dirty white coat opened the box.

He took from it an object: a half-burned, half-decomposed human head, complete with dentures, and laid it on the wooden table: the skull was shattered, plainly by a bullet, and had been clumsily repaired by some synthetic material.

The smell of formaldehyde filled the air.

The officer gazed unblinkingly at the shattered head, a very long moment.

The NKVD colonel asked him the question, very softly.

'Is that Adolf Hitler?'

The officer was a long time answering: his eyes were full of tears. He blinked them back: he was not going to give these bastards the benefit.

'Ja,' he said, stolidly. 'That is the Fuhrer.'

ACKNOWLEDGEMENTS

In the writing of this very long and detailed Biographical Novel, I am indebted to, first of all, those anonymous Germans who knew Adolf Hitler and were prepared to talk about him, but refused, even at this late date, to be named. I preserve their privacy but thank them. Some insights in the book, that look like mine, are really theirs. My German Researcher, Marion Dill, has been of enormous assistance to me, as have various libraries, including the Weiner Library and the British Library and various newspaper archives and the assistants who work there, including the Dokumentation Editor of *Der Spiegel*, and others.

I would like to pay tribute to, amongst others, the authors of many works on the Nazi Period. They include:

The Speeches of Adolf Hitler (Ed. Norman H. Baynes)
Hitler Directs his War (Ed. F. Gilbert)
My War Memories (by General Ludendorff)
Adolphe Hitler, Legende (by Werner Maser)
Failure of a Mission (by Sir Neville Henderson)
I Paid Hitler (by Fritz Thyssen)
Hitler Speaks (by Herman Rauschning)
Hitler as War Lord (by Franz Halder)
Der Fuhrer (by K. Heiden)
Berlin Diary (by W. L. Shirer)
The Last Days of Hitler (by H. R. Trevor-Roper)
The Life of Neville Chamberlain (by K. Feiling)
Hitler and I (by Otto Strasser)
The Second World War (by Winston S. Churchill)
Farewell Austria (by K. von Schuschnigg)
Mein Kampf (by Adolf Hitler)
Defeat in the West (by Milton Shulman)
Hitler and His Admirals (by A. Martiennsen)

Hitler the Pawn (by R. Olden)
Panzer Leader (by Heinz Guderian)
Austrian Requiem (by K. von Schuschnigg)
I Knew Hitler (by K. Ludecke)
Hitler's Words (by Gordon W. Prange)
Hitler's Table Talk (Edited by H. R. Trevor-Roper)
Hitler's Youth (by Franz Jetzinger)
Hitler, the Missing Years (by Ernst Hanfstaengl)
Memoirs (by Franz Von Papen)
Who's Who in Nazi Germany (by Robert Wistrich)
Hitler, the Man and the Myth (by Roger Manvell and Heinrich Frankel)
Inside The Third Reich (by Albert Speer)
The Yellow Star (by Gerhard Schoenberner)
Hitler (by Norman Stone)
The Rise and Fall of the Third Reich (by William L. Shirer)
A Social History of the Third Reich (by Richard Grunberger)
Hitler's War Directives (Edited by Hugh R. Trevor-Roper)
A Dictionary of the Third Reich (by James Taylor and Warren Shaw)
The Death of Adolf Hitler (by Lev Bezymenski)
Hitler's Words (by Gordon W. Prange)
The Bormann Letters (by Martin Bormann)
Das Ende des Hitler-Mythos (by Josef Greiner)
Young Hitler (by August Kubizek)
Hitler Privat (by A. Zoller)
Hindenburg, the Wooden Titan (by J. W. Wheeler-Bennett)
Hitler and I (by Otto Strasser)
The Ribbentrop Memoirs (by Joachim Von Ribbentrop)
Hitler's Interpreter (by Paul Schmidt)
The Final Solution: and *SS Alibi of a Nation* (by Gerald Reitlinger)
The Kersten Memoirs (by Felix Kersten)
The Face of the Third Reich (by Joachim Fest)
Hitler, a Study in Tyranny (by Alan Bullock)
Eva Braun, Hitler's Mistress (by Nerin Gunn)
Hitler Was My Friend (by Heinrich Hoffmann)
Last Witnesses in the Bunker (by Pierre Galante & Eugene Silianoff)
In the Face of the Gallows (by Hans Frank)